The CAT WHO
CAME *for* CHRISTMAS

The CAT *and*
the CURMUDGEON

The BEST CAT EVER

Also by Cleveland Amory

NONFICTION

•

The Proper Bostonians

The Last Resorts

Who Killed Society?

Man Kind?

FICTION

•

Home Town

The Trouble with Nowadays

EDITOR

•

Celebrity Register

Vanity Fair Anthology

To Jeane

The CAT WHO CAME *for* CHRISTMAS

The CAT *and* *the* CURMUDGEON

The BEST CAT EVER

CLEVELAND AMORY

BOOK-OF-THE-MONTH CLUB
NEW YORK

Printed in the United States of America

CONTENTS

The Cat Who Came for Christmas 1

The Cat and the Curmudgeon 241

The Best Cat Ever 545

The CAT WHO CAME *for* CHRISTMAS

ILLUSTRATED *by* EDITH ALLARD

To the biographee,
the best cat in the whole world —
with the exception, of course,
of yours.

The author wishes to acknowledge the help of his peerful editor, Fredrica Friedman, and his defatigable researcher, Susan Hall, as well as that of his severest critic, P. Bear.

Contents

I · *The Rescue* 3
II · *The Decision* 19
III · *The Great Compromise* 34
IV · *His First Trip* 50
V · *His Roots* 71
VI · *A Difficult Matter* 91
VII · *His Hollywood* 114
VIII · *His Fitness Program* 145
IX · *His Foreign Policy* 175
X · *His Domestic Policy* 207
L'Envoi 238

The Cat
Who Came for
Christmas

I ◦ *The Rescue*

To anyone who has ever been owned by a cat, it will come as no surprise that there are all sorts of things about your cat you will never, as long as you live, forget.

Not the least of these is your first sight of him or her.

That my first sight of mine, however, would ever be memorable seemed, at the time, highly improbable. For one thing, I could hardly see him at all. It was snowing, and he was standing some distance from me in a New York City alley. For another thing, what I did see of him was extremely unprepossessing. He was thin and he was dirty and he was hurt.

The irony is that everything around him, except him, was beautiful. It was Christmas Eve, and although no one outside of New York would believe it on a bet or a Bible, New York City can, when it puts its mind to it, be beautiful.

And that Christmas Eve some years ago was one of those times.

The snow was an important part of it — not just the snow, but the fact it was still snowing, as it is supposed to but rarely does over Christmas. And the snow was beginning to blanket, as at least it does at first, a multitude of such everyday New York sins as dirt and noise and smells and potholes. Combined with this, the Christmas trees and the lights and decorations inside the windows, all of which can often seem so ordinary in so many other places, seemed, in New York that night, with the snow outside, just right.

I am not going so far as to say that New York that night was O Little Town of Bethlehem, but it was at least something different from the kind of New York Christmas best exemplified by a famous Christmas card sent out by a New York garage that year to all its customers. "Merry Christmas from the boys at the garage," that card said. "Second Notice."

For all that, it was hardly going to be, for me, a Merry Christmas. I am no Scrooge, but I am a curmudgeon and the word *merry* is not in the vocabulary of any self-respecting curmudgeon you would care to meet — on Christmas or any other day. You would be better off with a New York cabdriver, or even a Yankee fan.

There were other reasons why that particular Christmas had little chance to be one of my favorites. The fact that it was after seven o'clock and that I was still at my desk spoke for itself. The anti-cruelty society which I had founded a few years before was suffering growing pains — frankly, it is still suffering them — but at that particular time, they were close to terminal. We were heavily involved in virtually every field of animal work, and although we were doing so on bare subsistence salaries — or on no salary at all for most of us — the society itself was barely subsisting. It had achieved some successes, but its major accomplishments were still in the future.

And so, to put it mildly, was coin of the realm. Even its name, The Fund for Animals, had turned out to be a disappointment. I had, in what I had thought of as a moment of high inspiration, chosen it because I was certain that it would, just by its mention, indicate we could use money. The name had, however, turned out not only not to do the job but to do just the opposite. Everybody thought that we already had the money.

Besides the Fund's exchequer being low that Christmas Eve, so was my own. My writing career, by which I had supported myself since before you were born, was far from booming. I was spending so much time getting the Fund off the ground that I was four years behind on a book deadline and so many months behind on two magazine articles that, having run out of all reasonable excuses, one of the things I had meant to do that day was to borrow a line from the late Dorothy Parker and tell the editor I had really tried to finish but someone had taken the pencil.

As for my personal life, that too left something to be desired. Recently divorced, I was living in a small apartment, and although I was hardly a hermit — I had a goodly choice of both office parties and even friends' parties to go to that evening — still, this was not going to be what Christmas is supposed to be. Christmas is, after all, not a business holiday or a friends' holiday, it is a family holiday. And my family, at that point, consisted of one beloved daughter who lived in Pittsburgh and had a perfectly good family of her own.

On top of it all, there was a final irony in the situation.

Although I had had animals in my life for as far back as I could remember, and indeed had had them throughout my marriage — and although I was working on animal problems every day of my life — I had not a single creature to call my own. For an animal person, an animal-less home is no home at all. Furthermore, mine, I was sure, was fated to remain that way. I travelled on an average of more than two weeks a month, and was away from home almost as much as I was there. For me, an animal made even less sense than a wife. You do not, after all, have to walk a wife.

I had just turned from the pleasant task of watching the snow outside to the unpleasant one of surveying the bills when the doorbell rang. If there had been anyone else to answer it, I would have told them to say to whoever it was that we already gave at home. But there was no one, so I went myself.

The caller was a snow-covered woman whom I recognized as Ruth Dwork. I had known Miss Dwork for many years. A former schoolteacher, she is one of those people who, in every city, make the animal world go round. She is a rescuer and feeder of everything from dogs to pigeons and is a lifetime soldier in what I have called the Army of the Kind. She is, however, no private soldier in that army — she makes it too go round. In fact, I always called her Sergeant Dwork.

"Merry Christmas, Sergeant," I said. "What can I do you for?"

She was all business. "Where's Marian?" she asked. "I need her." Marian Probst, my longtime and longer-suffering assistant, is an experienced rescuer, and I knew Miss Dwork had, by the very look of her, a rescue in progress. "Marian's gone," I told her. "She left about five-thirty, saying something about some people having Christmas Eve off. I told her she was a clock-watcher, but it didn't do any good."

Sergeant Dwork was unamused. "Well, what about Lia?" she demanded. Lia Albo is national coordinator of the Fund for Animals and an extremely expert rescuer. She, however, had left before Marian on — what else? — another rescue.

Miss Dwork was obviously unhappy about being down to me. "Well," she said, looking me over critically but trying to make the best of a bad bargain, "I need someone with long arms. Get your coat."

As I walked up the street with Sergeant Dwork, through the snow and biting cold, she explained that she had been trying to rescue a particular stray cat for almost a month, but that she had had no success. She had, she said, tried everything. She had attempted to lure the cat into a Hav-a-Heart trap but, hungry as he was and successful as this method had been in countless other cases, it had not worked with this cat. He had simply refused to enter any enclosure that he could not see his way out of. Lately, she confessed, she had abandoned such subtleties for a more direct approach. And, although she had managed to get the cat to come close to the rail fence at the end of the alley, and even to take bite-sized chunks of cheese from her outstretched fingers, she had never been able to get him to come quite close enough so that she could catch him. When she tried, he would jump away, and then she had to start all over the each-time-ever-more-difficult task of trying again to win his trust.

However, the very night before, Sergeant Dwork informed me, she had come the closest she had ever come to capturing the cat. That time, she said, as he devoured the cheese, he had not jumped away but had stood just where he was — nearer than he had ever been but still maddeningly just out of reach. Good as this news was, the bad news was that Miss Dwork now felt that she was operating against a deadline. The cat had been staying in the basement of the apartment building, but the superintendent of the building had now received orders to get rid of it before Christmas or face the consequences. And now the other workers in the building, following their super's orders, had joined in the war against the cat. Miss Dwork herself had seen someone, on her very last visit, throw something at him and hit him.

When we arrived at our destination, there were two alleyways. "He's in one or the other," Sergeant Dwork whispered. "You take that one, I'll take this." She disappeared to my left and I stood there, hunched in my coat with the snow falling, peering into the shaft of darkness and having, frankly, very little confidence in the whole plan.

The alley was a knife cut between two tall buildings filled with dim, dilapidated garbage cans, mounds of snowed-upon refuse, and a forbidding grate. And then, as I strained my eyes to see where, amongst all this dismal debris, the cat might be hiding, one of the mounds of refuse suddenly moved. It stretched and shivered and turned to regard me. I had found the cat.

As I said, that first sight was hardly memorable. He looked less like a real cat than like the ghost of a cat. Indeed, etched as he was against the whiteness of the snow all around him, he was so thin that he would have looked completely ghostlike, had it not been for how pathetically dirty he was. He was so dirty, in fact, that it was impossible even to guess as to what color he might originally have been.

When cats, even stray cats, allow themselves to get like that, it is usually a sign that they have given up. This cat, however, had not. He had not even though, besides being dirty, he was wet and he was cold and he was hungry.

And, on top of everything else, you could tell by the kind of off-kilter way he was standing that his little body was severely hurt. There was something very wrong either with one of his back legs or perhaps with one of his hips. As for his mouth, that seemed strangely crooked, and he seemed to have a large cut across it.

But, as I said, he had not given up. Indeed, difficult as it must have been for him from that off-kilter position, he proceeded, while continuing to stare at me unwaveringly, to lift a front paw — and, snow or no snow, to lick it. Then the other front paw. And, when they had been attended to, the cat began the far more difficult feat of hoisting up, despite whatever it was that was amiss with his hips, first one back paw and then the other. Finally, after finishing, he did what seemed to me completely incredible — he performed an all-four-paw, ears-laid-back, straight-up leap. It looked to me as if he was, of all things in such a situation, practicing his pounce.

An odd image came to my mind — something, more years ago than I care to remember, that my first college tennis coach had drilled into our team about playing three-set matches. "In the third set," he used to say, "extra effort for ordinary results." We loathed the saying and we hated even more the fact that he made us, in that third set, just before receiving serve, jump vigorously up and down. He was convinced that this unwonted display would inform our opponents that we were fairly bursting with energy — whether that was indeed the fact or not. We did the jumping, of course, because we had to, but all of us were also convinced that we were the only players who ever had to do such a silly thing. Now when I see, without exception, every top tennis player in the world bouncing like cork into the third set, I feel like a pioneer and very much better about the whole thing.

And when I saw the cat doing his jumping, I felt better too — but this time, of course, about him. Maybe he was not as badly hurt as at first I had thought.

In a moment I noticed that Sergeant Dwork, moving quietly, had rejoined me. "Look at his mouth," she whispered. "I told you they have declared war on him!"

Ours was to be a war too — but one not against, but for, the cat. As Sergeant Dwork quietly imparted her battle plan, I had the uneasy feeling that she obviously regarded me as a raw recruit, and also that she was trying to keep my duties simple enough so that even a mere male could perform them. In any case, still whispering, she told me she would approach the fence with the cheese cubes, with which the cat was by now thoroughly familiar, in her outstretched hand, and that, during this period, I apparently should be crouching down behind her but nonetheless moving forward with her. Then, when she had gotten the cat to come as close as he would, she would step swiftly aside and I, having already thrust my arms above her through the vertical bars of the fence, was to drop to my knees and grab. The Sergeant was convinced that the cat was so hungry that, at that crucial moment, he would lose enough of his wariness to go for the bait — and the bite — which would seal his capture.

Slowly, with our eyes focussed on our objective, we moved out and went over the top. And just as we did so, indeed as I was crouching into position behind Sergeant Dwork, I got for the first time a good look at the cat's eyes peering at us. They were the first beautiful thing I ever noticed about him. They were a soft and lovely and radiant green.

As Sergeant Dwork went forward, she kept talking reassuringly to the cat, meanwhile pointedly removing the familiar cheese from her pocket and making sure he would be concentrating on it rather than the large something looming behind her. She did her job so well that we actually reached our battle station at almost the exact moment when the cat, still proceeding toward us, albeit increasingly warily, was close enough to take his first bite from the Sergeant's outstretched hand.

That first bite, however, offered us no chance of success. In one single incredibly quick but fluid motion, the cat grabbed the cheese, wolfed it down, and sprang back. Our second attempt resulted in exactly the same thing. Again the leap, the grab, the wolf, and the backward scoot. He was simply too adept at the game of eat and run.

By this time I was thoroughly convinced that nothing would come of the Sergeant's plan. But I was equally convinced that we had somehow to get that cat. I wanted to get over that fence and go for him.

The Sergeant, of course, would have none of such foolhardiness, and, irritated as this made me, I knew she was right. I could never have caught the cat that way. The Sergeant was, however, thinking of something else. Wordlessly she gave me the sign of how she was going to modify her tactics. This time she would offer the cat not one but two cubes of cheese — one in each of her two outstretched hands. But this time, she indicated, although she would push her right hand as far as it would go through the fence, she would keep her left hand well back. She obviously hoped that the cat would this time attempt both bites before the retreat. Once more we went over the top — literally in my case, because I already had my hands through the fence over the Sergeant. And this time, just as she had hoped, the cat not only took the first bite but also went for that second one. And, at just that moment, as he was midbite, Sergeant Dwork slid to one side and I dropped to my knees.

As my knees hit the ground, my face hit the grate. But I did not even feel it. For, in between my hands, my fingers underneath and my thumbs firmly on top, was cat. I had him.

Surprised and furious, he first hissed, then screamed, and finally, spinning right off the ground to midair, raked both my hands with his claws. Again I felt nothing, because by then I was totally engrossed in a dual performance — not letting go of him and yet somehow managing to maneuver his skinny, desperately squirming body, still in my tight grasp, albeit for that split second in just one hand, through the narrow apertures of the rail fence. And now his thinness was all-important because, skin and bones as he was, I was able to pull him between the bars.

Still on my knees, I raised him up and tried to tuck him inside my coat. But in this maneuver I was either overconfident or under-alert, because somewhere between the raising and the tucking, still spitting fire, he got in one final rake of my face and neck. It was a good one.

As I struggled to my feet, Sergeant Dwork was clapping her hands in pleasure, but obviously felt the time had now come to rescue me. "Oh," she said. "Oh dear. Your face.

Oh my." Standing there in the snow, she tried to mop me with her handkerchief. As she did so, I could feel the cat's little heart racing with fear as he struggled to get loose underneath my coat. But it was to no avail. I had him firmly corralled, and, once again, with both hands.

The Sergeant had now finished her mopping and become all Sergeant again. "I'll take him now," she said, advancing toward me. Involuntarily, I took a step backwards. "No, no, that's all right," I assured her. "I'll take him to my apartment." The Sergeant would have none of this. "Oh no," she exclaimed. "Why, my apartment is very close." "So is mine," I replied, moving the cat even farther into the depths of my coat. "Really, it's no trouble at all. And anyway, it'll just be for tonight. Tomorrow, we'll decide — er, what to do with him."

Sergeant Dwork looked at me doubtfully as I started to move away. "Well then," she said, "I'll call you first thing in the morning." She waved a mittened hand. "Merry Christmas," she said. I wished her the same, but I couldn't wave back.

Joe, the doorman at my apartment building, was unhappy about my looks. "Mr. Amory!" he exclaimed. "What happened to your face? Are you all right?" I told him that not only was I all right, he ought to have seen the other guy. As he took me to the elevator, he was obviously curious about both the apparent fact that I had no hands and also the suspicious bulge inside my coat. Like all good New York City doormen, Joe is the soul of discretion — at least from tenant to tenant — but he has a bump of curiosity which would rival Mt. Everest. He is also, however, a good animal man, and he had a good idea that whatever I had, it was something alive. Leaning his head toward my coat, he attempted to reach in. "Let me pet it," he said. "No," I told him firmly. "Mustn't touch." "What is it?" he asked. "Don't tell anyone," I said, "but it's a saber-toothed tiger. Undeclawed, too." "Wow," he said. And then, just before the elevator took off, he told me that Marian was already upstairs.

I had figured that Marian would be there. My brother and his wife were coming over for a drink before we all went out to a party, and Marian, knowing I would probably be late, had arrived to admit them and hold, so to speak, the fort.

I kicked at the apartment door. When Marian opened it, I blurted out the story of Sergeant Dwork and the rescue. She too wanted to know what had happened to my face and if I was all right. I tried the same joke I had tried on Joe. But Marian is a hard woman on old jokes. "The only 'other guy' I'm interested in," she said, "is in your coat." I bent down to release my prize, giving him a last hug to let him know that everything was now fine.

Neither Marian nor I saw anything. All we saw, before his paws ever hit the ground, was a dirty tan blur, which, crooked hips notwithstanding, literally flew around the apartment — seemingly a couple of feet off the ground and all the time looking frantically for an exit.

In the living room I had a modest Christmas tree. Granted, it was not a very big tree — he was not, at that time, a very big cat. Granted, too, that this tree had a respectable pile of gaily wrapped packages around the base and even an animal figure attached to the top. Granted even that it was festooned with lights which, at rhythmic intervals, flashed on and off. To any cat, however, a tree is a tree and this tree, crazed as he was, was no exception. With one bound he cleared the boxes, flashed up through the branches, the lights, and the light cord and managed, somewhere near the top, to disappear again. "Now that's a good cat," I heard myself stupidly saying. "You don't have to be frightened. Nothing bad is going to happen to you here."

Walking toward the tree, I reached for where I thought he would be next, but it was no use. With one bound, he vanished down the far side and, flashing by my flailing arms, tried to climb up the inside of the fireplace. Fortunately the flue was closed, thus effectively foiling his attempt at doing a Santa Claus in reverse.

When he reappeared, noticeably dirtier than before, I was waiting for him. "Good boy," I crooned, trying to sound my most reasonable. But it was no use. He was gone again, this time on a rapid rampage through the bedroom — one which was in fact so rapid that not only was it better heard than seen but also, during the worst of it, both Marian and I were terrified that he might try to go through the window. When he finally materialized again in the hall, even he looked somewhat discouraged. Maybe, I thought desperately, I could reason with him now. Slowly I backed into the living room to get a piece of cheese from the hors d'oeuvre tray. This, I was sure, would inform him that he was among friends and that no harm would befall him. Stepping back into the hall, I found Marian looking baffled. "He's gone," she said. "Gone," I said. "Gone where?" She shook her head and I suddenly realized that, for the first time in some time, there was no noise, there was no scurrying, there was no sound of any kind. There was, in fact, no cat.

We waited for a possible reappearance. When none was forthcoming, obviously we had no alternative but to start a systematic search. It is a comparatively small apartment and there are, or so Marian and I at first believed, relatively few hiding places. We were wrong. For one thing, there was a wall-long bookshelf in the living room, and this we could not overlook, for the cat was so thin and so fast that it was eminently feasible that he found a way to clamber up and wedge himself behind a stack of books on almost any shelf. Book by book, we began opening holes.

But he was not there. Indeed, he was not anywhere. We turned out three closets. We moved the bed. We wrestled the sofa away from the wall. We looked under the tables. We canvassed the kitchen. And here, although it is such a small kitchen that it can barely accommodate two normal-sized adults at the same time, we opened every cupboard, shoved back the stove, peered into the microwave, and even poked about in the tiny space under the sink.

At that moment, the doorbell rang. Marian and I looked at each other — it had to be my brother and his wife, Mary. My brother is one of only three men who went into World War II as a private and came out as a colonel in command of a combat division. He was, as a matter of fact, in the Amphibious Engineers, and made some fourteen opposed landings against the Japanese. He had also since served as deputy director of the CIA. A man obviously used to crises, he took one look at the disarray of the apartment. In such a situation, my brother doesn't talk, he barks. "Burglars," he barked. "It looks like a thorough job."

I explained to him briefly what was going on — and that the cat had now disappeared altogether. Not surprisingly, while Mary sat down, my brother immediately assumed command. He demanded to know where we had not looked. Only where he couldn't possibly go, I explained, trying to hold my ground. "I don't want theories," he barked. "Where *haven't* you looked?" Lamely, I named the very top shelves of the closet, the inside of the oven, and the dishwasher. "Right," he snapped, and advanced on first the closets, then the oven, and last the dishwasher. And, sure enough, at the bottom of the latter, actually curled around the machinery and wedged into the most impossible place to get to in the entire apartment, was the cat. "Ha!" said my brother, attempting to bend down and reach him.

I grabbed him from behind. I was not going to have my brother trust his luck with one more opposed landing. Bravely, I took his place. I was, after all, more expendable.

Actually, the fact was that none of us could get him out. And he was so far down in the machinery, even he couldn't get himself out. "Do you use it?" my brother demanded. I shook my head. "Dismantle it," he barked once more. Obediently, I searched for screwdriver, pliers, and hammer and, although I am not much of a mantler, I consider myself second to no one, not even my brother, as a dismantler. My progress, however, dissatisfied my brother. He brushed me aside and went over the top himself. I made no protest — with the dishwasher the Amphibious Engineer was, after all, at least close to being in his element.

When my brother had finished the job, all of us, Mary included, peered down at the cat. And, for the first time since my first sight of him in the alley, he peered back. He was so exhausted that he made no attempt to move, although he was now free to do so. "I would like to make a motion," Marian said quietly. "I move that we leave him right where he is, put out some food and water and a litter pan for him — and leave him be. What he needs now is peace and quiet."

The motion carried. We left out three bowls — of water, of milk, and of food — turned out all the lights, including the Christmas lights, and left him.

That night, when I got home, I tiptoed into the apartment. The three bowls were just where we had left them — and every one of them was empty. There was, however, no cat. But this time I initiated no search. I simply refilled the dishes and went to bed. With the help of a Sergeant, a colonel, and Marian, I now had, for better or for worse, for a few days at least, a Christmas cat.

II ◦ *The Decision*

I awoke early the next morning — the earliest I could remember since the Christmas mornings of my childhood. In those days my brother and sister and I were allowed whenever we woke up to open our stockings with their presents inside, all individually wrapped and dutifully stuffed by Santa Claus. It was one of the few times I envied my sister. She not only still believed in Santa Claus — my brother and I were under threat of receiving no stocking at all if we attempted to persuade her otherwise — but she was also given a grown-up girl's stocking that was more than twice as long as ours and thus held many more presents. Liberation came early to our family.

In any case, my standing Christmas morning record for those days was 4 A.M. On my first Christmas with the cat, I did not break that record, but I came pretty close. Nonetheless, I decided to get up immediately and conduct a search for him. But, as I sat sleepily up in bed, I saw immediately that there would be no need for this. For, only a few feet from my bed, standing in almost exactly the same position he was in the first time I ever saw him, and looking straight at me in almost exactly the same way, was the cat.

He had evidently been standing like that for some time, waiting for some signs of life from me. Now, seeing same, he spoke. "Aeiou," he said. "Ow yourself," I replied; "Merry Christmas." I reminded him that he was supposed to say "Meow." "Aeiou," he repeated. Obviously, he was not very good at consonants, but he was terrific at vowels.

As I got out of bed and walked close by him on my way to replenish his bowls, I noticed that he made no attempt to move away. Neither did he after he had finished eating and drinking. He just stood for a moment or two, licking and contemplating things. Then, slowly and solemnly, he began a tour of the apartment. When he went back into the bedroom, I followed him. In the corner, between the two windows, he paused and looked back at me. "Aeiou," he remarked once more. Obviously he wanted to get up on the windowsill and look out. And, equally obviously, this time he required some assistance, although the night before he had managed the same jump without any assistance — and at about thirty miles an hour.

I went over and lifted him. He looked around at me as I touched him but otherwise did nothing. Instead, after a moment, he continued his slow, solemn tour, this time of the windowsill. He spent some time looking down on the street below and out at the snow-covered Central Park.

Then he proceeded to jump across to the next window, which opens on a small balcony. This he regarded with such special interest that for some time he lay down, quietly moving his tail back and forth. He had, clearly, seen pigeons. Finally, he jumped down again and went back into the living room.

Once more I followed him and, for the very first time since I had seen him, he stretched out full length. Then he rolled over, put his head half under his shoulder and looked at me, meanwhile once again quietly moving his tail. Cats talk with their tails, and no cat ever expressed himself more clearly. "I'll take it," he was saying, in exactly the way a prospective new tenant, who had just made a complete tour of the premises, would agree to a lease. Satisfied, I went back to bed.

At about eight o'clock, the telephone rang. I could not believe anyone would call so early on Christmas morning. It was, as I might have guessed, Sergeant Dwork. "Merry Christmas," she said. "How's our cat?" "Fine," I replied, "just fine." I did my best to conceal the fact that, even at that stage of my life with the cat, I was not entirely happy with the "our." Apparently, I succeeded, because Sergeant Dwork went into high gear. "I've got great news," she said. "I have a woman who wants him."

"Terrific," I said. I did not, however, say this with enthusiasm, something Sergeant Dwork must have sensed, because she quickly added, "I know her and she'll give it a great home."

I told her I was sure she would. "But the thing is," Miss Dwork continued, "she wants it right away. She wants it as a Christmas present for her daughter. They lost their own, you know."

I didn't, of course, but I tried to mobilize, if not enthusiasm, at least acquiescence. When could they come and see it? Perhaps in the afternoon?

"Oh, no." Sergeant Dwork sounded shocked. "Not this afternoon. This morning. Right now. In fact, she's already on the way to your apartment. Her name, by the way, is Mrs. Wills."

"Whoa," I told her sternly. "Not so fast." I glanced to where the cat had settled himself at ease in the living room. "He's so dirty," I said, "and it seems so awful to move him again, just when he's beginning to . . ."

But Sergeant Dwork cut me off. "Nonsense," she said. "The sooner the better. If he makes himself too much at home with you — and you get too fond of him," and here a distinctly disturbing note crept into her voice, "well, it will be just that much harder for both of you when you do give him up. And, remember, you yourself admitted that a permanent animal made no sense at all for you, with the amount of time you're away and everything."

What she said, of course, did make sense, and I admitted as much. "Okay," I said, "I'll see Mrs. Wills. I'll call you afterward to let you know if she likes him."

As I hung up the phone, however, I could not look at the cat, although I could feel he was looking at me. Instead, I turned my head and looked out the window.

In short order, the doorbell rang. Mrs. Wills was a nice woman, but she was also a formidable one, and I am not at my best with formidable women early in the morning. Quickly I realized, however, that I was perhaps being unfair — one thing which made her seem so formidable was that she was carrying a large cat carrier.

"I'm sorry to be so early," she said briskly, as, in all senses of the phrase, she moved in, "but I wanted it for . . ."

"I know," I said, "for a Christmas present for your daughter." I turned to gesture toward the cat. But there was, of course, no cat.

"That's funny," I hedged. "He was here just a second ago." I looked around nervously. The thought of another search such as the one the night before and watched by Mrs. Wills had all the appeal of an IRS audit. Mrs. Wills looked around.

"Whatever happened in here?" she asked. "It looks as if you've been bombed. Did the cat . . . ?"

I had of course completely forgotten the total disarray of the apartment. "Oh the cat," I repeated, attempting a light laugh. "Oh no. It wasn't the cat. It was my brother. You see, my brother was here last night and we were looking for a book we couldn't find. My brother is a great reader, you know."

In explanations like that, one always adds one ridiculous note. Mrs. Wills' eyebrows rose slightly, as she surveyed the contents of the living room closet, which were still strewn across the foyer floor. "Hmmm," she said.

I asked her if I could get her some coffee. She shook her head. She obviously wanted only that for which she had come.

There was nothing to do but bite the bullet. "Here, boy," I boldly called, feeling not only idiotic, but knowing full well that the odds against his even being curious enough to acknowledge such a call, let alone come to it, especially with a stranger there, were astronomical. Nonetheless, I moved around the room, continuing my call while ostensibly straightening things but actually surreptitiously looking for him. Finally, just as Mrs. Wills had begun to tap her foot meaningfully, I maneuvered myself into the position I had first wanted to be in — i.e., pretending to straighten the rug by the sofa but actually looking underneath it. And there, sure enough, at the very back, against the wall, crouched and rigid, was the cat. "Oh!" I exclaimed, getting down on my hands and knees, "There he is! In his favorite place!"

Reluctantly, Mrs. Wills too assumed the position. "I can't see a thing," she complained. "Well," I volunteered, "I'll get a flashlight."

When I returned and shone the light upon him, his eyes glowed. The rest of him, however, had the look of a cornered hyena. "Oh," said Mrs. Wills. "Oh my. He's so wild-looking." "Oh, don't worry about that," I assured her. "He's just a little surprised."

"And he's so *dirty*," she went on. "Well," I answered stiffly, "remember, he's been a stray. On the street. He can be cleaned up in no time."

But the inspection was not finished yet. "Why is he crouched so crookedly like that?" she wanted to know. "Is there something wrong with him?"

"Oh that's nothing," I assured her. "He sometimes even stands like that. I'm sure it can be fixed. And anyway, remember, he's not really himself. He's nervous with both of us looking at him like this."

Mrs. Wills, however, was by now relentless. "There's something wrong with his mouth," she observed.

"He's got a cut," I replied. "A very little cut. Really just a tiny cut."

She maneuvered herself upwards and returned to her chair. "Oh dear," she said, as if talking to herself. "I really don't know. Now that I've seen him I'm really not sure.

I suppose I could try it. But Jennifer is just a little girl and this cat is going to take an awful lot of work."

I told her that I didn't think it would be that much. I had a suggestion for her. Why didn't she let me get him cleaned up and quieted down and then she could make her decision? I had in mind at least a couple of days.

The idea appealed to her — but not the timing. It had, apparently, to be a Christmas cat or no cat at all. She consulted her wristwatch. "I'll come back after church," she decided. "I'll leave the carrier here."

So, I reflected, that was that. I had at least tried to do what I thought would, in the long run, be the best thing for the cat. And while I realize that I could have acted a good deal more enthusiastic about the final outcome, the problem was that I just didn't feel very enthusiastic.

In any case, now there was nothing for it — Christmas morning or no Christmas morning — but to give him a bath. I went into the bathroom to procure soap and washcloths, over which I ran warm water, as well as a bath towel and even a bath mat.

When I returned to the living room, the cat was no longer under the sofa. He was back in the middle of the floor, just where, pre–Mrs. Wills, he had been before. It seemed to me that he understood exactly what the mat and the towel and all the rest of the paraphernalia were about, and knew exactly what I was about to do. But, at the same time, it also seemed that he simply could not believe I would do such a thing. His tail made an incredulous rat-tat. "Wash a cat!" he was exclaiming. "Boy, have I got my work cut out for me with this one!" He clearly felt that whatever my inexperience and limitations as a cat-keeper might be, surely even I would be familiar with the basics — and what could be more basic than the plain and simple fact that washing was his job, not mine?

He rose to his paws and looked up at me. I looked down at him. We were, in a sense, eyeball to eyeball — I at six feet three and he at six inches. Just the same, it was going to be, as it always is in such a confrontation, a question of who blinked first. And that would not, I had already determined, be me.

And it was not, really. All right, certain purists might cavil that I did not get right down to the job. They might even argue that I made a small blink. But they would be absolutely wrong and it would be utterly unfair to me to make any more of it than that. What actually happened is that, just at the moment when I was about to commence operations, and as his tail began to rat-tat ever more ominously, I suddenly decided, and quite on my own, having nothing to do with the fact that his back was slowly arching and he was making his ears flat, that it was entirely possible I didn't know enough about cat-washing, and should consult authorities.

Hastily, I laid down my washing materials, and repaired to the bookcase, where I had a whole shelf of books about cats. Like the other books, these were now in a state of sad disarray. Besides, I was looking for something very specific — not cats in general, but cat-washing. There were many references to the subject in the various book indexes, but as happens so often with thorny issues, there were also many disagreements. There were, in fact, two diametrically opposed schools of thought. One of these schools held that you should never, ever, wash a cat. The theory had it that not only do cats prefer to do the job themselves, but they also do it better than a human ever could, and furthermore, humans were likely to get soap in their eyes or in their fur, and this could be very bad for them. On the other hand, the other school believed that it was perfectly all right to wash your cat, and indeed was so essential that if you didn't, all sorts of bad things could happen to him.

I decided in view of the current situation, and weighing all the factors, to adhere to Theory Number Two, and thumbed through the books until I found one, entitled simply *You and Your Cat,* which seemed the most definitive on the subject. It was written by an English veterinarian, David Taylor, and, with high optimism, I began to read:

> The kitchen sink will probably make the best "bath." Before you start, make sure all the doors and windows are closed and that the room is free from cold drafts. Place a rubber mat in the sink to stop the cat from slipping.

So far, I decided, so good. The next paragraph, however, was another story:

> If you think your cat is going to struggle, put it in a cotton sack, leaving only its head visible. Pour the shampoo into the sack and lower the cat and sack into the water. You can then massage the cat through the sack and form a lather.

Put the cat in a sack! Maybe, I thought, my brother and his regiment could achieve that objective, but that I alone could do so was highly doubtful. True, the cat was quiet that morning, but remembering the whirlwind of the night before, and not being an Amphibious Engineer myself, I foresaw the possibility of something on the order of, if not Gallipoli, at least Dunkirk.

Nothing, however, stopped the aquatic advance of Dr. Taylor:

> Fill the sink with about 2–4 ins. of warm water. The water temperature should be as close to your cat's body heat of 101.4 F as possible. To lift the cat in, put one hand under its hind quarters and hold the scruff of its neck with the other. If your cat prefers, allow it to rest its front paws out of the water.

I was sure that the cat in question would not only so prefer, but would also seize the first opportunity to have a go with those paws at the alleged perpetrator of any such proposed ablutions. In any case, I had had enough. I replaced the book, went back to the cat, gathered up my materials, and with all the authority I could muster, spread the bath mat down beside him.

To my amazement, he promptly stepped over and stood upon it. Although I had taken the precaution of remaining standing for, if need be, a fast getaway, I soon realized that I had underestimated him. He had, apparently, made his point, but he had no intention of being churlish about it. If I was going to be fool enough to do somebody else's work — i.e., his — well then, so be it.

I could not resist him any longer. I knelt down beside him, took him in my arms and, ignoring how dirty he was, gave him a hug. I hugged so long that he let out a small and surprised-sounding "aeiou," but other than that, he did nothing. I'm sure it was the first hug, or sign of human affection, he had had for a very long time, if indeed ever in his life. After that, I began his bath and, without a sound or a hiss or a single pullback, he let me wash away to my heart's content — first gently and then, as I went through literally layers of dirt, harder and harder.

In good time, having made several trips to the bathroom to rinse out the cloths, I had scrubbed enough to make a startling discovery. Underneath all the dirt he was neither tan nor gray, the two colors which I had fully expected. He was, instead, white.

I could hardly contain my excitement — at which the now much cleaner tail for the first time in the operation, moved. "What color did you expect?" it was inquiring. "Purple?" Almost in spite of myself, I heard myself answer him. "But you were so *dirty,*" I protested. "White was the last color I expected."

After I had him reasonably presentable, at least for a first effort, and had towelled him dry, I stood up and inspected him. His green eyes with his by now relatively clean and pure white face made him look, for the first time, beautiful. Indeed to me, at that moment, he looked so beautiful that I had an urge simply to stare. I knew that few animals liked to be stared at, and that when a human being did so, they usually looked away. But he did not look away. He looked steadily back at me. Once more I bent and hugged him.

When the doorbell rang again, it was, of course, Mrs. Wills. But when I ushered her into the living room to review the subject at hand, the subject was, once again, not at hand. He had repaired, as usual, to his prepared position.

I handed her the flashlight. By now Mrs. Wills had grown accustomed to getting down on her hands and knees as part of the inspection tour, and she gamely turned on the flashlight and pushed her head under the sofa. "My God," she exclaimed suddenly, "he's white." Her head turned to me suspiciously. "Are you sure," she demanded, "that this is the same cat?" I assured her that it was, and indicated the pile of washcloths and towels lying on the hearth as proof. "I can't believe it," she said.

"It was nothing," I shrugged. "Just a matter of know-how and stick-to-itiveness. But you were right, Mrs. Wills. White cats do take an awful lot of work."

Mrs. Wills paid no attention. Instead, she was entirely concerned with making contact under the sofa. "Here, kitty, kitty," she called. She called it again — in fact, she called everything but kitchy-koo. Naturally, nothing worked. Mrs. Wills reached. The cat moved. Mrs. Wills reached again. The cat moved again. This stylized duet went on for some moments. Then Mrs. Wills pulled herself up and went over and sat down in a chair. She chose one, I noticed, directly across from the sofa. I sat down beside her.

"I've never had an animal in my life react to me like that," she said. "I've never even met one who wouldn't meet me halfway. I've always had a way with animals."

I told her that was just the trouble; he thought that she was going to take him away. Mrs. Wills ignored my bad pun. "I've never," she said firmly, "seen any animal *that* shy."

Once, I offered, I had had a schoolmaster who told us there was no such thing as being shy. He said that being shy was just being conceited, that you thought everybody was looking at you and thinking about you and of course they weren't.

Mrs. Wills now looked at me as if I had two heads. But she was still clearly considering the cat. "He's so pretty," she said. "Jennifer would love him."

It was time to pull out all the stops. Of course, I said, it might not be just shyness — you really never could tell.

But on the other hand, it might be something else. I reminded her that white cats were, after all, albinos — and often deaf.

"Deaf!" she exclaimed. "You mean maybe he can't hear me calling?"

I told her that it was entirely possible — perhaps he could not.

For the first time Mrs. Wills looked doubtful. "I don't really know much about white cats," she said.

I moved in swiftly.

"It's not just the deafness," I told her; "it's the skin problems, too. White cats, you know, can have terrible skin trouble."

Now she looked positively uncomfortable. "Well," I went on relentlessly, "I'm sure it's not contagious. How old is Jennifer?"

"Ten," she replied worriedly.

"Well, I suppose she could wear gloves," I suggested. "Of course, skin problems can make a cat edgy. Fortunately, he isn't very large. But he certainly can be fierce. And he sure can swipe." I indicated the scratches on face and neck. "He really got me one awful one. Fortunately, he didn't get near my eyes. Does Jennifer wear glasses?"

Mrs. Wills' own eyes were now riveted on me. "It was nothing, of course," I said, "and Ruth Dwork was quick at staunching the blood." I paused. "Just the same, I don't think it would be wise, at least in the beginning, to leave Jennifer alone with him."

She looked back down at the bottom of the sofa. "But anyway," I went on, "he'll probably be at the vet most of the first several months anyway. You were so right about that crooked way he stands. He'll need at least one operation, for sure."

Mrs. Wills said nothing for a long while. Then a smile slowly started across her face. "Mr. Amory," she asked, "are you planning to keep this cat yourself?"

It was my turn to smile. "Why, Mrs. Wills," I said, "whatever gave you that idea?"

She got up and picked up the cat carrier. "A little bird told me," she said. I started to apologize for her trouble in having to come to the apartment twice. "Don't," she said. "And don't call Ruth Dwork. I want the fun of telling her how it all happened." She paused a last time. "I wish you all the luck in the world with your cat." She grinned and got in a last jab. "From what you've just told me about him," she said, "you're going to need it. Merry Christmas."

It was by now close to lunchtime and I had an engagement. When I went back to say good-bye to the cat, however, I was spared the under-the-sofa routine. He was once more in the middle of the living room. On the spur of the moment, there and then, I decided it was time to initiate our first real man-to-cat talk. I told him that I had been for some time a bachelor. And aside from having an occasional stray animal for a short period, I had lived alone. At the same time, I realized that he had lived in the — I put it as inoffensively as I could — well, wild and was thus used to fending for himself and in a sense living alone too. We were both used to making our own decisions. But now if we were going to live together in any degree of harmony, there would have to be compromises on both sides.

I, for example, would have to learn that he had his needs and I would have to learn to distinguish when he wanted company and when he wanted to be alone. And,

I continued, he would have to understand the same things about me. There could be and should be, I said, give-and-take on both sides in almost all matters. But in matters where there was disagreement and a resolution would have to be made, there could only be one person to make it. And that person would be me.

At this his tail, which had begun a slow movement, suddenly began to move faster. It was my first encounter with expecting agreement from him and getting instead not disagreement but something curiously in-between. He was obviously considering it all but by no means entirely going along with it. I had no idea what was going on in his mind but somehow it seemed to me that what I was saying was so complicated that it was something he would have to take up in committee. And his idea of committee was first to look away and then to yawn and finally to start washing himself. The signs were unmistakable. That while his committee might be in session — indeed while it might at that very moment be taking the matter under advisement — in no case was it about to be rushed into a hasty decision.

Suddenly it seemed to me essential for our future that I not allow myself to be bogged down by his kind of bureaucracy. Sternly I told him that he might as well understand now and for once and for all something else. That bachelors have a reputation for being — and I emphasized this strongly — Very Set In Their Ways.

This time the answer, together with the tail rat-tat, came instantly. So, he was replying, with exactly the same emphasis, Are Cats.

The conflict was begun — and the issue joined.

III ◦ *The Great Compromise*

Some years ago the distinguished English author Aldous Huxley wrote a brief essay which he began as follows:

> I met, not long ago, a young man who aspired to become a novelist. Knowing that I was in the profession, he asked me to tell him how he should set to work to realize his ambition. I did my best to explain. "The first thing," I said, "is to buy quite a lot of paper, a bottle of ink, and a pen. After that you merely have to write."
>
> But this was not enough for my young friend. He seemed to have a notion that there was some sort of esoteric cookery book, full of literary recipes, which you had only to follow attentively to become a Dickens, a Henry James, a Flaubert. . . .
>
> . . . Did I keep a notebook or a daily journal? Did

I systematically frequent the drawing rooms of the rich and fashionable? Or did I, on thc contrary, inhabit the Sussex downs? Or spend my evenings looking for "copy" in East End gin-palaces? . . .

And so on. I did my best to reply to these questions — as non-committitally, of course, as I could. And as the young man still looked rather disappointed, I volunteered a final piece of advice, gratuitously. "My young friend," I said, "if you want to be a psychological novelist and write about human beings, the best thing you can do is to keep a pair of cats." And with that I left him.

If I had read this essay before I had rescued my cat, I would probably have thought that Mr. Huxley had gonc around the bend. By Christmas night with my new cat, however, I no longer thought so — specifically from the time, that very second night I had him, when, just before I had gone to sleep, he had suddenly jumped up on the bed, marched solemnly up to my head, and then stretched out by the back of my neck. After that, I was in no condition to make any judgments about Mr. Huxley. If he was around thc bend, I was most assuredly all the way up the river.

And, when I had the chance, I eagerly devoured the rest of Mr. Huxley's essay — one which bore the intriguing title "Sermon in Cats." In it, Mr. Huxley went on to give the young man specific instructions. He was, for example, to procure the "tailed variety" of cat — indeed, the man was firmly warned against getting himself a pair of Manx cats and thus, presumably, making his study more difficult. "The tail in cats," Mr. Huxley declared, "is the principal organ of emotional expression." The author also counselled his student not only to watch his cats "living from day to day" but also to do more than this — "to mark, learn and inwardly digest the lessons about human nature which they teach."

In any case, whether it was because, consciously or unconsciously, I was following Mr. Huxley's advice, or simply because I enjoyed what I was doing, the fact was that, in the first days after I had rescued my cat, I spent a great deal of time just looking at him. I even did so, indeed I particularly did so, when he was sleeping. These were the best times, I found, for wondering what his life had been. All cats sleep an amazing amount — close to three-quarters of the time, I would estimate, counting, of course, the kind of nap which they have made famous. But he slept those first days even more than three-quarters of the time — clearly to compensate for the many hours he must have had to stay awake and alert during his previous life. I also presumed that he was sleeping more now because he was now happy. I was already a firm believer in the theory that one of the ways in which cats show happiness is by sleeping.

During his sleep he was obviously some of the time dreaming. In these dreams, he would twitch, often gently but at other times violently, both front and back paws moving — sometimes indeed so violently that he woke himself. At such times, during these sudden wake-ups, he would be alert very quickly. Then, after a brief look around and a casing of all fronts, he would do a definite double-take. Finally, after satisfying himself that the waking, not the dream, the present, not the past, was the reality, he would blow out a little sigh — he never really heaved one — and immediately go back to sleep.

I have read a great deal about what animals dream, but

none of it has ever really satisfied me. I believe they dream exactly the way we dream, and about everything in their lives — that they have good dreams and bad dreams in almost direct proportion, as we do, to whether their lives have been more good than bad. Unfortunately, because the majority of animals have it so much tougher than we do, I believe that the majority of dreams, except in the most fortunate petdom, are bad.

Nor do I believe, as I have also read, that, because animals have shorter memories than we do, they do not remember things as well. In the first place, I do not think they have shorter memories than we do — I think they have, if anything, longer ones. And, in the second place, I think they remember their dreams just as well as we do, and perhaps even better. I, for example, am a terrible dream-rememberer. If I don't concentrate on what I've been dreaming the moment I wake up, it is a very rare dream indeed that gets remembered past breakfast. On the other hand, I can tell by the manner in which my cat assumes his thinker position — front paws under him, head looking straight ahead, but eyes half shut — that he can certainly remember his dreams long after breakfast. And the only reason he is not thinking about them before breakfast is that, at that time, he is just thinking about breakfast. His thought process is very orderly.

As to what he dreamed about in those early days, I can easily imagine. To begin with, I knew from his teeth and other indicators that he was about two years of age when I rescued him. I was also fairly certain, from his cuts and bruises, his paper-thinness and generally poor condition, that he had been on the street if not all his short life, at least for most of it. But how long had he led a solitary life, the way he was when I found him? Surely he must have some time before been with other cats, at least back when he himself was a kitten? Or had he been someone's pet and perhaps gotten out and gotten lost and become a stray? Or had he perhaps been abandoned deliberately and, in that awful phrase, "gotten rid of"? These were all questions to which I would never know the answer.

Of some things, on the other hand, I could be fairly certain. One was that he had never been in a pound. There are only two ways out for animals at pounds — being adopted or being killed. And cats have such a low rate of adoption that many pounds, even in some large cities, don't bother to take them in at all. Not for nothing is it always the "dog pound" and never the "cat pound." And even at the best shelters, the adoption rate for cats is sadly low.

On the street, as strays, it is true that cats have certain advantages over dogs. They are quicker and can get away from trouble faster. They are smarter about locating hide-aways, and, being smaller, can fit into them less visibly. They can also forage for food more adeptly and, when they find it, have far better sense about what will and will not make them sick.

But here the advantages end and the disadvantages begin. Cats are notably clean animals and are sensitive, even fastidious, about their surroundings. A life in dirt and noise and confusion is hard on them. And, in this street life, they have a far more difficult time defending themselves. Stray cats, like stray dogs, often band together for safety, but being more individually territorial, they are more inclined than dogs to fight among themselves. Also, unlike dogs, although they may hide together, they almost never run in packs or actually fight together against common enemies. And these enemies, after all, include for them not only all the enemies dogs have but, for them, the dogs as well.

Then too, although as many people like cats as like dogs, there are far more people who don't like cats than who don't like dogs. There is no one go-away word for dogs as there is for cats — that curious expletive "scat!" There is some prejudice against dogs among non-animal people, but the prejudice against cats runs much more deeply. Some children tie tin cans and firecrackers to dogs' tails, it is unhappily true, but they only go so far for fear of being bitten. A cornered cat, however, is not regarded as dangerous and is considered fair game. Even kittens are not immune from such sport. By no means the worst of their torments, albeit it is probably the most stupid, is being picked up and dropped from heights to see if they really do always land on their feet.

Besides the fact that he had been thrown at and hit with things and had been severely cut, what else, I kept wondering, had been done to him? I found myself thinking of a film I had seen many years ago about a day in the life of a stray cat. The film had been made by the Pasadena Humane Society, and I have always remembered one scene — shot at cat's-eye level. It was of the cat trying at night to cross a California freeway. He was looking for any possible way to get across all those lanes — in the midst of all the screaming noise, the blinding headlights, the whizzing cars, and the monster trucks.

The film made you wish that we all, at one time in our life, would have to get down — really lie down — to the eye level of a small animal and have to look at the world from that perspective, to see how huge everything is and how terrifying. I even allowed myself to think about how enormous I must have seemed to my cat on that very first night when I rose to my feet and stuffed him in my coat.

His attitude toward me in those first days was fascinating. He showed me over and over, not just by happy tail talk, but, even more definitely, by delicate brushing against my legs, that he was, and apparently always would be, extremely grateful that I had effected his rescue. But at the same time he showed me in various other ways — by disappearances and actual yowlings if I had left him alone for too long — that the gratitude he felt toward me should in no way be construed by me as having anything to do with what was, to him, becoming every day more painfully obvious — that I had an incredible amount to learn about the art of living with him in any sort of civilized manner.

As anyone who has ever been around a cat for any length of time well knows, cats have enormous patience with the limitations of the human mind. They realize that, whether they like it or not, they are simply going to have to put up with what to them are excruciatingly slow mental processes, that we humans have embarrassingly low I.Q.'s, and that probably because of these defects, we have an infuriating inability to understand, let alone follow, even the simplest and most explicit of directions.

As if this weren't enough for them to cope with, they must also deal with what, for them, is almost equally frustrating — our tremendous physical shortcomings. The fact is that, to cats, we humans are, for all our grotesque size, unbelievably slow and clumsy. We are totally incapable of managing a good leap or jump or pounce or swipe or, indeed, almost any other simple maneuver which, at the very least, would make us passable fun to play with. It is not difficult to see how they arrive at these conclusions. Any self-respecting cat can, for example, leap with ease, from a standing start, to the mantelpiece — a leap some seven times or more his height. And yet the human record for the high jump, for pity sakes, for which we get a running start, is barely twice our height. Furthermore, since cats see at eye level so much of where this puny power of ours comes from — our ankles — they are obviously not averse to comparing our ankles with their own dainty and tiny-tendoned back legs.

Carrying this thought a step further, is it not possible that cats equate our pathetic slowness afoot with our slowness amind? If we are so handicapped physically, in other words, how could we expect it not to affect us mentally? Whether it does or not, they seem to realize, early on, that their task of training us is not going to be an easy one and can only be accomplished with extraordinary resolution and dedication on their part. They sense that it is absolutely essential for them to seize every opportunity for education and correction. Otherwise, as befitting our slothful natures, we will slip back immediately into our most incorrigible old habits. Their job in this regard is something, I'm told, like a wife's. The fact that I have been repeatedly told it, as well as the fact that, as I have said, I am a fairly recent bachelor, is something on which I am much given to speculation.

Not to put too fine a point on the matter, the fact also is that, having always had dogs myself, I had long held the theory that, in general, men prefer dogs and women prefer cats. I had even, pre-cat, defended this position with what I had always considered unassailable logic — male, of course.

To begin with, I started with such a basic as the cat's use of the litter pan. To women, this was proof positive of the advantage of the feline over the canine — not to mention that it obviates the necessity of a walk in inclement weather and ruining their hair. To men, on the other hand, it was something one knew about cats, but hardly more than that. Indeed, I had taken it for granted that my cat would, as he did, use his litter pan the very first night I had him. I did not even consider that the makeshift version, filled with torn-up newspaper, which Marian and I had contrived, may well have been the first one he had ever seen.

Besides this there is, for women, the added lure of the ability of the cat — something which is totally beyond the powers of the dog — not only to be able to clean himself, but also to want to do so and, in fact, do so repeatedly. To women, many of whom I have known who prefer a bath to any other engagement they can think of, and, indeed, give it precedence over any other — this appeal is irresistible.

But integral as were all these points to my theory, they were still relatively minor surface issues. The cutting edge of my theory and the crux of my logic involved something far more important. This was that the main reason women preferred cats over dogs was that they identified with, and much more strongly than men appreciated, the cat's independence. And that they did this because, up until fairly recently, at least, they had so little of it themselves.

Men, on the other hand, not only did not appreciate the cat's independence, they thoroughly detested it. Indeed, they immeasurably preferred the image of the devoted dog curled at their feet, the faithful companion who would obey without question his master's slightest whim, who would accompany him anywhere — at a walk, a jog, or even a run — and who would, above all, come when he was called no matter what he was doing, even if he were chasing a cat.

The fact that the cat, in contrast, would not even acknowledge the simplest command, let alone deign to obey it, and would seldom, if ever, come when called, even if doing nothing else — all this to men was not only disturbing, it also could mean only one of two things. Either the cat did not love them or, worse, the cat was part and parcel of the kind of revolution which, in the end, would result not only in anarchy in the street but right in their home and hearth.

I had, as I say, long held this theory. But, all of about twenty-four hours after I had had my cat, I was suddenly not so sure. And, if there's one thing I do not like to be, it is to be made suddenly less sure of something which, only a matter of hours before, I have been absolutely sure. In any case, I decided that I owed it to my cat to make a clean breast of it — at least to let him know, pre-him, where I was coming from.

Curiously, at about the same time as I made that decision, my cat, already constantly on the alert for opportunities to educate and, if need be, correct me, was coming to a decision of his own. We were on collision course.

The matter came to a head the day after Christmas. It came about, as a matter of fact, because of a present Marian had brought back to him on Christmas night — a yarn ball which she had brought over from the pile of presents given to our office cats. Although he had undoubtedly played with many things in his young life, I could tell right away from the way he went at that ball that he had never had a real toy before.

All that evening he batted it and bit it and tossed it and squashed it — and, of course, lost it. And, after he had done this, it was clearly up to me to get it back for him, even though I had the feeling he knew perfectly well where it was and even when this place was somewhere under the sofa, from which he could have retrieved it far more easily than I.

It was on approximately my eighth service as golden retriever that I conceived the first of my masterly notions on how to train him. I had once read an article by a man who had apparently trained many cats and remembered that the man had counselled, among other things, that with cats, in preference to the dog commands of "Sit," "Lie Down," and "Play Dead," the roommate of a cat should use "Sit," "Flop," and "Sleep." And also that, even with these changes, it was sometimes necessary to give what the man suggested was a "slight touch." Armed with this information and also with the determination to turn our play period into not just play but into a learning experience — something which gave me the good feeling that I was in the forefront of modern educational theory — this time, when I brought the ball back, instead of throwing it to him I threw it a little way from him. "Go get it," I told him earnestly. "Fetch." To which I not only added the masterly "slight touch," which in this case was a slight push, but also at the same time patted my leg. My meaning was crystal clear. He was to go and get the ball and bring it back to me.

His answer to this plan — one which was designed both to con him into being the one to do the retrieving and at at the same time to establish a clearly defined chain of command — was disconcerting. Instead of, for a single moment, entertaining the slightest idea of actually doing what I wanted, he had obviously and instantly decided to turn my whole master plan into a learning experience, all right — but one, equally obviously, not for him but for me.

First he sat down and looked at the ball and then sternly at me. He thumped his tail slowly, not once but twice. Cats, he was patiently but firmly trying to get into my head, do not fetch, or retrieve, or do any of those other unbelievably undignified things which might, in fact, be done by other animals whose name he obviously preferred not to mention in the present company.

I must have looked completely taken aback because, as he kept his green eyes fixed on me, his tail tone seemed to gentle just a little. And, he went on, in what was nonetheless a more patient manner, it was up to me to understand that it was not that cats did not like games. They did indeed enjoy games and as a matter of fact put more into their games and got more out of them than any of those selfsame animals he had declined to mention before. However, these games must be games that *they* wanted to play, and must be games initiated by them — after which, of course, if the pace of action could be improved or perhaps speeded up by the enlistment of outsiders (here he clearly meant me and my ability to get down on my knees and reach under things) — well, that, of course, could be considered. But it could only be considered on that basis, and in that order and never — and here the tail beat a final rat-tat — the other way around.

Obviously, it was time for another of our man-to-cat talks. "Come here," I told him. "Come," I repeated, lest there be any mistake.

This time he looked at me as if it was not possible for him to have heard what he thought he had heard. Even allowing for my obviously brief attention span, to have talked about fetching and retrieving and then, almost in the next breath, to have uttered this "Come" — it was really much too much. He was clearly working with a person who, in the words of the wise old saw, was not playing with a full deck. He was a tolerant cat, and he would do what he could to improve my behavior patterns. And, just to avoid any possibility of misunderstanding, he would ask me one more time what I had said. But that, his tail warned, would be that.

I told him that it was indeed what I had said. And, I went on, as far as I was concerned, the only question now before the house was — would he do it?

Cats do not shake their heads. They do not need to. They do, however, shake their tails, and this he did, with what I can only describe as finality. Cats, he was clearly saying, do not come when called. Aha, I said. *Never?* What about when it was something they wanted — like dinner?

He visibly sighed. That, he was trying to explain to me, was an entirely different matter. And, as usual, I was bringing up a total irrelevance. If there was going to be any purpose whatsoever in our discussion, would I please stay on track?

It was my turn to sigh. Without for a moment conceding that dinner had nothing to do with the case, could he forget that for a moment and simply answer one single question. Why would he not come?

This time his answer could not have been clearer if he had said it in words. It was, he implied, the principle of the thing.

This was, to me, the final straw. Principle my foot, I said, knowing full well that he is not particularly fond of feet. I told him I had known many cats in my life, and, whether he liked it or not — indeed, whether he liked them or not — I had also known a very great many of that other animal which he did not care to name. And, I concluded firmly, the kind of animal I liked best was the kind to whom, when you said a simple thing like come — well, came.

To this he said nothing for some time. Indeed, it was such a length of time that I seriously considered that I had done permanent damage to our relationship or, much more probably, he was simply mulling over the horror of a person like myself having had to spend such a large segment of my life in the company of what he clearly regarded as a lesser species. In any case, I was soon faced with the end of our discussion, and what amounted to an ultimatum. Gracefully and lazily, he rose, walked past the ball, and settled down again on the far side of the room. Cats, he said, as distinctly as I ever heard him say anything, Do Not Come.

It was my turn to be patient. All right, I told him. It seemed to me that we were, once more, in an area of compromise. After all, if, through no real fault of my own, I had happened to have spent a large portion of my time with a subspecies which had resulted in my developing certain mind-sets and attitudes, and if, as a result of those said mind-sets and attitudes I was more comfortable with a friend who, when I said, "Come," well, came, wouldn't it be possible for him to realize the stress it visited on me to have to change those mind-sets and attitudes virtually overnight? And wouldn't it be possible for him, with that recognition, to make an occasional concession to my limited mental state and when I said, "Come" to — well, once again . . .

He yawned and started to take a bath. Obviously, our discussion was at an end, and the matter had gone to committee. Equally obviously, a decision would not be immediately forthcoming. Indeed, from the lack of vigor with which he was pursuing his bath, the committee was undoubtedly going to be in session all night.

As things turned out, I never did get a clear-cut decision. I did, however, come away with a compromise.

The way we worked it out was that I was never to say, "Come" or "Come here" or anything like that. Along with this, I was never, when I wanted him to come, to do anything to offend his sensibilities, such as slapping my knee, clapping my hands, whistling, or making clucking noises with my teeth. However, I would be permitted more subtle indications that his presence was requested — such as directing an inquiry to the world at large, or asking the room in general, where he was.

For his part, he agreed when he heard such general inquiries, not totally to ignore them. On the contrary, after a suitable period of time had elapsed — one long enough so that it could be clearly construed to be a moot point as to whether it was his decision or mine — he would, in a dignified and orderly manner, proceed in my direction.

In this way, and to the world at large, it would be clear that he had not failed his hallowed ancestors, who had fought so long and so gloriously the sacred fight for independence. He had not abdicated his responsibilities and he had not turned in either his badge or his union card as a cat. Nor had he defected, or become a mole. All he had done, in the interests of the pursuit of happiness, to insure domestic tranquility and to preserve a more perfect union for both of us, was to allow this previously seriously disadvantaged person to consider a small part of him — a very, very small part, to be sure — to be something like the animal which he did not care to dignify by mentioning by name. But it was to be completely understood, and indeed an integral part of our agreement, that the matter was now to be considered settled, for once and for all, and was never to be brought up for discussion again.

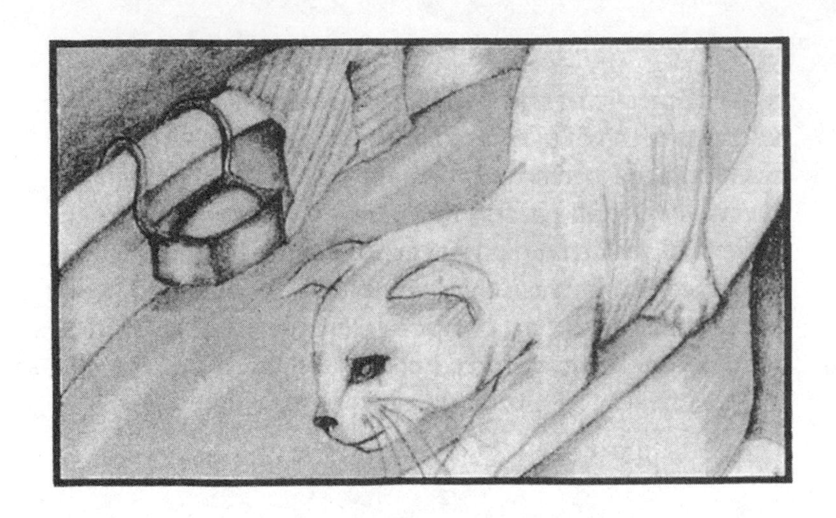

IV ◦ *His First Trip*

In my Society writing days I once wrote a story about the late Mrs. E. T. Stotesbury, premier hostess of Palm Beach, who one day went to meet her husband, who had been on an extended European vacation. Mrs. Stotesbury had used the time he was away to have extensive work done on their Palm Beach castle, and she had somehow neglected to inform Mr. Stotesbury of the magnitude of this. But it was now obviously necessary to do so, and thus, just before entering the driveway, she broke, in her own way, the news.

"E. T.," she said, turning to her husband, "I have a surprise for you." Warily, Mr. Stotesbury turned and looked at his wife.

"Eva," he said, "husbands do not like surprises."

Somehow that story reminded me of my cat. For, in

this respect, cats are more like husbands than wives. They too do not like surprises.

Cats do, however, like routine — in fact they love it. And, in the days — and nights — which followed the rescue my cat and I worked out many routines. Or rather he worked them out, and I, as dutifully as I could, worked at following them.

Some of these routines necessarily involved compromises. My cat, for example, liked to get up early — in fact he liked to get up at 3 A.M. That was, of course, all right with me. His hours, it had been one of our understandings, were his own. The trouble was that, at 3 A.M., he liked a midnight snack of Tender Vittles. Again, seemingly, no problem. Simply leave out a bowl of Vittles before he went to bed.

But unfortunately there was a problem. I could not just leave out a bowl of Vittles before I went to bed. He would eat them before he went to bed. He did not have, when you came right down to it, either any good old-fashioned Boston discipline — as I would have thought he would have at least begun to learn from me — or, for that matter, my good sound sensible Boston foresight. No matter how large a bowl I filled of Vittles before he retired, the bowl was empty before he retired.

His hours in this routine thus became my hours. And so we compromised. Before going to bed each night, I put out an empty dish on the floor by the bed and a package of Tender Vittles on my bedside table. At 3 A.M. — and he was extraordinarily accurate about this — he would wake up, roll over, and wake me up. At 3:01 I would roll over, put some Vittles in his dish, or at least reasonably near it, and go back, or at least attempt to go back, to sleep.

In the real morning we had to have another compromise. This one was about water. Actually it is a fallacy to think all cats hate water. As a matter of fact, most large cats love water. A British friend of mine, John Aspinall, who has a privately owned animal park near Canterbury, had, in this park, both tigers and also a swimming pool. The tigers on hot days regularly took dips in the pool and often, when they wanted more company, would come up to John's front door, scratch, and give a tiger's version of a miaow — after which John would hastily don his swimming trunks, open the door, and then they would all make a beeline for the pool. Normally the tigers just went into the water any old way, but as time went on and they observed John diving off the board, they too would get up on the board and do their version of John's swan dive.

Small cats too are not averse to water, at least on hot days. Another friend of mine, Marti Scholl, a former New York model who had a television show in Las Vegas, used to take her two cats out with her to her swimming pool. One particularly hot day, after she had taken a dip, she detected what she thought was unusual interest in the proceedings from her cats. Without further ado, she took one cat under each arm and walked from the steps end of the pool out to where they were just above the water. Then, little by little, just as you would teach a child to swim, keeping one hand under them at first, she placed them in the water. In no time at all they were swimming away from her, back and forth to their hearts' content. Indeed, after just a couple of lessons, they were soloing — swimming the whole length of the pool up and back.

My cat was by no means as into this scene as were the cats of Mr. Aspinall or Ms. Scholl. At the same time, neither did he actively dislike all water. He just disliked vertical water — as in rain or shower baths. He did not mind it coming down in small quantities as out of a faucet — in fact he was very fond of it that way. But it had to be small quantities. If it was to be in large quantities, then he firmly insisted on his water being horizontal. This he was especially fond of when I was in it — as in a regular tub bath. He did not like the shower at any time, whether I was in it or not.

So, again, we compromised. Although I had always taken showers, I gave up showers and took tubs instead. Baths, I decided, really get you much cleaner than showers do anyway. Also, whether this was true or not, I very much liked the additional routine which he had developed, and which I had followed, which went with the bath. What he would do, once I was in the tub, was to jump up on the edge of the tub — a precarious leap, considering his game hip — balance himself, and then make a slow solemn trip around. He would start first toward the back of the tub, stopping at each point when he got to my shoulders. Here he would lean toward me, give me a head nudge and a small nip, and then proceed on. When he got to the business end of the tub, he would carefully investigate the spout, and, if I had not turned it on just enough for him to drink a few drops, he would turn and tell me to do so. And, of course, I would.

I enjoyed our bath routine as much as any we did. One day, however, I read an article in, I think, *Cat Fancy* magazine, in which a woman wrote that one of the most charming things her cat did was to take a bath with her. She then proceeded to tell the story of her baths with her cat and tell it almost exactly as I have — even including the nudge and nip of the shoulder and neck and also the investigation of, and drinking from, the spout.

At first, thinking my cat and my cat only had ever done such a wonderful thing, I was extremely annoyed by the article. Nonetheless, on second thought, I consoled myself by thinking that if there were only two cats in the world who ever did it, my cat and that writer's cat, then it wasn't really too bad. And, after all, that writer had at least thought it was remarkable enough to write an article about it.

I still did have, however, a gnawing doubt — enough so that one day I approached a cat friend of mine and asked her right out if she had ever taken a bath with her cat. "Oh, yes," she at once replied, "and you know, when we're taking a bath together, he does the cutest thing. He jumps . . ."

I know, I said, sternly stopping her, so does mine. There were now, I thought, not just two but three, and how many others? Perhaps, I harbored the sneaking suspicion, there were hundreds of thousands of cats out there who all did it, and had been doing it for hundreds of years or at least ever since bathtubs were invented. For all I knew it had gone out over the cat grapevine that, if you do the bath thing, humans are so dumb they will think you're the only cat who does it. Perhaps the grapevine might even have added that even if humans don't think you're the only one who does it, and you do it in the morning, it's bound to put them in such a good mood that at the very least you'll be assured a bigger and better breakfast.

It was, I decided, not something on which I wished to dwell. Speaking of breakfast, however, I want to make clear that my cat and I did not have, by any stretch of the imagination, your normal morning repast. Indeed, perhaps the most remarkable of all the routines which we developed was here involved. For the plain fact of the matter is that, before its development anywhere else, and long before its adoption by the upper echelons of big business, my cat and I pioneered, all by ourselves, the power breakfast.

This too began with a compromise. My cat was very fond of breakfast, and, after he had eaten his, he was very fond of eating mine too. In vain I remonstrated with him that he was being selfish and inconsiderate. In vain also I lectured him that I had been brought up in a home where animals were not allowed in the dining room at any time, even when no meals were being served. As for his habit, without so much as a by my leave, of getting up on the table and taking a bite here and a bite there, of anything he pleased, from cereal to eggs or whatever, it would have to stop. It simply could not or would not be tolerated by me, and that was that.

So, once more, we compromised. I agreed to let him up on the table if no other guests were present, and he in turn agreed not to eat anything at the same time I was eating it. The gray area in this compromise was the question of when I had my spoon or fork in my mouth, and he was not sure whether or not it was going back to where it came from or was finished: whose turn, then, was it — his or mine? Eventually we worked this out — if the spoon was still in motion, it was still my turn; if it wasn't, it was his.

All in all, it was a power breakfast all right, and a great deal was accomplished. For one thing, when I was late and/or he was particularly hungry, I am sure we several times broke the standing Guinness record, and possibly the Olympic as well, for a single breakfast totally consumed by two partners.

It was, as a matter of fact, at one of these power breakfasts, when I got well ahead of him, that I noticed, for the first time close up, that his hip was still not well. The cut on his mouth had healed nicely, and his hip was some better, but it was by no means perfect. It was, in other words, high time that I took him to the vet. I had purposely put this off as long as I could — I did not want his settling in to be interrupted by the trauma of having to put him in a carrier and take him off to what I was sure he would think was away for good. But now the putting off could go on no longer. The hip was only part of the reason. He needed to be checked over, he needed an inoculation, and — worst of all — he would have to be neutered. Whether he did not go out or not, and whether or not he had any association with other cats, I, who had preached neutering and spaying for years, could simply not have a cat of my own which was not so "fixed."

Besides all this he was vigorously shaking his head a good deal. At first I thought it was just at some of my ideas, but, as it went on, even when I had not imparted any particular piece of advice, I realized that he was actually having trouble with his ears. This was not surprising. As I had told Mrs. Wills that first day, most white cats do. But it was again reason for taking him to the vet.

Another reason I had put off taking him to the vet was perhaps a subconscious one. In those days — and it was, after all, less than ten years ago — few veterinarians were at least publicly in sympathy with animal activists, or, as we were then called, "humaniacs." Although the veterinarian, like the doctors' famed Hippocratic Oath, took his oath too — "to use my scientific knowledge and skills for the relief of animal suffering . . . ," etc. — to the animal activist this oath, at least judging by the veterinarians' attitude toward us, seemed less Hippocratic than hypocritical. And some veterinarians, in turn, returned the favor. Indeed, some of the most vehement criticism I personally had taken came direct from their headquarters — from the American Veterinary Medical Association. I do not mean that I did not have vets as friends, or that some vets did not side publicly with me in some of my fights — I did and they did. But it does mean that these vets were the exception, not the rule.

To people outside the animal field, this might seem incredible. They read books about, and by, kindly vets who go around, at all hours of the day and night, doctoring animals and dispensing words which exude their love for them, they see animal movies and television shows in which the vet is the hero up against seemingly hopeless odds — albeit never against hunters or laboratories — and they may even have a child who loves animals very much and, when he or she grows up, wants nothing more than to be a vet and help animals. They are certain that all these kindly vets work hand in glove and on almost a daily basis with animal people and animal societies.

These same people outside of the animal field would sometimes drive into a city with which they were not familiar and, seeing more than once, the sign "Animal Hospital" — in fact thinking they saw more of these signs than for other hospitals — would immediately conclude they were in a very animal-oriented city, and would say something like, "This place seems to care more about sick animals than it does about sick people." Unfortunately, few of such people ever had the experience of picking up a sick or wounded animal by a roadside in or outside of such a town and then taking it to one of those "Animal Hospitals." If they had, they would often find that the "kindly" vet who ran the place would refuse to take the animal unless they met two conditions — first that they pretended it was their animal, not a stray, and second that they produced, in cash, at least fifty dollars.

One area in which the animal activist and the doctrinaire veterinarian of yesterday have long crossed swords is the matter of low-cost spay and neuter programs. While such efforts are surely an important attempt to do something about the cruel stray overpopulation problem, all too often in those days the veterinarians fought them tooth and nail. Such programs meant quite simply a loss of revenue, and, besides, they took the position that if they didn't keep spays and neuters, like their other services, at a uniform level, then well-off people who could afford to pay the regular price would simply take advantage of the lower fee, which was supposedly meant for poor people.

In fairness, there was some truth in this — an accurate gauge of who should pay the regular price and who the reduced was difficult to come by. But the net result of this opposition was that too often only humanely inclined veterinarians took part in such programs, and this in turn meant that these vets were intolerably overburdened. Today, with the success of such programs as Los Angeles' "Have A Heart," as well as the fact that more and more shelters are insisting that all pets be spayed or neutered before adoption, or at least as soon as possible thereafter, the situation is improving. And by no means the least of the reasons for this is the change in the mind-set of the veterinarian profession, particularly among its younger members. Where once vets had enjoyed a good laugh at the appearance, as far back as 1968, of the Fund for Animals' button "Animals Have Rights, Too," there is today a full-fledged and highly respected society called the Association of Veterinarians for Animal Rights.

Today indeed there is even reason for the same kind of optimism in the venerable struggle between activist and vet in the largest and most emotionally highly charged field of all — that of laboratory experimentation. A few years ago it was no easy task to get a veterinarian on "our side" who was willing to testify at a hearing in Washington or even in a state capital — the "other side," on the other hand, always seemed to have an endless supply of them. Nowadays, it's still not even-Steven, but we're gaining and this turnabout is, in at least this writer's opinion, long past high time. And for no animal more so than for the cat — the animal which, as any veterinarian should know, probably suffers more in the laboratory, because of his intense sensitivity, than any other.

There is, to begin with for the cat, the matter of his inherent cleanliness. In the early days, when the Fund for Animals was just beginning, I saw in laboratory after laboratory cage after cage which was just wire. It apparently made them easier to clean. And, for the people, I suppose it did. But for the cats, who had no way to stand except balanced on these thin wires and no way to sit or lie in any comfort at all, it was unbelievably heartless. On top of everything else — literally so in this — since there were cages above and below — urine and feces passed down through the cages on top of the cats below. No one apparently had considered litter boxes — indeed, most laboratories today still do not have them.

But the matter of his physical discomfort in the laboratory is, for the cat, just the beginning of his misery there. For this animal has the terrible bad luck of having a brain which, for all its small size, is not only, save for the ape, the most highly developed on the evolutionary scale, it is also the one most like the human brain. Actually, indeed, the cat's brain is so like ours that the only real difference the scientists have been able to find are in the memory association areas and the speech centers.

It is hardly surprising, then, that this remarkable little brain has, literally for centuries, been pried into by man. In the days before anesthesia the animals' agony must have been beyond imagination, but even today, when you see in virtually every major laboratory in the world hundreds of cats undergoing hundreds of brain experiments — all with the telltale electrodes firmly implanted not onto but into their little heads — it is an unnerving and indeed heartrending sight.

And, speaking of nerves, the cat has another and equally terrible piece of bad luck — his whole nervous system. Indeed, if his brain is so close to ours as to give us, in more ways than one, pause, his nervous system is so close as to be almost eerie. And so, of course, for the cat and the cat alone are reserved the most horrendous psychological experiments the mind of man can conjure up — and be paid for. So widespread, in fact, is this kind of experimentation that it is not by any means limited to bona fide laboratories. A twenty-year experiment, for example, involving millions of dollars of research grants, was recently spent to study, of all subjects, the effects of mutilation of tomcats on their sex life. The locale of the study was, of all places, at the American Museum of Natural History in New York, where, among other things, the experimenters blinded cats, deafened cats, and destroyed the cats' sense of smell, not to mention removing parts of their brains and their sexual organs.

Although these experiments were eventually stopped, they were not stopped because the museum itself disowned them — they were stopped because, as the president of the museum himself informed me, they had lost one-third of their membership over them.

Although few cruelties in the animal field any longer surprise me, the psychological experiments on cats still do. Two of them particularly stand out in my mind. One took place at Stanford University, where a Dr. William Dement achieved a certain stardom among his colleagues by establishing what I believe is still the standing world record for keeping a cat deprived of sleep. Dr. Dement kept one cat so deprived, on a brick surrounded by water, for seventy days.

The other experiment took place at the other end of the country, at the Veterans Hospital in Northport, Long Island. Here the researcher had at his disposal a wide variety of mother cats and their kittens. His procedure was to separate the mother cat from her kitten and then, when the kitten approached the mother, to give it electrical shocks through a device attached to its leg. These shocks increased in intensity as the kitten approached its mother, and the researcher began giving the shocks seven days after the births of the kittens and continued doing it for thirty-five days, right through the nursing period.

During this time he became, he wrote, interested in the behavior of the mother cats, although, he said, they were not part of the experiment. These mothers would, he noted, do everything possible to "thwart," as he put it, the experiment. They both bit and used their claws. They also tried to bite the electrode wires. And they of course tried to run over and comfort their kittens. But when this only got the kittens even more severe shocks, the mothers eventually pulled away and even tried to keep the kittens from them by striking at them.

The researcher was obviously fascinated by all this, and

all the time he was studying, his paper made clear, juvenile delinquency — the same subject, incidentally, which the Museum of Natural History was supposedly studying with the tomcats.

The veterinarian I chose for my cat was one who I knew felt as I did about such outrages. Her name was Susan Thompson and, among other distinctions, she had, twenty years before, been the only woman in her class at vet school. Before entering private practice, she had been on the staff of a shelter in which I was on the board, and I knew she was both extraordinarily professional and also had a rare combination of firmness and gentleness, and yet had the quickness that made it possible for her to do something which might be momentarily painful for the animal but was usually all over and the animal being petted before he knew what had happened. That, with a cat, is no mean achievement.

I called her and informed her of the high honor for which she had been nominated. She told me to bring the cat in the next morning and then listened to my diagnosis, as well as to my recital of all the virtues of my cat, with polite but I felt increasingly flagging interest until I got to the matter of his being "fixed." "If we're going to neuter," she interrupted, "I'll have to keep him overnight and I don't want you to give him anything to eat or drink after six o'clock tonight."

I knew she would have to keep him overnight, but I had not figured on the other matter. It was bad enough that I had to take him for the first time out of the apartment and entirely discombobulate him — just when he had become so settled and secure and happy — but that I also had to add to this putting him on a no-water, no-food regimen for all evening, all night, and even no power breakfast before his ordeal — well, it seemed doubly grim.

Nonetheless, there was nothing for it but to do it. And so all that evening, while he fussed for food, I did my best to distract him by telling him it wasn't my idea, it was other people's. I also did my best to distract him by extra fussing over him — by petting and playing. I even tried to get him to finish a baseball game we had developed with a Ping-Pong ball and which had ended in a dispute over a hit which he claimed was a home run and I claimed was a foul bunt. Unfortunately we had no instant replay available, and so my job was to get him to agree to actual replay. But over and over he would "aeiou" away, put out his paw, grab my leg, and attempt to move me toward the kitchen. When I refused he resorted to the most piteous "aeiou" I had ever heard. And, when bedtime came, he refused to get up on the bed.

At last, late that night, he finally gave up, jumped up on the bed and, not by my neck as he usually did but far down by my feet, lay down with an exaggerated and exasperated thump. At 3 o'clock, as usual, he awakened me, but when, even then, I made no move to deliver the Vittles, though he could clearly see the box and in fact had his eyes fixed on it, he had reached his breaking point. Obviously I had lost my mind, and from now on he would have to take matters into his own paws. With one agile leap, he was over me and on the bedside table, with one swift cuff he had the box overturned, and then, just when he was about to settle in, I made my move. I too swooped over and up and grabbed.

He looked at me with a look that said we have met the enemy and it is you, but I ignored it. Instead, I put the Vittles back in the box and the box in a drawer. As for him, he turned his back, jumped to the floor and, for the rest of the night, stayed there.

The next morning I settled the matter of the power breakfast with, if I do say so, a bold and masterful maneuver. I decided I would not, that morning, have breakfast either. No one, after all, needs breakfast every morning.

I went instead to the closet and brought down a carrier — one which Marian, with her usual foresight, had surreptitiously brought in and placed, out of his sight, on an upper shelf. The trouble was that the moment I took it out, although I was sure he had never seen a carrier before, the jig was up. He somehow knew something was going on about which he was highly suspicious, and that whatever this something was, it had to do with whatever that stupid thing — i.e., the carrier — was. Immediately it became apparent to me that not only did he not have the slightest intention of getting into the thing, he would not come anywhere near it.

As I was pondering how to handle this situation, I remembered reading somewhere that, before you tried to get your cat into a carrier, you should be sure he is both properly introduced to it and also has a chance to make friends with it — that he should be given the opportunity to play around it and even in it, by putting one of his toys in it — and that all this should be done well before you even think of taking him somewhere in it.

Of course I had not done this, and now it was too late. I also remembered the experience of a friend of mine, Pia Lindstrom, of television fame. Ms. Lindstrom at that time had two cats, and, she told me, she made her first trip to her vet with one cat in her carrier and the other cat under her arm. The first cat, she said, didn't mind the carrier at all, the second did. He would not be enticed in, and he would not — even with two people, one to hold him and the other to hold the carrier — be forced in. Thus she went to the vet as she went everywhere else — with one cat in and one cat out.

When she arrived, the vet assumed that either her cats didn't get along or that she thought two were too many in one carrier, or perhaps she was just a typically careless celebrity. In any case, he was all help. "Here," he said, "I'll take that one — I have another carrier in the other room." Ms. Lindstrom pulled away. "Oh no," she said, "don't bother. He won't get in." The vet demanded to know what she meant. Ms. Lindstrom repeated what she meant. But the vet wouldn't hear of it. "Nonsense," he said. And, with that, he seized her cat and started for the other room — and the carrier.

Ms. Lindstrom watched them disappear and heard the door shut. That was not, however, the last thing she heard. For what she next heard, she reported objectively, as she was trained to do, was the outbreak of World War III. She heard what sounded like chairs being overturned, possibly even tables, and various things landing on the floor. She also heard unmistakable human swearwords alternated with equally unmistakable cat yowls. And finally she heard total silence.

In a moment the vet, carrying his carrier, appeared. His shirt was ripped and there was blood on his arms. The carrier was fine, but, inside, there was no cat. Finally, like a streak of lightning, her cat went by the vet and leapt into her lap.

The vet put down the carrier, but at a respectable distance from both Ms. Lindstrom and the cat. "I don't think," he said, still panting, "he likes carriers." "No," said Ms. Lindstrom, trying not, at that particular moment, to pat her cat, "he doesn't."

After I finished thinking about that story, I started thinking about the task at hand — getting my cat into the carrier. I was, of course, determined not to use brute force, and so, after studying him for a moment, I decided to make a game of it. First I put the carrier as close to him as I dared, got down on my hands and knees, opened it, and showed him how terrific it was — how you could even see from inside it. To illustrate this I put my face right in it and looked out at him from under the isinglass cover. I even thought of pretending to eat something in there. I decided, however, that, under the circumstances of his enforced fast, this would be too cruel, and so, instead, I concentrated on attempting to show him how interesting it was in there — particularly with the nice soft blanket underneath and everything. He, however, evinced not the slightest interest in my interest and, in any case, whatever interest he did have he was determined to take my word for. One thing he would not do was come one step closer to it.

I looked at my watch — there was no more time. With one swooping motion with my hand I reached out, scooped him up, and put him, almost before he knew what was happening, inside. At the same time, with the other hand, I closed the cover and locked it.

He looked at me from inside with a look which, woebegone as it was, nonetheless clearly asked at least three questions. Was it not enough that I had tried to deceive him? Did I also have to resort to that typical human reaction of using total force? And finally, did I, after the ultimate betrayal, have, beyond it, a still darker plan?

I refused to answer any of the questions. Instead, I bravely looked away. I put on my coat, picked up the carrier, strode to the door, opened it, and marched to the elevator. The worst of it all — the ride in the elevator, the walk to the garage, the wait for the car and then putting him in — was that I was sure he felt he was now going to be put back where he had come from. To counteract this, when we were on our way in the automobile and he was in the seat beside me, I opened the top of the carrier and put my arm on top of him. I wanted him to be able to see that at least we were not going where he had been before, but at the same time I had not the slightest desire of letting him out of the carrier and investigating the scenery better. I was sure I could never get him back in.

Fortunately I found, near Dr. Thompson's office, a pretty good place, at least by New York standards, to park. A ticket, in other words, wasn't an absolutely sure thing.

One interesting thing about Dr. Thompson's office is that, while you have a day appointment, you do not have a time appointment. That is run on a strictly first-come, first-served basis — except, of course, in case of emergency. The other, and more interesting, thing is that in Dr. Thompson's office there is not an office manager. Or rather, there is an office manager, but it is not a person. It is a cat.

The cat's name is Blacky. Blacky came to Dr. Thompson from an owner who was tired of Blacky being sick and, though he was not old, decided to have him, in that euphemism, "put down." Dr. Thompson, however, decided otherwise, and, after reaching an agreement with the owner, kept Blacky.

Almost at once Blacky took over the office and has

remained as manager ever since. He was literally "on the desk" as I walked in. I immediately went up to him and explained my business. He listened attentively, and, I could have sworn, checked his list. Anyway, whether he did or not, when I put down the carrier, Blacky rose up and solemnly peered down at my cat. My cat equally solemnly peered back. Even through the isinglass there was, I could see, immediate rapport.

It was a good start, and since Blacky all but indicated where I was to sit, I went over and sat there. In the circle of seats there were two cats, one small dog, and one enormous Great Dane — all with their people. Blacky had indicated a seat in the cat section, the farthest distance from the Dane, but the woman who owned the Dane was, unfortunately, the most interested in me. She was complimentary about my animal work, but the more interested she became in telling me about this, the less she controlled her dog. And, since I had once more opened the top of the carrier, the next thing I knew he was eyeball to eyeball with the Dane. "AEIOU," he hissed, just as I put my hand between him and an animal for which he would make, at best, an hors d'oeuvre. Fortunately the woman at that moment got ahold of her dog, but she was now by no means as enchanted with me. "Surely you of all people," she said sternly, pulling her dog away, "should know that Danes are the gentlest of all big dogs."

Surely I did, I told her, but somehow I had neglected to inform my cat of that fact.

The rest of that wait was by no means my favorite — and I am not a good waiter under the best of circumstances. One of the cat women was the next to take an interest in me — or rather my cat. "And what is our name?" she asked, sticking her fingers in at him. I told her he didn't have a name yet — what with Christmas and all. She looked at me as if I were some distance from her concept of a fit owner. "Oh dear," she said.

After what seemed an eternity — when all of the previous arrivals had been attended to, and a new group assembled — I was at last called. As if on cue, as I carried my cat in to Dr. Thompson, Blacky got up and walked with us. I had not believed Dr. Thompson when she told me that Blacky actually went in with new patients — but now I did believe it. And, when I took the cat out of the carrier and put him on her examining table, I noticed that Blacky had jumped up on one of the stools and was looking at him almost as intently as Dr. Thompson.

"Oh, he's a beauty," Dr. Thompson said — as I was sure she told all owners. But I noticed that as she ran her fingers over him, he did not tremble.

Once more I blurted out my diagnosis — of the mouth and the hip and the ears. Dr. Thompson is very used to patients' diagnoses, and she paid polite interest — but she did not stop her examination. She said nothing for some time, then gave it to me all at once. "The mouth is almost well," she said, "and the hip is coming along fine. I'm going to let it heal its own way. I want to clean out his ears, though, but we can do that when we do the shots and the other thing. I also think we've got a little skin problem. He's got some allergies, but we'll do that another time."

I was almost glad he had some allergies. So many doctors, at the first sign of their patients having allergies, immediately prescribe the eviction of their cats. I felt it was nice cats could have some allergies of their own. Maybe, I suggested to Dr. Thompson, to doctors.

Dr. Thompson smiled. "Well," she said, "I'm going to

put him in the other room for a while until I finish with my other patients."

I was instantly all suspicion. Where? I wanted to know. Dr. Thompson showed me. "In here," she said, as she picked him up and I followed her into that other room. There were a lot of cages in there. She opened one and put him in.

I had not figured on cages — or on his being all alone. Dr. Thompson sensed what I was thinking. "Don't worry," she said. "Blacky will hang out in the room with him."

But what about food and water? I wanted to know. I told her he'd had nothing since the day before, and who would be there to give him Vittles at 3 A.M.? He'd want them, I knew, and Blacky was hardly up to that. Wouldn't she be there?

Dr. Thompson smiled once more. "No, I won't," she said, "but neither will he want them because he'll be sound asleep too." She opened the cage again. "Now give him an upbeat pat," she said, "and tell him you'll pick him up in the morning — first thing."

I did as I was told. I only hoped he'd believe me. But, before I left, I also patted Blacky. I was so glad he was there.

V ◦ *His Roots*

Dr. Thompson had called me and told me that my cat had come through his operation fine, but, just the same, that night, when he was away, my apartment seemed the loneliest place in the world. It was hard to believe that a small creature whom I had not even known a few days before could, by just not being there, have made it so. But he had — and did.

I resolved to use the time that evening reading everything in my library about cats. I started with famous quotations about them. And, early on, I found one which has since become my all-time favorite. It is by none other than Leonardo da Vinci. "Nature's Masterpiece," he called the cat.

It hardly seemed necessary to go further. Surely that description, by arguably the greatest artistic talent that ever lived — as well as one whose drawings of the cat have never been surpassed — comes at least close to saying it all. But the fact was I soon found others which would become favorites too. One was from, curiously, our own country's preeminent humorist. "If," Mark Twain said, "man could be crossed with a cat, it would improve man, but it would deteriorate the cat."

The English humorist Jerome K. Jerome had roughly the same point of view as Mr. Twain, but he gave his from the animal's angle. "A cat's got her own opinion of human beings," he said. "She don't say much, but you can tell enough to make you anxious not to hear the whole of it."

Here I could not help admiring not only the thought but also the use of the "she" instead of the invariable "he." If Mr. Jerome, 1859–1927, was not talking about a specific female cat, I decided, he was certainly a man in advance of his time.

In any case, to an English art critic, Philip Gilbert Hamerton, I accorded first honors for making what to me seemed the most memorable comparison between those age-old adversaries, the cat and the dog.

"If animals could speak," Hamerton wrote, "the dog would be a blundering, outspoken, honest fellow — but the cat would have the rare grace of never saying a word too much."

When it came to countries, it was not easy to choose which was foremost in praise for the cat. Eventually I decided that France deserved the prize, if for no other reason because it was a Frenchman, Théophile Gautier, poet and novelist, who, albeit immodestly, reduced the contest to totally nationalistic dimensions.

"Only a Frenchman," he wrote, "could understand the fine and subtle qualities of the cat."

A small host of French philosophers were not far behind Monsier Gautier. "Gentlest of sceptics," Jules Lemaitre described his cat, while the oft-quoted Montaigne made the lasting assessment of the cat at play. "When my cat and I," he wrote, "entertain each other with mutual antics, as playing with a garter, who knows that I make more sport for her than she makes for me?"

Still another French philosopher, Alain, was more difficult to understand. "Two things," he wrote, "are aesthetically perfect in the world — the clock and the cat."

I was willing to go along with the cat. But the clock stopped me.

One of the most interesting things I learned that night was the two most common expressions we associate with the cat — that he has nine lives and that he can look at a king — go far back in history. The nine lives, indeed, is one of the oldest of proverbs and has been repeated for centuries. It crops up, for example, in Shakespeare, in no less a work than *Romeo and Juliet.* There Tybalt asks Mercutio, "What wouldst thou have of me?" only to have Mercutio reply, "Good king of Cats, nothing but one of your lives."

A half century ago, a Scottish professor, Sir J. Arthur Thompson, professor of natural history at the University of Aberdeen, wrote a book entitled *Riddles of Science*. In it he devoted an entire chapter to the cat's nine lives. Sir Arthur's thesis was that each of the lives stemmed from one of the cat's lifesaving abilities. The first, for example, Sir Arthur believed came from the fact that the cat always fell on his feet, and that this was the result of his ancestral ability to climb. The second life came from his whiskers, which were a vital part of his ability to operate in the dark and were, indeed, so important to him that to cut them close was, at least temporarily, to incapacitate him.

The third of the lives, Sir Arthur went on, came from the cat's extraordinary ability to smell at great distances, the fourth from the animal's equally remarkable hearing. Despite his small ears, a cat, the professor noted, had proven to be able to turn in the direction of any sound at least twice as fast as the best watchdog.

Sir Arthur declared that the cat's fifth life derived from the animal's amazing visual powers — these eyes having both the legendary ability to see in the dark and also being, in relation to the size of his body, the largest of all animal eyes. On the other hand, Sir Arthur credited the cat's sixth life not to any astounding physical attribute but to the animal's homing instinct — his apparently infallible ability to find his way home, often from long distances and even after a purposeful dislocation. This instinct, the professor felt, was, when the cat lived in the wild, obviously all-important to survival — both from the point of view of the cat's own safety and also that of any newborn kittens which might have been left unattended in the den.

By the time Sir Arthur had reached the cat's seventh life, he, not the cat, was clearly laboring. In any case, he ascribed that seventh life to the cat's ability to make his fur stand on end — more hairs in proportion to body size than can, for example, the gorilla — and thus appear much larger, as well as more frightening, to a larger adversary.

If Sir Arthur was having hard going with his seventh

cat life, he had nothing left at all for the eighth and ninth lives or, for that matter, even what these last two lives were. Having said at the beginning of his treatise that the cat had more than nine lives, he nonetheless leaves us with only seven. Some veteran cat scholars have conjectured that this might have been purposeful — pointing out that while the oriental mystic number is nine, the occidental is only seven. This cat scholar, however, who is no mystic, felt shortchanged.

The saying that "even a cat can look at a king" has, I found, never had the exhaustive treatment accorded to the legendary nine lives, but it too can be traced to an ancient proverb. It has, however, at least one basis in more modern historic fact. In the fifteenth century, the story goes, Maximilian I, of the House of Hapsburg, King of the Romans and soon to be Holy Roman Emperor, was deep in conversation with a friend of his named Hieronymus Resch, a maker of woodcuts. During this conversation, the king looked over and saw that Resch's cat, stretched out on a table, was staring not at Resch but at him. From this rather less than earth-shaking occurrence came, apparently, not only the actual proof of the proverb but also its rather less than happy future connotation — at least as far as kings are concerned. For Maximilian, who spent a good deal of his reign embroiled in turmoil, intrigue, and warfare, always declared that the cat had looked at him with, as he put it, "deep suspicion" — a comment which, once again, will come as small surprise to all the cat-owned, before Maximilian's time, and since.

And, years later the cat and the king confrontation became the basis for one of the famous "Fantastic Fables" of none other than the late Ambrose Bierce:

A Cat was looking at a King as permitted by the proverb.

"Well," said the monarch, observing her inspection of the royal person, "how do you like me?"

"I can imagine a King," said the Cat, "whom I should like better."

"For example?"

"The King of Mice."

Actually, through the centuries, cats have, I discovered, not only looked at kings, they have also lived with them. And, although among kings and emperors as well as among common folk, there has apparently always been both the ailurophile and the ailurophobe, the balance, fortunately for the cat, has been highly in favor of the phile over the phobe. In our own country, while comparatively few of our Presidents have had cats, those who have — notably Abraham Lincoln — were extremely fond of them. Lincoln indeed, on a trip to Grant's headquarters in the dead of winter, and finding there three half-frozen kittens, adopted them on the spot and took them back to the White House.

The other best-known presidential ailurophiles were also, curiously, all Republican — Theodore Roosevelt, Calvin Coolidge, and Herbert Hoover — and, if the latter two at least were perhaps our most conservative Presidents, it should be borne in mind that this trend was not broken by Ronald Reagan. Although it is his dogs which have received most of his animal publicity, the fact remains that he has three cats at his ranch and all three, he maintains, get along not only with each other but also with his dogs.

In other countries, I learned, heads of state have come in both the pro and the anti cat camp. Neither the Kaiser nor Hitler liked cats, but Mussolini, the Tsar, and, curiously, Lenin, were all extremely fond of them. Farther back, Julius Caesar and Napoleon both detested cats, while both Louis XIV and Louis XV loved them. The latter, indeed, having been won over by his queen, Marie Leszczynska, was persuaded to give them the run of Paris.

On the other hand, Henri II, Henri III, and Charles IX were strictly in the phobe camp — indeed, when Charles came to the throne, he is reputed to have several times lost consciousness just at the sight of a cat. Moreover, one of Charles' ministers, Ronsard, went so far as to record his revulsion. "I hate," he wrote, "their eyes, their forehead and their gaze." As for George Louis Leclerc, Comte de Buffon, the famous French botanist who is generally credited with having been the first modern to attempt to embrace all knowledge, one thing he refused to embrace was the cat. "The cat is a faithless domestic animal," he wrote, "that we only keep from necessity in order to use it against another even more inconvenient enemy that we do not wish to keep at all."

But, harsh as these opinions were, I noted that they were strictly minority ones. Popes such as Gregory the Great and Gregory III, Leo XII, and Leo XIII, not to mention Pius VII and the late John Paul, were all pro-cat, and there are many stories of their affection for the animal. When Gregory the Great and Gregory III, for example, renounced all their worldly possessions, each refused to renounce one thing — his cat. And Leo XIII not only befriended a stray kitten born in the Vatican, but made it his companion for life — much of which the cat spent literally curled up in the folds of the papal robes.

In England the cat has long fared very well among the high and mighty. Napoleon might have hated cats, but his conqueror, the Duke of Wellington, was extremely partial to them, as were both Queen Victoria and Winston Churchill. Indeed, under Victoria, England was considered so ailurophilic that, when the Italian ambassador was once asked what he would like to be if he had his life to live over again, he quickly replied, "A cat in London, or a Cardinal in my country."

In point of fact, three of the most famous cardinals in history were also three of the most famous ailurophiles. Cardinal Wolsey, for example, carried a cat in his arms wherever he went and had one eat with him whether he ate alone or sat at a state function. In more modern times Cardinal Newman was, if more restrained, almost as similarly smitten. As for France's Cardinal Richelieu, he was undoubtedly the greatest friend of the cat in history. He had from childhood loved cats and, when he became virtually head of state, he not only made the cat an accepted part of the court but also kept two servants who served no other function but to take care of all his cats. And, on his death, the cardinal provided in his will for the future care of no less than fourteen of them.

Over and over in cat histories I read that, in comparison to other animals, the cat was a very late arrival on the animal scene. Over and over in cat histories, too, I read such a sentence as "The early history of the cat is shrouded . . ." and then, not, as usually ends such sentences, "in antiquity" but rather, of all phrases, "in mystery."

As one now owned by a cat, I hardly found this surprising. So, I irreverently wanted to ask, what else is new? One does not have to be cat-owned for long to know that, if there is one thing a cat loves better than anything else — save, possibly, making a large mess out of something which had been carefully arranged before he got there — it is a mystery. And if he can, as he so often does, make a large mystery out of where he has been when you go to look for him, even though he was right there a moment ago, surely it must have been mother's milk for his ancestors to make a mystery out of where they originally came from.

In any case, I discovered, late he was. The dog, the horse, the bear, and the reindeer had, the authorities told me, been on the scene not just for a short time before the cat but for a very long time — in fact, for millennia. Furthermore, these authorities point out — and they apparently include the trained bear and the harnessed reindeer in this assessment — that all of these animals had become, long before the appearance of the cat, not only the companion of man but also his servant.

The authorities profess their inability to find a satisfactory answer to account for this. Once more, however, even I, a relative newcomer to the cat-owned ranks, could see clearly that the answer was staring them right in the face — the dead giveaway being that word "servant." Indeed, no self-respecting member of the cat-owned fraternity would wonder for a moment why the cat's appearance was so dilatory. Their only wonder would be why, in view of the situation, he ever showed up at all.

Archaeological authorities point out that, in paleolithic times, in caves, rock carvings, bas-reliefs, etc., there are relics and representations of all kinds of animals — from deer to boar to birds — but not so much as a tooth, a vertebra, or indeed a trace of the cat. And if this is not hard enough news for the archaeologists, consider for a moment the plight of the anthropologists, who have literally gotten almost nowhere in trying to determine the ancestry of the cat. For centuries they were certain that his ancestor must have been some kind of wild cat but were never able to come up with exactly which kind. Fairly recently, however, flying in the face of the well-worn line that "God created the cat so that man might caress the tiger," they have decided that the First Cat was not any sort of wild cat at all, but might have been some other kind of animal. Indeed, the most recent anthropological evidence to be assembled points to the conclusion that the cat's ancestor was, of all animals, the fox.

One certainly means no disrespect to the wily fox — and it would seem that there are indeed physical as well as behavioral similarities between cat and fox. Just the same, the line "God created the cat so that man might caress the fox" doesn't seem to get the job done.

When and where, then, did the cat first appear? The when was, I learned, no earlier than 3000 B.C. — which is not yesterday as you and I may think of it, but was indeed yesterday when measured by the appearance of a wide variety of other animals. The where was, of all places, Nubia — a word which, ironically, is derived in the Nubian language from *nob,* or slave. Nonetheless, it was in neighboring Egypt, conqueror of Nubia, about five hundred years later, or 2500 B.C., that the cat first came into his own. His first name, in Egypt, was, curiously, "Myeo" — a fact from which, once more, the cat-owned would surely deduce that he named himself. In any case, his rise was rapid. He went from hunter — then, as now, at the low end of the social scale — to guardian of the temple, and, finally, to deity. It was, even by cat standards, remarkable.

The Cat-Goddess was known by a wide variety of names — Bast, Bastet, Ubastot, Bubastis, and Pasht — but whatever she was called, there was no question but that she was very high up in the Egyptian pantheon. She was not only the daughter of Isis, great and good friend of the great God Ra, the principal God of Creation; she was also, in her own right, Goddess of the Sun and Moon. And, although she had to share the sun part of her job with Ra, she was still vital to it — if for no other reason than that the Egyptians believed that, when they looked into a cat's eyes, the fact that those eyes glowed meant that they held the life-giving light of the sun, and this in turn meant that the sun would return the next day. To the Egyptians, who were by no means big on the dark, this made Bast, if not superior to Ra, at least very close to being his equal.

But Bast, aka Bastet, etc., was something else, too. Besides being the Goddess of the Sun and Moon, she was also Goddess of Love. Furthermore, she served in this capacity for both maternity and virginity. And if, in those pre-pill days, this must have taken some doing, she was in any case well rewarded for her trouble. She had her own temple in which she was surrounded by other cats, all of whom were not only also considered to be sacred but who were, in turn, surrounded by priests. These priests both watched over the cats and made predictions and prognostications from them — from, as one historian puts it, "the slightest purr, the faintest meowing, the most discreet stretch or the least alteration of posture."

All in all, it must have been one of the best jobs any animal lover could ask for, but at the time one of the most difficult — particularly since the priests had to give their forecasts to government officials as well as to any and all passersby who merely wanted their fortunes told. One can assume that, good at their jobs as these priests may have been, at least some of the time they must have had to go pretty much on a hit-or-miss basis, just as we do when, for example, our cat disappears and we cannot be sure exactly what is the reason. We do not know, for instance, whether the doorbell is about to ring, or a thunderstorm is coming, or we have just thought of doing something that the cat does not want done — such as giving him a pill or cutting his toenails. And if these speculations are what we have to go on from our cat's complete disappearance, imagine what it must have been like for those priests. Their cats apparently never disappeared — they just occasionally changed positions.

Such a distinguished historian as Herodotus tells us that not only was there a statue of the Cat-Goddess in the various temples, but that there was also a small statue of her in virtually every Egyptian home. "The Goddess," says another historian, "was a disturbing creature whom every Egyptian woman wished to resemble — in the strangeness of her gaze, her slanting eyes, her supple loins, her noble posture and her animal abandon." "Women," says still a third historian, "would rather go out of their way to move slinkily . . . rather like our present-day 'vamp.' And," adds this historian, "Cleopatra herself indulged in this fad."

All of which was to entice, in turn, both Caesar and Antony and which, judged by the success of the musical *Cats,* is still not without its charm today. In any case, Herodotus also tells us that when a cat died in a public place, bystanders would get down on their knees protesting that they were not responsible. Whether this was an act of love or expedience, however, is not clear — the killing of a cat was a crime punishable by death. Cats, like people, were embalmed and mummified and placed in sarcophagi.

It is not surprising, in view of ancient Egypt's attitude toward the cat, that the country's enemies could take advantage of it. When, in 500 B.C., for example, Cambyses, King of the Persians, laid siege to the Egyptian city of Pelusium, his initial attacks were foiled by the ferocity of the Egyptian resistance. Whereupon Cambyses called a halt to these tactics and ordered his men to comb the area outside Pelusium for eight days and pick up, but not harm, every cat they could find. For the next attack, Cambyses had each of his men, as he approached the Egyptian lines, hold up in front of him a live cat. One look at this new development was enough for the Egyptians. Rather than harm the cats, and without any further fighting at all, the Egyptians simply surrendered the city.

It was indeed, I discovered, a cat who was responsible for the ultimate subjugation of Egypt by Rome. A Roman soldier in Caesar's army killed a cat — albeit accidentally. However, an Egyptian mob immediately fell on the man, lynched him, and then dragged his body through the streets. Caesar himself warned the Egyptians of severe reprisals for this action — but the warning only served to further enflame the situation. Virtually all of Egypt rose against Rome in a resistance which continued, off and on, until the deaths of Antony and Cleopatra and until Egypt became a Roman province.

Rome itself was ambivalent about the cat. On the one hand, in the ruins of Pompeii not so much as a single bone of a cat was ever found, and in upper-class Roman homes, although there were all kinds of animals as pets, there were few if any cats.

On the other hand, cats were allowed in the inner sanctum of the temple of Hercules and in performance of the ritual dances to the Goddess Diana. The Daughters of Diana, as they were called, were masked and robed as cats. The Romans did, in fact, recognize the cat's aristocratic aloofness, independence, and freedom from authority. The cat was emblazoned on the standards of many of the Roman legions, and in the Temple to Liberty, dedicated by Tiberius Gracchus, the Roman Goddess of Liberty is represented, somewhat like our own Statue of Liberty, holding a cup in one hand and a scepter, if a broken one, in the other. At the Goddess' feet, however, in contrast to our statue, lies, carefully and gracefully rendered, the sculpture of a cat.

The cat's early history in other countries was also curiously interwoven with legends surrounding the country's religion. In Arab countries, for example, the cat was far better off than most other animals because of a cat named Muezza. The latter, it seems, was the favorite cat of Mohammed, and one day, when he was sleeping on Mohammed's sleeve and the prophet had to leave for a meeting, rather than disturb Muezza, he cut off that part of his sleeve on which the cat was resting. Later, when Mohammed returned, Muezza thanked him and bowed, whereupon Mohammed was so touched that he stroked Muezza's back three times — something which, according to legend, not only gave the cat its eternal ability to land on its feet after a fall, but gave it its three times three or nine lives.

In India, in contrast, all animals were protected by Buddha except the cat — the reason for this being, according to legend, that, when Buddha was dying, all animals were ordered to be present. And all obeyed, except for one — Buddha's own cat.

Here, there are two versions of the story. One has it

that Buddha's cat simply overslept and was late. The other version holds that Buddha's cat was among those present, all right, but that, at just the crucial moment when Buddha was ascending to Nirvana, a rat ran across the temple grounds and the cat, his attention diverted to more earthly matters, pounced on the rat and killed it. This was, of course, an unforgiveable social solecism at an extremely inopportune time. Nonetheless, the cat was eventually forgiven, and today in India the orthodox Hindu religion not only prescribes that each of the faithful "feed at least one cat under his roof," but also rules that, for anyone who kills a cat, "he withdraw to the middle of a forest and there dedicate himself to the life of the animals around him until he is purified" — surely an excellent piece of advice for all "sportsmen."

In Burma and Siam — two areas from which come two of our most famous cat breeds — there were, as in Egypt, cats who had to do with guarding temples and, more importantly, with the transmigration of souls. The soul, it was believed, relived, for a time at least, its existence in the body of a sacred cat before going on to total perfection in the next life. In Japan this belief went farther. The cat had religious significance even after death, and the geisha girls of Tokyo went so far as to raise a fund for a ceremonial service for the souls of the cats which had been killed to provide the catgut for samisens — the banjo-like instruments which they used to entertain their customers. Remarkably enough, before 1602 Japan kept its cats on leashes. In that year the Kyoto government passed a law ordering them released, the idea being that city cats needed their freedom in order to take care of the rats which were destroying the silkworm industry, and that the temple cats needed theirs to keep mice away from the papyrus rolls. Presumably, like all cats before them, and since, they had had, in between mice, a high old time with those rolls.

Ancient China did not actually worship the cat, but cats were strictly bringers of good fortune, because they were living assistants to the Hearth God, the household protector whose image was in every home. One cat was collared and tied in the home, but kittens and other cats were free to go in and out as they wished. Even the collared cat fared well, however, because, true to Chinese tradition for people, the older he or she was, the more he or she was venerated. The Chinese peasant, like the Egyptian, believed in the glow of the cat's eyes at night to ward off evil spirits, but the Chinese carried the Egyptian's fascination with the eyes a step farther. They believed it was possible to tell time this way — that from dawn the pupil in the cat's eye gradually contracted until it became, at noon, a perpendicular hairline. And then, during the afternoon, the hairline's dilation gradually increased until it was bedtime for people and guard time for cats.

Generally speaking, the cat came through ancient history with flying colors — and even through what, to two-legged creatures, were the Dark Ages. The cat's Dark Ages, however, were Europe's Middle Ages. All of a sudden, it seems, all the Eastern superstitions and the legends, even the religious veneration accorded him in the East, were, in the West, turned against him. He became, literally, the creature of the Devil. The Bible, for example, which refers to almost every other animal, has practically no reference to cats, either in the Old Testament or the New. The theory, in regard to the Old Testament at least, is that the Hebrews, having suffered the terrible bondage and persecution which they did under the Egyptians, had no appetite for even the mention of an animal their persecutor had so liked, let alone one which had been so venerated.

When it comes to the New Testament, its ailurophobia is part and parcel of the worst of medieval Christianity. In any case, this kind of Christianity not only removed the cat from its ancestral pedestal but condemned him as the embodiment of the Foul Fiend Incarnate, the intimate source of all manner of witchcraft and sorcery, of voodoo and vampirism, of black magic and even the Black Mass. Along with the Inquisition went just about every cat phobia in the old wives' handbook. Indeed, the Devil's Bible, published in, of all places, France, contained the statement "Only imbeciles do not know that all have a pact with the Devil."

Even the popes were part of the horror, and, all over the Roman Catholic world, as well as through a large part of the Protestant, men and women were tortured and even hanged just for helping or giving shelter to a sick or wounded cat. The superstitions themselves seem to have had to be cruel to be believed. One had it that only the burial of a live cat in a field would insure a good crop, another that only the walling-up of a live cat in a new building would insure the stability of its foundations. Nor was all this stupidity confined to Europe. In the American colonies, no fewer than two thousand accusations of witchcraft involving cats were legally upheld in court.

The black cat, of course, fared worst of all. As the personification of Satan, he suffered the tortures of the damned — literally. An incredible number of black cats were massacred in various ways — not excluding being killed at Mass itself. Cat-burning, indeed, became such an accepted rite that, long after it was a thing of the past, it was defended by Jacques Bossuet, one of the seventeenth century's most famous theologians. Furthermore, his defense was by reasoning which was, unfortunately, typical. Since the practice of torturing cats would have existed in any case, Bossuet maintained, it was better to have it happen during a Christian rite than during a pagan one.

Fernand Méry, French veterinarian and cat historian, managed to find in Brittany one lovely piece of good news for the black cat — a legend which dates from those terrible times but which still exists to the present day. The legend holds that on every black cat there is one hair, and only one, which is perfectly white. If you can find this hair and remove it without being scratched by your cat, you will have a unique good luck charm — one which can render you, whichever you choose — either rich or lucky in love.

But not, apparently, both. In any case, Dr. Méry, in his fine book *The Cat,* concludes his story with a touching comment:

> I particularly like this last legend. It implies that you have sufficiently gained the sympathy of your cat for it to allow you patiently to search through the whole of its coat for this one famous hair. The happiness that can come from this unique white hair is symbolic. It is recognition and reward for whoever can prove so much understanding and goodwill towards an animal that has been for so long despised and ill-treated.

The all-white hair in the black cat legend also sent me scurrying for stories about all-white cats, such as mine.

Once especially venerated, as in ancient times he had been, how had he come through, well, the Dark Ages? I presumed not well because while, in those terrible times, all cats suffered, the all white was so different that, like the all black, there surely must have been ridiculous superstitions associated with him. I did not, however, find any, and in any case, coming out of the Middle Ages, the white cat was soon again, if not a God or Goddess, at least by the time of Louis XV, a court pet. Later Queen Victoria would have her white cat and, in China and Japan, where medieval Christian cruelty had not penetrated, both the Chinese and Japanese emperors had white cats at the same time. Indeed, as recently as 1926, when a new king was crowned in Siam — the grandson of the king of *Anna and the King of Siam* fame — a white cat was carried in the procession. The soul of the king's predecessor was, the belief ran, at least temporarily embodied in him.

For my favorite story of the white cat I am again indebted to Dr. Méry. It happened during World War II in Burma at a time when the fortunes of the Allies in general and the British Army in particular were at a low ebb. The chief British problem was that, to build the strategic roads which they required, they were in dire need of Burmese labor and were willing to pay high wages to get it. But the Japanese, with their superior knowledge of Burmese beliefs and customs, were able to convince these laborers that, in the end, the British would lose anyway. And, the Japanese emphasized, in the meantime, the uncouth British would be making a mockery out of everything the Burmese held sacred — in particular the white, or, as the Burmese called it, the "immaculate" cat. So the roadbuilders began quitting their jobs in droves:

This went on until an English colonel with considerable knowledge of local beliefs had an original idea. First of all the order went out to all ranks to collect the greatest possible number of white cats. In the meantime, the silhouettes of white cats were stencilled on all the army vehicles, jeeps, trucks, tanks, etc. as if this were the emblem of the British Army. It certainly proved a lucky one. The rumour swiftly spread that the English aerodromes were unassailable, for they were the refuge of the immaculate cat. The same applied to the rolling stock. No more was needed. The native population ignored the Japanese propaganda and gave the full weight of their support to the Allies.

The next morning I was at Dr. Thompson's before any other client. Blacky, I noticed, was not "on the desk."

"No," Dr. Thompson once more anticipated me as I appeared. "Blacky is still with your cat."

As we walked down the hall, she said, "He's fine, but you're going to find he's a little unsteady."

I went in and marched right to the cage. Dr. Thompson was correct. My cat was indeed unsteady — in fact, I would have called him groggy. But, just the same, he had clearly recognized me and was staggering to his feet just as I opened his cage. "Aeiou, *aeiou*," he said.

"Aeiou, aeiou, *aeiou*," I replied, taking him in my arms. "We're going home now."

On the way out, I stopped, either to thank Blacky and hug Dr. Thompson or the other way around — I was too excited to know which. All I did know was that I had my cat again.

VI ◦ *A Difficult Matter*

A few days after the trip to the vet, the cat and I had our first real disagreement. Or at least it was the first since our Mexican standoff over the question of whether or not he would, on occasion and without the introduction of such an impossible variable to the experiment as food, come when called.

It came over something which, to those of the non-cat-owned persuasion, would seem ridiculous. It would not, however, so seem either to any of the veteran cat-owned or, for that matter, to any veteran cat.

What it was, in a word, was what — entirely irrespective of the question of whether or not he would come to it — to call him.

Frankly, I was growing heartily sick and tired of telling people about him and having to do so without the attachment of a name; of having people see him and ask what his name was and having to tell them, as I had that woman at Dr. Thompson's, that what with Christmas and all, and one thing and another, I had just not gotten around to it; and, finally, of not myself having anything by which to address him properly. I had been using that awful "you" — which is bad enough for a person whose name you have forgotten but is even worse for an animal and is, for a cat, totally impossible.

I was under no illusion that the job would be easy — which, curiously, was something I learned primarily in reverse. In other words, I learned it from the only people who had not bothered me about why I had not yet named my cat or who, when they asked about it, did not ask me its name. They were, of course, the veteran cat-owned and they were far too polite and much too wise to ask such a fruitless question. From them, indeed, I picked up valuable lessons as, little by little, I met more and more of these people and saw firsthand some who had returned, bloody but unbowed, either from the battlefield of an unsuccessful naming war, or from the neutral zone of one in progress. The naming of a cat, like marriage to a person, was obviously not to be undertaken or entered into lightly. On the contrary, it was, as T. S. Eliot, who wrote a whole poem about it, noted, "a difficult matter."

The late Mr. Eliot, I was soon to learn, understated. Indeed, in short order I would also learn that, compared to the naming of a cat, the naming of a baby, a dog, or a book, a battleship, a ball team, or, for that matter, a king, a pope, or a hurricane, is child's play.

Start with a child. You may, for a child, it is true, run into a few minor difficulties. You and your spouse might, for example, be in disagreement, in the case of a boy's name, about the use of Junior and Junior's possible future offspring, of III's, V's, etc., if direct or, if collateral, via an uncle, II's, IV's, etc. You may decide, in other words, that you either don't want to number him or you do. Or you and your spouse may disagree about the use of family names or even about naming your child after a family member — which will depend, of course, upon your liking or dislike of the party in question, or perhaps even upon such an ignoble consideration as that of a potential will. You may also have a second thought about some name you at first liked because of the possibility of a highly unsuitable nickname which might later be bestowed upon the child because of it by some unfeeling schoolmate.

But, as I say, these are basically small problems, and you and your spouse have, after all, nine months in which to talk them out, discuss them with wiser heads and, ultimately, solve them. And, best of all, after you have made your choice, you will not face even the most remote possibility of a squawk from your namee — at least not until long after it is far too late.

So much for the child.

Next take a dog. Even to consider comparing the difficulty of naming a dog with that of the naming of a cat is a waste of my valuable time, and yours too. Your dog will accept any name. Furthermore, he will recognize it almost at once and on the second or at most the third call will not only come to it but actually run to it. Above all, your dog will never, either by look, sniff, sneer, or innuendo, criticize your choice. You, as his master or mistress, as the case may be, have made your decision and he will abide by it. If that is what you want, then it is what he wants, too, and that is all there is to it.

The naming of a book can be a bit trickier. But, once again, to think of it in the same breath with naming a cat is — well, you can simply take my word for it that I have done both and there is no comparison. Many years ago, I was fortunate in having as my literary agent Miss Bernice Baumgarten, one of the most distinguished in the book field. One day I addressed to her the question of how important she thought a book's title was. She answered peremptorily that it was of virtually no importance. I next addressed to her the question of what she thought was a good title. "Any title," she replied, equally peremptorily, "of a good book." After that, I decided not to bother her any more about the matter.

The other examples I cited also fail to measure up in difficulty to the naming of a cat. Battleships and ball teams are, after all, named, if the former, for individuals or states; if the latter, the first part of the name reflects location, while the second part is usually concerned either with such mundane matters as a local occupation (cowboys, oilers, brewers), or evoking the image of something fierce (giants, bears, raiders), or even something as simple as the color of their sox. As for kings and popes, they are not really named at all — rather, like the juniors previously considered, they are numbered. Finally, although hurricanes used to present a reasonable challenge when female names only were employed and when there was the danger, in years in which there were a lot of hurricanes and the difficult letters toward the end of the alphabet were approaching, of running out of names not previously used, nowadays, with the addition of male names in deference to male liberation, anyone could do the job — even that awful new weather man on your local TV.

The naming of a cat, on the other hand, is something entirely else again. A cat who dislikes his name can, and

I am reliably informed, often does, go through his entire lifetime without ever, even by a careless mistake, acknowledging that he has ever heard it before, let alone recognizing, in any perceptible manner known to humankind, that it could in any way have any possible connection with him.

Early on in my name quest, a friend of mine who, with her husband, lived with a dozen or more cats, told me that, when all her cats were together and she or her husband called one of them, the others would often turn and look at the cat called — but, at the same time, while that cat would occasionally return the stare of the other cats, he or she would never look at or respond to her husband or her. The story was proof positive, she maintained, that cats have no real objection to other cats' names, they just object to their own. Another friend of mine, the copyeditor, as a matter of fact, of this book, well recalls two Siamese cats she once had, each of whose sole acknowledgment of their own names was to register extreme jealousy when the other was even discussed, let alone called.

All the cat-owned will agree that cats can be finicky about a great many things — about their food, for example, about certain people they either like or dislike, about noise or weather or almost anything else you or, more importantly, your cat can think of. But all of these are basically finickinesses which develop over a period of time and which therefore at least allow you the opportunity to develop your defenses against them. Your cat's persnicketiness over his name, however, begins with the very first time you are rash enough to try it on him.

An extraordinary number of cats indeed seem to harbor the firm belief that they should be able to exercise strict editorial control over their names and to employ, if need be, wartime censorship. Nor is this belief confined to the question of whether or not they like or dislike certain names. Rather it is based on a far more fundamental matter — and that is, in sum, that they are by no means sold on the idea that they should have a name to begin with.

Actually, I learned there was only one rule of thumb you could really count on about a cat's attitude toward your choice of name. And this was that, whatever you expected its attitude to be, it would be precisely the opposite. Some years ago a friend of mine, Jane Volk, rescued, in Palm Beach of all places, where her husband was a distinguished architect, one of the toughest tomcats I ever saw in my life — a fighting tom who had one eye, one and a half ears, half a tail, and a battle-scarred face. Of all her cats, her friends were sure, this would be the most difficult to name. Mrs. Volk, however, elegant and serene, promptly dubbed the cat "Mother's Precious Treasure." Not only did the cat not object, he took to the name immediately. It was always my belief that he knew it was funny too.

Some years ago, Eleanora Walker, a distinguished cat rescuer, wrote a whole book about the subject, entitled *Cat Names*. Mrs. Walker asks in one chapter, "Do our cats name us?" She answers this in the affirmative, and then states that these names probably have to do with humans as providers. "My former husband," she writes, "swore that Humphrey and Dolly and Bean Blossom called me The Big Hamburger."

In another chapter, however, Mrs. Walker goes a good deal farther. In this, entitled "The Tibetan Way," she tells us that she asked a friend of hers who was, as she puts it, "more spiritually advanced" than she, to work out a "method of meditation" which would "help someone bring forth the cat's name."

The friend dutifully did so:

> Relax yourself by lying on your back on the floor with your knees raised and your feet firmly on the ground. Breathe gently and regularly, concentrating on the exhale, and try to clear your mind of clutter. . . . If you are new to meditation and distractions continue to bother you, repeat the following mantra silently to the rhythm of your breathing. *Ham/Sah. Ham* on the inhale and *Sah* on the exhale.

This was apparently the method by which Tibetan mystics who "want to attain the qualities of a particular deity" got themselves in shape for the task ahead — in other words, for trying "to reproduce the image of the god in all its complexity inside themselves." And Mrs. Walker tells us encouragingly, "If you've ever seen a Tibetan deity, you'll realize that this is no mean feat. A cat is easy by comparison."

I was willing to take her word for it. The second and final step was just around the corner:

> My friend recommends that you look closely, intently and lovingly at your cat, observing every little whisker and eyelash and the details of his markings. Then, having relaxed yourself and cleared your mind as much as possible, close your eyes and try to visualize your cat in perfect detail. Sooner or later the essence of your cat's personality will reveal itself to you, and a name will rise from the depths of your subconscious to fit it, and that will be the best possible name you could have chosen for your cat.

Mrs. Walker's book was published some time after I had to name my cat. And so, unfortunately or perhaps fortunately — as a Bostonian, my long suit has never been Tibetan mysticism — I did not have the advantage of it. Nor, for that matter, did I have her list of possible names for white cats. These were, in two columns, as follows:

Whitey	Vanilla
Snowy	Whitewash
Snowhite	White Cloud
Snowflake	Blanche
Snowball	Bianca
Snowdrop	Daisy
Snowflower	Ivory
Snowfire	Rinso
Snowman	Soapsuds
Ermine	Marble
Eggshell	Crystal
Eggwhite	Jack Frost
Eggcream	Oyster

I have no wish to offend anyone who owns a white cat with one of those names, but frankly I didn't see the slightest chance of my cat sitting still for a single one of them.

What I did carefully consider, on the other hand, was an historical name. After all, I was primed with research on the subject, and I saw no reason why my cat should not be the proud bearer of the name of one of his ancestors.

I started with Bast the Egyptian. The trouble was that Bast was not a God but a Goddess. I didn't want to be sexist about the matter of naming, and Bast sounded as if it could be male, all right, but still, there was something a little unnerving about unisexing a Goddess. Leo XIII's cat curled up in the papal robes also appealed at the outset. The pope had named that cat Micetto — a name I liked. But here I was stymied by the fact that it was not only a long story to tell anytime anyone asked me why I had picked that name for my cat, it was also an odd one for a Boston Episcopalian. My Episcopalianism is High Church, all right, but it is hardly in Micetto's class.

The third name I considered was Mohammed's Muezza. Once again, however, the story I would be forced to tell over and over was a long one. And, more important, although I was partial to the Prophet himself, I was considerably less so to many of his present-day followers who, among other failings, have failed utterly to follow his teachings on the matter of kindness to animals.

The names of two of Cardinal Richelieu's cats briefly appealed — Perruque and Racan. They had been named by the cardinal by virtue of the fact of having been born in a wig — i.e., perruque — one commandeered for the occasion by His Eminence from the head of the Marquis de Racan. But the marquis, I learned, was, besides being a friend of the cardinal, not only a minor poet but a bad one at that. If my cat was to be named for a poet, it would only be, I decided, either for a major one or at least a good minor one.

Two other famous cats in history were intriguing. One was the cat owned by Shakespeare's patron, the Earl of Southampton, who was imprisoned in 1602 by Elizabeth I in solitary confinement in the Tower of London. The cat, a large black and white fellow, had been the earl's constant companion and somehow made his way to the Tower and, by climbing down the chimney, to the earl's cell. From here he refused to move and, when the earl was finally released, one of his first acts was to commission a window in Welbeck Abbey. The window is still viewable today, and it shows the earl, alone in his cell, with, beside him, his faithful cat.

The other cat was perhaps Italy's most famous feline — one who had lived in the late 1880s and the early 1890s in a café in Venice in the square facing the church of Santa Maria Gloriosa dei Frari. Not only was this cat an all-white cat, but he was also so well known that a book of his friends was kept in the café, and in it were such signatures as Pope Leo XIII, the king and the queen of Italy, Prince Metternich, and Tsar Alexander III. Furthermore, after the cat died he was immortalized by a sculpture which, like the Earl of Southampton's window, still exists.

There were just two troubles with these cats as possible purveyors of a name for my cat. They were, in order, first, that there was no known name for the Earl of Southampton's cat, it having been lost in history, and second, although the name of the cat in the Venetian café had not been lost, this name turned out to be Nini. And this was one I could see my cat rejecting out of hand.

Two more recent English cats also seemed worthy of consideration. One was Queen Victoria's best-known cat, which, once more, had the additional appeal of being white. The good queen had even found a name which was, apparently, to both her and the cat's liking — White Heather. I could not, however, see it for mine. The other possibility was Winston Churchill's well-known wartime companion Nelson. Much to his owner's chagrin, however, during the London blitzes, Nelson was invariably to be found, if at all, ensconced under the farthest corner of the nearest bed. "Despite my most earnest and eloquent entreaties," the prime minister commented, "I failed most utterly in persuading my friend before taking such craven action to give even passing consideration to the name he bore."

There were many interesting stories about the cats of literary giants — but few, alas, had apparently taken enough time in their naming to suit my purposes. Samuel Johnson, for example, was so fond of one of his cats that, according to Boswell, he invariably left the house to get the cat oysters each afternoon, rather than order one of the servants to do so. Johnson was apparently convinced that, had he so ordered the servants, one of them might well have exacted some sort of vengeance on the animal for having to perform such a menial task. Evidently, despite what you read about servants in those good old days, all was not always beer and skittles between upstairs and downstairs. In any case, the cat's name turned out to be Hodge — one fine, perhaps, for an English butler, but not, in my judgment, for an American cat.

The name of the cat of Alexandre Dumas the Younger came closer to my ideal. This cat, whose name was Mysouff, would every day walk with M. Dumas to a point halfway between his home and his office and then return home. And always he would come back to that place to meet his master and walk home with him. More extraordinary, on days when his master had another engagement and was not going to be there, Mysouff somehow knew and, according to Dumas himself, would never leave the house for the rendezvous.

Mysouff was, I decided, a name I would try on my cat — long story or no long story. Another possibility was one of Charles Dickens' cats, or rather kittens. When Dickens was working late in his study, this kitten would climb up on his desk and, with her paw, snuff out the candle. Dickens would usually relight it, whereupon the kitten would immediately snuff it again — after which Dickens would cease work for the night and devote his attention to her. The trouble was that, once more, I could not find out the name of the kitten. Along with two others, she had been born in Dickens' study to a cat whom, when he first saw her and before he found out she was a female, Dickens had named William. After learning she was about to become a mother, he renamed her Wilhelmina.

Alas, I decided, I could not have a namesake of my favorite author. Dickens would have to go. I did, however, find another possibility. It was a cat owned by H. G. Wells, and its name was Mr. Peter Wells — one which Mr. Wells, the author, not the cat, always insisted be used with the "Mr." included. In any case, Mr. Peter Wells was assuredly one of the most remarkable of cats. When a guest talked either too loudly or too long, it was his, Mr. Peter Wells', custom to jump down from his favorite chair, and then, making as much noise and getting as much attention as possible, proceed to leave the room. This surely must have added a dimension of suspense that has rarely been equalled in any salon, and I would, I decided, at least try on my cat the name Mr. Peter Amory.

Of all authors and cat-lovers I found, Mark Twain certainly has the distinction of having given his cats the oddest names. Among these were Apollinaris, Zoroaster, Blatherskite, and Sour Mash. The idea was, Twain maintained, not to be mean to the cats but, since they were so difficult about names anyway, to go all out and give them names which would be good practice for children learning the pronunciation of long and difficult words. Twain also had a cat named Tammany, one of whose kittens provided in Twain's poolroom the same appraisal service offered by Mr. Peter Wells in H. G. Wells' drawing room. It was the habit of the kitten to hole up in a corner pocket, thus adding, by her blockade, a new dimension to any game. To this tactic she added a second with her habit of not always, but occasionally, when the mood struck, swiping out with her paw and redirecting a ball headed toward the other corner pocket. In these cases, Twain recalled, house rules called not for any condemnation of the kitten but merely for putting the ball back as closely as possible to the original position and reshooting the shot.

Last but not least I uncovered the startling fact that undoubtedly the greatest cat-lover of all authors — the French writer Colette — was also one who failed so miserably at the naming of her cat that she ended up calling her *La Chatte*. It was, of course, merely the feminine of the French word for cat. While Colette always frankly admitted to having tried and failed to find any other name satisfactory to La Chatte, she was nonetheless highly pleased and always stoutly defended her cat's eventual choice. "I believe," she said, "that all cats like to think they are the only cats in the world. If this is true, then La Chatte at least has the firmest nominal claim on the honor."

Colette's name for her cat made another point. Our word *cat* is actually closer to other languages — and in those languages closer to ours — than perhaps any other common noun. He is *chat* in French, *Katz* in German, *ga'ta* in modern Greek, *cattus* in Latin, *gato* in Spanish and Portuguese, *gatto* in Italian, *kat* in Dutch and Danish, *katt* in Swedish and Norwegian, *kot* in Polish, *kut* in Egyptian, *kat* in parts of Africa and *katsi* in others, and *kott* in Russian. Even in languages in which he is a little different, he is still close — as in *kedi* in Turkish and *gatz* in Armenian — and elsewhere where he is different, the word for him comes from the sound he makes — as in *mao* or *mio* in Chinese, *neko* in Japanese, *biss* in Arabic, and, perhaps simplest of all, in Indonesian, *puss*.

There were at least possibilities here — of giving him the name for himself in another language — and, after some consideration, I placed on my list both Chairman Miow and King Kut. I also made a last run at literary catdom, all the way back to the first known reference to a domesticated cat in literature. He belonged to an Irish scholar in the ninth century, and his name was Pangur Bán. I liked the P and B — good easily recognizable consonants — and I put Pangur Bán on my list too. Elsewhere, however, the pickings were slim. There were, among non-fiction cats, Poe's Caterina, Thoreau's Min, Hemingway's Puss, and D. H. Lawrence's Puss Puss, and there were also, in fiction, Saki's talking Tobermory, Don Marquis' alley cat friend of Archie, Mehitabel, Gallico's resurrected goddess Thomasina, and even H. Allen Smith's Rhubarb, the cat who inherited a ball team. But none, unfortunately, filled the bill.

I also gave due consideration to the names of the great cartoon cats of history — among them Felix, Tom (of Tom and Jerry fame), and Garfield. If Garfield was my favorite name, however, the story of Felix interested me the most. Drawn by Pat Sullivan, an Australian cartoonist who came to this country in 1914, Felix' name, which derived from "felicity," was specifically chosen to counteract cruel superstitions about cats. Also, Sullivan admitted, he had based Felix in no small measure on the movements and humor of Charlie Chaplin. In any case, Felix became so famous that when Walt Disney created his Mickey, whom he had at first wanted to be a cat also, he soon decided that rather than compete with Felix, he would make Mickey a mouse.

Alas, Felix was black. But in the course of my search I did discover a truly remarkable white cat, who also had an equally remarkable name. He was Don Pierrot de Navarre, and he was owned by the French author Théophile Gautier, the same man whom we have previously met as the author of the statement that only a Frenchman could appreciate a cat. Gautier wrote movingly about this animal, who must surely rank at the top of all the literary cats in history:

> Sitting close to the fire, he seemed always interested in the conversation, and now and then, as he looked from one speaker to another, he would give a little protesting mew, as though in remonstrance to some opinion which he could not bring himself to share. He adored books and whenever he found one open on the table, he would sit down by it, look attentively at the printed page, turn over a leaf or two and finally fall asleep, for all the world as if he had been trying to read a modern novel. As soon as he saw me sit down to write, he would jump on my desk and watch the crooked and fantastic figures which my pen scattered over the paper, turning his head every time I began a fresh line. Sometimes it occurred to him to take a part in my work, and then he would make little clutches at my pen, with the evident design of writing a page or so. . . .

Now there was a cat I could identify with — and so, I hoped, could my cat. Or that at least he would do me the courtesy of giving to the name of Don Pierrot de Navarre the consideration it so richly deserved.

The cat was lying in my lap with his head on my knees sound asleep. But since it was getting late and I had no idea how long our naming session would take, I decided to wake him up and get on with the job.

Gently I turned him around with his head facing me. Then, after giving him a moment or two to pull himself together, I began, slowly but firmly, our discussion.

All animals, I explained, when they are domesticated and live with people, have names. Even birds who have lived with people, I continued, have names. I wanted to get his full attention as quickly as possible, and he is very interested in ornithology.

Just the way, I went on, people have names. The way, I proceeded a step further, I had a name. My name, for example, I told him, is Cleveland.

He gave me a long look which seemed at first to be full of concern, but, I soon realized, also contained advice. It was clear he felt I should, and as quickly as possible, seek professional help.

I ignored this. Instead I told him, just as firmly as I had started, that if he would keep an open mind about the whole thing, having a name would not only make him feel more comfortable around people, it would also make him feel so around other animals.

Even animals who were not domesticated, I pointed out, who just lived near people, such as animals in zoos, had names. Very large animals like elephants and lions and tigers and leopards. In fact, all large cats had names. And so, I said, did — well, smaller cats.

I paused meaningfully and then proceeded. All cats who lived with people, I pointed out to him, had names. Not just some cats, not just most cats, but *all* cats. Indeed, I concluded fearlessly, if he could name one single solitary cat who had ever lived with any person anywhere and who did not have a name, I would agree not to name him. Furthermore, I would even give him a reasonable time to think of such a cat.

And I did, too. I played it absolutely straight. But when he did not come up with a solitary example, as I knew he would not, I moved ahead to my peroration. In most cases, I told him, people just decided on a name they wanted to give a cat, and the cat itself had nothing whatever to say about the matter. I told him that I was not one of those people, and I would certainly never do a thing like that — I had much too much respect for him. Instead, what I was going to do — in fact what I had already done — was not to name him anything until I found a name that I — and here I almost slipped but managed to catch myself — that *he* and I, I quickly amended, *both* liked.

His tail began thumping on my knee. He wanted me to get to the point. The point was, I said, that I was going to give him fair say in the matter. In other words, I was going to try various names on him and get his reaction to them. And here I gave him fair warning. If he was willing to cooperate, well and good. But if he wasn't, so be it. In that unhappy event, I would just have to take the one which he appeared to dislike the least.

With that I put him down. All right, I told him, I am now going to turn my back on you and walk a few steps away. And when I turn around, I want to see what your reaction is.

I did so. "Here, Don Pierrot de Navarre," I said. "Here, Don Pierrot de Navarre." I then turned around to see the reaction.

I couldn't believe my eyes. If it is possible for a cat to

look daggers, then my cat looked daggers as perhaps none of his brethren had ever looked daggers before. I could not imagine what could be the matter. Certainly Don Pierrot de Navarre was a beautiful name, stately and imposing, fully worthy of any cat's dignity, almost royal . . . and then I stopped. It was, of course, nothing to do with Don Pierrot de Navarre. What had happened was that, in my enthusiasm to try and sell him the name, I had used the forbidden word "here." I had indeed marched straight into the anti-come danger zone and thus I had broken our previous compromise agreement.

I apologized profusely. I told him that I fully understood it would be impossible for him even to consider the merits of any name which had been prefaced by such an offensive and obnoxious word as *here*. But would he listen to it again? Without, of course, that word?

He would — and did. This time I just said, "Don Pierrot de Navarre" as persuasively as I could, and then once again repeated it.

And this time his look was just plain blank. And a blank look on a white cat is, I assure you, a very blank look indeed.

I decided to abandon Don Pierrot, at least for the moment, and move on to the works of Alexandre Dumas. Once more I turned my back. "Mysouff," I said, "Mysouff." I liked the *f* sound and was sure that he would, too. "Mysouff," I announced a third time, and emphasized the *f*.

I got a reaction, all right, but not the one I had been hoping for. Instead, the cat made a beeline for the kitchen. Obviously to him I was discussing dinner. When I had persuaded him to return I abandoned literary pretensions and chose, for my third try, the first of recorded domestic cats. "Pangur Bán," I informed him. "Pangur Bán."

For the first time I got a reaction. Not a large reaction, mind you, but a small one. I made a mental note of it, but forged ahead anyway. "Mr. Peter Amory," I intoned as if I were a butler announcing a guest; "Mr. Peter Amory."

What I received this time was a very slow, very large, and, I thought, very deliberate yawn. Alas, I regretfully concluded, I was not destined to have a cat named for such a stern editor of guest conversation. But the attempt to get Mr. Peter at least partway by him had given me the idea for another possibility. For some time I had been known as a curmudgeon. And the more my cat and I had been together, the more I detected unmistakable signs of curmudgeonly behavior in him. Whether he was modelling himself on me I couldn't yet be sure. But I flattered myself that he was, and anyway I thought Curmudgeon deserved at least a try as a name.

There were, however, a couple of difficulties here. For one thing, I had learned at first hand that *curmudgeon* is a word the meaning of which is a mystery to a large number of young people nowadays — who are, of course, the very people most in need of such a man. And I say "man" advisedly — a curmudgeon is one of the last things in this world a man can be that a woman cannot be. I had one aunt who tried all her life to be a curmudgeon and who never succeeded. All she did succeed in doing was making my uncle a curmudgeon. In any case, when I once asked the studio audience during a television appearance what a curmudgeon was, the first definition I received was "a medieval weapon," and second was "a kind of fish."

There was also that matter of the prefix "cur" — which was bad enough from a dog's point of view but from a cat's obviously totally unsuitable. And then it came to me. Why not change the "cur" to "purr." Purrmudgeon — surely an excellent name for a cat of mine and never mind if some young people thought it was a weapon or a fish.

Eagerly, I tried it on him. "Purrmudgeon," I said, pronouncing both *r*'s, and then, lest he think I was gilding the lily, I tried it again without any emphasis on the second *r*. "Purmudgeon."

He rejected it, of course. And the most maddening thing was that he had never seemed to me more curmudgeonly than when he did so. Discouraged, I returned to the drawing board. Perhaps, I mused, I was too abstruse in my choices, and the whole process should be simpler. It was a long way from the kind of thing I had been throwing at him, but I decided to have a go anyway. What about the name of Christmas for him? The night I had found him had, after all, been if not actually a white Christmas, at least a white Christmas Eve.

I tried it, as usual, twice, "Christmas. Christmas." Again, nothing. I had the uncomfortable feeling that he was now too bored even to yawn. And I was beginning to get very cross. What on earth could he have against Christmas as a name? Furthermore, Christmas was a terrific name because it was full of easily understood consonants and *s*'s — which any cat worthy of the name would understand by, if nothing else, the hissing sound.

"Christmas," I hissed. "Christmas."

He understood, all right. His ears went straight back and he hissed right back at me. I decided to concede.

I had, however, one more suggestion to make. Would

he consider the name Santa Claus? That was a name, I told him frankly, that even someone as persnickety as he was could not possibly have anything against. Santa Claus was, I explained, not only a jolly fellow, full of good cheer who brought joy and gifts, but he was also someone — something which I knew would appeal to him — about whom everybody made a great mystery. Older children, for example, were not allowed to tell younger children there wasn't any such person. And, as a final inducement, I assured him, if it would make him more comfortable with the name, we could spell it Santa Claws.

It was no use. He didn't want to be Santa Claus no matter how it was spelled. With some deliberation he rose to his feet, stretched himself paw by paw, and then, with a look which said more clearly than words that he had taken as much of this nonsense as he could reasonably be expected to absorb at one sitting, he marched sedately from the room.

I stayed where I was. I had been determined to have a new name for him by nightfall or know the reason why. Now I knew the reason why.

I plunged into thought. History had failed, humor had failed, the holiday season had failed. What was left? For some reason I started to think what some of my very favorite animals were — perhaps I could get a name from among them. I was in no mood to include the cat, but I did include the dog, the horse, the donkey, the tiger, the dolphin, the otter, the beaver, and the bear. There were many others but, suddenly, with the bear I stopped. Bear would be a good name for him, I thought — he looked like a little bear. And, since he was white, what about Polar Bear? As I thought of it, I remembered that he had at least reacted slightly to the name of Pangur Bán. It was an omen. They were both P. B.'s.

I tracked him into the bedroom, where he had curled up comfortably on the counterpane. I did not come right out with the name. I had learned a good deal from my previous earnest attempts. This time there would be no big deal. "Oh, Polar Bear," I remarked, "there you are." I said it so casually that he could not possibly have had a clue as to what I was up to. I sat down on the bed and began to scratch him. "Well," I said with the same casualness, "how's Polar Bear?" I went on from scratching to scrubbling and scrumping.

What I was doing, of course, was making it a fait accompli. And although I would like to tell you that he looked directly at me and solemnly nodded at me, he of course did nothing of the kind.

I would also like to be able to tell you that from that moment on he knew his name and that, if he doesn't always come to it, he does at least some of the time. As I say, I would like to be able to tell you that, but it would not be the truth.

Finally, I would say that, whether he knows it or not, Polar Bear has turned out to be the perfect name for him. But that too would not be the truth. There is only one perfect name for a cat. And, as T. S. Eliot has told us, it is one we will never know:

The Naming of Cats is a difficult matter,
    It isn't just one of your holiday games;
You may think at first I'm as mad as a hatter
When I tell you, a cat must have THREE DIFFERENT NAMES.
First of all, there's the name that the family use daily,
    Such as Peter, Augustus, Alonzo or James,

Such as Victor or Jonathan, George or Bill Bailey —
All of them sensible everyday names.
There are fancier names if you think they sound sweeter,
Some for the gentlemen, some for the dames:
Such as Plato, Admetus, Electra, Demeter —
But all of them sensible everyday names.
But I tell you, a cat needs a name that's particular,
A name that's peculiar, and more dignified,
Else how can he keep up his tail perpendicular,
Or spread out his whiskers, or cherish his pride?
Of names of this kind, I can give you a quorum,
Such as Munkustrap, Quaxo, or Coricopat,
Such as Bombalurina, or else Jellylorum —
Names that never belong to more than one cat.
But above and beyond there's still one name left over,
And that is the name that you never will guess;
The name that no human research can discover —
But THE CAT HIMSELF KNOWS, *and will never confess.*
When you notice a cat in profound meditation,
The reason, I tell you, is always the same:
His mind is engaged in a rapt contemplation
Of the thought, of the thought, of the thought of his name:
His ineffable effable
Effanineffable
Deep and inscrutable singular Name.

VII ◦ *His Hollywood*

To this day it is not quite clear to me why I decided to take Polar Bear with me on that trip to Hollywood. One reason was that I was going to be gone at least a couple of weeks — which was actually longer than the total period I had had him. Although Marian would, I knew, come in and not only feed him but play with him as well, still he would be alone a good deal of the time — and at the very time when he should be fortifying his security, not feeling deserted.

The second and more important reason for taking him was one which I would not admit, even to myself. It was the simple fact that I had become so fond of him that I simply could not handle being without him that long.

I was well aware of the difficulties attendant on my decision — indeed, I had been made so by every cat friend I had. One and all imparted such dire warnings about feline foraying that, after listening to them, I became convinced that a cat, unless trained at kittenhood, ranked as a fellow traveller on long trips somewhere above alligators and orangutans, but well below cross servants, quarrelsome children, sick goldfish, and compact automobiles.

There were, these friends were quick to inform me, many reasons for this. In the first place, they pointed out, cats, perhaps more than any other species, were territorial creatures — their home was their castle, their hearth, their heath, and even where their heart was. In the second place, these same friends emphasized, cats were creatures of conservatism and tradition. My friends did not go so far as to claim all cats were Republican, but the fact is that I had for some time suspected it of Polar Bear. For one thing, he didn't like anything happening that had not happened before. And although this had little to do with political party affiliation, it was a prejudice which, of course, flew fairly in the face of trip-taking — particularly on a plane to a place where he had never been before.

I patiently listened while my friends informed me that, in the third place, I would soon find that a cat regarded anywhere he had never been before, even a relatively simple hotel room, as strictly uncharted wilderness, around any corner of which lurked dangers which would put to shame a Chamber of Horrors in a wax museum on Hallowe'en. By no means satisfied with a total tailing, tracking, and sniffing of every nook and cranny of such a place, my cat would, they assured me, remain stiffened with terror until he had been there for a long enough period to have monitored every single sound from outside the room as well as inside, and to have carefully cased all comings and goings, both by day and night. They added, as a kind of minor afterthought, that during such a period my cat would, of course, not eat anything for as long as it took to convince me that he would never eat again — as being his way of administering fit punishment for the worries to which I had subjected him by taking him to such a place to begin with.

In the fourth and final place, my friends firmly abjured me, I would have the problems of the actual trip itself. Cats, I was informed, love scenery and seeing things, but these sights must be contemplated while they themselves are stationery. When they themselves are being fast-forwarded, they do not have the slightest interest in even the most engrossing visual fare — such as birds flying by outside the window of a car, train, or, for that matter, even a plane. If forced to watch same, I would, in fact, find not only disinterest but actual distrust and distaste, both of which would undoubtedly culminate first in severe motion sickness and finally actual vomiting.

As if all this was not enough, manuals on cat travel were presented to me which were crammed from beginning to end with a veritable litany of peregrinational pitfalls. One manual advised that the worst thing possible before taking one's cat on a long trip was to take him on a short or trial one. "This," I read, "will only make you worry more." Another manual declared that no trip with a cat should be undertaken without water, a non-spill water container, a litter pan, litter, air freshener, disinfectant, a whisk broom, and a supply of moist tissues. The latter, this work advised, are "for you, not the cat."

The worst possible thing, I read, was even to consider taking one's cat either to a friend's house or a hotel room. Dazedly I wondered what other alternatives there were. In any case, I was advised, the house of a friend, particularly a friend not sympathetic toward cats in general, let alone the specific problems of a cat on tour, could prove a nightmare. As for a hotel room, I read that literally no hotel room could be secured, that, sooner or later, a maid or a bellboy or an errant room service waiter or engineer would open the door and your cat would fly out, both to escape the new enemy and to find you — and while he would indeed be looking for you, your chance of finding him, when he could literally be anywhere, would be infinitesimal.

To all such reasoning and advice, I turned the deafest of ears. Pish, tush, I thought. Polar Bear was different. To one of my friends, who was most severe on the subject of the perils of the road, I addressed the question as to whether or not he happened to be aware of the fact that a kitten had once climbed the Matterhorn. A kitten, I repeated. He looked at me as if I had two heads, but he did not stop me from telling him the story.

It had happened some years ago. Matt, as he has since been renamed, was at that time a ten-month-old kitten — a black and white one, I was pleased to note — who had been with his owner the night before the climb in a hotel at the bottom of the mountain. The next morning Matt's owner awoke before dawn, and, weighed down with climbing equipment, departed the hotel room, leaving Matt behind to await his master's return. Step by tortuous step, Matt's owner and his party, together with guides, compasses, and a full complement of mountaineering tackle, including ropes, pickaxes, food, water, and emergency medical kit, made their long trek toward the summit. Finally they reached it and, as they were basking in their achievement and congratulating one another on their collective hardiness, the celebration was suddenly interrupted by a loud and querulous meow. Up the 14,780 feet behind them, also every step of the way, including up sheer rock, but with of course no equipment, food, or water, had come Matt — who, they soon learned, was very hungry and very thirsty but otherwise not the slightest the worse for wear.

I pointed out to still another skeptic some other extraordinary travelling which cats had accomplished. The best-known story, perhaps, was that of the "incredible journey" described in the great book of that name by Sheila Burnford. Miss Burnford, it should be remembered, not only wrote movingly of the trip across three hundred miles of Canadian wilderness of two great dogs — the young Labrador and the brave old English bull — but also told the tale of Tao, the Siamese cat who more than once saved all three of them, including both dogs. Indeed, on one occasion he saved them from a large and furious mother bear whose cub they had disturbed.

Finally, I told my skeptic friends of what I believe is still the all-time record for the longest journey ever made by a deserted animal. This was that of a cat owned by a New York veterinarian. The man lived with a friend and, when he had to move to California, he left his cat, believing that the animal would be better off staying with his friend in his old and accustomed quarters. The cat had been to the new house, in California, just once, but, five months later, that vet, like the Matterhorn climbers, heard a familiar meow. He opened the door and although his cat was indeed the worse for wear, he nonetheless dignifiedly entered the house, made his way to the familiar armchair which had been in the previous house, clambered up onto the cushion, and promptly fell asleep.

Surely, I told my friends, if one cat, as a kitten, could climb the Matterhorn, another could help two dogs make it to safety across the Canadian wilderness, and a third, alone, could travel the three thousand miles from New York to California, I could at least take Polar Bear along with me on one measly little trip to Hollywood.

Today, looking back, I would like to say how right I was. And, of course, how all the people who had warned me had been wrong. The only trouble is that it did not turn out that way. They were right and I, hard cheese as it is for a man of my mettle to admit, was wrong.

Actually, the trip started out fine — although I would like to make it clear that I have never understood those ridiculous airline rules which allow for only one animal in the first-class section and one in tourist. Are they afraid of barking, or meowing, or fighting, or people tripping over them, or what? The animals are, after all, in carriers, and provided each is separated by a row, having at least a few more per flight would hardly seem a major menace to air travel — at least not on a par with having the person in front of you putting his seat back in your lap, or having four armrests for each row of three people.

Although I had once done an imagined interview with the designer of airplane tourist sections — a charming fellow, albeit one only three feet nine in height and with only one arm — the fact was that I was hardly in a position to make a fuss about the animals in the passenger section. The Fund for Animals had, not long before my flight, been one of the leaders in the battle to force the airlines to redesign their baggage compartments so that they would be more humane for animal travel — which, up until our fight, they had not been — and for me now to carry the fight immediately to the passenger sections, with my own personal cat, seemed a bit much.

The long and short of it was that I had no alternative but to obey the regulations — and so I had obediently, and well in advance, secured one reservation for Polar Bear and one for me. I also had the proper kind of carrier, which, though a tight fit, could just make it under the seat. And the flight attendant could not have been nicer. Before takeoff, she allowed me to open the carrier enough so that she could have a quick pat, and she generously ooohed and aahhhed over how beautiful he was. She also promised that I could, after takeoff, open the carrier again.

However, not only did Polar Bear not return the young lady's generous advances, he pointedly and unceremoniously turned away from her. This is a peril, I was learning the hard way, of introducing your cat to anyone when you and he are in transit. The fact is that most cats, most of the time, have already met everybody they care to meet. And when they are travelling, make no mistake, all cats have. It thus behooves the cat-owned, on the road, to have at the ready a small arsenal of excuses, not excluding anything from little white lies to large black ones.

I made use of one of the latter. I told the flight attendant that ordinarily Polar Bear was the soul of friendliness, but having had the tranquilizer and all — well, she would understand. She didn't, of course, and he hadn't, but at least I had tried.

I was lucky in one respect. I had secured the window seat and there was no one in the middle seat. There was, however, a large man in the aisle seat and he had watched with interest Polar Bear's meeting with the stewardess. "He isn't much of a traveller, is he?" Once more I lied. I informed the man that Polar Bear was a great little traveller on short flights, but on long flights — which, I explained, he apparently suspected this was going to be —

he was inclined to get sick. This information, I was fairly sure, would minimize the man's interest when I would later be able to get the carrier up on the middle seat between us. And it did.

As we roared down the runway, Polar Bear gave voice to a steady stream of woeful "aeiou" 's — all of which were clearly audible even above the roar of the plane. I reached down and poked a finger through one of the airholes in the carrier to reassure him. But I doubt if it did much good. At that moment, compared to air travel, he would clearly have opted for a Conestoga wagon climbing through the Brenner Pass. To him airplanes put too many people into too small an area, and in the particular area where he was, there were many too many feet, which is his least favorite part of people at any time. Besides, it was all terribly noisy, cramped, and uncomfortable and, in his opinion, dangerous.

When I finally had his carrier up on the seat beside me, with the top partly open and my hand inside and resting on him, I tried to reassure him about the danger. But I wasn't very convincing. As an old pilot, I don't like takeoffs either — and I know they are, with the ghastly exception of running into another plane while airborne, the most hazardous part of flying.

I tried to interest him in the clouds outside the plane window, but he found them poor visual fare. It was obvious that everything my friends had said about cats not liking to be moving while doing their sightseeing was right on target. Even if Polar Bear had seen a bird, I knew it would not have had the slightest appeal. As far as he was concerned, everything out there was for the birds.

The arrival of food, I hoped, might at least distract him from his current dim view of the world in general and me in particular, but once again my friends were right. Though the flight attendant brought him his own little dish of food when the peanuts and drinks came, he wouldn't even get close enough to it to see what it was. As for the rest of the meal, he just wasn't buying. Airplane food was, to him, airplane food — and its appearance served only to reinforce the fact that the fast about which I had been warned, and which I dreaded, had, in fact, begun. I realized that I should have had a can of his own food to tempt him with, and indeed I had several such cans with me. But where were they? Like a selection of his toys, of course, they were in my suitcase — in the bowels of the baggage compartment. I think of everything.

The worst part of it all was that he had clearly not only gone on a hunger strike, he had also gone on a sleep strike. And when a cat does that, you can be sure the news is all bad. That trip lasted five and one half hours, and it seemed, at a minimum, like that many days.

At last, however, it was over, and I was met at the airport by Paula Deats, a screenwriter and former Fund coordinator. Paula is a cat woman from way back and she was over Polar Bear like an enthusiastic tent. Polar Bear, on the other hand, while better than he had been during the flight — anything, after all, was an improvement on that — was reserved. We were not even out of the airport yet, Paula was the first California girl he had met, and frankly, he seemed to feel, it was all, as it so often is in California, a bit too much too soon. Once more, it was time for an excuse. "He hasn't slept much," I told her, "and he's got a little jet lag."

Paula had managed to park close by, itself a feat at the L.A.X. Airport, and we were soon on our way — albeit in an automobile which, I was too polite to mention, could easily have fit inside the ancient Checker which I drive in New York. I have always regarded it as interesting that California girls who apparently feel very deeply about the necessity of having their own "space" somehow have so little regard for it in their vehicles. Nonetheless, crowded as we were, I opened the carrier and let Polar Bear out. I made no effort, however, to lift him onto my lap and show him the sights of L.A. Indeed, I was determined not to do so until we had turned onto Sunset Drive and left the horrors of the Freeway behind us.

"When are you going back?" Paula inquired. "Oh," I replied, "in a couple of months." It was an old routine between us. It had long been my experience that nowhere but in California do people ask you about your return immediately upon your arrival. Californians in general, I have noticed, are at least somewhat prone to this practice, but with California girls it is nothing less than second nature. They have, after all, been trained at birth that if they fail to insert this question into the conversation well before any plans are made, an out-of-towner, ignorant of local customs, might actually be tempted to stay through one of their sacred weekends — and hence interfere with either meditations or hot tubs, est or Rolfing, windsurfing or hang gliding.

Polar Bear, during this exchange, was alternately thrashing around or pretending he was dead. However since Paula, like most animal activists, had been known to house the worst-behaved animals imaginable — particularly her cats — I decided that rather than try to make further excuses for him, I would instead take the offensive. I told her that a fellow author, Richard Smith, had recently written an entire article about the difference between East

Coast cats and West Coast cats — and that, in his opinion, East Coast cats were less concerned about their looks than West Coast cats and preferred to be valued for their minds rather than for their bodies alone.

Paula refused to rise to the bait. I was, however, not finished. I told her that while Smith also stated that having a meaningful, caring, and nurturing relationship might be more important to West Coast cats than meeting a cat with a great body, the fact remained that East Coast cats *always* preferred to select their partners on the basis of personality and shared interests.

Paula said nothing. I only hoped, I further ventured, that Polar Bear's neutering would not interfere with any future inclinations he might have toward nurturing.

But Paula, being, like Marian, used to my bad jokes and worse puns, still refused to rise. I tried to get her to hold hands with me with her free hand, but she made a fist. I repeat — California girls are very strange.

As for Polar Bear, getting him, on this drive, to rise to anything was no easy task either. Finally, once we had swung onto Sunset, I was reduced to picking him up, planting his bottom on my lap, and putting his paws on the closed window. "Look, Polar Bear," I exhorted. "California! Beverly Hills! Movie stars!"

To Polar Bear this was once more evidence that I had gone around the bend — in this case some three thousand miles around. In any case, he did not see any movie stars, but he did see many people selling maps to movie stars' homes, as well as a steady stream of well-manicured lawns and an occasional well-manicured native either getting in or out of a well-manicured foreign automobile. He also saw a number of joggers and runners and was, like all sightseers in that area, interested in the fact that it is all right to run or jog in Beverly Hills, but you can be arrested for walking.

The Beverly Hills Hotel, toward which Polar Bear and I were headed, was a hostelry to which I had regularly repaired since the days of *High Society*, the first movie script I had ever worked on. Originally, the area where such late notables as Will Rogers, Spencer Tracy, Douglas Fairbanks, Sr., and Darryl Zanuck had played polo — from which derives the title of its famous lounge — both the hotel and the town around it were named after, of all places, the obscure Boston resort of Beverly Farms. Why it should have been so named — as well as why the "Farms" part became lost — is not clear. Nor, to an old Bostonian — one born, in fact, at the equally obscure Boston resort of Nahant — has it ever been quite clear why Californians, no matter how strange, chose to name their most select location, as well as their most renowned hostelry, for a Bostonian resort whose chief claim to fame is the fact that President William Howard Taft once stayed there. Certainly Beverly Farms was not even as famous as the Boston resort of Lenox — one forever memorialized by its headline of January 6, 1933 — "PRESIDENT COOLIDGE DEAD — MAY HAVE FISHED HERE."

But Beverly Hills is far from California's only example of curious naming. Indeed, I learned on the impeccable authority of my friend Maria Cooper, daughter of the late Gary, that the most famous of all California towns was named by a man who, visiting in London, was so taken with his host's name for his house that, upon his return to California, decided similarly to favor the area in which he owned land. The name was Hollywood.

Beverly Hills never became as famous as Hollywood,

but one of its hotels did indeed become better known than any of Hollywood's. And it did so despite the fact that it was, and still is, one of the strangest-shaped edifices this side of Xanadu — and was, and still is, painted pink.

The reason for its fame was simple. Early on, the hotel was not just a place to see, but, far more important by Hollywood standards, a place in which to be seen. All of this, too, started modestly. Indeed, there are still old-timers who recall the first of its mandatory sights — an elegant stallion being ridden down "The Bridle Path," as it was then known, by an equally elegant white-haired character actor named Hobart Bosworth.

Mr. Bosworth was not to remain for long in solitary splendor among the scenic sights. To the hotel repaired not only the Garbos and the Valentinos, the Barrymores and the Charlie Chaplins, the Barbara Huttons and the Howard Hugheses, but also royalty and Presidents, moguls and magnates. And while this parade of notables would, because of the worldwide penetration of the silver screen, have made any hotel famous, the Beverly Hills Hotel was made particularly so because of the penchant, on the part of a goodly percentage of its patronage, to choose the place not only for their regular visits but also for their irregular trysts. Following the footsteps of such as Clark Gable and Carole Lombard came, without benefit of clergy, either to the hotel proper or to its even more secluded bungalows, literally dozens of other celebrated couples. And yet, conversely, when other illustrious couples came unexpectedly with benefit of clergy, these often proved to the average sightseer, perhaps by sheer contrast, to be even more exciting — as, for example, when Mr. Howard Hughes suddenly appeared with an apparently bona fide Mrs. Hughes. And when Mr. Hughes and the former Miss Peters not only took separate bungalows but also ate all their meals apart, this only added to the thrill — particularly when it became known that the Hugheses, after ordering by room service, spent their entire mealtime talking to each other on the telephone.

What had always attracted me to the Beverly Hills Hotel was less the high jinks of the Hollywood hierarchy there than a far simpler and far more practical matter — the hotel had always, from its very opening, been known for hospitality toward animals. Indeed, in many cases its animal guests were almost as famous as were their human owners. Elizabeth Taylor holds, I believe, the record for having, through the years, brought the most animals to the hotel — she also holds the record for bringing the most husbands — but the one-visit record is held by Robert De Niro. Arriving for the filming of *The Last Tycoon*, Mr. De Niro brought with him seven cats.

In those days, animals had their own registration card at the desk and were accorded service on a par with all guests. The only time indeed when service faltered was when a maid refused to clean the bathroom of the fourteen-year-old son of the Ali Ipar of Turkey. In the bathtub, according to the maid, was a bear cub which was not only larger than she was but also had never been properly registered.

Today the policy of the hotel toward animals has, along with its changing ownership, altered. And it has done so not just with such animals as bear cubs but with dogs and cats. It no longer admits, let alone welcomes, them. I have never understood this — or indeed understand why any hotel refuses its guests the right to bring pets. If, for example, one has a dog which barks at night or menaces people in the elevators, it is reasonable to be asked to leave. But if, on the other hand, you have a well-trained dog, he should — perhaps for an extra fee and even the signing of an agreement to pay for any damage the pet might cause — be welcome. By the same token, if you have a cat which claws the furniture, you should, upon your departure, be charged for same. But if you have an animal which is not destructive, he or she should be welcome. All first-rate European hotels take pets, with this policy, as a matter of course. In this country, however, the current trend, with a few notable exceptions, such as the Holiday Inns, which take pets unless it is against a state law, is unfortunately in the opposite direction. One can only hope that in time and with the increasing respect being accorded pet ownership, this trend will be reversed. A possible sign is the success of the Anderson House, a hotel in Washaba, near Minneapolis, where not only are cats welcome but, if you have not brought yours and are homesick for him, the hotel maintains fifteen of them in a barracks dormitory with their names over their rooms, from which you can select a companion to share your room for the night. "It all started," Jeanne Hall, granddaughter of the hotel's founder, told me, "when a man from Pennsylvania, recuperating from a severe operation at the nearby Mayo Clinic, missed his cat so much I lent him one of mine. Now we have so much demand for them we need more. We even have honeymooners who ask for them."

Fortunately, when I arrived with Polar Bear at the hotel, it was still a pro-animal era. Actually, I was engaged in stuffing him into his carrier when Smitty, the doorman who has been there since before anyone (and sometimes even he) can remember, opened the car door. "Hello, Mr.

Amory," he said. "What have you got for us this time?" He peered into the carrier. "Oh," he said, "just a cat." I forgave Smitty. The last time I had arrived at the hotel for a Fund benefit, I had had with me a cheetah — one owned by the actor/writer Gardner McKay and one which, up on the dais, when suddenly flashbulbed from behind by an aggressive photographer, had whirled about so rapidly that, although my arm had been hit by just the very end of his tail, so quick was his motion that at first I had thought my arm was broken.

After the desk amenities were concluded, Wayne, my Bostonian bellman friend, came forward to take the luggage and, on the way to the room, to discuss with me the future fortunes, or lack of same, of the Boston Red Sox and the New England Patriots. Wayne, like me, is a lifetime sufferer.

Once in the room, after Wayne had gone and I had checked all screens, I opened the windows and let Polar Bear out of his carrier. I expected at least a bound around and "At last we are here!" sort of thing. Instead I got exactly what my friends had said I would get — total suspicion. His most motion was, in fact, owl-like — a swivel turn of his head toward the dark closet and under the bed. In vain I explained to him that no enemies could possibly lurk herein — they could not afford the prices. By then, however, he had lost all confidence in not only my judgment but also my credibility.

For some time he did nothing. And when, after what I regarded as a reasonable period, I could stand this no longer, I leaned down, picked him up, carried him to the windowsill, and plumped him down on it. Following this, I moved his head in the direction of the lush California greenery, the handsome pink bungalows across the way, the fascinating sprinklers, and even the interesting tennis game in progress on the courts below. He would have none of any of it. Indeed, except for one short nose wrinkle — which I took to mean he had at least deigned to notice that there was a different smell to California — I could not even get him to continue looking out. And the moment I released him he flew off the windowsill. Then, slowly and warily, he began his policing of the area. The telltale sign of this whole procedure was not only his tail itself — which wasn't up or even reasonably level but was, on the contrary, so far down it was close to dragging — as was indeed the rest of him. Indeed, he conducted the entire search as if he was crawling.

I pretended to scold him. There was absolutely no reason, I informed him, for his slithering around like a wounded bug. Of course he ignored me. When he had finally satisfied himself that there were no immediate enemies inside the room, however, he next did exactly what my friends had warned he would do. He went rigid — this of course to monitor every passing sound in the corridor outside the room, of which, unfortunately, there were many. From time to time, when there were definite evidences of such outside movement, as for example a hall carpet sweeper, he would turn and look at me. Was I just going to sit there, or would I do something about it? Was I an ally or was I at best a defector and at worst a mole? Why had I brought him to this den of iniquity anyway?

To distract him, I unpacked his food, prepared some for him, and put it down with a bowl of water. When I had done so, he again just looked — first at the food and then at the water and finally at me. Obviously he had not the slightest intention of eating or drinking anything. Was this then, I thought darkly, the continuation of the fast of which I had been warned and which he had begun on the airplane? I refused to believe he would do such a thing to me. I did not, however, refuse to believe it so surely that I did not resort to something of which I totally disapprove. I took him over to the water and literally slurped some into him. His look told what he felt. So now, he was saying, reeling back from the shock, you intend to drown me? I told him I had no such intention — he could go without eating for as long as he pleased — but he would jolly well not go without drinking and that was that. Even Gandhi, I reminded him, took liquids during his fasts. And with that I pointed to the water and gave him to understand that if he would not take a drink, I was fully capable of slurping him again.

Amazingly, he did take a drink — albeit a very small one. Actually, I thought, as I savored this small victory, I could use a drink myself. And so, without further ado, I moved his food and water to the bathroom, made a makeshift litter box, and then picked him up and put him in there. I was about to leave when he gave me one more of his looks.

This one was a truly remarkable one. It was the look that a boss gives a worker who is leaving at four-thirty. It was a look which also asked whether or not I, in all seriousness, thought that I was now going to put him in prison — to put him in a place from which he could not possibly even guard the door? Surely I must have taken leave of the last few senses I had left.

I refused to argue. His position, I told him, simply did not merit debate. I also informed him that where I had placed him was hardly a prison. After all, it had an open window from which, even with the screen, he could see all the sights outside and furthermore, there was even a telephone by the commode. He looked once more at me and then at the floor. Where was he expected to lie down? Surely not on that cold, bare floor? I decided to give in on this minor point, and reached for the bath mat. There, I said. And then, trying to make a big thing of it one way or the other, I closed the door.

"AEIOU," he said, and said it with fervor. Indeed, it was such a piercing remark that I was sure it could be heard on the tennis courts below. But I refused to be swayed by it. Instead, I took a sheet of paper from the desk. I was determined, as all the cat travel books had suggested, that there be not just one but two safeguards — both the "Do Not Disturb" sign, which I would place on the outside of the room door, and, on the bathroom door itself, a second and perhaps more potent sign. "PLEASE DO NOT OPEN THIS DOOR UNDER ANY CIRCUMSTANCES," I wrote. "DANGEROUS DOG INSIDE."

As I proudly propped the sign against the door, I could not help thinking that if the son of the Ali Ipar had come up with such a masterpiece, his bear cub might never have been evicted. I tried not, however, to think what Polar Bear would have thought about it.

Actually, with the exception of Polar Bear's attitude toward the entire experience, my trip could not have been more successful. The trip had two purposes, and both were connected with one of the Fund's major wars — against the clubbing of the baby seals. The event occurred each March in Canada off the ice floes of the Magdalene Islands in the Gulf of St. Lawrence and on the so-called Newfoundland Front. I had been on the ice many times and seen the clubbing firsthand. It took place only a few days after the birth of the snow-white infant seals and happened right beside their mothers, who, in a seal's natural environment, the water, would have been strong adversaries, but who, on land, where they had to remain until the seal pups were old enough to swim, were powerless to defend them.

It had become obvious that, in this battle, not only were we not getting anywhere in Canada, we were now actually losing ground because Canada was carrying the fight to us. The same government officials and Fisheries officers who either kept us off the ice entirely or who arrested us when we did manage to get there were now trooping to the United States in a public relations blitz which included radio and television appearances and meetings with the editorial staffs of influential newspapers. Over and over, these Canadian emissaries repeated the same message — that the poor people of the Magdalenes and Newfoundland were utterly dependent on the funds obtained from selling seal pelts, and, as for the clubbing itself, it was not only not cruel, it was actually much less cruel than the killing of animals in an American slaughterhouse. The facts of the matter, which these emissaries ignored, were, of course, much different. The poor people of the Magdalenes and Newfoundland got no meaningful money at all — indeed a mere pittance — from the clubbing compared to the profits reaped by foreign commercial sealers. As for the comparison with American slaughterhouses, this conveniently ignored the fact that non-kosher slaughter in this country, regulated by the Humane Slaughter Act, employs not clubs or hac-a-pics but stunning bolts to render the animals unconscious before death. Nonetheless, the blitz went on and indeed even grew in scope and intensity until it reached the point at which Brian Peckford, then Canadian minister of fisheries and later premier of Newfoundland, told a nationwide U.S. audience that, to Canadians, the clubbing of seals was much the same as was, to Floridians and Californians, the picking of oranges.

One thing was certain — that January we definitely needed some kind of victory in this war. So far the strongest thing we had going for us — and the thing which in the end would win the war — was film. Indeed, one of the Fund for Animals' firsts — and one which I particularly treasured — was that we had managed to get on network television some remarkable footage of the clubbing.

Actually, we had been lucky. The footage was so grim that, try as we might, we could not at that time even get it on a major local station, let alone a network. Finally, however, on the old ABC Dick Cavett morning interview show, I succeeded — primarily because the show was going off the air anyway, and either none of the network brass bothered to look at the film to see if it might be upsetting to the viewing audience, or if they did, didn't care. So air it did, and caused enough stir so that again mostly by luck, that night it was picked up and aired once more, as filler on a slow news night, on the ABC network news.

The effect of this film on millions of American viewers was extraordinary. Mary Tyler Moore, for example, one of the first notables to support us, told me that she remembered exactly where she was and what she was doing when she saw it. "We were at our beach house," she remembered. "I was standing outside the kitchen door and I was holding a pot of soup. I'm not exactly the flamboyant type," she continued, "but I was so horrified, and so angry, that I just threw that soup against the wall.

Then I called our local station and asked them how I could get in touch with you."

Miss Moore was not the only notable who felt that strongly. Another was her late Serene Highness Princess Grace of Monaco, who soon became the Fund's international chairperson. "I cannot stand the idea," she once told me, "that wild animals are killed to satisfy fashion." The baby-seal clubbing became a cause not only for her but for her whole family — the young Princesses Stephanie and Caroline even going so far as to take petitions out onto the streets of Monaco to try and get passersby to sign in protest against the killing.

Doris Day was, and still is, in many ways the most important supporter of all. The first national chairperson of the Fund, she would meet me at a health-food store in Beverly Hills for what she termed a "healthy breakfast." Doris would arrive by bicycle after her regular early morning round of looking for strays, and I remember, at one of these breakfasts, asking her if she believed that love of animals was inherited. "I know mine was," she told me. "My mother was in on the very first rescue I ever made.

"We were living in Cincinnati," she continued, "and I was very young. The people next door had a big, young dog outside in their yard, and I loved him very much. Then, one weekend, his people went away and left him, in very cold weather, to fend for himself without any food or water. I never forgot it, and I never spoke to them again. The dog cried and cried and the second night we took him in. And then, the next day before they got back, we took him away to my uncle's house and never said a word. They believed he had gotten out of the yard and run away, or maybe been stolen. And," she ended fiercely, "he had the greatest life with my uncle — that dog. He had the greatest."

Doris' first love then, and still now, is stray and unwanted dogs and cats, but she had also made for the Fund for Animals, along with Mary Tyler Moore, Angie Dickinson, Amanda Blake, and Jayne Meadows, our famous "Real People Wear Fake Furs" anti-fur advertisement, and she felt, if anything, even more strongly about the clubbing of the baby seals.

Altogether, we had put together quite a group of anticlubbers — a group which included Henry Fonda and Jimmy Cagney, Cary Grant, Katharine Hepburn, Dinah Shore, Jimmy and Gloria Stewart, George C. Scott and Trish Van Devere, Jack Lemmon and Felicia Farr, Glenn Ford, Burgess Meredith, Jonathan Winters, Steve Allen, Burl Ives, Art Linkletter, Beatrice Arthur, Jean Stapleton, Yvette Mimieux, and Joan Rivers.

Many of these stellar names turned out for the press conference which was my major reason for being at the hotel and, after it was over, a number of them worked with me to make anti-sealing public service announcements supporting our position. Moreover, those of them who were also painters — and an extraordinary number were — gave us one or more of their works for us to sell and raise funds for our campaign. Henry Fonda, for example, brought me a painting he had done — a beautiful study of a rose in a vase on an autumnal windowsill — wrapped in an overcoat. "It won't sell around here," he told me. " 'Round here they know I'm not that good. You'll get more for it out of town."

Mr. Fonda was far too modest. He was a fine artist, as no less an authority than Andrew Wyeth once told me, and we later sold his work for a large price. As for Katharine Hepburn, she not only gave us a painting to sell — a wonderful and lacy study of two young actresses in turn-of-the-century costumes — she also allowed us to make prints from it. It was, she told me, a picture she had painted in "a very happy time" — when she and Spencer Tracy, in between film-making, used to paint together.

I thought of Polar Bear often during the press conferences and visiting with our notables. Upstairs and alone, imprisoned in the bathroom, he had of course no part in most of the proceedings. But, with two of the notables, he did play a part. One was a remarkable animal activist named Paul Watson.

Paul and I had been corresponding for some time about the kind of activism we needed to let Canada know we still meant business in the war against sealing. What we had decided upon, in a word, was to paint the seals — to paint them with a red organic dye, one which would be harmless to them but would render them useless for furs.

Our meeting was to decide how best to do this. When Paul arrived, Polar Bear took an immediate liking to him — perhaps, I decided, because Paul looks rather like a bear. Large in size as he is, however, Paul is strictly the "Gentle Ben" kind of bear. And as he sat patting Polar Bear at his feet, he told me briefly the story of his life. A Canadian, he had, at the age of eight, written a letter to another Canadian friend of mine in New Brunswick, Aida Flemming. Mrs. Flemming had founded, for children, a "Kindness Club" and it was to this, for membership, that Paul had written.

He had grown up, it seemed, in an area where some

children regularly shot birds, tied tin cans to the tails of dogs and cats, and put frogs in the street to see how many would be hit by cars. First Paul would protest, then, if his protests were not successful, he would physically intervene. He was often beaten up, but he was never beaten down and, as he grew older, he thought a lot of other things were also worthy of intervention. In sum, not for him were the ways of the hunters who hunted, the trappers who trapped, or, now, the sealers who sealed.

At the outset of our meeting, we both agreed that because of the extraordinary protection the Fisheries officers and even the Royal Canadian Mounted Police gave the sealers — from the air as well as by ship — our options to accomplish our objective were few.

One was to go in by parachute. Both of us agreed, however, that this would be an extremely difficult and dangerous operation. Paul pointed out that it would involve parachute training for all the "painters," and also that they would have to come in at night — which meant not by helicopter but by fixed-wing plane. He felt that this could be done using the most modern "soft" landing chutes, which were capable of being accurately steered and could even hover, but he also pointed out that we would still face the possibility, if not the probability, of some of the painters landing not on the ice but in the ice-cold water, in which case their survival time would be minimal. Finally, it was my turn to note that even if we were successful in getting a team in by parachute, I didn't see any way of getting them out. The ice was too craggy and uneven and far too rapidly changing to count on a rendezvous point, and the seals were spread over far too wide an area.

In the end, we decided to rule out parachute-painting altogether, and went on from there to discuss our second option. This was to try to paint the seals from a plane — by using a crop duster which would be low and slow-flying. I told Paul we had located a pilot who felt, by flying in from Maine at night, that he could do the job, and that we had even gone so far as to have him make some practice runs on some tame sheep outside Denver. But, as with the parachuting, I told him, there were problems. At best, flying in and crossing in the Canadian border at night, with no filed flight plan, would subject the pilot to permanent loss of license — at worst, there was a good chance he would be shot down. I also told Paul that from the practice runs we had had, we had ascertained that both accurate control of the dye as well as its direction had proved next to impossible. We had not hurt any sheep, but there was a very good chance that, considering the winds and weather conditions over the ice at night, we could even blind some seals. And, even if we did not, after it was over the authorities would surely publicly announce that we had done so.

All in all, the plane option too was ruled out. This left us with only one final option — to go in by ship. The major problem here was that it would have to be a ship capable of getting through the ice, which could often quickly freeze, solid as granite, to incredible depths. The commercial sealing ships had their way to the seals literally carved through the ice for them by huge Canadian Coast Guard icebreakers — we would have to do it alone. I knew that the price of buying an icebreaker would be far beyond us, and I asked Paul if it would be possible to charter one. He shook his head. But I refused to give up. I told him, as an old salt from 'way back — one who had spent his boyhood summers in Marblehead, Massachusetts, birthplace of the Revolutionary hero General Glover, the country's first Marine — I simply was not convinced that somehow, somewhere, we could not get hold of some kind of ship which could, by hook or by crook, get through to those seals. I told Paul I wouldn't presume to tell him, a former Merchant Mariner, what kind of a ship it would be, but I did want him to tell me if my idea was at least possible.

Paul said it was, and for the first time I saw light at the end of our tunnel. Paul too became excited. He told me that he felt there was no need for us even to think in terms of an icebreaker. That we should, in his opinion, just buy a regular ship and make it into an icebreaker. How, I wanted to know. "By," he said firmly, "putting concrete into the bow, and a lot of rocks, too."

I like people with answers. What kind of ship was he talking about? Paul suggested a British trawler. The British fishing fleet, he said, was in deep trouble, and he felt we could pick up a trawler relatively cheaply.

I leaned over to pat Polar Bear, who was still at Paul's feet. What kind of money, I asked nervously, were we talking about? It was Paul's turn to pat Polar Bear again. "Maybe a hundred thousand dollars," he said, "maybe two hundred thousand."

Paul's long suit, I would soon learn, was not economics — and particularly not economical economics. The Fund for Animals had, at that time, a grand total of less than half that amount. I would have to raise a lot of money, and quickly, and — because we would have to maintain secrecy about what we intended to do — I would have to do it all without being able to tell people what their money would be going for.

It was not a pleasant prospect. Nonetheless, the success of our press conference had made me optimistic. After a moment's pause, I told Paul to go to England and get us a ship as fast as he could. Then, as we were shaking hands at the door, I added something else. I told him I would like to name the ship *The Polar Bear*.

Paul looked downcast. I asked him if he didn't like the name. He shook his head. Well then, what was it? Paul shuffled his feet. "I already had a name in mind," he said. "I wanted to call her," he went on, "*Sea Shepherd*."

I had to admit that his was the better name. I looked at Polar Bear. "But why," Paul asked, "don't you bring Polar Bear along? Every ship needs a ship's cat — you know, for good luck."

This was no time for travel lies — little white or large black. I told Paul I would talk to Polar Bear about the matter, but for him not to count on it. Polar Bear, as he surely could see, wasn't much of a traveller. If he wasn't any too fond of Hollywood and the Beverly Hills Hotel, he could hardly be expected to be thrilled at the prospect of banging through the Canadian ice, in a ship which wasn't designed for the job, in twenty-degrees-below-zero weather.

While we were still at the Beverly Hills Hotel, however, Polar Bear did at last get to meet a movie star, and it was eminently fitting that, when he did, it turned out to be one of the greatest of them all.

It was Cary Grant, and it happened in a curious way. I had for some years known Cary and occasionally saw him when I was in California. On this occasion I had invited him to have a drink with me in the Polo Lounge. I had assumed that this hallowed Hollywood room would have, through the years, had enough stars as to be in its way a "safe house" in which there would be no such thing as autograph seeking or other untoward events of that nature. But I had reckoned without the truly incredible appeal of Mr. Grant. Hardly had we sat down when at least three people had left their own tables, come over to ours, and were just standing there.

Cary never gave autographs, but his turn-downs of requests for them were such studies in charm that I often thought they served as come-ons even to people who knew they wouldn't actually get one. In any case, this proved itself on this occasion — and, as usual, Cary was up to the challenge. To one woman who gushed, "My friends will never believe I met you unless . . . ," Cary gently interrupted, "You mean you have friends like that? You really shouldn't." To a man who began, "I hate to bother you, but . . . ," Cary's interruption was firmer. "Don't ever," he advised, "do anything you hate." And finally, to a third man, who started, "My wife will kill me . . . ," Cary was also admonitory. "Tsk, tsk," he smiled. "You really shouldn't have that kind of a relationship — it's too dangerous."

Even when the autograph seeking had abated, we were not out of the woods. A woman suddenly appeared, glass in hand. "I just want," she said, on the way past me, "to sit in his lap." While I was sure that Cary would be up to a charming rebuff even to this request, there was, however, something about the woman that so irritated me that I rose, seized her arm, and made an effort to stop her. At this, the man who was with her at the table from which she had come and who was also doing well in the drink department, suddenly rose. "Take your hands," he shouted, "off my wife!"

Cary, who I am sure had been responsible for such scenes for well over half a century, thought the whole thing was funny. I did not. Nor did Nino, the Polo Lounge longtime maître d'. He hustled over and, with stern finesse, soon had the situation well in hand and the act over. Rather than risk a return engagement, however, I suggested to Cary that we adjourn our meeting to my room. And thus it was that Polar Bear got to meet his first movie star.

On the way to the room, Cary told me that he had always been a dog man himself and that frankly he always thought people who loved cats were a little "barmy," as he put it, on the subject. After we had entered the room, however, and Cary had sat down, and I had gone over to the bathroom to give Polar Bear his unconditional release, a remarkable thing happened. Polar Bear made a beeline for Cary and promptly jumped up in his lap. I gave Cary the age-old pet owner's story, which in this case was the truth, that it was the first time I had ever seen Polar Bear do that with a stranger. I also asked him if he wouldn't admit it was at least a better deal than the woman downstairs.

Cary, patting Polar Bear, proceeded to ask me some questions about cats. He wanted to know, for one thing, if I thought it was true that in general women like cats and men like dogs. I replied that it was the generally held theory but there was some evidence, a bit of which he was patting, that this situation might be changing. He also asked me if, again in general, male cats were more friendly than female. I said that I thought this was also true, again on the evidence before him, but I thought it was a theory we had best keep to ourselves. "It's the same thing, really, when you get right down to it," Cary grinned, "with people, isn't it?"

In his last years, Cary did have cats, and although people were inclined to attribute this to the fact that his wife Barbara was a cat person, I always thought Polar Bear deserved at least some of the credit.

VIII ◦ *His Fitness Program*

Polar Bear and I were, from the beginning, two very different individuals when we were sick. When I am sick, I want attention. I want it now, and I want it around the clock. Besides this, I wish everyone within earshot of my moans and groans, of which I have a wide variety, to know that I am not only at death's door, but also that I have the very worst case of whatever it is I think I have which has ever been visited upon man, woman, child, or beast since the world began.

If, for example, I have a slight cold and my cold has taken a turn for the worse, I wish people to gather around my bedside in respectful silence. For those with poor hearing, I wish them to gather especially close, and for those with poor memories, I wish them to bring pad and pencil — so that, of course, they can take down and transmit to posterity, exactly as I have uttered them, hoarsely and with extreme difficulty, my last words. In much the same manner I visualize my loved ones gathering, after I have gone to my final reward, to hear my Last Will and Testament. In this I intend to give them further instruction, after I have gone and they no longer have the benefit of my counsel, on how they are to conduct themselves.

If, on the other hand, my cold is a little better and there is now a fighting chance that I may, entirely due to my heroism in the crises, eventually get well, then I also wish them to gather around in the same manner and tell me how wonderful I have been through it all and how desolate they have been at the thought of coming so close to losing me. At such times I like to warn them that, during my convalescence, on pain of relapse, they must be constantly on call twenty-four hours a day — that they should think of themselves as army orderlies, always at the ready to bring on the double whatever it is of which I most have need — be it food or drink, books or magazines, a chess player or a chess computer, as well as, of course and particularly, Polar Bear.

When, in contrast, Polar Bear was sick, I could not fail to notice he was the exact opposite of this scenario. He did not wish either any attention called to his malaise or, for that matter, any attention, period — even from me. He would suffer it, the attention, not the sickness — he was very manly about the sickness — but that is all he would do. He wanted to be alone and he wanted to be completely alone. Compared to Polar Bear being sick, Greta Garbo was gregariousness itself and J. D. Salinger a publicity hound.

Needless to say, from the beginning, I could not abide this attitude of his. His wanting to be by himself conjured up in my mind all sorts of stories of elephant graveyards and animals wandering off to die alone. I became indeed so hypochondriacal about it that I was always and invariably certain that whatever it was he had would undoubtedly prove fatal unless I did something about it and did it right away.

More often than not, after either a visit or a call to the vet, such action on my part involved, on his part, a pill. This was not good news. Indeed it was such bad news that I really should change a preceding paragraph about his attitude toward attention. Kindly amend this paragraph to the next to last thing he wanted when he was sick was attention — the very last thing he wanted was a pill. When it came to pills, Polar Bear was not only a Christian Scientist, he wrote the book — and I say this without prejudice because I happen to be a very large admirer of their beliefs.

In any case, I remember well the first time I ever gave Polar Bear a pill. It was late in February, sometime after I had come back from California. As is my wont in such matters, before embarking on such a major enterprise as giving him a pill, I had decided, rather than embarrass myself with Dr. Thompson, I would consult other authorities on this subject. To my surprise, I discovered that there were many articles on either the general or specific topic. The fact that there were so many, I recognized, was hardly a good sign. But I tackled them anyway.

My favorite was an article by Susan Easterly entitled "How to Pill Your Cat." The reason this was my favorite was that Ms. Easterly seemed to address her work to those of us who had, as she put it, a cat of "the independent type" — one whom she identified as one "not prone to doing what you would like him to do."

That certainly, I thought, was Polar Bear. Indeed, he was so far from being "prone" to doing what I would like him to do in such a situation as being pilled that I decided the article could indeed have been written just for him. Without further ado I seized it eagerly.

"First of all," Ms. Easterly wrote, "do not advance upon your cat with feelings of abject terror. Think positively and have the pill ready."

Those were fighting words, and my thoughts harkened back to my Boston ancestor Colonel William Prescott and the Battle of Bunker Hill. If there was one thing I was determined I would not show, it would be terror, and certainly not "abject" terror. Polar Bear would never, I resolved, no matter how difficult the operation to come, see the whites of my eyes. As for thinking positively, my thoughts that first time I advanced on Polar Bear were so positive that I really felt, at that moment, I could have pilled a leopard. And my pill, though well hidden in the palm of my left hand, secured by my fourth finger — so that he would see the rest of my fingers normally extended — was just where I wanted it.

The trouble was that Polar Bear had apparently thoughts which were far from positive. They were, in fact, so negative that I was convinced that he had, by some dastardly subterfuge, where my positives were concerned, broken the code. Indeed, as I advanced on him he seemed to know that not only was I up to something but also that whatever this something was, it was not something he wanted to have anything to do with. And furthermore, some way, somehow, he knew about the pill. As he retreated as negatively as I positively advanced, there was no mistaking the fact that his eyes were riveted on what I thought I had so deftly hidden.

At this juncture I decided that not to advance farther was definitely the better part of valor. Rather I felt I should just hold the line at the ground I had already taken, and dig in. Meanwhile, I turned again to Ms. Easterly. I was sure she would have wise counsel for this kind of stalemate. And I was right. The only trouble was her advice was all too reminiscent of the advice I had received from another source, as all those of you with good memories will recall, about my cat's bath.

"Wrap your cat in a large towel," Ms. Easterly had written, "leaving only the head exposed. This prevents loss of your blood due to flailing claws." I was fully prepared to give blood in reasonable amounts, but I was by no means big on wrapping Polar Bear in a towel. And, I soon learned, after cornering him, neither was he. Nonetheless, I had vowed to follow Ms. Easterly's advice to the letter, and I proceeded to do so.

"Hold the cat firmly against you," Ms. Easterly's advice continued, "in the crook of your arm and on your lap. This allows both your hands to remain free."

Since one of my hands was limited by my arm crook, and the other one by the pill, they were hardly free, but I did my best. And I'm sure Ms. Easterly's advice worked like a charm with her cat — albeit I could not help suspecting that her cat must have been very small, very old, and very sick, if indeed alive at all, when she performed this maneuver. Or that perhaps she has a black belt in karate. In any case, her suggestion did not work with Polar Bear. He shot out of the towel like a dart out of a blowgun.

I am, however, no quitter. I caught him and recovered him — literally in fact with the towel — and this time, instead of my first gentle crook of the arm I held him in such a viselike grip that I elicited from him one of the most baleful "Aeiou" 's I had ever heard. I pretended, of course, that I hadn't heard it, meanwhile reading on by holding the article with my half-free pill hand.

"Place your hand over the cat's head," Ms. Easterly stalwartly continued, apparently at this time engaging a third hand, "using the thumb or forefinger, whichever is preferred, to grasp each corner of the cat's jaw. Apply slight pressure and its mouth will open."

Once more I took Ms. Easterly at her word as best I could, using the crook arm hand. I applied first, as she had suggested, slight pressure. Then I applied slightly more pressure. And finally I applied enough pressure to open the mouth of a crocodile.

The problem was that the mouth did not open. It did not open as much as a single solitary slit. Reluctantly I decided to modify Ms. Easterly's instructions. I took my index finger and, using it like an awl, worked my way into Polar Bear's mouth, a little back of his teeth. At last I had my whole finger in and across his mouth — like a bit in the mouth of a horse. And of course Polar Bear did just what a horse would do — he bit on the bit.

Go ahead, I told him, bite the hand that feeds you, the hand that's doing all this for your own good. He literally gagged on this line but I would not stop. Instead, at his very next gag, I used the opportunity to pop the pill into the back of his mouth.

"Close his mouth immediately," my instructions read, "stroke his throat and the natural reflex action will leave no doubt that the pill has been swallowed. Done properly and quickly, your cat will not even realize that he has ingested a pill."

I did the stroking perfectly. And then, just as I was congratulating myself on a masterful job masterfully performed, something hit me right between the eyes. Well, not exactly between the eyes but in fact on the nose — and it plopped from there to the floor.

It was, of course, the pill. Maybe some cats would not "even realize," as Ms. Easterly had put it, that they had "ingested a pill," but Polar Bear was not of their number. As a matter of fact he had, after firing his bull's-eye, once more jumped out of the towel to the floor and was quietly lying down licking his fancied wounds. From time to time, however, he would fix a by now extremely beady eye on me with just one obvious question on his mind. Would I, or would I not, be foolish enough to answer the bell for the next round? I stared right back at him. What did he think I was made of? Was his memory so short that it could not retain any of the saga of my past triumphs over his intransigence?

I took a deep breath and once more stood up. This time, almost in one masterful maneuver, I grabbed him, wrapped him in the towel, sawed open his mouth, and plopped in the pill. And this time also, after politely telling him to shut his mouth, then, with my hand, actually shutting it, I stroked his throat over and over until I was certain there was not the slightest possibility that he hadn't swallowed it. To make absolutely certain, however, I opened his mouth again, this time with surprising little resistance, I was pleased to note, and peered around inside. No pill anywhere.

I watched him as he went away to lick not only his fancied wounds but also, now, his pride. But I was a gracious winner. I went over, got down on my knees and scrubbled his ears and stomach. "You see, Polar Bear," I told him, "that wasn't so bad after all, was it?" I also told him he couldn't possibly have even tasted the pill. And surely he must realize that he couldn't set himself up as judge and jury of what was best for him. Only I, and his vet, could do that.

As gracious a winner as I was, Polar Bear was, I was glad to see, a gracious loser. I was thinking about this when, out of the corner of my eye, I spotted a telltale white object on the rug behind him. No, I thought, it couldn't be. But of course it was. It was the pill.

For a long moment I said nothing. I just looked at the pill and then, slowly, back at him. Finally he too looked at the pill and then, equally slowly, back at me. There was no doubt about what he was doing — he was smiling.

I rose to my feet with as much of what dignity I had left as I could muster. All right, I thought, if all-out war was what he wanted, all-out war was what he would get. But, I warned him — and he could go to the bank on what I was saying — the next attack would come when he least expected it. I would bide my time and then I would go all out.

And I did just that. I bode in fact for a good long time, because I had made up my mind that a nighttime excursion, under cover of darkness, was my best chance for success. And that night, after he had jumped up on the bed and was fast asleep — using, as usual, about three-quarters of my king-sized bed — I struck. With one single but incredibly rapid motion — one which would have done credit to the late George Patton — I sat up, seized him, plunged the pill into his mouth, and this time not only stroked his throat but, as I did so, all but did the swallowing for him. It was not pretty, but war never is.

The point is that he did indeed that night swallow a pill. But to say he was furious is putting it mildly. If cats can be livid, livid he was. He obviously considered my actions as the greatest doublecross since Brutus stabbed

Caesar. And to his way of thinking, even that dark deed, dastardly as it was, happened after all in broad daylight. What I had done to him had been done in the depths of the night.

Just the same, hard as it was to bear his wrath, the fact remained, from that day to this, or rather from that night to this, that is the way, with slight variations — as, for example, when he is sound asleep in the daytime — that I have administered all pills to him. Let sleeping dogs lie, they say. But where does it say that about sleeping cats?

Hard on the heels of our pill crisis, I was off for Canada and the painting of the seals. We had gotten the good ship *Sea Shepherd* in England and I was to join it in Boston.

Paul had no ship's cat aboard — he had kept that berth open for Polar Bear — but although I did not take him, I thought of him many times on that long and incredibly difficult voyage. Day after day and night after night we would shove ahead at the ice, stop, reverse our engines, go back fifty yards and then smash again — sometimes even riding up on the ice and then crunching down to clear water.

The low point was the fifth night — the night after the seal hunt had started — when a terrific storm had come up and we were icebound. That night I had lain down with my clothes still on, as totally discouraged as we were totally stuck. I must have dozed off when I felt a tugging at my coat. It was Tony, the second mate, a man who had volunteered to join the crew only two days before we had sailed from Boston. "The fog has broken," he said, "and the ship's sprung loose. I think we can make it."

I went up on the bridge with him and looked around. There was no more storm, no more fog, and ahead not even any more ice. There was a clear path to the seals. It was like a miracle. As full throttle we forged ahead I again thought of Polar Bear. He had indeed brought the Fund luck.

A little after midnight, we heard, for the first time, the barking of the seals. Then, suddenly, we saw one. Then another. And another. And another, until there were literally hundreds. On one side of the ship, they had all been clubbed and skinned. On the other, though, they were still untouched. Ahead the lights of the sealing ships were clearly visible, but their crews and clubbers were all apparently fast asleep, preparatory to resuming the next deadly clubbing.

They would have a rude awakening. First Tony stopped the *Sea Shepherd* exactly half a nautical mile away from the seals. I did not want the ship itself arrested, and Canada's so-called "Seal Protection" Act had decreed that nothing, ship or person, could come within half a nautical mile of the sealhunt unless engaged in the killing. It was surely remarkable seal protection.

Nonetheless, one by one, over the side, with their canisters of dye, went our brave, trained, and hand-picked ice crew: Watson, Matt Herron, Joe Goodwin, David MacKinney, Keith Kreuger, Mark Sterck, Eddie Smith, and Paul Pezwick. The Minister of Fisheries had assured the Canadian parliament that the *Sea Shepherd* would never get near enough the seals to see one, let alone paint one. Yet by the next morning we had painted, literally under the seal killers' noses, more than a thousand.

Today, looking back on the event, I realize that our painting of the seals was only one battle in the long war — but it was a victory and it came at a time when a victory was important. The most important battle would not come until four years later — the direct result of the brilliant strategy which was formulated and led by Brian Davies of the International Fund for Animal Welfare. It was Davies who persuaded me that the way to stop commercial sealing was to forget Canada, which was a lost cause anyway, and to concentrate instead on the European Economic Community — the countries which bought the pelts — and get these countries to ban the importation of the baby sealskin into Western Europe. And when this finally came about, what we all liked best was that the ban was put into effect under an already existing EEC law — one which banned foreign pornography.

But Canada, typically, did not give up and four years later resumed commercial clubbing, albeit this time limiting themselves to a 57,000 quota and going after just six- to seven-week-old seals, or, as they are called, "beaters." This time the sealers had apparently found a new buyer for their bloody pelts — Japan. Somehow it figured — Canada and Japan allied together, the seal killers and the dolphin killers.

Back at home at last, I found Polar Bear, having been well cared for by Marian, hale and hearty — in fact, too hearty. No matter how you looked at it, or rather at him, there was no gainsaying the fact that he was — and far too rapidly — gaining weight.

There is a canard about neutered and spayed cats, as there is about neutered or spayed dogs. And this is that they will, after the operation, invariably and almost immediately gain weight. It is not, of course, true. Cats and dogs gain weight from just one thing, and that is that they are eating too much.

At the same time, it is true that animals who were

former strays will often overeat. This could hardly be otherwise because, having gone through periods of intense hunger, they naturally have a tendency to regard each meal as possibly their last. Certainly Polar Bear fell into this category. On the other hand, he did not unfortunately fall into the category of the kind of cat for whom food can be left down in large portions and who can be left to eat whenever they wish to do so and never apparently eat too much. Polar Bear regarded any dish left out, no matter how much was in it, as something to be devoured there and then and that was that.

As if this was not enough, from the very beginning when I had just rescued him, he embarked on a devious and steady campaign of getting people, by hook or by crook, to refill his dish. After, for example, I had fed him his breakfast and had left for the office, he would wait until Rosa, the cleaning lady, would appear. Then, not all the time, because he was too clever for that, but nonetheless most of the time, he would entice Rosa to his by now thoroughly empty bowl — he made sure there was not a trace of food in it — and then, looking up at her, he would emit the most piteous of his remarkable repertoire of piteous "aeiou" 's. At which, of course, Rosa would invariably look at him and his empty bowl and, in a tone of great solicitude, attempt in Spanish to comfort him. *"Pobre gatocito,"* she would croon. *"El señor no te dió desayuno?"* Whereupon, I was sure, Polar Bear would reply, *"No, él no me lo dió."* When it came to food, I knew he wouldn't let a little thing like a language barrier stand in his way. In any case, Rosa would invariably assure him, *"Pobre Oso Polar, yo te lo voy a dar!"* and promptly fill his bowl to the brim. Thus, having finished Meal No. 1 less than an hour before, Pobre Oso Polar would now tuck into Meal No. 2.

In the late afternoon Marian would arrive, and she too would be greeted by a pathetic and forlorn-looking feline crouched beside an empty bowl. "Precious!" Marian would exclaim. "Didn't Rosa give you anything to eat?" No, not a nibble, Polar Bear, lying in his teeth, would reply — whereupon he would soon be attacking Meal No. 3.

Finally, when I came home, and he well recognized that I was a far tougher nut to crack and that for me neither of his previous performances would suffice, he would let out all the stops. No more would he try the beside-the-empty-bowl crouch, or thc pitcous "aeiou." Rather, I'd be on the receiving end of a full Broadway-style show — one that began with him flouncing around near the kitchen (but not so obvious as to be actually in it) all the time emitting not loud "aeiou" 's but rather the silent, heart-rending variety immortalized in Paul Gallico's *Silent Miaow*. If he failed to achieve the desired results with these — which, because of my innate suspicions, was often the case — they would be followed by what I can only describe as truly tragic Grand Opera yowls — delivered full throat, head thrown back, chest extended and voice aimed, in the finest operatic tradition, at the very last seat in the very last row of the fifth balcony.

When even this did not work, he would have still one last card to play. This was a series of unspoken but nonetheless clearly visible communications which were invariably accusatory in nature. An example was his all-purpose "If-you-don't-care-neither-do-I"; another was the more specific "If-your-imagination-is-so-limited-that-you-can't-even-picture-what-it-was-like-for-me-when-I-was-hungry-all-the-time" routine. Make no mistake, these were extremely difficult to resist, and, since I really couldn't be sure Rosa and Marian had fed him — something I think he well knew — all too often I also would bow to his multi-faceted manipulations. And that, of course, would be Meal No. 4. Finally, last but not least, would come that late late snack to which I have already alluded and which thus became Meal No. 5.

Looking at him, I realized I would have to call a halt to all this, and I would have to call it immediately. On one memorable Saturday morning, I began. First I took him to the window and held him up so that he could look down at all the people in the park, an extraordinary number of whom were either running, jogging, race walking, or just plain walking. I asked him if he knew what they were doing. He obviously did not because as I could see from the direction of his head he was not paying any attention to them. Instead his eyes were riveted, as they usually are when he is by the window, on pigeons.

I was annoyed at this. I told him that I was fully aware that he was interested in ornithology and in fact was an inveterate bird-watcher or, as the purists had it, birder. But could he not just once, I importuned, direct his attention away from the birds and toward the people? He could not. Finally, I literally had to turn his head. What did he think those people were doing? I asked him again. Did he think they were running or jogging or race walking or walking just for the fun of it? Of course not, I answered myself. What they were doing was keeping in shape.

When he would again be distracted by the pigeons, I would remind him that I had no doubt that even some of them had succumbed to the trend. In any case, I was warming to my task. Why, I went on, did he think there was so much calorie counting nowadays? So many no-cal drinks. So many sugar substitutes. The whole world, I told him sternly, was on a fitness kick. And, I assured him, it wasn't just a fitness kick for people, either. Animals too were involved in it. And not just the pigeons — cats too, I said, were. I always like to bring things home to him.

Furthermore, I went on, the idea of the whole thing was not just to be more attractive to the opposite sex— I did not want to dwell on that in view of his recent operation, and all — it was also, and far more importantly, due to a desire to be, just for oneself, healthier and more fit and to live a longer, fuller, and happier life. I was reaching my peroration now, and I began to raise my voice. Even if he understood nothing else, I stated firmly, I wanted him to get one thing straight — that Thin Was In and Fat Was Out. With this I actually turned his head back toward me and this time did shout a question at him — Did He Or Did He Not Want To Be The Last Fat Cat In The World?

He did not answer — something which I could easily have put down to the fact that he does not like loud talk, particularly when it involved personal criticism. I did not allow myself to dwell on this, however. Instead I decided to take his refusal to answer as a sign that no, he did not want to be the last fat cat in the world. Well, then, I concluded as cheerfully as I could, there were just no two ways about it — he would have to go on a diet. And, so that there could be no possible doubt in his mind, I repeated this. Diet, I said, diet.

I knew from the beginning, of course, that he would think very little of the idea. But I was determined. There would be no more badgering of Rosa and Marian and cadging of extra meals from them. Nor would there be any more heaping dishfuls — there would be smaller portions and they would occur at lengthier intervals. I also pursued what I thought were two excellent lines of approach to overcome whatever objections he might have. First, I reminded him, there was nothing to be ashamed of. He was not being singled out. Everyone, people and cats, was inclined to put on a few extra pounds as he or she got older — or rather, more mature. Second, I told him, even I myself had occasionally considered going on a diet. I knew he could certainly identify with this and I went to some lengths to tell him a story that had almost persuaded me in the dietary direction.

It had happened, I told him, only a few months before he came, when I had had occasion to visit a New York men's store — one in which, when the spirit, or rather Marian, moved me, I sometimes bought a new suit. The store was called Imperial Wear, I informed him, and it advertised itself as carrying clothes for the "Big and Tall." One day, however, I had had a nasty experience there. I happened to arrive at the store when my regular salesman was otherwise occupied, and I unluckily received a rank newcomer who stupidly took me to a section which I clearly saw was marked "Portly."

I was furious, of course. I am not fond of the word *portly* — in fact it is one of the very few old-fashioned words which I do not like — and in no uncertain terms I made my feelings clear to the young whippersnapper. Whereupon he nervously and rapidly informed me that the store used the word only for the style of the suit, and that actually "portly" was for thinner people than, for example, another of the sections, which he pointed out, was called, bluntly, "Stout."

I told Polar Bear that of course that made me feel a great deal better, and I actually even "My good manned" the young man a few times while he went on to explain that even the "Stouts" were divided into the "Long Stouts" and the "Stylish Stouts." But just the same the whole thing was, when you got right down to it, a close call. In fact, I told Polar Bear, I had not gone on a diet on that occasion but on the occasion of his diet, I would do so. In a sense, indeed, I explained to him, we would both be going on a diet together. I would do all the difficult part — the research, and the counting of calories and all that sort of thing — and all he would have to do would really be the minor part — after all my work was done — of just the not eating. I emphasized that I had always been a great believer in the idea of diets — the only trouble was that I had found, through experience, that I was much better at reading about them than I was at not eating them.

From that Saturday on I felt that at least we had come to some sort of understanding about the whole matter. I immediately cut down his portions and demanded that Rosa, on pain of never again being allowed to feed him, even when I was there, stop giving in to his performances. With Marian I had more difficulty. Marian is very bad at taking direct orders anyway, and, despite my remonstrances, was always giving him, as she put it, "just a tad more." In desperation I told her that she would either cease and desist or the next time I was at her apartment I would do something she never does — which is cut her cat's toenails. That did it.

Unfortunately it didn't do it for Polar Bear's diet. Smaller portions or no smaller portions, it was soon apparent that we were not only not winning the diet war, we were losing it. Polar Bear was still merrily gaining away as if there was no tomorrow — which, I stonily reminded him, there might well not be if he refused to buckle down. I would have to take more drastic steps.

What I decided upon this time was to put him on special food — diet cat food. Here the battle was joined with the very first can. Polar Bear did not like the look of it from the moment he saw me opening it. This was no fault of the food people. Polar Bear, as I have said, does not like anything new, and if there is one thing new which he especially does not like, it is new food.

I had purposely decided to try it on him on a weekend when I could be there all the time, and I was very glad of my decision that first Saturday morning when I put down the first bowl of it and saw he would not touch it, even though I knew full well he was hungry. All right, I thought sternly, if he wanted to play hardball I could play hardball too, and I promptly took it away. But I told him that when I was a small boy I had to eat everything on my plate or otherwise what I had left would be brought back again cold before the next meal and that if I didn't eat that first there would be no next meal. A great many Boston boys, I told him, had been brought up that way and they were all the better for it. In those days it was called "making a Hoover plate" — in honor of Herbert Hoover's relief program for the Belgian children. And although I didn't expect him to remember that, he could jolly well learn the same lesson because that was the way I intended to handle him.

Saturday noon I brought out the same dish again. Again, nothing. Once more I took it away. And, once more, I waited. This time I waited through an entire afternoon of caterwaulings. I ignored them. This was Valley Forge.

At dinnertime when, for the third time, I repeated the process and when, also for the third time, he stonewalled me, this time, before taking the dish away, in desperation and right in front of him, I put a finger in the food, licked it, and beamed at him. "Mmmmm," I said, "delicious." He watched me intently, but with an expression on his face of a medieval potentate watching a taster whom he had reason to suspect bite into a dish which he had purposely laced with poison.

I ignored the look and persisted. Even for his late night snack I brought back the diet food and told him it would be that or nothing. Again, nothing it was. And that night I underwent a steady rolling barrage of "aeiou" 's. Then, when I had finally managed despite these to drop off to sleep he promptly proceeded to flounce around on the bed until he was able to wake me again — a condition he had obviously calculated would bring me to my senses.

By the next morning when he had been twenty-four straight hours without food — and yet still refused so much as a morsel — I was frankly worried. But I knew I had only two alternatives — either bravely to stay the course or cravenly to give in to his blackmail. It was a measure of my mettle that, damning the torpedoes, I boldly marched to the icebox. This time, however, as I took down the same dish, before I even had a chance to put it down in front of him, he uttered a truly piercing "aeiou." And right here I want to make something perfectly clear about our battle — and that is that I did not give in, and he did not win. What happened was that, when he uttered that "aeiou," I happened to look carefully at that dish and I decided that it really might be spoiled or something and that if I made him eat it, it actually might make him sick. That and that only was the reason not to give him any more diet food but to go back to his regular food. But to say that he won, or indeed to place any other such interpretation on my action, is simply unwarranted by the facts. And, of course, it should be remembered that it was I, not Polar Bear, who made the decision.

I did so, as always, for a very good reason. This was because I had decided that, in the whole broad picture of any fitness program — I am very good at broad pictures — diet is only, when you come right down to it, a part of it. Equally important is exercise. A diet without exercise, I have always said, is only half a diet. I, for example, not only occasionally cut down on desserts but at the same time every weekend when the weather is clement, take out my bicycle and have a good hard ride. It takes me almost ten minutes to reach the chess tables in the middle of Central Park and, after a few hours there, I take a good brisk ride home. I credit this program not with any such nonsense as being able to get into my old army uniform — frankly, I think that is a ridiculous ambition — but with keeping me, both physically and mentally, in top shape.

For contrast, Polar Bear was, I realized, just lying around far too much of the time. And since he would obviously not do anything about this, it was equally obviously up to me. He was not fond of chess, and so I developed for him a wide variety of other games. In the living room I would first get out all his balls and any other toys which would roll and, one by one, I would entice him into, if not actually retrieving them — that would have been for him too demeaningly doglike — at least going after them on the double. Then, in the bedroom at night before going to sleep, I would stuff him under a thin blanket or sheet and begin a serics of slow-starting but fast-ending finger pokes. My favorite was one that started from behind him where he couldn't see it and ended right smack in the pit of his ample stomach. Whereupon he would then have a fair go, with all four paws and a bite to boot, at the offending digit. After this, it was understood that it was his turn to go on the offensive, and he would come out from under the blanket or sheet with fire in his eye and mayhem on his mind. I would meet his charge and this time we would really go to the mat and have a wrestling match — one which would put to shame those shams you see on television. Even when I finally got him down, he would not give up. Instead, he would just pretend to do so, hoping that I would, for a second, relax my hold. And, when I inevitably did so, it was San Juan Hill all over again. If his front paws, or rather claws, didn't suffice to do the job, he would call in the reserves. These were of course his back claws. And these, with his back legs used as battering rams and the claws as rotating rakes, were extraordinarily effective.

Finally, after a definite "uncle" had been cried, usually by me, and all falls and points tallied, he would jump up and take a victory lap — actually a victory leap — around the whole apartment. All in all, for him it was a pretty fair workout and was at least more successful in the fitness department than any of the diet experiments. For me, however, as the blood on my fingers and hands clearly attested, it was no walk in the Park. And one night, as I was watching his victory lap and was in fact actually thinking of the expression I had used for what it had all been for me, I realized that I had, inadvertently, thought of exactly what he did need — a walk in the Park.

Indoor exercise, fine as it was, was simply not enough. All Bostonians worthy of the name have always put a good deal of stock into taking good, old-fashioned walks or, as in happier times they were called, constitutionals — and I was no exception. All right, cats were not dogs, but it was nonsense, I decided, to say that you could not walk a cat. You could walk anything if the will was there, and the discipline, and you had that rare combination of know-how and stick-to-it-iveness which had ever been my hallmark in my relations with Polar Bear.

I did my usual faithful research, and, in short order, I put Operation Catwalk on my front burner. First, I procured a harness and then after doing my best to make it fit and get Polar Bear into it — neither of which was as easy as it sounds — I then turned to making a game out of the whole thing so that I could get him, if not to make friends with his new harness, at least to make a semblance of peace with the idea of being in it.

At last I was ready for in-house practice. I stood with the leash with plenty of play in it, as instructed, and waited patiently for him to decide where he wanted to go. Unfortunately, he didn't want to go anywhere. He just crouched and, with his tail moving ominously, looked at me. The look clearly said, "So now I'm going to live in a straitjacket?" I told him that this question was undeserving of a serious answer. He was, as usual, making a mountain out of a molehill — he could go anywhere his little heart desired. With that I gave the leash even more play, in the hopes that he would at least do me the courtesy of taking a step or two. But it was no dice. Finally, I myself made just the hint of a move in his favorite direction, at the same time quietly asking him if he wanted to go into the kitchen.

The moment that word *kitchen* was out of my mouth, he leapt. The next thing I knew he was in there, aeiouing, of course, for lunch — without me, without leash, and without harness. He had somehow gathered up both front and back legs at once and jumped through, under, or over it.

Now there was nothing to do but give him a snack — something which was, after all, hardly the idea of the entire program. And then, following this, for me and for the harness, it was back to the drawing board.

Finally I had that harness so that Houdini couldn't have gotten out of it. But, once more, I was just standing there and he was not moving. Indeed in all our in-house practice he moved only twice, once when the telephone rang — he likes it to stop ringing as soon as possible — and the other time when the doorbell rang and a chess player appeared. At this I decided to suspend our training exercises.

After the chess player had gone, I also decided that perhaps any more in-house practice was really a waste of time. There wasn't any real reason for him to move around inside anyway — it was time to move out.

I picked him up and carried him to the elevator. There was a woman going down and, as I put him down, she was very interested. "Oh," she said, "you're walking him. I didn't know you could, with cats. How on earth did you ever get him to do it?"

Practice, I told her, and persistence — it hadn't been easy. After this, when we reached the ground floor, I was looking forward to an impressive promenade across the lobby. So, of course, Polar Bear stayed in the elevator. And, while we were discussing the matter, the elevator, of course, went up again. This time we went all the way to the penthouse floor, where my rock group friend got on. "That's something," he said. "Walking a cat! I didn't know that could be done." I told him there was really nothing to it, once you got the hang of it. This time, though, once we had reached the ground floor again, I not only picked Polar Bear up, I carried him through the lobby, across the street, and well into Central Park. Then, after a last double-check of the harness, I gingerly set him down.

I must say he was very interested in everything — particularly, in order, the birds, the dogs, and the squirrels, and although I had the distinct impression that he regarded the latter as a very peculiar breed of climbing mouse, at least I felt we had made a start. With all his looking, however, he refused to budge so much as an inch. I waited and waited. He could get this much exercise, I thought, sleeping.

Suddenly, from behind us, I heard a loud woof. I spun around and, coming directly at us at full gallop, was an Afghan — one which, at that moment, looked to me like the largest one I had ever seen. I leapt for Polar Bear and at the same time delivered what I can only describe as the fastest hip check a man my age is capable of administering.

The next moment all three of us, the Afghan, Polar Bear, and I, were on the ground in an assembled heap. As I tried to get up, still shielding Polar Bear, a young lady, leash in hand, came running up. Ignoring me, she went straight for her dog. "Poor Alfie," she cried. Then, after putting the leash on him, and before she had even seen Polar Bear, she whirled on me. "I saw what you did," she said. "You attacked my dog. You ought to be . . ." She stopped because at that moment she had spotted, burrowing into my shoulder, a hissing Polar Bear. "Oh," she said, "a cat! Alfie hates cats!" I attempted to point out that, as she could surely see, Polar Bear wasn't all that fond of Afghans, either. The young lady ignored this and proceeded to deliver a stern lecture about the idiocy of trying to walk a cat anywhere, and particularly in Central Park. I protested that at least he had been on a leash and that, as Alfie had, after all, been off his, it seemed to me that I was hardly the only one at fault. I soon realized, however, that I was getting nowhere on that tack, and so I finally gave up, telling her merely that I would admit to the illegal block and would gladly accept a fifteen-yard penalty. With that, and with as much aplomb as I could muster, I moved off — hopefully to pastures new.

I went, as a matter of fact, quite some little distance, hoping that Polar Bear might, in the meantime, calm down. And this time I chose an area which I had thoroughly cased and determined to be one hundred percent dog-free. Then, and only then, did I once more lower Polar Bear to the ground.

And once more I waited — so interminably in fact that I was half asleep when, like a shot, Polar Bear bolted. And he bolted so fast and so unexpectedly that he took the leash right out of my hand. Frozen, I watched him fly over the grass after a squirrel. When I finally started after him, I was already so far behind that I could barely see the squirrel tear up a tree and, worse, see Polar Bear tear right up after him, his leash bouncing along behind him. Obviously it would catch on a knob or a small branch or something, and he would hang to death right over my head.

Amazingly, the leash did not catch — only because, by luck, the squirrel had quickly turned off to a branch and Polar Bear's leash was now not trailing behind him, it was hanging down. But the branch which the squirrel had chosen, though long, would in time become reed-thin. And, even if it could have held the squirrel, it could certainly not have held Polar Bear.

Whatever was going to happen, I realized, was better than hanging, but at the same time he was bound sooner or later to fall — and from a dangerous height. As I watched, the squirrel disappeared. For a moment I thought he might have leapt to another branch, but he had not. Instead, he had turned and run back underneath the branch. And, just when the squirrel ran under him, Polar Bear whirled.

He did not touch the squirrel, but he lost touch with the branch and lost his balance. As he fell, I jumped forward. Although I have always fancied myself as one of the greatest wide receivers ever to be overlooked by the Harvard team, I would have to admit that in this instance it was by pure luck rather than sheer skill that I caught him.

Sinking to my knees for a long moment, I just hugged him to my stomach. Then softly I spoke to him, I told him it was time to go home now. He obviously agreed and, as I carried him home, although I was prepared to admit we had probably had both our first and our last walk on a leash, I would still not admit it was any fault of mine, or, for that matter, his. It was simply because of forces beyond the control of either of us. It was, in truth, a jungle out there.

All right, the carpers and the nay-sayers could argue that up to now my diet programs and my exercise endeavors had not been howling successes. But, as I believe I have told you before and probably will again, I am no easy giver-upper or giver-inner. Long before Vince Lombardi or whoever it was said, "When the going gets tough, the tough get going," or Yogi Berra said, "It's never over till it's over," it should be remembered that I was saying, "If you can't play a sport, be one."

And the fact was, win, lose, or draw, I was determined to be a sport to the end about Polar Bear's fitness program. But I was also just as determined, for the good of his little soul as much as mine, to have some kind of clear-cut victory. So far, however, just how to accomplish this had eluded me. But one warm spring day, standing on my balcony, I had a brainstorm.

I have these brainstorms, if I do say so, with some regularity. But this particular one was special. I had gone out, as is my wont, to regard the world. And that lovely evening, as I was enjoying the scenery, it suddenly occurred to me that here I was, seeing all the sights in the street below and the Park beyond, and yet Polar Bear could not do this. He had to see it all from behind a window, which was not the same thing at all. It was wrong — he should be enjoying it just as I was.

But how, I thought — I'm very logical in my brainstorms — could he possibly do this? The only way would be to wire in the whole balcony. And the only way that could be accomplished would, even if the building were to allow it, only be unsightly from their point of view, but from mine it would ruin my actual view.

Your average inventor might have given up right then and there. But I was hardly your average inventor. When I am working on an invention I break it down step by step, as all the great inventors of the past have done. If you do not do this, you end with a stumbling block and your whole thing is half-baked.

As I thought of that, the answer came. There was no

need to wire in all the balcony — all that had to be done was just to wire in half the balcony. It was the perfect solution. But there was, still, one more step to overcome. There was only one door. If half of the balcony, unwired, included the door for me to get in and out, how would he get in and out of his wired half?

Again, this might have stopped your average inventor in his tracks. But it did not stop yours truly. Instead, I decided on a careful inspection of the site — always a crucial part of any great innovative idea. And, as I looked, once more the solution came — he could get in and out to his half from the bedroom window.

And so, step by step, I had climbed every mountain. There just remained the minor detail of getting the proper help for the job. A great inventor I might be and a great engineer as well — even, perhaps, a great architect, although up to this time I had never actually entered that field — but one thing I am not. And that is, as I have mentioned before, a great builder. Nor am I, if the truth be known, a great spender — in fact I have been called, I think much too loosely, the last of the small spenders. But I was certainly not about to go out and spend a small fortune for wirers, roofers, and heaven knows what else for what? For just a simple little job like that.

No indeed I was not, thank you very much. And, by pure chance, the very next afternoon a locksmith was coming to my apartment to install what a friend had recommended — a burglarproof lock.

Watching the man work, I started complimenting him. Not so lavishly, of course, as to be obvious. I simply told him that he was a fine worker and that a man with his talent must be able to fix or even build just about anything.

But did he not, I asked, sometimes get tired of working only on locks?

The man looked up at me expectantly. I pulled back. I told him it was nothing, I was just thinking of a tiny little job I had — one that was hardly worthy of his talents. There was more talk, of course, but the long and short of it was — the short being that, like all New York workmen, he charged me an arm and a leg. Nonetheless, the next morning, actually on time, the man arrived. With him he had yards of chicken wire, wood, bolts, and a wide variety of tools. And, by the following day, Polar Bear had his balcony.

Spring or no spring, that night, as it happened, snow fell. It was one of those rare but heavy snowfalls which sometimes blanket the city in late March. I realized, of course, I would have to postpone the christening of the balcony — there were at least five inches of snow — but Polar Bear would have none of it. He stood on the windowsill and practically banged his head against the glass to have it opened. In vain I remonstrated with him. He would not want to go out there now, I told him.

My arguments were useless — and so, as usual, I gave in. I opened the window and out he jumped. As he sank into the snow up to his stomach, he froze and made no attempt to move. Then, slowly, he swiveled his head and looked at me. "Well," the look clearly said, "you surely bleeped it up this time!"

Actually I took it as a compliment — obviously he now felt that I, at master control, was responsible for everything, even the weather outside. And as time went on and the weather improved, the balcony not only served him well — he could, in perfect safety, crouch down and lash around and be a big shot with the pigeons — it also, surprisingly enough, pleased the pigeons. Soon learning that he could not actually get at them, they in turn became big shots too. They cooed and chirruped at him to their hearts' content, ruffled their feathers within his vision, and promenaded boldly across his roof.

Besides this the balcony proved itself such an attraction that, in showing it off, I was able to expound on one of my many pet cat theories. This one concerned people who live in the country and regularly allow their cats to go out — often either at fatal peril from dogs or automobiles, to them, or at peril to the surrounding birds from them. Polar Bear or no Polar Bear, I feel that no cat owner has the right to jeopardize the right of his neighbor who may enjoy his birds just as the cat owner enjoys his cat. The ideal solution would seem to be something like my balcony — a good-sized outdoor, wired-in walk, one which could end, say, at a cat door at the kitchen. The cat could then go out whenever he wished — but he would be safe and so too would the birds.

I am very firm about this theory — so firm that I have actually dreamed of taking out a patent on it. I even dream of sitting back and watching such catwalks going up all over the country — with, of course, just a reasonable little royalty being divided, say, like the balcony itself, half to Polar Bear and half to me.

IX ◦ *His Foreign Policy*

Polar Bear's foreign policy, like that of some of our Presidents, left a good deal to be desired. On the domestic front, as we have seen, he had his ups and downs, but even when he was having the latter — when he was, so to speak, taking his lumps — he took them well. He was not the world's brightest cat, but he had unfailing charm and he was a great little communicator — not only with his tail but also with his grin, which was compounded of about equal parts of Morris, Garfield, and pure Cheshire.

When it came to his conduct of foreign affairs, however, the very qualities which had stood him in such good stead and had served so well domestically seemed here to fail him utterly. Again, like some of our Presidents, it was not that he did not like the idea of handling his own foreign policy — he did. Rather it was that he liked it too much and would not entrust it to people who knew far more than he did about the intricacies and nuances of it. And therein lay all the trouble. Because foreign policy is, when you get right down to it, something you either have a feel for, or something you do not. And, bluntly, Polar Bear did not. For one thing, diplomacy — the art of playing up to others and, even when you don't like them, never letting them know it — which is, in sum, the key to foreign policy, bored him. He was always going around it, or under it, or ignoring it altogether. For another thing, on the personal level, on which he was so effective domestically, no one, friend or foe, ever really knew where they stood with him. At times, particularly with small adversaries, he was the Rambo of the cat world and therefore seemed a bully, which he really was not. At other times, particularly with larger adversaries, although he spoke loudly and carried a very large stick — his tail really is enormous — he sometimes seemed nothing more than a feline version of Caspar Milquetoast, which of course he was not either.

But, not to beat about the bush any longer, he was one very prejudiced cat. He was, as a matter of fact, a mass or rather a morass of prejudices. Again, the parallel with certain Presidents comes, perhaps unfairly, to mind. In any case, I do not mean by this that all he cared about were equally fortunate fat cats. And certainly it is not right to say that all he cared about were just other white cats. But whether he would have, were it not for the fact that all cats are supposedly color-blind, is a moot point. In any case, I would not have bet on it, if for no other reason than because he had just about every other prejudice it is possible to have and still, in a changing world, survive.

I shall address first his foreign policy toward other animals. Frankly, it was terrible. Will Rogers once said he never met a man he didn't like — a saying I have always put down to the fact that the late Mr. Rogers must have had a very limited acquaintanceship. But whether he did or not, Polar Bear was assuredly the opposite of Mr. Rogers. I really don't think he ever met another animal he did like.

Some he disliked, it is true, more than others. Some he purely disdained and some he just ignored. In fact about the only animals I believe he didn't feel one of these ways about were horses. He thought they were too big, of course, and made too much noise and he felt that when they went on city streets, for example, they should wear sneakers. But they did not annoy him beyond that and he had basically a live-and-let-live attitude toward them.

It was not so with other animals. Take, for example, his foreign policy toward dogs. To a great many people, dogs are the best-loved animals on earth. Indeed the more fanatical of these people are particularly fond of the old saying that the very word "dog" is God spelled backwards. To Polar Bear, on the other hand, dogs, no matter how you spelled them, were, if not God's greatest mistake — he was not fond of serpents either — then so close to it that the difference was negligible. Furthermore he carried this prejudice against dogs to every single member of the far-flung dog family — even, I am certain, to those I have no evidence he ever met, except rarely, on television, and he did not like them there.

This for me was very bad news, not only because I had, prior to the coming of Polar Bear, always been, as I have already stated, a dog man, but also for another reason. This is that the Fund for Animals, like most organizations of its kind, is often and intimately involved in the rescue of and finding homes for strays. Although about half of these are cats, the fact remained that the other half are dogs. And, when these strays are rescued, in between the time when we pick them up and a permanent home can be found for them, it is often necessary to obtain for them temporary quarters. Thus, almost all of us have, at one time or another, used for this purpose our own abodes.

All in all, it was, therefore, only a matter of time before a stray would find its way to my apartment. While I had a fifty-fifty chance of it being another cat, I also had a fifty-fifty chance of it being a dog. It was, when you came right down to it, a toss of the coin. And, as bad luck would have it, the team Polar Bear lost the toss. The very first stray which appeared that spring was a dog.

The woman who would be bringing it one early Saturday morning had called me first, and she could not have been more apologetic. She knew I had a cat. But, she told me, she simply could not keep the dog she had found the night before even for the rest of the day, and certainly not for the whole weekend. She already had three dogs, and if she took in another she would, she said, be thrown out of her apartment, not only by her superintendent but also by her husband.

I had, of course, no alternative. And the woman was absolutely positive she would have a permanent home for the dog by Monday at the latest. "He's really," she said, "a darling dog."

When she arrived I stepped out to meet her and closed the door behind me. I had already planned my strategy in regard to Polar Bear, and it did not include that his first confrontation with this darling should be in front of this woman. If there were to be casualties, I should be first and darling second — they should not include either Polar Bear or a stranger.

At first look the dog seemed to me, after Polar Bear, the size of a Great Dane. He was not, of course. Unfortunately, however, he was by no means a small dog. Equally unfortunately he was, despite his size, obviously a puppy. And, equally obviously, as close to a totally untrained one as it is possible to imagine. Finally, and perhaps most unfortunately of all, uncertain as was his ancestry, one thing was patently certain about it — he was some kind of retriever mix. While there are in all of dogdom probably no more lovable animals than retrievers, at the same time they are also among the closest things in the animal world to a perpetual motion machine. This was the kind of dog which seems to have no walk — but rather to have just three gaits, run, leap, and bounce. In fact the woman had already named him Bouncer.

Once the woman had unbounced Bouncer and handed me his leash, I opened the door and proceeded to march, or come as close to marching as one could with such an animal, directly to my bedroom. During this march I kept a weather eye out for Polar Bear. I did not see him but I assumed that from wherever he was, he got at least one look.

The moment I closed the bedroom door, Bouncer leapt at it. I ignored this, however, and, after I had gotten him some water, I closed it again and went to see where Polar Bear was. He had repaired, as I might have expected, to the mantelpiece and, having obviously had his look, was on full alert. He was indeed so totally rigid that he looked exactly like one of my animal sculptures up there. It was clear that he was one of the last of the soldiers of Troy and I was the Greek who had brought in the Trojan horse.

Now, Polar, I told him in my best falsely confident voice, we will have none of this. Look at you, I continued. You would think I had brought in the Creature from the Lost Lagoon. Why, it's nothing but a little — I stumbled over that word *little* — friend. A friendly fellow, I added, who had no home. Polar Bear just looked at me, until I amended my explanation. Well, I went on, maybe he was fair-sized, but he was still, I emphasized, a puppy. I was trying desperately to get him to accept any part of my explanation as accurate.

I did not succeed. The thought that enormous as the dog already was, he was going to grow even bigger, obviously did not appeal to Polar Bear. I took another tack. It was not even my fault, somebody else had brought the dog to us — now it was up to both of us to be the hosts. Bouncer was our guest, and surely both of us had merely done what anyone with half a heart would do. We were not, after all, giving up our home, we were merely giving up a part of it — and at that temporarily — to a creature who was in dire need just as, he would surely remember, he had once been.

Polar Bear's answer to this line of argument was to go on the attack himself. He jumped off the mantelpiece and streaked for the bedroom door, where, knowing, of course, that he was perfectly safe, he proceeded to scratch and make warlike "aeiou" 's. This of course so excited Bouncer that he not only scratched back from his side of the door but began to bark loudly.

I sat down. I was well mindful of the fact that new dogs and old cats — or vice versa — should never be put together until they have been properly introduced, and that this should never be done until they have been kept separated at least for long enough to have gotten used to the idea of each other. Maybe, I thought hopefully, this was all part of that idea of getting used to each other. Maybe too, I hoped, the door could stand the gaff.

In any case, I let Polar Bear's scratching and aeiouing and Bouncer's bounding and barking go on as long as I could. Finally, when I could stand it no longer, I went over and picked up Polar Bear and carried him away from the door and into the kitchen. Then, while he was eating, I took the opportunity to prepare a bowl of dog food for Bouncer and take it into the bedroom. I assumed that Polar Bear would be too occupied to notice what I was doing.

I was wrong. He looked up from his food — a very rare thing — and watched me with an expression which made his previous attitude seem friendly. Now, he was saying, I was going to *feed* the monster. In his firm opinion, I had reached the depths of my treachery. I was not just the Greek in Troy, I was Benedict Arnold in Washington's tent.

After Bouncer had eaten, I decided it was time for a walk. Ignoring Polar Bear completely, I marched Bouncer to the door, stopping only to get my bicycle out of the closet, and in short order Bouncer and the bicycle and I were on our way.

Bouncer was surprisingly good on the leash, even beside the bicycle. And, when we arrived at the Park chess tables, although he really didn't sit at all, he was, at least for him, relatively placid while I had my chess game. He was also very popular with some of my chess friends and, by the time I headed home, I felt even more confident about the woman being able to find him a permanent home.

That night I decided it wasn't really fair to leave Polar Bear out there in the living room and have Bouncer with me in the bedroom. And so, carrying Polar Bear high enough to avoid Bouncer's highest bound, I reversed their room reservations. Although it was hardly a restful night — with the endless sniffings and chargings of both parties at the bottom of the door — somehow it was not as bad as I had envisioned it might be. At least it was not so bad that it dissuaded me from putting into operation the next morning my master plan for ending our ridiculous apartment apartheid.

It was to be a face-to-face meeting, and I worked out the details as carefully as if I were arranging a Summit. I did not actually prepare an agenda but I did just about everything else. I decided I would kneel between them at all times, would keep Bouncer on his leash in my right hand, and with my left would have a firm hold on Polar Bear. I would also pay close attention to all noises and, if there was a loud growl from Bouncer or a menacing hiss from Polar Bear, I would abort the mission. At the same time, I would ignore all minor threats and, if I could possibly do so, I would not allow the meeting to break up until there was, if not a lasting peace, at least a temporary Camp David.

I was so proud of the way I had planned it all that, after taking Bouncer for his morning walk, I came in brimming with confidence. I opened the outer door and, instead of turning left to the bedroom, moved briskly into the living room. The moment I missed the turn, of course, Polar Bear leapt to the mantelpiece. I could not allow this deviation from my plan for kneeling between them. And so, with Bouncer on the leash in my right hand, I reached for Polar Bear on the mantelpiece with my left.

I might as well have reached for quicksilver. Still holding Bouncer, I groped and groped. It was no usc. I could not touch Polar Bear, let alone grab him. Finally I was reduced to holding the entire meeting in a kind of bent-over-backwards stance, my left hand still groping and my right endeavoring, with the leash, to curb Bouncer's incurable desire to bound himself onto the mantelpiece. To make matters worse, Bouncer could not get a good fix on Polar Bear either. All he saw, all he could be really sure of, with each upward leap, was a constantly batting paw.

All right, I decided, so my Nobel Peace efforts were starting slowly — at least things could not get worse. And, in fact, they did not. I died hard, but after I had been between them for what seemed an hour and had seen not so much as one iota of change in Polar Bear's attitude, I had no alternative but to come to the reluctant conclusion that the chances of Polar Bear's ever recognizing Bouncer's right to anything, even to exist, were extremely nil.

Then, with as much dignity as I could muster, I took Bouncer into the bedroom and shut the door. But this time, instead of going back to stay with Polar Bear, I remained with Bouncer. I was determined to show Polar Bear just what I thought of his rotten foreign policy.

Later that afternoon, after I had taken Bouncer for another walk, I went into the living room to have a talk with Polar Bear. I was hardly pleased with him, but I realized that what had transpired had not, by any means, been entirely his fault. The dog/cat antipathy was deep-rooted, and the dog had, after all, come into Polar Bear's territory. And, when push came to shove — which it surely would — Polar Bear could hardly have been expected to understand that Bouncer's presence was to be only temporary.

As I entered the room, I called cheerfully to him, careful not to use the offensive "Come," merely to request his presence with my usual "Where's Polar Bear?" He did not respond. I called more loudly. Still nothing. I began to look for him. I looked all over the living room. I looked under the sofa and I looked under the desk. I looked in the closets. As I went on looking, the whole thing began to be all too reminiscent of that first night I had him. Which reminded me, of course, to look into the dishwasher. He was not there — he was nowhere.

Well, I thought, he was playing a game. If he was, two could play that game. This time, when I went in the kitchen, I opened the refrigerator door. That would get him, I knew, and on the run.

But the refrigerator door did not get him. I started to look again, and again I looked everywhere. Then, slowly but steadily, I felt a growing alarm. He had gotten out.

But how, I thought, could he? The door had not been opened. Thinking again, however, I realized that it had — it had been opened when I had taken Bouncer for a walk and again when I had brought him home. And both of these times, encumbered as I was with both Bouncer and the bicycle, and not really looking for Polar Bear because I had been so annoyed with him, it might indeed have been possible that he had somehow sneaked out and perhaps flown down the hall. On second thought, that really wouldn't have been possible. Surely I would have seen him.

I called again, loudly, and by now desperately. And this time, as I started to search again, I had still a third thought about his getting out. Either when I was taking Bouncer out or in, it *was* possible.

By now really worried, I went out in the hall. I knew the people in the apartments on my floor knew him but I wondered if he could have gotten off the floor — perhaps through the fire stairs door, when someone had opened it, perhaps through the door to the back elevator. Perhaps indeed he had gotten on the back elevator. Or even on the front elevator, when it had opened to let somebody off. But, I asked myself, wouldn't anybody who got on or off at that floor and seen him get on, have also seen that he was alone and stopped to pick him up, try to find out where he belonged, and bring him back to me?

Of course there was another possibility — a guest or a delivery man. They wouldn't have known where he belonged. They might even have thought he was used to getting on the elevator by himself.

I realized I was rapidly getting so wrought up that I was not thinking clearly. The first thing I would have to do was to stop and decide where, if he had gotten out, he might go. With that in mind, I took the elevator downstairs and told both George, on the front door, and Jimmy on the back, the bad news. Polar Bear, I told them, had gotten loose. Would they be good enough to pass the word?

Everyone was extremely concerned. Raymond, the maintenance man, offered to help me look up on the roof and also down in the basement — two possibilities I had not even, in my distraught state, considered. First we explored the roof. Fortunately, messy as it all was up there, there were not too many hiding places where Polar Bear could have been. But the basement was a different story. I do not know how many non–New York apartment dwellers have ever visited a New York apartment basement, but I assure you that, in even a relatively small building, there are more hiding places for a small animal than it is possible to imagine.

When Raymond and I had searched everywhere we could think of, and I had told everybody I could find of my loss, I went back upstairs and called Marian. She would come over right away.

With Marian I made another search, only this time, after our inside search, we also made an out-of-the-apartment search. I suggested that he might even have run into the Park — after all, he was familiar with it from our ill-fated walk.

We had no luck. Polar Bear was nowhere and night was coming on. Back upstairs we made plans. The next morning we would call all the animal shelters, we would take advertisements in the newspapers, we would place those pathetic "Lost" signs one sees on telephone poles and on trees. As we worked on our plans, I told Marian that I had no one to blame but myself. I had foisted another animal on Polar Bear and I had taken away his sense of security. He thought he was unwanted and he had done the only thing he felt he had to do — run away. He would be killed by a dog, hit by a car, or end up in a laboratory. And it would serve me right, because it had been all my fault. But he would be the one who would do the suffering.

Marian would not allow me to carry on in this vein. "I am still not satisfied," she said, "that he could really have gotten out in the first place. Maybe he's still right here." With that she started once more a search of her own. "Have you looked behind the books?" she asked. I admitted I had not, but I reminded her that Polar Bear was now so big that it would be almost impossible for him to fit back there. Nonetheless, Marian and I looked there, as we had that very first night I had rescued him, and shelf by shelf we pulled out and down and then looked behind almost every volume. We found nothing.

"Have you really scoured the closets?" Marian asked. I told her that I had. I reminded her that we had looked in every closet at least twice. Nonetheless, she was determined to do it once more. And this time, when she came to the last one, she asked me if I had looked on the very topmost shelf. By now I was so discouraged that I hardly heard her. But when she repeated her question, I pointed out that the topmost shelf, which was a good foot over my head, was at least seven feet from the floor, and that Polar Bear could hardly have made that. He was not, after all, a kangaroo.

Nonetheless, as I said, Marian is very thorough. Whether there was any way for him to get up there or not, look she would. We got out the kitchen steps and, from the top one, she literally chinned herself to peer at the back of that topmost shelf. Suddenly her eyes were looking directly into two other eyes.

"Aeiou," he said.

We were never able to figure out exactly how Polar Bear had managed to get up there. But the fact remained that he had. And one thing we were certain of — once there, he knew perfectly well we were going crazy looking for him. And he was determined to teach us, and especially me, a lesson, and one I would not forget.

It was one which, of course, I never did. Nonetheless, at that moment I was so glad to see him that I would have accepted any lesson. Everything was perfect. Monday morning the woman came and took Bouncer. "I have a wonderful home for him," she said, as she came in and I leashed him up and handed him over to her. I told her he deserved it — he was a wonderful dog. "By the way," she asked at the door, "how did he get along with your cat?" I turned my hands back and forth. So-so, I said.

There were, that spring, no more stray dogs. But there was, soon after, a stray cat — or rather a stray kitten. Again it happened on a weekend, and again on a Friday night. But the rescuer this time was a fellow tenant in my own building. He had found the kitten on the sidewalk only a few blocks away.

He knocked on the door. The kitten, a tiny, sandy-furred ball of mischief, was tucked under his arm. "Here," he said, handing her to me, "I've brought Polar Bear a girlfriend." To him apparently, that was that. Didn't he . . . ? I started to ask — but, no, he didn't. "I've got a dog, you know," he said. Oh, I heard myself starting to assure him, that would be no problem. His dog would . . .

It was no use. The man, who was evidently far wiser in the ways of the territorial imperative than I had been, would have none of it. "Oh, no, my dog wouldn't," he said firmly. "Anyway, the kitten would be much happier with another cat." And with that, and a final wave of his hand, he started down the hall toward the elevator.

But the arrival of the kitten, sudden as it was after the departure of Bouncer, did not really cause me the slightest apprehension. On the contrary, being one of the few animal activists having only one of anything — when there were so many needing homes — I welcomed joining the ranks of the multied. And I was absolutely certain that Polar Bear would be ecstatic about the whole thing. With our new tenant there would no longer be any question of the separation of Church and State, or dog and cat. Now there would be just happy togetherness from one end of the apartment to the other.

In this spirit, I rushed the kitten into the living room to meet Polar Bear. Look, I told him, as I put the kitten down beside him, look what's here. Wasn't she, I asked him, making sure to pat them both at once, just wonderful? Now he would no longer be alone and miserable when I was not around. He would have the kind of companionship he needed, every day and every night as well — with one who was not only of his own kind but also one with whom he could talk and play to both of their hearts' content.

Actually the kitten, I noted delightedly, wanted to play right away — and indeed to her heart's content. The only trouble was it was not to Polar Bear's. The new kitten's idea of heart's content was not just to play some of the time, she wanted to play all of the time — indeed, except when she was sleeping or eating, every single second of all the time.

She would move toward Polar Bear and, as quickly as possible, he would move away. If he moved away slowly, she would move forward slowly. If he moved away fast, she would move forward fast. And, when this began to bore her, she would vary the game. She would pretend, when he moved away, either slowly or fast, not to follow. Then, just when he was visibly sighing in relief, she would fly at him and pounce.

It was this variation of her game plan which led me to name her Pouncer. Pouncer was, I was prepared to admit, not the most original of names. In any case, it did not last long, for as I soon realized, the name Pouncer in no way did justice to her aerial skills. By the end of the first day I had amended her name to Kamikaze.

To say Polar Bear tired of their play is an understatement. Indeed it was soon all too apparent that the same Monroe Doctrine which he had enforced so vigorously when Bouncer was around would also be extended, and in no uncertain measure, to the Kamikaze Kitten.

When it was, however, whenever the kitten would give the signal to let the games begin, Polar Bear would move rapidly to take whatever high ground was at hand — the bed or a windowsill if they were in the bedroom, the sofa, the desk, a chair, or another windowsill if they were in the living room. This would, of course, be frustrating in the extreme to Kamikaze. Over and over, towards whatever refuge Polar Bear had chosen, she would leap and fall, then leap and fall again. Finally, when I could stand it no longer, I would pick her up and put her down beside him.

Polar Bear, who had enough problems with the kitten alone, did not, to put it mildly, take kindly to my entrance onto the playing field. Indeed, he would become so cross about it that he seemed totally to forget that I never fussed over Kamikaze in his presence without fussing, at the same time and even more so, over him. There were no more silent "aeiou" 's — now there were silent hisses and on occasion real ones.

I decided it was high time for another talk, and for this I took him to even higher ground — the mantelpiece. I did not want to be interrupted by Kamikaze and I wanted Polar Bear's undivided attention.

I told him that I was prepared, where Bouncer was concerned, to let bygones be bygones. But Kamikaze was, if he would pardon the expression, a horse of an entirely different color. How could he, I wanted to know, extend his stupid Monroe Doctrine to that darling little member of his own species? Was his heart made of stone?

His answer obviously was that, in this case, it was — or at least I took it so because my opening tirade was greeted with ominous silence. I decided to tone down my rhetoric one notch. All right, I told him, I would admit that Kamikaze could seem, particularly from a totally egocentered point of view, a bit much. But could he not do her and me the courtesy of managing to remember that he too had once been a kitten? What if nobody had played with him? Had he ever even thought of that?

This time his answer was to turn his back on me — a posture I never tolerated during our confrontations, whether he understood a word I was saying or not. Immediately I turned him round. I well realized he might have had a very difficult time as a stray and maybe very little play. I had no wish to rub a raw nerve, and I should not have brought it up. But, going back to my criticism of his behavior, I told him that I was not just faulting his awful foreign policy, I was also faulting his forever taking the short-term view of everything, and his seemingly utter inability ever to take the long-term view of anything. And this time, I warned him, he could be making a very large mistake. After all, this was not a case like Bouncer's of a temporary visit. Kamikaze was going to be with us permanently. All I was really asking of him was merely a modicum of patience. In no time at all, I told him, Kamikaze would outgrow wanting to play all the time. And, even more importantly, in less time than he realized, he would be an old cat and she would be a dignified adult cat who would surely remember how she had been treated by him when she was a kitten. All and all, it behooved him to mend his ways or the day would come when she would ignore him exactly the way he was ignoring her now and it would be a very unpleasant old age for him.

That was the end of our talk, and I really thought I had done a fine job of giving him the big picture and actually diagramming it as best I could without a chalkboard. Nonetheless, the situation after our talk not only grew no better, it rapidly grew worse. The nights were the worst — they were holy terrors. Polar Bear would leap up on the bed and Kamikaze would of course attempt to follow him. I would then have to reach down and pull her up, after which Polar Bear would attempt to jump back down. What it amounted to for me was trying to hold both of them apart, her from trying to start a game and him from running away. And, the moment I relaxed my hold on him, he was off for the living room and, for all I knew, the mantelpiece. Meanwhile Kamikaze would mew piteously to be allowed to follow him. But it was, of course, pointless to put her down, because she would trail him into the living room and just as piteously mew in there.

Finally, after three nights of almost total sleeplessness, I resolved to go back to the drawing board and begin again. The next free time I had I introduced games that the three of us could play together, everything from ball chasing — Kamikaze actually liked to retrieve — to more specialized endeavors in which, while the participants were primarily Kamikaze and me, Polar Bear could either join in or not as he pleased, but in any case would never feel left out. In addition to these efforts, I even stooped to bribery. Carrying Polar Bear, not terribly willing but at least inert, to Kamikaze's vicinity, I would, when I could manage it, try to place his nose right next to her soft fur. I asked him if she wasn't the sweetest, dearest little thing he ever felt.

He clearly did not think so, not even when I would accompany this special togetherness with a special treat of niblets — which, by literally taking them from right in front of her and giving them to him, I made believe were actually coming from her.

It did not work. Polar Bear, as I should have known, was far above this sort of chicanery. He had made up his mind, and no manipulative measure by me was going to change it. On one occasion he actually spit out a niblet. And even when he ate one, his baleful glance gave me to understand that, just as he would not give in to terrorism, neither would he bow to bribery.

I decided to have one last talk with him. I prefaced this by saying that Kamikaze was obviously such a charming little kitten that it would be easy, if that was what he really wanted, to get another home for her. It was now for him to decide. Did he or did he not care if he ever saw her again? Usually, he at least blinked a little during such talks, and thus I could get some kind of answer. But this time his eyes just stared straight back at me. No, he was obviously responding, he did not care if he ever saw Kamikaze again — in fact, as far as he was concerned, the sooner she moved onward, the better he would like it.

My second question was just as direct. Did he want to spend his whole life as an only cat? And before he answered this one, I reminded him that I had asked that question with all that that implied — one who would be much of the time all alone. Was that, I wanted to know, really what he wanted?

This time I could not vouch for any clear answer to that specific question. But I could hardly have missed the sure sign that being an only cat was indeed exactly what he wanted. Polar Bear did not dislike Kamikaze personally, and he certainly would never have hurt her physically — he was far too much of a gentleman ever to strike a lady cat — but he did very much dislike the idea of her. And it was not all a matter of possessiveness about me, either. It was a kind of possessiveness, it was true, but it was, to his way of thinking, not his for me but rather mine for him. Remember, in his view I didn't own him, he owned me, and it was just as beyond the pale for me suddenly to have another cat as it would have been for him suddenly to have another person. In sum, I was the one who had hurt him, not he me.

In the final analysis then, the whole thing really had nothing to do with Kamikaze at all. It was the fact that Polar Bear seemed to sense that she was to be permanent — and that he could not handle. And, irrespective of the whole thing's effect on him, it was patently unfair to Kamikaze. She deserved a home where she could be, if not the big cheese, at least one in which the big cheese would give her a better break than she had with Polar Bear. In the end I had only one course of action left. I passed the word that I had a kitten for adoption, and I did not hesitate to add to this word the further word that the kitten was, bar none, the darlingest one with which I had ever had anything to do.

When, a couple of days later, a young girl came to pick her up, the girl was, as I knew she would be, totally enchanted — so enchanted, in fact, that when she finally looked up from hugging Kamikaze, she regarded me with an accusing eye. "How on earth," she demanded, "can you bear to give her up?"

I told her that I did not want to, that if it had been up

to me I would have kept Kamikaze forever. But I told the girl I had to — it was a matter of policy. The girl looked blank. I informed her that it was a long story but perhaps the simplest way to explain it was that it was a policy I could do nothing about. It was, I concluded, as if I were in an army, and it was the policy of my superior officer.

The third stray that summer arrived early one June morning via an animal rescuer I vaguely remembered having seen before but could not immediately place. In any case, she had whatever she had rescued right with her in a cat carrier. Oh no, I told her, when I saw the carrier, not another cat. Polar Bear doesn't . . . "No, it's not a cat," the woman interrupted, as she opened the carrier for me, and I tried to peer inside. "His name is Herbert," she informed me. "He's beautiful, isn't he? See, he's lavender."

Actually I could see very little inside the carrier but I saw enough to see that Herbert was, of all creatures, a pigeon — and a very perishable-looking pigeon at that. Right away I remembered who the woman was — one of New York's legendary "pigeon women" — those who befriend the city birds who are so often friendless. I admired her and made an effort to restrain both lack of enthusiasm and incipient sarcasm. I did tell the pigeon woman that I really wondered, having been through a retriever and a kitten, if a pigeon was not just what Polar Bear and I really needed. "Oh, you don't have to worry about that," she said firmly. "I have cats and I've often had pigeons with them."

In that case, I wondered, why had she not had her cats with this one. I did not, however, say so. Instead I asked her what was the matter with Herbert.

The pigeon woman explained that the matter with Herbert was his left wing. She thought he had been hit by a car, she said, but whether he had or not, he would certainly have been hit by one soon if she had not removed him from the street. Herbert, she told me, would try to fly on one wing, but that with his very wounded other one he could not even flutter enough to get away from anything — not, for example, from her when she had gone to pick him up. She had, she said, carried Herbert home, put him in a carrier, and taken him right to the vet. The vet had done a fine job on the wing and had told her that what the pigeon now needed was R&R.

I did not need to hear the bottom line, but I was to do so anyway. "I thought the ideal place," she beamed, "would be your balcony."

You mean, I corrected her sternly, Polar Bear's balcony. My balcony was not wired in.

It was no use. Pigeon women and for that matter pigeon men are probably the most determined of all animal people. In no time at all I was following her — reluctantly — through the bedroom and to the window to the balcony. But, before arriving there, I pushed past her and reached in and removed Polar Bear, who, as we approached, was contentedly taking his morning sun. Although he did not like being ushered out and indeed did not, as he did not to all strangers, take to the pigeon woman, he was soon safely removed and replaced by Herbert.

As the lady busied herself in getting Herbert pigeon food she had brought with her, and building Herbert a makeshift nest out of a bath towel, I noticed that Polar Bear was watching intently from behind his only access route, the firmly closed window. At any moment I expected him to bat at the window, but he did not — in fact he showed, for him, remarkable restraint.

I put it down, however, not to discipline but to patience. I told the pigeon woman that I knew exactly why he wasn't making more of a fuss — what he was thinking was that what she was doing was preparing his lunch. Squab, I elaborated. Not exactly under glass, but close enough to it — behind glass.

The pigeon woman did not think that was funny. "You really don't believe they can be friends, do you?"

I told her I really did not. "You don't know much about pigeons, do you?" she pursued. I admitted to that charge also, but I told her I knew a great deal about Polar Bear. I told her that the day might come, and I really hoped it would, when the lion would lie down with the lamb, but that when the day came when Polar Bear would lie down with Herbert I would, if she would pardon the expression, eat it.

I also reminded her that, before the coming of Herbert, when Polar Bear was in residence in his balcony, other pigeons seemed to like nothing better, knowing that Polar Bear was safely enclosed behind wire and could do nothing about it, than to parade up and down in front of him and, indeed, as close to him as possible. I told her that this behavior would drive Polar Bear into a frenzy — he would crouch, lash his tail, and even leap toward the wire — but now that the tables were reversed and Herbert, not Polar Bear, was the prisoner, surely she could not expect Polar Bear, under these new circumstances and given his previous tormenting, to observe the Geneva Convention.

The pigeon woman did not agree. And, during the next

few days, while she came and went and I looked after Herbert, following the instructions with which I was plentifully provided, I saw no reason to change my mind.

In the times when she was around, I learned a great deal about pigeons. Among other things I learned that they were indeed remarkable birds. And not the least remarkable thing about them was that they and doves were, in reality, the same bird, that both were monogamous and usually mated for life. "I was sure I saw Herbert's mate," the woman told me, "watching me when I picked Herbert up. When he gets well, I'm going to take him to that exact same spot to let him go. Maybe she'll still be there."

The pigeon woman also informed me that pigeons were extremely bright birds, so bright, indeed, that they actually recognized people on the street and that this recognition was accorded not only to people who fed them, but also to people who were just nice to them, and even those whom they simply habitually just saw in a given area. She told me that to her one of the saddest things about them was that, because of the large numbers of pigeons, people almost never paid any attention to them as individuals.

Herbert, I could see for myself, was indeed an individual. He soon became very affectionate toward me as well as his rescuer, coo-cooing cheerfully when I came around and being friendly in his way whether I was coming to feed him or not. Although he spent most of his time in a hunched-up position, with his little head and almost nonexistent neck tucked into his body, as he began to feel better I noticed that he started to change from this position and would sit up, puff out his chest, and preen himself in front of me. One day, the third after he arrived, I found him lying flat on his back on the towel, taking a sunbath.

The pigeon woman was also a mine of information about pigeons as messengers. They could, she told me, fly incredible distances — one, for example, flew from Australia to New York, a distance of over nine thousand miles, and a trip which the bird managed, apparently, by island-hopping. But I was perhaps even more impressed with a World War II pigeon from Fort Meade, Maryland — one which, off on a training mission and becoming thirsty, had flown down to a pond. The pond, however, had been covered with oil, and the bird had become so soaked with it that he could not fly. Several days later, still soaked with the oil and still unable to fly, the pigeon had appeared at Fort Meade. He had walked home — for over one hundred miles.

The pigeon woman's favorite pigeon, however, was one named Cher Ami, the bird which was responsible for saving America's famed "Lost Battalion" in World War I. She told the story extremely dramatically — about how the battalion, surrounded by Germans and low on ammunition, was, as a final straw, being shelled by its own artillery, and its only hope was to get a message back to headquarters to cease the firing. An army major, having just seven pigeons, dispatched them one by one, but all were shot down. Finally the last, Cher Ami, went up. He too was shot and fluttered to the ground. Just before he touched the earth, however, he somehow righted himself and, with one wing shot through and one leg shot off and the all-important message tied to a dangling ligament, reached headquarters. After the war, the woman proudly told me, Cher Ami was awarded the Croix de Guerre by the French government, was sent home by General Pershing in the officers' cabin of a troopship and, later the mascot of the Signal Corps, was buried with full military honors.

By now I was really almost as intrigued with pigeons as my informant, but I still had not the slightest belief that Polar Bear and Herbert could ever be friends. Indeed, as the time went by, Polar Bear seemed to me to get crosser and crosser about the takeover of his balcony and more and more annoyed with me for not at least making an effort to become a white knight. The pigeon woman, however, would have none of such negativism. One day she came in from observing Herbert. "He's almost ready to be let go," she said, "but before I let him go, I want to prove something to you." I started to tell her that the only thing she would prove . . . but I did not even get to my point. As I said, she was a very determined woman.

One thing I insisted on — that at least I be in the balcony when Polar Bear would be allowed to enter. And thus, with Polar Bear still securely in the living room, and the door shut, I climbed out the bedroom window and got into the balcony with Herbert. Still feeling that the whole idea would end in total disaster, I nonetheless resolved to do my best. If I was to be in a United Nations peacekeeping force, I would at least give it the old college try.

At last, sitting directly between the pigeon and the open window, my hands ready to grab Polar Bear, I gave the lady the signal that I was as ready for her idiotic experiment as I would ever be. Listening carefully, I heard her open the bedroom door. The next thing I knew — it seemed less than a second later — I saw a furry whirr fly through the window directly at me. I did not have a chance even to slow it down, let alone grab it.

I am sure that any of you who have read this far could write the inevitable end to the story — of how, in that very next second, both the great experiment and Herbert were terminated and how, conscience-stricken and furious with the pigeon lady, I was forced to bury Herbert, like Cher Ami, with full military honors.

But, if indeed you would write it that way, you would be totally wrong — just as wrong as in fact, although I dislike having to admit it, I was about the whole experiment to begin with. Nothing like that happened at all. Polar Bear leapt past me, all right, using my shoulder as a way station. And then, turning in midair, he landed on Herbert's other side, just as I too spun around in the vain hope of warding off his attack — which was now behind me and would have been much harder for me to thwart.

But no such attack was forthcoming. Polar Bear merely sat down beside Herbert and proceeded to lick himself. Whether he was just glad to have at least part of his balcony back or whether he wanted to make friends with Herbert I could not be certain. Remarkable as was his behavior, however, Herbert's was even more so. Not only did he not move when Polar Bear overflew both me and him, he did not even do so when Polar Bear landed. He kept a beady weather eye on the new arrival — pigeons can see almost directly sideways without moving their heads — but he did not panic, he did not squawk, and he did not try to flutter away. He remained where he was, and for some time the two of them just sat and regarded both each other and the Park down below them, looking for all the world as if they were posing for a new version of *The Peaceable Kingdom*.

"See!" the pigeon woman exclaimed, as she climbed down from the window to be part of her triumph. "I told you so."

I really don't like people who tell me they told me so, particularly when they just happen to be right and I, as I seldom am, just happen to be wrong. And I was glad to see Polar Bear shared this feeling with me. For the fact was the moment the lady got down into his balcony with him, he promptly jumped out again, and took up a watching post on the windowsill.

It was not necessarily, I decided, that he didn't like the pigeon — he just didn't like the pigeon woman. As I told you before, you could never count on his foreign policy.

After Bouncer, Kamikaze, and Herbert, the next order of business on the agenda that summer was a piece of foreign policy of my own — or rather, that of the Fund for Animals. Once more it involved Paul Watson and the Fund's *Sea Shepherd*.

The *Sea Shepherd* had, after the painting of the seals, sailed to Bermuda. From there, Paul called me to ask if I would come down for a meeting. From the tone of his voice, I knew he had another plan.

When I arrived in Hamilton, I soon learned what this plan was — it was to "go after," as Paul put it, the most infamous of the pirate whaling ships, the ironically named *Sierra*. For more than ten years, this ship had broken even the extremely lax rules laid down by the International Whaling Commission, which was then, if not dominated by Russia, Japan, and the other whaling nations, at least rendered largely impotent by them. Operating under various flags of convenience, the *Sierra* had long made a practice of mercilessly harpooning every whale she came upon — mother whales, baby whales, even whales in such declared sanctuaries as the Indian Ocean. She had, among other things, killed virtually every whale around Bermuda.

What, I asked Paul, did he mean by going after her? "I mean," Paul said, "ramming her — putting her out of commission."

I hated the *Sierra* as much as Paul did, but I was taken aback by the idea of ramming another ship. I felt this was stretching animal activism to the limit.

Paul asked me at least to think about it, and that I told him I would do. In point of fact, I thought of little else until we met again — this time in my apartment in New York. Once again, Polar Bear was in on the planning of an operation — just as he had been at the Beverly Hills Hotel when Paul and I had planned the painting of the baby seals. And once again Paul was patting Polar Bear, just as he had been that previous time, while he told me exactly how he intended to do the job.

He pointed out that if we could put the *Sierra* out of commission, it would make it almost impossible for other pirate whalers — there were then five — to get insurance. And that with one blow it was not inconceivable that we could put the entire pirate whaling industry out of business once and for all. "Remember," he said, "we still have all that concrete in the bow — and the rocks."

Once again, as had happened before in our discussion about the seals, it was my turn to pat Polar Bear. I told Paul that I would agree to his plan if he would meet four conditions. I told him I knew he was not big on conditions, but I was going to tell them to him anyway.

My first condition, I said, was that he had to promise me that no matter how the *Sierra* was armed, he would carry no arms, not even a handgun. My second condition was that he also agree not to ram the *Sierra* in the open ocean, but only when she was close enough to the shore so that, if by some chance she sank, and they did not have enough lifeboats on board, or for that matter lifebelts, no one would drown. My third condition was that however he proposed to ram her, he was not to ram her in such a way that the two ships would become stuck together, and her crew could conceivably board the *Sea Shepherd* and injure or kill our crew.

My fourth and final condition was that he, and anybody else on the *Sea Shepherd*'s bridge, have a mattress with them. The *Sea Shepherd*'s bridge was at least forty feet over her deck, and, when the ramming occurred, I believed that the whole superstructure might fall forward to the deck. If they used their mattresses, he and the others up there would at least have the possibility of surviving the fall.

Paul thought about my conditions for a long time. Finally he spoke. "Okay," he said. At the door he picked up Polar Bear. "You know," he said questioningly, "we still don't have a ship's cat."

Taking Polar Bear from him, I told Paul sternly that he still didn't — at least not for that trip.

Early on the morning of July 17, 1979, Polar Bear and I were awakened in the apartment by the telephone. It was a reporter from the Associated Press. He informed me that they had had a report that the *Sea Shepherd,* which they knew was funded by the Fund for Animals, had apparently purposely rammed a whaling ship and did I have any comments?

I told my caller I would have but that first I wanted to

know if anyone had been hurt, and where the ramming had occurred. He told that first reports indicated no one had been injured on either ship, but that the *Sierra* had been badly damaged and that the ramming had occurred about a quarter mile from shore near Oporto, Portugal.

I breathed a deep sigh of relief. Then I told the reporter that, hard as it was for me to condone the ramming of a ship in the open ocean, he must remember that whatever illegality had occurred, it had not begun with us. The *Sierra* had been operating, totally illegally, for ten years and had illegally killed thousands of whales.

Later I heard from Paul the whole story — of how the *Sea Shepherd* had first located the *Sierra* off the Azores and that his crew had wanted to ram her then. But he had remembered my second condition and he had refused. Instead, he had followed the *Sierra* into Oporto, and then, to save our British captain and the British officers, had engineered a kind of voluntary mutiny. He had put the captain and officers off on the dock and then called for volunteers from the crew to go out and do the ramming. In the end, Paul, with just two others, engineer Peter Woof, from Australia, and seaman Jerry Doran from Hawaii, had done the job alone.

And what a job it was! The *Sea Shepherd* had made two runs at the *Sierra*. The first one, at her bow, had sheared off the harpoon and whale-killing gear altogether and then, after bouncing back and negotiating a 360-degree turn, the *Sea Shepherd* had undertaken a second run. This one ran straight at the *Sierra* amidship, and, while her crew scattered either toward the bow or the stern, was strong enough to stave in some fifty feet of her hull and rip open a huge gash in her hold — one which ironically revealed inside her load of illegal whale meat. Even this blow had been, as I had wished, a glancing one. In fact the only condition of mine which Paul had failed to meet was the matter of the mattresses. Paul and Jerry had, as I had requested, brought up two mattresses to the bridge. But when, just before the second impact, Peter had come running up from the engine room, Paul had given his mattress to him.

I forgave him. The *Sierra* never whaled again — nor indeed, shortly afterward because of the insurance cancellations, did any of the other pirate whalers. In the history of the long war to end commercial whaling, the ramming of the *Sierra* was only one battle. But it was a victory — one which, like the painting of the baby seals, had come at a low point in the war. And, widely reported as it was, played a by no means unimportant role in the eventual moratorium on commercial whaling.

As for Polar Bear, for the second time in the brief seven months I had had him, he had brought the Fund, in another extremely high-risk venture, almost incredibly good fortune. And both ventures had, after all, occurred in far-off foreign waters. Certainly for a local land cat, and one with as rotten a foreign policy as his, it was no small achievement.

X ◦ *His Domestic Policy*

Having addressed Polar Bear's foreign policy toward other animals, I shall now turn, in this final chapter, to his domestic policy — which was in reality his foreign policy toward people. I should like, however, to preface this with the admonitory note that it is one more example that, although Polar Bear and I were similar in outlook in many respects, in this case, as in the one previously discussed about when we were sick, we were two very different individuals.

I, for example, like new people. In fact my critics have been known to say that I am better with new people than I am with other people.

This is not entirely true, of course. My critics are prone to exaggeration and leaping to conclusions and not getting their facts straight. Actually I consider myself second to no one I know at being very fond of certain old friends who are good listeners and are not people who are constantly interrupting me. But at the same time I am prepared to acknowledge that there is, on the side of the critics, something to be said. As fond as I am of any of some of those friends I just cited, I am also extremely partial to almost all new people.

And why, may I ask, should I not be? After all, when you come right down to it, there is a great deal to be said for new people. You can, to begin with, tell them all your old stories without worrying whether or not you have told them to them before, and you can also tell them, as long as you can remember the punch lines, your old jokes.

Besides this, with old friends, even when you are just making polite conversation, you have to rack your brain every other minute worrying, when you ask them a question, whether or not you asked them that same question the last time you met them, or, when they asked you some question, what you answered at that time, particularly if it was something you didn't want to answer to begin with.

On top of it all, you have to remember their names and do so right off the bat — otherwise they will be offended. And even if you can come up with the name, which is by no means always possible, then you also have to remember the names of their damn wives. With new people, you're not expected to remember their names — after all, you just met them.

Finally, with old friends it is sometimes very difficult to convince them that you know more about whatever subject is being discussed than they do. One or the other of them, for all you know, may actually turn out to be an expert on the thing, and, worse still, the kind of expert who has the gall to challenge even your most basic credentials to be one. With new people, on the other hand, you can be an expert on any subject you please — who's to say you're not? — and you can just hold forth and impart your wise counsel, and, because you have just met and there is a certain politeness to be observed, you can do so without ever having the slightest fear of being convicted on some minor fact or date or something which has nothing whatever to do with the strong points you are making. All in all, other things being equal, it can't help but make for a far more interesting discussion — when it's your job to do the talking and it's their job to listen and learn.

Polar Bear, unfortunately, was never able to have this kind of satisfaction because he had never had, if I do say so, my gift of gab. Besides this, as I have said before, he didn't like anything new — and at the top of his list of new things he didn't like were new people.

The fact is he had a totally blind spot about them. Whoever they were and no matter under what circumstances they met him, he was always making one of those ridiculous unilateral decisions of his about them. The basic trouble, I always felt, was that he was simply not up to making any sensible assessment of just what was the difference between new people and people he knew. I could tell him until I was blue in the face that, if only he would give them half a chance, new people would become people he knew. But I was wasting my breath.

There were times, I admit, when the whole thing about new people and him was so frustrating that I more than once envied the person who, instead of having a cat like Polar Bear around, had, perhaps, a dog. Compared to Polar Bear, your average dog is, with new people, the emcee of the Miss America Pageant. Such a dog will run out and greet the new person as if what the dog wanted most in life was to meet either him or her. And that person, of course, will be immediately and highly flattered. And he or she will probably stay that way — particularly if you add to what the dog has done by saying the line so many dog owners are prone to say, that they've never seen that dog that way about anybody before. It is a line which I have often thought should, because of its obvious phoniness, stick in the craw of the dog owner, but it rarely does. As for the new person, because of the general conceit of people regarding their ability to attract any animal's affection, he or she will almost usually swallow it whole. And as for you as the dog's owner, you will right away have the new person eating out of your hand — at the same time, it goes without saying, your dog will soon be eating out of his or hers, and probably something that is very bad for him too.

But no matter. The cat person, or at least a person who is owned by a cat like Polar Bear, has no such easy row to hoe. Not for him is there the remotest possibility that his cat will serve, with a new person, as any kind of icebreaker or even a topic of conversation, let alone one who will become a lasting friend — and all for the simple reason that your cat will be nowhere around.

When, for example, a new person would enter my apartment, the first thing Polar Bear would want to do is to know what possible excuse whoever it was could have for interrupting him at such an hour — and for him such an hour included, of course, all twenty-four. The second thing he would want to know was if there might be anything in the outrageous disruption of his routine which could conceivably be of a positive nature where he was concerned — someone, for example, who might be going to sit down and have, say, with a cup of coffee or a drink, something to eat which would give him a chance for a snack. But this possibility was, in his mind, invariably far outweighed by the negatives — that the new person would be someone who was either loud, hearty, and boisterous and would take entirely too much interest in him, or else someone who had come to take me away from him.

No matter who it was, particularly if it were someone who was going to stay any length of time, Polar Bear wanted equal time to observe them and make up his mind about them. While he was doing this, his two favorite observation posts were, if the person was in the living room, under the sofa, or if the person was in the bedroom, under the bed. And make no mistake about it, he would get to either of these posts posthaste — not only long before they did but also before they had ever seen him.

I am well aware, having mentioned the bedroom, and having already said that I am a bachelor, what some of you are probably thinking — that in such a situation, Polar Bear might be something of an impediment to some romance or other. But I shall not, I assure you, dignify such thoughts of yours in this delicate matter by stooping to give them any answer at all. I shall, however, state only that this is a family book and you should, while reading it, mind not only your manners but your mind as well.

But, to proceed. If a new person did indeed stay any length of time, there was always the possibility that he or she would, sooner or later, spot Polar Bear — at a time when either he partially appeared or else perhaps, from his hiding place, had decided to go to another room or to his balcony. At such times it behooved me, as indeed it behooves any person owned by such a cat in such a situation, to have a veritable litany of excuses ready for recital. One of my favorites has always been "He's a little shy with strangers" — albeit I have found it to be singularly inappropriate on such an occasion as, when for example, Polar Bear had been under the sofa and then would emerge, literally, right beside the newcomer's feet, and scoot like a streak as far away as possible. In any case, others I have used are almost anything to do with the vet, such as "He's just back from the vet" or "He's just had his shots" or even the general "He hasn't been well." Besides these, I also favor an excellent all-purpose one, which is "He's just not himself today."

At first I used to think Polar Bear's attitude toward new people was due to the fact that he had been a stray and had had bad things done to him by people and that therefore he was suspicious of anybody who hadn't proved themselves to him. But I soon learned that this was not necessarily true. Rather it was just a characteristic of, not all, but some cats — and this whether they are purebreds or whatever. We, for example, have had two strays right in the Fund for Animals' office for some years before Polar Bear came. One of them is a beautiful green-eyed coal-black cat who was found, as a kitten, in the lower branch of a tree in the New Jersey woods during a thunderstorm, with none of the rest of her family anywhere around. We called her Little Girl, although this turned out to be, as she grew older, a singularly inappropriate name — for reasons I shall not mention because she is sensitive about it. In any case, Little Girl is as awful as Polar Bear about new people. Whenever she is around and anybody she has not seen before comes into any one of our offices, the next thing you know, she is not only not around, she is not to be found anywhere. The other stray, however, is a large black-and-white male who looks like a tuxedo and should have, in my opinion, been named Tuxedo. Unfortunately, I was overruled, and somebody else, who shall be nameless, decided that his name should be Benedict.

In contrast to Little Girl, Benedict is the soul of friendliness. He welcomes all newcomers to the Fund office as if he were the official greeter, and once they have stated their business and he has escorted them to whichever office they were heading for, the next thing they know, he is in their lap. Benedict is particularly in his element when there are a lot of people around, as at a board meeting, a Christmas party, or even a press conference. If, for example, there is television at the press conference and he has not been invited to appear, he simply waits until the red light goes on and then jumps up into the lap of whoever is on camera. People get to be stars on television by different routes — Benedict knows the shortest, and best.

Benedict particularly likes making friends with people who do not like cats. At one time we had a bookkeeper who admitted he was scared to death of them. Benedict had apparently given some thought to the problem and had come up with a solution. One day he watched, well hidden, while the man, seated in one of the offices and attempting to do his work, was at the same time nervously keeping a lookout for him. Benedict outwaited him and, when the man eventually relaxed his vigil, he crept in from behind his chair, shot up and leapt into his lap. He had apparently decided that the cure for the fear of cats was, like hiccups, a matter of a good surprise.

At first we were ready to scratch one accountant. But this turned out not to be necessary, because, as he so often is, Benedict was right. From that time on, the bookkeeper made his peace with cats. As for Benedict, to this day he continues to like everybody — with one exception. And that is Little Girl. But then, even with the friendliest of cats, you cannot have everything. They are, after all, cats.

The irony of Polar Bear was that, with people he already knew, he was as friendly as Benedict. With Marian, for example — he was extraordinarily affectionate — he would sit on her lap for hours at a stretch, and even when she had to join me in doing something which to him was unforgivable — such as helping me give him a pill — he would afterwards, and in no unmistakable manner, take it out on me but, pointedly, never on her.

There were other people of whom he was also genuinely fond. Most of these were other animal people who either stayed at my apartment when I was away or came in and looked after him when both Marian and I were away. One of his particular favorites was Alex Pacheco, who had crewed on the *Sea Shepherd,* and, although he had not yet founded People for the Ethical Treatment of Animals, was already distinguished as one of the up-and-coming young activists who would shortly revolutionize the animal rights movement. Another was Jeanne Adlon. Jeanne was a former office worker of ours who loved cats so much she soon had a whole business of just looking after them when their regular persons were away. How she did it I never knew, but she sometimes managed as many as twenty calls a day, during which she not only fed each cat on her rounds, but stopped and played with them.

Polar Bear made little trouble too about my chess-playing friends, even when a new one would arrive. Polar Bear was ambivalent about chess. He saw some virtues in it, such as the lack of noise associated with it and also that it usually involved only one other person besides me — which, second to no one, was his favorite number. But there were also two things he did not like about chess. One was what, to him, was the interminable length of it, the other the ridiculous seriousness with which people took it. When, for example, he had a rush call for an appointment on the windowsill to see a pigeon, or some equally important errand — and the shortest way to his destination was directly over the board — he never could understand why everybody made such a fuss about a few little pieces being knocked to the floor, particularly since they were pieces which he knew from experience didn't roll around very well and didn't have anything even remotely interesting, like a bell, inside them.

Other than these people, however, I can count on the fingers of one hand the new people whom, from the beginning, Polar Bear really liked. One was my granddaughter, Zoe. When Zoe first arrived, however, she did so with both my daughter, Gaea, and her husband, Sam, and since this made three people and Polar Bear's outside limit was two, he immediately repaired to his post under the bed. Whereupon Zoe promptly climbed right down there after him and pulled him out — and, to my amazement, he seemed to like it.

The other was Caroline Thompson, a producer and personal friend who had gone with us to Canada to paint the seals. Late one night when I was away, Caroline came to meet Polar Bear for the first time and spend the night there. The next morning, when she had gone and I had returned, I saw that Polar Bear was still asleep. And, when he woke up, he did something I had never seen him do before. He rolled around with an idiotic smile on his face.

Sometime later I was able to figure out why Polar Bear had been so immediately attracted to Zoe and Caroline. With Zoe, I put it down to the fact that she was, at that time, just four years old and was hardly bigger than he was. With Caroline, it was a sterner story. She had gotten him hooked on catnip. I called her immediately and reminded her that Polar Bear was a minor and that she could go to jail for what she had done. I told her I had decided, however, not to press charges. All I was going to do, I told her, was to send him, at her expense, to Betty Ford's.

Ironically, not the least interesting part of Polar Bear's domestic policy was his policy toward a domestic — Rosa, whom we have met before when discussing his diet. In any case, from the moment she first saw Polar Bear, Rosa loved him. She made a great deal of fuss over him and he, in turn, made an equal amount of fuss over her. He made so much indeed that he would permit her to clean and wash and mop and dust virtually anywhere. Not only would he not object, he would happily follow her around and take as much part in her activities as he could. He would even allow her to move him off the bed when she made it, and he particularly enjoyed, as a sort of game, making her also move him off the piled blankets and bed sheets before she remade the bed.

There were, however, two of Rosa's operations at which Polar Bear drew the line. And it was because of these, at least when she was actively engaged in them, that he immediately demoted her again to new person. One of these operations was carpet sweeping, and the other vacuum cleaning. When Rosa brought either of these machines of mayhem out of the closet, it was, for Polar Bear, the signal that diplomatic relations had been broken off and that the lights were going out all over the apartment. War was in fact already in progress and, the moment Rosa turned the machines on, these were, to him, no longer just machines but tanks which had crossed the border. The invasion had begun and he was Rome against the Visigoths, the Allies against the Central Powers, the U.S. against Russia, or simply us against them.

He did not like the carpet sweeper. He did not like the idea of it, or the way it moved. But with it, at least, first running in front of it and then moving to the side to swipe at it with his paws, he had a chance to slow it down and in any case it was reasonably quiet. The advance of the vacuum cleaner, the big tank, was something else again. He purely loathed it. The noise was ear-splitting and it was no longer a fair fight. His only hope was to rip open the bag and get at the infantry inside, but with Rosa constantly moving away from him and at the same time yelling at him above the din, it was all but impossible. He could not hear, of course, that all she was saying was *"Pobre Oso Polar! A tí no te gusta el aspirador, verdad?"* All he heard were command shouts above the noise of the battle. To him, the vacuum symbolized the full horror of modern war, and now it was no longer a matter of just *Amerika* on television. It was a case of infidels in his lair.

On occasion, at lunchtime, I would come home and, if I happened in during the middle of the war, neither Polar Bear nor Rosa would at first notice me, and I would watch the proceedings in amazement. Finally she would see me — Polar Bear was much too busy — and then, of course, she would stop the vacuum cleaner. It was at this time Polar Bear's turn to notice me, and he would run over and give me a terrific welcome. To him, I was the Home Guard, the Seventh Cavalry, the Marines. And I had come up just in time to save the day.

Afterward, however, when Rosa would of course continue with her vacuuming, and when I would obviously be doing nothing to stop her, the whole thing was now, in Polar Bear's eyes, a totally different story. He could not believe I would just sit there. This time I was not merely a traitor, I was far worse — I was someone who, with the war all but won, had snatched defeat from the jaws of victory — who, for some unaccountable reason, had shown the white feather. He would fight on to the bitter end and his inevitable defeat, but, after it was all over and the armistice declared, it would be a long time before he would have anything to do with me again.

As it happened that first summer, I was away from him much of the time because the Fund had begun a domestic war of its own — one which would last for many years — with, of all adversaries, the National Park Service. It broke out first in the Grand Canyon, specifically over the wild burrows there, which we wanted to rescue. To that end we had placed the down payment on a property in Texas, one which I had named after the book which was my favorite as a child. I called it the Black Beauty Ranch, and, though it was at the time small, it at least gave us a place from which, after we had rescued the burros, we would be able to adopt them. The sign at the gate said "Home of the Abused and Unwanted Equine" — but it also had, under this, a quotation from the last lines of *Black Beauty* — "My troubles are over, and I have found a home."

The burros in the Grand Canyon were not the mules which take visitors down to the canyon's floor. Rather they were burros which had been running wild in the canyon since Gold Rush days. The prospectors, not having found gold, had often simply abandoned their pack animals, and through the years their numbers had grown. Before we began our rescue, the National Park Service authorities had estimated their number at between 250 and 300. Actually, as we were soon to learn, government figures were rarely accurate, and there were 577.

At the same time, these same Park Service authorities had in their hands a report from a wildlife biologist which stated that the only answer to the problem of too many burros in the canyon was to shoot them. We were, of course, accustomed to the fact that wildlife biologists in general believe that the answer to almost anything is, if you have a problem, shoot it. But what made this report especially infuriating was that we were told it had been prepared by the same man who was also going to be paid to do the shooting. That was too much — and we were determined to do something about it.

We well knew, to begin with, that the burro is a very difficult animal to shoot. For one thing, he is an extremely intelligent animal, and the minute the shooting starts, he can be counted on to find every possible hiding place in particular in a terrain far more familiar to him than to his prospective killers. For another thing, he has only two vital areas — his brain and his heart — and the gunners, who obviously had little experience with either, would certainly wind up wounding many more burros than they would kill outright. A friend of mine had personally witnessed one burro shoot in which he saw, he told me, "one burro who had ten bullets in him trying to die."

In the century and a quarter the burros had been in the canyon, a number of removal operations had been tried.

All had, for one reason or another, failed. The Fund was determined that ours would not. To begin with, we put together a roundup team which included cowboys, horses, specially trained dogs, and even, ironically, mules — which, since their fathers were donkeys, were smarter than horses and could be counted on not to fall on the perilous rocks and ridges. The team was led by a man named Dave Ericsson, who was not only a world-class roper, but who, I was assured by one of his men, had once roped a rabbit. This was later confirmed by Ericsson himself, who told me, I was certain to reassure me, that he had not hurt the rabbit.

Besides this team, we also decided not to try to herd or lead the burros up the seven-thousand-foot climb to the canyon rim — a tactic which had been previously tried and had invariably ended in failure. Instead we were determined to fly out every single animal — in slings under helicopters.

The first day of our rescue was almost the last. We had been promised by the park authorities that we could use the main, relatively wide, tourist trail to get our team to the canyon floor. At the last moment, the Park Service reneged on this promise and gave us an alternate trail which, in some places, was nonexistent and in others straight down. Still within sight of the top, two horses slipped and several others started to panic — only incredibly quick thinking on the part of our lead riders saved them, and our rescue.

That first day too the temperature at the bottom of the canyon was over one hundred degrees — so high that even if we had found a burro, which that first day we did not, we could not in that heat have, without danger to the horses as well as to him, either rounded him up or roped him. And, even if we had done so, we could not have flown him out — the helicopter, in that heat, would not have had enough lift.

We learned to work in the early dawn hours, when it was cooler, and as late in the afternoon, before dark, as possible — and, one by one, the burros started to come out. At the beginning the cowboys had a lot of fun with the "Bambi-lovers," as they delighted in calling us. One day, at the end of the first week, however, when I had come from another part of the canyon, I noticed a group of them standing around the helicopter. As I came closer I saw that they had that day, for the first time, captured both a mother and a baby burro. I also learned that a spirited debate was in progress about this — one which concerned whether the mother or the baby should be lifted by the helicopter first.

One cowboy was adamantly insisting that it would be better to lift the baby first. The mother would then, he said, at least see what was happening and would be relieved when the helicopter returned for her. Another cowboy, on the other hand, was equally adamant that the mother be lifted first. That way, he said, she would at least know she wasn't being hurt, and that maybe her baby wouldn't be either. Finally it remained for Ericsson himself to settle the matter. First he asked the helicopter pilot what was the heaviest male burro we have lifted so far. "One was close to six hundred fifty pounds," the pilot replied. Ericsson next asked the weight of the heaviest female burro he had carried. "About four hundred pounds," came the response. "Okay," Ericsson said, "how much does a baby weigh?" "I'd say a hundred fifty," said the pilot. "Hell," said Ericsson, "let's build two slings and lift them together."

Our Bambi-loving had, apparently, spread. In any case, it was, we were told, the first helicopter rescue in animal history when a mother and baby had been lifted together. As the summer had waned, and the canyon had cooled, our rescue had speeded up, and we had begun to pick up burros of all sizes, shapes, and colors. One of them, in fact, was white — the first of that color we had seen. He was also a young burro with very much a mind of his own. For me, he was the easiest of any to name. I called him Polar Burro.

Back at the ranch, or rather back at my apartment, there was a problem. It had all come about because of something I had noticed that spring when we had had our first bad thunderstorm. Polar Bear had been terribly frightened. He had had an equally bad time on the Fourth of July, when there were all sorts of fireworks going off in Central Park. These lit up my entire apartment and made so much noise that he was convinced it was, if not the Second Coming, at least the opening of a second front. But a thunderstorm was, to him, even worse. Long before it began, or even I, as an old salt of much rough-weather experience, could see any signs of a storm coming, I would know there was one brewing somewhere because Polar Bear would disappear. Then, when the storm actually did break, nothing I did could comfort him. I could take him as far from any window as possible, to the farthest reaches of the kitchen closet, I could shut the closet door to shut out as much of the audio and video special effects as possible, and even cup my hands around his little ears. But it was to no avail. At best he went totally rigid, and at worst berserk.

One of my friends, who had stayed with Polar Bear when Marian and I were in the Grand Canyon and who had experienced a thunderstorm with him, told me in no uncertain terms when I came back that I would have to do something about the situation. She suggested a cat psychologist.

Before I had had Polar Bear, I had never met a cat psychologist. I had met animal behaviorists, who gave your pet obedience training, or who got him or her over bad habits. But a psychologist who would refine the discipline just to cats — that was, for me, a new experience. I told my friend that if such a person existed and he thought he was going to put Polar Bear through analysis or something like that, he should have another thought coming. I could see Polar Bear analyzing him, but not the other way around.

But my friend, like the donkeys I had been working with in the canyon, would not take no for an answer. "In the first place," she said, "it isn't a he, it's a she. And in the second place, I have already told her about Polar Bear and thunderstorms, and she is ready and willing to handle it."

I was still reluctant. I told her that I was brought up in Boston and the Bostonians I knew didn't put a lot of stock in analysis and psychiatry and all that sort of thing. Frankly, I told her, we thought it was for other people rather than for us — perhaps, I added solemnly, to make other people more like us. My friend just looked at me. Nonetheless, I promised her that if she would give me one last chance to take care of the problem myself, then, if it didn't work, I would agree to seeing the psychologist.

As I had done so often before, I repaired to my growing cat library. In *Your Incredible Cat*, by Dr. David Greene, I came upon something hopeful. Perhaps I could cure Polar Bear of his fear of thunderstorms by ESP.

The first thing I had to do was, apparently, to find out if Polar Bear was right-pawed or left-pawed. "If your cat is left-pawed," Dr. Greene stated, "the chances are good that he possesses psychic ability." Dr. Greene didn't tell me how to do this, but with my usual inventiveness I decided to have a game of ball with Polar Bear and see if he swiped at it more with his right paw than with his left paw. I threw the ball ten times. There were six left-paw swipes and only four right-paw swipes. I was elated. There was no question but that we were on our way. Now the only job left was how to transmit my pro-thunderstorm message to his anti-thunderstorm mind. Dutifully I read on about how I was to transmit and he was to receive. I was apparently, according to Dr. Greene, to do this when he was sitting, not lying down:

> His front legs should be completely straight with his hindquarters placed firmly on the ground. In this position he is most likely to be reasonably relaxed but still sufficiently alert to pick up a telepathic message. He should be facing away from you, with his head turned between 90 and 120 degrees, making it impossible for him even to glimpse your expression or posture, both of which could provide clues which would interfere with the test.
>
> If the cat is looking in the wrong direction, shift your own position rather than attempting to move him, since this inevitably increases his alertness and research suggests that an aroused cat is far less receptive to ESP signals than a relaxed cat.

I did my best. It was awfully hard for me to get him facing away with his head turned between 90 and 120 degrees — I am really no mathematician — but the way I handled it was with the same inventiveness I had used on the left-pawed thing. I got him near the window where he could see pigeons. He was terrific, he never looked at me once.

The second step was, I realized, entirely up to me:

> Sit down, make yourself comfortable, unwind physically and clear your mind. Let your thoughts dwell on some pleasantly tranquil image, perhaps a quiet country scene or a soothing color. At first you may find it difficult to banish distracting ideas from your mind, but this will come with a little practice.
>
> Once you feel mentally and physically at ease, glance at your watch to obtain the starting time and then stare hard at your cat for exactly ten seconds. It is essential not to make any movement or sound at this stage to avoid attracting his attention by other than telepathic means.
>
> Focus your mind as intensely as possible on some shared and pleasurable experience, a friendly game or a session of affectionate petting, which you both enjoyed.

Actually what I focussed on was the opposite of a thunderstorm — a nice, sunny day on the balcony playing ball with him. But one day apparently wasn't enough:

> Over the next few days or weeks, repeat this test on a further nineteen occasions, varying the time of day at which it is carried out. This is important but investigations have found that ESP seems to be stronger in some people during the evening and more powerful in others first thing in the morning. These changes seem likely to be due to the body's natural, circadian rhythms and the biochemical changes which they bring about in the functioning of mind and body.

I was, frankly, not aware of my circadian rhythms, whatever they were, but I decided to cut down on that idea of nineteen more tests — just a couple more, I felt, would do the job fine.

In any case, at last I was ready to transmit him the message. I beamed it full blast. I told him he wasn't scared of thunderstorms anymore, was he?

I had to wait, of course, for my answer, for the next thunderstorm. Unfortunately, there didn't seem to be any thunderstorms for quite a while. When, finally, one did come, my answer was loud and clear. Not only was he not any better, he was, if anything, worse. I called my friend and told her about my ESP efforts and I reported the unfortunate results. I told her that Polar Bear no longer even waited for a thunderstorm in New York to disappear from sight. Now he would lowtail it for the kitchen closet if the weatherman said it was raining in Baltimore.

I was, I admitted, ready for the cat psychologist. "Good," she replied; "I'll make an appointment for her to come next Saturday morning." There was a pause. "And by the way, I don't want you to be put off by her. She's not very good with people, but she's marvelous with cats."

The woman, when she arrived, was large and formidable. She was also extremely businesslike. Advancing into the living room, she fixed me with a steely eye. "Where," she asked, "are we?" We're in the living room, I told her. "No, no," she said impatiently. "We. We. Where's the cat?" She was, obviously, one of those "we" women so likely to be found lurking by hospital beds in the wake of uncomfortable operations who delight in asking groggy patients if we would like our orange juice now.

Polar Bear had of course, immediately attendant upon

the woman's appearance, repaired to his post under the sofa. I told her he was right under her legs. "Aha," she said. "Well, I don't need us right now. The first thing I would like to do is talk to you, then I will talk to us, and then finally I will want to talk to you both together." She paused and looked down again. "With us out," she added.

I told her it sounded a lot like a divorce or something — that I didn't want to get a divorce from Polar Bear, all I wanted was for him to get over how he felt about thunderstorms.

"As you perhaps know," she said, "I am a structural psychologist. Are you familiar with the work of Dr. Watson?" I told her only through my acquaintanceship with Sherlock Holmes. She ignored this. "Well, it doesn't matter," she continued. "What he believed is that by introducing the verbal report method, he would be able to deal with such common mentalistic phenomena as thinking and feeling — which of course, up to him, had always been in the stronghold of our structural psychologists."

I nodded. "What I will be trying to do," she continued, "is to combine his discipline with my own discipline. And what we will basically have to do here is to decide between an adjustive adjustment and a non-adjustive adjustment, because what we basically have here is clearly a situation neurosis which is undoubtedly induced by a traumatic response which results from a personality disturbance in childhood — or rather, I should say, in kittenhood. I understand we were a stray, so you probably don't know much about our kittenhood, do you?"

I told her I didn't. "A character neurosis can," she went on, as if she were addressing a class of particularly backward students, "like a traumatic situation, induce a situation neurosis."

I started to bridle. I told her Polar Bear had a perfectly good character. "Aha," the woman said again. It was clear that "Aha," second only to "we," was her favorite expression. In any case, she suddenly reached into her handbag and brought out a cassette. "This is a thunderstorm," she said. "Do you have a player?" I told her I did. She handed it to me and then got down on her hands and knees. "I want to get our reaction to it," she said. "Do you have a flashlight?" I procured her one, and then before turning on her cassette, I had a clear sense of déjà vu. It was very reminiscent of that Christmas morning with Mrs. Wills peering under the sofa to see whether or not she was going to take Polar Bear away.

The cassette was audio only — like one of those sleep records people turn on to hear gentle ocean noises or soft music, only in this case it was the opposite. Almost at once the room was filled with a booming, roaring din, complete with claps of thunder and even loud crackles, apparently to simulate lightning. At the very first boom, before even the first crackle, Polar Bear bolted. He almost knocked the flashlight out of her hands, crack blocked one of her ankles and then headed full speed for the kitchen closet. "Oh dear," she said, rising quickly and watching him, "we don't like it, do we?" No, I said grimly, we don't. I tried to stop her but she went into the closet after him. She did not, however, catch him. No woman alive — and few male cornerbacks — could have. The next thing I saw was Polar Bear heading for the bedroom, with the woman in full pursuit.

Fortunately, in a moment or two, her thunderstorm was over and I did not have to wait long before she reappeared. "We went out the window," she said, "I saw where we went but I decided not to go down in there after us."

I told her she had made a wise decision — that Polar Bear had gone to his balcony, which he regarded as a sort of refuge, but that perhaps, after he had calmed down, that would be a good place for her to talk with him.

The woman agreed, after making me promise to stay where I was. In a very short time, however, she was back again. "Well," she said, sitting down, "we're not very much of a communicator, are we?"

Once more I bridled. What, I wanted to know, did she expect — Ronald Reagan? I told her Polar Bear was in his way, at least with me, a great little communicator. "Aha," she said. "And how, may I ask, do we communicate with you?" I noted an edge in her voice, but I was firm, nonetheless. We talk, I said.

"We talk?" she questioned. "You mean *you* talk." No, I said firmly again, both of us talk. I talk to him and he talks to me. "You mean, *we* talk to you?" she repeated. This time I detected an even sharper edge.

I told her we certainly did, particularly when I was talking to us about something I wanted us to do and we were talking to me about what we didn't want. To do, I added lamely.

"Mr. Amory," she said quietly, "cats don't talk."

I wanted to say that she had certainly come into the book at a hell of a time to give me that piece of news — but I refrained. Instead I asked her why, if that was true, had she gone out to the balcony to talk with Polar Bear?

"I talked," she said sternly, "we didn't. We don't talk. What we give me are verbal pictures — images, if you will."

Then it was, I said, sort of like television? She nodded. "I've been meaning to ask you," she said, "if we watch television?"

I shook my head and for the first time smiled at her. I said I thought television was maybe too prejudiced for him — that there were all kinds of dogs in programs, and they even had shows of their own, but never cats — that there weren't even cats in family shows. All cats ever got to do was to appear in commercials and sell cat food.

"Do we spend much time in front of the mirror," the woman asked, "looking at ourself?" I told her he did nothing of the sort — that he wasn't at all vain and anyway what he thought he saw in the mirror was another cat. And he didn't like that, because he wanted to be an only cat. The woman picked up on this right away. "You mean," she asked, "he won't tolerate any other cats?" Not very well, I admitted.

"Aha," she said. "And you live alone, I understand." I nodded. "I think," she said, "we're beginning to get to the bottom of this. You know the visual image I got from us out there was a very clear red."

Red? I inquired. I told her I thought all cats were colorblind. She shook her head. "No," she replied. "The latest data suggest that they're not. They see in several colors — and red denotes something very specific."

I wanted to say that if Polar Bear saw red, he was, in my opinion, angry. And why shouldn't he have been? After all, she had turned on a thunderstorm and then chased him out on the balcony, where he never went when there was a real thunderstorm, and then when he got there, he found there wasn't any thunderstorm at all, but she had just made one up.

As I was thinking this, I had missed some of what the woman had been saying, but I came in on the end of it. "The color red," she said, "is usually an indication that what's bothering us has to do with our owner. I want to ask you something. Are you afraid of thunderstorms?" I told her that of course I was not afraid of thunderstorms and that if she thought I had given a fear of thunderstorms to Polar Bear, she was barking up the wrong tree. "You may not have given it to us," she said quietly. "We may have gotten it in our kittenhood. But what you have done is to bring it out and reinforce it."

How had I done that? I wanted to know. "You probably don't realize it," she said, "but you do fear thunderstorms. You fear them if for no other reason than that you know they will make us afraid." I said nothing. The cat psychologist stood up. "Well," she said, "I think that's enough for our first appointment. I've definitely decided we are not going to make an adjustive adjustment. We are going to make a non-adjustive adjustment. The next time there's a thunderstorm, I don't want you to pay any attention to it and above all I don't want you to pay any attention to our reaction to it."

My friend had supplied me with a psychological dictionary and, after the woman had gone, I looked up adjustive and non-adjustive adjustments. I did not understand them but shortly after them I came upon the definition of the "Aha" or "Ah-ha" experience. It was, the dictionary said, "The reaction accompanying the moment of insight in problem solving situations."

It was my turn to say Aha. And my problem-solving with Polar Bear involved one last compromise with him. If he would promise to try to be a little better during thunderstorms, I would promise never to have the cat psychologist back again.

I kept my promise, too. I did not, however, agree to cease and desist from another activity over which Polar Bear and I had constantly warred. This was the simple question of my, upon occasion, throwing a party. Parties were Polar Bear's particular bêtes noires. He could sense a party coming long before the arrival of the nice young couple who would usually be catering it. I have never understood how he did this — whether it was a sudden increase in phone calls, whether it was Marian rearranging furniture and bringing in flowers, or whether it was an extra-long war with Rosa and the vacuum cleaner. Whatever it was, by the morning of the party itself, and the coming of the caterers, Polar Bear was ready to go into his act.

I, of course, was well aware of exactly what was going on in his little hermit's mind, but whether I was or not, it made no difference. He wanted to show me that he was already a nervous wreck, and he also wanted me to know that he held me personally responsible for his condition. In any case, the first thing he did was to let the caterers know he also knew precisely what they were up to, and that it was something up with which he had not the slightest intention of putting. This already irritated me because the caterers were very fond of him and in fact did everything they could to win him over. But he would have none of it — indeed he gave them the strongest insult possible, which was to ignore their blandishments to entice him into the kitchen for an hors d'oeuvre.

Next it was my turn. As the caterers busied themselves in the kitchen, and I sat in the living room giving them helpful advice, he would walk back and forth in front of me, pausing only long enough on each turn to give me a look of withering disgust. "You know perfectly well," he would say, to begin our colloquy, "what happened to me the last time you gave a party."

Having heard the same speech several times before, I would be in no mood to hear it again, and would interrupt what I knew he was going to say next. I did indeed know what had happened to him, I would inform him. He had gone under the bed the moment the first guest had arrived and had not reappeared until the last guest had gone.

It was his turn to interrupt. "I am not talking about where I was fortunate enough to find refuge," he would say. "I am talking about what happened afterwards. You have probably forgotten, but I was at death's door for at least three days."

I told him that he was talking arrant nonsense. He had been in perfectly good health, he had just pretended to be sick because, in his warped little mind, he believed that I had purposely given the party to make him sick.

"And which, whether you know it or not," he would interrupt again — and this time in such a way as to point out that he had not heard a word of my previous statement — "was probably responsible for shortening my short little life."

Whenever he referred to that, I really felt that he was hitting below the belt. I told him that we were not discussing the shortness of anybody's life. What we were discussing, or at least should have been discussing, was that occasionally I gave a party because I happened to wish to pay back the people who had been kind enough to invite me to their parties.

Of course he made no effort whatsoever to understand that. As far as he was concerned, there was no need for me either to be having parties to thank people who had invited me to their parties, or, for that matter, for going to their parties in the first place. Instead, I should have at least the outward courtesy, if I was incapable of any inward understanding, to spend what were probably the last few evenings he had left on this earth in my home, alone, with him.

I would then tell him that I would simply not countenance any more of that self-pitying drivel. I would also add that he was, at most, two years old and should live perhaps ten times that long unless, by his total intransigence, he was determined to induce a wide variety of nervous disorders which could indeed bring him to an untimely end. But, I would warn him, if this did occur, he would be the one responsible, not me.

Finally I told him that for this particular party, I had at the very least assumed that he would take, if not a completely different attitude, at least not such a ridiculous one as he had about my previous parties. It was, after all, the first anniversary of the night on which I had rescued him, and I did feel that on this of all nights I had a right to look forward to something more than one of his infuriating disappearance acts. I admitted freely that there would be some people at the party who might be new to him, but there would be many with whom he was already acquainted — people such as Sergeant Dwork, my brother and his wife, and even Mrs. Wills, who had, in a sense, rescued him in reverse. Besides these, there would be people he knew much better because they had actually stayed with him at the apartment — my daughter, Gaea, my granddaughter, Zoe, Jeanne Adlon, and Caroline Thompson, the catnip provider. There would be even be a couple of his old friends from California, like Paula Deats, who would be coming all the way to New York to celebrate Christmas because they didn't have it out there.

I mapped it all out for him very carefully, and as the first guest arrived, I still had hopes. But by the time the second couple rang the doorbell, these hopes were dashed. Polar Bear had disappeared.

Marian and I devised a system whereby we kept an eye on the door as people arrived and departed to insure that he did not do likewise. And on occasion, and as inconspicuously as we could manage, we surreptitiously peered under the bed, to make sure that he was still there. Unfortunately, my checking was not surreptitious enough to escape the sharp eye of that redoubtable newsman Walter Cronkite. He had come upon me while I was assuming the couchant position by the side of the bed and, with an unerring nose for news, demanded to know what I was doing.

Turning and looking upward, I confessed that I was checking on my cat. Walter loves cats, and at that time had a cat of his own named Dancer — one who had been left with him on a temporary basis by his daughter but to whom he had grown so attached that he had permanently purloined it. "Cat?" he now queried. "You have a cat? What's his name?" And assuming the couchant position beside me, he also peered under the bed. "Hi, Polar Bear," he said coaxingly. "Come here, Polar Bear."

I would like to be able to say that Polar Bear rose to the occasion, but the sad fact is rise he did not. Walter Cronkite might, that very year, have been voted the Most Trusted Man in America by a large majority of the television viewing audience, but to Polar Bear such a distinction signified nothing. He was simply a new person, and Polar Bear backed, if possible, even farther into the farthest wall.

As Walter and I, defeated, rose to our feet, however, we managed to bump into the chessboard, which I had set up in the bedroom and at which Mr. George C. Scott was deeply engrossed in a titanic struggle with an opponent I had especially chosen for him — a young woman who was highly ranked as a tournament player. George, who had met Polar Bear, was suddenly interested and demanded to know where he was. I gestured futilely under the bed. "What the hell do you mean he's under the bed?" George said. "He can't spend the entire party cooped up under there!" And without further ceremony, and in the same famous rasp with which he had roused the Third Army in *Patton*, he gave Polar Bear his marching orders. "Polar Bear," he growled, "come here."

I smiled at George pityingly. Cats, I informed him, don't do that. Dogs do that. George's own dog, the mastiff Max, probably did that. But cats never do it, and certainly not Polar Bear. He simply wouldn't . . .

"He wouldn't what?" George inquired blandly. Because at that very moment, and looking nonchalant in the extreme, Polar Bear had materialized from under the bed. He walked unconcernedly over to George, stretched, and then in front of everyone all but saluted.

It was just one more illustration, if one were needed, that his domestic policy, like his foreign, had its exceptions.

When I awoke the following morning, Polar Bear was standing on the rug beside my bed, regarding me intently. I saw at once that he was not giving me his usual after-party, death's door act. Either he had forgotten to do it or he was, miracle of miracles, actually getting used to an occasional party.

He was, in fact, I thought, standing in almost exactly the same position as he had stood on that Christmas morning one year ago, and he was looking at me in almost exactly the same way. But he was now a very different cat. Instead of the thin and injured and frightened stray who had decided to try his luck with me, there stood a cat who was breathtakingly beautiful, glossy, and fat — well, I amended, possibly portly — and whose soft green eyes gazed into mine contentedly. If my ears did not deceive me, he was purring.

I lay and looked at him for a long moment — and thought of the incredible difference he had made in my life. But then, as I continued to look, his purring stopped. His eyes slowly narrowed and his tail began to twitch. Sentiment was all very well, he was clearly saying, but adult individuals did not wallow in it. Life goes on, parties or no parties, holidays or no holidays, and was I or was I not going to get out of bed and fix him his breakfast? In case I did not grasp his meaning fully, he spoke.

"AEIOU!" he said.

"Aeiou yourself," I replied, as I scooped him up on the way to the kitchen. "Merry Christmas."

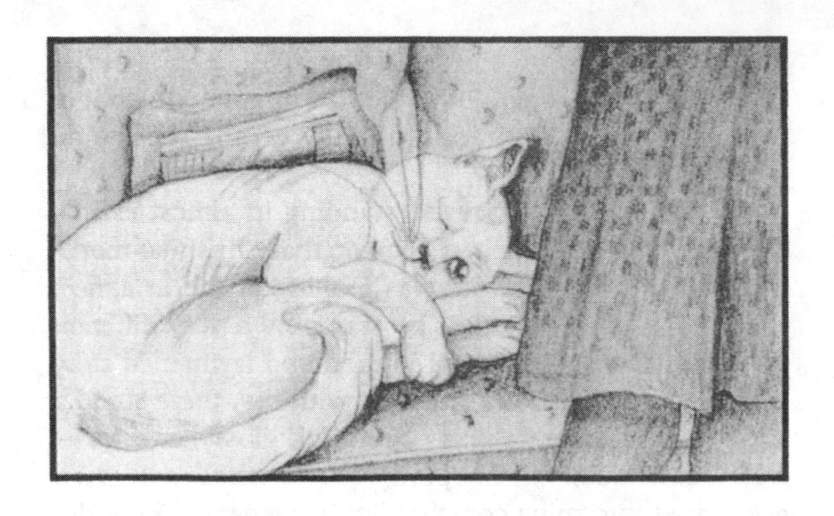

◦ L'Envoi

The events in this book all took place, as I have indicated, during Polar Bear's first year with me. That was, as I write these lines, almost a decade ago.

I am well aware that in most books about individual animals, the animal dies in the end. I have never liked this — indeed that was one of the reasons why, even as a child, *Black Beauty* appealed to me so much. It is true there was misery and suffering in the book. But, in the end, Black Beauty has not died.

Neither, I am happy to say, has Polar Bear. He is very much alive, thank you. In fact neither he nor I even consider him an old cat. When some young whippersnapper comes along, and it is necessary to establish precedence, we may use the word *mature* — but never *old.*

What Polar Bear is today is a senior citicat — with all the attendant rights and privileges that this title implies.

He does not travel on buses for less or see movies at a lower price, but that is only because he does not like to travel at all, and he would not be fond of most modern movies.

In some ways he has become, through the years, as indeed perhaps his biographer has as well, steadily more curmudgeonly. He is very aware, for example, that many changes have occurred in our lives and that not all of them have been for the better. He has seen too many examples of inferior service, unnecessary regimentation, lack of respect for elders, and, in commercials, the everlasting use of kitten and young cat actors who have not learned their craft. But in some of the areas discussed in this book he has, at the same time, become less critical.

One of these is the matter of transient strays. I do not say that he welcomes them wholeheartedly, but at least he has a more philosophical attitude toward them than he had in that first year. Only the other day, for instance, he almost wagged his tail at a dog who was passing the night. It is true that I started the wag, but still he made an effort to complete it.

I have also noted some — repeat some — improvements in his behavior toward new people. If he is particularly comfortable on the sofa, for another instance, and a new person appears, he will very often these days not even bother to bolt down and hide underneath it. I would like to add that I have seen similar improvements in his attitude toward travel, toward diets, toward fitness programs, toward large and noisy parties, toward thunderstorms, and even toward the vacuum cleaner. Unfortunately, that would be paltering with the truth. About all of the above he remains firmly unconvinced.

It might be said that I have made a lot of fun of him

in this book — but then, so has he of me. The fact remains that, in making fun of each other, we have had so much fun together that I hope those of you who have undoubtedly had similar experiences with your own animals will share in it with us.

But I hope even more that those of you who have never had an animal will hie yourselves to the nearest shelter, and adopt one. If you do, you will surely find that that animal will give you, every day of his or her life, not only joy and companionship but also that very special kind of love which can be understood, as I said at the beginning, only by those fortunate enough ever to have been owned by one.

The CAT *and the* CURMUDGEON

ILLUSTRATED *by* LISA ADAMS

This book is dedicated,
with as much affection as a curmudgeon can muster,
to everyone everywhere who has ever been owned by any animal.
And particularly to those who came to be so owned by rescue —
either in the woods, in the fields, on the streets,
from a public pound or a private shelter.

ACKNOWLEDGMENTS

The author wishes to thank first of all Marian Probst, his longtime assistant, under whose incredible memory for irritating facts he has, with the patience of Job, long suffered. He also wishes to thank Sean O'Gara, whose love of computers and other modern nonsense was not only baffling to the author but also annoying to Polar Bear. Then too he wishes to express his appreciation to Lisa Adams, his illustrious illustrator, who proceeded at tortoise pace to produce the cover and drawings, meanwhile studiously ignoring every one of his masterly suggestions. Finally, he wishes to acknowledge the all too pointed criticism of two particular writing friends — Cynthia Branigan, who early understood that the best way to handle curmudgeons is at a distance, and Paula Deats, who pinpointed the distance at 3,000 miles.

Besides these, the author wishes to acknowledge the professional and personal encouragement of four colleagues at Little, Brown and Time Warner — Fredrica Friedman, his editor, whose belief in this book from the beginning was, even to Polar Bear, catalystic; Kelso Sutton, whose support was, at crucial times, critical; Jennifer Kittredge, whose charm was such that it overcame even her constant mention of other authors; and finally Glea Humez, copyeditor extraordinaire.

Finally, the author is grateful for permission to quote from the letters excerpted in the second chapter, as well as from the following works:

Kinship With All Life by J. Allen Boone. Copyright 1954 by Harper & Row, Publishers, Inc. Reprinted by permission of the publisher.

Cat Astrology by Mary Daniels. By permission of the author.

Catsigns by William Fairchild. Copyright © 1989 by William Fairchild Publications, Ltd. Reprinted by permission of Clarkson N. Potter Inc.

How to Learn Astrology by Marc Edmund Jones. By permission of the Marc Edmund Jones Estate, P.O. Box 7, Stanwood, WA 98292.

Linda Goodman's Sun Signs by Linda Goodman. By permission of Taplinger Publishing Co., Inc.

Your Incredible Cat by David Greene. By permission of Bantam, Doubleday, Dell Publishing Group, Inc., and Joan Daves.

"The Story of Webster" from *Mulliner Nights* by P. G. Wodehouse. Copyright 1930, 1931, 1932, 1933 by P. G. Wodehouse, © renewed 1958, 1959, 1960, 1961. By permission of the Estate of P. G. Wodehouse and Scott Meredith Literary Agency Inc.

Contents

I ·	*There Goes What's-His-Name*	251
II ·	*Cat Power*	282
III ·	*First Dog*	311
IV ·	*On the Cusp*	353
V ·	*You Ought to Be in Pictures*	389
VI ·	*Meanwhile, Back at the Ranch, I Read Him His Rights*	432
VII ·	*Romance à la Cat Blanche*	483
	L'Envoi	533

The Cat
and the
Curmudgeon

I ◦ *There Goes What's-His-Name*

"Some cats," Shakespeare said, "are born great, some achieve greatness, and some have greatness thrust upon 'em."

Actually, Shakespeare didn't say that about cats, he said it about people. And I suppose there will be some purists out there who will take me up on it. Technically they would have a point, but, frankly, it has always seemed to me that Shakespeare was overly concerned with people. His references to cats are really very poor. I believe if he had been more knowledgeable about them and had worked a little harder on his line, he might indeed have included them.

Note, though, that I use the world "them," not Shakespeare's " 'em." Cats are not notably fond of being referred to as "them," and they could hardly be expected to take kindly to " 'em." Ever ready as they are to pounce on even an unintended slur, they would consider the use of the shortened colloquialism on the part of a stranger — which to them Shakespeare certainly was — at the very least, unwarranted familiarity and, at worst, an affront to their dignity.

In any case I did not know whether or not Polar Bear was great when he was born. He was already a full-grown cat by the time I rescued him in a New York alley on a snowy Christmas Eve twelve years ago. But since the very first time I saw him and saw how, hungry and cold and wounded as he was, he had still not given up, that at least to me proved he had already achieved greatness, and he hardly needed any more of it thrust upon him.

He did not really get it, either. Because, however, of having had a book written about him and making the cover of *Parade* magazine and having hundreds of fan letters, what he did have thrust upon him, willy-nilly, was not further greatness but something which so often in our modern world passes for greatness. I refer, of course, to celebrity.

Once upon a time, before you were born, the world was very cold and dark. Just the same there were all sorts of creatures roaming the earth and in the ocean. There were, for example, dinosaurs. But one thing there was not, and that was celebrities. There wasn't so much as a one of them roaming around anywhere.

The word, you see, hadn't been invented yet. You could in those days say about one of the dinosaurs who was better known than the others that he or she had fame, or had celebrity, but if you said that he or she *was* a celebrity, that would have been just as odd as if you'd said he or she was a fame.

In the old days, too, people made a great distinction

between fame and what was then called notoriety. Fame was generally a good thing, but notoriety wasn't — in fact the word "notorious" was almost always very bad. A notorious dinosaur, for instance, may well have been a well-known dinosaur, but he or she would have still been a very bad dinosaur.

When the word "celebrity" as we know it today, however, came along, and you could both *have* celebrity and also *be* a celebrity, it seemed people just stopped making the old distinction between fame and notoriety, and from that time on it seemed a celebrity was a terrific thing to be. Just about everyone you could name wanted to be a celebrity. Gangsters wanted to be celebrities, and bank robbers, and stock manipulators, and real estate people, and even New York Yankee principal owners. Fathers and mothers wanted their children, if they couldn't grow up to be President, at least to grow up to be the very next best thing — a celebrity.

There was, though, one remarkable exception to this rule. His name, as you have probably already guessed, was Polar Bear. Polar Bear did not like anything about being a celebrity. For one thing, celebrities have to meet a great many new people, and Polar Bear did not like new people and he particularly did not like having to meet them. He had already met everyone he wanted to meet, and in fact he would have dearly liked to subtract some of these. For another thing, being a celebrity would mean a change in his life, and Polar Bear did not like change. He was, when you came right down to it, a very Republican cat — he did not like anything to happen which had not happened before. For still a third thing, Polar Bear would not, I knew, make the slightest distinction between genuinely famous celebrities and bad, notorious celebrities. To him any celebrity, good or bad, was a publicity hound — in all the bad senses of both words — and I knew if I argued with him about it, it wouldn't do any good. He would surely just have come back at me with the question of who ever heard of a publicity cat.

I could of course have come back at him and could indeed have given him a whole celebrity roster of Felixes and Garfields, Sylvesters and Morrises. But I did not do so because I knew what he would say to that. He always has answers for my answers. He would say that they were not real cats, and even if Morris was once real, the current Morris wasn't, and he would even probably add that he knew for a fact that the real Morris had died in 1978 — in his opinion undoubtedly from an overdose of publicity.

From the beginning I realized it was not going to be easy to open his closed little mind even to the idea of being a celebrity. But the way I went about it was, if I do say so myself, masterful. I did not start with the more difficult areas of celebrityhood. Instead I started with one relatively easy area — the recognition factor. I began with flattery. I couldn't very well start with professional flattery, but I knew cats liked personal flattery almost as well as celebrities liked both professional and personal flattery.

What I did, in a word, was point out how handsome he was — with his snowy white body (which it was after I'd gotten him all cleaned up after the rescue), his Winston Churchill–like lion head, his big expressive green eyes, and, at one end, his long, beautifully groomed whiskers and, at the other, his large lashable tail. I told him that just as he had some doubts about being a celebrity he should remember that many celebrities, too — and ones not half as handsome as he was — often harbored doubts.

In particular, I pointed out, they suffered from ambivalence in regard to the recognition factor.

On the one hand, I also pointed out, they liked to be publicly recognized and even enjoyed on such occasions the exchange of a few words and perhaps the granting of a reasonable number of autographs. On the other hand, there were also times when they did not like to be recognized, as, for example, when they were busy or going somewhere in a hurry or, for another example, when, though betrothed, they were eating in a restaurant with someone of the opposite gender to whom they were not. That is why, I told him, celebrities wore dark glasses. Then they could always be sure of some recognition as somebody or other but not necessarily recognition as somebody specific. Dark glasses also seemed to make it a little more difficult for people to approach them, in particular at those inopportune times when they did not wish to be approached.

I could sense that Polar Bear did not take to the idea of dark glasses at all — even when, although he knew we were just playing, I pretended to put a pair of mine on him. And so, to relieve his mind, I told him that, celebrity or no celebrity, I did not see any reason for his wearing dark glasses. In the first place, I said to him, they would probably not fit very well and he'd wear them all askew. And in the second place, I pointed out, frankly, he wasn't *that* famous. To make him feel better about this I told him that although I was the one who, after all, had made him famous, neither was I, and that the reason I didn't wear dark glasses was because I soon discovered that I was very rarely recognized and when I was it was too often a disappointment.

I gave him the example that, after two appearances on the Morton Downey Jr. Show, then at the height of its popularity, I had been recognized the next morning on the New York street by no less than four strangers in a row. All in all, by the time I met the fifth I was firmly considering running for President. With this person, however, after I was already halfway through my by then thoroughly practiced deprecatory wave, I suddenly realized that there was no necessity for it. Indeed, the man had nothing to say about my performance at all. Instead he made only a brief statement. "Your hair," he said, "looked fine." It was only then I at last realized who he was. He was my barber — a man who through the years had, as he often complains to me, apparently taken a good deal of criticism about my unwillingness to pay his growing rate for what he calls "hair styling." I really think if I let him have his way I would end up with my hair tied in a bow, and although I am a very secure person I am not secure enough for that, thank you very much.

In any case, after meeting my barber I decided not to run for President after all. But after telling Polar Bear that story I reminded him that, concerning this recognition matter, compared to any celebrity he would care to name he would undoubtedly be subject to meeting the least number of strangers. After all, I explained to him, he would never meet anyone on the street for the simple reason that he did not go on the street — except when he was being carried in a carrier or when he was on a leash on his way to the Park and even then, when we would cross the street, I would carry him in my arms and could take care myself of any necessary meeting or greeting people. As for the idea of his having to meet people on, say a trip, this was almost nonexistent. Basically, Polar Bear's idea of travel was strictly limited to my apartment — the kitchen on the south, the living room on the west, the bedroom on the north, and his balcony on the east — and these only when there was nobody else at any of these locations. When there was, he preferred being under the very middle of the bed, in the bedroom. And there he met no one but an occasional bug.

This balcony was, however, when you came right down to it, one place where he would have to learn to handle the celebrity recognition problem because he was, from it, highly visible to people on the sidewalk. Readers with good memories of my first book about Polar Bear will recall that the whole idea of this balcony was mine and mine alone. What I had done was to give up close to half of my balcony to him. I reached mine from a door, but his was reached only by bedroom window — and his half was securely chicken-wired in. The idea of this was so that he could pursue his lifelong interest in ornithology, but at the same time, while pursuing it — unfortunately, in all senses of the word — he would at least not fall off the balcony and plunge to the street.

Over and over I had told him that the whole thing was, if I did say so, superbly designed and entirely for his own protection. But he has, of course, adamantly refused even to try to see it from that point of view. In his blind little way he saw the balcony only as a prison — one which was not only no protection for him but also seemed to him solely for the protection of the pigeons — and furthermore he saw it as something which was manifestly unfair since it gave them total advantage over him. They could flutter around above him to their hearts' content and even let fly down on him their short-range missiles. Meanwhile he, of course, was utterly powerless to fight back — all because of something which in his opinion I had, in a moment of dangerously unwise strategical thinking, concocted — a unilateral nuclear freeze.

I realized that it was essential in my handling of his celebrity recognition problem that I overcome his prejudice about both his balcony and the pigeons and make him realize that, when it came to being a celebrity on this balcony, he would have to be on if not his best — I hesitated to say "party" behavior, because he was very bad at parties — then at least his best average behavior. He would have, in a word, to show the flag. The very least I expected, I told him, was that on the occasion when a stranger called from the sidewalk up to him he would give some kind of acknowledgment. A quick nod of the head or the wave of a paw, as long as it was done in deprecatory fashion, would do nicely.

I did not, of course, get what I wanted. If someone called his name he would either glare down at them — the very worst kind of celebrity recognition behavior — or, the next worst, he would totally ignore them. The problem was that he simply didn't have a single charming deprecatory bone in his body. It was just glare or ignore — that was his whole repertory. And on top of it, he would never even do me the courtesy of ceasing and desisting from his everlasting warfare with the pigeons. In vain I would reason with him that, no matter how he felt about its being his balcony and their being the aggressors, he could at least recognize the fact that a lot of people, myself included, not only liked our feathered friends but also found extremely distasteful his continuing to regard them as unplucked meals. There was, to being a celebrity, whether he liked it or not, a certain element of *noblesse oblige*.

That was a bad expression to use. It was hard enough to reason with Polar Bear in plain English. In a foreign language I might as well forget it. All in all I had to admit that, at the very simplest of all the jobs of being a celebrity, he had failed miserably.

Your average member of the cat-owned fraternity might have quit right there. But I am not, as any of you who know me know, your average member of any fraternity. It is just not in me to say "uncle" after one setback. All right, I said to myself, I had not yet won Polar Bear over on the celebrity recognition front. But I had really fought, when you came right down to it, only one battle, and I had lost it through no fault of mine. I had lost it through the pigeons, by having to fight on two fronts at once — something which has through the years tested the mettle of many another great commander. All in all, the way I assessed the situation — with, of course, my usual objectivity — was that I had lost one battle. I had not yet lost the war.

I had, it is true, lost many a skirmish with him — but these really had nothing to do with his celebrity. Once, I remember, when he wanted to go out on his balcony and he was, as usual, hollering "aeiou" at me — he has always been terrific at vowels but terrible at consonants — I decided that since it was snowing, and there was snow all over his balcony, I should put a sweater on him and fix little makeshift snowshoes. I did so. In fact I made the latter out of my own socks. Then he went out and was out there all of a minute, because, when I went back to his window to see how he was getting along he saw me and flew back in with his sweater and boots still out there. And, to top it off, he had the nerve to "aeiou" again over and over at me, clearly holding me responsible for the snow — which, for some reason, he obviously felt gave the pigeons one more advantage over him.

In any case, I started the next phase of my attack by freely admitting that I could see from his point of view that there was a down side to being a celebrity. I told him that I would be guilty of parting with something less than the unvarnished truth if I did not admit that from time to time he would have unwelcome intrusions from photographers trying to take his picture — I told him they were called *"paparazzi"* — and that there even might be gossip columnists prying into his private life. But, while admitting all that, at the same time I emphasized that there were many up sides to being a celebrity. Furthermore, I knew him well enough to know that many of these would surely appeal to him.

Patience, for example, never his long suit, would, I reasoned with him, now no longer be a problem. He would not have to sit and wait so much, not even in the place of all places he least liked to sit and wait — at the vet's. He would, on the other hand, shortly after arrival, be almost majestically summoned to the inner sanctum, and hence would not have to endure, in the outer waiting room, the disagreeable contemplation of other cats or, worse still, dogs. And there were many other up sides I mentioned. He could now get away with his seemingly everlasting bad habit of not recognizing people he ought to have known, because now people would excuse him on the grounds he must meet so many people he could hardly be expected to remember everyone. Also, he could with impunity now leave whenever he wanted to from any group anytime and from any place. He could pay no attention to people even when they were obviously talking to him. He could have, in other words, the same "celebrity fade" I had observed so often in the eyes of the many celebrities about whom I had so often written. Even, if he could believe it, when *I* was talking to them — and starting one of my best stories, too.

As if all this were not enough, I went on to point out that, as for strangers coming up to him and bothering him and using an inordinate amount of his time when he was busy looking out the window or washing or taking one of his morning, afternoon, or evening naps — well, this would no longer be the case. Such strangers would have to make an appointment in advance and I would handle all that. I would take care also of seeing that he had an unlisted telephone — even a cellular phone with an answering machine and speed dialing, if he so wished. But there was no need for him even to think of taking calls or making them. I would see to it that as far as any call was concerned, he was in a meeting. As for people who wanted to see him in person, I would make it my business to screen them thoroughly — particularly those who wanted to talk to him just to say they had. And, when it came to sending out his photograph, I would not only do it myself but I would also pay for the extra pictures and the postage as well. I even had an autoprint made for him and I did the stamping for him. He would never, literally, have to raise a paw.

Finally, although he was very bad at comparison, I endeavored to show him that, again, compared to any celebrity he would care to name, he would never have to give so much as a moment's worry to all the sordid financial affairs which so often beset such celebrities — the taxes, the agents, the endorsements, the requests for appearances, and so forth. I tried to show him how lucky he was to have someone like myself, for not even a measly ten percent, but for free, undertake all this for him. There was not even any necessity for him to lose any of his napping time for having to consider the ever-difficult celebrity decisions as, for example, what kind of new car to buy or whether to have a summer house in the country or on the shore, or even what to wear. After all, when it came to cars, he detested car travel, and when it came to homes, he did not like being anywhere except where he was. As for what to wear, he didn't have to give it a thought — he was always tastefully attired and could go anywhere just as he was.

Honestly, looking back, I really could not understand why he had not been able to see the whole celebrity problem in a more reasonable light — a problem which, for him, would be really no problem at all. I had done my very best, in my reasonable, optimistic way, to make him see the glass as half-full. But he, or course, in his irrational, pessimistic way, invariably saw it as half-empty. And, on top of it all, he obviously blamed me, of all people, for spilling the damned glass in the first place.

It was really, when you came right down to it, so unfair of him and showed so little gratitude. After all, all the time he was sitting around eating and washing and sleeping and enjoying himself, where was I? I told him just where I was — I was chained to a desk doing all the hard work in the trenches which had made his life of ease possible. I did not expect thanks, but I did expect an occasional paw on the back — and even, just once in a while, some slight recognition that he was at least trying to entertain the basic idea of being a celebrity. If I did not get this, frankly, I told him, I would have to take a different tack. I had played good cop long enough — I could also, I said, start playing bad cop, and if I did not get any recognition I would have no other option.

I did not get it, of course, and so, gently at first but with increasing firmness, I started to acquaint him with the possible consequences down the dangerous path he was taking. I said that, even if he could not warm up to all the aspects of being a celebrity, he could at least pretend to enjoy some of them. The public, I warned him, would not take kindly to his attitude. The public was by no means inclined to reclusive celebrities. There were exceptions, of course — a Garbo here, a Howard Hughes there, even a J. D. Salinger wherever — but, generally speaking, the public expected celebrities to be — well, celebrities. The public was also very fickle, I reminded him. The public knew it made celebrities, but the public also knew it could break celebrities. The public knew too that if it didn't get its way, all it would have to do would be to turn to some lesser celebrity and he would be consigned to oblivion. I even brought up the question of the "Where Are They Now?" columns. How would he like to be in one of those? I also mentioned the archetypical story of the five stages of Hollywood celebritydom:

(1) Who is Hugh O'Brian?
(2) Get me Hugh O'Brian,
(3) Get me a Hugh O'Brian type,
(4) Get me a young Hugh O'Brian,
(5) Who is Hugh O'Brian?

Polar Bear wanted to know who Hugh O'Brian was. I told him, sternly, never mind who Hugh O'Brian was, that wasn't the point. The point was, how would he like that story not to be told anymore about Hugh O'Brian but about Polar Bear? I said for him to make no mistake about it, he was dancing on a very thin edge.

Even that, I warned him, lowering my voice, wouldn't by any means be the end of the road. Sooner or later he would die. And that, I said flatly, would be no picnic either. Dying nowadays, for an uncooperative celebrity, wasn't, I told him, what it was in the old days. It was a whole new ball game out there. Once people knew he was where he couldn't sue anymore, the floodgates would open. He would be fair game and it would be open season on him. I would be willing, I said, to bet my bottom dollar there would be a whole raft of terrible books about him. The writers of these books might not be able to make him out something currently fashionable, like a Nazi spy — he wasn't born in time for that — or even for being a rotten parent — he hadn't, at least to my knowledge, ever had any kittens. But that didn't mean he was out of the woods. He had, after all, been neutered, and what those writers would do to that just didn't bear thinking about. They would really go to town. To begin with, they would want to know why he'd been neutered and, after that, forget it. The cat would be out of the bag, whether he liked the expression or not. And he shouldn't think they would stop with what he'd done before, either — they wouldn't. They would pry into both his before and after, and, in the end, his whole sex life would be an open book — and at that he would be lucky if it was just one book.

Finally, I told him slowly and sadly, the whole thing would, also in the end, reflect on me. I would be the one held responsible for not steering him on the right celebrity path to begin with, and, afterward, for not keeping him on the straight and narrow. Even if he didn't give a wash of his paw himself how he went down in history he could at least consider that what he was doing was dragging someone else down with him — someone who, surely, deserved better.

I hadn't painted a pretty picture, but then I hadn't meant to do so. All I had done was to give him the plain facts of celebrity life today. In the end it was up to him. He could take it or leave it.

And, if you can believe it, he chose to leave it. All my logic, after a lifetime of studying and writing about the celebrity field, fell on deaf ears — indeed, he never even raised an ear. Really, I had to admit, stubbornness was his middle name, and once he had made up his mind about something — something which, incidentally, took him at the most a few seconds — that was it. Emerson said, "A foolish consistency is the hobgoblin of little minds," and while my dictionary defines hobgoblin as "a goblin represented as being mischievous, or ugly or evil," it also gives, as a secondary definition, "a bugbear." And make no mistake, Polar Bear, when it came to changing his mind, was both bearcat and bugbear. To him, celebrity in any way, shape, form, or manner was strictly for the birds. And when Polar Bear feels something is for the birds, he knows, as we have seen, whereof he speaks.

In fairness I should say that he did have the graciousness to grant the grand total of one television interview. This occurred on Entertainment Tonight, on the Christmas Eve following the publication of my book. And it took place, of course, in the apartment — Polar Bear would not have considered it anywhere else. From the beginning, however, I was apprehensive. I knew the whole thing would be touch and go — and indeed that is literally what it turned out to be.

The moment the crew entered the door was, of course, the exact moment Polar Bear disappeared. I eventually located him in the very middle of under the bed and finally hauled him out. But there is something about being in front of TV cameras which is Polar Bear's least favorite part of being a celebrity. I believe it is the rat-a-tat sound they make. In any case, to get him to even look as if he is looking at the camera I have to hold him in an ironclad grip with two hands on both sides of his jaw. And during this, no matter how hard I try to smile and make light of the whole thing, I promise you he looks as if he doesn't know what a television smile is. His expression is that of someone in front of a firing squad. As for the little "clucks" and "nice kitty-kitty's" from the cameraman, these not only did not make things better but made him look as if he had already been executed.

In any case, somehow we managed to get through — me holding Polar Bear in my viselike grip, trying hard to smile, chattering away about what a fun cat he was, meanwhile all the time trying not to turn whiter and whiter from the fact that his front claws were digging deeper and deeper into my knees and his back claws, which were even worse, were earnestly proceeding into areas where no claws should ever be. At first the producer did his level best to pretend it was all going well, but finally, by this time obviously concerned for the fate of his show, he signaled that the interview was over. He then quietly suggested that they should really have one other shot in which there would be more action. I explained that if there was to be much more action, it would be very doubtful if I should ever have children. But he ignored this. He was already looking for his other locations.

The next I saw of him he was out on the balcony. And not on my part of the balcony either, but Polar Bear's. He came in with a look of triumph. "I've got it," he said. With that, he explained that, for a final shot, Polar Bear should leap from the bedroom window. A cameraman would be waiting for him inside the balcony, and it would be just what the show needed for a close.

As a plan on paper it looked fine. In operation, however, I knew it would be very different. I pointed out that Polar Bear would see the cameraman and not only would he not go out, he would go as rapidly as possible in the opposite direction. And, although I did not know how he felt about sacrificing cameramen in the line of duty, the chances of his having, in this instance, to — well, scratch one — were, in my opinion, excellent.

The producer, however, would not hear of such negativism. He suggested I simply put Polar Bear out by reaching from the side of the window so that he didn't see the camera until he was already in full leap. It was just what the show needed, the producer pointed out again, and he was sure it would be a terrific shot.

And terrific, all right, it was. At first everyone seemed to have the whole thing in hand. The rest of the crew, at the producer's direction, made much noise — for Polar Bear's benefit — while they went out the door as if they were leaving for good. Meanwhile, just one cameraman, with his camera, sneaked into the bedroom and went out the window into Polar Bear's own balcony, where, crouching down, he silently took his post. Then it was up to me. Still grasping Polar Bear firmly in both hands, I took him into the bedroom and up to the side of the window. Here I awaited my crucial cue. When I received it I reached out toward the window and, with a firm fast movement, hung a sharp right with both hands. I had made myself as invisible as possible and yet I had given Polar Bear a launch which would have done credit to Cape Canaveral.

Touch and go I had said it would be, and touch and go it was. When Polar Bear saw that his sanctuary had been invaded and he was literally leaping into the very jaws of the enemy, he somehow managed, in midleap, an extraordinary variety of different moves in succession — all done so quickly they seemed in one motion. First there was the whirl of his body, next the turn in the opposite direction, then the brief touchdown of his left paw, after that with his right paw, a lightning right to the cameraman's jaw, and finally the leap back straight into my arms. He even managed to give me one good left hook to the stomach, too, just to let me know what he thought of my duplicity. Fortunately for my public, if not his, this never did show on camera, but his lethal right at the cameraman was there for all to see. And, this, of all nights, on the night of Peace On Earth, Good Will To Men.

Actually, individual interviews with no TV camera present were, as a matter of fact, hardly more successful. The trouble was that sooner or later a picture would be involved, and by this time Polar Bear regarded even a still photographer as a man up to no possible good. One day, for example, a woman reporter arrived from the *Toronto Star*. At first the interview went reasonably smoothly. Polar Bear stayed right in my lap and did not even make an effort to disappear. It was, however, the calm before the storm. The doorbell rang and it was, of course, the interviewer's partner, her photographer. Before the man had even taken out his camera Polar Bear had flown by him and repaired to his refuge under the bed. Here, as I carefully explained to the man as we visited the bedroom, he was literally unreachable except by crawl.

"Don't worry," the photographer said, "I have a cat myself. I know how to get him out." In vain I cautioned him once more. Even veteran crawlers, I explained, such as my late soldier brother, had failed. I even went so far as to emphasize the *late.* "Nonsense," he said, "I'll have him out before you know it." And, without another word, over the top — or, rather, under the top — he went.

Immediately Polar Bear began a dangerous series of steady hisses. Occasionally I would catch a glimpse of his nose or one of the man's shoes, but for some time there was apparently no actual contact. Finally I heard the smack of what I knew was the man's hand on the floor — obviously an attempted grab. This was at once followed by an incredibly loud whacking thump, and this time I knew it was not the man's hand but Polar Bear's paw. Although it sounded as if he had hit the floor rather than pay dirt, I couldn't be sure. In any case, after the thwack there was a long, ominous silence. I frankly feared the worst.

Finally, slowly and extremely sheepishly, the photographer emerged. I looked him over carefully and was relieved to see he was not visibly bleeding and still had the use of all his extremities. "You know," he said, "what I think I'll do? I think I'll get my camera and flash and photograph him right where he is. It'll really be a much more interesting shot."

I told him I couldn't agree with him more.

From the beginning there was, it seemed, a lively demand for Polar Bear to accompany me on what publishers call a "book tour." As a matter of plain hard fact there was considerably more demand for him than there was for me. Nevertheless, I did my best to grin and bear it. It was, after all, I told myself, the way of the world. People never look up to the person behind the personality. They just look up to the personality.

I know people have said I went on the book tour without Polar Bear because I did not want the competition.

I suppose that, when you're trying to do something on the field, there will always be those kinds of people in the bleachers. But the plain fact is, nothing could be farther from the truth. I am not afraid of competition. Man and boy, I have had competition out there on book tours that the kind of people who said things like that wouldn't understand if their lives depended on it. Why, on my very first book tour I went head-to-head with a Southern author named Harnett W. Kane. The tour was in Richmond, mind you, and my book was about Yankee Boston and his a biography about, as he put it, "the one woman outside my wife with whom I have ever been in love — Mrs. Robert E. Lee." And, if that wasn't bad enough, Harnett was probably the all-time champion book autographer. I've seen him stop people in the street if they had a copy of his book and offer to sign it. Finally, on our last stop on the tour, after I had sold maybe two copies of my book and he had sold a hundred of his, I asked him to sign one for me. He gave me one but refused to sign it. "You've got something of real value there, son," he said with some pride. "An unautographed Kane is a collector's item."

So, I repeat, it was hardly the competition that kept me from taking Polar Bear on the tour. It was the plain and simple fact, as I patiently explained to the publishers, that going with him from city to city, plane to plane, hotel to hotel, and even cab to cab, would be not only perilous in the extreme for him, but for me would be perilously close to certifiable insanity. I told them that, in Polar Bear's opinion, that kind of travel might be all right for dogs, horses, birds, mice, or humans, but it was far from all right for him.

I gave the publishers two examples. One was the occasion when I considered taking Polar Bear to another apartment while mine was being painted — the ordeal had been so awful that, in the end, I gave it up. In the ten years I had had Polar Bear, I told them, I had had the living room and even the kitchen painted but never the bedroom. Polar Bear stayed in the bedroom all the time the painters worked, loudly hissing beside the locked door at the noises in the next room, sniffing distastefully at the paint smells, and from time to time looking at me for all the world as if I had sold not only my birthright but his, too.

The second example I gave the publishers was that, although I had at one time briefly entertained the idea of a vacation with Polar Bear by taking a small house in the Hamptons, I did not so entertain it any longer. One look at the house brought the realization that the only room in which he could be safely confined without some access to going out making meals of the fish in the ocean was one small, hot bedroom and so I had no recourse but to abandon my summer vacation. New York, I decided, was really a terrific place in the summer. After all, a lot of people go away at that time, and all New York has ever really needed, when you came right down to it, is for about half the population to go away in the summer and not come back in the fall.

The publishers' final argument was that, while they knew I would do my best to sell the book, they really felt that, to put it candidly, Polar Bear would be a far better salesman. I answered this by saying they could not be more mistaken, that Polar Bear was bad enough at meeting people on his own turf but that off it he was a holy terror. As for his being a salesman, the mere thought was ludicrous. I had not at that time read *The Leadership Secrets of Attila the Hun,* because it had not yet been published, but later, after it had, I used it as what I considered an extremely apt comparison. I told them that in any carefully scored man-to-man contest between the original author of that book and Polar Bear in terrifying customers and not selling books, my money would be on Polar Bear. When they pointed out with some sarcasm that Attila was not the author of that book it was my turn to reply, with some hauteur, neither was Polar Bear the author of mine.

In conclusion I told them that if what they wanted was not to sell books, Polar Bear would be their answer, but that if what they wanted was to sell books, they should get themselves another boy. And, I reminded them, the sales manager never lived who could stand what he would see after Polar Bear had failed. I even patiently described this — which was, unfortunately for me, one of Polar Bear's favorite expressions — his own patented combination of sniff and curled smile which actually said "I told you so" better than any words could do the job.

Anyway, in the end the publishers reluctantly agreed to let me go "on the road," as it is called, on my own. Book tours for authors, I have learned from hard experience, are never easy. One thinks when one embarks, fortified by publisher encouragement, that one is going to take the country by storm. If so, one is usually brought up short. Publishers wisely warn authors that, when they get to a city, they should stay as far from bookstores as possible. The reason for this is that the chances of an author having his book in a bookstore when he is on tour is about the same as having a New York cab driver get out and open your door. It has happened, but it is not likely to happen again in your lifetime.

The trouble is, authors are inclined to fly off the handle and blame their publishers for not getting books in the bookstores. This is very unfair. The publishers, after all, cannot just put the books in the bookstores; the bookstores have to do that, and the bookstores can't put the books in the bookstores until they have bought the books from the publisher. But it is very unfair for the authors to blame the bookstores for not buying the books and putting them in the bookstores, because the bookstores cannot buy the books and put them in the bookstores until they know whether or not the public wants to buy the book. But it is very unfair of the authors to blame the public, too. The public, after all, doesn't know whether or not they want to buy the books because there are no books in the bookstores.

That is why, of course, not only reviews of books are important but also why it is important for authors to go on television and radio. The idea of this is that the host or hostess of the show can then tell the public to buy the book and the public can then go to the bookstores and tell the bookstores they want to buy the book and the bookstores can then go to the publishers and tell them they want to buy the book and the publishers can then send books to the bookstores and in the end there will be books in the bookstores and everyone will be happy.

What authors have to remember, however, is that television and radio hosts and hostesses have an awful lot of books sent to them and very few of these get to them. The reason for this is that when the publishers send the books to the television and radio stations, they don't go to the hosts and hostesses of the shows; they go to the mailrooms of the stations. The important figure here is the mailroom boy. The trouble is, the mailroom boy is very rarely a reader. He can read but he doesn't read books. He reads headlines and sports and comic strips and he looks at television, but when he sees a lot of books, they make him very nervous, and usually he either throws them away or gives them away. Your hope here is that one of the ones he gives away will be to his girlfriend. Of course if he does this, your book is no longer at the station, but just the same, if the mailroom boy's girlfriend likes the book she may tell the mailroom boy to take it back to the station and give it to the host or hostess.

Never, in other words, overlook the mailroom boy's girlfriend. However, even if everything works and she has made the mailroom boy take your book back to the station and give it to the host or hostess, this, if it happens at all, is likely to happen about an hour before the author is due to arrive at the station, and therefore the only thing the host or hostess has to go on is the jacket of your book. Even this presents problems because, although hosts and hostesses have to be fast readers, and usually do have a go at trying to read the book jacket, they are told an awful lot of things to remember before the show and apparently what the author's book is about is not one of them. I know that many times on my tour I had my book introduced as a novel. I also had it introduced as a new Christmas game. And, worst of all, not once, but several times, I had it introduced as a children's book. Fortunately only one TV hostess who did that had the temerity to suggest what ages she thought it was for. She suggested, as a matter of fact, twelve. I did not argue with her. Frankly, she herself looked just that age to me. All I told her, as politely as possible, was that to me there were three terrible ages of childhood — zero to ten, ten to twenty, and twenty to thirty.

There are, of course, many other features of an author's book tour besides television and radio interviews. There are also lectures, and again let me tell you from long experience these too can be no walk in the park. If you enter your auditorium and there is a very small turnout, your hostess will almost invariably tell you grimly that she had told the committee that people nowadays don't really want to come to hear people, they want to come to see people, and the only people they want to come to see are the people they see on TV. If, on the other hand, by some fluke there is a large crowd, rest assured you will not get the credit. Many times you will hear in such a situation, with the same kind of hostess grimness, some such line as "I only wish you could know how hard all of us have worked to get these people to come."

As for "book-and-author" luncheons, as they are called, these usually involve your being just one of at least four speakers. And if you sometimes wonder which is the best position to speak at these affairs, at least for the future selling of your book, wonder no longer. I have spoken in all four positions, and in each case I have been solemnly assured by the person in charge that my position was by far the most important. When I was the No. 1 speaker my job was easy. "You're it," I was told. "You're our leader. You make or break the whole lunch — that's why we put you there." Then, on another occasion, when I was the No. 2 speaker, I was equally solemnly assured that No. 2 was the most important. "You see," I was informed as we walked in, "you're really our lead speaker." This was followed by the hushed "You really wouldn't want to be the Number One. The waitresses will still be clearing the dishes and most of the time no one can hear a word." The same woman whispered the disadvantages of being No. 3 or No. 4. "They're getting tired by Number Three," she said, "and by Number Four so many people have to go. Babysitters, you know."

On the other hand, when I was No. 3 I was told that

that was the key slot. Again, the person in charge gave me the dishes problem of No. 1 and the babysitters problem for No. 4. "Number Two," she said, "is always our weak spot, but we have to put them *somewhere*." Finally, on the rare occasions when I got to be No. 4, I never heard a word about dishes, weak spots, or babysitters. "You're our main event," I was told. "You're the one everybody came to hear." This time, though, No. 3 got a different downer. "They *never* listen to Number Three," I was told. "They're all just waiting for *you*."

It was pretty heady stuff, all right, and they certainly had it down to a science. I did wonder, though, what happened when, as it occasionally must, they had an author come back for a repeat performance and be given, say, a different position in the batting order.

Even when it comes to sitting in front of a pile of books after the speeches, don't for a moment think you're home free. You never know, for one thing, when the author beside you might be another Harnett W. Kane. For another, you are almost certain to have some experiences which you will not soon forget. I remember three of these. One was the appearance of a woman in the line who debated long and hard as she stood in front of me. "Yes, I will," she said, firmly putting her book down for me to sign, "but don't sign it to me. Sign it to Mabel. Mabel loves to read. Mabel reads anything." The second was a woman who also stood in front of me for some time but did not put her book down. Greedily I reached for it to autograph. "Oh, no, don't," she said, "don't put anything in it. I may want to take it back." The third experience was a meeting with a woman who had not yet bought the book but who was obviously debating the purchase carefully. In the end, she put the book back on the table, shaking her head. "I just can't," she said. "I promised my husband I wouldn't buy a single nonessential between now and Christmas."

A final memorable experience and one which I am sure was mine alone occurred in Detroit. This did not involve a speech, but was simply a bookstore autograph, arranged by Doris Dixon, the Fund for Animals' longtime Michigan coordinator. It started out, of course, when I arrived. I noted that there was a reasonably long line of people and there were, mercifully, plenty of books. Of course there were no books in the other stores, and that's why the people were here, but happily I didn't learn that until later. With a modest wave I went to my assigned seat and sat down and signed people's books as they took their place in line. I did this as rapidly as possible, but it took some time because people not only wanted their names in the book as well as mine but they also wanted the name or rather names of their cats. Most had two or three but several had more — one had seventeen. The most popular name, incidentally, was Samantha. I tried shortening this to "Sam," but that was not popular. Nonetheless, I did my best not only to tell stories about Polar Bear but also to think of other ways to keep the line from breaking into open revolt.

Suddenly I noticed two women who, having bought the book, were both reading it together while they waited in the line. Now I submit that there are few authors alive, and I daresay few dead, who can resist approaching someone who is actually in the process of reading his book. In particular you always want to know where in the book they're reading. I had been a lecturer several times on cruise ships, where I have most often had this happen. Cruise ships are, after all, very close to the Promised Land for an author because here you have, first, a captive audience to whom, after your lecture, you can sell your book, and second, you can then walk around the deck and look over the shoulders of people, at least some of whom will be reading your book in their deck chairs. I remember on one occasion when, earnestly engaged in this pursuit, I noticed that one woman over whose shoulder I had looked the preceding afternoon had made only two pages of progress from my previous day's surveillance. I asked her sternly what seemed to be the trouble. "I went to the movies last night," she said. I told her graciously that I would understand that time but to please not let it happen again.

On this occasion in Detroit, however, seeing both those two women reading together, I got up as if to stretch and rest for a moment and then surreptitiously sauntered a few steps in their direction. The women were, I was first pleased to see, suitably engrossed, but then, as I got a closer look, I was brought up short with the realization that, having obviously just purchased the book, they were reading it, not at the beginning but at the very end.

In a loud voice I asked everyone in earshot if the police number in Detroit was, as it was in New York, 911. Immediately the bookstore manager appeared. She wanted to know what the problem was. I pointed to the two women — they were, I said, out of order. Indeed, they were reading my book out of order. I told her sternly that I did not permit my books to be read out of order and that I wanted them arrested. I told them I was perfectly prepared to read them their rights but they had to recognize my writing rights.

Actually I did make the women come up for interrogation. I told them I knew exactly what they were doing — they were reading the end of the book first to see if Polar

Bear had died in the end. And if he had, I continued my interrogation, they would have taken the book back, wouldn't they? Sheepishly they admitted they would have. It is not true, however, that I preferred charges against them. What I did instead was to make them stand in the corner until I had signed all the other people's books first, meanwhile explaining to the other people exactly why they were there and warning them they would join them if they so much as skipped a page.

Standing in the corner, you know, is a good old-fashioned punishment and in my opinion should not be confined to just children in school, where it is so often wasted. It is also, as I proved in the case of these women, very effective for adults as well. Frankly, I don't think any one of the people in that line will ever read one of my books out of order again.

On normal days when I get home I make a habit of going and lying down on the bed. I lie with my head north, whereupon Polar Bear jumps up and lies with his head south, right on my stomach. He then begins to knead away to his heart's content, which is of course good exercise for him and I feel I'm getting a good workout too — without all the trouble of getting on a bicycle or doing aerobics or anything like that, which can be so time-consuming. In any case, after this I usually initiate one of our regular biting fights. In these, during the cold weather I cover him with a blanket and in warm weather with a sheet. And then, while I come at him with my fingers from different directions from above, he bites from below. If I get him down with one hand before he draws blood, I win. If he gets a good finger bite lockhold, however — albeit a bloodless one — it's a draw. Whatever happens, afterward we go to sleep — which I like to do with one hand on him, wherever he is. But before we do, most of the time, particularly if he's won, he gives me a good-night lick.

In a book called *You and Your Cat,* by David Taylor, I have read, "The rasp-like upper surface of a cat's tongue is formed by hundreds of backward-pointing, small protuberances constructed of virtually the same substance as fingernails." I don't go along with rasp or nails. The farthest I will go is sandpaper, and at that it's the most wonderful, soft-feeling sandpaper in the world. But then Mr. Taylor even challenges that a cat is "communicating its contentment" when it purrs. All I can say is he never heard Polar Bear purr. Polar Bear's purr is pure chocolate syrup — and, remember, he's a vanilla cat.

I am going to ask you at this point, Gentle Reader — at least for all of you who remember when readers were called gentle — kindly to file and forget the above paragraph. I have two reasons for wishing you to do this. The first is that, being a curmudgeon, I am fearful that my fellow curmudgeons, on reading what they would surely regard as such an unseemly public display of affection, might well have cause to challenge my curmudgeonly standing. Indeed, I can see myself being actually drummed out of the regiment, my buttons cut, my sword, insignia, pen, and, for all I know, even my credit cards removed.

The second reason I have for wishing you to file and forget that paragraph is that when I have been on a trip not a line of it holds true. After a trip, indeed, I could go in and lie down on the bed and it would be hours before Polar Bear even deigned to come into the bedroom, let alone lie down with me. He has, in fact, just two policies with me after I've been away. After a short trip he gives me a hard time for a short time. After a long trip he gives me a hard time for a long time. The time after my book tour trip, however, he really outdid himself. He not only walked away from me when I tried to pick him up, he refused even to eat a bite of the delicious meal I prepared for him. Instead he first looked down at it, then up at me, and finally gave me one of his patented sneers. With that, he did not even walk away, he literally stalked away.

Finally I went to bed and, after a suitable interval, pretended to be asleep, thinking that no matter how mad he was he would get up on the bed and go to sleep, too. He could, after all, do this with me asleep and still not give up his principles. I waited a long time. At last I heard his familiar "aeiou," and felt his leap up onto the bottom of the bed. I could hardly wait for what I knew would be his next move — his slow walk up the bed, and his final flounce down on my stomach. At which point, of course, I would grab him.

I never, however, had the chance. Rather, he proceeded across the bed to the farthest corner away from my head. He, too, apparently had his idea of corner punishment and, if he couldn't put me in one, he had decided, when he knew I wanted him most, to go in one himself and stay there. He would show me once and for all that just because he didn't want to go away on any idiotic trip was no reason for me to go on one without him. All I had to do, which even I ought to be able to understand, was to stay where I was supposed to stay and then we could both be together without either one of us having to go anywhere. It was, when you came right down to it, just simple cat logic.

II ◦ *Cat Power*

The only area of being a celebrity of which I ever found Polar Bear to be even remotely fond was the increase in mail. Before this he never took much interest in mail, and I am sure he would have continued this policy had we lived in the country and had the mail been delivered, as it was in the Good Old Days, to your door.

The trouble would have been, of course, that Polar Bear likes very few people coming to what he regards as his door. Indeed, you can count on the fingers of one hand the number he does, and you would as a matter of fact have a digit or two left over. And, rest assured, these would not have included any postmen. Polar Bear feels about postmen the way postmen feel about dogs.

I know this for a fact because, even in a city apartment where the mail is just dumped into your box downstairs and then you have to get it yourself as you do everything nowadays, Polar Bear does meet a postman every once in a while. He meets them, for example, when they come up to the door for a signature on a registered letter or, for another example, when they appear just before Christmas. This they do not once but several times — Christmas is apparently a very meaningful holiday for postmen.

One such pre-Christmas postman visit was memorable. That was the day when someone who was not very good at wrapping packages sent Polar Bear some fresh catnip from a farmers' market. The postman had to bring it up because it was special delivery. And so, when I opened the door for him, there he stood with the flimsily wrapped basket which looked like a bouquet of flowers. I had no idea it was catnip, but Polar Bear knew it practically from the ring of the doorbell. As he leaped, I tried to place myself between the postman and the nips, and I think I did pretty well. If there was ever, however, a literal example of something being nip and tuck, this was it, and when it was all over there was no question but that Polar Bear was the winner. He had the basket, but the postman appeared to me, on first glance, as a basket case — albeit one who I'm sure had learned from then on to prefer even a dog to a cat after catnip.

This was a special occurrence, but, with increased mail and with very few postmen to contend with, Polar Bear did begin to show, as I say, increased interest. And the area of the mail in which he took perhaps the keenest interest outside of edibles was the arrival of new books. These were sometimes sent to me for a favorable comment for later use in a newspaper ad — a comment which is called a "blurb." When I opened such books — indeed, many times when I had not had a chance to do so because he had already done it for me — he would sniff them from cover to cover. In fact he often sniffed the covers right off them, which always seemed to me in itself an extremely favorable blurb. Certainly there was no question about his being, when it came to new books, a voracious reader. At the same time it hurt me very much that he ignored the older books I had written just because they weren't new. He wouldn't even sniff the covers to see if he would like them.

Polar Bear also liked something else about the increased mail. Somehow he seemed to be fully aware of the large amount which was addressed to him rather than to me. His character, I have always felt, leaves much to be desired in many departments but particularly in any department which involves any kind of competition with me. I remember, for example, one day when I brought up two packages — one addressed to me, and one to him. He opened his while sitting on mine. Whatever he did, his ability to spot the packages which were addressed to him was remarkable. Nor did all of these contain the telltale catnip or some other edible which was readily identifiable by smell. There were many others which were not so identifiable — toys, for instance, or food in cans — and to this day I've never been able to figure out how he knew what was in them.

Spot them he not only did, however, he also treated them all, not just catnip but even simpler items, as if, if he didn't move in on them tooth and claw, they might get away. I guarantee that on more than one occasion, having pried open a package containing a can, he would then start "aeiou"-ing around, batting me and making short runs in the direction of the kitchen. I always have the feeling that if I do not immediately follow him to the kitchen and get the can opener and open the can for him, he would either get himself a smart lawyer and take me to court for withholding rightful property or, almost as sinister from my point of view, develop his own capacity to pry cans open himself. He really is a great little prier — not only into his own affairs, but also into other people's and particularly mine.

My usual modus operandi was to open all the packages first and then, when he had sniffed and eaten to his heart's content, I could count on the fact he would want a nap and I could then enjoy the luxury of reading the rest of my mail without his sticking his selfish little nose into a lot of things which, whether he thought so or not, were none of his business.

One of the first of these was a letter from Mrs. Josephine Vernick of Southfield, Michigan. It was a very nice letter with one, to me, remarkable qualification. What, in a word, Mrs. Vernick told me she particularly liked about my book was my punctuation.

I was glad Polar Bear was asleep for that. I could just see him figuring out from my reaction that I had gotten a bad one, and it would be just like him in his rotten little competitive way to be pleased as punch over it. I had to admit, though, that in this case he would have a point. I submit that there is a wide variety of main reasons authors would like to be remembered after they have gone to their final reward, but I doubt that high on the list of any of them would be their punctuation. Just the same, I told myself, punctuation was, when you came right down to it, a basic element of one's style, and I could, therefore, at least take some satisfaction for the fact that I had received praise for this.

My satisfaction was, however, short-lived. This was

due to the very next letter I opened — one from Ms. Betty Stein of Fort Wayne, Indiana. Ms. Stein, a columnist for the *Fort Wayne News-Sentinel,* enclosed a review of my book. It began as follows:

> If you can ignore Mr. Amory's compulsion to write convoluted sentences, as he does in two or three out of four in a row, and if you are in no hurry to go from the subject, which almost always is his cat named Polar Bear, to the predicate (that's the part of the sentence with the verb and the object, for those of you who have forgotten your courses in grammar, or maybe didn't have them because for quite a spell it was considered unstylish and unnecessary to teach how to parse), and you don't mind going back to the beginning to find out what the author originally intended the sentence to be about, you'll find . . .

Well, as I've always said, you can't win them all. But, hard as it is for me to admit, I should say that Ms. Stein was not the first to call attention to my predilection for convolution. My very first literary agent, Bernice Baumgarten, was also very narrow-gauge when it came to this. On one notable occasion, early in my literary career, she came perilously close to doing permanent damage to my writing psyche. First she gave me a stern lecture about style in general and then added that, of all her clients, I had the worst tendency to write, as she put it, "pretzel sentences."

How I have longed through the years to write just one book which would make her eat her words. Now, however, after Ms. Stein's words I had to realize that that time was not yet.

One letter in particular seemed to sum up the majority feeling about cats from my correspondence. It came from a woman named Jackie Kamoroff, of Berkeley, California:

> I sit surrounded by my Pervis, rescued at 3 weeks old from the jaws of a dog, Eloise, rescued from the cat incinerator known as the pound, and Bill, my 18½ year old senior citicat.
>
> I noted that you described cat people as "cat owned." Around here we call it "cat power." I'm not sure I can define it but I can see you are definitely under its strong influence, as is my entire family, particularly my dad.
>
> As for myself, since I got Pervis and Eloise my boyfriend and I are no longer able to stay at his house. We have to go to my house for a dose of cat.

I was not sure whether Ms. Kamoroff's boyfriend was un-under the influence of cat power, or may have had cats of his own who did not get along with Pervis and Eloise, or, failing both of these, perhaps Ms. Kamoroff's family would not allow Pervis and Eloise to leave and Ms. Kamoroff could not live without them. But one thing was certain: Ms. Kamoroff may have said she was unable to define "cat power," but she expressed the feelings of a very large number of other writers. Sandy Worley, of Spokane, Washington, for example, also like Ms. Kamoroff expressed the power in terms of a male/female relationship:

> My husband was not a cat lover, but it was a "love me, love my cat" situation. So he has learned to love the cat. Even though he is allergic to the cat, he still allows it to have full run of the house. It has been quite a learning experience for him, and the only conclusion he has arrived at is that we are "cat butlers," whose only existence in a cat's life is to feed, pat, protect and jump at any demand!

Other correspondents found examples of "cat power" in some of my favorite quotations about cats I had used, including those from Leonardo da Vinci and Mark Twain. But, one I had also used was from the French philosopher

Alain: "Two things," he wrote, "are aesthetically perfect in the world — the clock and the cat." I had said that I was willing to go along with the cat, but that the clock stopped me. It did not, however, stop Anne Strong, of Shingle Springs, California:

> Bluemoon, the cat I belong to, just asked me to send his picture to Polar Bear, but when I asked him if he would look at Polar Bear's picture he walked off, so that's alright. One morning, however, jogging around the pond, I was struck with the word "clock" and built some positive associations with it. This surprised me since for as long as I can remember watches and such have been a bore. Well, that evening I read Alain's quote and your remark. May I suggest that a clock links one with the environment by its sound. Also, presuming it is working properly, it communicates nothing but the Here and Now or rather the Now-Here, Nowhere, the source of it all.

Frankly, just as I did not understand Alain's quote I did not understand Ms. Strong's explanation of it. The trouble is, I guess, I come from Boston and Bostonians are not very good with the Here and Now, the Now-Here, the Nowhere, or even the Source Of It All. Just the same, that doesn't stop us from maintaining California girls are fun to talk to even if they are not easy to listen to.

Fortunately, many other letter writers gave me additional cat quotes which were far easier to decipher. I had one favorite — one which came to me from no less than four different correspondents. "Being owned by a cat," this read, "is a liberal's introduction to conservatism." Since Polar Bear is as Republican as they come, this quotation appealed to me very much. And, on top of this, it was fortified by Linda Upchurch, of Arlington, Virginia, who favored me with the extraordinary news that she had adopted a cat which she had decided to name, of all names, Liberal:

> I did not then know the quotation you mentioned. But I heartily subscribe to it. My cat is black and white. At first I wanted to call him BW, but that was too rednecky for me. So I decided to go the reverse and let my cat make a statement of my own politics. I admit I fudged a little by nicknaming and calling him Libby, or just Lib, but I stopped this when a friend said you should never nickname cats — that they don't like the lack of formality in it. The irony of it all is that Liberal may make a statement for me, but his name has not made the slightest impression on him. Frankly, he is Old Guard to the core. A few months ago when I moved to another apartment he was sick for a week and angry with me for a month and now, in the new apartment, he will not permit any change at all. The other day I timidly attempted to move just a few pieces of the living room furniture but he literally went into a funk and just sulked and skulked around until I put back every single piece I had moved.

Second only to Liberal's introduction to conservatism was a quotation sent to me by Mrs. Schuyler Pardee, of Winter Park, Florida, who informed me it came from none other than the late Adlai Stevenson. "Cats do not practice witchcraft," Stevenson said, "in areas where people do not believe in it."

My third and final favorite came from Aida Zinc, of Malvern, Pennsylvania. "Cats," she said, "are like Baptists. They both raise hell, but you never catch 'em at it."

Until I received that letter I never knew what religion Polar Bear was. I feel I do now, if for no other reason, because more times than I wish to tell you in the dark of the night when I am sound asleep he goes into the kitchen and, with dastardly quiet, upsets everything, even carefully wrapped garbage. Then, in the morning when I go into the kitchen with him I of course find the carnage. He gives me a look which I promise you contains nothing but a remarkable combination of surprise and innocence — both mixed with what I can only describe as a firm determination to join with me and search the premises to find the perpetrator.

Polar Bear, after eating his mail, spent, as I mentioned, a good deal of time sleeping through most of mine. And, as I have also said, when it came to difficult letters this was fine with me, because I was certain, deep in his rotten little soul, he would be very fond of these. The letters were, after all, part and parcel of the whole celebrity thing which he detested. And, if some of them were critical, then, from his point of view, I had received, also from his point of view, my just deserts.

And some of the letters, make no mistake, were indeed critical — beginning, if you can believe it, with what I had named him. "This is not meant to be a carping letter," began Auriel Douglas, of Los Angeles — another California girl, and one who then, of course, proceeds to carp — "but rather one which aids and instructs someone who desperately needs guidance and lessons in the art of naming a cat. I do concede you did attempt to link your cat's color to the word 'Polar' inasmuch as those regions are generally covered by white snow, but to name a cat after another animal! No, no, never! It's not the done thing."

Not the "done" thing — now, really. But unfortunately Ms. Douglas was not done yet. "When naming a cat," she went on in her infuriating way, "if one's imagination is totally at a loss, start with a good encyclopedia. Look up names of emperors, empressesses, kings and queens.

Cats, particularly male cats, like very strong names which link them to majestic feats."

Empres*sesses,* indeed. Another thing about California girls is that they never finish school, on the theory presumably that, since out there there are no finishing schools, there is no point in it. Anyway, Ms. Douglas suggested that if I did not find anything desirable in royalty I should have moved on to artists. She mentioned Renoir, Modigliani, and Cézanne and then added patronizingly, "Picasso is a very nice name for a multi-colored cat, while Mondrian would suit one with two or three different colors. As for other names, there's absolutely nothing wrong with — in fact there is something quite distinguished with — a simple 'John,' or 'James' or 'William.'

"I do hope," Ms. Douglas concluded, patronizing to the end, "these tips will help. What must your cat's friends *think* when they hear him called 'Polar Bear?' I'd rather you called him 'Roly-Poly,' which, judging by your description, he is fast becoming."

That last personal remark seemed to me totally uncalled for — particularly since at the time I read it Polar Bear, having each day for more than a week eaten a hearty mail, was definitely more out of shape than ever. And, as I looked at him, still stunned to the quick by Ms. Douglas, I had an almost eerie feeling that he was hugely enjoying my discomfort. I might have been making it all up, but I doubted it. After all, he has never been fond enough of his name to deign to recognize it in the company of anyone else — which he well knows is especially embarrassing to me — and the fact that he now seemed to know I had received at least one especially critical letter for the name was surely not out of the realm of possibility.

The next letter, I was happy to see, was far more civil.

It was from Emily Johnston, of Westminster, Maryland, a woman who, while obviously not enamored with Polar Bear's name, rather gently suggested the name "William the Conqueror." She added that she too had a white cat whom she had named "Wilfrid Hyde-White." At the same time, she also admitted she had what she described as "a 16-pound cowardly red tabby." To him she had affixed, of all names, "Truman Kapuddy." However, the names suggested by Sarah Bizzell, of Fayettesville, North Carolina, to me deserved the prize. She named one of her cats Samuel Moses Beauregard Napoleon Bonaparte King Tut I. "Moses," she added helpfully, "for short."

Finally, Eugene Sheehy, of New York, favored me with a passage from Ivy Compton-Burnett's *Mother and Son* about a cat named Plautus:

> "Why do you call him 'Plautus?' " said Miss Burke. . . .
>
> "Oh, because he *is* Plautus," said Miss Wolsey. "Because the essence of Plautus is in him. How could he be called anything else?"
>
> "Who was Plautus in real life?"
>
> "Who could he have been but the person to give this Plautus his name?"
>
> "He was a Latin writer," said Miss Greathcart, as Miss Burke left a second question unanswered. "I think he wrote plays; not very good ones."
>
> "Why did you call the cat after him?"
>
> "Well, he has not written any good plays either," said Miss Wolsey.

Second only to my naming mistakes I was criticized for one particular error of my ways with Polar Bear. And this was one in which I knew he would take the greatest pleasure. It was, not to beat around the bush any longer, my ineptitude in getting pills down him and my final reliance on a sneak night attack when he was sound asleep. For this I was even taken to task by a stern memorandum which arrived right from my own Fund for Animals office. It was signed by Lia Albo, who is chief of the Fund's New York rescue service and a veteran of many cat-owned years. "The trouble is," she wrote, "you did not psyche yourself. You must first psyche yourself to believe you're going to be able to get the job done. Then, after you're all psyched up your psyche will spread to the cat."

I tried to explain to Ms. Albo that we Bostonians had a very poor record when it came to psyching ourselves, let alone spreading our psyche around to other people. Nonetheless, when she graciously offered to come to my apartment and do the first psyching job on Polar Bear herself, I could hardly refuse on his behalf. And so, on the very next day, Ms. Albo appeared. With some misgiving I picked up Polar Bear and placed him in her arms. She held him firmly, and I did not interrupt her while she was obviously at work in the psyching department. Then, when this was apparently concluded, she next deftly plopped the pill in his mouth and, as she did so, I noticed she blew hard on his face. "Blowing hard on his face," she explained, "is very important, too. Now, you'll see, he will *have* to swallow."

Polar Bear, however, whether psyched or not, had apparently never had anybody blow hard on his face. To say he did not like it was putting it mildly. What he did, in a word, was blow right back in Ms. Albo's face. Furthermore he did so with his mouth pursed, so that he managed a foreshortened but still remarkable replica of a Ubangi blowgun. Suffice it to say that his aim was perfect. The pill was returned to Ms. Albo directly between the eyes.

Afterward, I thanked her for her trouble but said that, all things considered, whether my critics liked it or not, I intended to return to my sneak night attack when he was fast asleep.

In fairness to Ms. Albo I should say that there were several other believers in the blow-to-swallow method. One was Rosalie Gleim of Florence, Kentucky, who also advised me not to get discouraged. "I have had cats since my childhood," she wrote, "but I did not learn to pill one until I was forty. The worst advice," she added, "was to put the pill on the eraser end of a pencil."

That was helpful, at least in reverse. On the other hand, Roberta Little, of Carmel, California, a long time Manx-catter, wrote me at some length of what she said was a foolproof method — which apparently had worked with the toughest of all her cats, one named, aptly enough, "Thumper":

> What is it about white cats? The Thump is a copper-eyed white Manx who suffers from lockjaw every time he hears me uncork a pill bottle. But after years of suffering, I have finally found a way to pill him effectively. You have to be smarter than they are and that's not easy. I literally have to sit on him! You don't want to try this when any other people are around because it's not a very dignified position to be in. Kneel on the floor and stuff your cat between your knees, facing the same way you are, with just his head poking out between your thighs. Behind you, make sure your feet are crossed to prevent a rear exit. It took me a couple of tries at this before I realized cats have a reverse gear, too. Then "sit" on them gently, just enough to keep them where you want 'em. You can confuse them by pretending this is a new game, but that only works a few times. If you can catch them in the middle of a plea for help, grab the scruff of the neck, thereby freezing their mouth open, you can stuff that pill in, then slam their

> mouth shut and stroke their throat . . . if you have more than one cat I think it's best to do this away from the others. I think it makes them laugh, and that could be embarrassing for the cat you're pilling.

Finally, the simplest advice of all came from Lenore Clifton, of Carmichael, California. "Our vet," she wrote, "fills a syringe with vitamins and, in front of Shaddow, and before giving it to him, takes some of it himself." Mrs. Clifton did not, however, say whether or not her vet administered pills to Shaddow in the same manner, but she certainly implied as much. And, frankly, ever since she sent me that letter I have been very curious to know what Polar Bear's reaction would be if I decided to emulate Shaddow's vet. Somehow, however, what with one thing and another, I have never gotten around to trying.

There were many letters which named other errors I had committed in my first year with Polar Bear — the year which the book encompassed. But one letter stood out because it did not stop with just one error. Instead it contained a veritable litany of them. Furthermore, it came on the letterhead of none other than a doctor of sociology:

> I have read your book and I want you to know that you have managed, in one short volume, to violate every known cat taboo. Indeed, you forced P. Bear into a situation of ceremonial uncleanliness that must have driven him almost into a nervous breakdown. People don't realize that cats come from a "pride" culture full of rigid taboos that cover face-to-face interaction and rules governing statuses based on age, sex, profile, long or short hair, color and pattern. Their social structure is identical to that of the Navajo people in that it is matriarchal and contains extremely strong taboos.
>
> Cats hunt with the lead cat, who is female, bringing

down the prey. Only after that do the other cats participate because if they jumped in on the chase they would interfere with the timing of this. When you tried to get P. Bear to fetch the ball of yarn, you interfered with his role as lead cat and, naturally, he backed off and allowed your gross bad manners to appropriate his work. In the future, your proper role should be to stand back admiringly while he brings down the yarn, and only then approach it.

Also, when P. Bear didn't provide a welcome for Kamikaze, the kitten you took in, your attempt to force him to "be nice" (1) violated his role behavior *vis-a-vis* a younger, female, different color animal where the adult must be passive and long-suffering but dignified until the other cat has calmed down enough to be trained, and (2) you violated the strongest taboo in the cat world when you forced him to look you in the eye while you explained things to him. The most hostile thing a cat can do is look another animal in the eye, and you forced P. Bear not only to violate his taboos over the kitten but to make eye contact with his best friend when all he was trying to do was to obey the deepest set of norms in the cat world. Shame on you.

Sincerely,

Curtiss Ewing
Arlington, Vermont

First "Shame on you" and then "Sincerely" — really, it was too much. I simply could not believe the unmitigated gall of such a terrible woman. I am a very fair-minded person and have always, even in difficult circumstances, been able to mitigate my own gall. Nonetheless this drove me to my limit. Furthermore, when I reread the letter, I decided that it fairly reeked of pro-female, antimale prejudice — the "matriarchal Navajos," "the lead cat, who is female," "the role behavior *vis-a-vis* a younger female," and all the rest of it.

I did have, however, one consolation about the letter. It arrived on a day when Polar Bear was away on business. He was, as a matter of fact, in the other room engaged in extremely manly business — the manning of the barricades against Rosa, the cleaning woman, and what Polar Bear regards as an enemy-filled armored personnel carrier: i.e., the vacuum. I really was very happy he did not see my reaction to that letter — I don't think I could have borne the satisfaction he would have taken in it.

What I did do was to devise a plan of action which would put Dr. Ewing in her place and at the same time not descend to her level and put the whole thing on a male-versus-female footing. In a word, I resolved to comb every letter I could get my hands on to find examples of men being just as damned capable of looking after their cats as any "matriarchal" Navajo she could find.

Frankly, it took a little time because there were only two or three letters on my side as opposed to perhaps a hundred or so on hers. But I saw no necessity of counting or even taking votes. When I am right about something I am right and that is that. I wasn't, after all, running a poll, and if I did, I'd do it the way they do those idiotic television polls and charge fifty cents for every call.

In any case, the letter I chose to use as the best example of cat husbandry being superior to cat wifery came from Lynn Goldsmith, of Oneonta, New York. I quote the letter at the same length I gave that awful Ewing woman:

Dear Mr. Amory:

On February 14, 1975, my husband of seven months brought me a Valentine's present in his pocket. It was a tiny white kitten with the biggest pair of green eyes, and the biggest ears I had ever seen. She was from the humane society, and since Rob had never owned a pet I suspected from the beginning that the present for me was really for him.

I wish I could say that it was love at first sight, but nothing could be further from the truth. I didn't like cats after a childhood trauma of watching one devour a chipmunk. Our apartment didn't allow cats, so we were in danger of being evicted if our landlord saw her. I was trying to write my Master's thesis, and the kitten had an annoying habit of mistaking my legs for a tree, and trying to climb on my lap that way. Once there, she would bat at my moving pen, scatter my notecards, and otherwise cause havoc and chaos in my already chaotic notes. Besides, she kept us awake at night, not crying for her mother, which I could have sympathized with, but trying to entice us to play.

Weren't cats supposed to sleep a majority of the time? I presented my case to my husband, explaining that we could have a pet, preferably a dog, once I was out of school, and we had a place of our own. She was a cute kitten, and I was sure that she would be very quickly adopted. Rob doesn't very often refuse to compromise, in fact I can get my way a surprising amount of the time, but he refused to return the kitten. I attributed his decision to sleep deprivation, and assumed that he would eventually see the logic in my argument.

Well, we were eventually evicted for having a cat, and I finished my thesis in the University library. Abbey became firmly ensconced as a member of our family, and eventually grew to fit her large eyes and ears — in fact I venture to say that she rivaled Polar Bear in size. She lived for ten years, and I can't imagine what our lives would have been without her. We do have another cat now, as well as a child who has learned responsibility and respect from our dignified, and somewhat less tolerant, elder statescat.

Having, with the assistance of Ms. Goldsmith and her persistent husband, put Dr. Ewing in her place, I now turned to the task of putting Polar Bear in his. The very next time we opened the mail together I pointed out to him letters about cats who regularly did all kinds of things I had tried in vain to get him to do. The first and foremost of these were letters from people who regularly walked their cats on leashes with harnesses — letters which indirectly criticized me for the fact that I had failed in my efforts to make Polar Bear ambulatory. I told him the next time I went to play chess in the Park he would jolly well go with me and, whether he liked it or not, on a leash. He gave me, of course, a look that all the cat-owned know — the look which says, so very clearly, not only lots of luck but also that you will need it.

I showed him letters too about cats who regularly watched television shows with their owners. I tried to do this with Polar Bear but I had noticed that as he grew in age he grew more and more critical of television fare. The more he saw of young cats in commercials the more he obviously disdained them. They simply, he obviously felt, had not learned their craft. As for shows in which there were other animals, these also receive poor ratings with him. As far as I could see, he liked only bird shows and fish shows, and this not only made me annoyed because he clearly liked them for the wrong reasons but also afforded us extremely slim pickings on the tube. He never even made an effort to understand why I liked so many sports on TV. The only sport I ever found him really interested in was Ping-Pong. My feeling about this was that he liked not only the quick back-and-forth of it — which he followed intently — but also felt the sound of the ball was just the right amount of noise. The trouble was that Ping-Pong was just big on TV during the Olympics — which gave us a good watch all right but one that came on, after all, only every four years, and certainly wouldn't help them in their sweeps.

I felt so sorry for Polar Bear about this that I was very glad when another letter writer, Geri Colloton, of New York, wrote me that I should get some videos which were specially designed for cats and which Polar Bear and I could watch together. I did this, and was pleased to see the first one which came was called *Video Catnip*. This I felt would do the trick because Polar Bear could, like the rest of us, both watch it and enjoy a snack with it. The video, put out by PetAvision, however, had no catnip. Instead it came in three long sections entitled, in order, "Cheep Thrills," "Mews and Feather Report," and "A Stalk in the Park." I was not crazy about those titles but I immediately sat Polar Bear down and turned it on. Actually I enjoyed it very much — birds chirping around and eating, squirrels chattering around and eating, chipmunks clucking around and eating — but frankly, I did get sort of hungry. So I went to the kitchen and got a snack for both Polar Bear and myself. When I brought it to him, though, I realized he hadn't been watching at all — he was fast asleep. I woke him up immediately. I didn't mind him sleeping through regular TV, I told him, but what he was watching was what I'd bought and whether he knew it or not this was pay TV and he could jolly well watch it whether he liked it or not. Whereupon, of course, after my outburst, he went back to sleep again.

I had almost exactly the same experience with the second video I tried, entitled *Kitty Video* and put out by Lazy Cat Productions. Finally I realized the trouble. I am not good at reading instructions, and, sure enough, I hadn't read the pamphlet which came with the *Kitty Video*. The first part was entitled "How to Teach Your Cat to Watch

TV." "Most cats," it began, "are not accustomed to watching television and will need some assistance to learn this human skill."

I'm not an easy man to stop once I've started reading something but I want to tell you this time I came close. "Human *skill?*" They had to be kidding.

But they were not:

> Loud music, too many people in the room and other animals can be disrupting and can cause a lack of concentration on the cat's part. Next, place your cat on your lap and begin the tape. Pet the cat and position his head toward the television screen (strategically scratch under the right cheek to aim head left). Never force a cat to watch the TV. He will have to discover it on his own. Tapping gently on the TV screen can help bring the cat's attention to the video.

I tried everything they said on Polar Bear — even that "head left," which I didn't understand. But nothing worked. Maybe, I thought, he should be watching the television alone, without me. But a large "caution" on the instructions quickly disabused me of that:

> Do not leave your cat alone while the video is playing. If the cat should leap at the screen, it could cause damage both to furnishings and to the cat. Your cat will need to learn to watch TV passively. With practice, your cat can become a harmless couch potato.

Polar Bear was their boy for that, all right, except for one thing — this time he was asleep before I even finished reading the instructions. Finally I put aside the cat video. And, I was relieved to find, my very next letter revealed there were far more than couch potato cats out there. There were cats who actually Did Things. There was even one cat, owned by Florence Davis, of Willow Grove,

Pennsylvania, who not only played the piano but also, when Ms. Davis played a selection of which he was not fond, would jump up and sit on her hands until she stopped.

Ms. Fields' cat was not the only one who took matters into his own hands. My favorite of these was a cat named Bogart, who, his owner, Carol Clausen of San Jose, California, wrote me, was so impossible that when she and her husband took in a stray he forced them to pay an extraordinary price. "We ended up," she wrote, "having to keep them separated and my husband and I had to sleep in separate rooms so that each cat had someone to sleep with."

This was meaningful stuff for a bachelor like me to read, and, as I looked at Polar Bear, knowing all too well how awful he could be about other cats, I wondered if he realized to what sorry ends his selfishness could lead. Just when I was trying to get through to him about this — which was difficult because his eyes were fixed on the balcony — suddenly he jumped up, raced around through the bedroom, flew out the window to his balcony, and smashed right up against the wire at a darling pair of pigeons — pigeons who were, mind you, billing and cooing.

He was, I decided, incorrigible — nothing to him was sacred, not even true love. My only recourse was to turn to a group of letters I'd filed under the heading "Cat Smartness." If there was anything on cat earth about which Polar Bear prided himself it was how smart he was, and I thought it would do him good to learn that there were cats out there who, when it came to smartness, could give him cards and spades.

To me the most remarkable of these was a letter from

Lenore Evans, of San Diego, California, about her cat named José. Mrs. Evans, an elderly widow, wrote me that one fall she was, as usual, engaged in stripping off the dead leaves from her fruit trees preparatory to raking them up when she realized she could not reach the top leaves. "Well," she said aloud to herself, "I can't reach those — I guess I'll have to wait for them to drop naturally." With that, and without hesitation, José, who had been watching the process, immediately ran up to one of the top branches of each tree in turn and, holding on with his hind legs to the trunks of the trees, proceeded with his front paws to reach out and shake the branches until all the top leaves had fallen. "Does this cat know the English language?" Mrs. Evans asked. "Is he a reincarnation of someone I once knew? Do you know I lowered my intelligence secretly to ask who he was? With that question, he just rubs his head on me but doesn't tell me anything."

Judging from the rest of Mrs. Evans' letter, however, José may have had good reason not to answer:

> When he tries to awaken me for his breakfast, I play a game with him by pretending I don't hear him "meowing." He does something different about this each time. But one day, when he had finished reaching under the blankets and tearing at me, he suddenly stopped jumping up and down on me and rubbing his face against mine. Instead he very carefully put his mouth into my ear, took a deep breath, and positively screamed his loudest. How did he know my hearing was there? At night, when he wants in with me, he jumps on the screen — I leave a big window open all night — and "meows." Once I decided he didn't need to come in right then, so I tried ignoring him. I looked at him and said, "there's nothing you can do to get me out of bed." With that he raised one foot,

> extended his claws, and brought his nails slowly down the screen. It was the old "nails-on-the-blackboard" bit, and of course I couldn't stand it. I got up and let him in.

I certainly didn't want Polar Bear to get one of his big ideas from that letter. A big boy at school used to do that, and I *still* hate it.

But again, just when I finished that letter Polar Bear, back from his pigeon breakup, happened to push on the floor — he loves to push things on the floor — a letter I had not yet filed under "Cat Smartness." As I looked at the letter I noticed it was one not addressed to me but to him — one purporting to be from a cat named Chris Kitty. Ms. Kitty parted with the information that her veterinarian had said that in all his years of practice he had come across the occasional dumb dog but never once in his life a dumb cat.

Polar Bear ate that up, of course — even though, as I recall, there was no cat food or catnip in it. But I would not be deterred from my effort to prove that he was far from what he thought he was — the smartest cat in the world. It really was curious that, as little interest as he had in being the most famous cat in the world, he had a terrific interest in being recognized as the smartest cat in the world.

But to do this, I realized, I would have to call up my big guns and all my ammunition. This meant, in a word, going to my Siamese file. From even a cursory reading of this file there was no question but that most Siamese owners consider Siamese the smartest cats there are — there was just the question of whether they or their cats should write the letters proving it.

My favorite letter on this subject did come, though, from

a person — Mary Ruth Everett, of West Chester, Pennsylvania:

> For twenty years we had a Siamese named Arthur (with his approval), and the only thing that cat could not do was speak English. While he lived he, of course, ruled the household. This fact was accepted by everyone. There are dozens of Arthur stories I could tell, but one I think especially you would enjoy is about what he did to visitors.
>
> Our unique old house (called the Gingerbread House in West Chester) was planned and built well over a hundred years ago by an eccentric university professor, and above the huge high mantle is a captain's-walk type railing with a central curved-out area in which, we think, he undoubtedly kept the bust of Shakespeare. Against the chimney it is warm and perfectly sized and shaped for Arthur to be curled up in. It was his place. There he stayed until someone knocked on the door. In an instant he sat up, perfectly straight and perfectly still — a statue. No *new* person ever spotted him. He waited until people were settled, drinks in hands, nibbles being nibbled and conversation going nicely, to his satisfaction. Then, with a Siamese rebel yell, he would leap down into the center of the room. Even the most dignified (sometimes stuffy?) victim/visitor jumped out of their seats, scattering food and drink and uttered, among their screams, some of the most undignified expletives on record. We smiled and said, "Oh, you haven't met Arthur" — which turned the conversation, no matter how serious previously, to Arthur-talk, which was just what he wanted. He then sat, calmly, washing and loving every minute of it, sizing up the people and spotting unerringly a *non*-cat loving one; into that one's lap he flatteringly (?) jumped, curled up, and purred loudly.

My second favorite letter on the Siamese came from Mrs. Althea Huber, of Bourbonnaise, Illinois, a lady who lives with a husband and nine cats, seven of whom are strays and two who are Siamese. She claimed the latter, Biggety and Cinderella, not only ruled the roost but regarded all other cats as, in their opinion, servant cats:

> I am really not sure that Siamese are smarter, but they certainly talk more and they are most likely to behave in a "human" way. Biggety can open any door, even difficult kitchen cabinet ones. As for Cinderella, she not only thinks the sun rises and sets on my husband, she regards him as the person who, in the morning, is responsible for turning on the sun. If Charles doesn't do it, and it is a dark, cloudy day, Cinderella accepts it — but only after that special Siamese look of distaste, accompanied by a stream of conversation which clearly says, in extremely patronizing fashion, "It really is so hard to get good help nowadays."

Convinced as I was of Siamese smartness, there was one large exception I would make to their being the smartest of cats. This included almost any female stray of any breed with kittens. My mail brought me several remarkably convincing examples of this, of which I shall choose just two. The first came in a letter I received from Jeanne Baggot-Guise, of Mystic Island, New Jersey, a woman who rescued, one winter's night, an extremely wild stray whom she named Lady Jane:

> One night I heard a kitten's distress call; I thought it was a bird at first. I went out front to look, and there was Jane. About eight feet away was a kitten, eyes open but not yet walking. "Jane," I said, "is this your baby?" "I never saw that kitten in my life," she replied. "Jane, there's no other cat around right now, and this kitten did not get here by itself." "Nope," she said, "not mine." So I sighed and took the kitten inside. A little while later, as I showed my husband The Latest, I heard that piercing cry again.
>
> I went outside again. This time there were two more kittens, and Jane was much closer to them. I looked at

> her, she looked at me. I said, "Jane, if you think I'm going to nurse three babies when you have all the facilities right at hand you're nuts." I picked up the kittens, picked up Jane (the one and only time she let me) and marched into the house. Jane said, "Oh, there's my other baby!" Mother and children took up residence in what was then our green room (you'll never guess what color it's painted now) and, in a word, throve.

The second example came from Donna Hess, of Palm City, Florida. Her husband's and her story also began with a wild stray, this one named Shadee. At the beginning, however, Shadee was not about to give up her freedom. She would appear at the Hess home for an occasional meal and would once in a while allow herself to be groomed, but that was all. She would not stay overnight. Soon, however, it became clear to the Hesses that Shadee was pregnant. Then, one night, she disappeared. Finally, many nights later — and four hours late for dinner — she reappeared once more, this time slim and trim. And, again, each night after dinner she would disappear again, obviously going to her kittens.

The Hesses searched everywhere for Shadee's kittens, but with no success:

> As time passed we began to wonder if the kittens were even alive. Then, exactly six weeks after her delivery, Shadee arrived at our house at a very unusual hour, 8:45 AM. Following closely behind her was the most beautiful, fat, fluffy and furry female kitten we had ever seen. She brought her offspring directly to us, meowed for breakfast, and ultimately decided to spend the afternoon. And that evening, after leaving her kitten, she once more disappeared.
>
> My husband and I came to the conclusion that there was only one kitten. Time would prove us much in error.

> The next time, she brought two more kittens. The final time, three more. At long last Shadee, too, stayed for good.

The Hess story was not, however, over. Two of the kittens were deformed. One was missing a right front leg, the other a right hind leg. The Hesses' veterinarian declared that the two deformed cats were not adoptable, and should be destroyed. The Hesses went to another veterinarian — in fact they went to four other veterinarians — and then ended up with five unanimous opinions. The deformed kittens should be destroyed. The Hesses did not agree. They placed ads in the local newspapers, and put up posters everywhere:

> One of my clients at the beauty shop where I work noticed one of our posters with a picture of the two deformed kittens. She called and agreed to stop by to see them.
>
> She informed me that she and her family had recently moved from a "no-pet" condo and were looking for a small pet for their twelve-year-old daughter. They arrived as promised, and fell in love with Peg and Chester. At this point, after a family discussion, it was decided to adopt both "unadoptable" kittens. We later learned that the husband in the family is an amputee. He had only one arm, and the daughter who wanted Peg and Chester had never known the father any other way.

In the end, however, I rested my case on cat smartness on neither a Siamese nor a cat mother but rather on two tomcats of uncertain origin whose claim to cat smartness came from one single act. The first story was sent to me by Diane Benedetto, of Boca Raton, Florida. It concerned a tom whom she did not even own — he was instead owned by a friend of hers. The cat, it seemed, regularly disappeared every Tuesday night and at exactly the same time, 7 P.M. Then, at exactly the same time each Tuesday — midnight — he returned and meowed to get in. Ms. Benedetto's friend became more and more curious about his cat's Tuesday nights — so much so that he decided, one Tuesday, to follow him, thereby becoming perhaps the first man ever to put a tail on his own cat:

> It was not easy, as the cat went through backyards, over fences, and down alleys until he came at last to a large two-story building. He then went up the fire escape of this building and settled down by a window. Somehow his owner managed to keep up with him but finally with the cat just sitting there on the fire escape and looking inside the owner decided that his cat had a friend in there and was waiting for it to come out. In any case he decided that was the place for a stakeout and he waited, too. He looked at his watch — it was ten minutes to eight. The wait seemed to go on and on. Suddenly the cat's tail began to twitch. The man looked at his watch — it was exactly ten minutes past eight. Almost immediately a voice from inside the room rang out. "Bingo," it said.

The second story was perhaps even more memorable. It was sent to me by Frederic Wyatt, of North Hollywood, California. His report was brief:

> We bought our home in California in October, 1965. With the purchase we acquired a lovely, affectionate cat who had obviously resided there for some time. Our relationship was ideal until the day of the California earthquake in the San Fernando Valley. During it, our cat disappeared. In time he reappeared — but not at our house. Instead he took up residence across the street. Never again did he darken our door.

Obviously that cat had gone to his final reward before the major San Francisco earthquake of 1989, but it is entirely possible that one of the smaller quakes following the '65 one may well have necessitated still another move for him. In any case, as I thought of these two stories I wondered what Polar Bear would do in similar situations. I did not play Bingo, but I wondered if I did and he came to watch me he would not find it a very dull game when compared to one of my good, crisp two-hour chess matches. As for the earthquake theory, I knew that Polar Bear did not regard me, as the Siamese cat Cinderella regarded Mr. Huber, as the person responsible for turning on the sun in the morning. On the other hand he did hold me responsible for every kind of weather he didn't like. If it was too cold in the winter, and there was snow on the balcony, it was my fault. If it was too hot in the summer, and there was a thunderstorm, it was my fault, too. All noisy holidays were my fault — the Fourth of July and firecrackers, Halloween and people at the door in crazy costumes, St. Patrick's Day, and Memorial Day, Labor Day and any other day when they had parades with brass and drums were my fault. Was I really sure he would not regard an earthquake too as my fault? And even if he did, would it then be possible for him, in his hard little heart, to forgive not just the earthquake but such an awful pun?

III ◦ *First Dog*

One thing I have never known about Polar Bear, and do not know to this day, is how old he is. Since I rescued him ten years ago he has not gotten any younger but, I repeat, I do not know his age exactly. I do know, however, that whatever age he is, he doesn't act it. He jumps and pounces around and plays with his toys and bats the ball of yarn under his scratching post almost the way he did when he was a kitten. I presume this, because of course I did not know him when he was a kitten.

That actually is one of the fascinations of cats — they play practically their whole lives the way they did as kittens. But, frankly, I think some of Polar Bear's behavior nowadays is, for a cat of his years, on the unseemly side. I sometimes wish, indeed, that he would spend a little more effort trying to emulate me in learning how to age gracefully.

At the time I rescued him, Susan Thompson, his vet, thought he was about two, but she has lately amended this upward and she now feels he could have been, at the time of the rescue, as much as five. Therefore, as I write this, as I say ten years later, he is somewhere between twelve and fifteen.

I on the other hand, am somewhere between sixty and seventy. I am very secure about my age. I tell close friends exactly how old I am except of course for the irritating kind who are always adding a year on you behind your back — the kind who will tell you that if you were born, say, in 1920 and it is now 1990, you're seventy. You're not, of course. You weren't *one* in 1920, for Pete's sake, you were *zero* in 1920, and you weren't anywhere near one until 1921. And so you're not seventy, you're sixty-nine. It's just simple mathematics. A child could figure it out.

The only time I take a year or two or even a few years off my age is when I'm with some younger woman, and I want to make her feel more comfortable. Of course I'm careful — you have to be nowadays. Some women will go rummaging around on or in your dresser for your passport or driver's license or go prying into some old article about you which, it will be just your luck, will turn out to be one which is full of inaccuracies about your age.

Actually the only thing that makes my blood boil about this whole age business are those television and radio people who mention your birthday when it comes around every year. They wish you a happy birthday, which is very nice of them and all very well, but then, for Crow Mike, out of a clear blue they blab out exactly what birthday it is. That really gets my dander up — and I'm sure it would get Polar Bear's up, too. Of course they're probably very young children themselves and don't know the first thing about age, but to be allowed to get away with doing that on the public airways is just beyond the pale. What is the FCC for? — after all, you and I are paying for it.

Anyway, as I said, I'm very secure about my age. And I only wish Polar Bear would be more like me and not go charging around the apartment when I have company as if there was no tomorrow. I had even hoped that, as he grew older, he would grow more mellow. The trouble is, he has not grown more mellow, he has grown less mellow. In fact he has become a curmudgeon, and even if you know very little about curmudgeons you should know that the word "mellow" is not in the vocabulary of any self-respecting curmudgeon you would care to meet in this world or the next.

Actually at first I thought it was very interesting that Polar Bear had become a curmudgeon. I remember very well just where I was when I first noticed it, the way we do about famous historical events. I was in the kitchen, in fact, and I had just taken his can out of the refrigerator — the same one he had refused to eat in the morning. And, instead of the cross "aeiou" I expected with the usual argument I knew we'd have to follow, I heard instead, unmistakably, a growl. I turned and looked at him. I told him that I could not believe my ears, whereupon, as if he knew perfectly well what I was saying, he looked first at the food and then at me and then, if you please, he growled again. This time I was totally nonplussed, and, frankly, I am never totally nonplussed. Once in a while I may be a little nonplussed. But usually, if I do say so, I am plussed. But this time I wasn't. The fact was incontrovertible. He had growled — and since he was a cat and not a dog, there was only one thing he could be. And that, of course, was a curmudgeon.

As I said at first, I thought it was very interesting that he had become a curmudgeon. Frankly, I'd never heard of a curmudgeon cat, and I thought it added to his uniqueness. But, as I thought about it some more, I also realized that it posed a problem. This was that, since I was already a curmudgeon, it meant there were now two curmudgeons under one roof. And that was, I knew, basically an untenable situation. I will tell you very candidly that two curmudgeons under one roof is one curmudgeon too many — and this holds just as true when one curmudgeon is a curmudgeon person and the other is a curmudgeon cat as it does when both are curmudgeon persons or, for that matter, I would assume, when both are curmudgeon cats.

I have had personal experience with two curmudgeons under one roof and I have never forgotten it. They were two Boston uncles of mine and they lived in the same apartment house. But even though they did not live in the same apartment, it still didn't work. They didn't speak to each other. And they hadn't spoken for years.

In fairness, on family occasions such as Thanksgiving or Christmas, they would occasionally speak through a third party such as me. If the salt, for example, was in front of one of them and the other wanted it, they would ask me — Mother always had me sit between them — to ask "your uncle" please to pass the salt. They never, I should add, split infinitives. And it worked fine — the other uncle passed the salt — not to the first uncle, of course, but to me, and then I passed it to him. In fairness, too, one of the uncles at least tried to set up some operative public ground rules when they passed each other on the public street. One day outside Boston's Somerset Club, that venerable institution to which both of them of course belonged, one broke their then-standing ten-year no-talking streak, which I believe was the Boston record at that time. "Sir," he said to the other uncle, "do we bow when we meet or not? It is a matter of complete indifference to me — it is for you to decide." The other uncle was taken so totally aback by this river of conversation after so many silent years that he apparently made what the first uncle construed as, if not a whole bow, at least a curt nod. In any case, from that time on they did, on passing, indeed curtly nod to one another. But they never did speak to each other and, shortly before their deaths, they established what I believe is the still-standing Boston record — one in which my entire family has taken, and quite pardonably I believe, quiet pride.

The Boston in which I grew up was a fertile ground for the breeding of curmudgeons, as well as for their care and feeding. I do not remember exactly when I became one, but I believe it was in the latter years of my late marriage. I also believe the reason for it was that it suddenly dawned on me one day, when I was reading in the paper about a woman wrestler, that being a curmudgeon was the last thing in the world that a man can be that a woman cannot be. Women can be irritating — after all, they are women — but they cannot be curmudgeons. Nowadays they can be truck drivers and weight lifters, hammer throwers and jockeys, firepersons, frogpersons, and even, I presume, Teenage Mutant Ninja Turtlepersons. But they cannot be curmudgeons. This is not to say that women have not tried to be curmudgeons — they have indeed. In fact I personally knew one — my aunt Lolla, who was, as a matter of fact, the wife of my Uncle Bagnalls, one of those uncles I mentioned. Aunt Lolla tried all her life to be a curmudgeon, but all she succeeded in doing was making Uncle Bagnalls a bachelor.

Even the dictionary defines curmudgeon as "a gruff and irritable elderly man." This is, of course, not entirely accurate. All right, maturity is part and parcel of decent curmudgeonry, but *elderly,* for Pete's sweet sake, that's nonsense. The reason is simple — dictionaries are obviously written by young people — who else would have the time? But you would think some older person would have caught the error and also taught them that there's a world of difference between being elderly and being mature. Many's the time I have asked a young person if he or she has the slightest idea of what a curmudgeon is, and you simply cannot believe some of the answers I've received. I remember one young man who told me he thought it was some kind of medieval weapon, and another one who thought for some time and then blurted out he thought it was a large fish. For all I know, they both worked on the dictionary.

Nonetheless, giving the devil his due, the dictionary does at least have the decency, where curmudgeons are concerned, to confine them to men. But when Polar Bear became a curmudgeon, I could not help wondering if curmudgeonry among cats was confined to male cats. Frankly, between you and me and the gatepost, now that I think about it I've met more unfriendly female cats than I have male cats, and it may well be that many of these were trying to be curmudgeons, too, just like my aunt Lolla. Whether they would be successful at it, of course, is another story. The fact is it takes, if I do say so, a lot of hard work to become an all-round curmudgeon. And, although Polar Bear took to it like a duck to water, I very much doubt if your average female cat would be able to master the art — if she would excuse that expression — as well as he had. They well many have, within the limits of their gender, but so far, until I see one with my own eyes, and watch her in operation, I'm from Missouri.

Anyway, to go back to where I was, I'm not from Missouri, I am from Boston. And, as I said, Boston has many curmudgeons and in particular it has many curmudgeon writers. I have often wondered why this is so, and one reason I have come to is that they get sick and tired of answering people who ask them how they write.

For myself, I don't mind telling people how I write except I am not inordinately fond of other writers telling me how *they* write. Indeed, over the years I notice I've come to prefer dead writers to living writers. I am particularly irritated by young writers who tell me they write on word processors. As a person who began his difficulties with the modern world with trying to operate a Venetian blind, I feel that to try to take up a word processor would be, for me, both foolhardy and probably dangerous. I did have a woman who came to my apartment one day and who, for a charge of $50, tried to explain to me the operation of a memory typewriter. I got as far as watching that typewriter grab the paper and roll it around when I asked her to please take it away. It was not only frightening me, it was also frightening Polar Bear. He doesn't like anything working by itself, and, frankly, he's not much on working in general.

Actually, the way I write is in longhand. I don't know how many people are still familiar with longhand — from the letters I've received I would gather very few. But I find it the best way to write a first draft because, since even I can't read some of it, it is at least not too definite and I do not get discouraged by it. Later I try to put it on a typewriter but not on any word processor or memory typewriter or anything like that. It is an old-fashioned typewriter where you can at least see every word you put down, and not one of those awful little ball things where you can't see anything until it's too damn late to do anything about it.

People also ask where I write. The best place for a writer to write, my friend the late Ring Lardner once said, is in a hotel room that is too expensive for you. I have tried this and I agree with Ring up to a point — but this point comes when all these modern hotels decided to have all their windows permanently sealed. The idea, as I understand it, is not to keep writers from jumping out the window — which is, after all, none of their business — but rather to keep down the air-conditioning costs in the hot weather, when people open up their windows and forget to turn off the air conditioner. Whatever it is, it's an outrage. I think writing in a sealed-windowed hotel room might be satisfactory for writing a history of submarine disasters or perhaps a new ending for the opera *Aida,* but otherwise I would not recommend it.

There are many other reasons why writers become curmudgeons. First and foremost of these are editors. The first letter I received from the first book I ever wrote came from the very first editor I ever had, at the old *Saturday Evening Post.* His name was J. Bryan III and he has since become a fine writer and, I presume if he still edits, is still a terrible editor. In any case, he wrote me a single-sentence criticism of my whole book. "The world 'only,' " he wrote, "is an adverb and should immediately precede the word it modifies — it should not be thrown into a sentence at random." To this day I'm terrified of the word, and only use it on only the rarest possible occasions.

At the present time I have another editor, Walter Anderson of *Parade* magazine, who is equally terrible but for an entirely different reason. All editors, I have noticed through the years, have a plethora of phobias and Mr. Anderson is no exception. His particular phobia is length. I do not know whether this was because, as a child, he was not allowed to wear long pants until after the other boys in his class wore them, or whether, in growing up, he aspired to the basketball team, but I do know that whatever you give him to read he would like it better if there was less of it.

It is extremely difficult to work for such a man, but through the years what has sustained me is that I have found numerous instances of far more illustrious writers than I who have also suffered under this same heartlessness. My favorite example of this was the late, great James Thurber. In his early days as a reporter, Mr. Thurber was forced to labor in the vineyards of a newspaper editor in Ohio who wanted every article as short as possible. Furthermore, he wanted both the opening paragraph that way and even the opening sentence. Dispatched one evening to cover a murder, Thurber dutifully turned in his story within the requirements. "Dead," he wrote. "That's what the bullet-ridden body of the man found outside the Elm Street Saloon last night was."

There is, I would believe, only one thing worse for a writer than having such an editor. That is having an editor who edits at the source. I have now two of these. The first, as all faithful readers of my last book will recall, is my assistant, a woman named Marian Probst. Ms. Probst came to me during the Spanish War and, as far as I'm concerned, is still on trial. And, make no mistake about it, a trying woman she is. As I've told you, I write my first drafts in longhand, and in the old days I used to give them to Marian to type. If Marian did not like a sentence or some line, she had three policies — one was to change it, the second was to leave it out, and the third was to leave out the whole paragraph. Worse, she never gave me back my first copy at all — I think, like Polar Bear, she ate it. In any case, one day, after finding wholesale changes, I said to her, "Women are better at simple, repetitive tasks." In those happy days, I hasten to add, we men could sometimes get away with saying things like that. But not, even in those days, with Marian. "Yes," she replied, "like listening to simple, repetitive jokes." Marian really is one of the many crosses I have to bear. Fortunately I have the patience of Job.

And, as if this were not enough, Marian is not the only editor-at-the-source with whom I have to cope. The second is none other than Polar Bear himself. Polar Bear sits, you see, on the shelf of the typewriter table on the left side of my old-fashioned typewriter, where the bar goes out as you type. And, as he has gotten older, he has become less and less inclined to move even when the bar runs into him. Remember, I do have a bell on the typewriter, and the bell is supposed to ring toward the end of the line and well before the bar runs into him. But either Polar Bear's hearing isn't as good as it was or he doesn't like bells. Whatever it is, he doesn't move, and what I have is not only the messiest right-hand margin you could imagine but also, on occasion, the necessity of actually having to change to a shorter word to accommodate him. If that is not editing at the source I do not know what it is — really, it's a wonder this book gets through to you at all.

Being, as I am, put upon so much of the time during the week, you may be sure that when it comes to my week-ends I do what I please. This is not only not writing but it is also actually doing something which is as far from writing as possible. This is playing chess. It is only a short walk from my apartment to a place in Central Park which is called the Chess House. It is on a hill near the old Carousel — which plays, incidentally, just three awful tunes over and over — but it is otherwise a very pleasant place. It features stone tables with chessboards on them which were donated by the late New York philanthropist Bernard Baruch. Of course some people of lesser mentality also use these tables to play checkers and make entirely too much noise while they are doing so, but what we regular chess nuts do is to bring our own chessmen in bags and meet there and play. There is also an inside house to which in very inclement weather we repair, but very seldom. Often I have played outside with rain pouring down, and if you're ahead you don't notice it and ignore it. Your opponent, of course, if he's behind, does notice the rain, and always wants to declare a draw or quit. But you just have to ignore him, and make your move.

In any case, on one particular Saturday I was, as usual, determined to go to the Park and I was also determined, after reading all those letters from people who had successfully taught their cats to walk in harnesses on leashes, to take Polar Bear with me.

The minute he saw me take the harness out Polar Bear decided he didn't want to go and, as usual, went under the bed. Afterward, when I had routed him out, he lay around gasping and feigning various illnesses such as having swallowed several huge hairballs. I am used to this, however, and, taking no prisoners, soon had him in harness — whereupon I picked up both him and my chess pieces and went down the elevator and across the street and into the Park. Here I put Polar Bear down and gave a gay little skip which I thought would indicate to him that it was now walking time. Instead, he just glared at me as if he hoped nobody else was looking.

In vain I pointed out joggers and bicyclists and all sorts of people doing all sorts of exercise. We were in a world, I told him very firmly, which every day grew more and more conscious of fitness — even I walked back and forth to my chess every Saturday and Sunday, rain or shine, and yet there he was, just like a prairie dog or a mole, not willing to make anything but a tiny little circle around the end of the leash. All right, I said, if that was what he was going to do, he could jolly well just spend the rest of the afternoon sitting on my lap and watching chess and getting fatter and more out of shape by the minute.

One of the exciting things about playing chess in the Park is, you never know until you get there with whom you're going to play. You know their faces and their styles of play and even some of their first names — after all, you've been playing with them for years. But you really never learn much else about them because chess is so engrossing that there's really no place for unimportant social amenities like last names or occupations. Once in a while you look forward to playing someone in particular — he might have lucked out on you last week and won a game — and then when you get there you can't find him and you ask around and find he died. It really can be very irritating, especially if he won that last game from you, but of course there's nothing you can do about it except play someone else. Once in a while one of us regulars will even take on a newcomer, if we've just won a game from a regular and we're in a bonhomous mood. Of course we know it probably will be a very short game, but at least it gives the new fellow a chance to learn something.

On this particular Saturday, still carrying Polar Bear, I walked up the ramp to the Chess House and, to my amazement, I saw nobody outside at the stone tables. I couldn't believe it — on a Saturday afternoon, too. I knew they couldn't all be inside the Chess House because it wasn't raining. And they couldn't all have died at once.

I realized I had to find out what was the matter, so I proceeded right up the Chess House door. There they all were, inside, rain or no rain, and there was also a young woman from the Parks Department. She told me that the reason everyone was inside was that there was going to be a special Park event — a Hungarian Grand Master would be coming who had agreed to play us all simultaneously. As she asked me if I wanted to participate, I noticed that she had a curious smile on her face.

I told her I would indeed like to participate. I also implied that she could wipe that smile right off her face — I would give that Hungarian Grand Master a game he would not soon forget. Meanwhile, at the same time I informed her that I would like to make a call to my assistant, because Polar Bear did not like to be inside the Chess House and, anyway, I saw no reason to give that Hungarian Grand Master the advantage of my having to hold Polar Bear and play him at the same time.

I went and called Marian and told her there was an emergency. A Hungarian Grand Master was coming to play me in the Park and I had Polar Bear with me and she would have to come and hold him and take him until I got through. I told her that it shouldn't take me too long. The fellow might be a Grand Master but I was at the top of my game.

Marian was reluctant — she has never understood that, in the Good Old Days, everybody worked half a day on Saturday. And everybody was happier, too. I had to wait quite a while, but at last Marian appeared and I gave her Polar Bear and went inside and joined the others at the long table which had been set up with perhaps twenty boards. There were seats for all of us beside the boards on one side, and on the other side there were no seats because the Grand Master would walk from board to board playing us all.

As I waited for him to appear, I realized I had something of an advantage over him. He would probably think he was up against just an ordinary player, but he would not be — he would be up against Yours Truly. I do not say I am a Grand Master, or for that matter a Master, but I am an Expert, which is the next category, and I surely could have been a Master if I had started my chess career earlier and had had time to read all those damned chess books which those awful young Masters I'm always running into at tournaments are always reading. Remember, too, I'd gotten sidetracked into getting married, which can be a terrible time-waster.

Not that I wanted to make any excuses. There is no luck in chess. You start even and you can't say that the wind was against you or you had the sun in your eyes or anything else you can say in practically any other sport you could mention. Even the excuse that you haven't played for a long time is perilous — an experienced opponent will know soon enough whether there is any truth in this. As for saying you are suffering from some kind of illness, the establishment of this as a preamble for a match was put to rest for all time by the great English champion, Alexander. Late in life Grand Master Alexander was faced with a young whippersnapper who said he was sorry, he didn't believe he would be able to give him a good match — he had been ill. Alexander fixed a steely eye on the young man — the steely eye is very important to this story — and spoke slowly. "Young man," he said, "in forty years of tournament play I do not believe I have ever defeated a wholly well man."

One thing I did resolve to tell that Hungarian fellow, whoever he was, was that he should know he was up against a man who had played not one game but two games with Bobby Fischer. Actually the match had not occurred in a tournament, but I saw no reason to stress that fact. What had happened was that Fischer, then sixteen years old, had come to the office of Norman Cousins at the *Saturday Review* at a time when I was also there. So, too, was Fischer's mother, who had decided that Mr. Cousins was the person to persuade her son to go to college — something which Fischer did not, apparently, want to do.

Mr. Cousins undertook his task with his usual determination. "I understand, Bobby," he began, "you don't want to go to college." "Nah," replied Fischer. "Bobby," Cousins pursued, "is there some reason none of us may understand that you don't want to go to college?" "Yah," said Fischer. Cousins smiled — he was zeroing in, he knew, on the crux of the matter. "Why, Bobby?" he asked gently. Replied Fischer, "Too much homework." Still Cousins refused to give up. "Bobby," he said, "I think you don't understand college. College isn't just books and study and homework. College teaches us who we are. Wouldn't you, Bobby," he asked, "like to know who you are?" Fischer looked at him curiously. "I know who I am," he said. "Who are you?"

The discussion was over. But afterward, as I said, I played two games with the then-new champion. As it happened I didn't win either one. But then, I hadn't played in some time and, as I recall, I was not feeling well.

At long last the Hungarian appeared. I could not believe my eyes. Immediately I knew why the Parks Department woman had smiled when she asked me to play. "Your opponent," she said, as the introductions were made, "is twelve years old." But that was not the final straw. The twelve-year-old was not even a *he* — he was a *she*.

The whole thing was too ridiculous. I am a very broad-minded man about women taking up chess. I think it's good for the game and I have several times gone out of my way to play one and help her with her strategy or in any other way I can. But a twelve-year-old — really, that was going too far. Just the same, I had agreed, and to back out then would not only be ungentlemanly but for all I knew might cause some kind of international incident.

Dutifully, albeit reluctantly, I sat down and waited until the child approached my board. I tried not to be patronizing or too smug but it wasn't easy. Honestly, she was an infant. She could hardly see over the table and her eyes were on a level with the pieces.

Anyway she moved pawn to King 4. And as I waited — you do not make your move until she comes back to your board — I decided on a traditional Sicilian, to which I would later add the fianchettoing of not just my king-side bishop but also my queen-side — so that I could later sweep the diagonals across the board. There was no doubt in my mind that before the game was over I would make that little girl mind her *p*'s and *q*'s. And I didn't mean the old-fashioned *p*'s and *q*'s, either — I meant pawns and queens.

Something — I don't know what it was — went wrong. First I lost a pawn. I wasn't happy about that, but I attributed it either to overconfidence or condescension or perhaps both. Anyway, I quickly pulled myself together. Surely I could spot that child a pawn, and somewhere in the middle of the game my male logic would come to the fore. But somehow, in the middle of that middle game, I suddenly and unaccountably lost a knight. I really couldn't believe the predicament I'd let myself into. It was some kind of mental aberration, I felt, caused undoubtedly by my subconscious being sorry for my little opponent. Finally, out of the blue, on her nineteenth move, I heard a tiny-voiced squeaky whisper say something like "shah," by which I assumed she meant "check." And, sure enough, it was a perfectly good check. Then, as I moved out of check, on her twentieth move she reached what seemed her whole arm length with her queen and, still in that ghastly voice, said gently, "Shah mat." I couldn't believe it. I had been checkmated by a twelve-year-old girl.

Now, I want to say here and now that I am as good a sport as the next man when it comes to losing a chess game. In other words, I do not throw the pieces or strike my opponent physically. I may, after a game in which I made a blunder and lost — we always lose, the other person never wins — kick a few trees on my way back from the Park, but I try to do it so that nobody sees it. This time, in view of the situation, I was the soul of chess sportsmanship. I even stood up and shook hands with that damned little twerp. And, afterward, I stood around graciously and watched, one by one, all my pals also lose. I don't say I was hoping for this to happen, but Somerset Maugham's statement did cross my mind: "All of us like to see our friends get ahead," he said, "but not too far."

It is true that, as I walked outside the Chess House, I did kick the door — but the plain fact was, the door was in my way. And, once outside, I put my mind on doing some good, sound positive thinking. What *was* chess, after all, I asked myself. It was just a game, for heaven's sakes. It was just plain damned foolishness to think it was a test of intelligence or logic or anything like that, or even — I hesitated to admit this on that particular occasion — a test of one's masculinity. And, I went on thinking, when you come right down to it, a child has a huge advantage over an adult. A child has nothing else in his rotten little mind except winning, whereas a person like myself has dozens of other far more important things to think of. And, as far as the him being a her, well again, carrying the whole thing to its logical conclusion, that just added to the strength of my argument. Being a girl, she undoubtedly had even less on her mind than a boy would have.

In other words, as I thought the thing through, I felt, if not all myself again, at least better. At this moment I saw Marian sitting with Polar Bear at one of the tables in the sun. "I went in and watched for a while," she said, "but you never saw me. You never even saw Polar Bear." I told her chess was like that — you never really notice anything when you're playing chess. "How," she asked brightly, "did you come out?"

Marian is always asking things like that brightly because

she's not bright enough to know not to ask them. It's really infuriating. She should have known that if I'd won I would have told her. Reluctantly I grunted something about losing. And Marian wouldn't let it go. She never lets anything like that go, which is why I should have let her go long ago. "You lost!" she exclaimed. "To that little girl! The one playing you all at once!"

I asked her to please keep her voice down. There was no necessity for broadcasting the whole damned thing all over the Park. And anyway, I told her, it wasn't really playing all of us at once. It was what was called "simultaneous," which was very different. I started trying to explain it, but I gave up. I wasn't feeling very well, I told her. I think I'm sick. But Marian, of course, wouldn't let that go. "Well, at least," she said, "you didn't say that before you started. And so she couldn't say that in forty years of tournament play she'd never defeated a wholly well man. She wasn't old enough."

One of the really terrible things about Marian is her memory. She remembers everything. I have never really seen why God gave so many women so many good memories and so many men so many rotten memories. They not only don't need them as much as we do, they are also always remembering things that are very embarrassing to us. What happened that day was a perfect example. It's bad enough Marian remembers every one of my favorite stories by heart, but to bring one of them up at a time like that — particularly when she has never learned the first thing about chess — was really too much. If women have such good memories, why in heaven's name can't they use them to remember when *not* to remember things?

In any case, on the walk out of the chess place, I tried

to explain to her that playing a group of players simultaneously is actually an advantage for the man — or, in that particular case, a woman — player. In the first place, it meant that the person gets the white pieces and therefore had the first move, which is an advantage. In the second-place, that person doesn't have to make a move until he or she gets to your board, whereupon you have to make your move the minute he or she arrives. In other words, the pressure really is on you and not on the person playing you.

I was just warming up to my explanation of the whole thing — it was not easy, because Marian just does not have my kind of logical thought process — when, all of a sudden, with one bound and one bounce, something leaped into our midst which at first seemed, not only to Marian and to me but also, I'm sure, to Polar Bear, a huge sheep.

All right, we were at that moment at a part of the Park which is called Sheep Meadow, but there hasn't been a sheep in Sheep Meadow since anyone can remember. Actually what had jumped into Marian's and my lap was not, of course, a sheep. It was, in fact, an Olde English sheep dog — an almost exact replica of my very first dog. As I hugged and patted him, I did so with some difficulty, because as the dog had leaped, Polar Bear had also leaped and had taken up a position literally on top of my head with both paws digging, respectively, into both my ears. Nonetheless, I could hear well his steady stream of hisses. I think that the real trouble was that he had never in all his life seen anything like an Olde English sheep dog and he had not the slightest idea of what it was. But to him, whatever it was, there was entirely too much of it, and it certainly did not belong with any civilized cat. Indeed, I had the distinct impression that he regarded it as a very bad cross between a giant sloth bear and the Creature from the Lost Lagoon or whatever the name of that movie was.

Certainly lost the creature was, and whether or not Polar Bear regarded it as belonging to some kind of remote wilderness, and the more remote the better, our immediate problem was to try to locate its owner. Marian suggested that, since the dog did not have a collar or a leash, I use my belt for both of them. I protested. Despite my fitness program, which I've already said entailed regular walks to and from my chess, I very much doubted that my trousers could be counted on to hold up without my belt, particularly when I had both hands on Polar Bear.

Marian would not hear of this. Taking Polar Bear from me, she motioned me to proceed with the makeshift collar and leash. And so, in short order, with the Creature leading the way — we hoped in the direction he had come from — and with me hanging on for dear life, with one hand on the end of my belt and with the other on my trousers, we began our journey. On the way I gave Marian, for her edification, a brief synopsis, based on the memories of my first dog, Brookie, of the wonderful qualities of the Olde English sheep dog. I mentioned how friendly they were, how good with children, and how, because they didn't have any tails, they invariably wagged their whole back ends. I also pointed out that, while they didn't seem to have any eyes in their face underneath all that hair, they really did see very well or at least were supposed to. I did tell her, though, that actually Brookie never did see very well and was always barking or growling at good things he came up on or were coming at him and was always panting happily and licking at bad things. Finally I mentioned how brave they were, and loyal to their people, but that despite this they were terrific wanderers and were always going long distances and getting lost. I also reminded her that the "Olde" in Olde English sheep dog was always spelled with an *e,* which showed how really old they were. This one was not, however, olde at all. He was, in fact, still a puppye.

The good news was that since we knew there weren't many Olde English sheep dogs in the Park we stood a very good chance, even if we did not locate the dog's owner, of at least locating somebody who knew the dog and would lead us to his person. The bad news was that it was starting to get dark, and Central Park is a very large place, and it became clearer and clearer that we had less and less chance of finding either the dog's person or even someone who knew him or her. Actually all we found were critics. One lady was very cross — "You ought to be ashamed of yourself," she said to me. "That leash is too short for a big dog." And one man was not happy about Marian and Polar Bear. "That cat is terrified of that dog," he said. "You ought to take him home."

In the end we decided to take that man's advice. The owner, we decided, might well be, for all we knew, home, too, and already calling up shelters and reporting a Lost Dog. We too should probably be back in my apartment reporting a Found Dog.

For Polar Bear the next-to-final straw was entering the apartment building, going up in the elevator, and realizing that the huge beast, which to him was at best an outside dog, was now going to be admitted into his sanctum sanctorum. But the last final straw for him came when we actually entered. Marian still had Polar Bear in her arms and I still had the creature by the leash, but neither of us had either for long. The dog leaped off the leash from me and made a beeline for the kitchen. First, with one slurp, he drank all of Polar Bear's water and then promptly moved on to Polar Bear's favorite — his bowl of niblets. At that point Polar Bear let out one loud hiss and, using Marian's breast as a springboard, dove, both claws extended, for wherever he assumed would be the sheep dog's eyes — if indeed he had any.

I want you to know that here was another crisis, and here again I was not found wanting. Not for nothing had I been one of Milton Academy's great catchers — the catcher who, if I do say so, was always called upon to warm up our great pitcher, Slim Curtiss. All right, they might use another catcher in the actual game, but when it came down to seeing how much "stuff" Slim had on that day and to handle those warm-up pitches when he was fresh, you can imagine on whom they called. And this crisis, I knew in a flash, was no warm-up — it was a game situation. The game was on the line, and there was going to be a play at the plate — the crucial test for any catcher worth his salt.

I forgot my trousers completely. I dropped down and with all my instincts working threw one leg out. This was to guard the plate — i.e., the dog's head — still down in the bowl. At the same time, I put both hands out in a ball-catching position to meet the onflying runner — i.e., Polar Bear. And, as I say, I did my job. Polar Bear never reached that plate or bowl at all — he was out by a mile, and only my leg mashed into the sheep dog. And remember, I caught Polar Bear without even one of my trusty old catcher's mitts in my hands. When you came right down to it, I caught a Bear bare-handed. And, make no mistake, I paid for it in the palms of both hands.

Of course, as I raised Polar Bear over my head, I told

Marian it was nothing — just a scratch. I did not even receive my proper moment of triumph, because the dog, having finished the niblets, was obviously determined to leap up and have a turn at bat, with both his paws, at Polar Bear. I had done my duty, however, and, with my trousers still in a precarious position, I graciously allowed Marian to do the mopping up. She did a very good job, too — for her — of placing herself between the dog and me. "You take Polar Bear to the bedroom," she commanded, taking the sheep dog again by the end of the belt and hauling him over in front of the fire. "I'll keep the dog here and start making some calls about him."

At this, almost docilely, the sheep dog made a typical dog circle in front of the fireplace and lay down. I honestly think he was fast asleep before Polar Bear, watching from my shoulder, could believe what he was doing. Actually, I think in some ways his going to sleep infuriated Polar Bear even more than the attack on his provisions. In any case, Polar Bear not only resumed his hissing but also, if I was not mistaken, began spitting with rage. Still holding him firmly, I told him to mind his manners — that, whatever the situation, he was still the host and the dog was our guest. But this time I was just going through the motions. Where Polar Bear and the Olde English sheep dog were concerned, what you had was Iran and Iraq. I know a lost cause when I see one, and without further ado I took him to the bedroom and shut the door. There, leaving him to fuss and fume at the door, I went over to the bed and lay down. I could feel a nap coming on. Chess is very tiring, you know — particularly when you lose.

Almost immediately, it seemed, I was in Dreamland — literally. And here I would like to say a word about my dreams. In my younger days I didn't always have good dreams, in the sense of their coming out right. I don't know anybody who always does have them that way unless they're some damn saint or something. But what I almost always did have were good dreams in the sense of well-written dreams. They had a beginning, and a middle and an end. You had somebody to root for — usually yourself — and they didn't skimp on the production. You had a large cast and you went to interesting places and you had attractive girls and particularly one *very* attractive one. You didn't always get her in the end, but so what? You can't win them all, and at least you got a good run for your money. Indeed, in some of those dreams there was so much going on you got what amounted to a double feature, and not one of those one A, one B jobs, either. Often you got two straight A's.

Today, like so many things nowadays, at least to my experience, dreams are not only not as good as they used to be; most of them are not worth dreaming. They're just a waste of good sleeping time. Maybe they think they're trying to make us old-fashioned "escape" dreams, because they think that's what the public wants. Whatever they think, they're not doing the job. What they're making are dreams which are always putting you somewhere where there is no way out, or where you're trying to get up a wall with nothing to get a purchase on. My guess is they're just trying to turn them out too fast to meet some deadline for some production schedule or something. Whatever they're doing, what you get is one little low-budget job after another. The casts are minimal and the acting, what there is of it, is nothing but overacting. Frankly, I haven't dreamed a single dream in years that couldn't use more work and a complete rewrite, a new director, and probably a new producer as well.

That afternoon's dream was typical. I expected to have one about chess, but I wasn't looking forward to it because I knew they'd probably spend the whole dream on my blunder in losing to that damned twelve-year-old girl. In the old days, of course, they wouldn't have done that. They wouldn't have mentioned that blunder, and they would have given me a good old-fashioned dream I could get my teeth into — like playing Bobby Fischer for the World Championship, for example. I could even help them with the dialogue, if they didn't know chess.

I didn't get that, of course — in fact I didn't get a dream about chess at all. What I got instead was a dream about my Olde English sheep dog. That would have been perfectly all right with me if they'd done me the courtesy of giving me a good old-fashioned dream. But I didn't get that either. What I got instead was a dream that from start to finish was nothing but a comedy of errors. It would have been funny if it was meant to be a comedy, but it wasn't. What it was was really libelous, not only about me but about Brookie, too. All in all it was just a perfect example of rotten dreamworkmanship and probably no dream research department. For all I know, they probably economized on them, too.

Anyway, the dream started with Brookie jumping off the back of a truck and knocking me down and attacking me. Attacking me, mind you! A dog who never in his life attacked me or anyone else who didn't deserve to be attacked and whom I loved from the very first moment I saw him, every day of his life and for that matter still love. What the dream was obviously trying to show was what happened the day Brookie first arrived, but it didn't happen anything like the way they showed it. What really happened was Brookie arrived in a big crate on the back of a pickup truck one Christmas morning when I was eight years old. My grandmother had given him to me after I had picked him out from a picture book she had of dogs. When she and I and the whole family ran out to see him and when I saw the man prying off the slats of the crate with a hammer and screwdriver and got my first sight of Brookie, I was so excited that I had an asthma attack. My mother made me lie down, and the next thing I knew Brookie was on top of my stomach licking my face. But an attack, really! It just wasn't like that at all. It was, as a matter of fact, the happiest moment of my childhood.

The next scene I remembered in my damned dream was just as off-base and in my judgment perilously close to libel. Anyway, what it showed was my brother and me robbing the cook in the kitchen at gunpoint, and right after that we were being tried in court for stock fraud — as if we were Ivan Boeskys or Milkens or something.

This was really outrageous. The trouble was, the people who wrote the stupid dream didn't take the trouble to give any background to whoever they thought would dream the damned thing in the first place. And their writers didn't know the first thing about Boston, or the textile business. The fact is that the textile business in Boston, in which my father worked, was in those days either a feast or a famine. When it was a feast we had a gardener and a chauffeur and maids and a cook. When it was a famine we had boarders. The dream picked one of the feast times, of course — you'd know they would — but to have it that, my brother and I went around robbing the servants like reverse Robin Hoods or something. Really, it was so far from the truth that when it wasn't libelous it was ludicrous.

In the actual facts of the matter, my brother and I were blameless as the driven snow. What happened was that we were low on funds one summer and, knowing my father was flush that year, we went to him to get a bigger allowance. But Boston fathers, then or now, aren't New York fathers — what my brother got was thirty-five cents a week and what I got was twenty-five cents. And we didn't get our raise, either. So, after that, we decided to take a trip into Boston and see my uncle who was a stockbroker to see if he could do anything about the problem. He suggested various stocks for us to buy, but on thirty-five and twenty-five cents a week we realized it was going to be a long haul, particularly when my uncle explained that stocks could go down as well as up. We thought our uncle looked as if he was doing pretty well, so we asked him what stocks he bought — we thought that might be quicker. But when he confided to us that he made money whether stocks went up or down, that did it. There and then we decided that that's what we wanted to be — stockbrokers.

The only trouble was, of course, we didn't have any stocks to sell, so we did the next best thing — we made up stocks. But for the dream to imply that we went out and robbed people was really below the belt. We spent a lot of time painting up certificates and even went to the trouble of putting out stock listings, which we gave out to all our customers free. We even had some of the stocks paying dividends — Family Foods, for example, a stock which we put up or down depending upon whether or not we liked our dinner, paid one cent a week, and we paid it right out of our own pocket. We also had a stock called Pet Food, in honor of Brookie. We started putting that up or down, too, depending on whether or not he liked his dinner. But since Brookie always liked his dinner, we decided to put that up or down, too, depending upon whether or not we liked our dinner. After that, we had a whole raft of other stocks — Weather, and Good Housekeeping, and General Automobile, and School, and we even had the Red Sox and the Braves and the Bruins, which were the easiest to put up or down.

Naturally we had to have customers for our stocks and, far from the way the dream had it, instead of robbing the servants we gave them the chance to get in on a good thing on the ground floor. We sold the cook, for example, Family Foods — she learned very quickly what we liked best to eat — we sold the gardener Weather, and the chauffeur General Automobile, and we even got the upstairs maid into Good Housekeeping, even though she took a lot of persuading because she'd never heard of stocks before. As for our friends at school, we got several of them into School, and even more into our sporting stocks. And in less time than it takes to tell about it, we had no measly thirty-five or twenty-five cents in our pockets — we were rolling in dough. Every now and then some spoilsport would want to sell his or her stock and, although we carefully explained to them that this was not how America was built, we always let them if they absolutely insisted, as long as they sold it to someone else and didn't bother us about it and we got a small commission. Meanwhile, we didn't behave like a couple of nouveaux riches with our money — we just bought necessities. I remember, for example, the time we bought, C.O.D., two new baseball gloves. We were out having a catch with Brookie that evening when my father drove up and saw the new gloves and asked us where we'd gotten them. We told him the truth — we told him we'd sold stock for them.

What the dream really made a mess out of was the ending. What really happened, when you came right down to it, was just plain rotten luck. The upstairs maid, the same one to whom we had so much trouble selling Good Housekeeping, had an emergency in her family and came to my father for a small loan. Like any good Bostonian, my father asked her why she hadn't saved for a rainy day — whereupon she burst into tears and said she had, but that it was all in the stock. He patted her on the head and told her not to worry, she could sell the stock. Whereupon she burst into tears again and said she had tried to, but no one would buy it. Then my father asked her who had sold it to her, and that was when she had to mention us, and that we wouldn't buy it back from her.

She had no business bringing that up, of course — and that's where I suppose the damned dream got its Ivan Boesky idea, but I repeat we never robbed anybody — not even after we decided, after consultation with our father, to give the servants back their money. My father's attitude toward this was very poor, we thought, particularly after we'd explained to him that what he could be doing was to start a crash which could spread to our friends at school. At that point he made us give them back their money, too. The final straw was when he made us sell our gloves. This time we told him frankly that what he was doing was killing private initiative. Even today, looking back, the way the dream told the story of robbing the servants — that seems to be really rotten journalism. Actually, what we had done was to teach those servants, firsthand, the economy and to make them a part of a real dream — the Great American Dream, in fact.

But, to get back to that dumb dream of mine that day, I want to say here and now that the third part of it was just as bad as the first two. This part had Brookie and me at sea — in fact it had me ramming an enemy ship, one which was moored and anchored — and Brookie falling overboard. This was just plain slander. In the first place, the boat I rammed was a powerboat, and since as a sailing man I hated powerboats, wherever it was, even moored, it was still an enemy ship. In the second place, Brookie never fell overboard. He almost did, it was true, but he didn't. The dream was really sloppy here. In the third place, I didn't just purposely ram a moored boat — I was much too good a sailorman for that. There was a reason I did it. I did it to save Brookie, and there was just simply no excuse for the dream not giving me the credit for that.

The real story began at Peaches Point, near Marblehead where, again in one of our flush years, we went in the summer. My father had a large racing yacht, a "Q," as that class was called, which came complete with a man who polished the brass on the wheel and the winches and the turnbuckles. I, on the other hand, had a tiny catboat — a Brutal Beast, as that class was called. And that summer I had made a bet with another Brutal Beast captain that, whoever won the next race, the other would have to be his man for the rest of the summer. And, to make a long story short, I won.

Even after I won the race, however, and had won my man for the summer, I was still not out of the woods. The trouble was, there was no brass on my boat for my man to shine. To a lesser skipper this might have seemed an insoluble problem, but not to me. With Brookie on board

I hoisted sail on the *Eagle,* as I had named my boat, and set out for Marblehead harbor and its famous Graves Yard.

As I pulled into the dock, Selden Graves himself, the owner of the Yard, came down to greet me. He was the archetypical Marbleheader — tall and taciturn, lanky and laconic, but with a hint of a smile lurking in a granite face. "Hello, Cap'n Amory," he said, patting Brookie. "What can I do you for?" I told him I wanted a wheel on *Eagle* with a lot of brass on it because I had won a man in a bet and there wasn't anything for him to shine. Solemnly, Graves looked over all twelve feet of the length of *Eagle.* "Well," he said, "I don't think we've ever put a wheel on a Brutal Beast, but I see no reason why it can't be done. You and Brookie, though, will have to mind the wire. It'll cross right here." He showed me where the wire in the center of the boat would cross *Eagle*'s entire beam and feed right back along the sides to the rudder. I told him that I would mind the wire, and I was sure that Brookie would, too.

That very afternoon I had my wheel, and was sailing back with a good stiff breeze behind me and with Brookie, sniffing the wind as usual, wedged into the small space between one of the forestays and the mast. Frankly, I felt like the captain of a Cup Defender. By the time I reached Peaches Point, however, the wind was really strong and, as I turned into it with my sail flapping, I realized for the first time that it wasn't quite as easy to steer with a wheel as it was with a tiller. I also realized that with the wind that strong I wasn't going to make it to my mooring, and I had to veer off and try again. The trouble was that, as I did so, I was headed straight for a large powerboat which was owned by the richest inhabitant of Peaches Point. I don't know what its real name was, but it was orange and we called it the Tangerine Terror.

But for the dream to say I purposely rammed the Terror was an outrage. I didn't have any alternative. If I'd tried to slack off and go around the stern of the Terror, with those gusts of wind I'd never have made it. And if I'd tried to tack, Brookie, wedged up there as he was on the leeward side, would have fallen overboard. Anyway, what happened was we hit the Terror. You have no idea how hard a sailboat in a good breeze can hit — particularly since a wave from another damned powerboat rode under us just before we hit, and *Eagle* was riding down that wave so we hit the Terror right at her waterline. Brookie bounced first into the Terror, and then back toward me. He would have hit the wire, too, if I hadn't grabbed him. In any case, as I held him and we kept bobbing and banging into the Terror before drifting astern of her, I had a chance to assay the damage. There was no doubt but that *Eagle* had placed a hole in the Terror — and not a small hole, either. In fact, water was gurgling in.

Like any good sailorman, I knew my duty and headed straight for the dock. Dropping sail, I did not hit the dock too hard, but at this point I couldn't have cared. I just threw my bow line around a cleat in the dock and, with Brookie racing beside me, ran for the house of the owner of the Terror.

He himself came to the door. "Oh, hello, Clippie," he said genially, using my childhood nickname, "and Brookie too," he said, giving him a pat. "Why don't you come in and have a cold drink?" And, he added, "I'll see that James gets Brookie some water." I told him quickly that I wasn't thirsty, and neither was Brookie, but I had to talk to him about something that was the matter. He patted me on the head. "Oh, that can wait, Clippie," he said. I told him it couldn't wait, and while he was telling James about the drink, I blurted out that I had put a hole in his boat. Even that didn't seem to concern him. "Oh, don't you worry," he said. "I'll tell my man, and he'll fix it in the morning. Here, sit down." This time I did more than blurt. "Sir," I said, "it can't wait. Your boat is sinking!"

At this he ran to the window and looked out at the Terror, which, by this time, was indeed, if not actually sinking, at least listing very badly to port. "God!" he said, ignoring me and running for the dock. At this moment James, having brought some water for Brookie and put it on the porch, handed me some orange pop. Frankly, though, I wasn't all that thirsty, and neither was Brookie. Brookie knew when something was the matter, and the dream never gave him credit for that any more than it gave credit to me.

The fourth part of the dream was just as inaccurate as the rest of it, but this time they went too far. They showed Brookie and me on Death Row, and the reason we were there, apparently, was we had both been convicted of murder. And the person we were supposed to have murdered was, of all people, our governess.

Again, the dream didn't give any background to the whole thing. I hadn't murdered the governess — all I had done was to try to put her out of commission. The background was very important. What had happened was that my parents had decided, after our last governess had left, to get a new governess. My brother and I could not abide the decision. Governesses, we felt, were all very well for sissies, and even for my sister — she was four — but for two grown men of eight and three-quarters, which I was, and eleven and a quarter, which my brother was, it was an insult.

The way my parents went about getting a new governess was to interview them in the living room, and so, after my brother and I held what we called a Council of War, my brother decided that what we had to do first was to send a reconnaissance party down the stairs, close to the living room, where we could hear the new governess being interviewed. "We've got to listen for Achilles' heels," my brother told me sternly. "They've all got Achilles' heels. All we have to do is find them."

I didn't know what an Achilles' heel was, but I felt that if I could get the governess running, and I had Brookie with me, I could sic Brookie on her because he loved to run after people and nip at their heels. If the governess had a bad one, I figured, Brookie, with a little practice, could at least make it worse.

Anyway, our war plans worked out perfectly with the first two governesses. One left after one day. We had learned from our reconnaissance that she was afraid of dogs, so what we did was to tell her she ought to stay away from Brookie, because he didn't like women, and he'd been a War Dog. The second governess took us longer. She didn't mind Brookie, but she told my parents while she didn't mind working in the daytime, she wanted her nights to herself and didn't want us bothering her. Our war plan for this one involved a friend of ours named Joe Burnett, who had had a disagreement with his family and had decided to run away. He was going west, my brother explained to me, and he was going to have to live off the land but he was going to stop at our house first and it would be up to us to provision him.

Even though it was a long way from Southborough, Joe's home, to our house in Milton, Joe was going to be there very early in the morning, and if we weren't up yet, he was to throw a pebble at our window to wake us. What my brother, who was very versatile in his war planning — he would later become Deputy Director of the C.I.A. — decided to do was instead of telling Joe which window was ours, to give him directions to the governess' window.

The plan worked beautifully. My brother hadn't overlooked a single detail — he had found out, for example, that the governess was a very sound sleeper — and, just as he figured, when Joe got tired of throwing pebble after pebble with no one waking up, he finally threw a rock. Right through the governess' window, too. And though sadly it was very bad for Joe's escape, because our family called his family, it was perfect for us. That governess was out of the house by noon. It was all careful planning, my brother explained to me, and having Right on your side.

The third governess, though, was a tough one. She was English, and her name was Miss Quince, and she didn't seem to have any Achilles' heel at all. She didn't even dislike Brookie. Indeed, the only thing Miss Quince did really dislike, we learned from our reconnaissance, was playing games. And, though hour after hour we Parcheesied her and dominoed her and mah-jongged her and chessed and checkered, and even croqueted her, it did no good. But again, to get back to that dream, that Brookie and I had killed her and that's why we were on Death Row, was just plain absurd. What actually happened was that late one afternoon, just before supper, my brother and I were playing croquet with Miss Quince, and I had just knocked her ball into the bushes and had two shots for the last two wickets on the stake. At that moment — Miss Quince was really a very poor sport — she suddenly announced it was suppertime and the game was over. All I did was tell her what I thought of her decision, when she started running at me, and that was when I took my mallet — we had just gotten nice new ones, with heavy heads — and swung it around my head, and let fly at her. I didn't aim for her head at all — what I was aiming for was her Achilles' heel, but since she was coming at me I could hardly have been expected to hit it. Anyway, my mallet kind of whirled around, with its heavy head making it pick up speed, and where I hit her was just below the knees. She went down like a stone. She just stayed there, too, face down, right in the way of my wicket. My brother and Brookie reached her first. My brother just looked at her for what seemed an awful long time. "I think," he said matter-of-factly, "you've killed her."

Well, I hadn't, of course. The dream just blew the whole thing out of proportion and it totally ignored the all-important fact of the whole matter — that Miss Quince may have lost the battle, but my brother and I had won the war. Miss Quince left the next morning, and my parents decided that they would just get a governess for my sister — that my brother and I were really too old for governesses. All right, on the short side of the whole thing I did get the worst spanking I ever had, but that was a whole lot better than being executed. And as for Brookie going to be executed, as the dream had it, that would have been a terrible miscarriage of justice. While my brother and I just looked at Miss Quince when she was down, it was Brookie who dug around and tried to find her face.

And that was what finally got Miss Quince up. As I said, she didn't dislike Brookie, but she didn't much like his idea of artificial respiration.

The finale of the dream was really the worst part of all. This time, once again Brookie and I were going to be executed — the writers of those dreams must have had sequels on their brains. But this time, if you please, we were being executed in front of a whole firing line of nuns. They were all dressed in black, and one of them was coming up to us with two handkerchiefs to tie around our eyes.

The dream had it that she tied those handkerchiefs, too — which was absolute nonsense. In a spot like that, neither Brookie nor I would have ever accepted those handkerchiefs. We would have just shaken our heads with sardonic smiles the way we'd seen the hero in *Beau Geste* and lots of other movies do it, and then we would have looked the firing squad right in their eyes.

And, once more, they missed the whole background and the whole real conflict. The problem was that this dream occurred at my first school, the Brush Hill School, one which was not only right near my house — that was why Brookie was always down there — but it was also right near a convent. And that was the problem — the nuns were always complaining about the noise we made at recess. The whole thing came to a head one day in our regular game of prisoner's base. Brookie and I had just made a heroic dash down to our prisoners without being tagged — which meant we had rescued them as they were reaching out, hand to hand from the goal line, and we had brought our team dead even. Then suddenly there was this Mother Superior and those nuns talking to our recess teacher, and the next thing I knew the recess teacher was telling us the game was over.

Of course, the dream didn't go into any of that. And, remember, it was now a tied ball game. I'm not talking extra innings here, mind you, I'm talking a flat-out tie in regulation time with two minutes left on the clock before the end of recess. And they had the gall to call the game over.

All right, our side had made some noise, but so had the other side. What are you supposed to do in a close game like that — take the Vow of Silence? Anyway, since I was the captain of my team, it was up to me to lodge a protest. The other captain, as I recall, didn't do a damn thing. Whether he was a very religious person or just some idiot who was satisfied with a tie, I don't remember. In any case, in no time at all Brookie and I were surrounded by nuns and Brookie was barking — no dog likes being surrounded by people in black — and I was giving my side of the whole thing, but before I could even marshal my arguments, the next thing I knew we were in Miss Pitts' office — the Mother Superior and all the nuns and everybody except Brookie. They wouldn't let Brookie in.

It really was a kangaroo court in there, and that dream was just as kangaroo as they come. It had terrible writers, too, because they let a great character slip right through their fingers. That character was Miss Pitts, the head of the school. Man and boy, I've known my share of formidable women in my time, but I'll tell you here and now I've never known one of them who could hold a candle — if you'll pardon the expression in this particular situation — to Miss Pitts. I don't want to make personal remarks, but I'll tell you Miss Pitts' breastworks would have made the Army Corps of Engineers want to get into some other line of work. And, when she looked down at you over them and through her glasses, which she wore 'way down over her nose with long black tapes around her neck, she was really terrifying. You felt awful small in front of her — many's the time I saw even Brookie look like a Chihuahua.

But Miss Pitts should have been ashamed of herself, the way she conducted that trial. She believed anything and everything the Mother Superior and those nuns said and wouldn't take my word for anything — even when I asked her, as politely as possible, who the hell's field they thought it was. They also said, not counting that time, that I'd taken the Lord's name in vain nine times. I didn't argue about that. All I argued was that it shouldn't have been in vain — that of all times in life when you needed to appeal to a Higher Authority, certainly one of them was when you'd had a rotten decision called on you for no reason at all. Remember, in those days there was no such thing as Instant Replay. The final straw was when one of the nuns said I had said something about kissing her. I never said a word about kissing her — all I said was that a tie was like kissing your sister, and of course I meant your sister sister, not a nun sister.

I was ten, as I recall, when it all happened. And I certainly learned then there are times when there is no justice in the world. But the whole execution thing in the dream was, as I say, just ridiculous. I do know, though, where they got that handkerchief idea from. They got that because Miss Pitts decided my punishment would be that every single day before recess I would have to go to her office and she would tie a handkerchief around my mouth and I would have to wear it every day until Christmas.

But the point is, it was never over my eyes. And I really didn't mind it over my mouth once I got used to it. It made it a little difficult for me to give commands to my team, but they soon learned to come up close, which I particularly didn't mind when they were girls. Actually what I told everybody — and particularly the girls — was that I had a very sensitive mouth and I wasn't supposed to let the cold weather get on it. I didn't do it for sympathy or to be a hero or anything like that. I did it because I wasn't going to let Miss Pitts or that Mother Superior or those nuns walk all over me.

As I woke up, I seemed to be pushing something away from my eyes or my mouth, I don't remember which. In any case, I looked around and saw Polar Bear still obviously pawing at the door. For a while I just lay there wondering how long he'd been doing it — I had heard you can dream incredibly long dreams in an extraordinarily short time. If so, this was at least one good thing about that dream. I certainly wouldn't have wanted to waste a lot of time on a dream that had blown as many opportunities as that one had.

At that moment Marian came in. She was very excited. It turned out that among the calls she had made about the sheep dog had been one to the Fund for Animals hotline, and the woman who owned the sheep dog had later called that line about her dog being lost, and Marian had called back, and now it was just a matter of time before the woman would come and get her dog.

Marian suggested she would stay with Polar Bear until the woman came, and why didn't I go in and say goodbye to the sheep dog? I thought it was a great idea, particularly after the dream had done so much injustice to sheep dogs. The only trouble was that, in the course of our Changing of the Guard, Polar Bear saw his opportunity and, in a flash, he was out the door, around the corner, and after the sheep dog. I rushed out there, but I knew he would reach the dog long before I did, and I was also sure that there would now be another *mano a mano* with no me to thwart the first *mano*.

But, amazingly, nothing like that happened. As Polar Bear charged toward him, the sheep dog merely raised a playful paw. At this, Polar Bear put on the brakes and slid to a stop. The sheep dog sighed and gave every indication of continuing his sleep. Polar Bear surveyed him crossly for only a brief moment, then with a sigh of his own — which I was sure he meant to appear resigned but which I actually think contained more than that — he turned around and snuggled, his back up against the stomach of the sheep dog, stretched out, and, to my astonishment, closed his eyes, and went to sleep too.

For a long time I just stood and watched them. Then, very quietly, I lay down beside them, and gently, so as not to wake them, I began patting them both at once. I thought about the wonderful times Brookie and I had had together, but I also thought how wonderful it was that Polar Bear should now decide to make friends with this sheep dog. I also made a firm resolution that sometime in the future I would once more have a dog like Brookie and a cat like Polar Bear. But I would get them both at the same time, or as near to it as possible, and have them grow up together.

As I watched them, both the sheep dog and Polar Bear were obviously in Dreamland. The sheep dog's paws started moving, and so did Polar Bear's. I just hoped they were having good dreams and that theirs at least weren't full of the kind of sloppy modern workmanship that ruined so many of mine. But of course I couldn't be sure. For all I knew their dreams, too, weren't what they were in the old days.

IV ◦ *On the Cusp*

There are three kind of door cats. There are indoor cats and there are outdoor cats and there are also indoor and outdoor cats. Indeed there is probably every kind of door cat except shut door cats. I have never yet met a cat who liked a shut door. Polar Bear dislikes shut doors so much that I have even seen him start a two-front war against both my closet doors at once. He won the war too, of course, because I opened them knowing full well what he wanted to do was see if there was any new footwear in there which needed being whipped into biting shape.

But, I digress. Of the three kinds of cats I mentioned, Polar Bear is strictly an indoor cat. Except for forays to his balcony and an occasional trip with me in his carrier he stays indoors. Nonetheless I know, of course, that there are also outdoor cats. By this I mean cats who are looked after by people who feed them — cats who live outside and have only inside access to some barn or other shelter. I admire these cats and I also admire the people who look after them and, hopefully, get them neutered or spayed.

Besides indoor and outdoor cats, however, there is that other kind of cat I have mentioned — the cat who is both an indoor and outdoor cat. These are cats who basically live indoors but who go outdoors whenever they feel like it. I object to these indoor-and-outdoor cats — or rather I object to the people who have them, because they do not confine them in chicken-wired runs on the order of the balcony I had built for Polar Bear. All right, his balcony isn't the biggest balcony in the world, but neither is mine — and remember, he took half of that.

I object on two grounds to those of you who do not confine your cats. One is that they kill birds — yours and, worse still, your neighbors', people who, after all, are entirely entitled to like their birds as much as you like your cat. The second ground I object on is that the chances of your cat getting injured or killed either by automobile, dog, or other animal are not only good — they are, in your cat's lifetime, an odds-on bet.

People have written me that my chicken-wire-run idea is too confining for the cat. My answer is that it does not need to be — it can be a long and interesting run and even include a tree or two. Indeed, it can be anything you want it to be as long as your cat can't get out any way but the same way he got in — the best way being a swinging door to your kitchen. The important thing is that not only are your birds and your neighbors' birds safe, so is your cat or cats. And again, not only from automobile, dog, or other animal but also from disappearance. This can be just as bad as the other fates which befall your cat, because you will, in all probability, never know what happened to him. All you can do is guess and hope — and, once more, your hope is a long shot. Barbara Diamond, in *Cat Fancy* magazine, printed the stark statistics. She put the average life of the indoor cat at twelve to fifteen years, the average life of the outdoor cat at two to three years.

Which brings me to another point — the matter of declawing. On this I am as adamant as I am about the indoor-outdoor matter. Cats should not be declawed, period — end of argument. I know there are veterinarians who maintain that, if they do not declaw the cat as the owner wishes, the owner will "get rid of it" — my very least favorite expression — and therefore they do it. My answer to this is they should not do it. They should keep the cat, and get a home for it and get rid of the owner.

I say this even about cats who, people will tell you, never go out and therefore seemingly have no need of their defenses — i.e., their claws. But the fact is there is always the chance your cat will get out. Maybe it is not a very good chance, but it is there all the same — the ill-opportuned opened door, the ill-screened window, the carrying case which flew open, or that automobile trip when you stopped and someone got out the door and so, unnoticed, did the cat. Your cat may even get out, ironically, at your vet's. And, when and if one of these occasions happens, your cat is not just virtually defenseless, your cat is hopelessly so.

I say this knowing full well cats are destructive of furniture. All the scratching posts ever produced and all the remedies ever devised to stop cats scratching to the contrary notwithstanding, sooner or later your cat will scratch your furniture. You can cut his nails, even his back nails, to your heart's content and even to his hissing discontent, but some day, some night, he will have a go at your favorite antique.

But do you then declaw him? Of course you don't. You don't even punish him. Punishment not administered at the moment, and most of the time even then, is, with a cat, not an option. Instead you should just stop and think one thought — is that piece of furniture or even all of your furniture put together as important as your cat?

The answer is, of course, a simple one. And, in my case, therein, as they say, hangs a tale. This tale, as you have probably already guessed, was about Polar Bear having a go at my own favorite piece of furniture. It is, or rather was, a beautiful chess table which was sold to me by an antiques dealer in Charleston, South Carolina. It also was, or at least so the dealer assured me, the chess table owned by that late great Confederate, Robert E. Lee.

In any case it is a table so important to me that I do not ever use it for play with my regular chess friends — the kind who might spill something on it or, worse still, burn it with a cigarette. I use it only when I am by myself, working out some chess problems. From the beginning, however, Polar Bear never understood how important to me this table is — I think he is a Yankee at heart. And, one day, as I was working out a chess problem, he leaped upon the table and skidded — i.e., dug — his way to a stop. I looked at the table in horror. I do not know how many of you remember, in the good old days of marble-playing how, if you didn't yell "No Roman Roadsies" before your opponent yelled "Roman Roadsies" — well, your opponent dug a road all the way to the hole. In this case Polar Bear had dug a Roman Roadsie in Robert E.

Lee's chess table. But did I do anything about it? Of course not — I did nothing.

Actually I am not being entirely accurate when I say I did nothing about it. What I did was think about something — about the time when I too had been in a somewhat similar situation to Polar Bear's at that particular moment. It all happened many years ago when I was visiting in Scottsdale, Arizona, at the home of the father of Miss Nancy Davis.

I had met Miss Davis in the early fifties at a time before she had met Mr. Ronald Reagan. She was at that time an actress living in New York and was a close friend of the late Betsy Barton, a writer friend of mine of whom I was very fond. Miss Davis and I started seeing each other from time to time, and one day after the publication of my second book I chanced to mention to her that I was about to go on a book tour. Immediately she wanted to know if I was going to Arizona. I said yes, as a matter of fact I was. She wanted to know if I would be in Phoenix. I consulted my schedule — I told her I would indeed be in Phoenix. And, as a matter of fact, for a weekend. "Well then," she said, "you'll have to stay at my father's house. He has a home in Scottsdale."

The very next day Miss Davis called, told me she had called her father, and said that, although he could only see me on Friday night — he had to go back to Chicago that weekend — he had insisted that I come and stay the whole weekend because the maid and cook would be there and they would have nothing to do and the house would be mine. In vain I protested all the trouble she and her father were going through, but she would not hear of it. Her father, she said, was looking forward to it.

I had never met her father, although I knew he was an

extremely eminent neurologist who had, among other achievements, raised millions of dollars for his Northwestern University Medical School. When I arrived at his house late Friday afternoon, he himself met me at the door, and I could see immediately that he was an exceptionally formidable fellow. Nonetheless he greeted me cordially and, as we talked about his daughter, he not only introduced me to what he said would be my room but also took the trouble to show me the rest of the house. Although Scottsdale would later become one of the nation's most fashionable suburbs, in those days it was just a relatively simple place out in the desert. The Davis home, however, was far from simple. Indeed, as one of the showplaces of Scottsdale, it was both luxuriously furnished and also had an extraordinary collection of both fine art and antique furniture. Dr. Davis was particularly proud of the desk in the den — one which he told me had once belonged, as I recall, to Alexander Hamilton.

Over cocktails I soon learned that Dr. Davis himself also seemed to belong to Alexander Hamilton — at least as far as his politics were concerned. And by dinnertime our conversation had begun to flag. Indeed, before the soup course was concluded, I had the distinct impression that, as a dinner partner, to interest Dr. Davis for very long, I was neither bright enough, successful enough, famous enough, rich enough, nor Republican enough. Suffice it to say that in ensuing years I was not in the least surprised when Dr. Davis would join a group of Californians in the inner circle of the country's right-wing conservatives. During that dinner, however, I remember that he seemed to have much curiosity about my relations with his daughter — relations which, he seemed very relieved to find, had not progressed to the point at which he surely would have become exercised. Indeed, before retiring, he bid me both a cordial good night and also what seemed a rather final good-bye, explaining that he would be leaving early the next morning but that I was to enjoy myself and that the maid and cook would be at my disposal.

Accordingly, when I arose the next morning I immediately headed for the kitchen. Here the maid informed me that Dr. Davis always took his breakfast in the den, and would I like to do that also? I said that would be fine and, in short order, she brought me a tray. In short order, too, I fell to the fine breakfast. I also began, however, to make some phone calls which the publisher had instructed me to make, and soon there were incoming calls as well. Altogether, accepting and turning down engagements, I was in the midst of that brief period of celebrity that authors on book tours enjoy to the fullest. And, meanwhile, with the pressure and excitement of it all, I was smoking like a well-fired chimney.

All of a sudden, after finishing a phone call and starting to light up another cigarette, I noticed that my previous cigarette, which I had totally forgotten, had missed the ashtray. It had also missed the breakfast tray. It had not, however, missed Alexander Hamilton's desk. It was not a minor burn, either — it was a Roman Roadsie.

For a long moment I just stared at it in horror. At that moment the maid appeared with more coffee. As she approached, I had only one option. This was to drop head down with my arms extended over the charred battlefield. "Oh, Mr. Amory," she said, "you must be so tired — all those calls." Without moving from my position, and trying to look as weary as it was possible to do at that early morning hour, I nodded wanly. I told her it wasn't easy being on a book tour — it was really exhausting.

After the maid had gone, I worked on other options. I could, of course, summon the maid and admit what I had done, but she was not a young maid and I feared a possible stroke. I could also have covered the whole thing up, stayed over until Dr. Davis returned on Monday morning, brought myself to my full height, and said, "Sir, I have something terrible to report. I have burned a furrow in Alexander Hamilton's desk. I am terribly sorry, sir. I shall of course pay every cent of the repairs."

I did not even consider this option. Dr. Davis was not the sort of man to whom you could say such a thing. He would have only one answer, which would have been to summon his chauffeur, march me out to the desert, and shoot me. There was actually only one possible option — somehow to get the desk repaired before the return of Dr. Davis. But this demanded getting rid of the maid and the cook. Bravely, first once more assuming my supine position, I summoned both of them. I told them that I was going to be away all that day and probably all Sunday too and they should take those days off. I wouldn't need them back until Monday. Immediately they protested that they could not do that, that Dr. Davis had instructed them to take care of me. I argued with them. I told them that it was absurd for them just to stay there and sit around when I would not even be there.

Our discussion went on and on, but finally they agreed, saying they would be back first thing Monday morning. Please not the first thing, I entreated. I might be coming in very late Sunday night, and I would like to sleep Monday morning. I told them I would be terribly tired by then — even more tired than they could see I was now. Nonetheless, no matter what I tried, the very latest I could get them to agree to appearing was Monday at 9 A.M.

The moment I heard their car go out the driveway, I grabbed the Yellow Pages. I tried Furniture Repair after Furniture Repair. There was no answer after no answer — it was, after all, Saturday morning. Finally I found one that was open. I have a desk here, I said as casually as I could, which I saw seemed to need a small repair. They asked me to explain. "Sounds to me," they said, "as if we'll have to sand it down and refinish the whole top." I said they could do whatever they had to do, but they had to have it look as close as they could to the way it was before. "OK," they said, "we'll pick it up Monday and have it back within the week." I told them they didn't get the picture at all. They would have to pick it up today, I said, and return it on Monday. Early Monday, I emphasized. Very early Monday. Crack of dawn Monday. "Two overtime days?" they exclaimed. "Do you have any idea what kind of money the boss would be talking?" I told them money was no object. I did not even haggle, although the price we finally agreed upon would have allowed me a weekend penthouse at the Arizona Biltmore. A condemned man in the desert does not haggle with the proprietors of an oasis.

The moment I put the phone down I made an exact diagram of everything on the desk. I then placed each item, carefully marked, on another table. When I had finished, sure enough I heard a truck in the driveway, and two large men arrived to pick up the desk. Before one of them started to pick up his end, however, he whistled. "Whew," he said, "what we've got here, Sam, is a torch job." I ignored this but made them promise, torch job or no torch job, dead or alive, the desk had to be back by the crack of dawn Monday. They looked on their order slip. "Right," they said.

Furniture Repair was as good as its word. Literally at dawn Monday, the same men in the same truck chugged up with the desk. I looked at it carefully. The furrow was not only no longer visible to the naked eye; it would not have been visible to Dr. Davis even with a neurological X-ray eye. What had obviously been done was that the whole top of the desk had been reduced by the exact size of the furrow. But the matching and coloring were really remarkable. By the time the maid and the cook appeared, I was sitting behind the desk with every item as it was. The maid asked me if I would like breakfast. I told her indeed I would — a large one. She noticed that I did not have an ashtray. "I'll get you one," she said. I shook my head. I told her I'd given up smoking, and she should, too — she might burn something if she wasn't careful.

Ever since then I've watched the career of Miss Davis with keen interest. I am always saddened when a woman I once dated sees fit to be so unwise as to settle for a secondary choice as marriage partner rather than me, and I often think how sad it is that in later years they are consigned to live to regret their ill-considered decision. When I read about Mrs. Reagan going on to be first First Lady of California and then First Lady of the Country, I had to admit that, under the circumstances, she'd done as well as could be expected for someone not at that time farseeing enough to see the possibilities in me. Often as I read about her, however, and particularly after Dr. Davis's death, my thoughts kept returning to Alexander Hamilton's desk. Did it go back to Chicago with the Davis family there? Or did it go with the Reagans to their ranch in San Ysidro? Or did the desk stay with them all the time and go first to Sacramento and then to the White House and finally to Bel Air?

Wherever it went, I often thought about someday having a chance to see it again — at which time I would tell Mrs. Reagan the truth about it. Not the whole truth, mind you — Mrs. Reagan is too much like her father for that — or even nothing but the truth. Rather I would choose to tell her just some of the truth. Something casual, say, like Mrs. Reagan, you certainly have a beautiful desk there, but, frankly, I know furniture and I think I should tell you that I just don't believe the top of that desk is the original top.

For years, as I say, I have wanted to do that and finally I thought the time had come when, a few years ago, I was asked by Walter Anderson, the editor of *Parade*, to go to Washington and interview Mrs. Reagan. I accepted with extraordinary alacrity. At last, I thought, I would have my chance to speak my piece to her about — well, the piece. The interview took place, too, but somehow, what with one thing and another, I never got the chance to do what I had set out to do. It was not that Mrs. Reagan was short with me. She was not — in fact, I was granted a full hour. But what I had envisioned — some airy persiflage and then a casual walk around the rooms until I spotted Alexander Hamilton's desk — never came to pass. It did not even come close to pass. Throughout the interview I was not only not alone with Mrs. Reagan but in the additional company of two of her secretaries as well as a Secret Service man and a stenographer who took down every word either she or I said, not to mention a video cameraman. When I quietly asked him what he was there for, he did not answer. The stenographer, however, quickly and quietly explained to me that he was there so that if, for example, I wrote that Mrs. Reagan had laughed and she had not, they would then have evidence of my error. Altogether, to have suggested a short stroll in search of a piece of missing furniture in such surroundings would have taken the kind of nerve which, against the Davis family, either *père* or *fille,* I just never seemed able to muster. It would have taken, I guess, a trained actor, which probably explains why she chose Mr. Reagan.

After the interview was over, reluctantly I realized that my great opportunity had come and gone and I had been found wanting. There was no question but that I had failed. Nonetheless, I simply could not go to my final reward with the secret of Alexander Hamilton's desk locked away forever. Before I left the White House I stopped at the desk of Mrs. Reagan's secretary and told her the story. Would she, I asked her, when she had the chance, please tell Mrs. Reagan the story and would she also mind asking her where the desk was now? The secretary agreed. And, in a few days I had a letter from her. "In regard to the Scottsdale story," she wrote, "Mrs. Reagan has asked me to inform you that she has no recollection of such a desk being in that room."

No recollection! Could it be possible, I wondered, that I had dreamed the whole thing and that it was just one more dream I had had which, like so many of the others, needed more work? Or, on the other hand, could it be true and was Mrs. Reagan unwilling to admit that one of her priceless antiques was ersatz? Or, for a third possibility, could she have consulted one of her astrologers, and had the astrologer told her to give me that answer? Or, for a fourth and final possibility, could I have uncovered still another White House cover-up — one in which the desk had been destroyed but no one would admit the fact? I finally decided that this was my favorite answer to the riddle, but somehow, deep down inside, I sincerely hoped the whole affair would not end up in court. I just could not picture Nancy Reagan having to testify, like Fawn Hall, that she had shredded Alexander Hamilton's desk.

I was not thinking of Alexander Hamilton's desk when I received one of the most curious letters from my first book about Polar Bear. I was, however, thinking about Mrs. Reagan, if for no other reason than that the letter concerned astrology — a subject of which Mrs. Reagan was not only perhaps the country's most famous devotee, but also one in which she saw fit to devote the whole first chapter of her latest memoir. In any case, the subject of the letter I received was that I should see to it that Polar Bear had his horoscope done. The woman who wrote the letter obviously knew not only a great deal about astrology but also a good deal about the character of Polar Bear. She suggested in fact that if Polar Bear did not like his horoscope being done by an outsider, I could do it myself. There were many books about cat astrology which could help me.

Frankly, before I got that letter, I didn't know there was such a thing as cat astrology and I certainly didn't know there were many books about it. As a matter of fact, despite my relationship with Mrs. Reagan, I didn't know much about astrology, period. It was true, of course, that there are people in the Fund for Animals offices, as I guess there are in most offices, who talk a lot about astrology and ask their friends what sign they are and so forth, but, as I think I had mentioned previously, I am not very big on things like that and indeed am on the small side with most ologies which have to do with making decisions, romances, and other problems. We Bostonians just don't seem to have problems like that. We just have problems with other people.

Actually one of the problems I had with other people was with a young lady in the Fund's New York office. She was a very strong believer in astrology. One day she announced to us that she had cast her own horoscope, and she also parted with the information that she would have to leave us. The horoscope, she said, clearly indicated that the best place for her to live would be in Oregon. We were trying to work out the possiblity of transferring her to Roger and Cathy Anunsen's Fund for Animals office in Oregon when, not long after, she informed us that she had decided not to move there after all. She told us that she had done another horoscope, and this one had produced the information that Oregon, as well as California — and indeed everything west of the Mississippi — was going to fall into the sea. She had, therefore, decided to stay with us in New York. It is not easy nowadays, as I believe I've said before, to get good help.

The experience, however, had left me somewhat soured on the subject of astrology, and I had put off the matter of answering the woman who wanted me to have Polar Bear's horoscope done. Finally, though, I bit the bullet. Indeed, I had already planned a letter in which I proposed to tell the woman that as for her having doubts about an outsider doing the job, she could not have been more right — I had never yet found anything Polar Bear liked an outsider doing except going away. As for my being able to do the job, I also proposed to tell her that in this she could not have been more wrong. I had never understood astrology even when people took extreme patience trying to explain it to me.

In the middle of putting off writing this letter, however, I received a call from the woman. I told her I was sorry that I had not answered her letter sooner and then explained what I was going to say. "I told you," the woman said sternly, "there are many books. You don't have to know the first thing about astrology yourself."

That made me cross. I do not feel I know everything, but I do feel I know the first thing about everything. As a matter of fact, most writers know the first thing about everything — the trouble comes when they have to go on to the second thing. In any case, to prove my point, I told her I very well knew that the first thing I would have to know to do Polar Bear's horoscope would be the exact date and time of his birth. I informed her that even the vet couldn't pin down the date of his birth within three years and, as for the time of it, we didn't have the faintest idea. He had been, after all, a stray.

Nonetheless, the woman persisted. "You don't have to know the exact date or time of birth," she said. "You'll see — just go get yourself some of the cat astrology books I mentioned." She paused — I had already learned she was a very meaningful pause woman. "And while you're at it," she continued, "you might pick up a couple of astrology books for yourself. Honestly, I think they might help you."

I ignored what she was irritatingly implying, but I couldn't stop her. "I've looked you up," she went on, "and you're a Virgo. I also know that your birthday is September second. The thing I don't know is what time you were born." Two A.M., I said. She wanted to know what authority I had for that. I told her my mother was the authority because I had asked her. I did not tell the woman that it was also because this was not the first call I had had on the subject.

"Aha," she said. I didn't like the sound of that because I was pretty sure what was coming next. "What year was it?" she asked. I pretended I hadn't heard her, but it did no good. "Aha," she said again, "remember, I can find out. They did you last year on your birthday on the radio and they said what year you were." I told her that if they did, they were wrong, and if they did it last year they were wrong by a year — which by my count was at least two years wrong now.

That at least stopped her. Just the same, after her letter and her telephone call I was intrigued enough by the idea of there being books about cat astrology that I decided the very next morning to go out and get some. And, because I was right there in the bookstore, I also picked up some people astrology books. I did not do so, I wish to make it clear, because the woman had told me to. I did it only because I had made up my mind that the next time that woman or somebody like her called they'd soon find out they didn't have an amateur on the other end of the line — they'd have Yours Truly.

That very afternoon, in fact, I turned to one of the people astrology books I had picked out. It was called *Sun Signs*, by Linda Goodman. I turned first to the list of "Famous Virgo Personalities":

Prince Albert	Lyndon Johnson
Lauren Bacall	Elia Kazan
Robert Benchley	Joseph P. Kennedy
Ingrid Bergman	Lafayette
Leonard Bernstein	D. H. Lawrence
Sid Caesar	Sophia Loren
Maurice Chevalier	H. L. Mencken
Theodore Dreiser	Walter Reuther
Queen Elizabeth I	Cardinal Richelieu
Henry Ford II	Peter Sellers
Greta Garbo	Robert Taft

Arthur Godfrey
Goethe
John Gunther
William Howard Taft
Roy Wilkins

Actually, I didn't think much of that list, not just because I wasn't on it — I could see the list wasn't up-to-date — but also because, as far as I could see, there was only one well-known cat person in the whole lot. And that one, after all, was Cardinal Richelieu — a man who certainly was a big cat person in France but was a pretty tough baby in other ways. Nonetheless, I plowed on — into a chapter, apparently written for women, called "The Virgo Man":

> We may as well get this out into the open right away — don't pin your hopes on a Virgo man if your heart is hungry for romantic dreams and fairy tales, or you'll find yourself on a starvation diet. . . . A pleasure-seeking, selfish, mentally lazy woman will never make it with a Virgo man, even if she's fairly oozing with sex appeal. This is the very last man in the world you can expect to find running off with a Go-go girl, though he might loan her his sweater if she's chilly.

That really infuriated me. It was, I felt, close to libelous on all us good Virgos. And what about Joseph P. Kennedy, for Pete's sake? Can you picture him loaning a topless Go-go girl a sweater? At any rate I decided at this point to give up *Sun Signs* and have a go at a book called *Moon Signs*, by Donna Cunningham. "This book," said the introduction, "with its Moon Sign tables and Moon descriptions, can help you prevent lunar burnout and keep you from baying at the Full Moon."

Frankly, I didn't see how I could have lunar burnout when I'd just started on the damn subject, and I couldn't imagine either Polar Bear or myself going around baying at the Full Moon, but I doggedly kept on. And, I soon learned, it was not just a question of baying at the Full Moon, it was meditating on it — indeed, Polar Bear and I should apparently not just meditate on the Full Moon but on the New Moon as well. I didn't know what Polar Bear was to bay at or meditate on, because after all I didn't yet have a sign for him, but what was evidently expected of me to do, as a Virgo, was what Ms. Cunningham described as "Meditations and Affirmations for the Lunations":

> I AM COMPASSIONATE TOWARDS MYSELF AS WELL AS OTHERS.
> I LET GO OF IMPOSSIBLE STANDARDS OF PERFECTION.

I saw no reason why I couldn't have a go at baying at that. Indeed I had already decided, when I started on this astrological exercise, that I wasn't going to try to set any impossible standards of perfection for myself, but neither was I going to give up easily. And so, with firm resolve, after *Sun Signs* and *Moon Signs* I went on to another of my books. This one was called *Astrological Guide for You in 1990.* It was by Sydney Omarr, but it had an introduction by Raymond Mungo, a man who in turn was introduced by Mr. Omarr as having "Pisces sun, Scorpio Moon and Cancer rising sign — a grand Water trine." Mr. Mungo, in his turn, was equally flattering about Sydney. "You've chosen your guide well," he wrote. "Omarr is Mr. Astrology to the world, perhaps the cosmos." Mr. Mungo warned us, however, not to try to bother Mr. Omarr in person. "Sydney Omarr's whereabouts," he wrote, "are not for public knowledge."

If Mr. Omarr was as tough on Virgos as some of the others, I could well understand why he was on the lam. But, however he felt about Virgos, I was relieved to find he had something nice to say about us in a chapter he had included by another astrologist, Marsha Rose Emery, Ph.D. The chapter was entitled "Your Erotic Nature in 1990," and I really don't know how I chanced on it — the book just seemed to open to it. In any case, Dr. Emery had this to say about us Virgos and — well, our nature:

> Anyone you allow to get close to you this year will find out that Virgo is anything but a puritanical virgin. . . . This year people see you as far more sexually dynamic than anyone could have realized from your outward conservative stance.

That was more like it, and I eagerly embraced more of Mr. Omarr — particularly what he had to say about what was going to happen to me in 1990. At that time, he had done my whole 1990 month by month. For June, for example, he said, "Now is the time to dig in and deal with details. Read between the lines, if necessary."

That sure brought me up short. Reading between the lines is not an easy thing to do in your own book. Under August he said, "You'll pull strings from behind-the-scenes." Frankly I just don't think he had any idea how hard that would be for me to do with Marian and Polar Bear around. Nonetheless, under November he had good news: "One page of your life," he wrote, "is coming to an end while another more fulfilling chapter is beginning."

One thing I did hope — that it would be a more fulfilling chapter than this one had been so far. For the plain fact was, as far as getting Polar Bear's horoscope done, I wasn't getting anywhere. But that did not stop me. As I've always said, when the writing gets tough, the tough get writing. And some of us are not only tough but smart, too — smart enough to know that when we're not getting anywhere, we ought to get some help.

The help I got, through a friend's advice, was to call a woman named Robyn Ray — one who, my friend told me, was a consulting astrologer. Normally I'm a little leery about consulting consultants but in this case, astrology being a pretty leery subject to begin with, I decided to put my leeriness aside. I called Ms. Ray and asked her if we could do lunch. In New York, you will recall, we don't have lunch, we do lunch.

Ms. Ray was, it turned out, a charming woman — one who, before doing lunch with me, had been doing what she called a "power breakfast" with what she described as "a spiritual support group." I told her spiritual support was just what I needed at this stage, and I was sure we could really do a terrific power lunch. I also told her she seemed to me to be just what the doctor ordered. "It's funny you should say that," she said. "Nostradamus, you know, the most famous of all astro-predictors, was a doctor as well as an astrologer." She paused. "So were all doctors until just before the beginning of the seventeenth century — they were all astrologers as well as doctors. Nostradamus, in fact, avoided the Inquisition by writing his predictions in astrological terms. Otherwise he would have been accused of consorting with the Devil, and would have been executed."

I told her I would be careful to write my predictions in astrological terms, too. I knew there were millions of believers in astrology out there who might not execute me but they would certainly not take kindly to anyone making fun of them. Anyway, I next told Ms. Ray what my problem was, and I asked her if she had ever done such a thing as a cat horoscope. "No," Ms. Ray told me, smiling, "but I did do my dog's." How, I asked her nervously, did he like it? I reminded her Polar Bear was very critical. "He liked it fine," she said.

Relieved, I proceeded on to my difficulties about solving my problem — that I didn't know what year Polar Bear was born, let alone what time. Ms. Ray sighed. "You'll miss a lot," she said, "because you won't get the ascendant." It was my turn to sigh. I didn't want to admit I didn't know what an ascendant was. But I did tell her I was finding astrology very complicated in general and in particular I was getting pretty fed up with what they said about Virgos. "Don't get discouraged," Ms. Ray smiled, "Virgo is a sexy sign — particularly if you've got the moon and eight other planets affecting you."

I told her that was good news indeed and I would try to be on the lookout for the affections of any of those planets, and also would try to reciprocate them. I did mention, however, that I was concerned with reading lists of other Virgos — there seemed to be a lot of them, I said, with whom I didn't have anything in common. "Don't worry about that either," she said. "Other Virgos have different planets and different signs in different houses." Oh, I said. Finally I told her that I really didn't understand signs, or planets, or houses or even cusps. "Don't worry about cusps," she said; "they're just the edges. Remember it's not just the planetary influence on us — it's how we realize it. The problem most people have with astrology is that they think everything is predetermined, but it's not. That's my approach to astrology. I'm not taking responsibility for your own life away from you — you always have the choice. If somebody says something personal to you, you can either be insulted or you can take it in stride. For example, if an astrologer tells you that you seem to have a need to be destructive, you can handle this by going out and helping people tear down old buildings."

I told her that I had never thought of that, but New York was surely the right place for it. There were half a dozen buildings being torn down right on my block. I added that Polar Bear was pretty destructive around the apartment, but I didn't know how he'd be about going after a whole building. Ms. Ray smiled again. Then, gently, toward the end of our lunch, she explained to me that the astrology books I had been trying to read were too difficult for me at this stage of my astrological development. And, suspecting that that might be the case, she said she had brought along a book she thought I could handle. As we said good-bye she handed it to me.

The book was called *How to Learn Astrology,* by Marc Edmund Jones. And, later that very afternoon I started on it. The first thing I was relieved to find was that it was not a children's book — I had been a little nervous about that from what Ms. Ray had said. It was, however, a beginners' book — indeed, Mr. Jones mentioned beginners in his very second paragraph. Moving on for a moment, I went to see what he had to say about Virgos. "The symbol is the Virgin," he wrote, "represented by the 'M' of primitive matter, with an added stroke to suggest a chastity girdle."

A chastity girdle! Was there no limit to the insults to us Virgos? And even in a beginners' book! What if some child got ahold of it? How would you like to be a Virgo father and have to explain a thing like that to your child? Or, for that matter, how would you like to be a Virgo child asking your father what his "M" meant? Just the same, by this time pretty well inured to Virgos having to take so many slings and arrows of outrageous fortune, I just rose above what Mr. Jones had to say about us and went on trying to find out what "houses" and "planets" had to do with everything. "Most simply," Mr. Jones wrote, "a 'house' is a place where someone lives and in the horoscope it is a place where a planet, or group of planets, is located."

As I understood it, the planets were getting into our houses and the houses were getting into our signs, and that was why all Virgos, for example, weren't the same. But don't think for a moment there are just a couple of houses or anything like that — there are, apparently, twelve of them. Mr. Jones suggested that I learn each of their "fundamental meanings." The "First House," he explained, for example, had as its fundamental meaning "personality." The "Second House" had "resources and money," while the "Third House" had a whole slew of fundamental meanings, which he said were "Environment, Brethren, Communication and Short Trips." Yet not until the "Ninth House" did you get to "Understanding, Religion and Long Trips."

It really wasn't easy but I plowed on, because once I had those houses down pat, Mr. Jones suggested that I go on to the planets and what he called their "Simple Meaning." He had arranged these, he wrote, "in order of practical convenience":

Sun	Purpose
Moon	Feeling
Mars	Initiative
Venus	Acquisitiveness
Mercury	Mentality
Jupiter	Enthusiasm

Saturn	Sensitiveness
Uranus	Independence
Neptune	Obligation
Pluto	Obsession

Mr. Jones then proceeded from houses and planets to aspects and ascendants, conjunctions and oppositions, quadralures and sextiles, and even T-crosses and trines. If this was a book for beginners, I began to feel, Mr. Jones had the wrong boy. He stopped me, finally, on page 162:

> The beginner is learning to use an ephemeris and a Table of Houses without any necessity of mastering the mathematics behind them, and in the same fashion he can use the special type of logarithms prepared of astrological operations without need to concern himself over the mechanics of applying geometrical proportion to irregularities. He has been dealing on the one side with the daily or twenty-four hour motion of the planetary bodies, and on the other with the extent to which each planet must move to reach its horoscopic position. He has seen that the factor determining the latter is the time elapsing from midnight or noon of the ephemeris to the moment of birth, and by the simple device of adding the special logarithm of this lesser time span to the special logarithm of the zodiacal movement of a particular planet in a whole twenty-four hours he has the logarithm of the zodiacal span the planet in question must traverse to reach its horoscopic place.

For beginners, mind you. In the end, reluctantly, I had to say that astrology was just too tough for me. But I had not yet given up on it for Polar Bear. Polar Bear is tougher than I am — frankly, he's one tough cat — and remember, I hadn't yet tackled so much as one cat astrology book. But neither that nor the fact that I did not know what year Polar Bear was born, much less what time of day, did not now worry me. The main reason for this was that the more I read of astrology the more I realized that an awful lot of it is backward. East in astrology, for example, is west, and west is east. North is south, and south is north. Planets and houses don't move clockwise, they move counterclockwise. Indeed, the more I read the simple horoscopes in the astrology books, the more I realized that what the astrologers had really done was to take the lives of famous people, the details of which were well known, and then fit their signs and houses and planets and ascendants and all the rest of it into those already known facts — so this too was really backward.

If they could do all they did backward, I suddenly thought, in one of those flashes of inspiration for which I wish I were better known, why couldn't I? Maybe I too had another career ahead of me — after all, Nostradamus had been dead a long time and how many people are there out there who can name the No. 2 man in the field? Maybe also, of course, I wouldn't make it, but, whether I did it or not, I wasn't getting too far in my astrological studies going forward — I could hardly do any worse going in the opposite direction. One thing was certain. There and then I determined that was the way I would do Polar Bear's horoscope — with no holds barred and the Devil take the hindmost. I realized this was hardly an apt expression, considering the problem Nostradamus had with the Devil as well as the direction in which I was now determined to go, but my die was cast. I would start by taking Polar Bear's traits of character, both the good and the bad — I wanted, after all, a true astrological portrait, warts and all — and then I would go back and find out into which sign, with similiar character traits, he best fitted. And, in the end, I would know exactly what sign he was.

And, who knows? By the time I got to the ascendants and the aspects, conjunctions and oppositions, quadralures and sextiles, the T-crosses and the trines and even the cusps, I might be able to pinpoint the exact day and even the time he was born. Greenwich Mean Time, of course, is what I mean. Those astrology books give you not only Greenwich Mean Time but also Sidereal Time, and, frankly, at my age, I really didn't have the time, either Mean or Sidereal, for that kind of thing. That could be done, after all, by some child with a computer or something.

I had four books on cat astrology. And the very one I turned to first was easily the most remarkable — if for no other reason because it was written by a cat. It was called *Horoscopes for Pussycats,* and its author was a cat named Bootsie Campbell. The brief "About the Author" section told us that Ms., or for all I know Mrs., Campbell "had a father who was an all-white Maine Coon cat named Snowball," and a mother who was a "beautiful tortoiseshell." Bootsie herself, this section said, was "a Gemini." There was also a picture of the author which seemed to be taken front-on at night, and showed her looking out a window, deep in concentration, presumably at the stars.

I showed Bootsie's picture to Polar Bear, to which he gave his usual "so what" sniff. He really is very bad about other cats' pictures. This time, though, I did not let him get away with it. I pointed out to him in no unmistakable way that, while he was going around eating books, this Bootsie was writing them. I felt I did not have to add that, while I was hard at work doing all the writing of these books, what he was doing when he wasn't eating them was lying around living off the fat of the land from them.

The second book was called *The Cat Horoscope Book* and was written by a man named Henry Cole. He was described as "a nationally known astrologist." "Not only will this book," the jacket promised, "answer your most pressing problems, but it will also present you with a complete personality file on your cat based on privileged information."

This was particularly good news, because it would mean I would now have not just a complete personality file on Polar Bear but I would as well have one based on privileged information, which, if I could keep him from either digging around or prying into, I was determined to keep that way. I knew I had one thing going for me. In strong contrast to Bootsie, when Polar Bear went out on his balcony at night he was so interested in the pigeons that I would be willing to bet he didn't give the stars, let alone what they could be telling him, so much as a passing thought.

The third book was called *Cat Astrology.* This one was written by Mary Daniels, who was both a friend of mine and also a feature writer for the *Chicago Tribune,* as well as the author of a book about the cat Morris. Mrs. Daniels wrote in her introduction of a "chance encounter with a young Buddhist priest in a dark and dusty bookstore." She recounted the incident as follows:

> "Buddhists believe pets are in their last incarnation before becoming human and probably will reincarnate in their next life as humans; they are learning how to become more like people by associating with them.
>
> "All living things have karma (one's fate in one's

existence as determined by behavior in a previous)," continued the gentle Buddhist priest.

"Animals' perception of right and wrong is 'very dim,' " he added, "and their capacity for choice is less than ours. But if they respond to it properly, the general trend is upward."

Whether doing Polar Bear's horoscope, even if backward, would be an upward trend toward his perception of right and wrong I couldn't be sure. As for helping him on his way toward being a person in his next incarnation, I wasn't at all certain that that would be, for him, an upward step. I was, after all, as all faithful readers of my first book will recall, a Mark Twain man where this sort of thing was concerned. "If," said Mark, "Man could be crossed with a cat, it would improve Man but it would deteriorate the cat."

It was, in the introduction to my fourth cat astrology book — one called *Catsigns,* by William Fairchild, an English novelist and playwright — that I at last found something into which I could get my teeth. In fact here I found the first real backup I had yet had of my whole idea of doing Polar Bear's horoscope backward. I want you to remember, though, that I had the idea first, before I had read this. In any case, here's what Mr. Fairchild said on the subject:

> If you haven't the vaguest idea of his birthday, or, if he's a stray who's walked in without any identity papers and adopted you, just decide on his principal characteristic, find it under one of the Signs, and then read the rest of the information contained therein. If it doesn't check out for him it could be that he's been putting on an act to fool you, or that love has partially blinded you to his true strengths and weaknesses. Take a long cool look at him and try again. His Moon Sign won't tell you everything

> about him. . . . It *will* tell you, however, a very great deal that you will *need* to know for your mutual wellbeing and accord. After you've read it once for yourself you might try reading it a second time to him.

I knew this wouldn't be easy. Polar Bear is hard enough to read to the first time, and frankly, I had never tried doing it a second time. But I did try it anyway. And, of course, it didn't work. For Polar Bear, nothing works when it's something that to him is too much like working.

One thing I did learn from Mr. Fairchild was his dos and don'ts about how to handle cats of different Moon Signs. If, for example, you cat was an Aries cat, his "do" was to develop a keen sense of humor; his "don't" was not to question his belief in his own brilliance. If, on the other hand, you had a Cancer cat, your "do" was to smile at your wife/husband when he's looking, and your "don't" was to be a martyr — one is enough, Mr. Fairchild said. If, on the third hand, you had a Leo cat, your "do" was to let him think he's on the throne, whereas your "don't" would be to let him treat you as a devoted subject. Finally, if your cat was a Sagittarius, your "do" was to realize he thinks he's a genius, and your "don't" was to admit you're not a genius.

I thought a lot about these suggestions as applied to Polar Bear, but, helpful as Mr. Fairchild was, the fact remained I still did not have Polar Bear's sign. Accordingly, I proceeded to put all four cat astrology books in a row. After that I took their comments on the characters of the different cat signs, and compared them sign by sign with what I knew of Polar Bear's character. It wouldn't be easy, I knew, but then, what about astrology was?

I decided to score Polar Bear sign by sign — on a 0 to 5 basis, and then the sign on which he scored the highest would be his. I started with Aries (birthdates March 22 to April 19) because I had learned by this time that astrology books never started with something like Capricorn (December 22 to January 19), which would coincide with the year as we know it. Instead they always started with Aries. Frankly, I had my suspicions that the reason they do this is that this way they include April Fools' Day, but, putting these suspicions aside, I went along with it.

Actually I found much unanimity of opinion on Aries cats. Mr. Cole, for example, called the Aries cat "the egoist of all felines. Don't," he advised, "try too hard to adapt your Arian to the human condition for he views humans as merely a means to an end — his own." That sounded like Polar Bear. Mrs. Daniels called the Aries cat the "Godfather" and the "boss cat," and pointed out that he was ruled by Mars, "the red planet of War." There was a lot of Polar Bear here, but what Mrs. Daniels said made me concerned about female Aries cats — of whom I had a nervous picture as Amazons. "This is the cat," she went on, "that heads unerringly toward the very guest who hates cats." Again, she was right on the money about Polar Bear. As for Mr. Fairchild, he declared that the Aries cat's habit of "continually fizzling out of great enterprises can be ascribed to the effect of the Moon (water) on the fire sign (Aries)." Finally, when it came to the cat Bootsie, she spoke directly to Arian cats. "Your heart is easily moved," she said, "although you don't show it quite so intensely." She also gave these cats some party advice. "Don't arch your back," she said, "and ignore guests."

That last and the boss cat idea, as well as several other points, made me at least consider Polar Bear as a possible Aries — in fact, I was about to give him a 4 out of 5. But what stopped me in my tracks was the fact that Mr. Cole had called the Aries cat not only the "egoist of all felines," but also the "hippie of the cat kingdom." Polar Bear a hippie! The very thought was intolerable — he wasn't even a long-haired cat. Without further ado I scored Polar Bear only a 1 as an Aries.

Taurus (April 20 to May 20) was, according to Henry Cole, "the sign of the Bull — a naturally female sign" — something I found totally mind-stopping — but which he went on to say was "a fixed sign ruled by Venus." One thing was certain — that part of it, at least, ruled out Polar Bear. Nonetheless, when Mr. Cole went on to refer to the Taurian as a "hibernating bear," and a cat whose favorite sound was "the click of the refrigerator door," I wondered if my initial judgment had been too hasty. Mrs. Daniels went along with the refrigerator door and in fact called the Taurian a "gallumping gourmet. But," she continued, "if you're looking for an intellectual companion, quite frankly this is not the cat for you." This made me almost cross enough to give up the sign for Polar Bear — he is a terrific intellectual companion. However, when Mr. Fairchild said Taurians would "burrow into a blanket whenever the emotional climate became charged with tension," I reversed gears again. If there ever was a cat who hated any kind of climate being charged with tension more than Polar Bear, I have yet to meet him or her. He's really terrible about thunderstorms. Finally Bootsie had her direct advice: "Don't let unpleasant news of other pussy-cats," she said, "get you agitated and unsure of yourself." Frankly, it didn't seem to me that having unpleasant news of other cats would bother Polar Bear at all. What he would mind would be pleasant news of other cats. All in all, my final score for him as a Taurian was only 2 out of a possible 5.

Gemini (May 21 to June 20), the sign of the Twins, came next — one which Mr. Cole defined as a "somewhat masculine sign." At first I felt this sign might well be the one I was looking for — Polar Bear had, after all, been neutered — but Mr. Cole's next words were far from Polar Bear indeed. "The Gemini cat," he said, "will thrive in a houseful of creative people who are inveterate party-givers. He will then adopt your desk as his own and in his most ingratiating manner see to their every desire." Since Polar Bear's party behavior begins with a dawn attack on the caterer, and ends with an Achilles' heel charge on the last one to leave, I could hardly think of a more opposite description. Mrs. Daniels, on the other hand, piqued my interest with a reference to chess. "Your Taurian cat," she said, "will fall asleep while you play chess, while a Gemini cat would be right in there kibitzing, hardly able to contain his excitement, while patting with a paw the next piece you should move." Perfect as such a cat would be for me, I again had to admit it was not Polar Bear. His idea of excitement in a chess game is to knock the pieces off the board — something which, in a game in which you're ahead, would drive even a player in good health to an early grave. Mr. Fairchild said his Gemini cat entered his parties "on the heels of the first arrival and proceeded to stand about with an aristocratic air waiting to be introduced. . . . Eventually she made her departure along with a bunch of new friends and, as she went out of the front door, gave us a 'such-fun-do-hope-we-meet-again-soon' look." This was so far from Polar Bear I didn't even have the heart to think about it. As for Bootsie, she said flatly of Geminis, "You are of a dual nature. You are generous, just, changeful and fickle —

none may trust your love." I considered this, where Polar Bear was concerned, libelous and, combined with the party goings-on, I ended up giving him, for Gemini, a flat zero.

Of Cancer (June 21 to July 22), the Crab sign, Mr. Cole had this to say: "One minute a ball of fun, the next moody," and warned that your guests "might even find her sulking in the corner for no apparent reason, unapproachable, and even you whom she best knows could risk a handful of claw or, worse yet, a faceful of hiss." Upon reflection, thinking about Polar Bear and this assessment, I decided to take the Fifth — and by that I did not mean a 5. Cautiously I moved on to Mrs. Daniels. She called the Cancer a "Fraidy-Cat," and added that they had "a scuttling walk." I had to admit that, although Polar Bear was hardly a fraidy-cat, where things he was afraid of were concerned — things like thunderstorms, firecrackers, too much rain, and the vacuum cleaner — he did indeed scuttle with all four legs bent so low they barely kept his body from touching the floor. Mr. Fairchild told of the Cancerian cat's special look, the "see-how-I'm-suffering-but-far-be-it-for-me-to-complain" look. In extreme emergencies, he noted, "they will use its companion piece, the 'of-course-no-one-understands-me-I'm-just-a-cat' look." Polar Bear, I had to admit, was a master of both of these. Bootsie's advice to Cancer cats was also intriguing. "You must remain open minded," she said, "and allow others to influence you in the right directions." Once again, I liked the idea of trying that one on Polar Bear, but it was really a bit much to tell him to *remain* open-minded when, after all, the only open-mindedness I'd ever seen in him was over something about which he had not yet made up his mind. Nonetheless, Cancer came closer to him than any other sign I had studied so far, so I ended up giving him a 3.

Leo (July 23 to August 22), the sign of the Lion, looked at the start a good bet for Polar Bear — after all, what he looks like, second only to a bear, is a lion, and Henry Cole got the bet off to a good start. "All cats," he said, " 'own' their humans, but your Leo, of all cats, possesses them totally." And Mrs. Daniels added to the idea of this being Polar Bear's sign. "The Leo cat," she stated, "is the most catly of cats, felinity raised to its highest power." Mr. Fairchild, however, had a warning. "He's a big cat," he declared, "who does everything in a big way. Beware, though, of making promises you can't keep. He's also an idealist and if you once slip from the pedestal on which he's placed you, it will be a long time before you're able to reinstate yourself in his good books." If this wasn't right on target, I didn't know what was. But so was Bootsie, whose advice to Leo cats sounded as if it had been written for Polar Bear. "Don't be afraid," she wrote, "of thunder or lightning. Remember, you occasionally make loud, lonely, frightened sounds and frighten people too." There was no question in my mind but that Leo went even beyond Cancer for Polar Bear's possible sign. I gave it a 4.

I approached Virgo (August 23 to September 22), my own sign, with high hopes, not the least of which was that Mr. Fairchild had given the Virgo People's Sun Sign as one of the best suited for Virgo cats' moon sign. I decided to ignore that he had also included in this category Gemini, Leo, Capricorn, and Pisces. In any case, Henry Cole bolstered my hopes further. Moving by the fact that he said Virgo was "the sign of the Virgin, a naturally female sign," I moved right on to something else. "The

6th House of the Zodiac," he pointed out, "symbolizes 'I analyze,' " and if there was ever a cat who analyzed everything more than Polar Bear, I believe you would have to go into analysis yourself to find him or her. Even if I permitted him to chase mice, which of course I did not, I am sure he wouldn't have had to kill them — all he would have had to do would be to analyze them to death. Mr. Cole also went into Virgo's endless critical proclivities as well as their "fussbudgeting" and "worrywarting. While cats are creatures perfect unto themselves," he said, "your Virgo doesn't realize this; the major consequence being that she continually seeks a higher level of faultlessness." Ignoring the "she" here, I took a moment to bask in this praise for both of us. Mrs. Daniels pointed out that Virgo was ruled by the planet Mercury, which governs communication. I basked in this also. Both Polar Bear and I were terrific communicators. In fairness, I should point out that Mrs. Daniels did go into our fussiness and finickiness. "Alas," she wrote, "this is not one of the easiest signs with which to live." But how, I wanted to ask her, could it be otherwise? As I've always told the people I work with, it is never easy to live with someone who is always right.

Nonetheless, it remained for Mr. Fairchild to put the finishing touches on my placing Polar Bear in Virgo. "Your Virgo Cat," he said, "critical and choosy from birth, reserves the apogee of his suspicion for pills and will go to almost any lengths, including biting your finger, in order not to swallow one." That surely was Polar Bear all the way. And, if I needed a finale, I had it from Bootsie. "The pupils of your eyes," she said, "grow larger and larger at the sound of a pigeon." Not even the sight, mind you, just the sound.

There was no question but that I had achieved what I had set out to do — Virgo was Polar Bear's sign. I gave him a 5 on it, and refused even to look at the Libras, Scorpios, Sagittariuses, Capricorns, Aquarians, or Pisceses. Indeed all that was left now was for me to figure out his exact day of birth in Virgo. I know there are people out there who will say I just chose September 2 because that was my birthday, but they will be wrong. By now an expert in astrology, I did it in a way which I am sure would have made even Nostradamus proud. First I figured out that Polar Bear had to be nearer Leo, which was ruled by the Sun, the most powerful planet in the solar system, and one to which I had given a 4, than he was to Libra (September 24 to October 23), and Libra, for heaven's sake, was just one more of those damn signs ruled by a girl — again, the planet Venus, if you please, the planet of Beauty, and Love and Harmony. All right, I didn't mind her coming after Virgo, but sure not *in* it. Anyway I didn't need her, not with that fine Leo before Virgo. And, remember, I didn't ignore the cusps and the ascendants or the trines or anything else either. And it all came out September 2 — 2 A.M. September 2, to be precise.

Of course there will probably be a few of you out there who will want to know, besides the time and the date, the year. I am not going to tell you. Frankly, Polar Bear is just as sensitive about his age as the next man — and if that man happens to be me, I see no reason why I should go around blabbing it all over the place. If you want to write me about it, go ahead — it's a free country. But, I warn you, I am now a famous astrologer and, like Sydney Omarr's, my whereabouts are not public knowledge.

V ◦ *You Ought to Be in Pictures*

One of the most exciting pieces of news a writer can have about a book he has written is that it is going to be made into a movie. When this happened to my first book about Polar Bear, however, I did not get as excited as you might expect.

It is true that I harbored for a moment a passing dream, which I hoped would be well written, about a house in Bel Air and a swimming pool — in fact two swimming pools, one for me and one wired-in, like his balcony, for Polar Bear. But nothing elaborate, mind you, like having Perrier water in our pools or anything like that. In other words, swimming pools or no swimming pools, I kept my feet on the ground.

The reason I could not get more excited and that I kept my feet on the ground is a simple one. This is that, despite having heard that one or more of my books are going to be made into a play or a movie, I have a very poor track record of having it actually happen. Not that I haven't come close, I want you to know, but, at the end, no cigar.

On the very first day after the publication of my very second book, *The Last Resorts,* for example, I entered a friend's party and was quickly ushered to his television set. His set was not only on but was on with the then very popular Sunday night broadcast of none other than the late Walter Winchell — at that time the be-all and end-all of gossip columnists. Mr. Winchell's lead item that night was an announcement from Mr. Irving Berlin that Ethel Merman's next musical, with Mr. Berlin doing the music and lyrics, would be my book. Everybody congratulated me and treated me as if I was sum punkins — an expression you probably don't know but which would be good for you to look up in your dictionary. A word looked up, you know, is a word remembered. I looked it up, as a matter of fact, and it wasn't there. As I told you, dictionaries are written by children.

In any case, the very next morning, I had a telephone call from Mr. Berlin himself. He asked me if I had seen the broadcast, and, when I said that I had, he asked me if I would come to see him. I said of course I would, after which he explained he was in the hospital but that I was to come there anyway.

When I arrived at Mr. Berlin's bedside he shook hands and then looked sharply at me. "Do you," he asked, "have anything against Flo Ziegfeld?" I shook my head. I did not tell him that Mr. Ziegfeld had died — something I later looked up — when I was twelve. "Good," he said. Then came another question. "Do you," he asked, "write dialogue?" This time I nodded my head as sagely as I could. "Good," he said again. "We'll get started tomorrow morning." He paused and looked out the window. "I want to start," he continued, "with 'Alexander's Ragtime Band.' " He paused again and then looked straight at me. "But," he said, "we'll have to hurry — my health is not good. I'm a very ill man, you know. Frankly, I'm at death's door."

The door was a long time opening — Mr. Berlin was then sixty-one and he did not pass on until forty years later, at the age of one hundred and one. We never, however, went to work on our project. The trouble was that Mr. Berlin had neglected to inform Ms. Merman about his plans before the Winchell show, and that very day Ms. Merman issued a statement that she did not appreciate Mr. Berlin announcing her shows without his having the courtesy to inform her of them in advance, and that therefore she would not do *The Last Resorts.* Mr. Berlin next tried Ms. Mary Martin, but Ms. Martin curtly replied that she was not in the market for Ms. Merman's rejects. Therefore, that was not only the end of Ms. Martin but, as it turned out, Mr. Berlin also.

I do not wish to go into everything that went on from there. Suffice it to say that the Messrs. Howard Lindsay and Russel Crouse took over from Mr. Berlin and, after they finished a "book" of my book, they sent it to Mr. Cole Porter. Mr. Porter, however, replied that he did not want Mr. Berlin's rejects, and that was the end of not only Mr. Cole Porter but also of the Messrs. Lindsay and Crouse. Altogether, *The Last Resorts* was optioned by eleven different producers, including Mr. George Abbott and Mr. Harold Prince, and had eleven different books of it written, including ones by such distinguished dramatists as Jean Kerr and the late John Patrick. Indeed Mr. Porter once told me that he alone had received no fewer than five books of my book. In the end, though, it was never produced. Nonetheless, it was announced so many times that a friend of mine from Texas came all the way from there just to see it. I did not see him, but after he went back to Texas he wrote me that he had liked the show very much. To this day, however, I have never been able to find out what show he did see that he thought was it.

I have had a few other somewhat similar close misses — albeit not so highly publicized ones — with other books I have written being optioned for plays or movie rights. Therefore, understandably, I did not go to the bank on the news about my cat book. Indeed, this time my dream about Bel Air and a swimming pool was, as I said, a very short dream — one which was marred at the beginning by the fact that I knew Polar Bear wouldn't be too crazy about a swimming pool anyway.

The producer of "The Cat Who Came for Christmas" was to be Mr. Pierre Cossette, a man whom I had never met but who was the producer of what, I was told, were the terrific Grammy shows. Although I had never seen a Grammy show, I was also told he would do a terrific job on my cat story. In any case, one of Mr. Cossette's first efforts was to give a press interview in which he announced there would be a nationwide contest to choose the cat who would play Polar Bear — one which, he said, would be the biggest search in Hollywood since the search for Scarlett O'Hara. He also said that not only would there be "kitty kasting kalls" all over the country to find "the proper catidates" — Mr. Cossette is very big on puns — but also that the final contest would be held in Madison Square Garden.

At the prospect of a Scarlett O'Hara search, I was considerably less enthusiastic than Mr. Cossette. I visualized hundreds of cats running all over Madison Square Garden and thousands more outside, and I could see almost endless possibilities of cats fighting, getting hurt, and even getting lost. Mr. Cossette said I simply didn't understand the value of "free pre" — which he explained to me was free publicity. I said that I did, but that what we would undoubtedly get would be "post mort" — which I did not explain. In the end we agreed on an entirely different kind of contest — one by appointment only.

Actually, the more I thought about the whole idea of a contest, the less I thought of it. I have, you see, a thing about contests — one which goes way back in my childhood to my first teenage summer. That summer there was an advertisement in a Boston newspaper about a contest — one which was to see who could make the most words of three letters or more out of the letters in the words "Pierce Arrow." The contest was limited to New England, but it was being run by the national Pierce-Arrow company, maker of the automobile of that name which in those days was a very big thing — bigger, indeed, than the Cadillac or Packard or in fact any competitor.

The first prize was to be a Pierce Arrow — a vehicle whose cost, as I remember, was $2,000 — an astronomical sum for those days. The second prize was a $1,000 ticket on a Pierce Arrow, and the third prize was a $500 ticket. The ad ran in June, as I recall, and all entries had to be in by the end of August. There was nothing for me and my faithful Brookie to do but give up a summer of swimming and sailing and baseball and tennis. Instead, with Brookie beside me, day after day, night after night, I typed line after line of word after word on sheet after sheet. At thirteen, one has incredible persistence, and if

Brookie, at eight, did not have quite as much as I did, he at least tried his best by sticking beside me. I worked from a dozen or more dictionaries and typed and retyped the words, single-spaced, on the same line, way over in the left margin. If I came to a word that was not included in at least two dictionaries, I added a note about it on the same line — over and over again, the same kind of entry, such as "foreign word not in most American dictionaries," or "Australian bird, only in English dictionary, not in American."

Finally, late in August, I finished. I sent in my hard-worked pages. I waited patiently but hopefully. I did not see how anyone could have found any more words unless they had used more foreign dictionaries and had borne down more heavily on foreign words. In any case, sure enough, in early September the paper announced the winners and, even more surely enough, there was my name. I had won, the paper said, third prize.

The whole family, including Brookie, shared in my excitement. And when I received from the company not only a letter but also a check for $500, my happiness was complete. All I had to do, the letter said, was to take the letter and the check down to the nearest Pierce Arrow dealer.

Brookie and I went together, and although at first they did not want to let Brookie into the showroom where all the cars were — Brookie was never very good about tires — I took him in anyway. I found the man apparently in charge and showed him my letter and my check. He looked at them both for some time but then gave them both back to me. "Well?" he asked. I told him if it was OK with him I would like to have the money instead of the check. I told him politely that I had nothing against Pierce Arrows, but I was only thirteen and therefore would have to wait three years just to drive mine out of the showroom — and this, I pointed out helpfully, might be pretty inconvenient for him. If he would just give me $495, I said, I would be happy to call it square. He shook his head. "No," he said, "we can't do that. The check is only good *on* a Pierce Arrow — toward the purchase *of* a Pierce Arrow."

I considered this development for some time. Well, I asked him, how much would he take for my check? "I can't take anything for it," he said. "We don't cash checks." I told him that then, I guess, I would just have to cash it somewhere else — at, say, a bank. Once more he shook his head. "Look at your check," he said. "It's not a cashable check except *for* a Pierce Arrow." By this time I was getting pretty discouraged, and Brookie was getting restless. I did, however, have one last idea. Well, I suggested, if he didn't mind, I would just wait there until the first customer came along to buy a Pierce Arrow and then I would give him my check and the customer could just give me, say, $490 for it. The man shook his head a last time. "You can't do that," he said. "You check is nontransferable. It says so, right on it. Look at it."

The last thing I wanted to do right then was to look at that check again. Instead, I called Brookie over and pointed to the white-walled tire of the nearest brand-new Pierce Arrow. Before the man could do anything, Brookie rose to the occasion. Then, together, we turned on our heel and paw and made our exit.

When I got home I realized that not only had I been had, but I also began to have my doubts about the whole contest. My doubts centered on the first and second prize-winners. If nothing else, I wanted to know how they had gotten more words than I had and, if so, how many more.

Their names were listed in the paper with their addresses. The first prize winner had an address in Portland, Maine; the second, in Providence, Rhode Island. I called information for their telephone numbers. Neither, apparently, had a telephone.

Nonetheless, as I said, at thirteen one is persistent. An older friend of my brother who had a driving license drove me first to Portland. There was no such person at the address — in fact no one at that address or around it had ever heard of such a person. Next we went to the address in Providence. The same situation obtained there. I had, at last, proof. The whole contest had been a fraud. I had really been the winner, but I had won nothing. Later that fall I learned that the company, having already decided to go out of business, had used the contest to get people to buy their last cars in the dealerships.

To say the whole experience soured me on contests is to put it mildly. Once bitten, I was not only twice shy — I was permanently so — and as time went by not in the least shy about it either. To this day, if I see people in line to buy lottery tickets I endeavor to dissuade them. I am not saying lotteries are frauds — they're not — but the odds are astronomical, and the payback, even if you do win, after the state and the federal government and everybody else, including the person who sold the ticket to you, get their cuts is hardly more than fifty percent. Even the worst slot machines pay over sixty percent.

All in all, when Mr. Cossette came up with the idea of a contest to find a cat to play Polar Bear, I did not believe he had any intention of staging a fraud, but at the same time I wanted iron safeguards. In answer to this he reiterated that the contest would be on an appointment-only basis and furthermore he said I could be one of the judges. The other two, he said, would be the director of the movie and himself.

Alas, this too rang a bell — and again not a good one. The only time I have ever been a judge in a national contest was an experience which paled even my Pierce Arrow debacle.

The date was 1972, and the occasion was the Miss U.S.A. Pageant — one which was held, that year, in a hotel in Puerto Rico. At first my selection had seemed a high honor — indeed, the person who informed me of my selection told me it was really a very high honor because, he said, the final show was not only going to be televised live but would be one of the first live national television shows to be carried via satellite and therefore would be seen by over seventy-two million people. Every single one of us connected with the show would be, he said, looking at me sternly, vitally important to the success of the whole thing. And, he concluded, no one would be more so than I, as one of the judges, would be. "In front of seventy-two million people," he said looking me right in the eye, "the last thing we want is a bomb."

As a matter of fact, a bomb was just what we did have. But I am getting ahead of my story. Hardly had I arrived in Puerto Rico when I was greeted by a real greeter type. "I'm Mitch Potter," he said, holding out his hand. "I'm in charge of handling the judges." I raised my left eyebrow at this — I can only raise my left eyebrow because I have very little hair on my right eyebrow, but I do it, if I do say so, very effectively. "You will have complete freedom," Mr. Potter said. "Complete freedom," he repeated. Obviously he had read my eyebrow.

Mr. Potter then explained what our job judging the

girls — I remember he never used the word "women" — would be. We would have to pick Miss U.S.A. from the fifty-one winners of the states' pageants and that then Miss U.S.A. would go on to compete against "girls" from other countries to be Miss Universe. I asked him why Miss Universe — why not Miss World? "Because," he explained patiently, "there already *is* a Miss World contest." He paused. "As a matter of fact," he continued, "there is a Miss Universe contest, a Miss World contest, a Miss America contest, a Mrs. America contest, a Miss Venus contest, a Miss International contest, a Miss Black America contest, a Miss Teen-Age America contest, a Miss Junior Miss contest, a Miss Pre-Teen-Age America contest . . ." I held up my hand. I had heard enough. The thought that one is not as special as one thought one was is never easy to take. "The difference between the Miss America contest and the Miss U.S.A. contest," Mr. Potter explained, "is that the Miss America contest has a talent competition. We don't." Mr. Potter was obviously very proud of this. Pride was apparently a big thing with the Miss U.S.A. Pageant. "Over the years," he continued, "we've had some of the most famous names in the world as judges. Why, we've even had *ambassadors*." I wanted to know what ambassador. He paused a moment, obviously thinking, then brightened. "The ambassador," he said, "from Thailand to Sweden." Oh, I said. At this point he began to look us over critically. "I would also like to say," he said sternly, "that over the years every single one of our judges has entered into the spirit of the thing — with two exceptions. They were two glamour boys from Hollywood who were more interested in chasing the girls than in judging."

I was going to tell him that I supposed there would

always be rotten apples in any barrel — even among Miss U.S.A. judges — but I didn't get a chance, because once again he seemed to be looking at me critically. "For your information," he said, "every three girls have a chaperone who is either with them or knows exactly where each one is at all times. The girls are all on the fourth floor of the hotel — no one is even allowed on that floor except the chaperones. Not even their fathers or their brothers. At the elevator doors they have police."

That very evening, Mr. Potter told us, concluding his not-so-brief briefing, would be our first judging. "It's the Semi-Finals," he said, "Evening Gowns and Swimsuits. I suggest that, as the girls go by, you use abbreviated symbols, like 'O' for outstanding, 'S' for so-so, and 'D' for dog." With that he started to leave us, but before he did I told him I would never use that final symbol — it was an antianimal expression.

The next morning, I went to see a rehearsal for the television show. If you've ever seen one of the many "Miss" shows, you may find it hard to believe they have a rehearsal, but they do. In fact, for three days they do. Then, you may well ask, why isn't it a better show? You may well ask this, but I, as a former TV critic, do not feel that I am the one to give you the answer. Suffice it to say that the rehearsals are, if such is possible, worse than the actual show. In any case, sitting in the rehearsal hall, I was spotted by Herb Landon, the executive director of the pageant. "You're not supposed to be here," he said sternly. "The girls aren't supposed to be looked at by the judges except when they're being judged." He paused. "But," he continued, "as long as you're here you might as well stay, and I want to tell you something. If there is one thing I resent it's the implication that these are hard, tough kids.

We take great pains to see that our girls are good girls. We are really beyond reproach.

"It's all gone now," he went on, warming to his task, "the whole idea of a girl with a great body swinging down the runway. She may not even have a great body — why, we've had Phi Beta Kappas. Our girls meet *kings!* It's a matter of breeding — look at them! They're not hard. They're nice, neat, clean girls from good families. Notice how they're dressed — just for rehearsal! Even if they're wearing shlumpy clothes, they're clean!"

I went next to the swimming pool, where I had been told I would find a man named Sid Sussman, who, my informer informed me, had been responsible for an enormous number of girls getting to the Miss U.S.A. and other national pageants. I found Mr. Sussman sunning himself with a large cigar in his mouth. "I've been called the Vince Lombardi of this racket," he said. "It's a hard thing to live down. I just handle D.C., Maryland, and Virginia now, but I've also handled Pennsylvania and other places. I used to handle Florida, but I took a bath there. I run close to three hundred pageants a year, and I work all year long. I've got a 'farm system' — Miss Teen-Age, Miss Pre-Teen, Miss Junior Miss. You name it, I run it. I'm the creative type. I like to take a kid off the street and make her something."

Make her *what?* I wanted to know. He thought for a moment. "Well," he said, "I had the kid who later was married to Richard Zanuck." Mr. Sussman puffed his cigar. "In my local contests," he said, "I wouldn't presume to tell a judge who to pick. All I do is pick the judges." He smiled. "I don't mind doing a little indicating — the only thing I mind is when someone says a girl is my girl. I resent that. I may be a bachelor, but with eighteen thousand girls a year in my pageants, I'm not hard up for female company. But the fact is, I've got to like my winners. Remember, you pick them for one night. I have to live with them."

Before interviewing the girls, the judges were given biographical sheets about them. On these the girls had entered their lives' ambitions, as well as why they had entered the Miss U.S.A. contest. A surprising number, I noted, had answered both of these questions together — that to be Miss U.S.A. *was* their life's ambition. There was also the question of who do you think is the most important man in the world today. It was very close. The winner was Billy Graham. He had four votes, followed by President Nixon and Bob Hope, who had three each. An extraordinary number of the girls, I learned, had been in dozens of contests. Miss Georgia, for example, had been in seventy-nine. She had been Miss Peach Queen, Miss Rhododendron Queen, Miss Labor Day Queen, and Miss North Carolina Motor Speedway Queen. Miss Minnesota had been Miss Hibbing (Minn.), Miss Iron Range, and Miss City Courts Employees Queen of St. Paul. Miss Kansas, I noted, was Pep Club President. What, I asked, is a pep club? "I work with the cheerleaders," she told us. "I'm responsible for the pep of five hundred girls." Miss Indiana was peppy, too. "I love being a cheerleader," she said. "I've been a cheerleader for six years. It's been practically my whole life."

Just the same, some of the girls had memorable answers to our questions. My favorite was Miss New York, a remarkable young woman named Alberta Phillips, the only black woman in the contest and the one who I thought should have won it — if for no other reason than for the way she answered my question as to how she got into it in the first place. She smiled. "During my interview," she said, "I lied about my color."

The final afternoon I played golf. Coming back to the hotel, I found it surrounded by hundreds of picketers of the Puerto Rican Socialist Party. "¡FUERA YANQUI! ¡FUERA MISS U.S.A.!" their signs read. Their leader, Florencio Merced, explained to the media their objections. "The pageant," he said, "represents a vile utilization of women as sex objects."

That evening, when the show was on the air and just before the winner, Miss Hawaii, was announced, there was a tremendous rumbling sound. Not until later, however, did I learn what it was. We had, indeed, bombed. Or, rather, I should say, we had been bombed. Still another Puerto Rican party, the Independencias, had attempted to knock the show off the air by getting at the electronic equipment on the seventh and top floor of the hotel. Since there were police there, they couldn't get to the seventh floor, so what they did was bomb the sixth floor — the floor where all the judges' rooms were.

I did not, I want you to know, take it personally — there was, after all, no way they could know that I felt about the pageant just the way they did. The bomb actually went off in room 663 — *my* room was 662. When I was finally allowed in there by the police, the room was a shambles of broken glass. The whole porch had been blown off, and with it — nowhere to be seen — were my brand new swimming trunks, which I had put on the porch to dry. Gazing at the wreckage and thinking of the Coronation Ball, which was still to come, I tried, as I always do, to look on the bright side. Swimsuit was, for me, now out — the fact is, I wouldn't have had a chance in Swimsuit anyway. The way I saw it, I would just have to score heavily in Evening Dress and Personality.

Nervous as I was about again being called on to be a judge, I had to admit there were seminal differences between being a judge of an international beauty pageant and being a judge to pick a cat to play Polar Bear in a movie. For one thing, in this contest there would be no Swimsuit competition at all. And this was just as well. Although I have known many cats who liked to swim, Polar Bear is not one of them. Indeed he is very much not one of them — something I indelibly deduced one morning when, as is his wont, he was circling my bathtub and managed to fall in. Unfortunately, despite the nice warm water, he not only completely lost his cool, he also managed his fall directly adjacent to what I shall delicately describe as the lower part of my stomach. Before I could do anything, after several desperate attempts to claw the water, he then proceeded to claw until he reached what to him was shore, but to me was something else. I shall not say more except to say that, despite my quick capsize and masterful rollover, Polar Bear wasn't the only one who lost his cool that morning.

If there would be no Swimsuit competition, neither would there be Evening Dress. All cats in the competition would, like Polar Bear, be dressed alike — in fact, they would all be formally evening dressed, resplendent in their white whiskers and tails. There remained, however, two other important competitions. The first was Personality. Unsatisfactory as this word is for cats, who, after all, have more of this than any "person" I have met, this would indeed be undoubtedly the quality which would be key to the one who would get the part. Nonetheless, side by side with Personality would be the equally crucial one of Talent — the very qualification the Miss U.S.A. Pageant so prided itself on not having, if you'll pardon ending on a preposition, any of.

And, judging — if you'll also pardon that word — from the letters and pictures which poured in, there was certainly no lack of talent among the potential contenders. Before I even got to the matter of Talent, however, as I read the letters I was amazed, to begin with, by how many white cats there were. You don't see that many white cats in people's homes but, make no mistake, there are hundreds, thousands, and, I would guess, even hundreds of thousands of them. Not a few people even offered white female cats for the contest and, admitting this in their letters, wanted to know if the gender of their cat would exclude them. To these I immediately replied that it would not — that Lassie the Dog was, after all, a male and why should not Polar Bear the Cat be female? There would be, I assured one and all, no sexism in any contest of which I was a judge — it would be E.R.A. all the way.

Surprised as I was at the number of white cats, I was even more surprised by the number of these cats who, as their owners expressed, "did things." These "things" seemed indeed almost endless. There were people who had cats who could tell the time of day, who could wake them with a paw on their face, who could tell there was someone at the door before the doorbell rang, who could tell the telephone was going to ring before it rang and who could turn off the answering machine when it annoyed them. There were also people who had cats who could shake hands, who could sit up and beg, who could walk on their hind legs, who could retrieve and who could jump through hoops, and even who could lie down and roll over and pray. There were other cats who could turn on the faucet in the sink, who could use the toilet, who could open closet and kitchen cupboards, who could even open heavy doors by repeatedly jumping up and turning the doorknob, even cats who could open lightweight windows and close heavy ones. There were cats, too, who could play the piano and even pick out tunes, who could read books — or at least picture books — who could watch TV and turn it on as well as off, who could look at themselves in the mirror and even primp, who could type, and not only on a typewriter but also on a word processor. Finally, there were cats who could empty the trash or garbage.

Just the same, the more I read what these cats could do, the more I realized that Polar Bear, too, "did things." In fact he did an awful lot of those very same things those other people's cats did. He couldn't tell time in general, but he could certainly tell when it was time for something he wanted. He, too, woke me with a paw on my face, although when he was particularly hungry, he preferred, depending on his mood, a tail tickle or a full tail swipe. And he too knew when there was someone at the door before the doorbell rang — indeed, he could tell they were coming to my apartment the moment the elevator stopped and they got out.

As for many other things those other cats did, like shaking hands and sitting up and begging and walking on his hind legs and retrieving and jumping through hoops and lying down and rolling and praying — all of these weren't necessarily things he couldn't do, he just wouldn't do them. He could turn on faucets, he could open and close closet doors and cupboards, and, if he couldn't open lightweight windows and close heavy ones, this was again not because he couldn't — he just didn't do windows. Finally, when it came to emptying the trash or the garbage, Polar Bear not only could do that — and regularly did so when he was looking for something he wanted — he also went a step further. He put things in the trash or garbage when they were something he did not want, such as boxes of medicine I had for him, or the nail clippers I used on him or a comb he didn't like. He did this, and in fact he did so much of this, that, when I couldn't find one of those things, the trash basket or the garbage can was one of the first places I looked.

There remained, just the same, one large question. The fact that there were cats who could do, and sometimes did, remarkable things did not mean they would or could do these things on command or on some specific occasion. And, even if they could or would, could or would they perform them on a set — in a totally strange place with dozens of total strangers around and dozens of distractions such as lights, dollies, whipping wires, and even traveling cameras over their heads and zooming in on them? Could or would they, too, perform without their own "person" giving them their commands — without even their own person being there at all and being left with a total stranger trainer?

One thing I did know — Polar Bear would not do those things, not even things he did regularly, when anybody else was around, no matter who was telling him to do them, and that included me. And, as for doing those things on a set with all the distractions and the strangers, I could only advise any movie company which planned on such an operation to take out a catastrophic policy — one which should be carefully written to include not only equipment and people but also the pun.

Not that I ever harbored any illusion of Polar Bear being able to play Polar Bear to begin with. A cat who, after all, didn't even want to be a celebrity when the whole job of becoming one had been handed to him on a platter, and who didn't have to do anything about being one because it was all done for him, certainly would have about as much desire to be a movie star as your average armadillo. Just the same, as I compared what he was doing with his life with what other cats were doing with theirs, I had an uncomfortable feeling. I do not mean that I was in the least dissatisfied with him the way he was. As a matter of fact, my thoughts didn't concern me at all — something which is very unusual for me — they concerned only him. I just wondered if he wasn't missing something that could make his life more interesting. Too much of his life, after all, it seemed to me, was spent napping, and the only time his napping seemed to be interrupted was when he was getting ready for a real sleep.

Therefore, without further ado, and again not with any idea that he could do many or even several of those feats the other cats could do, but merely that he might like to learn at least one of them, I resolved to get down to the job of training him. The only trick he had ever learned to do in all the years I had had him was to walk — or at least stay — on a leash. Surely there had to be something he could learn to do besides that.

My first job, I knew, would be to get some good books on the subject. And, embarking on this, the very first book I came upon had a good piece of news right on the cover. It was called *The Complete Guide to Training Your Cat*, by Ray Berwick, and even above the title was the line "Who says you can't teach an old cat new tricks?"

I didn't want Polar Bear to see that — he is very sensitive about the word "old" — but for me, as a mature teacher, it was as I say very good news. It meant that, when it came to training, you didn't have to start your cat from scratch — or, rather, at kittenhood. The second book I came upon, by Paul and Jo Loeb, also had an encouraging title — *You* CAN *Train Your Cat,* it was called. And, if the capitalized "*CAN*" seemed a little defensive, it was still, I decided, basically positive. The third book I came upon, however, had far more disturbing news, and this news too was, if you please, right in the title. It was a book by Leon Whitney, a veterinarian, and it was called *Training You to Train Your Cat.*

Frankly, I had never realized that I had to be trained before I trained Polar Bear. Ever since my Brush Hill School days, let alone the Army, training has never been my long suit. I've always thought I was very good at training other people, but I have never felt other people were worth a damn training me. But, obviously, this time I would have to bite the bullet. It was really maddening, though. Apparently I would have to be professionally taught how to communicate with an animal I had been communicating with just fine, thank you, for more than ten years. But, for Polar Bear's sake I resolved to do it.

One thing I did not need was anyone telling me what was the best book on the art of communication with an animal. It was one given me many years ago by none other than my longtime friend Doris Day. It was, Doris told me then, her favorite book, and I know that it still is. It is called *Kinship with All Life,* by J. Allen Boone, and it was published as far back as 1954. To me, at this time, faced with the possibility of a movie cat, it was particularly fascinating because it began with a movie dog. The dog was, as a matter of fact, the most famous movie dog of all time — more remarkable even than the various Rin Tin Tins and Lassies which followed him. His name was Strongheart, and he made his first film, *The Silent Call,* as far back as 1921 — two years before the first of the Rin Tin Tin movies and a full seventeen years before the first of the Lassie films.

As compared to the many Rin Tin Tins and Lassies, there was only one Strongheart, but what a dog he was. Originally trained as a military dog and for police work in Germany, he was brought to Hollywood as a three-year-old by the screenwriter Jane Murphin and her husband, Larry Trimble, a director. Up until Strongheart, no animal of any kind had ever been given a leading role in a film, but with his very first film, *The Silent Call,* Strongheart was catapulted into becoming not only Hollywood's top-ranking star but its top box-office attraction of all stars, people stars included. In between a couple of his films, and more or less by chance, Mr. Boone, a writer and film producer — a man who up until the time he met Strongheart knew, as he wrote, "practically nothing about dogs" — was given the job of looking after the dog while the Trimbles were away.

Mr. Boone was also given, he records, just three basic instructions on how he was to treat Strongheart. He was not to "talk down to him," not to use "baby talk" with him, and, most important, not "to say anything to him with my lips that I did not sincerely mean in my heart." With just these three injunctions, Mr. Boone soon realized that Strongheart was not only able to understand human talk but also to read "human thinking." As time went on, however, Mr. Boone also realized that everything in their communication "moved," as he put it, "in only one direction — from me to him." Determined to change this, Mr. Boone embarked on a program which included, among other things, instead of his taking Strongheart for a walk, Strongheart taking him. He would indeed do nothing when they started a walk except just stand there until Strongheart decided where they would go.

Reading this was very encouraging to me because, as I have already mentioned, when I put Polar Bear down with his leash and harness in the Park, I didn't pull him — I let him decide where he wanted to pull me. I wouldn't have admitted to Mr. Boone that the reason I didn't pull him was that it wouldn't do any good, but at least I didn't anyway. The trouble was, of course, Polar Bear never wanted to go anywhere except stay where he was — but still, the point is I really was following Mr. Boone's teaching to the letter even if I couldn't follow it to the extent of Polar Bear going somewhere.

Mr. Boone never, apparently, worked with cats. But, after Strongheart, he did communicate with a wide variety of other creatures. Indeed, toward the end of *Kinship with All Life* he even attempted communication with an army of ants. These ants had invaded his porch, and brandishing both a broom and poisons over their heads, he addressed them as follows:

> "You ants may not be aware of it," I said, "but I am in a position to wipe most of you out of existence within the next few minutes with this poison and this broom. But that doesn't seem to be the right answer. We humans have been killing one another off in matters of this kind for centuries and we are worse off today than we were when it started."
>
> Then remembering how every living thing likes to be

> appreciated I began sending all the complimentary things I could think of in their direction. I told them how much I admired their keen intelligence . . . their zest for living . . . their complete dedication to whatever they happened to be doing at the moment . . . their harmonious action in a common purpose . . . their ability to work together without misunderstandings or the need to be constantly told what to do.

At this juncture Mr. Boone paused to take a look at the ants through his magnifying glass. Since the situation was, as he described it, "worse than ever," he decided to bring his broadcast to a close:

> "That's all I have to say to you ants," I said. "I have honestly done my best in this situation. The rest is up to you fellows. I am speaking to you as a gentleman to a gentleman."

Sure enough, that very night Mr. Boone went out on his porch and there was not an ant in sight:

> Not one! The icebox door was still wide open, with inviting food inside and there was some food on the nearby table. But not an ant in sight . . . those little fellows had actually kept their part of the Gentleman's Agreement. This happened several years ago. Since then I have never been bothered by ants in any manner, at home or abroad. Occasionally a scout ant passes through on his way from outdoors to outdoors and pauses just long enough for us to exchange a friendly, silent greeting with each other.

Finally, in his last chapter Mr. Boone decides that when a fly decends on him instead of shooing it away or grabbing a Flit gun he will make friends with it. He noticed, again with his magnifying glass, that when the fly paraded on his finger, he would begin to rub his legs over his head, causing his head, as Mr. Boone puts it, "to bob briskly up and down in my direction":

> Assuming that this could be his way of expressing appreciation, and not to be outdone in good manners in my own house, especially by a fly, I began bowing just as politely back to him. I was grateful that none of the neighbors could see me through the windows.

A few days after making friends with his fly, Mr. Boone gave him the name Freddie — one which made me a little nervous because that is the name of my peerless editor at Little, Brown, and I was afraid she would think I was making fun of her. I was not, of course — Mr. Boone named the fly. I had nothing to do with it, honest I didn't. In any case, one day while Freddie was standing in the palm of Mr. Boone's hand, getting his wings stroked, Mr. Boone decided to begin, as he puts it, "silently talking across to Freddie as a fellow being just as I had learned to do with Strongheart":

> I would ask the little fellow in my hand a question, and then give careful heed to all freshly-arriving mental impressions. . . .
>
> Unexpectedly, every question that I sent across to Freddie was followed, through the medium of these returning impressions, by a silent counterquestion. I asked Freddie what he was supposed to be doing in my world; back almost instantly came a demand to know what I really was supposed to be doing in *his* world. I asked him why it was that flies treated us humans so badly; right back came the question: why had we humans always treated flies so badly.

If Mr. Boone could have a "dialogue," as he called it, not only with Strongheart but also with ants and Freddie the Fly, surely I could have one with Polar Bear. After all,

I had been having, if not silent dialogues, at least out-loud dialogues with him for a decade. Just the same, if as a former amateur in this communication business I was now about to turn pro, I realized it was probably high time for me to consult other professionals. Accordingly, following Mr. Boone I decided on Beatrice Lydecker, a woman who once told me she had communicated with more animals than anyone else.

I first met Ms. Lydecker some years ago in California. I did not yet have Polar Bear — or, rather, Polar Bear did not yet have me — but I well remembered Ms. Lydecker told me at the time that, although she first got into communciation with animals by talking with horses, she had also had great success with dogs and cats. One of her first customers, I remembered she had said, was a lady who had two cats, one of whom was always spraying her furniture. The lady wanted to know which one was doing the job and had turned the problem over to Ms. Lydecker. I asked Ms. Lydecker how she had solved it. "I just asked them," she replied. "Right away the guilty one admitted it." I told her I was, if I might use such an expression in animal communciation, dumbfounded. "The one who is doing it *always* admits it," Ms. Lydecker explained. "Animals are very honest if you ask them directly about something."

Frankly, at that time I had had some doubts about this. And, since I had Polar Bear I now had many more. Often I had asked him directly about something he did — such as upsetting the garbage to get something he wanted — not only did he not answer me directly, instead what he did was indirectly, as I have said before, to offer his assistance to search for the alleged perpetrator. In any case, now with my new-found resolution to establish more successful communication with him, I decided to make an appointment with Ms. Lydecker the next time she was in New York.

When Ms. Lydecker arrived, with her assistant, at my apartment, it was of course too much for Polar Bear. He immediately low-tailed it to the bedroom. Embarrassed, I started to go get him but Ms. Lydecker stopped me. "No," she said, "I'll tell you just where he is. It'll save you time." She closed her eyes and went into what I thought was meditation. In a moment she opened her eyes and spoke to me. "I see him near water," she said. Helpfully I suggested the bathroom, but Ms. Lydecker shook her head. "No," she said, "he's near water but not that near." I pointed out that there was only one other room, and that was the bedroom. Perhaps he was there? Ms. Lydecker brightened. "That's where he is," she said. Again I started to go get him, but Ms. Lydecker again stopped me. "No," she said, "I don't need him. I'm going to talk to you about how you communicate with him."

Ms. Lydecker told me she had been communicating with animals since she was a young child. Children, she told me, communicate better than adults with animals because they understand, as she put it, "nonverbal language" and also because they have not yet learned to think of animals as "something different from themselves." At school, she pointed out, the children lose their nonverbal skills when they acquire verbal skills. Ms. Lydecker also clearly believed that women are better at trying to communicate with animals than men because, she told me sternly, "Men close off this kind of thing by their logic and statistical thinking."

This was again bad news for me — trying to train myself

to train Polar Bear and now being told that women and children would be better at it. I took some comfort, though, in the fact that I am actually so rotten at statistics maybe I could be a terrific communicator even if I were just a man. Also, I was basically a subscriber to Ms. Lydecker's belief that one of the reasons most grown-ups have so much trouble with communication with animals is that they interpret everything about animals from what they would feel is their position instead of from the animals' point of view. "When animals go out and start sniffing around," Ms. Lydecker told me, "we usually think they are just going around planning where they're going to the bathroom. They're not doing that at all. What they're doing is reading their daily newspaper."

For a moment I wondered if this was why paper-training with some animals was so difficult. I decided, however, not to explore this further with Ms. Lydecker. One thing I did find she was extremely firm about is that all animals can read our minds. Certainly, knowing Polar Bear, I went along with that. And, for that matter, the corollary to it — that the trouble we have comes from our not having the ability to read *their* minds. Ms. Lydecker clearly believed that the way we should do this is by the use of "visualization," or "mental pictures." She explained that the best way to do this would be for me to take a picture of Polar Bear in the position I wanted him after he had done what I wanted him to do. For example, if I wanted him in what she called the "stay" position, I should photograph him in that position and then memorize that picture until the image was clear in my mind. Then I was to put the picture away and, with practice, I would be able to create that mental picture at will, so that the next time I wanted him to stay somewhere, all I had to do was bring up that picture in my mind while I was telling him to do it.

While I was doing this, Ms. Lydecker went on, what I would really be doing was having ESP with Polar Bear. I'd be conversing with him in his language and, she said, "Chatting with him will seem natural to you."

I could hardly wait for my next real "chat" with Polar Bear. Before she left me, however, Ms. Lydecker used an example from her first love, horses. "If you're trying to teach a horse to go over a jump," she said, "what you do is mentally visualize the horse taking the jump with complete ease."

Curiously, when I came to my next authority for training myself to train Polar Bear, he turned out to be the well-known English psychologist David Greene, author of *Your Incredible Cat*. And, in his section called "How Fast Does Your Cat Learn," there sure enough was jumping training.

Dr. Greene suggested using a child's toy or constructing one's own hoop from a "stiff plastic tube, formed into a circle and held with a wooden peg." Frankly, I'm not good at this sort of thing and I never seem to have things around that everybody else seems to have when they want to work on something — and these certainly included plastic tubes and wooden pegs. But I did my best by taking off a tire from my bicycle and not bothering with a peg at all. When it comes to ingenuity I'm no genius, but I am ingenious.

Nor did I stop there. What I did was put the hoop in the doorway to the kitchen and block the spaces around it and then put Polar Bear's dinner on the other side of it. He went through the hoop like a shot. He did it so well, in fact, that I decided I didn't need any more intermittent steps but was ready for what Dr. Greene called the "final stage" of the I.Q. test. But for this stage, according to Dr. Greene, I had to scratch Polar Bear's supper:

> The final stage of the training consists of holding up the hoop and calling out "Come On!" without showing the cat any food. Just extend your hand as if offering a reward and give the command. The idea is to link this instruction with the desired action so firmly that the words are sufficient to produce an eager leap. . . . The test is completed when the cat jumps through the hoop correctly on at least two out of three occasions. Now rate his IQ using the chart below:

Number of Commands Given	*IQ Rating*
60+	Below Average
50–60	Slightly Below Average
40–49	Average
30–39	Above Average
29 or Less	Very Intelligent

This time I was not successful. In fact, without his supper on the other side of the hoop, Polar Bear was awful. Frankly, I am not going to give you his final score. All I will say is that as far as his jumping through the hoop, "correctly in at least two out of three occasions," he never did it — in fact, the only time he ever did it was when he felt it was the best way to get away from both me and the hoop altogether. Finally, as far as the number of commands I gave, I lost count at 100. When it came to mastering supposedly the simplest of all tricks Polar Bear was not just below average, he wasn't even on the chart. And, if the truth be known, by the time I finished, Polar Bear was so heartily sick of anything that even looked like a hoop that I think if at this point he had seen a kid with a Hula Hoop you could have scratched one kid as well as his hula.

One thing I did learn from Dr. Greene — this was that it was apparently very important what position you got into before you talked to your cat. For years I had just talked to Polar Bear any old way — close to, head-to-head, from a distance, or even from another room, and I got his "aeiou" 's back fine, too, wherever I was — and I had no trouble interpreting them. But if I was going to turn pro at this talk game, Dr. Greene made it clear that positionally I would have to get down to business. And down to business was just what Dr. Greene had in mind. Above all, he pointed out, I was not to look at Polar Bear's face:

> Instead, while the cat is looking at your face, gradually sink down on your heels so as to come close to his level. . . . Now look slowly away from the cat, before allowing your gaze to return to his face. As you do so, half close your eyes before restoring eye-contact. Then, when you are looking at one another, blink several times. . . . Once your approach has been accepted, the cat may acknowledge this trust by lowering his lids and blinking or by using one of the greeting signals already described.

I found, I am sorry to say, the opposite. Instead of "lowering his lids and blinking," Polar Bear gave me a look which clearly stated that I should do nothing until the men in the white coats arrived and after that I was to stop doing what I was doing and get up and go along quietly with them. But nothing stopped Dr. Greene:

> To get on even better terms, use the head rub by placing your forehead against his and rubbing your head and chin against his head. This is a warm and affectionate greeting message used between two friendly cats.

Here Dr. Greene was going too far. I yielded to no man alive, and few dead, on how to "get on even better terms" with my cat, and I had no intention of allowing somebody else to tell me how to snuggle and scrubble him. I also wanted it understood that nowhere, despite the disappointments I had had, did I believe that Polar Bear was dumb. Obviously, when it came to training, *I* was the dumbbell. But reluctantly I did have to admit that, under my direction as a trainer, when it came to stacking up as a trickster against those other white cats, Polar Bear didn't have a prayer.

Reaching the end of my tether on this training thing — where patience is concerned I have, it is true, often been accused of having a very short tether — I called a friend of mine, Linda Hanrahan, a fine trainer, and asked her to come over and make a firsthand assessment, not only of me as a trainer but Polar Bear as a possible candidate to play himself in the movies. When she arrived I told her my tale of woe — that the only trick I had ever gotten Polar Bear to do, outside of staying on his leash, was to lie down — and that, frankly, was only when he was already lying down.

When Polar Bear came in Mrs. Hanrahan took one look at him and told him to lie down. Whereupon, amazingly, Polar Bear lay down. After that Mrs. Hanrahan herself sat down. "The first thing you have to do to train a cat," she said, "before they do their first trick, is to trick them into thinking it's not something you want them to do for you, it's something they want you to do for them." I didn't understand this very well, so Mrs. Hanrahan went on. She explained to me that she and her husband, Joe, had no fewer than three trained cats, and that all of them only did what they were supposed to do because of what happened afterward. Tyrone, for example, she said, was a remarkable gray tabby who did extraordinary things. Nonetheless, although he had been doing tricks for years, he still had to be tricked to get him into his carrier even to go for a "shoot," as she called it, and then he only did his work for a reward of special vitamins he liked which came in a tube. Her other two were just the same — Rhedd Butler, a beautiful red, would perform only if at the end she knew she could make a beeline for her favorite fake fur puff; while Sally of the Soaps, as she was known for her soap opera work, would perform only if at the end she got special scratching and brushing.

Mrs. Hanrahan asked me to stay in the living room while she took Polar Bear into the bedroom. "I want to try a couple of things," she said. Lots of luck, I wanted to say, but I did not. Nonetheless in an extraordinarily short time Polar Bear came flying back into the living room, closely followed by Mrs. Hanrahan. "I want to tell you something," Mrs. Hanrahan said, sitting down. "He won't make it." Then, thinking I would be upset — when actually I was very relieved — she added, "Don't worry about it. The hardest thing any trainer has to cope with is the fact that practically everybody who has a cat thinks he or she should be in the movies or on television, and they insist on bringing them over to show Joe and me what they can do. What they can do, in a word, they don't. Their cats can do things at home, but not in a studio." She paused. "The best Hollywood trainer I know, a man who works with lions and tigers and bears and elephants and kangaroos and everything else — and has most of them able to do incredible things — told me that the most difficult animal he's ever had to train was the common house cat."

* * *

After Mrs. Hanrahan had left, relieved as I was about the whole thing, I was not sure how Polar Bear would feel. I knew he really wouldn't like even the idea of being a movie cat, but I also knew him well enough to know that in that inscrutable little contradictory brain of his he might still be harboring the illusion that he at least ought to be considered for the part, even if in the end, of course, he would turn it down. And so, without further ado, and at least to make me, if not him, feel better about it all, I carefully pointed out to him that if I, the one who had made his career possible, was not even being considered for the part of playing me, why on earth should he, ill qualified as he was, be considered for playing him? I at least had real acting experience. In fact, I had played a memorable rug shepherd in a Brush Hill School Christmas pageant — or at least I had until they brought in a real sheep and Brookie the sheep dog decided to herd it.

I also went a step further. I carefully compiled a list of people, if not cats, who never got to play themselves in movies made about them. Did Charles Lindbergh, I asked him, play Charles Lindbergh? Did Glenn Miller play Glenn Miller, or Monty Stratton play Monty Stratton? He did not know who Monty Stratton was, but the answer was obvious. Of course, none of them did — my friend Jimmy Stewart played all of them. Did Thomas A. Edison play Thomas A. Edison, or Clarence Darrow play Clarence Darrow? Again, of course not — Spencer Tracy played Edison and Darrow. And there were countless other examples I had for him. An actress like Frances Farmer was played by Jessica Lange. A singer like Loretta Lynn was played by Sissy Spacek, and even boxers like Rocky Graziano and Jake LaMotta were played, respectively, by Paul Newman and Robert DeNiro. At least a dozen actresses, I pointed out to him, had played Jacqueline Kennedy, and as for Charlton Heston, a man who after all had played pretty nearly everybody else, when it came down to him being played by somebody after he'd gone, my guess was that their choice would be Ronald Reagan.

Anyway, just when I felt I had all the bases covered with him and the whole thing totally nailed down — so that there would be no misunderstanding between us — an extraordinary thing happened. Hollywood, as they say, called.

I will, as they also say out there, take it from the top. I was doing an article on the late John Huston and, in the course of it, I naturally wanted to interview his children. I had done Anjelica and Tony, but somehow I had missed his director son, Danny. When I called Danny he suggested I come over that very day in the late afternoon because he was casting that day and was going to England that night. He named the place — a loft far over on the West Side of Manhattan.

When I arrived, there were half a hundred actors and actresses. Some I knew well, including Dina Merrill, Teresa Wright, Tammy Grimes, and Katharine Houghton, Katharine Hepburn's niece. Some others I knew, too, as one does with actors and actresses, not by their names but by their faces. All of them, it seemed, were engaged in reading scripts — some were even reading in low voices to each other.

I gave my name to the young man who seemed to be handling it all, chatted briefly with some of those I knew, and then sat down and waited. After some time the door opened and someone called my name. I went in and there, in another room, at the end of a long covered table, sat Danny Huston, a producer friend of mine named Steve

Haft, an associate producer, and a casting director. Behind them were half a dozen other people, and what they were doing, obviously — I learned for the first time — was casting a movie. In front of the table was one stool. Equally obviously, that was where I was supposed to sit, so sit I did. As I did so, however, I decided that since this was not the kind of one-on-one interview with Danny I was after, I would at least start with a joke. My leg was bothering me that day, and I had brought a cane, and so, without further ado, I banged my cane on the floor. "This," I said, "is an outrage. Every single person out there but me has a script — I wasn't even given the courtesy of being given one. I don't even know what part I'm up for. I don't even know whether the damned movie is a comedy or a tragedy. All I know is, whatever it is, I can do it."

Everybody seemed to stir uncomfortably. My jokes have a way of taking a little getting used to — which is one of the problems with them. Two people in the back of those seated even started to come toward me as if there had been a call for a bouncer. Danny, however, stopped them. Instead he looked at me directly. "Do it again," he said. I don't like repeating my jokes. Few of them, when you come right down to it, bear repetition, but if there's one thing I can't stand it's my jokes falling on deaf ears. In any case, assuming Danny was perhaps a little hard of hearing, I said it again, loudly — loudly enough, indeed, to make the two who had started forward believe they were right in the first place. But this time Danny himself rose and, telling the others to take a short break, motioned me to come around the table. For some time we sat together and discussed his remarkable father. I took some notes and afterward took my leave.

I thought no more about the whole thing until I had

finished my article and, several weeks later, was out in California. There Marian called me, very excitedly, from the Fund for Animals' New York office. "Guess what?" she asked. I could tell from her voice it was something good. My first guess was that someone had left the Fund a million dollars. "No, not that," Marian said. My next guess was that they had found a cat to play Polar Bear. "No, not that either," Marian said. "What they've found is the cat to play a part in a new movie. And," she added, "guess what — *you're* the cat."

I told her she must be kidding — at the most, they might want me to try out for some part. "No," Marian said firmly, "you've *got* the part." What part? I wanted to know. "It's a part in the movie *Mr. North,*" Marian continued. "You'll be playing an elderly butler." A *mature* butler, I automatically corrected. Marian ignored this. She told me I would have to be in Newport, Rhode Island, a week from Tuesday night — that the movie was based on Thornton Wilder's last novel, called *Theophilus North,* that John Huston would be starring in it, and that Danny would be directing. Marian also said that they had sent over a script, and did I know what my first line would be? I did not. "Well," she said, "you're asleep, and somebody says something about Newport, and you're meant to wake up and bang your cane on the floor and say, 'Newport, damnable place! No lady here ever heard the beginning of a concert, or read the end of a book.' "

For the first time I got the idea of how it all happened. Then what do I do, I asked — by this time as excited as Marian. "You go back to sleep," she said. I didn't like the sound of that, but, in a moment, I was all actor again. How many "sides," I asked her, did I have? Marian didn't even know what "sides" were — good help is *so* hard to get nowadays. All right, never mind, I said. How many lines? "Six," she said, "not counting the one I already gave you."

Well, I wasn't to be Hamlet, but then one had to start somewhere. One thing I now knew — how I got the part. By pure luck, with my joke in front of those people, I had come up with something very much like the first line of the butler. And Danny, who was on his way to England to look for, among other things, an English-born butler, and who, like his father, was always on the lookout for someone who would come cheap, had decided I, with practice, would do. Back in New York, however, I wondered how I would handle the matter with Polar Bear. Here I had maintained that one of the reasons he wouldn't be in the movie was that I wouldn't either, and now here I was, behind his back really, about to tread the boards without him. One idea I had was to take him to Newport with me and show him, firsthand, how he wouldn't like making movies, but this plan dissolved when Marian informed me that we would be staying at a motel.

Polar Bear and I had only once stayed at a motel, and he didn't like it at all. That particular time, when I tried to order his midnight niblets, I knew the jig was up when I not only had to explain what niblets were but also what room service was. Apart from Polar Bear's feelings, however, the idea of where I would be staying was unbelievable. Maybe I was not going to be a star but surely there was some distance between that and staying in a motel. In Newport, of all places — a place where, in the days when I was there, even staying in a hotel was beyond the pale. As for staying in a motel, to think that this was going to happen to someone who in his better days had stayed at The Breakers with the last granddaughter of

Commodore Vanderbilt, and who attended the last private dinner party at Marble House, given by Frederick H. Prince, the last private owner of Marble House and the owner of forty-one railroads — really, it was so unthinkable I decided not to think about it.

All in all, I was glad I had decided not to take Polar Bear with me and subject him too to such humiliation. But very soon, too, I decided something else. This was that, from the time Marian and I arrived, we had a wonderful time. Make no mistake, the smell of the greasepaint and the roar of the crowd is heady stuff. All right, the makeup is, if not smelly, at least itchy and irritating, but for me the roar of the crowd, particularly since it was in reverse — we were shooting outside, and they stopped all traffic — was very exciting. Acting, when you came right down to it, is not just more fun than writing — because anything is — it is also more fun because you're not so damn alone. You're a *team*, I tell you. John Huston was too ill to do his part and had been replaced by Robert Mitchum, but if, for example, Lauren Bacall went up on her lines in my first day's shooting, why, I was there to calm her down. And, if Anjelica Huston came to me for guidance, I was there to give it to her. If Robert Mitchum was having an off day — as a matter of fact he wasn't there any day when I was there — I was there to fill that breach, too.

Within a few hours I even felt capable of trying out a bit of business with Harry Dean Stanton, who, as the Cockney sidekick of the hero, Tony Edwards, was the funniest man in the show. I even refused to take offense when he suggested that I not look at the monitors during the shooting, nor see the rushes at night. "If you do," he said, "it'll throw you off for tomorrow." Frankly, by that time I felt nothing could throw me. I particularly enjoyed the alfresco luncheons with the extras who were bus-loaded down from Boston. Some of them had stories going back to Garbo and Rudolph Valentino. Only at one lunch did I sit alone, and that was at my own insistence. I had to, I explained — I was working on my line.

It was true — I had one line that afternoon. Nonetheless, by then I felt like such a seasoned actor that I was not surprised when Marian came over and asked me if I was willing to do an interview with a camera crew which was shooting a film on the making of the film. When the crew appeared, the interviewer turned out to be a young woman who looked to me to be a child. She told me Mr. Huston, as she called Danny, had suggested me — and, as she mentioned him, sure enough I spotted Danny lying down in the grass and pretending he wasn't there. Immediately I decided to give the young woman, and Danny too, their money's worth.

Her first question was not difficult. "What," she asked, "do you think is the main trouble with Hollywood today?" Looking as pensive as I could, I told her that the trouble with Hollywood today was that the actors didn't learn their craft. At this, the young lady looked up. "Frankly, Mr. Amory, I'm not familiar with your career. How long have you been in the movies?" It was my turn to ask a question. I asked her what time it was. Surprised, she looked at her watch. "It's a quarter of five," she said. Young lady, I told her sternly, I have been in this game since seven o'clock this morning. "Do you," she asked, "like making movies?" It's a living, I told her, but it wasn't all beer and skittles. How would *she* like to be my age and taking orders from a twenty-five-year-old whippersnapper? I pointed over at Danny, but it didn't do much good — she just wasn't able to make the necessary age translation. "Do you," she asked, "plan to make any more pictures?" I nodded sagely. "What kind of movie would you like to make?" she continued. I'd like to make a Western, I told her, with Charlotte Rampling. I did not tell her that I had been in love with Charlotte for years but I had never gotten to meet her because she had stupidly married somebody else and gone to live abroad where it was easier for her, I suppose, than living where she might meet me.

In any case I did tell her that after Charlotte and I had made our Western I intended to buy a home in Bel Air with two swimming pools. "Two!" she exclaimed. Yes, I said firmly, one for me and one for my cat. "Your cat!" she exclaimed again. "I thought cats didn't like water." I told her Polar Bear didn't mind horizontal water, he just didn't like vertical water, and that was why I couldn't take showers anymore; I had to take baths. As for swimming, I pointed out, he wouldn't actually go into his pool, but then neither did most Hollywood people. They just had to have a pool so they could sit around it, talk about their tans and their fans. Polar Bear didn't have a tan, but he would want a pool just the same, so he could talk about his fans.

After I had made two movies, I told her, I intended to go right into politics. "Why?" she asked. Because, I explained to her, if you are going into politics in California, you had to be a movie star first, otherwise you couldn't get in. "Why?" she asked again. "Why" was obviously her favorite word. I patiently explained to her it was because a movie star got to meet so many people and therefore they could best find out what the little people were thinking. I did not mention her, but I pointed over to Danny. There was one of them over there, I told her. Why didn't we go over and find out not only what he was thinking, but also if he was.

Months later, when the movie was out, the mail of course poured in. Well, I'm exaggerating. Perhaps I should say it just came in. No, I'll be more accurate, it trickled in. Actually, there were two letters, and one of them, if the truth be known, didn't think I was very good. But, as I've always said, a star can't judge his performance from fan letters. The other letter said I was terrific. Of course some people said it was from my sister, but people are always saying things like that when you get big. It wasn't from my sister at all — it was from my sister-in-law.

I waited faithfully for William Morris and ICM and all the other big agencies to call me for other pictures. But not a single one of them did — not for a Western or even an Eastern. No one even wanted me to play myself in the movie about Polar Bear. The way I figured it, they had all decided I would now be too high-priced. And so, in desperation, I started trying to figure out who, next to me, would do a good job in the movie about Polar Bear. Eventually I settled on George C. Scott. George C. Scott wasn't me, but then, after all, who was? And he did have possibilities.

Accordingly, the next time I was in Hollywood, I paid a call on George. When he and I get together, we like to play chess. And this time was no exception. Midway through our final game I took the bull by the horns — one of my least favorite expressions — and asked him if they made a movie from *The Cat Who Came for Christmas* would he be willing to play me? I carefully did this, incidentally, when it was my turn. George thought for a moment, looking at me. "You can tell them," he said, "I would be interested." We proceeded with our game. Then, shortly before the end — which George was winning — he looked at me again. "Don't tell them I'd just be interested," he said. "That doesn't mean a damn thing. Tell them I'd be very interested."

I thanked George and, afterward, when I went out to dinner with George and his wife, Trish, and another friend, I was determined to show my appreciation by at least getting the check. We were at The Ginger Man, a restaurant owned by Carroll O'Connor, and when the others were talking and I got the waitress' attention, I told her that I would like to get the check, if that would be all right. "Oh, no sir," she said, "Mr. Scott has already told me he wants the check." That was apparently that. I had, however, another opportunity to talk to her a few minutes later. Listen, I told her, I'm a friend of Mr. O'Connor's and he told me to tell you that I was to get the check. "I'm sorry, sir," she said again, "Mr. O'Connor didn't tell me and I don't know you, and Mr. Scott is a regular customer." I had still another chance — this time I was stern. I want you to know, I told her, lying in my teeth, I'm Carroll O'Connor's chief writer in New York. I wrote *In the Heat of the Night.* "I'm sorry, sir," she said a third time, and once more that was that.

But, before dessert, I had one last chance. This time I spoke to her conspiratorially. The reason I want the check, I whispered to her, and Mr. O'Connor wants me to have it, is because today is Mr. Scott's birthday. "Oh," she whispered back, equally conspiratorially. "I understand." And, sure enough, some time later, she slipped me, unnoticed by George, the check.

As George and the rest of us started to get up, however, the restaurant suddenly darkened and through the door came, glowing with candles, the largest birthday cake I have ever seen. Immediately the entire restaurant not only burst into applause but, standing up, started to sing — looking directly at George — "Happy Birthday to You."

At the third "Happy Birthday" line, when the lights from the cake reached our table, I saw George's face. It was a bright and furious red, and it was glowing straight at me. The man who had refused an Oscar was not a man who liked his birthday celebrated in a public restaurant. He lives in a house high in the wilds of the Malibu hills with an unlisted telephone number and an unlisted address on an unnamed street, with all his neighbors carefully instructed, on pain of execution, not to reveal its location. If somehow you do manage to find the house and have the temerity to ring the bell, you will be greeted at the door not by George and Trish but by two mastiffs who are the size of small dinosaurs.

In any case, as the cake was put down on our table, over the din of the last line of "Happy Birthday" and the clapping of the restaurant guests, I could hear, addressed to me, in George's patented Patton voice, various expressions of fury which ended with "DAMN you, Amory — it's in OCTOBER!"

George had, as usual, a factual point — his birthday was in October, and our dinner was in May. In vain on the way out, I tried to explain to him that I didn't know when his birthday was and that I had tried over and over, but that it was the only way I could get the check. My explanation did no good. I didn't hear from George for almost a year.

And, come to think of it, I haven't heard hide nor hair of a movie called *The Cat Who Came for Christmas*. Which, I might add, to Polar Bear's way of thinking, was the best news he'd had since the book came out.

VI ◦ *Meanwhile, Back at the Ranch, I Read Him His Rights*

When I was a small boy — if a large one — I had a favorite aunt. I pronounced this, of course, sounding the *u*, as befitting the proper Bostonian wife of one's uncle, and not what has been corrupted by the rest of the country into a small bug. Her name was Lucy Creshore, and one of what were then regarded as her peculiarities was that she rescued a large number of stray cats and dogs. A sizable number of these she kept right in her own home with her.

I loved my Aunt Lu, and I loved to go to her house and have, as she called it, "stray play." On one occasion, however, I was not at her home alone. I was there for a large Thanksgiving dinner — which in those days regularly included an extended family — and when at this dinner one of her stray cats ventured toward an older cousin of mine, he kicked it. I first picked up the cat and then I kicked my cousin. I got him a good one, too, right in the shins, and afterward I asked him how he liked it. He didn't, and so I put down the cat and we had a fight.

It was a good fight, too — one in which, anyway, there was no more kicking. I really don't know whether I won or not, but I do know that before dinner he and his sister and his father and mother all left — which I took to be an indication that at least he didn't want to fight anymore.

It was a large family of many aunts and uncles, and I never could keep track of everybody and so, on the way home, I asked my father what relation the boy I fought was to me. "He's your second cousin once removed," I remember my father saying, and he then proceeded to explain what that was. I did not, however, pay too much attention to this, because I was already working on one of my bad jokes — which I didn't say but which was on the order that I was glad I had removed him before dinner.

Unfortunately my cousin was not the only member of the family who did not like Aunt Lu's ménage — or as some called it, her menagerie. They thought her house was a mess and they criticized her for it. This only made me more fond of her, and somehow years later, when my college time came around, this relationship came full cycle. This was because that time coincided with some of the worst years of the New England textile business, in which my father was engaged, and it was my Aunt Lu who paid my way through my first three years of college. In my last year, as president of the *Harvard Crimson,* I made enough money to pay my own way. In such office, however, I learned a hard truth. If you have been president of the *Harvard Crimson* in your senior year at Harvard, there is very little, in after life, for you.

In any case, many years before college Aunt Lu had given me as a Christmas present a book. It was a copy of *Black Beauty.* It had immediately become my favorite book. I learned it practically, and almost literally, by heart — that remarkable story of man's inhumanity to horse. I learned, too, the almost equally remarkable story of its English Quaker author, Anna Sewell. *Black Beauty* was the only book Miss Sewell wrote in her life. She was in her fifties when she wrote it and so ill when she did so that it took her seven years and she had to dictate the last chapters because she was in too much pain to hold a pencil. She sold her book outright for just twenty pounds and, dying within a few months of its publication, never lived to see its incredible success — to become indeed the sixth largest-selling book in the English language.

I was also brought up on the story of how *Black Beauty* first reached the American public. Ten years before its publication in 1868, two trotting horses, Empire State and Ivanhoe, each drawing two men, had raced forty miles over rough roads from Brighton to Worcester for a purse of a thousand dollars. Both horses averaged a speed of more than fifteen miles per hour — and both, after the race, died. They had literally been driven to death.

The next day a letter appeared in the *Boston Daily Advertiser*. It read as follows:

> It seems to me that it is high time for somebody to take hold of this matter in earnest, and see if we cannot do something in Boston as well as others have in New York, to stop this cruelty to animals. . . . I, for one, am ready to contribute both time and money, and if there is any society or person in Boston which whom I can unite or who will unite with me in this matter, I should be glad personally or by letter to be informed.

The letter was signed by a great-great-uncle of mine by the name of George Thorndike Angell. He was also a great-uncle of my Aunt Lu. In any case, as a prominent attorney and well-known philanthropist, he soon had a formidable group of leading citizens who responded to his letter, including not only well-known Boston merchants but also some distinguished literary figures. Even before Angell, Emerson, Thoreau, Dr. Oliver Wendell Holmes, and John Greenleaf Whittier had already spoken out against cruelty to animals. But Angell went further. The American Humane Education Society, which came about after his letter to the paper, was the first of its kind in America, and the first publication of the Society was *Black Beauty*. Called by Angell "the 'Uncle Tom's Cabin' of the Horse," the book soon found its way to some three million American readers and virtually every school library in the country.

The book made such an impression on me that it was a boyhood dream of mine to have, some day, the kind of refuge to which the horse Black Beauty finally comes. And today the Fund for Animals has indeed such a refuge — one which not only bears the title, the Black Beauty Ranch, but also has under its entrance sign another sign. This reads as follows:

> I have nothing to fear
> And here my story ends.
> My troubles are all over
> And I am at home.
>
> — Last lines of *Black Beauty*
> Anna Sewell

Actually, our Black Beauty Ranch, which is located in Murchison, Texas, in the fine nonprairie verdant grasslands of the eastern part of that state, came about not only from my boyhood dream but also from a rather more practical matter. This was that, after embarking on the rescue of animals, we sorely needed our own place to keep — and from which later to adopt — these animals. In the case, for example, of our rescue of the Grand Canyon burros, we had hoped, after first rounding up and then lifting them by helicopter, to adopt them from corrals right on the canyon's rim. But this had proved impractical for two reasons. The first was that we brought up far too many animals — 577, in fact — to do careful on-site adoptions. The second was that many of the burros were in no shape to be adopted right away and we had to have a place to take them, vet them, and either get them into such shape or continue to keep them.

As time went on we began to rescue not just wild burros but also wild horses and wild goats as well as a wide variety of other animals. Indeed, as I write this, Black Beauty is now home to over 600 animals which range over 605 acres and include everything from racehorses to raccoons, from mules to monkeys, from elephants to foxes, and from llamas to such luminaries as Nim, perhaps the world's most famous "signing" chimpanzee, and Shiloh, the last of the infamous Atlantic City "diving" horses — horses which were made to dive six times a day, seven days a week, into a pool ten feet deep sixty feet below them.

I really don't know what possessed me to take Polar Bear to the ranch. I knew all too well how he would be about any exception to his feelings about traveling, but I also felt that, in this particular instance, I had to take exception to his exception. As is my wont — which I like to reserve to myself because I am not fond of other people's wonts — I rationalized my decision in various ways. Polar Bear had, after all, learned to walk on a leash — or at least stay on a leash while I walked around him — why should he not also be able to learn to walk around the ranch, particularly when it was a walk on which I intended to carry him?

When I am going away I always take care not to pack the night before and let Polar Bear see the suitcase and therefore give him less time to be, as he always is, when he sees it, first cross, then mad, and finally furious. Even if he is going with me I do this, because, unlike some of the more fortunate members of the cat-owned fraternity, I am not at liberty to bring out his carrier and show him he is going, too — for the simple reason that wherever I am going is not going to be where he wants to go, for the even simpler reason that he never wants to go anywhere.

So, as usual, quickly and invariably forgetting something, I packed the very morning of our trip, coaxed Polar Bear with a grip of iron into the carrier, and took off for the airport. To say he was better than on previous trips would not be true. Neither would it be true to say he was worse. He seemed worse, but that was only because I had purposely put out of my mind how bad he had always been before.

What brought it all back was the fine-tuning of his "aeiou" 's. These he started the moment we were in the taxi and worked to full pitch when we entered the airplane. Here, after first telling me with a particularly piercing "aeiou" that he wished to be taken out of the hated carrier so that he could at least die where he pleased, and then, when partly out, or rather half in and half out, he began his truly operatic "aeiou," which meant he wanted to leave the plane entirely. Suffice it to say that he was so bad that the flight attendant actually spent considerable time commiserating with me. "Isn't there anything," she asked, "he likes about flying?" I assured her there was not. In Polar Bear's opinion, I told her firmly, an airplane was nothing more or less than a submarine and, furthermore, it was a submarine which, to his way of thinking, had dangerously oversurfaced.

Once off the plane, with Polar Bear still securely in the carrier, I proceeded by bus to the rental car establishment. I do not like to have someone from the ranch have to come to meet me. Everyone at the ranch is busy, and the drive from Dallas to Murchison is close to two hours, and therefore anyone coming to meet me and taking me back would have at least eight hours of driving.

Our trip was in the summer, and it is hot in the summer in Dallas — albeit less so where we were going. In the automobile, after carefully seeing that all windows were secured, I turned on the air conditioner and let Polar Bear out of his carrier to roam and jump the car at will. He was surprisingly good — much better than he was in the plane — and interested in everything, particularly as the verdure became greener and less the desert kind of plains so many people think of as everywhere in Texas. Soon we were not only in green hills but also in horse and cattle country. Polar Bear knows all about horses from the carriage horses in Central Park, but cattle were something else again. Strange creatures as they were, they seemed, from his point of view I'm sure, to have a most desirable way of life. When they weren't actually eating they were chewing, and when they weren't eating or chewing they were lying down and obviously resting up for more eating and chewing.

The nearest town to the ranch is Athens, Texas. Nearby,

however, are both Paris, Texas, and, of all places, New York, Texas. I have often wished that latter could have been the location of the ranch — there are so many people I would like to write to from that address.

In any case, as I turned down the dirt road leading to the ranch, I felt, as I always do, a growing feeling of excitement. Usually, taking people down this road, I insist upon a game — the first one to see one of our burros gets a dollar. But this time I didn't — even though Polar Bear was so glued to the window I think he would have won easily. At the ranch gate I first stopped, as I always do, to check the Black Beauty sign, and then pulled a little way inside, stopped the engine, and just looked around. There were animals visible everywhere. There, off in the distance, reared the huge head of Conga the elephant. Farther off, a herd of wild mustangs were running. And, closer at hand were all kinds of animals whose troubles, indeed, as the sign on our gate said, were all over and who were at home.

In short order one of the ranch hands drove up in the ranch pickup. With him, running alongside the pickup, was Lady, a mutt husky who is, as we call her, our ranch "foredog." Polar Bear was about to think very little of Lady when she somehow communicated to him that she was a guard dog not of people but of animals. The ranch hand had seen pictures of Polar Bear but he had never seen him in person and so, proudly holding him up, I asked him what he thought of him. "Well," he said, "I never expected him to be so what." I could not make head or tail of this and I took immediate umbrage at what the man said. Polar Bear, after all, is far from a so-what anything, least of all a so-what cat. And then, in a flash, it came to me — it always takes me a while to accustom myself to the Texas accent — his "what," of course, was "white."

After exchanging the rental car for the man's pickup, Polar Bear and I took off for a tour. On the way to our first pasture I kept thinking about that East Texas accent. It really has to be heard to be believed. I am not just talking here of "all" for oil, or "are" for hair, or "arn" for iron, or "ass" for ice — remember, I am still in the "a's" — I am also talking "bard" for buried, "kain't" for can't, "dayum" for damn, "fur" for far, "griyuts" for grits, "hard" for hired, "hep" for help, "lags" for legs, "own and oaf" for on and off, "pap" for pipe, "poly" for poorly, "rass" for rice, "stars" for stairs, "tahm" for time, and "tarred" for tired. As if this wasn't enough, all the time they are convinced they are talking the "Kang's Ainglish," and it is other "paypull" who have turned the language around with "ever what" for whatever, and even "ever whichaways" — which, incidentally, is one of their favorite expressions.

I also thought about a call I had one day from a man at the ranch to my New York office. "Cleveland," he said, "I know how you feel about adopting just one burro and that you always want two of 'em to go together." I told him I did indeed. "Well," he said, "there's this fella here from Hogeye, Arkansas, who wants to adopt just one. But, Cleveland" — the man paused — "he's a real nass fella." Nice, I automatically corrected. "Well," the man went on, "I toad him how you felt, but he says he's got a pony and a goat and he jes wants one. He's in the barn with it rat now and he's already named it. He wants to call it Ben Wheeler."

Ben Wheeler was the name of the nearest town to the

ranch, "Pop. 477," as the sign reads. I still hesitated. "Cleveland," the man said again, "I tell you he's a *real* nass fella." I gave up correcting and agreed. There was a long pause. Finally the man spoke again. "Cleveland," he said, "is there a paper in New York called the *New York Times*?" I told the man there was indeed a paper in New York by that name, and they sure would be disappointed that he hadn't heard of them. But I was curious why he wanted to know about it. "Because," the man went on, "this fella says he rats for it, and he wants to rat about the ranch for it." I was very excited. I told the man to be sure to be nass to him — I said it exactly as he said it this time, so there would be no mistake. "Of course I'll be nass to him," the man said. "I told him I was really busy, but if he wanted to follow me around and ask questions that'd be just fine." There was another long pause. "Cleveland," the man said, "tell me something. What would a fella from Hogeye, Arkansas, be doin' rattin' for the *New York Times*?" This time I was firm. I told him never mind what he was doing, just be nass.

The long and short of that story is that the following Christmas Eve the best story that was ever written about the Black Beauty Ranch appeared in the *New York Times*. The writer was Roy Reed, one of the *Times'* most distinguished writers, and a man who now indeed lives in Hogeye, Arkansas. That very afternoon, through directory assistance, I found his telephone number. The woman who answered the phone was, I presumed, Mrs. Reed. In any case, I endeavored to tell her, in the best Texas accent I could muster, that I aimed to talk to Mr. Ben Wheeler. "I'm sorry," she replied, "Mr. Wheeler cannot be disturbed right now. He's eating his Christmas dinner." She then asked me if I wanted to speak to her husband. Before her husband came on the line, however, I had the chance to tell her not only what I thought of her husband's article but also that I knew that Mr. Wheeler had found a wonderful home.

On the way too I thought of another memorable visitor to our ranch, one etched in all our memories. He is the distinguished prizefighter, the Reverend George Foreman, a man who has a church not far away. After touring the entire ranch he asked the man who took him if he could adopt some burros. The man agreed and asked if he would like to pick out his choices. But he did not want to do that. "No," he said, "I'd like you to pick them. I'd like you to pick the four burros on the whole ranch who you think have the least chance of ever getting adopted."

The man did so, well knowing that those burros, too, like Mr. Reed's, would have the right kind of home.

I have one animal I always visit first when I go to the ranch. This is a very special burro named Friendly. When we arrived at the main burro pasture, I got out of the pickup, first putting up the window to see that Polar Bear didn't follow me. Before I spotted Friendly in the pasture, however, she spotted me and came not running — burros rarely run — but trotting, which for a burro is full speed for anything but flight. As Friendly came close and I reached to pat her I looked over to the pickup and saw that Polar Bear was not only looking but scratching to get out. Immediately I went back and picked him up and carried him out to meet what I was sure was the first burro he had ever met. Friendly is tough on animals her size or larger but with something smaller, particularly one as small as Polar Bear, she is a perfect lady — so much so that in this case Polar Bear was not even jealous. And while Friendly plowed her head into my stomach and Polar Bear began exploring her neck with his paw I thought, as I always do, how much this burro had meant to our first major rescue.

Friendly had come up in a sling under the helicopter in the very first batch of burros we rescued in the Grand Canyon. I was in the corral when she was lifted up over the rim and delicately dropped to the ground. I was also one of the crew who untied her. Friendly did not, as all the other burros had done, trot immediately and rapidly away from us — instead she just stood and looked at us in that contemplative and philosophical way I was soon to learn was her trademark. Whatever had happened to her — the roundup, being tied in a sling, being picked up and fastened to a roaring helicopter overhead, being carried seven thousand feet up in the air, and then finally being let down among all of us and hundreds of onlookers — it had all been sudden and uncomfortable and ridiculous and even crazy, and she surely thought that was what we must all be. But she also realized, I felt then and still feel, that no one had really hurt her, and therefore we were not all bad. That first night, after dusk, I had gone out to the corral again. For the first time I walked through what had been, only a few hours ago, those "wild" burros, and I was looking for her. Behind me, sitting on the fence, I heard some of the cowboys who had taken part in the rescue laughing at me. I turned to look at them and suddenly I saw what they were laughing at. All the time I had been looking for Friendly there, in the dark behind me, quietly plodding along and knowing full well, I am sure, how funny it was, was Friendly.

We had already publicly said that wild burros would make good pets — better pets, indeed, we had claimed, from the point of view of temperament, than horses — and we had also said that, rather than get your kid a pony, get him or her a burro. We said that because we needed to get homes for our burros, but at the same time we didn't really know just how good they would be, and we certainly hadn't had it proved to us. The burro who proved it was Friendly. That was why, then and there, in those first moments at the corral when she stood and looked at us and had not trotted away, I had given her her name. In a way I felt Friendly was responsible not only for the successful Grand Canyon rescue and adoption program but also for the much larger later rescues at the Naval Weapons Center at China Lake and Death Valley — more than five thousand burros in all.

I did not see whether Polar Bear would become jealous when, still holding him, I gave Friendly the kind of all-out bearhug, if in this case a one-armed one, I was used to giving her. I did remember, though, as I was doing this, what had happened on another occasion when she, not Polar Bear, was watching me hug another burro.

It had happened more than ten years before. Friendly, you see, at the time of the Grand Canyon rescue, was pregnant. Later, at the ranch, she had her baby, which we named Friendly Two — and always spelled it that way. The first time I ever saw her baby she had trotted over with her from a distance in the pasture. That time, when she had started to put her head into my stomach, she had suddenly stopped, moved back, and instead — with some pride — pushed her baby toward me. I had hugged and hugged and gushed and gushed over the baby until, suddenly, even more quickly than she had stopped before, she pushed in, pushed her baby away, and pushed her own head back into my stomach. It was just as if she was saying that she wanted to show me her baby, and had wanted me to hug her, but enough was enough. I was never to forget that she was Friendly One and her baby was Friendly Two.

This time, though, it was Polar Bear's turn to decide that my hugging of Friendly One had gone on quite long enough, thank you very much. In fact he squirmed so meaningfully that I had to stop patting Friendly and let him give me a push in the stomach, Friendly not withstanding.

It was time to move on anyway, because there were many other burros to whom I wanted to give personal attention. One in particular was one of those rare cases in which a burro, after an adoption, had come back to us. Adoption policies at the Fund for Animals are strict. Our contract reads that any animal may be taken back by us if "in the subjective judgement of the Fund the animal is not properly cared for, watered, fed, looked after, etc. even including the word 'happy.' " Ed Walsh, the Fund's peerless New York lawyer, without whom there would be no Fund, said that what I wanted wasn't very legal, but I told him to put it in anyway for the good of my soul. Ed complained that my wanting it and the good of my soul didn't make it any more legal, but Ed doesn't understand Episcopal souls very well. Frankly, I don't think he thinks Episcopal souls are completely legal anyway. In any case, this particular burro was returned to us because he was, his former adopters said, "too wild," and that they "couldn't do anything with him." He arrived back at the ranch at 2:00 one afternoon, and by that evening he was not only eating out of a ranch hand's hand, he was also nuzzling all visitors, even total strangers.

After the burros came the mules. There are dozens of

these at the ranch, and one of the reasons we have so much affection for them is that our more difficult rescues could not have been made without them. When, for example, burros had to be driven down from the high ground to which they regularly repaired when being chased, the cowboys mounted mules, who are both craftier and more surefooted in difficult high-ground open situations.

There was justice in this, of course, because the reason a mule is smarter than a horse is that its mother was a burro. If the father was a burro and the mother was a horse, the result is a hinny. The ranch people maintain that a hinny is even smarter than a mule for the very reason that the father is a burro, but, as I have many times told them, they might very well get away with saying something like that in Texas but I had to live in New York. As we looked at the mules, however, I had to admit they were extraordinary animals. My personal favorite is Ghostly — an all-white fellow who has such a remarkable combination of smartness and gentleness that he has won the hearts of all of us, and even did Polar Bear's when I tried a picture of a white mule and a white cat together. It wasn't easy with one arm around Polar Bear and the other on Ghostly, and the picture didn't come out. But then my pictures rarely do since they stopped making Brownies. I was terrific with a Brownie.

After the mules we went looking for horses. There are so many different kinds of horses on the ranch that it is hard to pick either stars or favorites. All in all though I think Polar Bear's favorite was a small, stunted, lovable little guy who was perhaps the most awful starvation case we had ever encountered. He was rescued on a Thanksgiving

Day, so we named him Pilgrim. On the day when he was found he could hardly move at all but was desperately trying to inch his way toward what would have been his Thanksgiving dinner — the bark of a tree. At first trusting no one, he now seems to trust everyone, and Polar Bear was no exception. As I stood with Polar Bear in my arms, Pilgrim came forward and started what I knew to be a friendly whinny, to which Polar Bear first responded with at least one of his tentative "aeiou" 's and then, to my surprise, reached out a definitely friendly paw.

Our next horse stop was with a white horse named Cody. I did not let Polar Bear near him because, of all the stories on the ranch of man's inhumanity to horse, his is perhaps the most outrageous. His former owner, an Atlanta doctor, became so angry that he would not come to him as he would to a boy who looked after him that one day, in a fit of anger, he shot the horse in the knee. Not satisfied with this, he then rigged a block and tackle with weights and left Cody shackled with no medical attention for ten days. A group of Atlanta women took the doctor to court but, although the prosecution was successful, they were unable to gain custody of Cody. Nonetheless they persevered to the end, and after first buying Cody at an auction — which would have led to a slaughterhouse fate — next raised the money to have him transported to Black Beauty Ranch.

The first time I saw Cody trying to hobble around on an all but useless front leg I was certain he was in such severe pain that he should be put down. The vet, however, asked me to defer such a decision until that afternoon. And, that afternoon, the next time I saw Cody he was in one of the pastures, far off from where he had been before. If he had been in as much pain as I thought, the vet pointed out to me, why would he have hobbled all that way? I had no answer, but I was still worried that, with wild mustangs around, when it came to grain-feeding time he would not have a chance. A ranch hand answered that by having me watch him at feeding time. Cody not only got his share, but, with ears laid back and teeth bared at any horse who tried to take any food from him, even the wildest of the wild mustangs soon saw there was little percentage in trying to get Cody's share. Needless to say, when I brought Polar Bear to see Cody, I too kept our distance. The way Cody swings that head of his, I have learned, the only way to approach him is to keep someone he sees regularly between you and him.

Only one of my favorites was missing — Whitey, the horse we almost got. Whitey became the symbol of countrywide carriage-horse abuse when, a few summers ago, he staggered for a moment on New York City's Sixty-second Street, then, literally delirious from the heat, he suddenly fell over on his side. There he would have died had it not been for the quick reaction and expert first aid administered by a registered nurse and two visiting Californian veterinary students. Although New York City carriage horses are supposed to be off the streets when the temperature reaches 90° — one of the few victories the Fund for Animals had then achieved for these animals — a woman who went to see Whitey noted that this was the same horse who, six weeks before, she had seen collapse from the heat and had observed being first kicked and then whipped to his feet by his driver.

Led by the New York radio commentator Barry Gray, the Whitey case created a furor — one which, although Whitey's owner refused the Fund for Animals' offer to buy him, did at least lead to Whitey's being removed from the city entirely. It also led to tough new carriage-horse legislation which bars the carriage horses from operating in traffic during rush hours and basically confines them to Central Park. Remarkably, the New York City Council passed this bill 31 to 3, and although vetoed by Mayor Ed Koch, it became law when the council overrode the mayor's veto 28 to 4 — the first time a mayor's veto had been overriden in twenty years. Just why Mayor Koch saw fit to veto the measure is still a mystery. The only explanation would seem to be that he apparently turned the same blind eye toward the misery of the carriage horses with which he watched the incredible corruption within his administration — something which led to his later well-deserved defeat at the polls.

Our last horse engagement was to visit the far pastures — the domain of the Fund's wild horses. For no animals has the Fund for Animals fought harder than for these. I personally had high hopes for the wild horses when President Reagan first came into office. He had, after all, once made the stirring statement that "the best thing for the inside of a man is the outside of a horse." President Reagan's feelings, however, were apparently limited to Republican horses. Although fewer than seventy thousand wild horses ever grazed our public lands — yours, by the way, and mine — in comparison with some four and a half million cattle and sheep, all of course grazed by the ranchers at ridiculously low fees — nonetheless, the western ranchers and their toadying politicians had their way.

Roundup after roundup was authorized by Congress, and the Bureau of Land Management in the 1980s alone was voted millions upon millions of extra dollars to do their brutal work. This work, incidentally, they almost never did themselves, but instead ladled out to cronies.

On one of their feedlots in Nevada, when I asked the man who ran the place if I could see his cripples, he replied, "Oh, you wouldn't want to see them — and you sure wouldn't want them. Some can't even walk and some have their eyes out." That man, by the way, ran his infamous corral with no veterinarian and received ten thousand dollars a day.

When it came to the Bureau of Land Management's adoption policies, these were almost as cruel as their roundups and holding pens. Although under the Wild Horse and Free-Roaming Burro Act they were not supposed to adopt out more than four horses to a person, by the use of phony fee-waivers and "powers of attorney" they would often give out as many as a thousand horses to one person. And, although the act specifically said the horses were not to go to slaughter, they gave away, as our lawsuits proved, hundreds of animals knowing full well they would.

Here it should be noted that wild horses are not "broken" at Black Beauty — the word is never used. What they are is "gentled." Nor, during this process, are they ever approached by truck or even on horseback, because that is how they were originally driven and captured. They are approached only on foot. After the personal approach comes the personal delivery of some grain — just dropped and left. Then, a day or so later, an apple or a carrot is presented, this time by hand. Finally, when this has gone on for several days, there comes the first and very gentle pat. From that time on, the ranch hands maintain, a child could do the rest. And in the case of my granddaughter Zoe, age twelve, a child did.

* * *

By this time I felt Polar Bear was up to meeting the largest of the ranch's lodgers — the elephants. As we approached Conga, and Conga approached us, I held Polar Bear back a little — not so much to add to his apprehension but so that I could sneak a backward glance at his eyes. These, I was glad to see, contained, along with their usual travel-weary owlishness, a by now practiced, if not totally resigned, agreement to look over whatever manner of monster I was next placing on his menu. Conga, I must say, mountainous as she must have seemed to Polar Bear, was at her gentle giant best. Holding Polar Bear as I was, with a fence between him and Conga, even as Conga's trunk came over the fence toward him, he was far more fascinated than he was frightened. And, I am sure, what he found most fascinating about elephants was that they seemed to have tails at both ends.

Actually Conga is friendly to all residents and visitors, both people and animals, and even welcomes one and all to her pasture — albeit she does not want anyone but regulars to sit on her fence. As for her neighbors in the next pasture, before we had a companion elephant for her, she took such a shine to one particular burro that every evening she would take some hay over and, dumping it close by, first put her trunk over the fence and hug the burro and then, moving away, would proceed to do the one trick she knew, kneeling on one front knee, with one back leg extended.

At the ranch we do not encourage ex-performing animals to "do their thing," but in this case we had made an exception. We had also noticed that the old saw that elephants are afraid of small animals does not hold in Conga's case. She is not in the least afraid of field mice, and dogs as well as cats go in and out of her pasture with impunity. Knowing all this, I was certain, as I held Polar Bear reasonably close to her, that she would not alarm him. And she did not. I did have the feeling, though, that Polar Bear thought there was entirely too much of her, but since he feels that way about virtually every animal larger than himself, I did not let it worry me. Normally, when I am on one of my regular ranch visits without Polar Bear, I go right under the fence and under Conga, too, and pat her everywhere including under her stomach. I also reach right into her mouth and pat her tongue — she loves that. On this visit, however, I drew the line at both of these intimacies. Just the same, after putting Polar Bear back in the pickup, I gave Conga some special pats specially edited for Polar Bear's benefit.

In short order Conga's companion, Nora, arrived. Nora, in comparison to Conga's fourteen, is a six-year-old African, and I was sure she would appeal to Polar Bear. For one thing, she is less than a third of Conga's size. But if I had assumed the meeting would be easy, I certainly assumed wrong. I should have realized that Nora is a very young elephant, and Polar Bear, bad as he is with new adults, is even worse with new children. Elephant children, I soon learned, were no exception. Nora didn't make things any easier either because, among other things, she is a lot faster with her trunk than Conga. In any case, Nora expected the kind of food we generally bring around — apples, oranges, bananas, watermelon, sweet potatoes, and such — and, seeing Polar Bear, seemed to make the immediate decision that he was something between a banana and a sweet potato. She made a very sudden and very rapid trunk reach toward him. Immediately and bravely out flew Polar Bear's paw. It was touch and go there for a second but, looking back without the benefit of Instant Replay, I had to give Polar Bear the round, and I was proud of him.

Both elephants came to us in all-too-typical ways. Conga came from a roadside zoo in Florida where, about to be replaced by a younger elephant who knew more tricks, she faced either being sent, in zoo parlance, "down," or, literally, being put down, or killed. Nora, on the other hand, came to us from a circus — one which was successfully prosecuted for cruelty by a long-time friend of the Fund, Bettijane Mackall, who then sent Nora to us. As we stood with Conga and Nora I was, as always, brought back to my first relationship with elephants in such places as Kenya, Tanzania, and Mozambique. Even before the days of the mass poaching, among the Fund's earliest gifts to other societies were Africa-bound infrared equipment and other sophisticated antipoaching weaponry. Today, after the cruel carnage, and despite the far too long deferred ban on the ivory trade, we still are far from sanguine about what continues to go on. Dick Lambert, for example, husband of Florence Lambert, one of the Fund's most stalwart elephant supporters, became so incensed at governmental corruption that, after offering to give his own airplane for antipoaching work, he eventually took back his gift. "We weren't satisfied," Mrs. Lambert says, "that the governments were doing enough."

Nor are all of the elephants' troubles confined to Africa. If anyone thinks so, perhaps he or she should pause for a moment, as I did there at the ranch, and think of an incident which occurred at the San Diego Zoo — one which, at least up to that time, had long been considered one of this country's most respected. It began when

Dunda, an African elephant like Conga and Nora, was transferred from her long-time "home" at the zoo itself and taken to the zoo's Wild Animal Park, where she was to go into a "breeding program." Here, lonely and frightened, Dunda, according to the zoo, swung her trunk at a keeper, although this was never proved. Afterward, the head elephant keeper, Alan Roocroft, ordered what he called a "disciplinary session." What happened at this session — which did not become public for months — was that, a full day later, after her alleged trunk-swinging, Dunda was stretched out on the floor with a block and tackle and, while Mr. Roocroft yelled voice commands, other keepers, positioned on each side of her head, alternately beat her at varying intervals for two days with ax handles.

Just how the zoo was able to cover up this story would seem incredible unless one was familiar with both the zoo and its highly organized publicity network. Even Dunda herself, her head a mass of welts and bruises, was hidden. Finally, however, primarily because of two zoo elephant keepers, Steve Friedlund and Lisa Landres, the story did break. And, when it broke, it broke in all particulars, including the fact that Dunda was a gentle elephant and never had done the trunk-swinging of which she was accused. From then on the hero of the story was Dan McCorquodale, a remarkable California state senator and chairman of the Senate's Natural Resources and Wildlife Committee. Despite opposition from not only the San Diego Zoo but also from virtually every zoo in the state, he demanded and chaired a hearing on "the Dunda case."

The zoo brought out witness after witness, from their board members to their curators and from their veterinarians to Joan Embry, all of whom had a vested interest in the coverup, and all of whom, it seemed, made three claims — that the beating had not been severe; that severe discipline was necessary in the handling of elephants; and that the Dunda case was an isolated incident. None of these claims was substantiated, and as for the beating of Dunda being an isolated incident, it was soon apparent that such beatings at the zoo were routine, if for no other reason than that they made it easier for the elephants to perform tricks. One of Mr. Roocroft's favorites, we learned, was to conclude a Wild Animal Park tour by having thc visitors seeing him lying down on the ground on his back and having an elephant stand over him with one foot just over his face.

I was to be the first speaker on Dunda's side. But before I even testified, I was subjected to much pressure not to do so, including being called by the chairman of the board of the zoo. Then, literally just before I was introduced, Mr. Roocroft himself came over to me and said that he was "authorized" to offer me the zoo's "best bull elephant." This, he said, he would personally take, at the zoo's expense, to our Black Beauty Ranch and, "no matter how long it took," would breed him to Conga and that we could have the baby. I was so flabbergasted that for some time I didn't even answer, but when I did, I did so in a voice which I hoped would be heard by Senator McCorquodale. I told Mr. Roocroft that the Fund for Animals had never been in favor of breeding animals but that now, knowing him, I was not sure we were in favor of breeding people.

Fortunately, we had witnesses on our side who were far better able to keep their tempers than I was, and, not long after the hearing, despite the opposition, Senator McCorquodale's bill to ban the beating of elephants passed the California legislature by a wide margin.

After the elephants we headed back to the ranch house and supper. Here Polar Bear was to visit the animal I wanted him to meet most of all, one of the ranch's most loved creatures — a cat. By no means young in age, she is, in point of residence, the oldest animal on the ranch, because she was already there when we bought the place. Her name is Peg and, if Lady is the foredog of the ranch, then Peg is assuredly the forecat — if, for no other reason, than that she has only three legs. Her fourth, her right front, is off at the shoulder — lost, we were told, to a leghold trap on neighboring property.

From the moment Polar Bear and Peg met there was an understanding between them I had never seen with Polar Bear and any other animal. Perhaps it was the fact that, after a day spent with so many others, he was at last face-to-face with one of his own kind. Or perhaps it was that he seemed immediately to recognize Peg's infirmity and not only respected it but felt he would not be offered the kind of challenge he might have expected from barging into another cat's domain. In any case, it was extraordinary. Almost immediately Polar Bear leaped up on the sofa and went into his Buddha meditation pose — gazing directly at Peg, who was seated across the way. Then, slowly, Peg arose, looked around for a moment, and then hopped over toward Polar Bear. Just before she leaped toward him she turned a little sideways and so landed beside him. As Polar Bear turned to look at her, she too turned to look at him, but neither look from either one of them betrayed even the slightest hint of the typical hostile cat stare.

And, not immediately but in good cat time, Polar Bear slowly turned over on his side and reached out with all four paws. So did Peg — albeit with just three. In a moment all seven paws were actually touching each other's stomachs and in that position first Polar Bear, who had, after all, had a very long day, closed his eyes and then Peg closed hers and both were fast asleep.

For some time I just sat and looked at Polar Bear and Peg together — particularly at Peg. To me, Peg has long been the living symbol of the cruelty of the fur business. No animal, with the exception of the ape, the raccoon, and the otter, uses his or her frontal extremities more deftly than the cat. To go through the rest of a life without the use of a front paw — in Peg's case, a whole front leg — was tragic enough, but at least Peg was just one animal. When one thought from her to the literally millions of other animals whose only escape from the awful leghold was to gnaw off their own leg, one could easily realize that trapping was one of the worst of all man's inhumanities to animals.

My own fight against the fur trade went back even before I founded the Fund for Animals. I remember particularly an exhibit I had at the New York World's Fair in 1965. We had live animals behind glass in various showing rooms. The most popular of these had been the final room, called The Den, which featured a beautiful model in a cloth coat together with her three friends — a German shepherd, a coyote, and a wolf. Barbara Walters came out from the Today show and interviewed me. "Cleveland," she said, "do you really think you're going to stop the women of American from wearing furs?" I told her I didn't know, but that I was sure as hell going to try and that particularly I was going to try to make them relate the fur on their back to the cruelty involved. I remember well Barbara's surprise, and I did not blame her — at that time it seemed so far off. Today, however, it does not seem so.

Not just in this country but all over the world the fur industry is under attack. My particular favorite antifur slogan is that of the Friends of Animals: "Get the Feeling of Fur — Slam Your Hand in a Car Door." I am also partial, however, to my own way of handling someone wearing a fur coat. This is to walk behind them and say to someone beside me, in a loud voice, "It's just what I always told you — it makes her look so fat." I like to do this so much I do it even when there is no one beside me — I just pretend there is.

For years the furriers have countered antifur arguments with truly extraordinary logic, as witnessed in the following quotation from *Fur Age Weekly:*

> The first tool, as anthropologists use the term, was not the first stone to be hurled or the first stick to be wielded. Lesser anthropoids can do that. The first precision tool requiring nimble fingers was probably a bone needle used to sew hides together. . . . Thus it is not unreasonable to assert that the fur industry is largely responsible for the extraordinary adroitness and coordination of the human hand — particularly that crucial, uniquely human device, the fully opposable thumb. The ability to stitch rabbit pelts together ultimately became the ability to assemble transistor radios, perform delicate surgery and play the music of Chopin.

Furriers also have a remarkable ability to distance themselves and their business from the cruelty. When, for instance, as far back as 1972 I showed a Fund for Animals trapping film on Walter Cronkite's Evening News, two of the country's leading furriers told me personally it was the first time they had ever actually seen animals in traps. Furriers still do not admit traps are cruel, but at the same time they do their best to convince the public that they trap very few furs but instead ranch almost everything. The reality, of course, is far different. Actually an enormous amount of all furs, even mink, are trapped, and only chinchilla is totally ranched. In any case, make no mistake, fur ranches can be almost as gruesome as traps. I shall never forget one experience I had with a ranch in Idaho — one of, of all animals, beavers. It was supposed to be a "model" beaver ranch, but whatever it was, it had gone bankrupt. The receivers turned out to be Teresa Kloos and Alexia Reynolds, two extremely humane young women, who, when advised to have the beavers killed, refused to do so. Instead they contacted the Fund for Animals.

The first time I saw the beavers I couldn't believe it. If this was a "model" ranch — their only water was their own urine — I wondered what a bad ranch was like. Nonetheless, we went to work. We took out advertisements asking for people who wanted to adopt a beaver — or, rather, two beavers — and in short order, in a state which at that time had been almost totally "trapped-out," as they call it, of beaver, we soon had hundreds of applicants. Many Idahoans, it seemed, had sorely missed that wonderful animal and had either ponds or a river on their property. The "expert" wildlife biologists we spoke to told us that our beavers, who had been more than three generations in the ranch, would not survive three days in the wild, but thankfully this proved almost totally false. Out of 905 beavers we lost less than half a dozen — through road kills or other accidents — and most became almost as highly regarded by their owners as the owners' own pets.

As for myself, to this day I keep — facing the desk in my office — a picture of Blackie, as I called the first beaver we placed. He is a beautiful animal, with a silvery shine in his black fur, and his eyes seem to be looking at me just the way they did when I pushed him toward his first pond. There is a special glint in those eyes — one which I've always taken as a last quick "thank you." To this day when I see a woman — or, for that matter, a man — in a beaver coat, I am disgusted.

I also keep on my desk a letter from a fur rancher, albeit a pretty impersonal one, since it was addressed, "To All Anti-Fur People." Nonetheless I found it fascinating. "God," the man had written, "was the first furrier. This was because," he later continued, "God told Adam and Eve to clothe themselves in skins." And therefore, the man concluded, what he was doing was, "following in God's Footsteps and doing God's Work."

My answer to that man was that I did not believe many furriers would go to heaven, but that if by chance he should be one of the few, I felt entitled to hope that, when he got there, God would turn out to be a very large, and very cross, beaver.

Actually, strained as through the years have been my relations with furriers, they are no more so than my relations with hunters. The reason is simple. Hunters have never seemed to understand what I have tried to do for them. As far back as 1963, for example. on the Today show I announced the formation of a new club — one to be called the "Hunt the Hunters Hunt Club." All the club ever tried to do was to define the word "conservation" for the hunters the way they have always defined it for the animals. We were shooting them, in other words, for their own good. But from the beginning the hunters made no effort to understand this, even though we made clear we never used words like "shooting" or "killing." Instead we used the hunters' own words — words with which they would feel comfortable — "culling," "trimming," "harvesting," or just "taking." We wanted them to understand that if we didn't take them, in no time at all there would be too many of them. They would be crowding the woods, and the fields and the roads, and they would be breeding like flies.

All we really asked of the hunter, when you came right down to it, was for him to take the long-term view of the whole thing and not the selfish short-term view. In the end we both wanted, after all, the same thing — we both wanted a stronger herd. We even asked them directly if they had ever seen a hunter out there in the middle of the winter, starving in the woods. It was not a pretty sight.

The hardest criticism we had to take was that the "Hunt the Hunters Hunt Club" had no season on hunters. Nothing could have been further from the truth. The club's very second rule forbade members to take hunters — and I quote — "within city limits, in parked cars or in their dating season." And the third rule clearly stated that, after harvesting their hunter, members were not to — and I quote again — "drape him over the automobile or mount him when they got home." Mounting the cap or jacket, we felt, was in better taste.

The next hardest criticism we had to take from the hunters was their claim that we were out to exterminate them. This was unfair, and really was, we felt, hitting below the belt because, as we made clear from the beginning, when the hunters' numbers fell below a certain level we had another whole program to deal with that — we would breed our own hunters. We called this program "Hunters Unlimited." It is true that not many of our members had experience with hunters' children, but from the ones they did know they were certain that, with a little practice, they could do as well. Naturally, though, we wanted to breed the kind of hunters who would jump about and flush properly and make sporty game. We were certainly entitled to that — after all, it was our money which was paying for the whole program.

An extraordinary number of people wrote me after the broadcast asking to become members of the club, which I found very gratifying. And, more than a quarter of a century later, the syndicated columnist Roger Simon wrote a column which to my mind highly qualifies him to be at least an honorary member. Mr. Simon's work was occasioned by the Fund for Animals' challenge to the so-called "hunter harassment" laws — which some state legislatures, pressed by the NRA and other hunter advocacy groups, had passed despite the fact that the law's constitutionality was widely questioned. Mr. Simon wrote, in part, as follows:

> We all know that many odd things are legal in this country. You can burn the American flag. You can march around wearing sheets and burning crosses. You can exhibit dirty pictures at government expense.
>
> You can also shoot an arrow into a deer's eyeball. That's legal. It is *illegal* to speak the words: "I don't think you should shoot that arrow into a deer's eyeball."
>
> Five people were arrested in Maryland for doing this

> last weekend. . . . Forest and Wildlife Supervisor Joshua Sandt, who supervises the state deer herds, defended the hunters. "I think the biggest problem people have is that they tend to believe that animals think and feel the same way we do," Sandt said. "First off, they don't think and, second, their nerve endings are not the same as ours."
>
> Well, first off, Joshua Sandt couldn't be any dumber if you cut off his head. And second, if Sandt really believed that animals "don't think" and have different "nerve endings" then I guess it would be OK if people went out and shot arrows into dogs and cats, too.

The next morning at the ranch we were up betimes. This is an expression I not only wish more young people knew the meaning of but also made more use of — particularly since so many of them, at least in the morning, are chronic somniacs. Polar Bear, I am glad to say, is always up betimes. He was so even when I first knew him and now, in his more mature years, continues to be. I was particularly glad he was so that morning, because it was to be a very special morning for him — one in which he would meet, if he would pardon the expression, a fellow animal celebrity, one who is indeed one of the world's best-known animals.

He is a chimpanzee, and his name is Nim. Born in 1973 at the Institute for Primate Studies in Oklahoma, he was, at the age of two weeks, at the direction of Dr. Herbert Terrace, a psychologist at Columbia University, taken from his mother and brought to New York City. Here, at the home of one of Dr. Terrace's students, Stephanie LaFarge, Nim would not only live in a house with a human family, he would also sleep in a crib at night and, in the daytime, wear clothes, sit in a high chair, eat at the family table, and be trained to use the toilet.

Just like any other baby, Nim was bottled and burped, diapered and rocked, tickled and played with, and, in turn, just like any other baby he smiled and laughed, yelled and cried. From the beginning, however, from his very first giggles, all the humans around Nim talked to him in sign language, the language of the deaf. And, in the very same way a baby begins to understand words, Nim began to understand signs.

One day, still in the very early life of Nim, something happened which related very strongly to the fact he was about to meet Polar Bear. One of his teachers, ever on the lookout for something which would excite Nim, brought with her to his "class" one day something in a carrier. Peeking through the hole Nim saw that inside was a white cat. Nim was very excited. "Open me," he signed, pointing to the box. "There's a cat in the box," the teacher signed back to him. Nim of course knew that, but seeing the teacher would not immediately open the carrier he began a whole variety of other signs, including "Open cat," "Cat hug," and "Cat me."

Eventually Nim, squealing with delight, was allowed gently to play with and hug the cat. There was only one problem — whenever the teacher held the cat Nim got jealous. At first the teacher did not know whether he was jealous of her because she held the cat or of the cat because that was what Nim wanted to hold. Nonetheless the visit went well, and at the end of it Nim had very gently hugged and kissed the cat good-bye.

At the end of almost four years of schooling Nim had become the most famous of all the "signing" chimps. He had appeared on the covers of numerous magazines and had had two books written about him. But Nim was once again separated from those he knew and loved and was returned to Oklahoma. Then, from there, Nim was sent to a New York laboratory. Here was a chimpanzee who had not only already done more than his share of service to humanity — more than a score of his student teachers had either written theses about him or had otherwise bettered their careers through their work with him — and yet that apparently wasn't enough. He would now undergo experimentation.

This was totally unacceptable to us, and we resolved to go all-out for Nim. Many other like-minded societies joined us and, finally, threatened with what would surely be a highly publicized lawsuit, the University of Oklahoma agreed to remove Nim from the New York laboratory and take him back once more to the place where he was born. While Nim was there, he would once again be under the care of his first owner, Dr. William Lemmon.

I knew that Dr. Lemmon had had many large offers for Nim — from well-known zoos all the way to circuses — but I also knew that I had one thing in my favor. This was that Dr. Lemmon was no admirer of circuses and not even one of most zoos. Finally, after I had an all-day session with him in Oklahoma, Dr. Lemmon agreed to let us have Nim under one condition — that the Black Beauty Ranch would indeed be his permanent home. It was my turn to make a condition. I told Dr. Lemmon that Black Beauty was like the Ark — we wanted two of a kind, and he would have to find us the right companion for Nim.

Dr. Lemmon met his condition well. He came up with an ex-circus chimp named Sally, one who was over breeding age and who was as even in temperament as Nim was uneven. The day she arrived at the ranch to join Nim was a memorable one. If it wasn't love at first sight, it was certainly love after first bite. And, from the very beginning,

Sally proved that even at Nim's worst she was able, if not to charm him, at least to calm him.

As we approached the porch of Nim and Sally's house, both of them had, from far off, their eyes glued on Polar Bear. And, as we got closer, I could see that this would not be the all-too-often situation that it is with strangers approaching — of a visitor poking at chimps. This would be the opposite — the chimps wanted to poke at the visitors. I did not want this, however. I knew that Nim had a terrific memory for almost everything that had happened in his childhood and, while I wondered whether he could recall, back in his past, that first white cat, I took no chances on any gentle touch. Fortunately, I did not have to worry. Nim immediately grabbed his tire and started showing off and, after waiting for Sally to calm him down, I cautiously moved forward with Polar Bear. As we came closer I noticed Polar Bear's eyes moving back and forth, following Nim as he rode the tire.

Suddenly Nim rode over to us and gave his sign for "toothbrush." Obediently Polar Bear and I went for his toothbrush and paste. I handed them to him, but still there was apparently something missing — he was making a sign with which I was unfamiliar. Suddenly I remembered. Nim wanted his mirror. I went and got it and handed it to him and, while Polar Bear watched in amazement, Nim first held up the mirror, then brushed his teeth, and finally and very politely offered to do the same for Polar Bear. Fortunately, though, Polar Bear pleaded a previous engagement. Even I have a very difficult time brushing Polar Bear's teeth, and he wasn't about to stand still for the job being done by a chimpanzee.

I had wondered if, when Polar Bear and Nim were face-to-face, Nim might not have a go at his old signs of "Me cat" and "Me hug," etc., but he did not. I know some of Nim's sign language, and others at the ranch know much more than I do, but none of us are inclined to make a big thing of it. Actually most of the time Nim understands so much of human language that signs are not even necessary. Usually I will ask Nim something such as if he thinks it's going to rain. He will immediately look up and around at the sky and then either nod or shake his head as the case may be. Signs in such instances do seem superfluous. And, if there is one thing all of us at the ranch want for Nim, it is that he have no more pressure in his life. If he wants to sign, he signs. If he doesn't, he doesn't — and that's that.

Close contact with Nim, who, although I wouldn't say it in Polar Bear's presence, is undoubtedly the smartest animal I have ever known, always makes me think of just how close he came to being just one more laboratory animal. This was vividly brought home to me at the time of Polar Bear's visit, because at that time, I was working on an "Op-Ed" article for the *New York Times* in which I addressed two laboratory cat experiments which I found particularly reprehensible.

The first of these occurred at Louisiana State University. Here, under an eight-year two-million-dollar Department of Defense contract, cats first had parts of their skulls removed, then, put in vises, were shot in the head. The experimenters' purpose, they said, was "to find a way to return brain-wounded soldiers to active duty. Basic training for an Army infantryman costs $9,000," they stated. "If our research allows only an additional 170 men to return to duty . . . it will have paid for itself."

The second experiment I wrote about occurred at the

University of Oregon. There, under a seventeen-year million-and-a-half-dollar grant, psychologists surgically rotated the eyes of kittens, implanted electrodes in their brains and forced them to jump onto a block in a pan of water to test their equilibrium. This experiment had resulted in one of the country's most famous laboratory "break-ins" — and the subsequent indictment of one of the animals' "liberators." During the trial not only were the experimenters unable to cite a single case in which their experiments had benefited humans but, in the end, the cruelty the kittens had endured was too much for Judge Edwin Allen, who presided at the trial. The testimony he had heard, he said from the bench, had been "disturbing to me as a citizen of this state, as a citizen of this city and as a graduate of the University of Oregon."

I concluded my article by stating that a judge was just what was needed — a judge first, and then a jury — and that the experimenters had been both long enough. When, however, the *Times* came to print letters in answer to my article, they chose two highly critical ones from the opposite ends of the country — one from Stanford and one from Harvard. The Stanford letter was from Thomas Hamm, Jr., director of Stanford's Division of Laboratory Animal Medicine, a man who spoke at length of the "elaborate protocols in place" to protect Stanford's laboratory animals. He did not, however, mention that all but a few of Stanford's sixty thousand laboratory animals spent their entire lives underground — under, in fact, a parking lot. Nor did he mention that when the Fund's California coordinator, Virginia Handley, complained that Stanford's dogs were never exercised, he replied, "There's no scientific evidence that dogs need exercise. We did try putting them on a treadmill but they didn't want to stay on it."

The second letter, from my own university of Harvard, was in its own way even more remarkable. It was written by Dr. David Hubel, a man who said I was threatening the search for cures to "all the diseases that blight human life and happiness." Like Mr. Hamm, Dr. Hubel failed to mention several matters, chief among which was the fact that, on taking on a new job in 1989, he had written a letter to some thousands of doctors and members of his society — one which began as follows:

> If I accomplish nothing else as President of the Society of Neuroscience I want to try to mobilize the doctors of this country to fight the Animal Rights Movement. If even a minor fraction of our doctors would say one sentence to each patient ("Don't forget that without research on animals we wouldn't have been able to treat your disease, and such research is being seriously threatened by the Animal Rights Movement"), the result might be impressive. If posters could be put on the walls of waiting rooms, and pamphlets on the tables in hospitals and in offices, it could make a huge difference. One small phrase or statement at the bottom of the doctor's bill or prescription form would help.

From such a man I could hardly expect sympathy to my laboratory cruelty charges. Nonetheless, Dr. Hubel's evident paranoia about "animal rights" struck close to home. Although I have a book in my office entitled *Animal Rights*, written by the English humanitarian Henry Salt as far back as 1892, the fact remains that the Fund for Animals played a major role in the phrase's more recent currency. Indeed, through the good offices of Mr. and Mrs. Edward Ney, we were in the very early days of the Fund presented by the Young and Rubicam advertising agency with a slogan: "Animals Have Rights, Too." This, which we promptly put on our T-shirts and bumper stickers, almost immediately achieved wide popularity. Early on, however, I was asked what we meant by it and, frankly, I was not sure — it hadn't, after all, been my idea. Nonetheless I attempted three short paragraphs, as follows:

> The right to freedom from fear, pain and suffering — whether in the name of science or sport, fashion or food, exhibition or service.
>
> The right, if they are wild, to roam free, unharried by hunters, trappers or slaughterers. If they are domestic, not to be abandoned in the city streets, by a country road or in a cruel and inhumane pound.
>
> And finally the right, at the end, to a decent death — not by a club, by a trap, by harpoon, cruel poison or mass extermination chamber.

Looking back on those lines, I think they still express what I feel today. But there are many times when the Fund is fighting battles for animals when I frankly find the phrase "animal rights" difficult — as, for instance, when we were fighting the timber companies in the Northwest for killing bears because they ate the sap in what the timber companies regarded as their trees. In fact, during this fight I realized that, to the timber company people, the mere mention of "animal rights" conjured up bears marching down the main street toward the Capitol and then marching in to take seats and raising their paws to vote. Nor have I always been happy about the way the phrase is sometimes construed by its more far-out adherents. In the matter of bears again, for example, when Sean O'Gara of the Fund for Animals reviewed a remarkable movie, *The Bear*, he was immediately brought to task by an animal rightist who wrote *The Animals' Agenda* magazine that he was "infuriated" by the "numerous injuries" to animals in the film. The man then went on to enumerate these — that "dogs were muzzled and tethered," "horses are saddled and ridden," and "bears eat real fish." The latter was his only concession. He was not, he said, "suggesting that bears should not eat fish," but that "the injury to the fish is not simulated."

Candidly, I was at a loss to answer that one — and left it to Mr. O'Gara. I was not, however, at a loss when, not long before Polar Bear's visit, a group of animal rights leaders came to the ranch one evening for dinner. Nervously I explained to the chef that our guests would be "vegans." The chef looked midway between blank and concerned, so I went on quickly to explain that veganism was beyond vegetarianism — that vegans did not eat milk, butter, eggs, or cheese, or indeed any dairy products. I told him not to worry, though, about it, because our guests said they would bring fake hamburgers and fake hot dogs with them. By this time I was sure the chef was beginning to believe in the idea of five loaves and two little fishes. I didn't, however, have the heart to tell him that wouldn't work either, because fish, too, was out.

We were all sitting around enjoying our meal at different tables in the main ranch dining room when, looking across at the chef, I saw him obviously biting, for the first time in his life, into a fake hamburger. I looked over at him and attempted to ask, as quietly as possible, how he liked it. Unfortunately at that moment, as so often happens in such situations, all other conversations suddenly appeared to die at once. The chef looked up after his mouthful. "Cleveland," he said, "do you want the truth?" I told him I always wanted the truth. He considered this for a moment and, then, after a quick look at the rest of his hamburger, looked up straight at me. "Cleveland," he said, "it just barely beats eatin' nuthin'." To the animal rights activists' credit, however, there was immediate laughter.

On Polar Bear's last afternoon at the ranch there were still dozens of different animals for him to meet. I started with a particular group who would normally run free in the ranch's wildlife area but who in this case were either too lame or abused to do so. These were several rabbits. To me rabbits are the animals God forgot. Indeed they seem to spend their entire lives in fear and stress. As pets — and they can, with understanding, make great pets — they all too often end up being dumped out not only after Easter, but also at other times of the year. In the laboratories they undergo truly awful experiments, not in the least of which is the infamous Draize test on their naked eyes for, of all purposes, cosmetic testing. And, in the wild, they simply lack the weaponry to be anything but easy prey to a seemingly endless array of foes.

Polar Bear was very good about the rabbits — and not just because they were, aside from Peg, the first animals he had met that were his size. They were also the first who were obviously more nervous about him than he was of them. It made me think of some day taking him to Simpsonville, South Carolina, where we have a whole rabbit sanctuary — the only one I know of in the country. It is run by a woman named Caroline Gilbert, who not only feels the way I do about rabbits but knows at least ten times more about them than I. She has hundreds of rabbits — everything from ex-pet rabbits to ex-greyhound-training rabbits to ex-laboratory rabbits. Her two favorites are Benny and Abbit-Rabbit. She discovered Benny at a rabbit show trying to defend himself against three men's efforts to remove him from his cage while a large group of spectators giggled at the "mean" rabbit. Abbit-Rabbit, on the other hand, was sold as a pet at a flea market to a mother with eleven children. A week later the mother called Animal Control because Abbit "wouldn't play anymore," but instead just lay on his side. She wanted to know if she could, as she put it, "trade this one in and get another."

Next on the agenda came a visit with the ranch's most recent arrivals. These were animals who had survived a nine-day period during which they were neither fed nor watered, and they had come to us, after a successful prosecution by Mitchell Fox and the Progressive Animal Welfare Society, all the way from the state of Washington. Polar Bear's favorite among these was, much to my surprise, a llama. He made our fourth llama, and we named him — after having already used up Lloyd, Llewellyn, and Llewis — LLD. If we get any more, please remember we are in the market for more "ll" names. I personally ran out with LLD.

Polar Bear, I knew, had never seen such an animal before, and I had never seen him show so much curiosity toward anything new. But his strong "aeiou" 's were unmistakably favorable. Accordingly, for his meeting with the llamas, I chose a face-to-face encounter rather than one at ground level. For, contrary to what we have been led to believe about llamas, ours do not spit. Once in a while, however, when they do not wish to get in or out of a truck or something like that, they can not only kick like a mule but, in some instances, can behave even more stubbornly. Nonetheless, at their best our llamas are the kissiest of all the animals at the ranch, and I was not in the least surprised when two of them came over and decided to kiss Polar Bear at once. But, partial as he obviously was to them, this seemed to him a bit much, and, after first flashing out his warning paw, he next ducked his head into my jacket. He was not about to let even new friends take such double liberties, no matter with how many *l*'s they were spelled.

There was still another group of animals to visit — our wild goats. As we approached their pasture I knew that Polar Bear had never seen a goat before. This was because, before we reached them, he heard them and pricked up his ears in that special way I have learned he greets a sound he has never heard before. Coyotes have their musical howls, burros their wonderful brays, horses and mules their infinitely variable whinnies and snorts, but, among all animals' sounds the "baa" of the goat is, if not the most musical, certainly the most incessant. By the time we reached them — and they were approaching us as rapidly as we them — their chorus was such that Polar Bear decided to join in and at least give them — or me, I wasn't sure which — one of the strangest "aeiou" 's I have ever heard from him. Afterward, though, he shrank back and, while still peering to some extent, also managed to continue to bury himself in my jacket. This was understandable. Goats are a herd animal. They rarely travel alone — and in Polar Bear's opinion there were, in the first place, too many of them and, in the second, they were too close at hand. Polar Bear likes better-mannered creatures who know enough to keep their distance until they are properly introduced.

Our goats are San Clemente Island goats — a rare breed of Spanish Andalusians whose problems began in earnest when, during World War II, the late President Roosevelt, in a burst of typical pro-Navyism, gave San Clemente Island outright, and apparently in perpetuity, to the Navy. The Navy immediately put the island to use as a shelling target not only from ships at sea but also for field trials of new weapons from the air — something they continued to do after the war. How the goats had been able to survive forty years of this is a mystery, and the terrain of the island, with its rugged and craggy protective cliffs, only partially explains it. More important was the goats' uncanny ability to find and take immediate cover once attacked. This prowess, we would soon learn firsthand, matched that of experienced troops in battle.

In all, during the Fund's rescue of more than five thousand of these animals, we were at war with the U.S. Navy, in court and on the island, for more than six years. To me, looking back at it, there were three particularly memorable incidents. The first began in the halls of the Pentagon itself. Here, with Dana Cole, our California lawyer, I made my way toward the office of Vice Admiral Tom Hughes, Chief of Naval Logistics and apparently also Admiral of the Goats. Among the offices we passed was that of Secretary of Defense Caspar Weinberger. He was a man who had preceded me by a couple of years as president of the *Harvard Crimson* and also one whom, through his assistant Benjamin Welles, we had long been trying to reach to get him to intercede for us in favor of the goats. Along the whole incredible corridor was oil painting after oil painting, apparently depicting famous sea battles, which pictured one ship after another blowing up other ships. All of these, I presumed, were enemy ships.

Finally we turned into the admiral's conference room. Here there was a full complement of captains, lieutenants, ensigns, and civilian personnel. Shortly thereafter Admiral Hughes appeared, introduced himself, shook hands, and sat down. First he lit his pipe and then, without preamble, rose and went to the large map of San Clemente Island on the wall. From here things began to go from bad to worse when the admiral, as well as his point man on the map, brought up the question of the endangered flora and fauna on the island. Whenever the admiral said anything, all the others at the table nodded and said, almost in unison, "Aye, aye." Finally the admiral went over and sat down. "You see, Mr. Amory," he said, "our hands are tied. We have to get rid of the goats. It's the Endangered Species *Law*."

I had been good so far, but bringing up the Endangered Species Act was too much. No one had fought harder for this act than the Fund for Animals, and for it to be used now against us, and on such flimsy grounds, was truly infuriating. I pointed out that, as I understood it, there were exactly three endangered species of fauna on the island and that, as I also understood it, two were birds and one was a lizard. I told the admiral that I was prepared to admit that an occasional goat might occasionally step on an occasional lizard, but I would certainly like him to name an instance of a goat eating a bird. I also asked him if his gunners, when they shelled the island, took care to avoid both the birds and the lizard.

There was a long silence. Finally I could stand it no longer. I looked first at the admiral and then at the others. Dana remembers that I called them a bunch of murderers, but I think I phrased it much better than that. I did, however, mention for the benefit of the Annapolis men present that what they were shooting was their own mascot. In any case, the result was predictable.

As we left the Pentagon, Dana suggested that, having failed with the Navy brass, we should now take our case to the media — which had been consistently favorable to us and the goats. We started with the ABC network. On the way I told Dana what I proposed to say — that I now knew why the Navy had botched the rescue of our hostages in Iran. "How?" Dana asked. It was because, I said, they evidently thought they were going over to shoot them — they didn't know they would have to rescue them.

"If you say that on the air," Dana said to me slowly, "you will have to get yourself another lawyer." Don't worry, I told him. And, as I look back, I really think I intended not to say it. But, when we reached the network, all the effort we had put into the goats somehow got the better — or worst — of me. "What do you think of the Navy turning you down?" the interviewer asked. I know now, I said firmly, why the Navy had botched the rescue of our hostages. They thought they were going over to shoot them — they didn't know they would have to rescue them.

"That's great," the reporter said enthusiastically. "We're going to lead the news with it." With that he went away, and I looked at Dana. He refused even to look at me.

It was almost time for the Evening News, and for some moments we just sat there waiting to see it. Suddenly, just before airtime, the reporter reappeared. "Here," he said, "look at this." He showed us a news clip. The clip said that Secretary Weinberger had overruled his admirals about the goats and that the Fund for Animals would be allowed to rescue them after all. "We're going to lead with this," the reporter said excitedly.

At first I too was so excited that I couldn't think of anything but our victory. But then, suddenly, I remembered what I had previously said. I asked the reporter if it would be possible not to use it. "I don't know," he said, disappearing again. "You'd better," Dana said, "hope hard."

Mercifully, they did not use what I had said. In any case, the second most memorable incident — the rescue itself — was shaping up in California. Our first job was how to take care of all the media who wanted to be in helicopters to take pictures of the country's first major helicopter "netgun" rescue. What Mel Cain, our peerless pilot, and New Zealanders Bill Hales and Graham Jacobs, inventors of the netgun, did that day on that island — with a dozen news helicopters buzzing around them — was truly extraordinary. The very first goat was run down on an up-run path — Mel always insists on either an up or level run, not a down one in which a goat captured in the net could hurt himself — and that first goat was beautifully and accurately netgunned. While Bill jumped to the ground to tie the goat's legs, remove the net, and put the animal in the sling, Mel made a quick circle. Then, when he returned, Bill quickly hooked the sling to a ring under the helicopter, and the goat was then flown back to the corral, where it was gently landed and untied. The whole operation had taken less than four minutes. In all that day more than sixty goats were rescued, some from very difficult terrain.

The third and final memorable incident of the rescue occurred when, later, we were allowed to enter the hitherto totally forbidden unexploded-shell area. Here I was alone with Donna Gregory, the Fund's corral boss, one morning down at the very end of the island. We had a truck there which we were using as a holding corral and were awaiting Mel and Bill's first morning run. All of a sudden, bouncing along the rough dirt road toward us we saw a Navy jeep with two naval officers sitting in front. As they turned up the hill toward us at full speed, I didn't know what we had done wrong, but I told Donna it sure looked as if we would shortly be headed for the brig.

Finally the officers arrived and jumped out of the jeep. "Mr. Amory," the senior officer said excitedly. I "aye, aye'd," "sir'd," and all but saluted him. "Mr. Amory," the officer went on, "have you or Miss Gregory seen any suspicious-looking ships in this area?" Ships? I automatically queried. "Yes," he said, "we've had reports of a Russian ship in this vicinity, and we wondered if you'd seen anything like that." No, I said quickly, adding, "No, sir." "All right," he said, "but keep your eyes open. And if you see anything at all, take your truck and drive right to the command post." With that both officers jumped back into their jeep and took off without another word.

It was all Donna and I could do to keep from laughing before they were out of earshot. Here we were, on a U.S. Navy–owned island, far out in the Pacific — an island bristling with every kind of radar and detective device known in modern warfare. And yet our entire national security apparently depended upon whether or not Donna, who wears thick glasses, and I, who on a good day might be able to see a hundred yards, saw a Russian ship. It gave one pause, all right — in fact, as I looked at Donna, I could see it gave us both pause.

One enduring dividend which came to us from the goat rescue was a whole new California shelter. In looking around for a place near San Diego from which to do our goat adoptions, we happened upon the Animal Trust Sanctuary in Ramona and its formidable founder, Patricia Nelson. Ms. Nelson not only insisted on us adopting our goats from her shelter but, upon her retirement, gave it to us — lock, stock, and barrel. To run this, we installed an eighteen-year Navy civilian executive named Chuck Traisi, a man who from the beginning was so outspoken against the Navy's shooting the goats that he first joined us in taking part in the rescue and then, refusing to wait two years for his pension from the Navy, joined the Fund itself. With his remarkable wife, Cindy, he now not only directs what has become one of the country's finest wildlife rehabilitation centers but also operates something which is particularly dear to my heart — a cattery which even Polar Bear would find difficult to criticize.

On Polar Bear's last night at the ranch he participated in what has come to be a regular ritual — the feeding of every animal a special good-night treat. This takes the form of, per animal, at least two large slices of freshly baked protein bread, a delicacy which is kindly donated by a local baker from their supply of miscut or damaged loaves. I have taken a fair amount of kidding about this — that I feed my animals on bread and water — but the fact is, it is actually the animals' very favorite food, outranking hay or oats or any other grain or anything else, and it even ranks so with Conga and Nora as well as Nim and Sally.

The way the horses and burros, the mules and the goats, the llamas and all the others gather for their daily, or rather nightly, bread is simple. The pickup is driven from pasture to pasture, and the animals, well knowing it is coming, gather on the double from whatever distance they are when they first hear its familiar sound. And, as they come up to the truck, they do so in surprisingly good order because they know from experience that even the bossiest will get no more than his or her share and that no one, not even the most timid, will go without. Seeing this on a beautiful, warm starry Texas night is, to me, the most memorable part of a trip to the ranch, and it has proved so to almost all our visitors. When, for example, the Fund's national director, Wayne Pacelle, saw it for the first time, he told me there and then it was the best sight he had ever seen in his life. Since it was pitch dark that night and he, out of Yale, had at that time just turned twenty-three, it was not exactly an observation on which a Harvard man of more reasonable years would want to go to the bank, but still it was nice to hear.

The animals are fed from the back of the truck, and the night Polar Bear was there, when our feeder got out to climb in the back, so did we. I have always been a bit skeptical about the theory that cats can see in the dark as well as in the daytime — if, for no other reason, because when Polar Bear flies in from the balcony, headed for the bed, some nights when the lights are out, he often bumps into either something fairly substantial he knows perfectly well is there, such as a piece of furniture, or me. In any case, on that particular night — which was a dark one — I had reason to wonder just how he would feel about all those open-mouthed animals within biting range, and I took therefore extra pains to shield him. But I soon saw I had little to worry about. He had by then become, at large animals close at hand, an old hand.

One thing Polar Bear did do, though, was to keep looking up at the man doing the feeding and, when the man looked down at him, he immediately looked at me. "I know what he wants," the man said. "He wants some, too." I told the man, a bit patronizingly I admit, that of course he didn't — cats didn't like bread. With that, the man immediately broke a piece of bread into cat-sized pieces and put the pieces into one hand. No, I told him again. Don't. It's no use. I know Polar Bear. He won't touch it.

The man was very stubborn, though, and, ignoring me, he offered the bread to Polar Bear anyway. And what did Polar Bear do? Guess.

You're right — and furthermore he did it with the mouth of a huge mustang also reaching for it. The thing is, Polar Bear is very stubborn too. It's not enough that he won't do what I want him to do — he won't even not do what I tell people he won't do, even when it's something he doesn't do all the time.

VII ◦ *Romance à la Cat Blanche*

When I first arrived in New York, after the publication of *The Proper Bostonians,* I stayed on Forty-fourth Street at the then Old Royalton Hotel, long the residence of two of my favorite authors, Dorothy Parker and Robert Benchley. I hasten to add that it is not that I felt that after the publication of my book continued residence in Boston would be dangerous, it was rather that I felt living in New York would be more broadening and something everybody in Boston sooner or later needs, even though they might not care, in Boston, to admit the fact. In New York I also frequented, right across the same street, the Algonquin Hotel, which had in the lobby the first of a long succession of cats — each of them, appropriately, named Hamlet.

The Algonquin dining room was of course celebrated for its famed Round Table, to which well-known authors repaired for well-known lunches. I was in no way eminent enough to be eligible for regular membership in that august group. However, I was occasionally invited on a sort of trial basis by two formidable curmudgeons of the day, George S. Kaufman and Alexander Woollcott. There I was privileged not only to absorb the rudiments of New York's idea of curmudgeonry but also to hear, firsthand and fresh off the table, some of my favorite stories. Two of these were about none other than Miss Parker herself.

The first of these concerned the fact that Miss Parker had on one occasion a man in her room and, in those more circumspect social times, was promptly taken to task for this by being called by the desk clerk. "Miss Parker," the clerk began, coming immediately to the point, "do you have a gentleman in your room?" Miss Parker also came immediately to the point. "I don't know," she replied. "I'll ask him."

The second story occurred when Miss Parker visited, on Long Island, the home of the publishing mogul of the day, Mr. Herbert Bayard Swope. Since Miss Parker did not drive, she took the train and was met at the station by Mr. Swope. As they approached the Swope house Miss Parker saw that on the house's spacious veranda there was obviously a party in progress — the ladies were in evening dress and the gentlemen in tuxedos. Furthermore, as Miss Parker and Mr. Swope mounted the long stairway, they could see that many of the ladies and gentlemen seemed to be doing a very odd thing — with their hands behind their backs they were bending over tubs of water. In these tubs, although Miss Parker could not yet see them, were apples — which these participants were intending to bite.

Finally, Miss Parker and Mr. Swope were close enough

to take a good look at what was going on. It was obviously something that Miss Parker had never seen before, and for some time she surveyed the scene in silence. Then her curiosity got the better of her. "Herbert," she asked, "what are they doing?" "It's the new craze, Dorothy," explained Mr. Swope. "It's called 'Ducking for Apples.' " This time Miss Parker's silence was very brief. "Herbert," she said firmly, "there, but for a typographical error, goes the story of my life."

I had made my transition from Boston to New York as gently as possible — out of deference to an unnecessarily dangerous shock to my system — and, in keeping with this effort, my next favorite regular haunt, second only to the Royalton and the Algonquin, became the Harvard Club of New York. Again, in keeping with my careful transition from Boston, this was also located on Forty-fourth Street. Here, too, as at the Algonquin, there was also a resident cat, and I liked that. But there was one thing about the Harvard Club I cordially disliked. This was that its walls were adorned with a wide variety of animals' heads. These heads are still there, and though as the years have passed I have learned to live with them, I am more and more concerned about what appears to me their growing resemblance to those of some of the more elderly members.

Fortunately my favorite room in the Harvard Club of those days had no heads. It was, however, concerned with hair. It was the barbershop, and it offered not New York–priced but rather Boston-priced haircuts. These, at least in my case, were ministered under the fine Italian hand of a barber named Louis Butrico, and with him I soon struck up a close friendship. Mr. Butrico was very complimentary about *The Proper Bostonians*, and, like most new authors, I basked in his approval. That is I did until, as our friendship firmed, I could not help being aware that the compliments, nice as they were, were as nothing compared to those Mr. Butrico bestowed upon another Harvard author. This author was none other than Mr. John Gunther, who was not only a very large man but an enormously successful one, and the author of a dozen or more best-sellers, at least two of which, autographed, Mr. Butrico kept right on his barber table. Again and again I was forced to hear not only the sales figures for Mr. Gunther's books but also the number of printings through which apparently all his editions went. Finally, unable any longer to stand for it — or rather sit for it — I resolved on a plan of action.

This action entailed my arrival for my next haircut armed with two copies of a *Reader's Digest* article I had recently written. As I climbed into the barber chair I did not show these to Mr. Butrico but instead hid them under the newspaper on my lap. When Mr. Butrico started, as I knew he would, on Mr. Gunther and indeed took time off from my hair to show me still another copy of an autographed book, I quietly but firmly put my game plan into full gear. First, apparently graciously, I took the Gunther book and opened it to the autograph, read it, and shut it. Then I looked up to Mr. Butrico. Does Mr. Gunther, I asked him, write just in English? Mr. Butrico looked surprised for only a moment, then added that he thought he did. Oh, I said meaningfully. And then, with some ado, I pulled out the first of my *Reader's Digest* magazines and opened it to my article. The edition was in Italian.

Mr. Butrico whistled. "Wow!" he said, grabbing the

magazine and holding it in front of him in wonderment. "I didn't know you could write in Italian." I smiled modestly and said I hoped it was OK — my Italian was not, I was afraid, what I would like it to be. But Mr. Butrico, by now reading, would not permit such modesty. "It's terrific," he said. "It's perfect." I sighed in apparent relief and then, after a suitable interval, asked him if he would like me to sign it for him. He was very pleased and, after I had done this, I again reached under my newspaper and fired my second barrel. Italian was hard enough for me, I said, but this one was *really* tough. With that I handed him another edition of the magazine, this one with my same article in Japanese. This time Mr. Butrico was so amazed he was not even able to whistle. He just looked and looked at it and then finally, in pure wonder, at me. I'll sign this, too, I told him, if you'd like to have it. And this time, with no ado at all, I did.

I never did find out what Mr. Butrico told Mr. Gunther the next time he came in for a haircut, but I do know that from that time on I heard considerably less about Mr. Gunther, and I had reason to believe that Mr. Gunther heard a good deal more about me. I am only sorry, however, that Mr. Butrico had retired long before the publication of *The Cat Who Came for Christmas*. For, had he not done so I would have had, for the first time in my life, a score or more books in different languages to show him. And not the least of these would have been the Japanese edition — one which to me was the most remarkable because among the few things we have which the Japanese do not have — and as a matter of fact do not even make — not the least of them is Christmas. My book in Japanese is called, simply, *New York Cat Story*.

* * *

From the publication of my book abroad I learned not only many things about cats in different countries but also just how large in almost every country is the literature of the cat. My favorite example of this was a letter from an American author, Gloria Johnson, of Virginia, who sent me a book called *A Cat's Guide to Shakespeare.* At first when she sent it to me, I wasn't sure whether it was a book for people who wanted to be guided through Shakespeare through the eyes of a cat or indeed whether it was a book about Shakespeare for cats. On opening it, however, I found it was neither. It was an art book containing drawings of cats illustrating various Shakespeare quotations, my favorite being a cat's quote from *Julius Caesar:* "I am indeed, sir, a surgeon to old shoes." Polar Bear, I should point out, is surgeon not only to old shoes but also to new shoes. Whenever he finds a pair of mine he likes, he whips them into biting shape in no time at all.

Among the things I learned from foreign cat books was that cat literature had its beginnings in fables which exist in the folklore of almost every country. These are particularly prevalent not only in the Scandinavian countries as well as Germany and Switzerland but are almost equally so in countries as diverse as Ireland and Russia and even Arab countries. I also learned that, while most of these fables are humorous, and the cat almost invariably the villain, the primary purpose of the fables, from Aesop to La Fontaine, was to demonstrate a moral precept. To me, to have chosen the cat, villain or hero, for such a task would seem an exercise in futility. Indeed, I am indebted to Jack Smith of the *Los Angeles Times* for what would seem to me to be a fairly definitive statement on this ticklish point: "I can honestly say," Mr. Smith writes, "that I never knew a moral cat."

I take, however, some umbrage at this. Polar Bear has a kind of morality which I firmly believe is in many ways more honest than mine. The New England conscience, I have often said, does not stop you from doing what you shouldn't — it just stops you from enjoying it. Polar Bear's conscience, on the other hand, not only doesn't stop him from doing what he shouldn't, it also doesn't stop him from enjoying it thoroughly.

Examples of this will shortly and in good time be painfully addressed in the matter of his breakup of not one but two romances of mine. Meanwhile I shall continue in the more important matter we were discussing — which, as I recall, was cat literature. On this subject it is clearly French literature which deserves first credit for having promoted the cat to something beyond a creature in fable. And this is, of course, as it should be, if for no other reason it was the French poet and novelist Théophile Gautier who reduced all international promotion of the cat to nationalistic dimensions. "Only a Frenchman," he wrote, "could understand the fine and subtle qualities of the cat."

A veritable host of French authors did their best to prove M. Gautier correct, including Montaigne, Chateaubriand, Balzac, Baudelaire, Zola, Cocteau, and Colette, as well as Alexandre Dumas, both *père* and *fils*. Of all of these Colette was easily the most prolific, perhaps because of her often-expressed belief that, as she put it, "by associating with the cat one only risks becoming richer."

Close on the heels of France, however, in the literature of the cat is England. Here the most celebrated feline is undoubtedly Lewis Carroll's familiar Cheshire — the cat who, at one time, is "a grin without a cat," and, at another, a cat to whom Alice finds no use speaking, " 'till its ears have come or at least one of them."

My own favorite character in *Alice in Wonderland,* though, is not the Cheshire Cat but the Executioner — the man who, ordered to cut off the Cheshire's head, argues in typical British fashion. "You couldn't," he said, "cut off a head unless there was a body to cut it off from: that he had never had to do such a thing before, and he wasn't going to begin at *his* time of life."

But Carroll was by no means the prime British satirist of the cat. That honor belongs to the late Scottish writer H. H. Munro, better known as Saki. Born in Burma, the son of a British army officer, Saki was sent at the age of two to live in England with two English aunts whose strictness and lack of understanding would become the basis for so many of his satires. In these Saki did not overlook cats, and in his short story "Tobermory," he produced one of the all-time cat classics.

This is the story of a man who discovers he could teach animals human language and after working with, as Saki puts it, "thousands of animals," finally decides to confine his work to cats — animals who, as Saki again puts it, "have assimilated themselves so marvelously with our civilization while retaining all their highly-developed feral instincts." Specifically, the man narrows his search for his perfect student to Tobermory, a cat he locates in the home of Lady Blemly, to whose houseparty we are introduced at the beginning of the story.

Right away, we know Tobermory is up to no good because his "favorite promenade," Saki tells us, is a "narrow ornamental balustrade," which runs not only "in front of most of the bedroom windows," but also from which Tobermory could "watch the pigeons" — something which immediately brought Polar Bear to mind — as well as watching "heaven knew what else besides." In any case, at the afternoon tea which begins the houseparty, the very first question Tobermory is asked, after the host, Sir Wilfred, goes to fetch him, is if he will have some milk. To this Tobermory answers, "I don't mind if I do." But to the second question — what does he think of human intelligence? — Tobermory has no answer. "It is obvious," Saki wrote, "that boring questions lay outside his scheme of things." But Tobermory has a question of his own. "Of whose intelligence in particular?" he asks. "Oh, well, mine for instance," says a guest, with what Saki describes as "a feeble laugh." "You put me in an embarrassing position," continues Tobermory, who then proceeds, without any embarrassment at all, "When your inclusion in this house party was suggested, Sir Wilfred protested that you were the most brainless woman of his acquaintance, and that there was a wide distinction between hospitality and care of the feeble-minded." Tobermory then proceeds with other observations and character assessments which, in the end, result not only in the end of the houseparty but also, sadly, the end of Tobermory.

Saki, one of the greatest satirists of all things English was, at the age of forty-six, killed in action fighting for Britain on the Western Front in World War I. But even before his time the cat had been used as a vehicle for satire by many authors in other countries. Japan, for one example, produced a master of satire who used a cat as the protagonist of his most famous work. The author, Soseki Natsume, a lecturer at the Imperial University, wrote his book entitled *I Am a Cat* in 1905. But it is still widely read today and its author is generally recognized, as the introduction by his translator reads, as "the best writer of prose to have emerged during the century since contact with the outside world was re-established in 1868."

The story concerns a nameless stray kitten who wins a place in the home of, as the book jacket describes the man, a "dyspeptic schoolteacher of many enthusiasms but mediocre ability." From kittenhood the cat grows to cathood and proceeds to give us his comments on the shortcomings of Japanese middle-class life, in which pretenses of the schoolteacher and his friends are almost invariably belittled by the cat in comparison with the cat's own friends, the "sleek and powerful Rickshaw Blackie" and the "elegant Miss Tortoiseshell."

This book too had made at times a disquieting impression on me because, as anyone who has ever been owned by a cat knows, what we want most to know about our cats is what they think about us. And more than once I felt the nameless cat's stern assessment of the schoolteacher as coming far too close for comfort to what well might be Polar Bear's assessment of me. I could even, in my darker moments, visualize that someday, after I had gone to my just reward, a book would come out by Polar Bear about me — or one by a writer using Polar Bear as the protagonist and me as some ridiculous kind of antagonist — only without so much as a mention of my patience, my fortitude, or my steadfast self-abnegation. I could even see a title — *Master Dearest.*

In any case, in *I Am a Cat* the schoolteacher's first words to his wife are, according to the cat, "I am a scholar and must therefore study. I have no time to fuss over you. Please understand this clearly." Later, after seeing the teacher fall asleep over a book every evening, the cat has the first of his many reflections. "Teachers have it easy. If you are born a human, it is best to become a teacher. And if it is possible to sleep this much and still be a teacher, why even a cat could teach." When the schoolteacher begins to fancy himself as an artist, and starts to paint his cat, the cat does his best to be a good model and stay still but finally has to go and relieve himself. At this his master shouts, "You fool!" and then threatens him — which again moves the cat to contemplation. "He had," he tells us of his master, "a fixed habit of saying 'you fool' whenever he curses anyone. He cannot help it since he knows no other swearwords." As for his master's threats, these move him to still more reflection:

> The prime fact is that all humans are puffed up by their extreme self-satisfaction with their own brute power. Unless some creature more powerful than people arrives on Earth to bully them there is just no knowing what dire lengths their fool presumptions will eventually carry them.

The cat even sneaks an occasional look in his master's diary, and indeed favors us with an excerpt from this, one concerning a stroll his master took with a friend:

> At Ikenohata, geishas in formal spring kimono were playing battledore and shuttlecock in front of a house of assignation. Their clothes beautiful; but their faces extremely plain. It occurs to me that they resemble the cat at home.

This of course provokes the cat to return to his favorite subject:

> I don't see why he should single me out as an example of plain features. If I went to a barber and had my face shaved I wouldn't look much different from a human. But there you are, humans are conceited and that's the trouble with them.

Still a third cat satire which, to my mind, belongs right up there with "Tobermory" and *I Am a Cat* is one written by P. G. Wodehouse, a British author who later became an American citizen. In my formative writing days I was so enamored of Mr. Wodehouse's "Jeeves" stories and other sallies at the British nobility that my schoolboy writing efforts owed much to him — so much so, in fact, that more than one came perilously close to plagiarism.

Years later, when Mr. Wodehouse became a friend of mine as well as an ardent supporter of animal causes, he gave me a book of his short stories. In this was included a tale which I believe was the only one he ever wrote about a cat.

It is called "The Story of Webster," and it opens with a group of typical Wodehouse characters discussing the shortcomings of cats — always, apparently, a popular subject with the English landed dog gentry. This discussion boils down, as one gentleman puts it, to the cat's "insufferable air of superiority":

> Cats as a class have never completely gotten over the snottiness caused by the fact that in ancient Egypt they were worshipped as gods. This makes them too prone to set themselves up as critics and censors of the frail beings whose lot they share. They stare rebukingly. They view with concern. And, on a sensitive man, this often has the worst effects, inducing an inferiority complex of the gravest kind.

An example of such cat gravity is shortly visited upon a young gentleman named Lancelot, one who, brought up by his uncle Theodore, a man described by Mr. Wodehouse as "the saintly Dean of Bolsover," had decided much against his uncle's will — and in fact severely placing in jeopardy his inheritance from his uncle's actual will — to enter the Bohemian life and become an artist. And at the time this story opens, Mr. Wodehouse tells us, "his prospects seem bright":

> He was painting the portrait of Brenda, only daughter of Mr. and Mrs. B. B. Carberry-Pirbright, of 11 Maxton Square, South Kensington, which meant thirty pounds in his sock on delivery. He had learned to cook eggs and bacon. He had practically mastered the ukulele. And, in addition, he was engaged to be married to a fearless young *vers libre* poetess of the name of Gladys Bingley, better known as The Sweet Singer of Garbridge Mews, Fulham — a charming girl who looked like a penwiper.

But into this idyll rain, of course, must fall — which it does when Uncle Theodore is "offered the vacant bishopric of Bongo-Bongo in West Africa." But to take on the post, he must part with his faithful cat, Webster, whose tender care he decides to entrust to Lancelot.

From the very first moments of Webster's arrival everything goes awry. Webster immediately engages in washing himself, rotating his left leg rigidly in the air. Upon seeing this, Lancelot is reminded of something one of his nurses apparently once told him — that if you creep up on a cat when its leg is in the air and give it a pull, and at the same time make a wish, in thirty days that wish will come true. This, unfortunately, Lancelot attempts to prove.

Webster immediately lowers his leg, turns, and instead of his leg raises his eyebrow. "Webster, it is true," Mr. Wodehouse tells us, "had not actually raised his eyebrow. But this Lancelot felt was simply because he hadn't any." In any case, from that first altercation everything Lancelot does is, if not in Webster's eyes hopeless, at least something which needs immediate improvement. When, for example, Gladys arrives to meet Webster for the first time, Lancelot begs her before the meeting to remove ink spots from her nose. When a friend lights a cigar Lancelot has to remind him that Webster does not like cigar smoke. As for Lancelot himself, no longer can he go about, when there is no company, in carpet slippers or sit down to dinner without dressing. He even has to explain to his friends that he is sure they have heard of a person being henpecked — well, he is catpecked.

Nor, alas, can he now even consider marrying Gladys. Webster has found her wanting, and in her place has chosen Brenda Carberry-Pirbright — a lady Webster has found eminently suitable by the fact that when she comes to see Lancelot he sticks his tail up, utters a cordial gargle, and rubs his head against her leg.

Lancelot, by now practically on his way to the altar — actually to one of Mrs. Carberry-Pirbright's "intimate little teas" — is stopped only by the appearance of Gladys and the delivery of her ultimatum. "If," she tells him, "by 7:30 on the dot you have not presented yourself at Six-A Garbridge Mews, ready to take me out to dinner at the Ham and Beef, I shall know what to think and shall act accordingly."

After Gladys has gone Lancelot rushes for a drink and, in his haste, spills it — something which Webster not only sees but, "in his eyes was that expression of quiet rebuke." At first Lancelot looks away but then, looking back, he beholds, in Mr. Wodehouse's words, "a spectacle of a kind to stun a stronger man than Lancelot Mulliner":

> Webster sat crouched on the floor beside the widening pool of whisky. But it was not horror and disgust that had caused him to crouch. He was crouched because, crouching, he could get nearer to the stuff and obtain crisper

> action. His tongue was moving in and out like a piston.
>
> And then, abruptly, for one fleeting instant, he stopped lapping and glanced up at Lancelot, and across his face there flitted a quick smile — so genial, so intimate, so full of jovial camaraderie, that the young man found himself automatically smiling back and not only smiling but winking. And in answer to that wink Webster winked too.

After this, when Lancelot has, as Mr. Wodehouse describes it, the "goods on Webster," we are assured of a happy ending, one in which Brenda Carberry-Pirbright will no longer be in the picture and Lancelot and Gladys are free not only to go off into the sunset but also, and in good time, to march down the aisle.

Here I feel I must point out that what my friend Mr. Wodehouse was engaged in writing — about Webster's campaign to break up Lancelot's romance — was fiction. What happened to me was far from fiction — it was nonfiction, in fact. And furthermore it happened, as I have said, not once but twice. Indeed, in my considered opinion, looking back over these several years when it all took place, Polar Bear was in both instances not only the alleged perpetrator but the actual guilty party — the first time indirectly, the second time directly.

The first instance began in California. Those of you with long memories may recall an earlier chapter in this book in which some of you may still harbor the feeling that I was unduly harsh in my assessment of certain California girls — in particular in the case of one who wrote me criticizing the name I had chosen for Polar Bear. You might even go so far as to accuse me of a certain bitterness. If so, such, I assure you, is far from the case. The only question, as in all such matters, is what did I know and when did I know it — and when I did, did I do the right thing? I did indeed, and on this score I am as pure as the driven snow. I was not then, and am not now, in the least bitter about the whole experience. It was, after all, a learning experience for the girl, and as for myself I was, like Mr. Wodehouse's Lancelot — a name with which, incidentally, I found myself identifying — saved in the nick of time.

It is true that years ago at about the time I got Polar Bear I myself was, if you can believe it, somewhat smitten with a California girl. I know it is going to be hard for many of my readers to believe this, but there it is. It all began, as such matters of the heart with curmudgeonly bachelors are wont to do, innocently enough. And for the most part it continued that way. It is not that curmudgeons don't have hearts — we do — but our heads, of course, come first. This is indeed the very essence of curmudgeonry, and is why curmudgeons do not, for example, fall "head over heels in love" or any of that sort of nonsense. No curmudgeon worthy of the name ever allowed his head to be on any comparable level with his heels, let alone his heart.

What did happen, and really all that happened, was that I happened to make the acquaintance of, as I believe I've already said, this California girl. She was also, I shall have to admit, so beautiful that she attracted not just California men, which is not hard to do, but also men from other states, other countries, and, I would guess, from a close-up look at some of them, other planets. As for her own looks, she had long black hair, big brown darty eyes, and a figure which would stop a clock — something which is particularly dangerous in California since out there people are, as you know, already three hours behind.

I shall shortly address this subject further — the matter of the time, of course, not the girl's figure — this is, after all, a family book. Meanwhile I wish to state here and now that what I did, and I might add all I did, on meeting this girl was immediately and totally unselfishly set myself to the task of protecting her from all the unseemly attentions she was getting from those forementioned men. Indeed, as I immediately pointed out to her on our very first meeting, these attentions were not attentions at all but rather intentions — and, to boot, they were intentions of an extremely doubtful nature.

But this was by no means all I had to do. Indeed I had to do something almost equally important. This was because, being a very observant person, I had immediately observed that this girl, besides being beautiful, was also both fun and funny and that, while this added considerably to her charm, it did not make my task any easier since, like so many California girls, she had never been taught when not to be funny. Thus, at this very same first meeting, I was forced to part — really long before I normally do such a thing — with one of my most cherished pieces of wisdom for the edification of the fairer sex. This is, simply, that there is, at crucial times, nothing that ruins romance like a sense of humor in a woman.

There was still another formidable obstacle to my objective. This was that she was, again like most California girls, heavily "into" — in that awful California word — all areas of the Women's Movement. Now, no one is a greater admirer than I of the strides this movement has made, for women, but this girl carried the movement into an area for which no self-respecting curmudgeon could for a moment sit still. What she did, if you can believe it, was to carry the movement into the field of romance. I first noticed this when she told me she didn't want to be called a girl — which of course I handled by saying I had no intention of not doing so but that if she wanted to call me a boy it would be fine with me. The second thing I noticed was the way she drew back when, out of pure affection one evening, I had patted her on the head. She said she didn't like to be patted on the head. I told her that she would simply have to get used to it, at least when we were standing up. She was shorter than I and, frankly, from that position I couldn't see any other place to pat her.

But the third and to me most diabolical thing that she did in carrying the Women's Movement into the field of romance was to treat the men in her life, if you please, the way men treat women. She loved them, mind you, and then left them. Thus it soon became all too painfully clear to me that I had not only the task of protecting her from other men — not to mention controlling, at crucial times, her sense of humor — I had also to put my shoulder to the wheel doing something for which, whether she knew it or not, she had an almost equally desperate need — to secure, in a word, her liberation from liberation.

It was not going to be easy, and my first problem was a lack of communication. I do not mean this phrase in the nauseatingly irritating way people supposedly in love use it — again, like humor, particularly at the wrong times — I mean lack of communication in the actual sense of the phrase and, in particular, telephone communication. I have already mentioned the time problem with California. You call before your lunch and they haven't yet arrived at their offices. Then when you do get there and get your message they call you and *you* are out to lunch. When you call them back they, of course, are out to lunch and then they call you back but by then you are gone for the day. This is bad enough for communication among people with regular business hours, but in the case of this girl I was faced with something else again. The girl was at that time working, but here I hasten to say I use the word "work" in the loosest California sense. It has been my observation that the only time California girls are working is when they are working out. In any case, what this girl did at least Monday through Thursday was to arrive at her office shortly before noon, get her mail, and go to lunch, and if she got back by 2:30 in the afternoon — which was, for her, a hard day — she left at 4:00. On Fridays she left before lunch and for good.

Telephone communication with such a girl was, from the East, obviously impossible during the week. That left only weekends. Business people faced with this sort of problem have, I understand, at least a reasonable chance of reaching each other over the weekends, but with California girls you can forget weekends. California girls are never home weekends save in the case of terminal illness. Whether they are est-ing or Rolfing, tennising or skiing, swimming or surfing, snorkeling or white-water rafting, backpacking or hang gliding — and this girl was into all of these — you cannot reach them except in their automobile, where they spend approximately half their lives and which is of course why cellular phones were invented. I could, and usually did, leave a message on her answering machine Friday, but since she never came back until the wee hours Sunday morning by the time she called me, if indeed she did, my hours — which, incidentally, she never learned — were even wee-er. In fact, it would be Monday morning.

In short, I had to give up telephone communication entirely. Instead I did my best to stay in touch with her by mail. At least I had the benefit of a distinctive name. And, make no mistake, I needed it. I was with her once when she was opening her mail, and in it I happened to see a postcard from a man named Michael, protesting undying love. "I don't see," she said, "why men don't put in their last names. I know three Michaels." Nonetheless, as I say, I was luckier and, in one of my first letters, I was so curious as to how she could have possibly managed to get a job I asked her to send me a copy of her résumé. The résumé was hard to believe, even by California girl standards. Under colleges she had listed eleven. I later learned she listed every college she had attended, all right — but on dates.

I had never before in my entire life met a girl who had as many dates, and by this I do not mean dates per week, I mean dates per twenty-four hours. She had luncheon dates, cocktail dates, dinner dates, late dates, and, I presume, late late dates. As a matter of fact, the very first time I had what might be classified as a date with her I asked her when she had started having dates. She thought for some time — which was, in itself, unusual — and then said she couldn't remember. I suggested age twelve. "Oh, no," she said, "I was very dorky then." I had no idea what that meant — California girls have a language all their own — but since by that time she couldn't remember what she said — California girls also have both incredibly short attention spans and really no memories at all — I never did find out. "By the time I started going out," she said, "I always seemed to date older men."

I would have liked, at this point, just to bask in the first real sign of good sense I had ever noticed in her. Instead

I realized it was a golden opportunity to educate her on the virtues not only of older men in comparison with younger men but also particularly of older eastern men in comparison with California men of any age. California men, I pointed out to her, are not even interested in how their girls look — they are only interested in how *they* look. And frankly, I confided to her, they not only spend just as much time in front of mirrors as their girls do but, on average, more. The trouble was, I had talked at some length about this and I had lost her. She was thinking of something else. "My problem was," she said, "that my only real crushes were on unavailable men — like married teachers."

My brief period of optimism about her good sense about older men abruptly shattered, I went back to asking her about her colleges. I asked her why she dropped out of so many. "I did it," she said, "to get away from unfinished business. I mean, of course," she added, smiling, "unfinished exams and term papers and things like that." I ignored this, and asked her how long her average relationship had been. I knew that if I was going to give her the benefit of my advice I would first have to make her see the error of her ways until, of course, she had met me. But she just didn't seem to get the idea at all. "My average relationship," she said, "was six weeks — except when it involved travel. I love to travel. I've been to just about every country except India. I would love to go to India. Have you ever been to India?" I told her sternly that I had, but that she was changing the subject. At this she wanted to know what the subject was. Men and women, I told her — I even used the word "women" instead of "girls." "Men and women," she said, "are two very different things. They are alien nations. Putting them together is like putting dogs and cats together. I am a cat, you know. I love cats."

This was another good piece of news for me, and indeed I was later to meet her two cats. But I realized that if she had decided that men and women didn't belong together it was very important for me to find out why. It had nothing to do with me personally, I told myself. I was really doing it just for her and, one day when we were looking at her cats, I asked her to continue with her analysis of the whole men and women thing. "Men are like wild canids," she went on — she loved animal examples — "they're always nipping at women's heels and they love it best when we're running from them. When we're standing still they have absolutely no interest in us."

On another occasion I asked her point-blank how she broke off her relations with men. "Different ways," she said earnestly. "Usually I tell them I have no interest in romance beyond a certain point." She paused. "Another way is I ask them to please stop sending me poems. I tell them I have boxes full of poems and I don't have anyplace to put any more." I told her she could count on me on that score — I didn't write poems — but again she wasn't listening. "The real trouble is," she said, "men are more romantic than women — at least they are at the beginning. What they really do is go into a herd of us and cut out one of us. But they are certainly not as romantic at the end, when they always get so bitter." She threw up her hands. "That's why," she said, "I can't take them seriously and why I make jokes."

I knew she was a writer and I asked her sternly if, in her writing, she wrote jokes. "Oh, no," she said, "I just talk jokes." Once more I reminded her there was nothing that ruined romance more than a sense of humor in women. I knew I had said it before, but with California girls you have to say things at least three times to have even the hope of their remembering them.

Despite all the time I was taking, all my unselfish efforts, trying to give her the rudiments of respectability, I always seemed to be stymied by one seemingly unconquerable obstacle. In every conversation, just when I had her concentration, and had repeated what I had said at least three times, she would always, wherever we were, get a phone call. And I do not mean just one call — I mean phone call after phone call — she apparently let everyone she knew, at least all those of the male persuasion, know where she was at all times. Finally one day, when we were at the swimming pool at the Beverly Hills Hotel, and she literally had three calls in succession, I could stand it no longer. I admit I was not in the best of moods. I was well aware of two things: that the number of times one is paged over the loudspeaker at the Beverly Hills Hotel swimming pool is as accurate a measure of the size of one's celebrity as exists west of the Rockies, and I was also aware that on that particular day I had not had so much as one measly call. In any case, then and there I decided that, if I was going to make any real progress with my work with that girl I would have to get her as far away from California as possible. I considered Antarctica but finally narrowed my plan down to my apartment in New York. And so, casually, when she came back from her third phone call I broached the subject. How would she like to come to New York for a visit? "New York?" she said. "I hate New York." I reminded her that, hate New York or not, she had said she liked to travel and, I added pointedly, only in New York would she get to see Polar Bear. Whether it was this argument which prevailed on her, or whether she decided on the basis of what I am sure was a motley crew of other men she knew in New York, I do not know. I do know that, after a period of deep thought — which was difficult for her — she agreed to accept my invitation.

I prepared for her visit with mixed emotions. I was excited to have my eastern friends meet her but I did not want to give any of them the wrong impression. I therefore instructed her that it was extremely important, before she met anybody else, that she come to dinner quietly with me, where we could not only discuss her general education without interruption, but also her deportment with anybody else who might know me.

I did, it is true, take the liberty of having one of those New York services prepare a special dinner. But this, I hasten to add, was not for any reason except that my culinary skills, slow but excellent as Polar Bear finds them, are simply not up to very special dinners. I just thought it would be easier, with Polar Bear and all, to have the dinner all prepared and in the oven, ready to serve. I also wanted it to be a candlelight dinner. But this again was, I assure you, for no other reason except that my view over Central Park outside is much better with candlelight inside than it is with electric light.

Finally the day, or rather the night, came. And, late as always, she arrived. So, almost at the same moment, did Polar Bear. She even knelt to pat him just as I had long envisioned she would. But then, out of the blue — indeed the very first sentence she had uttered since she had come in — came the bombshell. "Oh," she said, patting away, "he's so fat!" And then, as if this weren't enough, she compounded the felony. "He's much too fat," she said.

Even Polar Bear did not believe it. To his way of thinking she had, on far too short an acquaintance, made far too personal a remark. He pulled away and instead of his usual "aeiou" he uttered just the very last part of it — what seemed to me a clear "ow." He had been hurt.

As for myself, knowing her, I believed what she had said, all right, but that did not make it any better. It is true that in those days, not too long after the rescue, when he had been so thin, Polar Bear had been putting on some weight. And, as I made clear in my first book, dieting was far from his long suit. But for me, who had worked so hard on his diet — even if he hadn't — her remarks were simply infuriating. I would not have expected her to know a good old-fashioned word like "portly" — as the good old-fashioned men's stores called their large-size sections — but I did expect something besides what she had said. I think, for example, if she had said something on the order of "He certainly is a large cat," or "He's getting a little heavy, isn't he?" I could have stood it. Indeed I would undoubtedly have put it down to the fact that California girls regard being thin as the most important thing in life next to their next date or the community property statute. But to say what she had, and not once but twice, it was just too much.

Frankly, from that moment on all my good intentions toward her seemed to disappear. We did indeed eat the candlelight dinner, and afterward we sat on the balcony with Polar Bear across on his. But even with her at last safe in my apartment, without the possibility of her getting a phone call and with plenty of time for the kind of consciousness-raising session that would be really meaningful — as California girls who have so little of it like to say — I did not even start on her improvement. The fact is, I had completely and irreparably lost my heart for the job. In a word, I gave up.

And, a short time after her New York visit, without the benefit of being in my custody, the California girl did just what, sooner or later, I knew she would do — she married beneath me. I mean, of course, she married beneath her. The man she chose was, of all things, a California entertainment lawyer — which, as I read it, is a contradiction not just in two terms but in three. And her marriage soon went awry, as I knew any marriage she would make except with me would.

However, to hold Polar Bear even indirectly responsible for the whole story is not quite fair. For one thing, it had for some reason the effect of inducing me to more manful efforts about his diet. For another thing the story, as it turned out for the girl, is not that sad. Now happily divorced, a sadder perhaps but certainly wiser woman, she is now a distinguished screenwriter. As for myself, if I am at times a sadder but a wiser curmudgeon, I did at least have the grace, after a suitable period of mourning, to resume if not her instruction — which I saw was hopeless — at least our friendship.

As for the occasional gossip I occasionally run into that I had been in love with that girl, nothing could be further from the truth. In the first place, curmudgeons do not fall in love with California girls. In the second place, I know people say that love is blind but if so, looking back on it all, compared to me a bat was a Seeing Eye dog. I kept my eyes open every single step of the way. All I ever tried to do was to give that California girl — one who, as ultimately was so amply proved, sorely needed it — the benefit of my wise, free counsel. And, I would like to point out, even continuing this work after the fact has not been easy. Let me give you a final example. The last time I saw the California girl we were at the Beverly Hills Polo

Lounge, and my friend Debbie Sunshine, the pianist, began playing one of my favorites, "It's So Nice to Have a Man Around the House." I was humming happily when, all of a sudden, the California girl looked up. "Damn," she said, "I hate that song. I'll bet it was written by some damn man."

Immediately I sprang into action. I told her I had hoped she had learned, after all we had been through, not to say things like that and that the song was undoubtedly written by a good old-fashioned girl and that, furthermore, I would be only too happy to take her up on her bet. We had some argument about this, including my use of the word "girl," but we finally agreed that if the song was written by a woman she would have to mend her evil ways and spend a whole weekend with me. If, however, the song was written by a man, I would have to spend a whole weekend writing anything she wanted for her.

The wager settled, we immediately repaired to Ms. Sunshine and explained our problem. Dutifully Ms. Sunshine rummaged around in her sheet music. Unfortunately she could not find "It's So Nice to Have a Man Around the House." The next morning, however, driven to the airport by two actor friends of mine, Ty Harmon and Leslee Ross, I again explained my problem, and Ty, who is a very knowledgeable fellow about show business — in between jobs he drives for a company called "Diaper to the Stars" — sent me, the next day, a fax. It was brief:

> Sorry. "It's So Nice To Have A Man Around The House" was written by Jack Elliott and Harold Spina.

Not one man, but two! Really, there was no end to the rotten luck I've had with that California girl. I should have considered the odds against me for the simple reason that the vast majority of romantic songs are written by men, because we are obviously more romantic than women. Nonetheless, I decided, after careful consideration of the whole thing, to make the best of my loss. I just wouldn't tell her. I knew she wouldn't bother to look it up, and it was at least an even bet she would forget it. Which would give me a chance, at some future time when the statute of limitations had run out, to point out to her how much people lose who don't remember things. And in the end it would be just one more valuable lesson she had learned from me.

If Polar Bear was indirectly responsible for what had happened in the California matter, for what happened in the second instance when romance reared its ugly head he was, as I have said, directly responsible. And this instance happened with a woman who was as different from the California girl as chalk is from cheese — which is an expression none of you young people have probably ever heard, until now, but now you have.

A tall blonde girl with blue eyes and a lovely smile, she was from Boston and had there learned, either at her mother's knee or in a good Boston school, never in the presence of boys to demonstrate even the possibility that she had as much intelligence, judgment, or humor as they did — as a result of which, of course, she was extremely popular. She was, in fact, an Old Flame of mine. Indeed, we had for some time gone together, although that phrase, along with such later editions as "going steady," or that awful modern "significant other" were at that time happily unknown. All in all, she was eminently suitable — in all senses of the word — as the California girl was not, and was the kind of girl you could without qualm or advance warning take home to your mother — of whom nowadays there seem to be a precious few. Indeed we might well have married had it not been that somehow, for some ridiculous reason she had, just like the California girl, married someone else — a mistake which I was sure, particularly when we ran across each other, she had sorely regretted.

In the fullness of time, however, this Boston girl had, as the California girl later had, a divorce. Since I had also been divorced, this meant that there was now no reason why we should not see each other. And, to make a short story long, when she wrote me she would soon be making a business trip to New York, I was very pleased about it, particularly since it all happened after that California girl had made her extremely poor choice and I was still worried about her. This woman, I sensed with my usual foresight, could easily turn out to be what the doctor ordered to get over any scars the California girl had left on me. And in fact, even before she arrived, I could visualize her sobbing on my shoulder about how she ever could have made such a mistake as not to marry me.

As in the case of the California girl, I had decided on a candlelight dinner. But, as the service and I bustled about in our preparation, I suddenly realized that I had overlooked one important detail in our scenario. And this detail was, of course, Polar Bear. Right away he knew something was up and when Polar Bear knows something is up, his first reaction is to go down. Indeed, he goes into his Buddha meditation pose. This is, of course, to enable him to think exactly how he is going to handle it, and since he does not know what the *it* is going to be, this can entail on his part a very long think. I have observed this enough to know that basically what he is planning is one of two possible courses of action. With the California girl he had obviously decided on a frontal assault and an immediate appearance. On the other hand he could just as well have decided on the exact opposite — a rearguard action and no appearance at all. In this case I had no idea which he would do.

Actually, when the woman arrived she didn't mention Polar Bear and we were indeed already eating our dinner before the subject came up. Then suddenly she looked around. "Where," she asked, "is Polar Bear?" I made one of my typically lame explanations — I don't really remember which one — that I was sure he was in the other room, that he had been poorly lately, or that he had just been to the vet. Whatever I said, right after it she announced blithely — or at least as blithely as Boston women are likely to get — that she was very glad he wasn't around.

At this, of course, I took immediate offense. Instead of saying anything, though, I just looked at her. As I have previously mentioned, I have only one eyebrow that I can raise. But still my one-shot is, if I do say so, very effective. Nonetheless, she just ignored it. "You know," she went on, "you never had cats when I knew you — you always had dogs." She paused meaningfully — Boston women do pause very meaningfully. But for this pause I had a knowing answer, which, as I remember, was a wise nod. She too nodded, in answer to my nod. "Anyway," she continued, and once again blithely, "I'm so glad he's not around because I'm allergic to cats."

For a long moment I said nothing. I had, of course, totally forgotten that in the days when we were going together I not only did indeed have dogs, but also did not have a cat. Now however I was torn. If I spoke my mind I would not only be forgetting my Boston manners, and with, after all, a Boston guest, I would also be kissing good-bye — to use in this connection an unfortunate phrase — another candlelight dinner. If, on the other hand, I politely said something like "Oh, that's too bad," I would be completely untrue to everything I believed — or, rather didn't believe — about being allergic.

My dilemma was solved by the immediate appearance of Polar Bear. Polar Bear is, in his way, the exact opposite of those good old-fashioned children — who, as few of you may recall, in the good old days were supposed to be seen and not heard. Polar Bear likes not to be seen but to be able to hear everything. In this case, he had obviously chosen a nearby hiding place and when he left it, he did so extremely rapidly, as if he couldn't wait a single other minute to meet her — to him up to that time, remember, a total stranger. He first slid to a stop, then made a beeline for her ankles. These he started, tail up and in his most affectionate way, rubbing back and forth.

At this the woman seemed to move as fast as he had. She jumped out of her chair, stopping only to pull a Kleenex out of her purse, and then, standing, looking down at Polar Bear, alternately sneezing and wheezing, gasping and coughing.

This time I was on the very horns of the dilemma. I could do nothing or I could do what had to be done. What I did, of course, as all who know me would know I would, was what had to be done. Scooping Polar Bear up from his unseemly ankle ogling I carried him to the bedroom and deposited him on the bed, after which — and after a brief attempt to explain to him that what I was doing was for his own good — I then left, closing the bedroom door behind me, and went back to see if my guest had expired.

She had not. But what she had done was to retire to a nearby chair. In this, although her gasping and coughing had stopped, she continued wheezing and sneezing and had even added some weeping.

My whole action of taking Polar Bear to the bedroom had taken less than a minute, but in that minute I had done a lot of thinking. Again, I could do nothing or I could speak my piece about allergies. I did the latter. But I should like to make clear that I did this not because I realized that whether I did it or not my candlelight romance was undoubtedly, at least for that evening, over and done with. I did it because, if there is one thing that makes my blood boil — and, being a curmudgeon, there are at least a dozen of these things a day that do — it is people saying they are allergic to cats, and then going to some doctor and having him tell them to "get rid" of the cat and finally taking the cat to the shelter, where of course it will be "put down" — when, instead of all this, there are many alternatives.

I realized that this was not going to be any walk in the park handling this woman in this matter, but I was bound and determined to give it the old college try. Since she was in no condition to talk I at least had on my side my favorite kind of audience — not only a captive one but one which would not be interrupting. I told her that in my life I had had every kind of allergy known to man, and certainly every kind known to woman. I told her that, even as a small child, I had hay fever, asthma, eczema, and hives, and I had in fact been allergic to so many things that they gave up testing me for them. I was, I continued, still probably allergic to most of the things to which I had been allergic then. But if there was one thing I had learned about allergies, it was that if one does not give in to them, one will in time either outgrow them or so immunize oneself to them that it amounts to the same thing.

I waited a suitable interval for all this to sink in. I then went on to state sternly that most of the time doctors tell people to get rid of their cats either because they don't like cats or because it is easier than getting to the bottom of the patient's other allergies. I told her that during my worst allergies, I had once been put for several months in a cabin with air conditioning — a rarity in those days — and existed on just six kinds of food. I didn't expect doctors to do that nowadays, but if they had the gumption to test their patients and find out exactly to what they were allergic, and inoculate them for that, they might well find out that all this handled the cat problem too. And, even if it did not, such doctors should be reminded that a patient can be specifically inoculated against cat allergies. I further said that while I would not recommend that someone who said he or she was allergic to cats actually sleep with one in the bed — at least until he or she had been for some time in another room situation with the cat — in time even that would be possible and would indeed speed up self-immunization.

Finally, after one more suitable interval, I reached my peroration. I asked her point-blank if she realized how often cat allergy had proved to be entirely mental. And, I added firmly, she should not overlook that patients were not the only ones who had this mental allergy to cats — so did some doctors. Indeed, in my opinion, patients often caught this from their doctors — and for this, I added even more firmly, there was apparently no inoculation.

Of course, nobody likes to be told anything physical is mental — particularly not people from Boston. And this woman was, Boston or no Boston, no exception to this. When at last her wheezing, as well as her weeping, had subsided enough so she could talk, she spoke firmly. "With me," she said, "it's not mental. I can't even go into a room where a cat has been." At this I moved in for the kill. As politely as I could, and with as little sarcasm as possible, I pointed out that she had just been in such a room — one, in fact, in which a cat spent most of his life and indeed in which he had still been, and not far from her, at the time she started eating dinner. Yet only when he came out to her and she had seen him did she have her attack. If that did not prove, once and for all, how large was the mental element of it, I would like to know what did.

I could have gone on, of course, but I did not. I really don't enjoy arguing with people who don't know enough about the subject, or don't know the facts or are always bringing up facts I don't know. And the woman was, after all, temporarily incapacitated and I did not want in any manner to seem to be taking advantage of her. I had to remember that she was my guest and, as her wheezing and sneezing had now come to a full stop, it did occur to me that I might well have too soon written off our possible romance. In any case, courteous as always, I gave her my arm and we went back to the dinner table. Over the dinner and even more so over the wine we talked about old times. Aside from the allergy episode the woman could not have been more charming, and as the evening wine on — I mean wore on — I suggested we walk out on the balcony.

We did so, and since it was a lovely summer evening the scene was clearly set for what it was supposed to be from the beginning. I had, in fact, just started to put my arm around her when suddenly she pulled back and once more proceeded to wheeze and sneeze, gasp and cough.

An alert reader with the layout of my apartment balcony in mind will of course immediately surmise what had happened. There will be some — albeit I hope not many — who will put it down to my lack of romantic appeal. But the majority will know that just at the moment when I was about to take the woman in my arms, and I was headed east and she west, Polar Bear made a flying leap out of the bedroom window onto his part of the balcony. The woman had not only seen him over my shoulder, she also had no way of knowing he could not, because of the wire, come all the way to her. One thing was certain — I had learned firsthand that, at crucial times, a sense of humor in a woman is not nearly as ruinous as a full-bore allergy attack.

A lesser man might, at this juncture, have given up. I am not, however, a lesser man, I am a morer man. There and then I conceived a plan which would have a twofold purpose. The first would be to prove to someone with an apparently severe cat allergy that there were not only other remedies than to "get rid" of the cat, there were literally dozens of others. The second would be — and I hasten to emphasize that this would only be second — that I would not be cheated out of a well-deserved romance. When I can do a good deed and at the same time get what I want, I feel all of my powers moving in harmonious cooperation.

I moved, as I always do when I have a battle plan, rapidly. As soon as her allergy attack had subsided and we were walking to the door, I told her I knew she was going to be in New York for three days and that if she would just come back for another night before she left — I suggested her last night, which would give me two whole days — I would not only deallergize my entire apartment,

I would deallergize Polar Bear, too. Surprised as she was that either or both of these were possible, she was also, like most Boston women, game, and she agreed. I next suggested, inveterate bettor that I am, a bet. At this, game though she was, she was also practical, and she wanted to know what the bet would be. I knew she was in advertising, so I said that if she had, during the evening in question, as much as one allergy attack, she would win and I would agree, at her direction, to work on as much as a full page of any ad or other piece of writing she wanted done. If, on the other hand, she did not have any such allergy attack, I would win. "What?" she asked, as I opened the door. Guess, I said, shutting it.

After she had gone I let Polar Bear out of the bedroom and, as I did so, I looked at the room carefully. I already knew enough about what I had to do to deallergize the living room without taking on the bedroom as well. The bedroom, bed or no bed, was out. Deallergizing the bed alone would, I was sure, be more than a two-day deal and, for all I knew, would involve a brand new bed. I certainly did not want to lose that particular bet on, of all things, a bed. I would do just the living room — and that would be that.

Frankly, at first I did not know exactly how much of a job I had ahead of me, but when I set myself to something my middle name is determination. I also made the decision that whatever it was I had to do it would be better not to try to do it all myself. I would, after all, be directing the whole operation and I needed to keep a clear head and not tie myself up with trivial details. Thus, early the next morning I called a couple of chess-playing friends of mine who are on the husky side — which is very rare for chess players — and told them to come over immediately. I mentioned casually that while we were playing chess there might be a little furniture to be moved, so they might want to wear old clothes.

While I waited for them, I decided to do some research on the subject. Even though I felt I knew practically everything there was to know about allergies I didn't see what harm refreshing my knowledge would do. In good time I found, in *Cats* magazine, a fine article by Barbara Kolenda entitled "Coping with Allergy to Cats." This I thought could be just what I needed, but I was worried about Ms. Kolenda's use of the word "coping." It sounded a little on the slow side and I had to move fast. Anyway, Ms. Kolenda advised four steps, and I immediately plunged into her "Step One." "The first thing you have to do," she said, "is to make your bedroom off limits to your cat." Frankly, I had trouble with this right away because if someone is allergic to one's cat I couldn't imagine not wanting to solve the problem enough to be able to have the cat on one's bed. That, in my opinion, is where cats belong. Nonetheless I did see what Ms. Kolenda was driving at — it was, after all, why I had already removed the bedroom from my list of what to do. And, when I came to her "Step Two," I believed I had struck, if I did say so in this connection, pay dirt:

> Perhaps the most useful thing you can do (second only from banning the cat from your bedroom) is to acquire something called a HEPA (High Efficiency Particulate Air) filter. These filters were originally developed for use in the space program and can clean the tiniest particles, including dander, dust and pollen out of the air.

The idea that I, a man who for all my abilities has not yet been able to master either a word processor or, for that matter, a memory typewriter, was going to go really high-tech — the space program, mind you — was heady stuff, and I resolved to get a HEPA posthaste. Furthermore, Ms. Kolenda had other good news about what I was sure would soon be my very own HEPA:

> A good one is capable of exchanging the air in an average room several times an hour, with each pass removing more and more allergens. These filters generally come with one or more prefilters for removing things like fur. . . .

That was really thrilling, and I resolved there and then to get myself a giant one of those babies. In my mind's eye I immediately conjured up giving a party with some damn woman waltzing in with either a whole fur coat or maybe just a fur hat or fur cape — *whoosh,* my giant filtered HEPA would suck it right off her and whisk it away. I even visualized getting a giant shredder for it. I could see myself standing there, watching it all, and with the woman standing there frantic, I would just quietly explain that I was very sorry, ma'am, but I was allergic to fur.

All in all, by the time my chess friends came in and we started to work on the living room I was in high spirits. It was hard work, but as I sat there directing them from the chessboard, I was very proud of them. They didn't miss a thing — the sofa, the stuffed chairs, the curtains, the rugs, and even the books. And what we couldn't totally deallergize with vacuuming — something, all the instructions said, which had to be done several times — we just moved. The way we — or rather, they — did this was to go down the hall and persuade a friend of mine to take "a few things," as I put it, into her apartment. It is true that as the few things grew into a lot of things she got a little worried, and finally when the sofa came and she didn't even have room to get to her door, she demanded to know what it was all about. Just spring cleaning, I told her cheerfully. She did not, however, let this pass. "Spring cleaning!" she exclaimed, "In August?" Oh, I said, so it is. How time flies.

Even after all this, and after sending one of my friends out to search for a HEPA — on a rental basis, of course — I still had two more steps of my own. And "Step Three" was far from my favorite. It was the problem of deallergizing Polar Bear himself. My best advice here came from a pamphlet put out by the Associated Humane Society. It was entitled "Being Homeless Is Nothing to Sneeze at!" The section in question sounded easy:

> Now we come to de-allergizing your pet. Comb and brush your pet well. Bathe in a good quality, watered-down tearless protein shampoo for pets — available in any pet store. Bathe twice and rinse VERY WELL. Next towel off excess water while the pet is in the tub or sink. Then pour over it, saturating the coat totally, a solution of one part fabric softener — like Downy — and four parts water. Work it into the coat and DO NOT rinse off.

Whoever wrote those instructions, one thing I knew — they did not know Polar Bear. Remember, the last bath I had given him was the day after I had rescued him and although he had a few baths at the vet in the years that had since elapsed, he had not had one from me. Nonetheless Polar Bear, once bitten, is not only twice shy, he is forever shy, and on top of this he has a memory which would shame an elephant. The last I saw of him was a full hour from when I first started running the tub. How on earth he knew this was not going to be just another bath for me, but one for him, I had no idea. Perhaps all the movement of furniture and vacuuming and dusting in the living room, none of which he liked, had made him suspicious. Whether it had or not, this time he did not do just one of his minor disappearances — he majored in this one. And, as I say, it took me a full hour to find him — indeed the only reason I did so in that time was that my chess-playing friends, after dusting the books, had not put them back too carefully. So, sure enough, between two of my favorite books, *John Brown's Body* and *Comfort Found in Good Old Books*, I located first the end of Polar Bear's tail and then, behind those books, the rest of him.

The finding of him, however, turned out to be the easy part. When I had to put him down in the tub in the "watered-down tearless protein shampoo for pets" and tried to keep him there, I immediately had not only my hands full but my chest and one of my legs as well. And since I knew full well by that time that this was not going to be just a bath for him but rather one for both of us, I only wished I had dressed — or rather undressed — for the occasion. All in all, by the time I came to the second part of our ablution, the "pour over it" part — in which I assumed the "it" was him — I was in need of absolution, if not from him at least from a Higher Source. We were not only head-to-head, we were toe-to-toe. His meows had become hisses and his eyes were blazing. As for the "solution of one part fabric softener to four parts of water," by then, I assure you, with him spitting foam I was in no mood for splitting hairs or for measuring. Finally, when I came to the last injunction — "work it into the coat and DO NOT rinse off" — capitals or no capitals, I decided, I had had it even if he still hadn't, and I had not the slightest intention of obeying the instruction to "bathe twice."

Once would do nicely, thank you, I decided, if I was going to be in any kind of shape to answer the bell for the big evening.

By the time I finished, one thing was certain. The whole idea of the bath, as I understood it, was to keep Polar Bear's dander down. But however well this may have worked, there was no mistaking that he now had the rest of his dander up. Before I let him out of the tub he was as near to total fury as I had ever seen him. But even in his rage I knew he was thinking of what he could do when he got out which would irritate me the most. What he chose was leaping from the tub and darting immediately for the bedroom. Here he jumped up on the bed and started rolling around — all the time watching me, since I had followed him, to get what he was sure would be a very bad reaction to what he was doing. But I know him too well to give him any such satisfaction. I simply ignored him, and I had a good excuse for this. I could not rest on laurels. With all I had done so far, in the deallergizing of the room and of him, there was still another job for which I had to prepare. And this was, or rather would be, the deallergizing, upon arrival, of the woman herself.

I learned what I had to do about this not from instruction books but from a chance meeting I had the morning after my first date with the Boston woman. The meeting occurred at the New York Athletic Club and was with a friend of mine, a distinguished magazine consultant named John Henderson. Mr. Henderson asked me what I was up to, and I told him if what he meant was what was uppermost in my mind that day, it was, frankly, a bet. I then related to him the whole stern story and told him, in no uncertain terms, that I was under the gun. "Do you really want to win your bet?" he asked me. I told him I did indeed. "Well," he said, "you've as good as won."

Mr. Henderson then parted with the story that he, too, was extremely allergic to cats and that sometime before, calling upon a friend of his, Pamela McRae, a rising young director at the Metropolitan Opera and a woman who had two cats, he had been severely smitten — and in more ways than one. "I was not only terribly embarrassed," he said, "I had to leave the apartment. I literally couldn't breathe."

Why, I wanted to know, did he think I was going to win my bet? "Because," he said, "I got over it — completely." Ms. McRae, I wanted to know, or the allergy? "The allergy," he said firmly. I told him I was all ears. "It's too complicated for you," he said. "Call Maryann."

I knew Maryann Lane was a telephone operator at the New York Athletic Club and I also knew she was a very charming woman who lived in Peekskill, New York, with nine cats and four dogs. I called her in the evening. Talking with her, I found out that not only had she once been allergic to cats, despite now having nine of them, but that so had her daughter Laura. Together with her daughter, she said, she had visited doctor after doctor. "We went," she said, "to Mount Sinai, to Ear and Nose, and literally dozens of private doctors. Every single one of them told Laura and me to get rid of our cats." Finally someone — she couldn't remember who — told her to go to the head of the pulmonary department of New York's Phelps Memorial Hospital.

This time, however, the advice was different. "Don't worry about getting rid of your cats," the doctor told them. "You don't have to. It's not them, it's you." He paused. "I'm going to take care of you." With that he handed

Maryann and Laura two bottles. The first was something called Proventil, the second Vanceril. Both were inhalants. The doctor instructed them to take two puffs of Proventil before they entered a house or apartment in which there were cats and to take two puffs of Vanceril when they were inside such a house or apartment when they sensed an allergy attack coming on.

Maryann and Laura did what they were told. And sure enough, not only do they rarely have to take the inhalants, but they have never, after taking them, had a severe allergy attack. Afterward, not surprisingly, both have become imbued with close to missionary zeal in their desire to get other people to try it. "I've had other people you know besides Mr. Henderson try it," Maryann told me. "Frank, who used to be the head doorman here at the club, and dozens and dozens of other people. I used to tell people that both inhalants are made by Schering and are available at most drugstores, and all they have to do is get their doctors to prescribe them. Now I don't even do that. I just tell people to call the Fund for Animals."

I next told Maryann and Laura, with some editing, the story of my bet and asked them if they were positive I would win. "Absolutely," Maryann said, "if you can make that woman take the medicine." I told her that I could make anything that walks take medicine — except Polar Bear.

Once I had the inhalants in my hand, my idea was that I would alert the doorman in my apartment building to buzz me on the buzzer when the Boston woman arrived, and I would then meet her in the hallway to see that, before entering the apartment, she took two puffs of Inhalant No. 1. I was prepared to do this, and indeed the dinner was in the oven when, all of a sudden, my doorbell rang. I refused to open it. You can't come in, I shouted. Stay there and get way back from the door, and I'll come out. Quickly I opened the door and saw, to my surprise, standing by the elevator, not my Boston woman but a messenger. He was understandably concerned. Nonetheless, he handed me a special-delivery envelope. Opening this, after he had hurriedly made his departure, I saw it was from Lia Albo, the Fund for Animals' chief rescuer. Her message, carefully typed out, was brief. It read as follows:

Chinese Herbal Remedy for Cat Allergies:

¼ ounce Korean ginseng
¼ ounce white jelly fungus
¼ ounce wei-shan

Boil above in *ceramic* pot with 3 to 4 cups of water until it's down to 2 to 3 cups.

Strain and drink.

Can drink hot or cold — can add sugar to taste

Drink daily.

For a moment I must admit it sounded intriguing but, alas, it had arrived too late for my purposes — particularly the part about "drink daily." Clearly it was something I would have had to have started earlier. Also, game though my Boston friend was, I didn't think she would be overjoyed at eating the "white jelly fungus." Nonetheless I was extremely curious to know if it was really Lia Albo's own remedy. I went back in the apartment and called her. "No," she said, "it's really not mine." Well then, I asked, whose was it? There was a long pause. Finally Lia spoke. "If you're going to put it in your book," she said, "why don't you just say it's from Lia's possible new boyfriend's sister's ex-boyfriend."

It was as good as done, I told her. With that I went back to my wait for my dinner guest. This time the doorman did his job and buzzed me on the buzzer and I was standing in the hallway by the elevator when the Boston woman came up. I told her she couldn't go in yet — she had to inhale a little inhalant first. She was surprised, but she was a good sport about it, and took two puffs of Inhalant No. 1 right away. I next presented her with Inhalant No. 2. She was getting a little antsy at this point but felt better when I told her she didn't have to take Inhalant No. 2 right then, but she had to keep it with her and had to take two puffs of it if she sensed an allergy attack coming on.

At last I opened the apartment door and with some ceremony ushered her in. She couldn't believe all the changes I had made. I not only spent a good deal of time showing off the deallergized furniture but also went to some lengths to make her breathe deeply as we stood together near the HEPA, drinking in the de-particulated air. It was, I told her, if I did say so, direct from the Space Center. A little exaggeration, I always feel, is a man's privilege when dealing with a dinner date.

Even the appearance of Polar Bear, pinch-faced as he still was from his bath, didn't for a moment shake my confidence. Nor did it, I was glad to see, shake hers. When, however, I saw her start to lean down and pat him, I insisted that before she did so she take two puffs of Inhalant No. 2. After that, when I went into the kitchen to get our first course, I didn't even bother to look over and watch them. My bet, I was sure, was all but in the bag.

I should have looked. For, all of a sudden, as I put the first course on the table, I heard all too clearly the telltale sounds of the beginning of a wheeze and a sneeze. For a moment I couldn't believe it. The table was between us and I couldn't see either my guest or Polar Bear. I just listened, stunned. And then, along with the wheeze and sneeze, there was not only a gasp, there was also an unmistakably coughed "AEIOU."

Before I even turned to look, I realized I did not need to do so. The sounds were not coming from my Boston friend, they were coming from Polar Bear. She had not pulled back from him, he had pulled back from her. She was no longer allergic to him. But he, even deallergized as he was and breathing in that rarefied air, was now allergic to her.

As I looked at him wheezing and sneezing, I could not believe it. And, curiously, neither could he. But one thing he did believe was who was to blame. And who or what do you think this was? My Boston friend? The deallergized apartment? His deallergization? Even his bath? Wrong, on all counts. Clearly, as usual, he blamed me.

For some time I looked at him and he looked at me. Then, without a word, as I had three nights before, I leaned down, picked him up, took him to the bedroom and shut the door.

By the time I returned, both my Boston friend and I knew that the die was cast and whatever chance we might have had for romance had gone up in, if not smoke, at least de-particulated air. Polar Bear, like Mr. Wodehouse's Webster, albeit in a different way, had called the tune. Both of us being from Boston, however, we did not waste the dinner. And, as we sat enjoying it, I was even emboldened to bring up the question of the bet. It seemed to me, I said, that, looking at the fact from all angles, I had not really lost. She smiled. "Let's call it," she said, "a draw." A draw, I replied almost automatically, is like kissing your sister.

Later that evening, after she had gone and Polar Bear and I lay in the bed, I was glad to see that his wheezing and sneezing had stopped. I also talked to him at length. He has a short attention span, but for once he did his best, before he went to sleep, at least to see, even if he did not understand, how concerned I was. As for me, I did not go to sleep for some time. Instead I went over in my mind everything that had happened, step by step. I like to do this after any controversy I have with anybody because I like to find out where the other person went wrong. And I particularly like to do this in, if I do say so, the very rare cases I've had in my life of unrequited love. I realize this is another expression that probably none of you young people have ever heard of because, as far as I can see, you always get requited love. But never mind — the point is that, as I thought about the whole thing, suddenly I brightened. Into my mind came a picture of the kind of allergy case I had just been through, of a man visiting doctor after doctor and asking them what to do about someone who loves his cat and wouldn't consider giving him up even though his cat was allergic to his girl. By this time I really was dreaming, and in the dream it was all happening to me. And, as I say, I was going from doctor to doctor to doctor. I was just hoping one of them would give me the only answer — get rid of the girl. But do you know what? Not even in my dream would a single damn one of them do that.

Actually, underneath all the romance — which is always at best a doubtful proposition — there was undeniable reality. At about the time of the breakup of my ill-fated amatory advances toward the Boston woman, one which you will recall fell hard on the heels of one of my extraordinarily rare lapses of judgment in the matter of the California girl — well, as I say, after these Polar Bear did, as some cats do, develop some allergies of his own. Unlike most cats who do this, however, and therefore have to go to the vet's for their shots — in his case the shots came to him. This came about through the fact that, with my usual conning artistry I was able to persuade his vet, Susan Thompson, to make, in his case, house calls. But even with all my artistry I was able to do this only upon giving her my solemn promise that I would not tell anyone that she did so. I agreed with alacrity since I knew, wonderful as Dr. Thompson is with animals, she is inclined to be on the forgetful side about her animals' people — specifically, among other things, what they do — and in my case she had neglected to mention that my promise was just not to tell people. It did not anywhere include anything about not writing about it.

On the surface the arrangement of her coming to him instead of the other way around looked like good news for both Polar Bear and me — Polar Bear because he would not have to make his very least favorite journey, to the vet's, and me because I did not have to suffer the slings and arrows of trying to get him into his carrier to begin with, and then the trip and all the rest of it. But under the surface it was not that good news for either of us. For Polar Bear there remained the stark fact that he still had to have, willy-nilly, his shot, and for me, as will in good time shortly be revealed to you, the whole thing had dire consequences.

In truth Polar Bear loves Dr. Thompson, but the fact

that she is a vet precludes him from any demonstration or even indication of this — otherwise he'd have to turn in his union card as a cat. Moreover, being as forgetful as he is about people, he did not realize on her first appearance that she was a vet. But the moment he realized that her appearance in the apartment did not mean she was just one more woman who was coming to see him but was instead someone who was going to give him a shot, all love was lost and she became an enemy. And this change came about not by any means in the fullness of time but on her very second visit. From then on, of course, he would disappear and I would have to locate him and carry him to her. During this endeavor he invariably put on an act which reached the height of his well-developed feline thespian operatics — he accompanied his piteous "aeiou" 's with caterwauling wails. In between, as I carried him to his doom, he was all but saying to my face how could I have possibly sunk so low as to turn him over to such a fiend incarnate for torture specifically outlawed by the Geneva Convention.

And all this, mind you, over a shot which was over and done with in a matter of a few seconds, which did not really hurt him at all and indeed was of such little consequence that afterward he not only didn't bother disappearing again but also shortly became, union card or no union card, positively affectionate toward Dr. Thompson.

Not so, however, toward me. In his curious little twisted mind he never even gave me the benefit of afterward deciding that the whole thing wasn't, after all, that big a deal. To me he was completely unforgiving. But, far worse than this from my point of view was the fact that, as Dr. Thompson began coming regularly, he began to harbor the darkest of suspicions toward any woman who came to my apartment for any reason whatsoever. He made indeed only one exception to this, and that was Marian. I firmly believe that the only reason Marian got off his hook is that Marian is such a softy with cats that not only will she not cut her cat's toenails, she will not even allow anyone else to do so. I do not know whether this intelligence had traveled the cat grapevine or whether Polar Bear made the judgment on his own. I do know, however, that some way, somehow, he knew for certain that Marian would never stoop to such indignity as inflicting a shot on him.

But, as I say, Marian was his sole exception. Any other person of the female persuasion who so much as darkened my door was to Polar Bear, when it came to the possibility of getting a shot in the posterior, a possible perpetrator. And to say that this has not considerably darkened for me the possibilities of any further romantic interludes would, simply, not be stating the truth. And, if you think I'm exaggerating, I am not, because another tragedy too is involved here. This is the fact that most of the women who come to my apartment do so not to see me but, hard as it is for me to bear, to see Polar Bear. And when, instead of seeing him the way they had imagined they would and having the opportunity to pat and play with him, all they see is, first, a disappearance act and, second, a reluctant drag-out, I can assure you it is a long hard road from there to even the possibility of a candlelight dinner. Indeed I think I can state without fear of contradiction that, under similar circumstances, Casanova himself might well have considered becoming a monk.

◦ *L'Envoi*

Some of you with good memories may recall that earlier in this book I stated that two curmudgeons under one roof — even if one is a person curmudgeon and the other a cat curmudgeon — was one curmudgeon too many. After all these years with Polar Bear, however, who is, if not a black-belt curmudgeon such as myself, at least a white-belt one, I now believe that I should have allowed, in my flat statement, some room for the possibility of a rounded exception. Clearly Polar Bear and I have proved that it is possible for two curmudgeons under one roof to get along famously — in at least most senses of the word — as long as one of us is occasionally willing to give in to the other. I am not saying which one of us does this more than the other — I do, after all, still have my pride — but I will just leave it that one of us does. But please, realize that I mentioned the word "occasionally."

I also believe, however, that when you have two curmudgeons under one roof you have, basically, two problems. And here I am speaking not just of Polar Bear and myself but rather about the whole broad field of person and cat curmudgeonry. In any case, the first problem is that it is very important which came first — the person curmudgeon or the cat curmudgeon. In my considered opinion, it is the cat curmudgeon who should come first, and then he can teach the person curmudgeon the finer points of the trade. If the person curmudgeon comes first, I believe this would be very difficult. This is because, as close observation of Polar Bear has forced me to conclude, cats can teach but they cannot learn.

The second problem concerns the age-old problem of — well, age. You cannot, for example, expect an old curmudgeon cat to teach a baby boy to be a curmudgeon any more than you should expect a young curmudgeon kitten to teach a grumpy old grandfather curmudgeon. Neither, conversely, can you expect your baby boy to teach your old curmudgeon cat or your grumpy old grandfather to teach your kitten. It just wouldn't work. What you are looking for here, in short, is a proper age balance between a cat's age and a person's age. In this connection you have probably heard that one year of a cat's life is like seven years of a person's life. Well, if so, you have heard wrong. Many cats, for example, live to be fifteen — how many people live to be one hundred and five? Some cats even live to be twenty — how many people live to be one hundred and forty? I am, of course, excepting those people whom you see on those irritating commercials eating yogurt and dancing up and down some mountain.

Frankly, I think the reason they say they're that age is that it's the only way they get to see television, which apparently otherwise they never get to see at all.

Anyway, to put you straight on the whole matter of a cat's age in comparison to a person's age I wish you to look at the following chart, one put out by the Gaines Research Center people. I've gone to a good deal of trouble to get this for you so I want you to look at it carefully:

Cat's Age	*Person's Age*
6 months	10 years
8 months	13 years
12 months	15 years
2 years	24 years
4 years	32 years
6 years	40 years
8 years	48 years
10 years	56 years
12 years	64 years
14 years	72 years
16 years	80 years
18 years	88 years
20 years	96 years
21 years	100 years

Now please don't get wandering off the track here on me and worrying about your own cat's age in comparison to your age. I want you to keep your mind on what we're talking about and look at the chart strictly from the point of view of person and cat curmudgeonry. Let us say, for example, that ten is the youngest age a cat can really become a recognized curmudgeon and fifty-six the youngest for any person. Again, please look at the chart and, translating the figures, you will see what I am talking about. Actually I became a curmudgeon at forty-nine but, as I told you before, I had damned good reason to hurry it along and I am, of course, if I do say so, precocious. But, even giving Polar Bear the benefit of cat precocity, he could not have become a curmudgeon until he was nine, at which time he was a mature cat and I, at fifty-two, was still a young man. But since he is now — as again I said earlier we don't know exactly how old he was when he was rescued — between twelve and fourteen, and I am now between sixty-four and seventy-two, give or take, as I am inclined to, a few years off, right now as I write this means we are reaching our curmudgeonly peak together and undoubtedly will continue to stay at this peak.

I figure indeed that when he is between sixteen and eighteen and I am between eighty and eighty-eight, we might even be said to have reached the Pike's Peak of person and cat curmudgeonry. On the other hand if, for example, you had a cat curmudgeon of twenty and a person curmudgeon of, let's say, just beyond seventy, you would have trouble, the same way you would if you had a person curmudgeon of ninety and a cat curmudgeon of eight. I know at this point some of you may be getting a little confused, but if you are go back and look at the chart again, and then read these two paragraphs again, it will soon become clear, and you will have learned a lot.

Of course there remains no question in my mind but that I have been a very good mentor for Polar Bear in all his curmudgeonly development and it is extremely gratifying to me that more and more I see him taking the same sort of umbrage I do at the very same totally infuriating modern idiocies. If he doesn't have the range of these which I do — because of his lack of travel — it does not mean that I do not believe that if he had my range he would not get just as mad as I do about such matters as hotel windows which don't open, airplane seats which are designed by one-armed people about four feet tall, and waiters, clerks, telephone operators, and taxi drivers who are all apparently from countries with which, at the time one runs into them, we are still at war.

I base all this on the unassailable fact that Polar Bear gets just as mad as I do about shoddy workmanship, slipshod service, defective cans and medicine bottles and even soda bottles which take an engineer to open, not to mention the disappearance of good old-fashioned heavy cream and cereal boxes which cost twice as much as they ought to and, when you finally do manage to get them open, you find are half-full. Indeed at certain modern outrages he is even less tolerant than I, and here I will include late-night or early-morning telephone calls as well as those endless and extra-loud television commercials, particularly those with cats in them who have not only not learned their craft but are not nearly as handsome as he is. He even shares my fury at sports announcers with their everlasting praise of sports figures who "stay within themselves." What do they think Polar Bear and I do, for heaven's sakes? Stay without ourselves?

The bald truth is that, frankly, it would take two curmudgeons working together even to begin to cope with all these things. And doing this in tandem has over the years brought us even closer together. I also believe that in these last years I have detected unmistakable signs that in certain ways Polar Bear has made a real effort to emulate me. This is very flattering, of course, and although I do wish he would concentrate less on my few faults and more on my many noble traits, I realize that I have got to take the bad with the good and that no man, as my friend Noël Coward once said, is a hero to his valet. I do not mean to suggest for a moment that Polar Bear is a valet. But I do wish he was. Valets are, after all, just one more example of good old-fashioned people who have very inconsiderately up and vanished. Many's the morning I could use one, and Polar Bear could, too. Frankly, he doesn't pick up anything, not even his toys. I'm really *his* valet — something which, for a mature, busy biographer, is really an absurd thing to have to be. Did Boswell, after all, go around picking up after Dr. Johnson?

What I do wish to suggest, on the other hand, is that when two curmudgeons have such a close personal relationship it is very difficult for either one to be a hero to the other. An example of this is the matter of our ailments. It is, after all, a fact of life that as one grows more mature one also grows in better judgment, superior mental ability, and in all-around good old-fashioned common sense. But it is also a fact of life that, unfortunately, all this increase in these mental areas is often accompanied by a decrease in the physical areas.

I, for example, have developed arthritis of the hip, and in no time at all Polar Bear developed arthritis of the hip also. And while I of course suffer mine in silence, he does not. When he wants, for example, to be lifted to the bedroom window so that he can jump out and see what the pigeons are doing, does he, as I would, manfully hoist himself up there without a word of complaint or a thought of asking for help? Not at all. He goes to the window, looks first up and then to me, "aeiou" 's his little head off, and just stands there until I go over and do the job for him. And this, mind you, when I have caught him when he is in a real hurry doing it himself with no trouble at all. And on top of this, and as if that weren't enough, he has the unmitigated gall — my gall, as I've said before, is always mitigated — to believe that his pain is the equal of mine. Time and time again I have pointed out to him how absurd it is for him to claim that in his little leg, hardly the size of my little finger, he could possibly have as much pain as I have in my leg. Frankly, the only possible reason I can imagine for him even thinking such a thing is probably that, when you come right down to it, it is all in his little mind — which is, again when you come right down to it, about the size of a tenth of mine.

I do not for a moment mean to put down Polar Bear's mentality, and if I seem to do this, I do so, of course, only in comparison to mine. Polar Bear is, and always has been from the day I rescued him, one very smart cat. He is also, in case I have not made this clear, one very beautiful cat. And, finally, he is one very lovable cat — if not toward everybody, at least toward me. Which to me at least proves that he is, besides being smart and beautiful and lovable, a cat with excellent judgment.

I say all this because at this point I should also like to say that I have recently got another cat — or, rather, another cat got me. It all happened on a trip to the hallowed Boston summer resort of Martha's Vineyard. There are, of course, other than Proper Bostonians who summer here — Washingtonians and even New Yorkers, who are made reasonably welcome as long as their money is not too new and they do not have too much of it or show it too much or they are not Yankees fans.

The reason for my trip was that I was to lecture on Martha's Vineyard and, needless to say, in this lecture I stressed the importance of being born, if not actually on the Vineyard, at least in Boston. That night after the lecture Marian and I stayed with an old friend, the distinguished artist Ruth Emerson, and we spent as much time as possible with Ms. Emerson's beloved raccoons and skunks — which every night she regularly feeds in a way which would do credit to the Black Beauty Ranch.

All in all, it was a delightful visit up to the dawn of my last day. That day, however, I made a serious error. At the behest of another devoted animal person, Anna Bell Washburn, I visited the local animal shelter. And there, as I walked by the cages in the cattery, I suddenly felt a large paw on the back of my head. As I turned around, I saw the perpetrator — his telltale paw still out of the cage. He was, as later described by Elaine Lembo of the *Vineyard Gazette,* an "orphaned white cat with a silly, blue-eyed buggy stare" — one which, she said, turned me into "mush." And, not satisfied with that — a word, for any curmudgeon, certifiably libelous — she then went on in the next paragraph to repeat the libel.

I did not sue, but only for the reason that I was, at that time, entirely too busy with the cat. I was, indeed, from the moment he reached out to me, had. Actually, as I was later to learn, the whole thing had been a put-up job. Mrs. Washburn and her friends had, I believe, all but trained the cat to reach out anytime any likely large sucker was about to pass. Clearly they knew — and I had to admit they were right — that this cat was the kitten image of Polar Bear when I first saw him that snowy Christmas Eve. The only difference was he had blue eyes instead of Polar Bear's green, and his two front paws six, not five, toes. Those women also knew that I would not be able to resist him, but not for any mushy reasons. I am not, after all, a sled-dog driver.

Polar Star, as I named him — and before, I should add, the recent novel of the same name — was a country stray.

His summer family had just abandoned him on the incredible theory such people seem to have — that a cat can just get along somehow. And somehow this one had, at least for a while, until a kindly person had found him and brought him to the shelter. If his looks are similar to Polar Bear's, however, his personality is not. He is as outgoing as Polar Bear is the opposite. He loves everybody, and right away. Indeed most of the time he seems more like a dog than a cat.

I know that the idea of my falling for another cat will offend many people, particularly those who will remember Polar Bear's very poor attitude toward other cats. I wish, however, to state my side of the case. In the first place I never had the slightest idea of bringing Polar Star to my apartment. Although Polar Bear has grown less hostile to the occasional stray who passes a night or a weekend with me, I really believe this is because he now knows through experience that they will be transient and not permanent guests. In the second place, the place to which I did take Polar Star was not to my apartment but instead to my office at the Fund for Animals, where he would join our other two permanent office cats, Benedict and Little Girl.

It was, I should admit, at first not an idyllic arrangement. Indeed, both Benedict and Little Girl immediately took very dim views of the whole idea and were, from the very first day, very mean to the then-small newcomer. In vain I warned them that, small as he then was, he would get bigger. And, by the size of those six-toed paws I could see he would be very much bigger than they were, and in fact this is just what has happened. And Polar Star now returns in full measure just what they, in the beginning, did to him. Maintaining even short periods of peace has not been easy, but the armed truces now outnumber the actual wars and, as my battle-scarred multi-catted friends Jeanne Adlon, Jane Volk, and Jennie Lester assure me, all will, in the end, work itself out.

One important lesson I've learned from Polar Star is that there is a large and basic difference between city strays and country strays. And this is that, generally speaking, the former are wary of people, since people are the ones who have usually done bad things to them. The latter, on the other hand, are most wary of other animals because it is with those other animals that they have had their problems. Certainly Polar Star, who loves people, does not love other animals — and this unfortunately, at least at present, seems to include other cats — but at the same time, no cat I have ever known is better loved by almost every person who comes across him.

I was well aware that no matter how I explained why I adopted Polar Star — or rather allowed him to adopt me — it would still not satisfy some people. One of these would, I knew, be Rosa, the cleaning lady. Since Rosa also cleans the office, she knows both Polar Bear and Polar Star intimately — and, totally possessive as she is of Polar Bear, she was at first almost as bad about Polar Star as the other office cats were. I remember well, on one of Rosa's worst days about the whole situation, she called me from my apartment. "Mr. Amory," she said in a voice which I knew boded no good, "Polar Bear is very difficult today — he won't eat a thing." I told her that Polar Bear was very difficult many days, and that that was what a curmudgeon cat was supposed to be. I also added that, as for his not eating that day, this was not bad but good news. Rosa, of course, was not about to buy my explanation. "The reason Polar Bear is difficult," she said, "is that he knows perfectly well you have another white cat down there. He's seen the hairs on your clothes." I told her that Polar Bear could not possibly know I had another cat, and that as for the hairs, that I had had hairs of various animals on my clothes since before she was born. "But," she added sternly and firmly, "what if he thinks you love another cat as much as you love him?"

This time, equally sternly and firmly, I told her there was no way he could think such a thing because he was a smart cat, and he was certainly smart enough to know it could not be true. I even went so far as to tell her that I did not believe I would ever, in my entire life, have another cat I loved as much as Polar Bear.

Rosa was, at last, at least partially satisfied. Nonetheless, she had one last question. "Mr. Amory," she asked, "are you going to write about Polar Star?" I knew immediately that she was going to be very cross if I said I was, and so I decided to beg the question. When it comes to a difficult question I am usually as brave as a lion but once in a while I think that begging is a better policy. This, clearly, was one of those times.

Just the same, after the conversation was over, I did some good hard thinking about the whole matter. And, as usual, I came to the right decision. I would indeed write about Polar Star, but I would not do so until the very end of the book. For there, I was sure, it would be safe from Polar Bear as safe can be.

He had sniffed and even eaten some of my first book, it is true. But he had never, after all I had done for him, done me the courtesy of finishing it.

The BEST CAT EVER

ILLUSTRATED *by* LISA ADAMS

For Walter Anderson

Acknowledgments

First of all, the author wishes to acknowledge the critical judgment of Marian Probst, his longtime assistant — a judgment which, hard as it is for him to bear, was amply and often demonstrated in these pages to be infuriatingly superior to his own.

Second, the author also wishes to pay tribute to the considerable contribution of his longtime editor at Little, Brown and Company, Fredrica Friedman. Although she has been singled out in the text as being two parts panther and one part Bengal tiger, it should not be forgotten that these qualities prove of particularly rare value in a book about a cat.

Third and finally, the author wishes to extend special thanks to Sean O'Gara, who somehow managed, on machines incomprehensible to the author, both to push the manuscript forward and at the same time to keep impeccable order in the office — with the exception, of course, of the office cats.

Besides this, the author is grateful for permission to quote from the following works:

"How Old Is Old?" by Ian Dunbar, D.V.M., published in April 1991 *Cat Fancy.* Reprinted by permission of the author.

The New Natural Cat: A Complete Guide for Finicky Owners by Anitra Frazier with Norma Eckroate. Copyright © 1990. Reprinted by permission of the authors.

Arthritis: What Works by Dava Sobel and Arthur C. Klein. Copyright © 1989. Reprinted by permission of St. Martin's Press, Inc.

Arthritis by Mike Samuels, M.D., and Nancy Samuels. Copyright © 1991. Reprinted by permission of Simon & Schuster, Inc.

Excerpts from the "Art and Dusty" videotape, produced by The Changes: Support for People and Pets Program at Colorado State University's Veterinary Teaching Hospital. Reprinted by permission of Carolyn Butler and Laurel Lagoni, codirectors of the program.

Courage Is a Three-Letter Word by Walter Anderson. Copyright © 1986. Reprinted by permission of Random House, Inc.

Contents

	Prologue	555
CHAPTER ONE	A Cat for All Seasons	557
CHAPTER TWO	My Harvard	582
CHAPTER THREE	First Jobs	623
CHAPTER FOUR	My Last Duchess and 4,000 Other Celebrities	664
CHAPTER FIVE	Polar Bear and Me and Your TV — Your Guide to the Medium Medium	717
CHAPTER SIX	The Miracles of Modern Medicine — and Some Exceptions to Same	753
	L'Envoi	786

The Best
Cat
Ever

Prologue

First, an apology. It is presumptuous of me to title this last book about the cat who owned me what I have titled it — *The Best Cat Ever.* The reason it is presumptuous is that to people who have, or have ever been, owned by a cat, the only cat who can ever be the best cat ever is their cat.

I understand this, but still I beg your indulgence. Please remember I am writing this only a short time after Polar Bear has gone, and writing about him is not now an easy task.

I guess it is never easy to write about a cat when he or she has gone. Of course, it is not so easy to write about them when they are around, either. Cats have difficulty standing still for portraits, whether in pictures or in a memoir, and they do so many different things and do them so quickly and change so fast that I really believe what we all should do when they are still around is to keep a diary.

Unfortunately, few of us do this, and although I have already written two other books about Polar Bear, I realize I missed much. But not, of course, anything like how much I miss him. I had already learned that writing about him was a much more difficult task than matters like either quickness of movement or of change. But I still had something else to learn — the awful truth that now when I write about the funniest things he ever did I do not want to laugh, I want to cry.

Nonetheless, I shall not inflict that, or anyway as little as possible of that, upon you. Polar Bear, who, just by being himself, did so much for so many stray cats — in twenty countries — deserves better. And I promise you, I shall do my best to see that he gets it.

I shall try, in other words, not to dwell on the present and the awful missing of him. I shall dwell, rather, on the past and the fun we had for the fifteen years we had together.

If I succeed in doing this I know you will pardon me for calling this book what I have called it, becausc one of the things I used to call him, in our special moments together, was the best cat ever.

In this book you will read that there is a small monument to Polar Bear at the Fund for Animals' Black Beauty Ranch in Murchison, Texas. The inscription on that monument states that that is where he is buried. Although I wrote that inscription, I do not want you to believe it. Where he is really buried, and where he is, and where he will always be, is in my heart.

CHAPTER ONE

A Cat for All Seasons

It has long been a theory of mine — and I am known, if I do say so, for my long theories — that authors, generally speaking, are rotten letter writers. There are good reasons for this. The good letter writer is writing privately, thinking of one person and writing intimately to that person. The author, on the other hand, who is not particularly accustomed to writing privately but rather to writing publicly, is not thinking of any one particular person except perhaps — and sometimes all too often — himself or herself.

And, speaking of that him and her, it is another theory

of mine that women, generally speaking, are better letter writers than men. There is a wide variety of good reasons for this, but the one which I believe has most merit is that women are superior in one-on-onemanship, if they will kindly forgive the male intrusion in that last word.

If authors are not that terrific at letter writing, however, they do appreciate good letter writing when they receive it. Indeed, one of the greatest pleasures authors have is reading letters addressed to them about what they write. I am no exception, and since my most recent books have concerned, among other things, my cat Polar Bear, I am particularly pleased about the number of people who write to me wanting to know more about him. Once in a while of course I wish that at least a few of these writers would also want to know more about me but, as I have often said, you can't have everything — particularly nowadays. You would think, though, that a reasonable number of people would take the time to figure out who did all the behind-the-scenes work, all of the dirty work in the trenches if you will, which made Polar Bear possible. But no, they don't. It's the star they want, and never mind the man without whom Polar Bear would never have been heard of, let alone been a star.

I was not the least jealous of Polar Bear, mind you, but I do want you to know that if the situation were reversed and more people wanted to know about me than about him he would not for a moment have been as philosophical about it as I was. As a matter of fact, I can see him now going right into one of his snits — and I tell you when it came to being jealous Polar Bear could go into the snottiest little snit you ever saw. Kindly remember that jealousy has often been described as "The Green-Eyed

Monster," and after you've done that just stop and ask yourself what color eyes do you think Polar Bear had?

There is, though, one question an extraordinary number of these letter writers asked which I found irritating for an entirely different reason from the ones who ignored me, and that was, very simply, the question they asked as to whether or not Polar Bear was still alive. I found these letters particularly annoying when he was still alive, and they are of course much more difficult to answer now. After all, I don't go around asking whether or not someone I know whom I also know that they know is dead yet. Just the same, that is the way "still alive" always sounded to me. In fact, still alive still sounds to me a dead ringer for dead yet.

Letter writers who were, to my mind, more considerate of my feelings were inclined to ask simply how old Polar Bear was. I liked that better, but I do believe that at a certain age, whether it is about cats or people, the question of how old one is has a certain annoyance to it. You do not meet someone you have not seen for some time and suddenly ask how old he or she is. It implies that they are not as young as they were. My answer to that is, who is?

The best answer to this question was given many years ago by a famous friend of mine — and also Polar Bear's — the late Cary Grant. Faced with a wire from a researcher from *Time* magazine which asked, "HOW OLD CARY GRANT?" Cary himself politely wired back. "OLD CARY GRANT FINE," he said. "HOW YOU?"

In any case, to answer my letter writers, I always made clear, at least until now, when he is gone, that Polar Bear was indeed alive and well. I rescued him, as I made very clear in *The Cat Who Came for Christmas*, on Christmas Eve,

1978, which made him in 1992, fourteen years older than he was when I rescued him.

There remains, of course, the sticky question as to how old he was in 1992. He was at least fourteen years more than when I rescued him, but how much more? In other words, how old was he when I rescued him? Remember, he was a stray, and strays do not come with birth certificates. Susan Thompson, his veterinarian, believes he could have been any age between one and three, but she is the first to admit that veterinarians have a very difficult time estimating cats' ages exactly. Horses, yes, apparently by their teeth, but cats no. Cats have very odd teeth anyway.

Marian Probst, my longtime assistant, believes Polar Bear was less than one, but I don't want you to go to the bank on Marian's opinion about his age, either. For example, Marian is always adding a year to my age for no reason at all, although I've told her a hundred times that because I was born in 1917 and it is now 1992 that does not make me seventy-five, it makes me seventy-four. After all I was *born* in 1917 — I wasn't *one* in 1917 — I was *zero* in 1917, and I wasn't anywhere near one until 1918. But it is no use talking figures with Marian — you might as well talk the economy.

Anyway, going along with Susan's doubt and ignoring Marian's mathematics, it is quite possible to assume that Polar Bear, who could well have been zero in 1978 was, let us say, zero until 1979. By the same figuring, I was sixty-one in 1979 — in the prime of life, if I do say so. Today I am a little past my prime, perhaps, but not much, mind you, just on the rim of my prime. On the other hand, in 1992, Polar Bear was, as I say, at least fourteen. Now,

I realize that when it comes to comparing cats' ages to people's ages an extraordinary number of people still believe that old wives' nonsense that seven years of your life is like one year of your cat's life. By that standard Polar Bear was, by a person's age, ninety-eight. How many people do you know who, at ninety-eight, are still alive? I know there are some, but I am asking how many.

And besides this I have literally hundreds of letters from people whose cats are in their twenties, and an extraordinary number whose cats are over twenty-five. That would make them, for a person, 175. The next time you see a person who is 175 please let me know, and while you're at it you might as well also tell him or her that, despite what Marian says, he or she is only 174.

I am, of course, not the only person who has called attention to the fallacy of that 7-to-1 cat-versus-person theory. Not long ago a veterinarian in the Gaines Research Center came up with a new chart — one which I have already published in a previous book but which I am now publishing again, for the benefit of those of you, and there are so many nowadays, who have poor memories. In any case, here it is:

Cat's Age	*Person's Age*
6 months	10 years
8 months	13 years
12 months	15 years
2 years	24 years
4 years	32 years
6 years	40 years

8 years	48 years
10 years	56 years
12 years	64 years
14 years	72 years
16 years	80 years
18 years	88 years
20 years	96 years
21 years	100 years

To my way of thinking this is certainly a lot closer to the mark than that old 7-to-1 theory, and it is rather remarkable how Gaines refuted that 7-to-1 by having the person go three years while the cat was going only from six months to eight months, and yet having the person at the advanced age of ninety-six go just four years to one hundred while the cat went only one year, from twenty to twenty-one. In any case, Gaines was not by any means alone in changing the 7-to-1 formula. In a British cat book, for example, I found the statement that some experts believe once a cat is nearing "feline old age" you should "multiply its years by 10 to get a true comparison with a person's age." And a British-born veterinarian now living in this country, Ian Dunbar, came up with a shorter revision:

Cat's Age	*Person's Age*
1 year	3 years
7 years	21 years
14 years	45 years
21 years	70 years
28 years	95 years
31 years	103 years

Shortly after the publication of his findings, Dr. Dunbar was challenged by Washington writer Ed Kane, who took him to task in three specific areas — of his cats' one to humans' three, of his cats' seven to humans' twenty-one, and of his cats' fourteen to humans' forty-five. Mr. Kane also recommended a study of cat-versus-human age by Dr. Tom Reichenbach. This, I learned, first appeared in *Feline Practice,* a veterinary journal, and in it Dr. Reichenbach went so far as to use a computer to compare the ages of some 480 cats and the data obtained from census records on human ages. He also completed a graph which demonstrated the comparison of one- to-seventeen-year-old cats with zero- to ninety-year-old humans. You may be sure I was very happy to see that zero recognized. In any case Dr. Reichenbach came up with these findings:

Cat's Age	*Person's Age*
1 year	17 years
2 years	28 years
3 years	31 years
4 years	41 years
5 years	45 years
6 years	45 years
7 years	51 years
8 years	58 years
9 years	61 years
10 years	61 years
11 years	66 years
12 years	66 years
13 years	71 years

14 years	76 years
15 years	81 years
16 years	81 years
17 years	89 years

I found some of these figures fascinating. For example, in the year when the cat went from five to six, the person stayed at forty-five, and in the year when the cat went from nine to ten, the person stayed at sixty-one. And still again, when the cat went from eleven to twelve, the person stayed at sixty-six. Finally, when the cat went from fifteen to sixteen, the person stayed at eighty-one. It was especially good to know that when Polar Bear was going from five to six and nine to ten and eleven to twelve, I was staying absolutely still. Who says everybody has to keep growing older? You don't, if you put your mind to it.

One thing was certain. If Polar Bear at fourteen was like me at seventy-four — I know the damned graph said seventy-six, but it could well have been a mistake — we were in a sense roughly the same age. At least we were both by no means old, but in the full bloom of what I would call our maturity. At the same time I realized I would now have to watch out for him more carefully. In just one more year, at fifteen, he would be like me in my eighties. Fifteen might not seem too bad for him to think about, but certainly the eighties were something I did not want to dwell on. What I did want to do was go back to some of the letters I had received from people who had cats over thirty. Dr. Dunbar had given a cat's age at thirty-one as a person's age at one hundred three. I was not really looking forward to being one hundred three, but from where I was sitting it was certainly a lot more appealing than Reichenbach's having Polar Bear being fourteen and me being just four years away from those damned eighties.

No matter. Whatever the age relationship between us, and whether or not I was in the prime, or on the rim, of my maturity, it was time for me to realize that, whatever I was, Polar Bear was no spring chicken. And so, whether he liked it or not, I had better get on with an entirely new health and fitness program for him. The first thing I did was to read everything I could get my hands on pertaining to older cats. One of the first was a book by Harry Miller entitled *The Common Sense Book of Kitten and Cat Care.* "Cats generally begin to show their age," he wrote, "at about 8 years." Frankly, that made me pretty mad. Polar Bear had not done anything of the sort at age eight and in fact at fourteen he still had not. But Mr. Miller went on:

> The elderly cat does not jump and run in play as he used to do. He is no longer capable of sustained exertion, and he may even tire after moderate exercise. He'll want to sleep more, and may be short-tempered about things he once put up with.

Again, that was not Polar Bear. He jumped and ran and played just the way he always did. He certainly did not tire after moderate exercise. It is true he wanted to sleep more, but I have never known him when he did not want to sleep more. Finally, as far as being short-tempered about things he once put up with, he never did put up with things he once put up with, for the simple reason that he never put up with them in the first place.

Frankly that opinion came too close to home for comfort. Finally, there was perhaps the most extraordinary opinion from my old friend Dr. Dunbar. He wrote in *Cat Fancy* magazine about a California cat named "Mother Cat" who, he said, had two hundred kittens and nonetheless lived to be thirty-one. She also, he maintained, liked both other cats and people, but she liked people more and more as she grew older. I could certainly understand that. At least I am sure by that time she liked people better than male cats. Dr. Dunbar, however, proceeded:

> As with Mother Cat, some cats like people more and more as they grow older. Other cats like people less and less, becoming increasingly intolerant of being disturbed and handled, especially by children and strangers.

Since Polar Bear was intolerant of children and strangers by the time I first saw him, he was, by fourteen, totally so. Nonetheless, Dr. Dunbar then went on with a suggestion about how to handle older cats when it came to what he called "even routine visits to the veterinarian."

> Do not wait for your middle-aged cat to become old and grouchy. Do something about it now. Prevention is the name of the game.

Dr. Dunbar was not kidding — and a game was indeed what he had in mind, as we shall see in a moment. First, though, he begins with how to prepare your cat for the experience:

> To prepare the cat to enjoy veterinary examinations, begin by introducing your cat to visitors. A simple and

> ultimately enjoyable exercise is to invite people over to the house to hand-feed the cat its dinner. Refusal to take food from a stranger is a sign that the cat is stressed. Your job is to remove this stress before your cat's next routine veterinary examination. Do not rush, however; let the cat do things in its own good time. Forget the cat's dinner for today, and have the stranger try again tomorrow. Remember, it is quite normal for wild *Felidae* to go several days with no food at all. With patience and perseverance, any cat will come around eventually.

With all due respect to Dr. Dunbar, I could visualize all too clearly what would happen if I were to try the very idea of giving Polar Bear his dinner by hands-on feeding from strangers. Even if they were relatively familiar strangers, I assure you, they very soon would have a lot more to worry about than whether or not wild *Felidae* had or had not eaten for days — such as, for example, whether or not they still had the use of their own extremities to eat with.

But Dr. Dunbar apparently had not had that much experience with cats who felt as strongly about strangers as Polar Bear. Because, after the hands-on feeding, he proceeded right on to his promised games:

> When the cat enjoys the company of strangers, it is party time — time to play Pass the Cat. One visitor picks up the cat, offers a treat, performs a cursory examination, offers a second treat, and then passes the cat to the next person. This game puts the cat in good stead for a visit to the veterinary clinic, especially if one or two visitors dress up as ersatz veterinarians — wearing white coats or surgery greens and sporting an antiseptic after-shave.

This one was, frankly, too much for me even to attempt to visualize. I just knew that when stranger A passed Polar Bear to stranger B, let alone on to strangers C, D, and E, that would be it because the stranger never lived who could handle a passed Polar Bear, game or no game.

As for the game preparing Polar Bear for meeting a white- or green-coated "ersatz veterinarian" sporting "an antiseptic after-shave" I think one visit from Polar Bear would, at the very least, persuade a stranger to part company with the white or green coat and the antiseptic after-shave as rapidly as possible. And my advice to said stranger would be, after carefully shutting the door behind him before the advance of Polar Bear, to enter, again as rapidly as possible, some other ersatz field of endeavor.

I do not wish to give the impression that Polar Bear was, in his latter years, more difficult than he was when he was younger. Actually, that would not be fair — in many ways he was less difficult. When, for example, two strangers came to my apartment, he would often not bother to move from the chair in which he was sleeping. When he was younger, one stranger was his limit. Two, and in a flash he was off under the bed or under the sofa, and woe betide the stranger who tried to "Here Kitty Kitty" him from under there. Polar Bear was better when he was older, I believe, partly because it was more trouble for him to move. But equally partly I believe it was because as he grew older he grew more philosophical.

In 1991 *Cat Fancy* magazine did a survey of older cats — approximately one-third of whom were from ages ten to twelve, another third from thirteen to fifteen, and still another third from sixteen to nineteen. An extraordinary number of even the oldest of these cats were still lively and, just as I found with Polar Bear, at least a little friendlier with strangers. I liked best the comment of Andrea Dorn of Nevada, Ohio: "I'm not sure whether my cat's personality has changed or not," Andrea said. "I'll think she has become friendlier, but then she'll meet a new person and make a bad impression, and I realize that she and I just get along better. She hasn't really changed; I've just become more like her."

The more I thought about that story the more I thought that through the years Polar Bear and I had gotten more and more like each other. But I do think I should say that, while I had made a real effort to emulate his good qualities and not his bad ones, I do not feel he made the same effort in that department toward me. All too often I found him not emulating my good qualities, but emulating my very worst qualities. For example, I found him growing increasingly short of patience. I know patience is not my long suit, but I saw no reason for him to emulate that minor fault of mine when he could have much more profitably been working on one of my many major virtues, such as my unfailing courtesy to my inferiors. Which, if I do say so, keeps me very busy indeed.

But no matter. The point is that, generally speaking, we got along famously and, as I have said, knowing Polar Bear was, as the age comparisons showed, aging far more rapidly than I was, I made allowances for his character failings just the way I kept a careful check on his health and fitness. I had particular trouble with his eating. After years when he was younger of trying to keep him from getting too fat, now when he was older I was suddenly faced with the problem of him getting too thin. In the early days he was fussy about food, all right, but only fussy when I tried to put him on a diet. In later days, however, he was just fussy, period. It made no difference what I put down. He would sniff it and look at me, and all but say "You don't expect me to eat this, do you?" So, naturally, I would try something else. I usually had the same response again, and indeed it often took a third choice for him to get interested. Too often his average meal took on the appearance of a smorgasbord.

I was relieved to learn it was not at all unusual for older cats to eat less and to lose weight. But it worried me, and I fussed and fussed over it. I called his vet, Susan Thompson, on the slightest provocation, and when I claimed, as I usually did, that he was too sick to travel to the vet's, she graciously made a house call. She kept reassuring me that he was doing fine, but she also told me the fact was sooner or later I should know he would get sick.

I hated her telling me that. I hated it when Polar Bear was sick when he was younger, but when he was older, and he was in the twilight of his years, I did not think I could stand it. Just the same, I knew it was inevitable, and I tried to be a good soldier and brace myself for it. I also did my best to do everything I could for him.

And then like a bolt out of the blue came the shock — the very last thing I would expect. Polar Bear did not get sick — *I* got sick.

It was really incredible. Me, in the prime or on the rim, as I said, of my maturity, being the one to succumb, while Polar Bear, despite being the one far more precarious on the cat-age versus human-age scale and the one of the two of us who, by any odds, should have politely led the way toward any infirmity, was fine and dandy. Honestly, it was so unbelievable I could hardly make any sense out of it, let alone start to live with it.

As I have tried to make clear from the first book about Polar Bear, he and I were from the beginning two very different individuals when we were sick. When I was sick I wanted attention. I wanted it now, and I wanted it around the clock. Besides this, I wished everyone within earshot of my moans and groans, of which I have a wide variety, to know that I am not only at Death's door but also that I have the very worst case of whatever it is I think I have that has ever been visited on any man, woman, child or beast since the world began.

I stated clearly that if, for example, I had a slight cold and the cold had taken a turn for the worse, I wished people to gather around my bedside in respectful silence. For those with poor hearing, I wished them to gather especially close, and for those with poor memories I wished them to bring pad and pencil so that of course they could take down and transmit to posterity, hoarsely and with extreme difficulty, my last words. In much the same manner I visualized my loved ones gathering around after I had gone to my Final Reward to hear my Last Will and Testament. In this I fully intended to give them further instruction, since they no longer had the benefit of my counsel, on how they were to conduct themselves.

All this, mind you, for a cold. But now I had something far more severe — a combination of an ulcer, a distorted aneurism, and what my doctor, Anthony Grieco, described, after a look at my X-rays, as a "curmudgeonly esophagus." I know I have often been described as a curmudgeon, but to hear one's esophagus described in this way — and by one's own doctor — was a bit unsettling. Furthermore, since I was struck with all these troubles at once, I did not even have the time or opportunity to settle down into my usual hypochondriacal ways heretofore described. Instead I was just another patient — and one who, unhappily, as I believe I have already mentioned, was born without any patience.

The most curious thing of all is what happened to my relationship with Polar Bear. Instead of my looking after him, he was now looking after me. No longer was he the rescuee, as had happened in the beginning when I had found him that snowy Christmas Eve, when I found him outside the garage, now he was the rescuer. It really was a total turnaround from what had been our relationship since that first day.

Of course, he was not the only one looking after me. And Polar Bear was never good at being one of a group doing something together as a team. He was either the captain, or he would not play. In this case, if he could not be chief cook and bottle washer, he wanted to be chief of everything else. During the daytime he would sit at the far corner of the bed nearest the door and monitor all comings and goings with the authority of Horatius at the Bridge. During the nighttime he would hunker down between my arm and chest, making sure the covers allowed him to keep at least one beady eye ready for examining any nocturnal visitor.

If the person entering was Marian, my daughter, a friend, or even a long-standing enemy whom I had returned to grace, Polar Bear would of course motion them through, acting for all the world like a traffic patrolman. On the other hand, if the person were a stranger, out would come not only the paw to stop traffic, but the rest of Polar Bear, too. He did not actually attack people, but he certainly gave every indication of not being above such measures if required.

Watching him, I could not help thinking of a story I had read of another protective cat. The cat's name was Inkee, and he was owned by a woman named Debra Lewis of Detroit. One day, Mrs. Lewis remembered, she and her husband were playing on the floor. Inkee was in another room. Suddenly Mrs. Lewis yelled, "Ouch!" Immediately Inkee arrived on the double. His actions were, she reported, in order, first to sit on Mrs. Lewis' chest as if to say "Are you all right?" second, when Mrs. Lewis assured him she was, to kiss her on the nose; third, to go over to her husband and bite him; and fourth and finally, to run out of the room.

I sincerely believe that, faced with similar circumstances and substituting Mrs. Lewis for myself, Polar Bear would have done all of the above. I am particularly sure he would have done so in the case of the most difficult person with whom he had to cope during my illness — the trained nurse. Polar Bear did not like nurses, trained or not, and nurses did not like Polar Bear. For one thing he is not fond of people in white — on the theory, I believe, that their people-caring is just a front and that, underneath, they are probably veterinarians preparing at any time for a surreptitious assault with a needle.

There was another reason that Polar Bear did not like this particular nurse, and that was that he did not like her voice. Whether it was what she said with that voice or whether it was the way she said it — her maddening use of the plural, the endless "How are we?" addressed, of course, to just me — I do not know. But it was certainly one of the reasons he did not like her. There was, finally, a third reason he could not stand the nurse, and that was that I did not like her either, and he was smart enough to know that, and also to know that the reason I did not like her was primarily that she did not like him.

Fortunately this round robin did not last long. Her stay, however, brief as it was, had a bearing on Polar Bear's crowning achievement as watch-and-guard cat. This was the day, or rather the night, he spent with me in the hospital. I shall not tell you which hospital it was. Actually, I was in two of them — in Texas, where the attack first came on, and also in New York. But to spare the attendants of both of them — none of whom, I wish to point out, I actually physically abused — I shall not mention the hospitals' names.

There was a reason Polar Bear was at the hospital. Marian, who could not visit me that day, had a friend bring Polar Bear down in his carrier to see me. The friend was supposed to return before visiting hours were over and take Polar Bear back, but unfortunately an emergency came up and she could not make it. Since that particular day and night the other bed in the two-bed room was unoccupied, I decided that if Polar Bear spent the night he would at least not be bothering anybody else. I even took the precaution of spreading some newspaper in the bathroom for a serviceable litterbox.

If I had asked Marian to leave Polar Bear with me for the night, I very much doubt she would have done so. Marian plays strictly by the book — not, I am sorry to say, always by one of my books — and when it comes to rules and regulations I am firmly convinced that she, not Robert, wrote those rules of order. All in all, I was fortunate that night to have the friend bring Polar Bear and then not be able to return, although I must admit that when it happened I immediately began practicing my favorite winning argument in any situation — that "they" said it would be all right. Those "theys" may have been entirely fictitious, but I promise you they have covered a multitude of sins in my life, and in this case they came through with flying colors.

I did, however, have a serious talk with Polar Bear. I told him that during the night an almost steady stream of people would be passing through our room because that is the way hospitals work — they were sort of like railroad stations. Furthermore, I warned him, most of the people who would be passing in or through the room would be dressed in white, but he would not in any circumstance regard them as veterinarians. Indeed, I told him, he was not to regard them at all because I wished him, from the moment he heard footsteps approaching outside the door, to get under the covers and stay there without leaving in view even so much as one of his beady eyes.

I could tell by his tone of listening — and do not fool yourself, Polar Bear did indeed have a tone of listening — that he did not go along with my idea about this. Clearly, he wanted to know that if this was how it was going to be in the hospital, how in the world could I expect him to do his job of protecting me?

There are all kinds of protection, I told him sternly, just the way there are those who also serve who only stand and wait. They also protect, I added to make it absolutely clear, who only lie and wait. But lie and wait, I added firmly, was just what I expected him to do.

I next told him our first trouble would be the arrival of my supper. The minute I said "supper," Polar Bear could not see what trouble that could possibly be. I explained that it would be trouble because it would probably be brought by a man or a woman in white, and before he started to jump out of bed and up on the tray it would be nice if he at least waited until the man or woman had put the tray down.

I was of course being sarcastic. I didn't want under any condition for him to appear until the man or woman in white had left not only the tray, but also the room.

Polar Bear had the clearest way of asking, "And where, may I ask, do I come in?" The way he did it was by coming as close as a cat can to a cocked eyebrow. I told him he came in because the minute the man or woman went, then and only then could he come out and share my supper. And amazingly enough, it all happened exactly as we discussed it. The minute I heard the wheels of the meal cart outside the door I swooped Polar Bear under the covers and the man came in, put down the tray, and left, all so quickly that Polar Bear did not have time to do anything about it. Once we were alone, however, out he came, and dove for the supper tray. And so, between us, as we so often did at home, we shared and shared alike, his idea of sharing and sharing alike being that he ate both his share and my share of what he liked and left me to have both my share and his share of what he did not like.

When we were through I again placed him under the covers until the man had come in and removed the tray. Afterwards, I warned Polar Bear that we were far from out of the woods yet. Still to come, I told him, were at least three more visits. I also told him that, from then on, one or the other of us should stay awake and that we should schedule watches the way they do on shipboard. Since by this time Polar Bear was already yawning his head off — which was a tendency he often had when I was starting on something important — I decided to teach him a lesson and told him I would take the first shift from ten to twelve, and he could then take what I explained to him was the beginning of the graveyard shift, from twelve to two, and then again I would take over from two to four. There were only two troubles with this beautifully thought-out plan of mine. For one thing, we did not have an alarm clock, and for another we did not know exactly what our battle plan would be when the one who was on watch called the other to action. Actually, Polar Bear was terrific at waking me when he wanted something, but I had no idea how good he would be at waking me when he did not want something or wanted something to stop.

Anyway, we were in the middle of all these plans when suddenly I heard footsteps and the door opened and we had our first visitor. She turned on the light, moved swiftly to my bed, and put down a tray with some water and a pill in a cup. "It's our medication," she said. So far she had not even looked at me or the bed and I was sure she had not seen Polar Bear. But now she was turning and would see Polar Bear. Polar Bear, however, was nowhere to be seen. He was back under the covers. What he had done of course was to see the pill — and all I can say is that if I have ever seen a cat show the white feather I saw it then. I knew perfectly well how Polar Bear felt about pills, but this was too much. When it was all over and he came out, I had to explain to him what showing a white feather meant. I told him that it was plain and simple cowardice. He wanted to know where it came from, and I told him never mind where it came from, he would not remember it anyway. Actually, I learned it came from the belief that a gamecock with a white feather in his tail would not be a good fighter, and I did not see any reason for bringing up such a sordid subject as cockfighting.

I really gave him a very good speech, but the last part of it fell upon deaf ears. He had fallen asleep again. This of course I could not permit. It was now his watch, and people who went to sleep on their watch were often shot. Also I told him I particularly did not want him to go to sleep again before the sleeping pill nurse came — because sleeping pill nurses get very angry when patients go to sleep on them before they have had a chance to give them their pills. I informed Polar Bear sternly I simply would not answer for the consequences if the sleeping pill nurse saw him under such circumstances — it would be bad enough if she saw him under normal circumstances.

Once more I dozed off, and once more it seemed only a short time before the door opened again and this time the lights came flooding on as well as the cheerful question, "How are we tonight?" All I could do was reply wanly that I was as well as could be expected. Once more there was, of course, no Polar Bear in evidence. He was under the covers again, sleeping on picket duty — really he was impossible — particularly since we were this time faced with the temperature-and-pulse nurse. First she put the thermometer in my mouth and then reached for my wrist. This was a mistake. Polar Bear almost invariably took exception to strangers attempting intimacies with me. Out came, all too visibly, one of his arms with its paw headed ominously for the nurse's hand. I had a brief thought that what we would now have would be a three-person arm wrestle, but unfortunately the situation was far worse than I thought. The nurse could not fail to see Polar Bear's arm appear from under the covers, but that was not the main trouble. The main trouble was that she did not think the arm belonged to a cat. What she thought it belonged to was far worse — she thought it belonged to a snake. In any case she shrieked her displeasure, jumped up and made a mess of everything, including the thermometer in my mouth.

At this juncture I could hear steps coming down the hall — probably, I thought, the nurses' guard. Immediately I took the thermometer out of my mouth and reached under the covers where, good as gold, Polar Bear still was. I pulled him out and held him up, in all his glory, for the nurse to see. See, I said, no snake, no snake at all, just a dear little cat.

By this time she did not know what to think, but it was Polar Bear who saved the day. He did not hiss at her or do anything threatening, but instead gave a definite purr and then one of his perfected silent AEIOU's. It won her over in an instant — in fact, before her nurses' guard appeared, she had actually helped me to get Polar Bear back under the covers. By the time they marched in I was having both my temperature and pulse taken as if nothing had happened.

Our third visitor was the sleeping pill nurse, and from the beginning we were off to a bad start. Despite what I had explicitly told Polar Bear not to do, he was sound asleep and so — ashamed as I am to record the fact — was I. When this truly ghastly woman banged open the door, turned on the top light, and uttered her war cry, "And how are we tonight?" it was all too much. I wanted to say, "We *were* fine," when, without so much as a by-your-leave, out came Polar Bear. Actually, he felt he had his leave — he thought she was the same nurse as the one before.

She was not, of course. I will say this, though, for the sleeping pill monster — she held her ground. But I knew she would not, like the other nurse, let it go. This was strictly a law-and-order nurse. I had to think of something and I tried once again. "They said it was all right" but to say it fell on deaf ears is an understatement. "And who may I ask *us*," she said, looking of course at just me, "is *they?*" The doctor, I said lamely. With that she moved to the chart at the foot of the bed. Oh, not that doctor, I said arrogantly, the head doctor. "Well," she said ominously, "we" — and for the first time not looking only at me — "will see." And with that she started to march out the door.

I tried to continue with the last argument about my "they" but it was no use. She was in such a state of high dudgeon that she had not even remembered to leave me my sleeping pill. And on top of her departure, out came Polar Bear who — I am not making this up — actually put on, for my benefit, if not for hers, a masterful imitation of a cat's idea of a human's high dudgeon.

In any case, it was masterly enough so she did nothing about him, and I never did know whether she tried to do something about him. All I know is that we had one more interruption, which came the next morning. It was the nurse who came to take blood. I was virtually sure Polar Bear would not stand still — or rather lie still — for this, and he did not. But in more than one way it was my fault. For some reason nurses always go for my left arm when they go for blood, and invariably in that left arm they cannot seem to find a good vein to work with. In vain I presented the other arm and begged my visitor to try it but, nurses being nurses, it was no use. After three tries, however, I had had enough. I pulled my left arm away and demanded she try the right one. She refused. We had come to a Mexican standoff — or at least we had one until out from under the covers came my champion. Out he came in full battle stance and, giving the nurse first the hiss and then a growl, he did his masterpiece — he held up a warning paw. It was his right paw, too.

Immediately the nurse knew she was outgunned. Without a word she moved around to the other side of the bed, took my right arm, and took the blood. And even more remarkable, before she left she at least tried a pat in Polar Bear's direction. "I have a cat, too," she said. "I won't say a word."

Later that morning when the men in white came to get us — and some women in white, too — Polar Bear and I went, as the saying goes, quietly.

CHAPTER TWO

My Harvard

Convalescence from being ill is, for most people, very different from the actual illness. But as you certainly know by now I am not most people. Actually, during my convalescent period I wished just as much attention as I wished during my illness. I liked people to gather around my bedside much as they did then, only this time instead of being sad and filled with impending doom I wished them to be congratulatory and filled with admiration for me. And I most certainly did not want them to keep these feelings to themselves. Instead, I wished them to express in their own words how wonderful I had been through all my troubles and how desolate they had been at the thought of coming so close to losing me.

At such times during my convalescence, of course, I liked to take the precaution to warn these people that, on pain of my having a relapse, they must show the same concern they showed when I was ill and be on call twenty-four hours a day. I also said that I thought it was best for them to think of themselves as Army orderlies, always on the ready to bring on the double whatever it was of which at that moment I had the most need — be it food, drink, a book, a magazine, a chess player, or a good conversationalist. If the latter, literally the last thing I wanted was somebody who talked all the time. When I say good conversationalist what I mean is a good listener. There is nothing that ruins a good conversation when you have really gotten going and launched into the subject — and then having the other person turn out to be a rotten listener. I want a person with a good long attention span, and I also want a person who agrees with me. He or she does not have to agree with me right away, but I naturally want him or her to agree with me after I have pointed out the fallacies in their arguments and they have understood the eternal verities in mine.

My assistant, Marian is, I have found over the years, a reasonably good conversationalist for a woman. She is not, however, what I would call — and so few women are — good at arguments. All too often she lacks the basic facts necessary to sustain her side of a question, and completely overlooks the careful marshalling of the facts which I have done on my side. Over the years I have done my best to help her with her logic, but it has not been easy.

Polar Bear, on the other hand, was only an average conversationalist. In the first place, he was far too inclined to be totally concerned with those parts of the conversation which pertained entirely to him — at a cost, obviously, of completely missing other and often far more important parts. In the second place, he could not seem to stretch his little mind into understanding that those parts of the conversation which to him seemed to pertain only to me could well turn out to be important from the point of view of his own deportment and general decorum. And in the third and final place, his attention span was, to be charitable about it, lamentable. The only attention span I can frankly compare it with was that of my second wife, of whom I hasten to add may she rest in peace — something, I assure you, she never gave me.

The reason I brought up the question of the conversational proclivities of Marian and Polar Bear was that I decided that the first trip I was permitted to take after getting ill would be a trip by motorcar to Boston to attend two different reunions — first of my Milton Academy class, and second of my Harvard class. I shall not tell you which number reunions these were because frankly it is none of your business. But they were not yesterday.

Before I was taken ill, Polar Bear detested trips. I really believe, however, that having gotten so used to looking after me during my convalescence, he made the decision that if it was between me going off and leaving him, and him being left behind, or him biting the bullet of a trip, he would take the bullet. Whether or not this is true, the three of us set out by automobile for Boston, and Polar Bear was, if not on his best vehicular behavior, at least not on his worst. Indeed we managed the whole trip with only two stops until we came to Milton, Massachusetts, the town in which the academy is located.

Milton Academy was founded in 1797. My father was partial to any century preceding his own, but he was especially fond of the Eighteenth. Actually, Milton was not the oldest, but it was one of the oldest, of a distinguished group of New England prep schools including Groton, St. Paul's, St. Mark's, and others which, taken together, became known as "The St. Grottlesexers." This was an odd sobriquet because if there was one thing these schools were not long on, it was sex. Only relatively recently did they admit girls at all — not even, in Milton's case, when the girl's school was, literally, just across the street.

What these schools had most in common was that they were extremely strict. One of the things I hoped about going back to the reunion was that I would still find this same strictness as it was in my day, and I felt that just being there and hearing about this strictness could not help but have a salutary effect on Polar Bear's behavior. It is the same way I feel about the behavior of schoolchildren in schools today. They just do what they please, right in the classroom — just the way Polar Bear did just what he pleased, right in the living room.

In any case, as we drove up outside the main building of the school, I could not resist informing both Marian and Polar Bear of what happened to me on my first day at Milton Academy. It was a very memorable day, at least for me. We had a history teacher named Reginald Nash who had been a major league baseball player years before and who was a very dramatic man for a schoolteacher. That day he stood in front of a large map of England with a long pointer in his hand, and he was telling us about a war between England and Holland. "Remember, boys," he said firmly, "this was before the days when England ruled the seas. In those days it was the Dutch who ruled the seas. Why, the ships from Holland even swept right up the English Channel." As he said this he pointed with his pointer to the English Channel on the map, and stared at us like somebody on stage. For some reason his standing there like that and pointing with that pointer reminded me of the picture on a container in the medicine cabinet in my bathroom. Why sir, I said, the Old Dutch Cleansers.

Although the Old Dutch Cleanser container was certainly well known to others of my classmates — and I would have thought that a couple of them would at least have chuckled, if not actually laughed — not a soul did. Instead, the whole room fell ominously silent. Despite all that roomful of new classmates I was left deserted — totally alone. Worst of all, because we were seated alphabetically, I was in the front row, only a few feet from the terrifying Mr. Nash.

Endlessly slowly, it seemed, he put down his pointer. Then, equally endlessly slowly, he took off his glasses and put them on the desk. Next, from his seat only a few feet from me he first delivered one of the longest glares to which I had ever been subjected, and finally, after what seemed an eternity, he spoke. "What," he asked, furiously biting off each word, "is your name?"

Clippie, I replied, supplying my childhood nickname. This sent him into a brand-new second round of fury.

"Your *last* name!" he shouted. Amory, I said. There was now an even longer and more awful silence than the first one. Then once more he spoke. "Master Amory," he said, his voice dripping with sarcasm, "you are, I believe I can say without fear of contradiction, the freshest boy who has ever been at Milton Academy."

I said nothing. "Do you know, Master Amory," he continued, "when Milton Academy was founded?"

Yes sir, I said, 1797. "Good," he said, "then you'll have no trouble studying out exactly how many years, how many classes, and even approximately how many boys you have managed to surpass in freshness since that time." He paused. "Meanwhile," he said, "to accompany you in your study I'm going to give you a far easier number to handle — I am going to give you six marks."

Six marks! I could not believe it. In Milton Academy's marks system one mark was bad enough, two very bad, and three horrendous. But six! I had never even heard of anybody getting that many — and all in one day, and on my very first day. There was only one way you could work off marks. This was by raking leaves Saturday morning — all morning to work off just one mark. My Saturday mornings would be gone until November.

At recess my older brother, who was three classes above me, sought me out. "How's it going?" he asked cheerfully. I told him it was not going very well. "Well," he said, "it's just your first day. Everything probably seems a little confusing. You'll get the hang of it." I told him it was not like that — I just hoped *I* wouldn't be hanged.

At length I told my brother what had happened — that I had been given six marks. "Whew," he whistled. "Six! What the hell did you do, murder someone?" I told him no, but I had made a joke. I then reported the story and the joke to my brother. "God," he said, "it wasn't even a good joke."

My brother was always pretty hard on my jokes. Actually it would not have made any difference if I had made a good joke. Milton Academy was almost a military academy when it came to discipline. The masters taught both with sarcasm and, if necessary, physical punishment. Many a master regularly threw chalk at boys who either talked in his class or fell asleep. And needless to say when the boy stopped talking or woke up it was well understood that he was on no condition to throw it back.

I can remember some of the sarcasm to this day. In that same first year, for example, in the class of a man who later became my favorite master, Al Norris, I whispered something to my friend Vasmer Flint. We often thought we could get away with things in Mr. Norris' class because he wore a green eyeshade and we thought he could not see us very well. Actually, I think he had a magnifying glass in that eyeshade, and his hearing was so acute that it seemed to us that he seemed to be able to hear us even when we just had an idea of talking. At any rate, after my whispering to Vasmer he talked not to me but to the whole class. "Master Amory," he said, "seems to have something of great importance to impart to his friend, Master Flint — something so important it is obviously of far more moment than anything I could possibly be saying. But I hope that Master Amory can be persuaded to part with this information so that the rest of us can be that much more enlightened. I see no reason for it to be reserved to Master Flint alone."

Then for the first time he spoke to me. "Master Amory,"

he said, "if you are not too busy perhaps you will do me the honor of coming up here." As I climbed up to his desk on the platform, Mr. Norris got up from his chair. "Here," he said, "you do not need to stand. Just take my seat. And I hope, if you do not mind, you will permit me to go down and take yours." With that, Mr. Norris and I exchanged seats. Nonetheless, he continued speaking from down there. "Now," he said, "Master Amory, do proceed. Please tell us not only what you told Master Flint but do go on from there. I am sure all of us would like to hear you conduct the class for the remainder of the period."

One thing was certain — after an experience like that, you never again so much as breathed unnecessarily loudly in Mr. Norris' class. But frankly I never thought that being taught with that strictness ever did us the slightest bit of harm. The fact is the majority of us ended up close friends with the masters early on we had feared the most — and furthermore we became friends for life.

Take for example Mr. Nash, the same master who had given me the six marks on my first day. I can remember vividly in the fall of my senior year when he was teaching us another history class at the final class of the day which ran from two o'clock to three o'clock in the afternoon at the exact time when his beloved New York Giants were playing in a World Series game against his detested New York Yankees. Mr. Nash, as I told you, was a former ballplayer and he also coached our baseball team, and he dearly wished at that time not to be teaching his class but to be listening to that game on the radio. Just the same, he knew his duty, and once more he was at his map on the wall and this time in his same dramatic way he was telling us about another war, the late unpleasantness between The States. Once again, too, he had his glasses and his pointer, and he jabbed away at first Vicksburg and then Atlanta. "Grant would make a jab here," he jabbed, "and Joe Johnson would rush to meet him. Then Grant would make another jab over here, and Joe Johnson would once more move to meet that."

Mr. Nash was obviously building to a climax, but suddenly he put the pointer down. Off came the glasses, and finally a long look — right at me. "Cleveland," he said, "the Giants just don't have the power." Almost immediately, however, he caught himself, grabbed his glasses and his pointer, and was back at the map. "And Grant," he went on, "would try again over here but Joe Johnson would get right over there too."

It had taken me six years but it was a long way from those six marks.

Polar Bear was by this time extremely bored with my Milton Academy reminiscences, and was ready to see some action. All reunioners were to be put up right in one of Milton Academy's dormitories. There were younger boys to help us with our luggage, and dutifully Marian and I and Polar Bear made our way to the room to which we had been assigned. I thought the room was very nice and extremely nostalgic, but Polar Bear thought the accommodations were extremely Spartan. He sniffed particularly at the hard chairs. I did not have the heart to tell him I had not had the nerve to tell people I was bringing him. Finally he settled on the bed.

Dinner was to be in the main dining hall with assorted classmates and wives. Obviously, since there was no lock on the door, this presented a problem for Marian and myself with Polar Bear. While we were both looking at Polar Bear and trying to figure out the situation, the same thing suddenly occurred to both of us at once — something we knew, at that moment, was also occurring to Polar Bear. Why didn't we just have room service? Polar Bear is very fond of room service.

Unfortunately, Spartan schools like Milton Academy not only did not have room service, they had obviously never heard of it. Finally, what Marian and I agreed upon doing was having me go downstairs, first to search for some portable food for Polar Bear and, second, hopefully to find some stray classmate who wanted to meet Polar Bear badly enough so that he would be willing to cat-sit for a little while, and thus give Marian and me a chance for a little socializing.

It all worked out, I am glad to say, excellently. I found some food, and also a classmate who agreed to the job. I do not say that Polar Bear took to him, but he took to the food and, afterward, by a general rubbing on his leg, indicated that he would not be adverse to a second helping.

I took advantage of this change for the better from Polar Bear's usual behavior to slip away with Marian and get down to enjoy at least some of the reunion dinner. The first thing I noticed was how terribly old some of my classmates were. Honestly, some of them looked old enough to be my grandfather, let alone one of my classmates. As for the headmaster, he looked like a child. I really could not believe we had been introduced to the right man. All I could think about, when I gradually made conversation with him, was the headmaster of my day — and, frankly, if you thought Mr. Nash and Mr. Norris were tough babies, you never laid eyes on William Lusk Webster Field. He had the largest ears of any man I ever saw. They were like satellites on the sides of his head, and if Mr. Norris could see everything in his classroom, Mr. Field seemed to hear everything, even in other buildings. And if anybody was doing anything wrong in one of those buildings, they were immediately apprehended and brought to Mr. Field. I can still remember from some infraction of my own, standing there in front of Mr. Field at his desk, and seeing nothing but those two enormous ears, which seemed to be reaching out to incarcerate me forever.

Compared to Mr. Field, the headmaster I was talking to could not, at least in my opinion, scare anybody — at least not until he grew up. As for my classmates, when I mentioned to them that I had brought Polar Bear with me, some of them expressed an interest in meeting him or rather, to be accurate, their wives did. My classmates' wives, I quickly learned, were far more discerning readers than my classmates. Immediately, however, I said that I would agree to take any classmate's wife upstairs to meet Polar Bear, or any classmate — provided it was not one who was a member of that original history class who left me to my fate without even a chuckle over the Old Dutch Cleanser. I know as you grow older you ought to let bygones be bygones but there are, after all, some bygones in life that you just simply cannot let be gone.

One classmate's ex-wife turned out to be, of all ironies, my very first girl. Needless to say I made a beeline for her. I had been really crazy about this girl. She was blonde and had pretty bangs and she was none too intelligent, which even then I was smart enough to appreciate. But afterward, when I was away at college or somewhere, she had up and married someone else. It is always discouraging when a girl like that marries beneath you, but what can you do? I put it down to willfulness and a lack of foresight but even that, at the time, did not help much. And even this time, so many years later, I could still remember it well. Indeed, the more we talked over old times the more I sensed how much she felt she had missed, and what a terrible mistake she had made in not marrying me. I could sense these things almost from the beginning of our talk, because I am a very sensitive person.

One of the things we talked about was the days when I was at the boys' school and she was at the girls' school — which I have already told you, and you should have remembered, was entirely separate even though it was just across the street. I discussed with her my opinion that it was far better than this modern nonsense of putting the sexes together before they know the first thing about sex. I went on to tell her all this modern living together had not seemed to improve anything — at least as far as divorce went. At this, to my surprise, she told me she had been divorced three times — which I found shocking, no matter how upset she had been over me. I know I have been divorced twice, but after all I am a man.

I myself took her up to meet Polar Bear. Marian had taken some other people up, too, and a few of them had just gone up by themselves and were introduced to him by the classmate who was looking after him. Actually, Polar Bear could not have been better. He never once retired under the bed or even sulked. And when he looked bored — which he did whenever more than one person approached at once — he did so in a way that was not totally off-putting — which, for him, was really exemplary social behavior. Indeed, during the whole evening he only bit one person, and that was hardly his fault. It was a friend of my first girl's, and the trouble was she had pushed her friend on Polar Bear before he had finished his food — and Polar Bear was never very good before he had finished something. Also, as I have already told you, my first girl was awfully pretty, but to say she was not very bright was being kind.

When it was finally all over and we were retiring for bed, I had to tell Marian and Polar Bear one last story about Milton Academy. This one concerned a catalogue. In my day almost all Milton boys went on to Harvard — at least thirty, and usually more like forty, out of a class of about fifty. When it came to football, Milton's proudest boast of my day was that either eight or nine, I have forgotten which, Milton boys started the Yale game in their senior year at Harvard. I doubt any single high school or prep school ever achieved that record at any time.

Despite these statistics I did not want to go to Harvard. At Milton Academy I had developed certain rebellious traits, and these broke out in full flower in the spring of my senior year. I wrote for catalogues to other colleges. It was just one of those wild crazy flings of youth — you see it today, on a lesser scale of course. In any case, when these catalogues came to me there was one in particular from a college called Stanford. It was located in the West. I was familiar with the West of course — I had an uncle in Dedham and an aunt in Needham — but this particular catalogue was a rather remarkable one. It showed tennis courts and swimming pools. It showed boys and girls studying together — always, as I have said, a doubtful proposition. And finally it showed the young ladies, at least those adjacent to the swimming pools, not by our Boston standards fully clothed.

I was gazing at this catalogue in rapt attention when my father chanced to see it over my shoulder. "Bah," he said.

So I went to Harvard.

On the way from Milton to Harvard I decided to go a roundabout way and show Marian and Polar Bear where I was born — what was then the Boston resort of Nahant. It is now more of a year-round residence, but one thing that has not changed about Nahant is the way it is pronounced. It is pronounced the way the Bostonian pronounces the wife of his uncle, and not what has been corrupted by the rest of the country into a small bug. It is, in other words, *Na-haunt* and not *Na-hant*.

As we drove over the causeway from Lynn into Nahant proper I started looking for the house in which I had been born — which, it is a source of some irritation to me, has never been properly marked. I explained to Marian and Polar Bear that Nahant was in some ways sort of like Milton Academy — it was Spartan and severe. "Cold Roast Boston," it used to be called. A resort, mind you. Just the same, as I also explained to Marian and Polar Bear, we had our good times in Nahant, darn it we did. We had, for example, Dutch-treat picnics. We also had Saturday-night croquet. Then, too, we had swimming. This was at a place called Forty Steps. Like my house, I had a hard time finding this, but I finally did. As we were looking at it, I pointed out to Marian and Polar Bear that to get to the water you had to go down forty steps —

which were not really steps at all. What they were, were rocks. They were slippery and slimy and seaweedy. And, when you finally got down to the water, you did not get to anything like a beach or sand or even pebbles. What you got were more rocks, and they too were slippery and slimy and seaweedy.

As for the water itself, when you got into it, you soon found that it was not just cold water, it was ice-cold water. I put Polar Bear's paw into it to show him how cold it was, and I told both him and Marian that I remember one day when Dad and I were swimming there, among the frigid icebergs, and I suddenly said to him, "Dad, it isn't much fun, is it?" My father turned his by then blue face in my direction. "It isn't meant to be fun," he said. "You feel so good when you get out. What do you want to do — go down on the Cape with the Kennedys?" I told Dad of course I did not want to do that, and I am certain Polar Bear wouldn't have wanted to either.

It is not a long run from Nahant to Cambridge and to Harvard, but Polar Bear went sound asleep anyway, and once we had arrived at Harvard and were ensconced in our reunion rooms, he was quite ready to sleep again. I expected a little more enthusiasm from him seeing, for the first time, his master's alma mater and at least hearing firsthand a knowledgeable history of the oldest college in the country. Honestly, seeing him go right to sleep like that before I had even begun talking made me think how many times in his life he has missed hearing some of my most important thoughts.

Actually, Marian missed some of my words of wisdom too because in no time at all she, like Polar Bear, having located the sofa in the living room, was fast asleep also.

Whereupon, of course, in the time I had before we were to go downstairs to join the reunion lunch I was left alone to think about my life at Harvard. Actually I do not remember whether or not I went to sleep myself and maybe dreamed the whole thing, but in any case there was something about being back in those old college rooms again that took me back to the first time I had entered such a room in my sophomore year.

My roommate then, and in fact for all four years of Harvard, was a Milton Academy classmate. His name was Bruce Foster. Freshman year we had roomed together in what were called "Halls." Next, as sophomores, we were in a "House." Bruce's father, like mine, had been to Harvard and he, like my father, was steeped in Harvard lore. "If a man's in that," Harvard's President Quincy used to say, tapping the Triennial Catalogue, containing a complete list of Harvard graduates, "that's who he is. If he isn't, who is he?" But make no mistake, Harvard's Twentieth Century presidents were equally formidable also. Indeed, of President A. Lawrence Lowell the story is told that a visitor to Harvard seeking to see Mr. Lowell stopped at his office only to be turned away by the secretary, who reported that her boss could not be seen. "The President is in Washington," she said, "seeing Mr. Taft."

One does not need to be a Bostonian at Harvard for long without being willing to concede that in some other cities' societies — New York for one — a certain cachet of social prestige derives from colleges near them — as, for example, Yale or Princeton near New York — but a Bostonian soon learns to attribute this to the fact that such cachet comes from the kind of boy who really belonged at Harvard, but went to some other college due to youthful indiscretion or lack of character. Major Henry Lee Higginson, for example, dedicating the football stadium, Soldiers' Field, which he had given to Harvard, drew this line of condescension as delicately as he could in what was described at the time as one of his "simple, manly addresses." "Princeton is not wicked," he told his audience. "Yale is not base. Mates, the Princeton and Yale fellows are our brothers. Let us beat them fairly if we can, and believe they play the game just as we do."

One thing Bruce and I resolved to do that very first day in our sophomore room was to take easy courses. My reason for this was simple. My brother, during his freshman year, had taken five general courses — four were considered tough enough — and got five straight A's, not even one A minus. He had then also gone on to finish Harvard in three years and gotten a *magna cum laude.* Boston brothers are notably competitive, but for me, as a C student or at best an occasional B, following in the footsteps of such a brother would have been the height of folly without at least trying to level the field.

I had another reason for taking easy courses. Having been editor of the Milton Academy magazine, *Orange and Blue,* I had decided to go out for the *Harvard Crimson* in my sophomore year. But while the *Orange and Blue* was a magazine and came out only once a month, the *Harvard Crimson* was a daily and involved endless evening work, if you did make it, not to mention endless competitions once you did. First there was a competition to be assistant assignment editor, then another to be assignment editor, then a third to be assistant managing editor, a fourth to be managing editor, and fifth and finally a competition to be President. In a nutshell, the amount of time left for your classes was modest indeed.

Bruce, who had no older brother and had not the slightest intention of going out for something like the *Crimson*, had no such excuse. What he did have, however, was something very rare in the Boston and Harvard I grew up in — a well-honed desire to have, during his college years, a grand good time. Bruce was not particularly handsome. He had a kind of narrow face and oversized ears. But he was a very, very funny fellow, and unlike some very funny fellows was enormously good fun to be around. He was as popular with girls as he was with boys, and before he finished at college he was president of the college club and had at least twice as many real friends as the chief class politicians had acquaintances.

Actually the hardest I think I ever saw Bruce work was in our quest to find those easy courses. To begin with we set very high standards, below which we were determined not to go. The first of these was that we would consider only courses which had no examinations. The second was that we wanted courses which met only once a week. Our third criterion was that it must be a course which did not meet before eleven o'clock in the morning. The fourth and final thing we demanded was that the course did not meet above the second floor.

Looking back I realize these last two criteria may seem a trifle picky, but I knew that the *Crimson* would keep me up late many nights, and as for Bruce, his social schedule, particularly in the springtime, was far too heavy for him to consider getting up before eleven. As for the course not being above the second floor, our room was on the third floor, and we got awfully tired of going up and down stairs.

Finally we had our schedules in order. I remember one of my courses was Introduction to Art, and another was Military Science, both of which I had been assured by knowledgeable friends were "pikes" — i.e., easy — and although I had to take one tough course on Chaucer because English Literature was my major, the fourth course Bruce and I came up with was our masterpiece. We really believed we had found the easiest course in the entire Harvard catalogue.

It was called The Idea of Fate and the Gods, a title which did not particularly appeal to us. But as we found out more about it, we were assured by the catalogue that if it was not to be offered that year, the substitute would be The History of Sacrifice, which appealed to us more. And basically either one was, title aside, to our taste close to perfect. There were no examinations, both courses met only once a week, on Fridays from 4 to 6 P.M., and they met on the second floor of the Divinity School. Bruce was a little annoyed that the course met from 4 to 6 P.M. on Friday, because he felt that might interfere with his Friday night dates. But I told him sternly that everything in life which was worthwhile entailed a little sacrifice. I assured him I meant no pun on The History of Sacrifice, but I was certain he would learn something from that, too. Bruce also grumbled a little bit about the Divinity School being a long walk, but I told him if worse came to worst we could take a taxi.

To get into either The Idea of Fate and the Gods or The History of Sacrifice, we soon found out, we would have to be approved by the professor. Dutifully we decided to pay a call on the man. As we walked toward the Divinity School Bruce complained once more about the distance. I told him to look at it this way: at least it was on the level and not up and down, like on the third floor or something.

Once arrived, we learned that the course was given by one of the world authorities on religion, Professor Arthur Darby Nock. Nervously we knocked on his door. Professor Nock himself jumped up and opened it. He looked us over. "What class are you?" he asked. I told him. "Sophomores!" he exclaimed. "Why, I've never even had an undergraduate in The Idea of Fate. I had one in The History of Sacrifice once . . ." he paused, "but we're not offering that this year. Just The Idea of Fate." Suddenly he looked at me. "Foster," he said — he had already mixed us up, and he never did get us straight — "why do you want to take this course?" I looked as earnest as I could. Sir, I told him, all my life I've been interested in the idea of fate and the gods. Professor Nock then turned to Bruce. "Amory," he said, "why do *you* want to take The Idea of Fate and the Gods?" "Same as him," Bruce said, pointing to me. I wanted to kick him. Make up your own ideas, I whisper-hissed to him — he's got us mixed up. Professor Nock was still looking at the papers we had brought him. Finally he looked up. "I guess just because we've never had an undergraduate in The Idea of Fate before doesn't mean we can't ever have one, does it? Or two of them," he smiled. Bruce and I both nodded.

Our first class was a memorable one. The room was filled with graduate students, Jesuit priests, rabbis, and all sorts of people from as far off as Chicago. From the moment Professor Nock began his introduction neither Bruce nor I understood a single word. On top of that, as I say, Professor Nock had mixed us up — a situation which, of course, Bruce immediately latched onto. He started talking to me as if we were not in class at all. "Amory," Professor Nock said, "stop that. You'll have to pay attention here." Bruce, of course, started again. "Amory!" Professor Nock said even more sternly, "I've spoken to you before. I have to have your attention." Again, I whisper-hissed to Bruce. You do that once again, I said, and you will regret it. Needless to say, he did do it again, whereupon I stood up and walked to the door. "Foster! Foster!" Professor Nock said. "Where are you going?" I am going for a walk, sir, I said. I did, too, and I did not return. But Bruce had at least learned his lesson. He did not talk to me in class again. Instead he went almost immediately to sleep.

Toward the end of the term Bruce and I made a very distressing discovery from a fellow classmate. This was in a word that, while there were no examinations in The Idea of Fate and the Gods, there would, however, be a paper due. Furthermore it was a paper whose subject had to be approved by Professor Nock. Frankly, neither Bruce nor I had the slightest idea what we would write about.

Somehow Bruce managed to solve his problem, primarily with the assistance of a friendly minister. But, as my deadline for approval neared, I was getting nowhere. One day, however, in the Chaucer class something happened which rang a bell. What it was, was that I learned that the Chaucer course too would require a paper. To the average person that might not have been anything to solve the problem. But not to yours truly. I rose, if I do say so, to the occasion.

I had, in this Chaucer course, become friends with a

fellow student named J. Sinclair Armstrong — in fact, I was lucky enough to sit beside him because of our Amory/ Armstrong juxtaposition. Armstrong later became head of the Securities and Exchange Commission, and as a student he would have been a match for my brother. He took notes in a big, rounded hand which was not only beautiful to see but very easy to copy. One day, shortly after I had copied copiously, I suddenly turned to him. Sinclair, I said earnestly, did Chaucer have much of an idea about the idea of fate and the gods? "Did Chaucer *what?*" Sinclair asked. He looked at me as if I had gone around the bend. No, seriously, I pressed, I really need to know because I have got this little problem. In fact if I do say so, Sinclair, it is now two problems. And there is really no need for it to be any problem at all.

In no time at all Sinclair wormed out of me the whole dastardly scheme I had cooked up — somehow to make one paper of two — both being, of course, Chaucer's idea of fate and the gods, and both being, as I thought of it, a joint effort by Sinclair and me, but unfortunately as Sinclair thought of it, a pretty one-sided thing. At this I took Sinclair into my confidence. I explained to him that I was in a difficult predicament — that I was up against one course that I could not possibly get through without him and another in which I did not understand a single thing. And when it came right down to it, all I was really asking was for him to go through our Chaucer book — I emphasized the "our" to indicate that I felt we were now really a team — and jot down any references which might conceivably concern either the idea of fate or the gods. For him, I said, the whole thing should be a snap. Honestly Sinclair, I promised him, a child could do it.

As I said this I realized I had perhaps gone a little too far. "Well then," he said crossly, "why the hell don't *you* do it?" I reminded him of the *Crimson*, working all night and never getting enough sleep, and still being cheerful with him every morning.

In the end everything worked out fine. The very day I was to give my choice of topic to Professor Nock, Sinclair met me in the morning with a proposed outline. In no time at all I was on my way to Professor Nock. What would he think, I asked him, of a paper on Chaucer's ideas about fate and the gods? He clapped me firmly on the back. "Chaucer!" he said excitedly, "the poet! We've never had a Chaucer. Go to it, Foster." Amory, I said sternly. I told him I thought he would like the idea, and had taken the liberty of preparing a small outline. Actually, I had seen no need to retype it — it was in such beautiful handwriting. "Beautiful handwriting," Professor Nock said, "beautiful, Foster — I mean Amory. Capital, capital," he said. Then he stopped. "But you understand you're going to have to flesh this out."

I nodded sagely. When I took it back to Sinclair, I told him first the good news — that Professor Nock thought our outline was terrific, and then I gave him the bad news — that he would have to flesh it out a little. Again, at first he was irritated, but in the end he agreed, except this time he would not allow me to hand in his writing. I would have to type it. I told him I thought he was being petty — that we were now a real team, and a team is only as strong as its weakest member.

The final step of course was to convince our Chaucer professor that just what he needed was a paper on Chaucer's idea of fate and the gods. But he fell for it hook, line, and sinker, so again I felt all I should have to do was to carbon a copy for him. There were no Xeroxes in those days. But again Sinclair was difficult and insisted on another typing. I finally, albeit reluctantly, agreed to that also. I have always felt it was important to let employees have a certain say in management. It makes them feel part of the decision-making process, and you never know when you are going to need them again.

There was, finally, an interesting sequel to The Idea of Fate and the Gods. When Bruce and I went to the Divinity School to get back our papers from Professor Nock there, in large letters on both papers, were huge D minuses. This was not good news. For me, it did not mean that I would go on probation, but for Bruce it did. Two C's and two D's was probation. Crestfallen, we went to see Professor Nock to explain the problem. He was his old self. He listened to us for a few moments, then jumped up and grabbed our papers. "Do you know," he said, "I had forgotten all about you being undergraduates?" With that he took a huge crayon, and through the middle of both our D's he drew a line, making them both B's. Then, after looking at them for a moment like an artist examining his painting, he drew two plus signs after them. "There," he said, "two B plusses. Capital, capital." We could not have agreed more.

When Marian woke up we had a consultation about Polar Bear — whether to bring him down to the reunion lunch, in his carrier of course — or whether, as we had done at Milton, get a cat-sitter and then after lunch invite friends who especially wanted to meet him to come up and do so. Unfortunately, however, Harvard had no undergraduates like Milton who were meant to help us old-timers with all sorts of problems, including cat-sitting. So we were finally reduced to the carrier route. All during lunch though we had to keep the carrier under our legs because Harvard's dining room had the usual nonsense about no animals — even for old-timers like myself.

In the old days Polar Bear would not have taken kindly to being at foot level in the carrier, with all sorts of strange people peering down to look at him and pet him. But, as I have said, as he grew older he grew more philosophical about, if not exactly taking what came, at least not constantly making mountains out of molehills. Also, once I had added snacks and even occasional solid food to his social interplay, he decided that being "on," as it were, even on underneath, was not too bad. Indeed, he was clearly enjoying himself when, all of a sudden, there was trouble.

The trouble was in the form of a Harvard house officer of some sort who told me, as if I did not know it, that no animals were allowed in the dining room. I wanted to know if it would be all right if we just shut the carrier top. The young man considered this but finally shook his head. "I'm sorry," he said, "but you're going to have to take him away." When I asked him where — which I did sarcastically — he had no suggestion. In my day, I told him, it was called "Harvard Indifference." I reminded him that we also had a saying, "You can always tell a Harvard man, but you can't tell him much." By this time we were going at it pretty hot and heavy, but for some reason he suddenly eased up. "My sister," he said, out of the blue, "likes cats." I told him I was glad there was someone in his family who did. He ignored this, however, and said that his sister was at the present time handling the coats in the coat room, and if I would take the cat to her he would see that she would handle him through the rest of the lunch.

Marian and I were not keen on turning Polar Bear over to strangers, but the coat room was just a short distance away — enough so we could keep an eye on him — and in short order we could see that not only was Polar Bear doing fine with the difficult man's sister, he was also doing fine with everybody else around the coat room. The woman had opened up the top of his carrier, and we could not believe it when we saw him rising up in there, preening himself, and looking for all the world like a coat room attendant asking for a sizable tip.

Meanwhile, back at our table, the old grads fell, as is their wont, into reminiscing. From the beginning I was amazed at the depth of my classmates' feelings about the good old days in general, and in particular about the good old days at good old Harvard. It was not that I did not understand this — I had seen too many generations at Harvard not to understand — but somehow I was beginning to understand why at Milton I had written for catalogues to other colleges. Finally I felt so out of it that I decided to pull them all up short by reminding them that "Fair Harvard," the Harvard anthem and alma mater, was played at my father's funeral. And, if I do say so, I really think this stopped them. The comedian in the class wanted to know if it was played by the Harvard band. I told him of course it was not — it was played by the regular church organist. At this the wag wanted to know how many verses were played. I told him, naturally, just one verse, but as a matter of fact my father's favorite verse was the last verse, the fourth. I also told him that the words were very memorable, particularly in that fourth and final verse. I added that my mother used to give my brother and myself twenty-five cents for every hymn we learned, and although there was some controversy when my brother chose "Fair Harvard" — I protested that it was not really a hymn — he ended up with twenty-five cents, and so did I. I reminded the class comedian that the words to "Fair Harvard" were written by Reverend Samuel Gilman, and that it was first sung at Harvard's Bicentennial in 1836, and the music was the old Irish folk song "Believe Me, If All Those Endearing Young Charms." If, I added without further ado, I could have the courtesy of some quiet I would be happy to sing it to them. Whereupon I proceeded to do so:

Farewell, be thy destiny onward and bright,
To thy children the lesson still give,
That with freedom to think and with patience to bear,
And for right ever bravely to live.
Let not moss-covered error moor thee at its side,
As the world on truth's current glides by;
Be the herald of light and the bearer of love
'Til the stock of the Puritans die.

I admit I am not the most accomplished of singers but, if I did not get applause, I did at least get a respectful pause. That is, until the class wag had still another question for me. "Are you," he asked, "going to have 'Fair Harvard' sung at your funeral?" I told him I was not, and for two reasons. The first was that although I liked that last verse I did not like that last line, because in my opinion the Puritans were never known as being that big on being bearers of love. The second reason was that I had already decided what I would have played at my funeral — it was the song "Bless the Beasts and the Children."

I told them that "Bless the Beasts and the Children" was Polar Bear's favorite song, too, and I intended to have it played at a memorial service for him someday. That, as I knew it would be, was too much for almost all of them. "A memorial service," the wag said, "for a cat! Now I've heard everything! Are you going to sing it?" I told him I was not going to sing it, but I would certainly have it sung by someone the way I knew not only I would like it best, but also Polar Bear would — with as little emphasis as possible on the word "children" and as much as possible on the word "beasts." Just to be sure they understood what I meant I sang them all that one line, so they couldn't miss it:

Bless the beasts *and the . . . 'ildren.*

The next most popular subject after Harvard in general at our reunion luncheon was Harvard fund-raising. This topic always seems to loom large at class reunions because Harvard is one very formidable university when it comes to fund-raising. For every class there is a Class Fund chairman, as well as a lot of Class Fund agents who always seem to go to every reunion. These gentlemen point out, in no uncertain fashion, the importance of your giving every year to the Class Fund, and are not above indicating that your last gift was hardly what they would have expected. And, in the event you did not give at all, they make sure you understand how impossible it is for them to meet their quotas when faced with such deadbeats.

Unfortunately I am one of these deadbeats. I have not given to my Class Fund for more years than either the Fund or I care to think, because of the simple reason that I have a charity of my own, the Fund for Animals, and this runs counter — at least to my way of thinking — to some things about Harvard I do not like, particularly its treatment of laboratory animals. When I am approached by a Class Fund agent, however, I am always polite and tell them that my late father always gave generously to his Class Fund, my late brother always gave generously to his, and my two nephews both not only give regularly but one of them was at one time actually employed as a fund-raiser by Harvard. All in all, I point out, it was hardly a bad show for a family, and he should think of it in the order of something of a record — four and a half out of five.

As for Harvard's record on laboratory animals, however, I found it fell far short. Not long after I had founded the Fund for Animals, one of the first laboratories I visited was Harvard's. I have never forgotten either how difficult they made it for me to enter or what they did once I had done so. Indeed it was something that I have never had happen in any other laboratory I have visited before or since. What they had right with me, besides the usual officials of the laboratory, was a man with a television camera, placed what seemed right behind my neck, literally photographing everything I saw. The idea of this was that if what I would later say was critical — and they could be sure some of it would be — they would have contradictory photographic evidence which would then bolster their usual claim that all the animals were well cared for, had plenty to eat and drink, and were happy.

Once upon a time Harvard had leaders who felt differently on the subject of laboratory animals. One such man was none other than Henry David Thoreau, Class of 1837. Mr. Thoreau one day had the misfortune to kill by mistake a turtle which he afterwards decided to send to his friend Louis Agassiz, a scientist at Harvard, to use as a specimen. But, after he did so, Thoreau was extremely troubled, and in his *Journal* wrote as follows:

> I have just been through the process of killing . . . for the sake of science. But I cannot excuse myself for this murder, and see that such actions are inconsistent with the poetic perception, however they may serve science, and will affect the quality of my observations. I pray that I may walk more innocently and serenely through nature. No reasoning whatever reconciles me to this act. It affects my day injuriously. I have lost some self-respect. I have a murderer's experience in a degree.

Thoreau was equally definite in his opinion on the subject when asked in person. Once when asked why he did not shoot birds to study them he replied, "If I wanted to study you, would I shoot you?" On another occasion, asked about college diplomas, he had a memorable reply. "Let every sheep keep its own skin, I say."

It is true that, nowadays, animal activists have finally been able to see that laboratories at least have what is called Animal Care and Use Committees. These are supposed to have at least one member who is not an experimenter but someone who represents the "community," and who can oversee the laboratory's practices objectively. In practice, however, this person is chosen by the experimenters, who regularly rubber-stamp each others' protocols as enthusiastically as they band together to defend each other on the rare occasions they are charged with cruelty. Harvard's Animal Care and Use Committee is typical. It meets only semiannually, and holds its meetings at breakfast in the Faculty Club. An Animal Legal Defense Fund lawyer finally managed to attend one such breakfast. He was not only received with what he reported was "universal hostility," but also found that all members of the Committee were even hostile to the idea of having an outsider, or "community member," present. When the lawyer finally asked if there were any philosophers present, one member of the Committee replied sarcastically, "We're all philosophers here."

Obviously none, sadly, of the stature of Henry David Thoreau. In recent years Harvard appeared front and center in the investigation of research fraud by Representative John Dingell's House Subcommittee on Oversight and Investigation. Indeed, the story of how universities get their grants by first adding everything to their request they can think of — including laboratory rentals, parking spaces, and even cleaning ladies' fees — and on top of that, adding what they call general "overhead," was the crux of the investigation. This was, in almost all cases, over 50 percent of the grant itself. In other words, if a university received a million-dollar grant — to, say, torture cats — they then billed the donor, the National Institutes of Health for example, one million five hundred thousand dollars. Harvard ranked first above all universities in such a practice, coming in at 88 percent, followed by Stanford at 64 percent and Yale at 60 percent.

For reasons I have already made clear I had not, as I said, given to my Class Fund for many years. But, make no mistake, it was not easy. Harvard does not give up on anybody. Year after year they keep after you. And finally, in my case, they produced their crowning achievement. It was in the form of a letter relating to my roommate, the aforementioned Bruce Foster. A Second Lieutenant, Bruce was killed at Kasserine Pass in North Africa in one of the worst disasters of American arms in the Second World War. His unit was maneuvered into a trap by German Field Marshall Rommel, and all but a handful of Americans were killed — Bruce was shot attempting the hopeless task of getting his men out from their crippled tank.

The letter from Harvard about him was, as I say, something of a masterpiece. It was from Laurence Johnson, a friend of mine and the captain of the football team, not even just at Harvard but before that, at Milton. He addressed me by my childhood nickname, as follows:

> Dear Clippie:
>
> It has been called to the attention of your Class Committee, several members of whom I know you know well, that you have not for many years made a contribution to our Class Fund. I am sure you understand the pride we have all had in the fact that our class had, last year, the second highest percentage of class givers of any class in recent history — save only the ones who now have only one member left,

and, of course, if he goes on giving that class now comes in at 100%. This was hardly a comparison rated against our percentage which happily has a much broader base. We came in, as I said, Clippie, the second highest percentage, based on 92% of givers who we were able to locate.

But Clippie, what I would like to tell you is a story which has nothing to do with numbers or percentages or even regular givers to our Fund. It has to do, on the other hand, with something which I know will have such a deep personal meaning for you that I could not, in all good conscience, let another day pass without informing you.

What it is in a word, Clippie, is that Harvard University has decided to establish a scholarship in the name of Bruce Foster. Bruce was a classmate who you, as his roommate and best friend, undoubtedly remember better than any of the rest of us — and also the memory of his tragic death at Kasserine Pass. I'm sure you know all of this, but what I do not think you know is the remarkable success we have had in our preliminary testing as to the probable success of such an undertaking. In fact, as I write this to you, the sum of $4,500 has already been raised or pledged.

Unfortunately, time is of the essence here because, as again you may or may not know, Harvard does not accept any scholarship under $5,000 and obviously all of us want to go "over the top" before Harvard makes its own decision to let this one go "by the board" — as frankly has been done in the case of many other scholarships.

With this time frame in mind, Clippie, I thought

first of you who would, of all Bruce's friends, want to step forward with a gift which would take care of this matter right now. I knew you would want to do this particularly since the names of a large number of Bruce's classmates who have already given, including Bruce's two sisters, are already known and I am sure you would not like to see any of these read a list of contributors and find you, as Bruce's best friend and roommate, not present.

I'm sure I do not need to say more. All of us here, and especially me, Clippie, await your reply with keen hopes.

Sincerely, your friend
Larry

Marian says I worked longer on my letter of reply than I worked on any other letter or article in her memory. Whether this is true or not, in any case my Class Fund Committee did indeed receive my response. It went as follows:

Dear Larry:

Thank you so much for your letter. You are indeed right that it has been some time since I anted up for my Class Fund. In fact, it has been such a long time that I am embarrassed about it. The problem, Larry, is that I too have a charity, called the Fund for Animals, and any extra money I have I feel should go in that direction, particularly since I have through the years become increasingly unhappy about a conflict between Harvard and the Fund for Animals involving laboratory animals.

I do not want you to be concerned about this, but I do want you to know about it. Now for better news for you. As one who got his feet wet in the field of fund-raising, I yield to no man in my admiration of how Harvard goes about it. Indeed, I believe that anyone entering this field should give his days and nights to a study of how Harvard manages to go on, year after year, raising its millions and even billions of dollars.

Indeed, if I may add a personal observation, I myself have had since graduation hundreds and hundreds of letters from my Class Fund and I sincerely agree that it would be almost impossible to graduate from Harvard and not give to your Class Fund. Sooner or later Harvard will discover, in even the most hardened of non-givers, an Achilles' heel, a chink in the armor — something which will in the end mean that they can no longer go on living without changing their non-giving ways. All of us realize such Achilles' heels or chinks do not have to be revealed by the errant non-giver himself, but may come from another person, a more loyal Harvardian, such as a father or mother, a child, a wife, or even a distant relative. But just the same, Harvard will sooner or later find someone who will bite the bullet, force the issue, and spill the beans.

Larry, I remember a classmate of ours who you too will remember, a man who tried for years not to give to his Class Fund. Finally he got so fed up with receiving letters that he gave up a very successful advertising career, family and friends, chucked it all, and at a very early age moved to the island of Bora Bora.

Here he took up with a dusky maiden and for some time tasted nothing but the fruits of total freedom. And then, suddenly one early part of one memorable evening, just as he and his maiden stood in the doorway of their little grass shack preparatory to going inside for the night she suddenly turned to him and said, "But Don, you haven't given to your Class Fund."

Larry, I cannot vouch for the authenticity of that story but I can indeed believe that our classmate did indeed stop giving up giving, and I feel that I, too, will undoubtedly have to follow in his footsteps.

Larry, what a stroke of genius for you and your committee to come up with a $5,000 scholarship in the name of Bruce Foster, to have Bruce's other friends and even his two sisters know who has given and who has not, and finally to tell me that you have $4,500 already raised, and that Harvard will not accept a scholarship less than $5,000. Really, it's perfect.

Larry, I honestly believe there are few men alive, and even few dead, who could in such a situation avoid bowing to the inevitable. Certainly I do not believe I am one of those men. Indeed I see nothing in the whole unhappy situation but for me to sit down immediately and write you a check for $500.

That was the end of the second page of my letter. I particularly wanted the first part of my letter to him to end at the bottom of a page. I had a feeling that the committee would be sitting around a table, and because of the difficult time they had had over the years with me, they would at least want to hear my letter of surrender read in full. And, when they came to that end of the first part, at the bottom of the page, and heard their chairman read that last line, I could see them all smiling and congratulating each other. I could even see in my mind's eye my old friend Larry pounding the table and saying, "There, I told you! I knew he was tough, but I knew we could get him. There's a way — there's always a way!"

Next I knew, however, they would have to turn the page. That was because I still had remaining my Page Three:

> Larry, you just had one terrible piece of luck. Do not please think it will ever happen again, and don't on any condition reassess your strategies. They are good strategies, in fact they are close to perfect. Larry, the bad luck is simply that you got me.
>
> Larry, I am not going to send you my check for $500 — in fact, I am not going to send you a check at all. I simply cannot. Bruce loved so many things about Harvard. He loved the friends he made. He loved where he lived, both in his Hall freshman year and in sophomore and ensuing years in the House. He loved luncheons at the club, afternoon sports, evenings walking on the Charles River, and looking for feminine company.
>
> But there was, Larry, just one thing Bruce did not like about Harvard. He did not like the books. He did not like the books or the studying. He knew how to stay off probation — that he needed three C's and a D — but, once when he received four C's, he was very angry. He felt he had obviously over-studied.
>
> Larry, I do not need to give you more examples. It

is unnecessary. For you to give a scholarship for such a man would be a blot on the escutcheon of Harvard forever. You and the committee would go down in Harvard history as the Committee of Sham and Shame. You would indeed have made a mockery of Harvard's own motto of "Veritas."

I realize that I have left you with a problem. You have $4,500 raised, and Harvard will not accept $4,500. What can you do? Larry, I have an idea. I note there are nine members of your committee. Forget the scholarship. Each one of you should take $500, get yourself a plane ticket, go to Las Vegas, and have yourself a hell of a weekend. Bruce would have loved that.

Sincerely, still your friend,
Clippie

If I do say so, for a long time I was not bothered by any more letters from our Class Committee. The class did, however, put on one memorable happening at the time of our Twenty-Fifth reunion. Harvard is very big on Twenty-Fifth reunions. For your Twenty-Fifth and Twenty-Fifth only, the entire class gets to go back with their families and spend time in the hallowed Halls and the Houses. As a member of the Twenty-Fifth you are even more important than the Oldest Living Graduate. Indeed, many people now feel that the whole Oldest Living Graduate competition is not what it was in the old days — that it is not, to be blunt about it, played the way it was meant to be played. Nowadays there are Oldest Living Graduate candidates who take practically no chances at all and hardly ever leave their room.

Fortunately such goings-on have never taken place in Twenty-Fifth reunions. The competition to give Harvard more money than any previous Twenty-Fifth class is fierce, but the game is played absolutely fairly and squarely.

Indeed the Twenty-Fifth is such a huge event that before our Twenty-Fifth reunion even started all the members of the class from New York, New Jersey, and Connecticut were invited to a dinner at the Harvard Club of New York. Here we would all be addressed by none other than the President of Harvard himself, Dr. Nathan Marsh Pusey.

Dr. Pusey did an extraordinary job in his talk. He told us all about the new Harvard we would shortly be seeing when we journeyed up to Cambridge for our reunion. And it was not an easy job, either. Many members of the class had, as in the good old days, entered their sons at birth to Harvard — and now even their daughters — and a large number of them had not gotten in. Clearly, Dr. Pusey's most difficult job was explaining to those parents of those children why they had not made it.

But, as I say, there was no question that Dr. Pusey was up to the task. He explained exactly what the new Harvard was. He explained the way, for example, Harvard scoured and scouted for new Harvardians all over the world. They would, for example, find one fellow in Tierra del Fuego, and maybe another in Madagascar, and possibly a third in Reykjavik, and on and on, until they had brought dozens and dozens more to Harvard to study. And Dr. Pusey went on to explain that these new students would not necessarily graduate as we had done — they would just stay on, and get M.A.'s and Ph.D.'s, and so on. But, he assured us, we would not be neglected, either. We would have the honor of supporting them — year after year. We actually would have the chance, at this reunion alone, Dr. Pusey went on, to give Harvard more money than any previous returning Twenty-Fifth class had ever given it.

Honestly, after that, we all felt terrible about the very idea of entering our own sons or daughters. All they could do was drag the place down.

It was almost over. Before it was, however, Dr. Pusey made one mistake — he asked for questions. But it was not really his fault. It was just one of those things that happened. What happened was that a classmate of ours, a man whom Dr. Pusey could not have known, rose to his feet at the back of the room.

Our classmate is a man who came over on the Mayflower, and frankly he has not done a great deal since. He has tried a lot of things, like selling stocks and bonds to his friends, or selling them insurance, or even automobiles, but what he really found he was best at was doing nothing. He is the kind of fellow who is very good at weekends but not very good in the middle of the week. He is, as I say, really a very nice fellow, but the plain fact is after seven o'clock in the evening he gets increasingly perilous. At lunchtime, at five o'clock, or even possibly six o'clock, Dr. Pusey could have asked for questions with him in the audience with no trouble at all. It would have been fine. But at nine o'clock it was far from fine.

Slowly our classmate rose to his feet and wove his way to a nearby microphone. Actually, for nine o'clock we thought he was doing very well, but of course we were used to him. "Dr. Pushy," he said, "I have a ques-shun. Whaddya gonna do about a fellow who came over on the Mayflower, and his shun went to Harvard, and his shun went to Harvard, and his shun went to Harvard . . ." Obviously our classmate was going to keep on through all the eleven generations his family had indeed been to Harvard. We did not want to stop him. All of us already knew if you tried to stop him you only got into more trouble. Slowly he intoned on, ". . . and his shun went to Harvard, and his shun went to Harvard, and his shun went to Harvard . . ." And then, at last, he concluded, ". . . and his shun can't get into Harvard. Whaddya gonna do about that, Dr. Pushy?"

To Dr. Pusey's everlasting credit, the silence was mercifully brief. He rose to his feet. "I don't know what we're going to do about it," he said. "We can't send him back. The Mayflower doesn't run any more."

CHAPTER THREE

First Jobs

Polar Bear was not a party animal. Actually, I never had a party which he even remotely appeared to enjoy. And when I say even remotely, I mean just that — he was usually under the bed or the sofa or in a closet.

For one thing, he was severely lacking in small talk — surely a part and parcel essential for any party. I often described him as terrific at vowels, but terrible at consonants. His AEIOU's, for example, might waken a wake, but they were hardly even passable party fare. When toned down they made a fine hello, and I have always believed they would work well on a telephone answering machine, although I never had any luck in trying to teach Polar Bear how to do this. But the trouble was, for a party these AEIOU's of his always seemed to have to do with him only, and nobody and nothing else — hardly a party plus. As for his attempts at genuine MEOW's, these were almost totally lacking in being a party asset. Indeed, because of the lack of an "M" in his vocabulary, they were hardly distinguishable from one of his gentler AEIOU's.

All in all, when there was a party invariably the cat seemed, if Polar Bear would forgive the phrase, to have gotten his tongue. He simply did not have that prime of all party essentials — the gift of gab. He did not either open a conversation, keep a conversation going, or even, for that matter, contribute to its graceful conclusion.

There was something else that Polar Bear lacked when it came to parties. Years ago my grandmother used to say that the trouble with the younger generation was that they had never been taught not to "look out loud." Her generation, she maintained, was always taught that, and was brought up on the idea that if they could not smile and say something pleasant, they could at least smile and think something pleasant and above all, as she put it, not "look out loud."

Frankly, Polar Bear was awful about not looking out loud. And it was not that I did not try to teach him not to do it, either. I did — but it's not an easy thing to teach — especially when he is looking out loud at you all the time and you are the one doing the teaching. And, make no mistake, when he looked out loud, it was not just a minor look out loud, it was a major, and where a party was concerned it was invariably critical. In fact, he almost invariably made a whole critical analysis of both the people, and what they are doing, and, worst of all, a totally unfavorable opinion of why they were there in the first place.

I really believe Polar Bear enjoyed working on his critiques long before the party began. Somehow he always seemed to know days ahead when there was going to be a party. Whether this was because of the extra goings-on in the apartment, the extra cleaning, the scurrying around in the pantry or the kitchen, or whatever, he somehow always knew. And, from that very moment that he knew, he had the very opposite of the good party-giver's desire to make a party go. He wanted to make the party stop.

He had, it is true, his side. For many years he made no secret of the fact that he had already met everyone he wanted to meet, and indeed, as a matter of another fact, he would like to subtract a by no means small number of those. In latter years, as I have pointed out, he was somewhat better, but whether this was just because his attitude years ago could hardly have been worse, or whether I had just gotten more used to it, or whether I was clutching at straws, I really did not know.

But one thing I did know — I never allowed this antisocial side of him to stop me from enjoying having my friends over — and this even though, in the early days at least, I paid dearly for it. When, for example, a large party was about to begin and the cook was about to begin cooking, and the caterer was about to begin catering, Polar Bear would immediately sink down and skulk and mope around as if he were an armadillo on his last legs. And when I would go to him to try to cheer him up it was no use. He gave me, in spades, that look my grandmother so disliked, and to say it was not out loud is an understatement. It was in fact out very loud — all the way from his half-shut eyes to his droopy tail. He made even his whiskers look bedraggled, and as for his nose, it was unmistakably sniffing around as if to smell something about to expire. All in all, every inch of him proceeded to give me warning that if I proceeded on with my idea of the party I might very well find him not only at death's door in the morning but very possibly actually through the door.

This is not to say that in my by no means large New York apartment I was constantly throwing parties. I would just try, as other people do, to reciprocate, and when friends had you over for cocktails, a lunch, a dinner, or whatever, you naturally wanted to do your best to return the favor. Actually I gave only one large party a year, which I have come to call my Marathon Party. I hasten to state that this was not a marathon party in the sense of size, even if it was somewhat in the sense of length. Actually the party begins when anybody wants to come. The New York Marathon begins on television in the late morning, and you see about twenty-five thousand or more runners starting out, jammed along the Verrazano Bridge. It then goes on until finishing time which, for the winners, is shortly after two o'clock, but for the stragglers goes on until late in the afternoon. Actually the finish is only a hundred yards or so from my apartment, and the runners having gone once around Central Park come down Central Park South and then finish around the corner. Since my apartment has an eighth-floor balcony, it is really a terrific place to see the race and, since Polar Bear had his own wired-in balcony just beside the main balcony he too could watch it all, were he in a party mood. Suffice it to say that I have had at least eight marathon parties and I cannot remember a single one of them for which he was in what I would call a party mood.

This was particularly galling to me because Polar Bear could well go out on his own balcony via the bedroom window and watch the marathon and not be bothered by a single guest who could not reach him there. The main balcony, you see, was reached by the door, and Polar Bear's was entirely wired as a safety measure from (1) his jumping off it, and (2) for pigeons. It was really a masterful piece of design by me which to my mind was not nearly as appreciated by him as it should have been — particularly since it was really only one day a year he had a constant stream of people standing out there beside him. At such a time it seemed to me he never even stopped to think that the whole rest of the year he could go out on his side of the balcony and sit and think in solitary satisfaction.

As usual my party was a mixture of old men friends and new girlfriends. No, I am joking of course. But it was a mixture of old and new friends — not to mention friends of friends. In other words, friends who brought friends. This is a typical New York habit — despite the fact that New Yorkers probably have on average fewer house guests, whom they would at least have an excuse to bring, than any other city in the country. In other words, they bring to you guests they would not think of asking to stay with them.

For this Marathon Party I made a special effort to include many people Polar Bear knew particularly well. And I also included several people who had never been to my Marathon Party before and yet were people I particularly wanted Polar Bear, if he would deign to do so, to meet.

Not the least among these were Mr. and Mrs. Primo Acernese, from Allentown, Pennsylvania. I had met Mr. Acernese under perhaps as unusual circumstances as I can ever remember meeting anybody. It took place in the early morning at Hegins, Pennsylvania, the site of the country's most infamous annual live pigeon shoot. Because of this particular shoot's country-wide publicity and egregious cruelty, the Fund for Animals had decided both to try to get as many animal activists as possible to the scene, and also to hold there the day before our annual national conference, one normally held in a more civilized location.

One thing was certain about the shoot. Although there would be hundreds and hundreds of animal activists from all over the country bravely opposing it, there would be thousands and thousands of local yokels violently supporting it. As for the thousands of trapped pigeons, most of them were pen-raised and, feeble from lack of food and water — many having never flown before — they were so disoriented that when suddenly released from the traps in front of the line of shotgunners they often did not fly at all, but just unsteadily walked out of thc traps. They were then blasted on the ground, literally only a few feet from the feet of the gunners. Around the shooters were the so-called "trapper boys." These are local kids who put the pigeons into the traps and release them by pulling the string attached to the trap when the gunners say "Pull." They are also supposed, in between the shooting, to break the necks of the wounded pigeons, but there are so many of these wounded that the boys often do not bother to break their necks but simply throw them into trash cans hidden from the crowd behind wooden screens. The lucky birds, in other words, have their necks wrung. The unlucky ones either bleed to death or otherwise die slowly and painfully.

Even the attempt to stop such sadism — for which some 250 shooters pay as much as $450 — would not, we knew, be easy particularly when it would all take place in one of the cruelest states in America. Indeed, of the Pennsylvania Game Department I had said many times that they would shoot their mother if she was on four legs. I had not yet seen the pigeon shoot when I had said that but after seeing it I felt that I was perhaps doing a disservice in not counting the shooting of mothers who had only two legs. Actually the area, we learned, would be patrolled by, besides the Pennsylvania Game Department, 170 State Police.

About one o'clock the night before, when Wayne Pacelle, our National Director, and I were discussing last-minute plans, my telephone rang. It was a longtime friend of mine named Syndee Brinkman, former head of the National Alliance for Animals, who wanted to come over right away. She had, she said, a special request. When Syndee arrived she told me that she had heard that some of the shooters were, as she put it, "out to get me," and would I be willing to get myself a bodyguard? She said she already had the man and that he was home, waiting for a phone call.

I should point out I told her that I had never had a bodyguard before and that I was neither a gangster nor a President and, furthermore, I did not believe in guns. Syndee is not a woman who takes no for an answer and, unknowingly, I had given to her a foothold. "This one I am thinking of," she told me, "doesn't use a gun. He runs a martial arts school and he's a God knows what degree black belt Cheonkido. That's beyond Taikwondo," she added.

I had never heard of Cheonkido or Taikwondo but I must admit I was intrigued. I was once a boxer, but now with arthritis and some other problems I had no desire to be mugged by the kind of person who would torture a pigeon. Her idea, I admitted, might be an interesting way to handle the thing. Meanwhile Wayne, an old friend of Syndee's, checked in firmly on her side. He asked Syndee to demonstrate what her man could do — whereupon Syndee said that she herself had held a board over her head, full stretch, and that from a standing start her man jumped up, hit the board with both feet, and broke it.

I told her I hoped she knew I did not want him to kill anybody, but I was too late. Syndee was already on the phone, telling Mr. Primo Acernese to meet us at the pigeon shoot. She then handed the phone to me. I expected at the least gruffness, but I soon realized the man whom I was talking to was a soft-spoken gentleman.

The next morning when I met him I was surprised again. I expected a large, powerful fellow with bulging muscles. Primo was small — about five foot six — slight, and weighed less than 150 pounds. He seemed to have no bulging muscles at all. Very soon I was to notice, however, that wherever you touched him he was hard as a rock. Actually the most suspicious thing I could see about him was that he was wearing dark glasses.

"You tell me where you want to go," he said quietly, "and I'll tell you whether you can go there or not." Suddenly I felt like a prisoner, or at least someone guarded by the Secret Service. I told him I wanted to see everything, and I wanted to start by going over to the shooting line. Without a word he went ahead in that direction and I followed him. "But when I want you to go somewhere else," he said over his shoulder, "you go immediately."

We did not have long to wait. As we approached the shooting line I noticed three men moving in my direction. "There's the guy," one of them said, "Let's get him right now." Primo had stopped and so did I. As the three men approached, however, Primo did not seem to be doing anything but watching them. Then he turned to me. "Over there," he said quietly, "in front of that wall." I looked where he wanted me to go. "Now," he said, this time less quietly. Why there, I wondered. This time I did not get any answer, but just a shove toward the wall. I later learned that Primo did not mind how many people were in front of me, but he did not want anyone behind me.

The approaching trio were now almost on top of us. I noticed how much larger they were than Primo. Suddenly Primo moved forward just a step. "Stop," he said quietly. Equally suddenly the men stopped in their tracks. I could not hear what else Primo said to them, but it was my impression that he had not said anything. They had just decided, on closer inspection, that there was something about him that made it clear to them that for them to do anything more was not going to be either profitable or healthy.

All day it was like that — anyone who approached who was not a friend never came beyond where Primo wanted them. Meanwhile, the appalling shoot went on. Despite the efforts of the animal people, who were kept from the shooters by the police, thousands of birds were shot. Nonetheless, the brave activists who broke through the lines were successful in rescuing some 500 birds — after which, of course, they were carried off to jail in buses. On the last bus of the day, clearly visible on the roof of the bus was one of the pigeons.

Once during the day I asked Primo if he wanted a Coke. "I never drink when I'm working," he said. Finally at the end of the day when I demanded he take some money for his work he shook his head. I started to press it on him, completely forgetting myself and by now totally confident. I told him kindly to remember that I was bigger than he was. For the first time all day he smiled.

Polar Bear never thought very much of a party which started before lunch. But since this one did, he at least expected it to end at a reasonable hour. This, however, was obviously not happening either. He then did something quite unusual for him — he made the best of it. He did this by responding to Primo and his wife, Carol, even though they were both obviously dog people. And if there was one thing Polar Bear well knew it was that there was a large difference between dog people and cat people. But he also seemed to know right away that although Primo and Carol might have had dogs, they were not just dog people — they were cat people, too, and in fact they were animal people in general. A good example of this, as Carol told us, was that both their dogs were strays — a huge Doberman type named Bill, and a tiny little guy named Fido of, she said, extremely uncertain origin. Who was the boss? we all wanted to know. "Fido, naturally," said Primo firmly. We also all wanted to know if Carol worried when Primo was either out guarding or competing with advanced students. Carol shook her head. "No," she said, "because he's so good at it." What if, we insisted, he was against someone as good as he was? "He wouldn't be," she said quietly, "and if it turned out to be that way, Primo would figure out what to do."

The next person who had never been to my Marathon Party before and whom I especially wanted Polar Bear to meet was a man named William Zinsser — with whom I went all the way back to my college days. I had, as a sophomore, applied at the Harvard employment office for a summer job as a tutor-companion. These jobs still exist today, but they have become more of a female pursuit — basically governessing young children. In my day the pursuit was primarily male. The boys we were to look after were older — Bill, for example, was fourteen — and despite the description "tutor-companion," few of these jobs involved any tutorial work. Instead, the operating word was "companion." You looked after your charge to the extent that you drove him around, saw that he got in on time if he was out at night, and during the day you played outdoor sports with him — tennis, golf, sailing, etc. — as well as, in the evening, a wide variety of indoor games. As for pay, I was to get a hundred dollars a month and a fifty-dollar bonus if I did a good job. I was not going to get rich on my first job, but I did have free board and lodging and no expenses, and for those days it was considered good pay and the jobs were extremely desirable.

When Bill and his wife, Caroline, came in and were introduced all around, particularly to Polar Bear, I suddenly realized looking at Bill that to me he was still fourteen and I was about eighteen or whatever I was then.

There is something about age differences so pronounced in those days they seem to stay that way when you suddenly go back to them. Actually a four-year spread, when you are both in your fifties or sixties, is meaningless, but when you are fourteen and eighteen it is a huge differential. I even had difficulty thinking of him as the distinguished author he had become. Indeed, after many years as a writer and editor on the old *New York Herald Tribune* and as a highly successful teacher of writing at Yale, he had produced one of the all-time classics about writing, called *On Writing Well*. But none of that would have been possible, I told everybody firmly, had I not rescued him from the shellac business where, when I first knew him, he seemed to be headed because his father was the owner of a shellac company.

This was not exactly true, of course. My stories in such circumstances, when I have a large audience, rarely are. Actually, Bill could not understand the first thing about chemistry, and he would have been a menace in the shellac business. It was his mother who had the literary inclinations that were later translated into his career. Nonetheless, I not only took credit for it all, I went on to describe, in glowing terms, my first night on my first job. It was, to say the least, a nightmare of an experience.

I should explain that Bill and I were in a third-floor room. Later, when his mother and father as well as his two older sisters went abroad, we would have separate rooms. In any case, like most college-aged students, I was sleeping incredibly soundly when all of a sudden, still three-quarters asleep, I felt a toe being tickled. Promptly I pulled my leg up under me. Somehow, though, the toe was found and the tickling continued. By now only half asleep, I realized that someone was doing this tickling, and I was focused enough to figure out that if this was Bill, I would have to take stern and immediate steps to discourage such behavior. And stern steps were just what I did take. Without further ado I pulled both my legs still further up under me and with both feet lashed out at the intruder.

Immediately I heard first a deep and ominous groan and, then, a tremendous crash. At this I woke up completely and to my horror saw Bill's father sitting on the floor, clutching his stomach — which of course I had effectively karated. For a moment neither of us spoke. I had at least started mumbling apologies, but even these were interrupted by his gruff explanation. "The telephone is for you," he said. "Whoever it is says it's very important. You'll have to come downstairs. The telephone is in our room."

As Mr. Zinsser led the way down the narrow stairs I again made apologies which now, after looking at my watch and seeing that it was exactly 2:30 A.M., I put into high gear. But the worst was yet to come. The telephone turned out to be right by Mr. and Mrs. Zinsser's bed. Indeed, it was right by Mrs. Zinsser's head. "Hello," she said politely, holding the phone up toward me. Once more I apologized and seized the instrument.

"Clippie!" a voice shouted, a voice which to my horror came from someone at least three sheets to the wind. I tried to hold the phone as high as possible — with one hand over the earpiece to cover the sound of his voice — but I did not believe I was totally handling this situation. I could only hope that the message from an old Milton classmate of mine, R. Bennett Forbes, Jr., was not getting through either to Mrs. Zinsser or to her husband, who had retired on the other side of the bed.

What this message was, in a word, was that Bennett was at a debutante dance at the Seawanhaka-Corinthian Yacht Club in Oyster Bay and he had learned, through my brother, who was teaching sailing there for the summer, that I had a job at the Zinssers' house in nearby Great Neck. The party was absolutely terrific according to Bennett, a connoisseur of such affairs.

Finally his voice stopped. In as even and serious voice as I could muster, and one that, considering my situation, would have done credit to learning of a death in the family, I stated firmly, entirely for the Zinssers' benefit, that then there was, Ben old boy, nothing I could do about it until the morning, was there?

This was of course a major mistake because it immediately sent Bennett off into a paroxysm of rage. "No, no, no!" he shouted while I earnestly pushed the telephone towards the ceiling. "Not in the morning — now! Hell, it's not even three o'clock!"

At this point I gave up. Don't worry, I repeated in the same voice in which I had earlier attempted to do the job, I'll call you first thing in the morning. With that, firmly, I hung up. I had taken a terrible chance that he would call back, but for the first time in the whole nightmarish experience I got a break and he did not. Before leaving I told the Zinssers that I was terribly sorry about the emergency — a word I had some difficulty with but which I nonetheless gamely tried — and said good night.

The next morning there was a postscript to the episode. At breakfast neither Mr. nor Mrs. Zinsser made any mention of the telephone call that night to the rest of the family.

But when we were all assembled at the dining room table, Mrs. Zinsser, who liked to give out the mail at breakfast and who made some ceremony of it — for which in this case I could hardly blame her — slowly passed a postcard addressed to me which at least two of the elder Zinsser sisters, as they took it on the way to me, could hardly avoid seeing. "This," Mrs. Zinsser said, "seems to be for you." It was indeed. "Mr. Cleveland Amory," the address said, "C/o Mr. And Mrs. William Zinsser, Great Neck, Hot Dog, Long Island."

It was of course from Bruce — and it somehow made a fitting end to my first twenty-four hours of trying to make my living in a cold, cruel world. Actually the job itself, as it developed, had both bad and good points. The first bad point was that when Mr. and Mrs. Zinsser and the two elder sisters went abroad, Bill and I and another sister did not stay in their house but went to Bill's grandmother's house. The second bad thing was that the grandmother had lived alone in that house, albeit with several servants, for a quarter of a century. Indeed, she was as set in her ways as any older woman I have ever known — and I have known my share. The third bad point was that the aforesaid servants of said grandmother were almost as set in their ways as their mistress and, besides, they took the view that whatever a tutor-companion was, it did not belong upstairs or at the family dining room table. It belonged below stairs with them, and should eat there as well. As for making my bed, they just did not do it. I made my own bed the entire summer.

The good point of the job was that however tough the grandmother and the servants made life for me, Bill and his sister June made up for it. If their grandmother criticized me for anything — and she did a great deal — they both took my side immediately. Indeed, sometimes they went well beyond the bounds of taking my side. I remember one day when their grandmother had lost her glasses. First at the table she asked June where her glasses were. June said she did not know. The grandmother next turned to Bill. When Bill did not know either, it was my turn. "All right, Mr. Amory," she said, as if I was already identified and convicted as the perpetrator, "will you please give me my glasses?" This was too much for Bill. "Oh, Grandma," he said, "I suppose every time Mr. Amory loses his baseball he says, 'All right, Mrs. Zinsser, give me my baseball.' "

The use of the word "baseball" — before tennis ball or any other kind of ball — was natural. Bill and I enjoyed sailing and tennis and golf and swimming, but our first love was baseball. Almost every evening we went out and had a catch or hit flies or grounders to each other, and indeed it was not long before we came naturally to a joint invention of what, if I do say so, was the very best two-man baseball game ever invented.

I know there have been many other two-man baseball games invented over the years by men and boys — and even nowadays I suppose the occasional one by girls — but I repeat, ours was the best. To begin with, we not only invented it on a tennis court, we played it on a tennis court. We did play our share of tennis — I was on the tennis team at school, and part of my job was teaching Bill tennis — which was not difficult because he was a very good player. But at baseball he was even better, and so, frankly, was our game.

In the back of the court, attached to the fencing, we

placed a rectangular board which defined the strike zone. Directly in front of it we placed a home plate. We then marked a pitching rubber just inside the net. When the pitcher hit the wood it was a strike — the wire, a ball. A line drive over the net, but not far enough to hit against the fencing at the other side of the court, was a single. A line drive which hit the far back fencing was a double. If it hit either the far left or the far right fencing, it was a triple. If it went entirely out of the court it was a home run.

There were several other refinements we made which I know all you fans are anxious to hear. A grounder, for example, hit toward the pitcher and fielded by him had to be either thrown over a bag we placed at first base or if picked up, the pitcher could run over and tag the runner before he got to the bag. If the pitcher caught a line drive and there was someone on base, it was a double play.

Of course I have given you just the bare outline of the game we invented. And remember we did not play just against ourselves — we played a whole team against another whole team. We knew the names of all the players on all the major league teams by heart, and whether they were right-handed batters or left-handed batters. If you had a left-handed batter you had to bat left-handed. The only exception we made was if you had a left-handed pitcher you did not have to pitch lefty. We tried it over and over, but we just could not get the damned ball over the plate well enough.

When it came to us being individually a whole team, we did have some arguments. Since Bill went to Deerfield and was reasonably Massachusetts he wanted to be the Red Sox and so, of course, did I. And we both of course detested the Yankees. What we did when we had to have them in a Series against each other was to ration them in reverse. In other words, if you had had them not long before, you did not have to have them. And we were very tough on the other guy for not trying when he had the Yankees. We had some terrible rows about that.

Sundays we always played doubleheaders. I will never forget one we had when I played the Red Sox against Bill's Detroit Tigers. Bill had Schoolboy Rowe and Tommy Bridges as pitchers, Mickey Cochrane as catcher, an infield of Hank Greenberg, Charlie Gehringer, Billy Rogell, and Marv Owen, and an outfield of Goose Goslin, Pete Fox, and Al Simmons. Meanwhile I met him with Wes Farrell and Lefty Grove pitching, Rick Farrell catching, an infield of Jimmy Foxx, Eric McNair, Joe Cronin, and Pinky Higgins, and an outfield of Heinie Manush, Doc Cramer, and Mel Almada. It was dark when we finished and everybody up at the house was yelling, but we kept on anyway and would have finished both games if we had not lost the last ball we had.

Of course our games took a toll of the tennis court. Finally, when the battering we gave the fencing behind home plate was too much we prevailed upon the gardener to fix it after carefully explaining to him what an honor it was to be the head of a grounds crew for a Sunday doubleheader. We also explained to him how important it was for him always to bring his dog, because his dog was really terrific at going after home runs.

I think one of the reasons Bill was so intrigued with Polar Bear was that in his classic book on writing, he devoted in his chapter on humor a large section on *archy and mehitabel,* by Don Marquis. "No formal essay, for instance," he wrote, "could more thoroughly deflate all the aging actors who bemoan the current state of the theater than Marquis does in 'the old trouper,' a long poem in which Archy describes Mehitabel's meeting with an old theater cat named Tom:

i come of a long line
of theatre cats
my grandfather
was with forrest
he had it he was a real trouper . . .
once he lost his beard
and my grandfather
dropped from the
fly gallery and landed
under his chin
and played his beard
for the rest of the act
you don t see any theatre
cats that could do that
nowadays
they haven t got it they
haven t got it
here . . .

Intrigued as Bill was with Tom, he had to admit that Polar Bear was more of a Mehitabel. Polar Bear, no anti-feminist, took this sexual transformation with, I thought, extremely good grace. As for myself, I still had another story to tell my guests. What happened was that many years later, looking back at being a tutor-companion as such a curious but interesting job, I ended up deciding to base a television series around the idea, or at least this is the way I thought of it in retrospect. Actually what happened was that I had a meeting with Douglas Cramer, the then director of TV programming for the ABC Television network. Mr. Cramer asked me if I had an idea for a television show. I told him I did. He wanted to know what it was. I said what it was, was to have a show called "Saturday Review," a real magazine of the air, one which would handle the arts, movies, theater, books, even television itself. Mr. Cramer said he had an idea, too — it was to have a show based on my writings in the field of Society.

So we compromised. We came up with an idea based on my writings in the field of Society. Actually, this was where my second idea, the story of the tutor-companion, came in. And as the idea took shape it was very exciting. Soon I had written the introduction for a treatment of the show, as follows:

> Once upon a time, I wrote — such as the TV season of 1965–1966 — there was a lovable old millionaire from Oklahoma named O.K. Crackerby, a man with a fortune in, in more ways than one, natural gas. He is a widower with three children (an older girl and two younger boys), a man who has come East to ply the Eastern resort circuit, since he promised his "missus," before she passed on, that some day he would stop just making money and do right by the kids. To do this, to make little gentlemen out of the little monsters, and out of the girl a "debbytant," he has acquired the services of something he has learned the Eastern resort families have — a "tutor-companion." The latter would be the star —

the man whose job it would be to teach the kids there is something more in the world than making money. He would teach them manners, how to play sports and, perhaps most important, how to be a good sport. Above all, the show would not only have the conflict between *nouveau riche* and *ancien régime* — it would also have, as a dividend, an ever-changing lush background of this country's great resorts.

Mr. Cramer leaped at it all, especially at the tutor-companion idea — and particularly the name I had chosen for the young man, St. John Quincy, pronounced "Sinjin Quinzy." In fact, everyone at ABC was so taken with the idea of a brand-new character in a job which nobody in Hollywood had ever heard of that they decided to forgo calling the whole show "O.K. Crackerby!" as I had — instead they decided to call it "My Man St. John."

In any case, soon the treatment was completed and the show went onward and upward to the final board meeting where the ultimate summit decisions are made. They are really thrilling, those final meetings. In a big room around a large table sit all the top network brass — Mr. Leonard Goldenson, the president in charge of all the other presidents, Mr. Thomas Moore, the president in charge of all the other presidents that Mr. Goldenson was not in charge of, and all the vice-presidents, too. Not to mention the vice-presidents themselves, men in charge of so many things it gave me a charge just thinking about it.

Then into this room, one by one, come the little people — the people with the new show ideas. Each one in those days was given just ten minutes to present his case for his show. My presentation — I ask my readers, could it have been otherwise? — was masterful. I grabbed them with my opening teaser, held onto them for dear life through my characters and projected storylines, and closed with a stirring epilogue that literally throttled them.

When it was all over, I already knew the verdict. A pilot would indeed be made — and with just network money, too. Mr. Leonard Goldenson even spoke to me directly. "Mr. Amory," he asked, "are you going to write this show for us?"

Here, if you can believe it, I made a mistake. I said no — that I did not think any one person could write the show every week. I said that I thought that at the very least it would have to be me and another guy.

The simplicity of it was devastating. All of those executives became, in that one moment, in the face of such childlike honesty, children themselves. And, for the first time in network summit meeting annals, I believe, they all smiled. Let us do the worrying, they promised. *They* would get the "other guy."

Today, being an older and wiser man, I realize that what I should have said was yes, I would write the show. If I had said that, those executives would promptly have crowded $5,000 or so into my pockets every week under the "writing budget" and then I, like any other gracious writer-in-chief, would have gone out and hired somebody at, say, $1.25 an hour, given him a few hours each week to do a script, and then I would have taken home, by my figuring, $4,997.50.

Ah, the pity of it. But, no matter. After the meeting I went outside the room and held a celebration — not only with Mr. Cramer, but also with Mr. Cramer's then assistant, Mr. Leonard Goldberg. We drank a toast to the success of "My Man St. John," and I of course made plans — to go abroad, buy myself a TV station, and get a new suit — all the things I had always wanted. Then very quietly Mr. Goldberg spoke. "Cleve," he said, "I'm just a poor boy from Brooklyn. But just between friends, what the hell is a 'two-door companion'?"

That's the way he said it — "two-door companion" — and I honestly think he thought it was some kind of automobile. He had been very busy, and he had not had time to read the outline or the treatment. But it was really touching. Here was a mere slip of a lad, but a network executive nonetheless, who had fought the good fight for the show — never failing, ever fighting — without even knowing what it was he was fighting for. That man would go far, I felt even then. And in truth he did. He went on, in fact, from show to show and is still doing it, year after year. As for the second "other guy" to write with me, it was not a long wait for only a few days later Mr. Cramer called me again. "What," he asked, "would you think of the idea of Abe Burrows?"

Mr. Burrows! I exclaimed. Mr. Burrows! The famous humorist and so-called Play Doctor of Broadway? The man who would go to Philadelphia or New Haven when a Broadway show was being tried out and in trouble and after one evening seeing it would fix it right up for Broadway? Naturally, I told him I thought it was a wonderful idea, but Mr. Cramer said, "Cleve, I want to warn you about something. If Mr. Burrows does decide to do it, it won't be quite all *your* show anymore."

He had emphasized the "your," but by now I had picked up the lingo. Let me do the worrying, Doug boy, I told him, you get Abe.

Meanwhile, just thinking of Abe Burrows as my other guy, I revised my plans. Never mind the trip abroad — I would go around the world. Never mind the TV station — I would buy *TV Guide*. And as for the new suit — well, I'd get the suit. I really needed it.

Mr. Burrows promptly wrote a first script using, I was glad to see, the same words I had used in my treatment of "My Man St. John," i.e., "He is not Hollywood's idea of a gentleman — he *is* a gentleman. He is a man who is very good at weekends, but not very good in the middle of the week." I was thrilled. And, not long after, Mr. Burrows himself called me. "Cleve," he said, "what do you think of the idea of Burl Ives to play Crackerby?" Mr. Ives! I exclaimed. Big Daddy himself! The great folksinger and humorist! I said I thought it was a wonderful idea. "But Cleve," Mr. Burrows continued, "I want to warn you about something. I don't know if we can get Ives, but even if we can it's going to mean giving up something. You see . . ." I cut him short. Let me do the worrying, Abe boy, I said, you get Burl.

To get Mr. Ives, however, it seemed we had to give up quite a bit — including, as it turned out, the show. For United Artists Television, who had Ives for a pilot about sailing the Caribbean, asked in return for their giving up Ives and their show, our show. Also Mr. Ives was not happy with the title of the show. He wanted the title of the show to be his. So in short order, "My Man St. John" became "O.K. Crackerby!" again.

Next came the fateful day when the pilot was actually being shot. I could hardly wait to get out to Hollywood to see it. I rushed to the Sam Goldwyn studios. The guard asked for my name. I gave it to him. He looked down a long list. "You're not on it," he said.

I smiled democratically. I know you have to be careful, I told him. I'm probably unlisted.

Finally when I did get in I learned the guard was not the only one who did not know I had anything to do with the show. Neither did anyone else. Eventually, though, I did get to meet somebody who introduced me to the executive producer, a man named Rod Amateau. He's a friend of Abe's, I was told. You see, it was explained to me, Abe won't actually be living with the show.

Mr. Amateau, it turned out, was evidently pretty busy, too. "O.K. Crackerby!" was just one of six shows he was apparently living with, including, I was sorry to learn, "My Mother, the Car." Nonetheless everyone was very excited about "O.K. Crackerby!" When it was tested by an audience rating system it tested the highest of all the year's new shows. No fewer than thirty-seven sponsors were lined up to sponsor it, and of the very first four to see it three bought it. To this day I often wonder what they saw.

But I put such thoughts behind me. The Number One New Show of the Season! Now even the trip around the world wasn't enough, not even *TV Guide*, not even my suit. Hang the expense — I'd get *two* suits.

I went to see the pilot in high spirits. With modest expectation I awaited my credit on the screen — that glorious line, "Created by Cleveland Amory." And there it was, all right — "Created by Abe Burrows and Cleveland Amory." Oh well, I thought magnanimously, Burrows did lend a hand, and anyway there would be other credits.

And sure enough there were — many of them, in fact. "Written by Abe Burrows," "Story Consultant, Abe Burrows," "Directed by Rod Amateau and Abe Burrows," and even "Theme by Rod Amateau and Abe Burrows."

Oh well, I thought, that's show business. And anyway, maybe now I was going to be so rich it would be imperative for me to remain anonymous. In any case, back in New York the new scripts began to roll in, by all sorts of writers. Evidently Mr. Burrows had gotten himself still another guy — and, in fact, another and another and another, as far as the eye could see. The only trouble was that, as these scripts rolled in and the shows appeared each week on the television, the one thing I could see was that any resemblance between them and the original idea of the show was purely coincidental.

The last one I remember before the show mercifully went off the air was evidently one of those scripts which Hollywood writers keep in their drawers — their desk drawers — to sell with appropriate name changes for any show. It told the story of a poor boy, the son of a man who owned a bake shop, who didn't seem to have any mother and who had therefore made up an animal, a griffin, to be his constant companion. The story also went on at some length into the story of the boy's schoolteacher and her relationship with his father.

At this point I left it, but at least for once in the "O.K. Crackerby!" experience I felt ahead of the game — they had written a show with an animal in it, even if it was a griffin.

If my first job had started poorly and had not, judging by "O.K. Crackerby!" on television, ended so hot either, my first real job, postschool, was a different story. And I had, at the Marathon Party, a friend whose family played the crucial part in my getting the job in the first place. Her name was Katharine Houghton, an actress and playwright, who was not only the niece of Katharine Hepburn, but had played her daughter in "Guess Who's Coming to Dinner," and was also the daughter of Ellsworth Grant, my closest friend, next to Bruce, at college. Indeed, he lived across from the Harvard house rooms Bruce and I occupied. Ellsworth, a bright and charming fellow and, like the Hepburns, from Hartford, had fallen in love with Katharine Hepburn's second sister, Marian. Meanwhile, in the course of meeting the rest of the Hartford Hepburn clan, as fate or propinquity would have it, I fell in love with the third sister, Peggy.

When Kathy Houghton arrived at the party I was still involved with the Zinssers, so Marian had the job of introducing Kathy around, and particularly to Polar Bear — to whom she took an immediate shine and, most extraordinarily, one which was equally immediately returned.

It was really amazing. Polar Bear had met three brand-new people at the party and he had batted three for three. He liked them all. I took immediate credit for this extraordinary occurrence, of course. What else could it be but the fact that I had chosen my guests so well.

Actually, in the case of Katharine, I really had no idea how crazy about animals she had always been. Indeed, I learned for the first time that she had had, as she put it, "cats and dogs and rabbits and birds and God knows what else, all of whom I liked more than people."

Polar Bear seemed to sense that Katharine was a real animal person. Although there were already far too many people for his taste in the apartment, and although the marathon was blaring over the television and the first runners were about to come by outside, despite all of this, all the noise and commotion inside and out, when Katharine went out on the balcony to watch the proceedings, to my amazement out on his balcony to watch beside her went Polar Bear. Even the helicopters flying overhead, over the runners, did not send him flying inside to his room and under the bed.

The arrival of Kathy Houghton like Bill Zinsser, sent my mind back many years. I had spent almost every college weekend either in the winter in Hartford or in the summer at Fenwick, near Saybrook, where all good Hepburns repaired. And, fascinating as I found Katharine and her sisters, I found equally fascinating their father and mother. Dr. Hepburn was a particularly forceful person to whom I loved to address questions just to hear his invariably memorable answers. One day, during a period in which Katharine was receiving very poor personal notices around the country and was in fact regarded as "Box Office Poison," I was reading one of the two Hartford papers in which there was a story about Katharine returning from Hollywood for a visit to Hartford. The article was written in such glowing terms it might well have been a society page story about Hartford's most prominent debutante. I spoke of this to Dr. Hepburn and then gently mentioned the contrast with the press Katharine was receiving around the country. Dr. Hepburn lowered the part of the paper he was reading and fixed his formidable face on me. "Young man," he asked, "do you know what kind of work I do?" No, sir, I replied respectfully, I do not. "I thought not," Dr. Hepburn continued, "so I shall tell you.

I am a surgeon, and I specialize in what is politely known as the 'old man's operation.' " Oh, I said, but Dr. Hepburn was not yet through. "I have operated," he continued firmly, "on half of the newspaper publishers in this city, and I confidently expect, in good time, to operate on the other half. Does that," he asked, pushing up his paper again, "answer your question?"

It did indeed. Playing golf with Dr. Hepburn on Sunday morning was also a memorable experience. There were the usual Sunday morning social conflicts between those who wanted to play golf on Sunday morning and those who wanted everybody to go to church, but the fact that in the little resort of Fenwick the little church, called St. Mary's by the Sea, was right smack in the middle of the fairway of the fourth hole added a whole new dimension to conflicts elsewhere in society. Almost every Sunday the church was bombarded at least once and sometimes several times a day and indeed more than once in the summer a window was broken. Finally the idea took root among the churchgoers to pass a rule that, at the very least, and particularly on the fourth hole, all golf should cease between 11 A.M. and noon. This was naturally infuriating to the golfers, and this new controversy was in full height on a day when Dr. Hepburn was to play. Immediately he became part of a legendary story. In any case, that morning as luck, or rather bad luck, would have it Dr. Hepburn, teeing off on the fourth hole, hit a fine drive which bounced directly toward the church. Since it was a warm day the back doors were open, and the ball on its third or fourth bounce went directly into the church and up the aisle. As the congregation rose part in wrath and part in amusement, Dr. Hepburn without a word strode into the church, located his ball, put down his little canvas golf bag, selected his putter, and with a long firm stroke putted his way back out the way he had come in.

Mrs. Hepburn was an equally memorable character. An early founding member and leader of women's suffrage, she was a lifelong feminist in a day when being such was rare enough so that two young men as conservatively brought up as Ellsworth and myself found her both fascinating and at the same time sometimes as terrifying as her husband. Mrs. Hepburn was also, in contrast to her conservative husband, extremely radical in her views toward social issues and politics — to the point where an extraordinary number of dinner table arguments would end with some guest being so upset that Mrs. Hepburn would have to clap her hands and simultaneously announce the end of that discussion, and the beginning of a game.

I remember the day when I told Mrs. Hepburn that I was president of the *Harvard Crimson*. Immediately she asked me what I was going to do after college. You did not win many conversations with Mrs. Hepburn. Just the same, I liked to try to tease her, and I told her that once you had been president of the *Harvard Crimson* in your senior year at Harvard there was very little, in after life, for you.

Nonetheless, I believe it was her prodding that had much to do with the fact that I did take steps regarding my future employment. What I did was to go to Little, Brown and Company on Beacon Street. I could also have gone to Houghton Mifflin Company. They are both what we in Boston call perfectly good Boston institutions. In other words, they are a little bit better. I went directly to the head man — in Boston we do not trifle with middlemen — I told him he was indeed fortunate, and that I was one of the great writers of our time, and I had come to start my career at Little, Brown and Company. The man gave me a curious look. Did I realize, he asked, I would have to read other people's manuscripts? I told him I had not had much time to do much reading outside of my own writing, but I would try to help him. Then he gave me another curious look. Was I not afraid, he asked, that Little, Brown would kill my creative ambition? I told him I guessed that was just a chance I would have to take. Finally the man had had enough. Young man, he said, there is no job for you at Little, Brown and Company. This was a blow — right there in the heart of Beacon Hill. I must have looked very crestfallen because for the first time a rather pitying look came into his eyes, and he said, "You know, one of our editors just went down to Philadelphia to join the staff of the *Saturday Evening Post.* They come out every week, you know. You could write every week for them."

I certainly was not going to take any haphazard suggestion from a man without the perspicacity to hire me. Nonetheless, I went home and decided to have a man-to-man discussion with my father. I brought up the suggestion about the *Saturday Evening Post.* My father considered the idea. Now, Philadelphia was not Boston — but then, what was? It was not New York — there was something to be said for it. Finally, I think what won him over was the fact that in those carefree, happy days the *Saturday Evening Post* printed on its cover "Founded A.D. 1728." It was the right century. Furthermore, after "Founded A.D. 1728" appeared the words "By Benj. Franklin." He was, after all, a Boston man even if he did take a rather extended trip to Philadelphia.

In short order I wrote a letter making an appointment to see the head man at the *Saturday Evening Post.* Before I heard from him, however, I went back to Mrs. Hepburn and told her of my experience with Little, Brown and Company. Mrs. Hepburn was very mad at Little, Brown and Company, but she was very excited about the *Saturday Evening Post.* "I have a friend there," she said, "Adelaide Neall. I'll write her about you."

I had forgotten all about this by the time I received a note from Wesley Winans Stout, editor of the *Saturday Evening Post,* in which he told me to come to the *Post* for an interview. When I arrived there I started out again that I was one of the great writers of our time — but Mr. Stout waved his hand. "Hm," he said, looking over my resume, "*Harvard Crimson.* You published a lot of humor, didn't you?" I could not make head or tail of this. Here was a man, the editor of the widest-read magazine in America, who simply did not know the difference between the *Harvard Crimson,* the undergraduate daily, and our hated mortal rival, the *Harvard Lampoon,* the undergraduate humor magazine. Obviously the man needed me. Actually, the *Harvard Crimson* had published very little humor — we took ourselves as seriously as it was possible to do and still survive in a changing world. But there was no time to quibble. "A lot of humor?" he asked again. I nodded vigorously. Enormous amount, I said. Just about every day.

In any case by the time the interview was over what I received was the job of Postscripts Editor. I was to be in charge of the short poem and prose pieces — the so-called

Postscripts — found on that particular page. I was also to be in charge of the cartoons on that page as well as the cartoons throughout the magazine.

For a young man just out of college to get such a job was almost incredible. All of the other editors — even if I was hardly then actually one of them — at the *Saturday Evening Post* had at least fifteen years' experience on a magazine or a newspaper. It was indeed so incredible that it was many weeks before I found out how it had happened. One thing was certain — it had practically nothing to do with either my resume, which in those days was rather longer than it is now, or my ridiculous line "one of the great writers of our time." What it did have to do with was three things. The first was that J. Bryan III, one of the editors and a distinguished man, had been doing postscripts for years and had become fed up with it, and that very morning before I arrived he had told the head editor as much. The second was, that as I mentioned, Mr. Stout had definitely confused the *Harvard Crimson* and the *Harvard Lampoon*, and thought at least he was getting a person with a lot of experience in humor. But the third and by far the most important reason was far more complicated. It concerned Mrs. Hepburn.

Mrs. Hepburn had indeed written her friend, Adelaide Neall, an editor at the *Saturday Evening Post* and a fellow Bryn Mawr alumna, about me. And though Adelaide Neall was an editor at the *Saturday Evening Post* her name as Adelaide W. Neall did not appear that way on the *Post* masthead. Although Ms. Neall was the only female editor at the *Post* in those days, it was felt that the appearance of even one female editor on the masthead might be disturbing to *Post* traditionalists and might even suggest a lessening of stature throughout the magazine. And so Ms. Neall's name invariably appeared, to the end of her life, as A. W. Neall.

When I thanked Mrs. Hepburn, and told her that story, her eyes flashed. "I knew they were conservative," she said, "but I never knew that." I knew what Mrs. Hepburn was thinking. I begged her not to write again, however, at least until I was firmly in harness. But I did want to know what she had said about me. "My letter was very short," she said. "I said, as I remember, 'Dear Adelaide, there is a man here who has taken a shine to Peg and the feeling seems to be reasonably reciprocal, and as for the rest of us, though we are not overboard on anybody his age, we are at least getting used to him. I understand he is going down to try to get a job at the *Saturday Evening Post.* I hope you help him. If you do not, I shall not allow your organ of privilege to enter this house again.' "

When Kathy Houghton came in from the balcony Polar Bear also came in. I thought about a story for which the Hepburns were responsible which involved considerable embarrassment for me. Actually, I had always felt Polar Bear enjoyed occasions when I was embarrassed. I think he did this because cats do not like to be embarrassed, and I had obviously been responsible for occasions which had been embarrassing for him.

In any case, the first of these stories concerned my being I believe as embarrassed as I ever remember being in New York. It came about at the time when I first came to New York and was actually for the first time being driven there in an automobile by none other than Katharine Hepburn herself. Just before she left me off where I was staying, at the Royalton Hotel, she asked me, since I was new to New York, if I knew many people. I told her not very many, whereupon she instructed me in a vague sort of way to call on her friend Tallulah Bankhead. "I'll call her about you," she said.

Of course I had not the slightest idea of taking her up on this. If there was a more formidable celebrity of that time in New York than Miss Hepburn it was certainly Miss Bankhead. Tallulah, as she was called by everybody, was a living legend not only for her talent and for her incredible voice but also for her temper as well as her temperament. All in all, she frightened even close friends, let alone total strangers.

Some days later, however, Katharine called me up and said I had not yet gone to see Tallulah. I was noncommittal. "You've got to do it," she said, "she's expecting you. Why don't you just drive up some Sunday lunchtime? Tallu loves people for Sunday lunch."

Now of course I had to go. Almost ill with nerves and worry I drove to Miss Bankhead's house in Bedford, New York, and arrived around one o'clock. The first piece of bad news was that there were dozens of cars parked in the driveway. The next was that even standing outside the door I could hear a bedlam of loud voices, raucous howls and gales of laughter. It took me literally minutes to get up the nerve even to press the bell. Even when I did I did it very timidly. Immediately, to my horror, the room full of voices I had just heard became absolutely silent. Finally the door opened, and the butler appeared. "Yes?" he said, somehow looking down on me although he was a full foot shorter. I am a friend of Katharine Hepburn's, I said earnestly. Miss Hepburn has, I believe, called Miss Bankhead about me.

The butler heaved a sigh as if he supposed that nowadays anything was possible and, after instructing me to wait, he left the door ajar and went back to the room. He obviously repeated what I had said because the next thing I heard was the unforgettably throaty sounds of Miss Bankhead's own voice. "Tell him," she shouted, "I'll be damned if I can see every damned one of Kate Hepburn's goddamned friends." At this there were roars of laughter which kept up all the time the butler was returning to me. "I'm sorry," he said, "but Miss Bankhead seems to be busy right now. Perhaps some other time."

I could scarcely believe my good fortune — I could get away. Immediately and gratefully I turned around to flee, but before the butler could shut the door there was one more terror in store for me. Once more Miss Bankhead's voice roared from the room. "Is he," she asked, "handsome?" I tried to move on out, but the butler caught up with me and once more took a survey. "Well," shouted Miss Bankhead, "what the hell are you doing? I asked you if he was handsome!"

At this I must have turned so bright red that even the butler was sorry for me, because as he moved away and back toward the room he said, rather pityingly, "Passably." I must have passed muster because this time he took me back inside.

Still beet red, I was marched around and introduced by Miss Bankhead herself. I never did enjoy that first visit very much, but in no time at all I either outgrew it or forgot it because Miss Bankhead and I became, if not fast friends — a dangerous phrase to use with her — at least good friends. Indeed, from that time on I had many memorable Sunday lunches with Miss Bankhead, as well as trips to the Polo Grounds to see her beloved New York Giants.

Also, although I did not marry Peggy Hepburn, I did through the years stay friends with the whole Hepburn family. My most recent meeting with Katharine was when her book, *Me,* came out. I went over to congratulate her on it, and in talking, as we often do, around each other rather than at each other — because there are usually so many others present — I asked her if it was not terribly sad for her that Peg had for some incredible reason chosen to marry a Bennington professor instead of me. Did she not realize, I teased, what her sister had given up? And if she could not realize it, why could she not think of Peg, and realize the wonderful life she could, as my wife, have had? Did she not ever think about it? "Not ever," Katharine replied, "and neither does Peg." Why, I demanded. "Because," Katharine said firmly, "you have no chacter." She made, in the New England way, only two syllables out of the word. I told her sternly I knew I was somewhat deficient in character, but I did not appreciate having one of the most prominent women in the world going around blabbing the fact. I paused meaningfully. And furthermore, I continued, I demanded to know there and then what evidence she had for her slanderous charge.

In response Ms. Hepburn asked me, for the record and in front of all those people, if by any chance I remembered one time late in the summer when Howard Hughes was visiting, and she and Howard were playing tennis every morning with Peg and me and golf every afternoon, how in between times Peg would often make me take a swim. And how, she added, on one particular occasion, when Mr. Hughes and she happened to be watching from the house with binoculars, they clearly saw Peg dive in and swim some fifty yards or so, and at the same time they also saw me do nothing but duck under the pier and then jump up and rub a towel around myself. I was clearly demonstrating, for their benefit, how invigorating it was. And, since I did not on that occasion so much as get a toe wet, I had no character.

It was my turn to take the stand. In the first place, I said, by spying on us and using binoculars, they were nothing but Peeping Toms and should not be believed. In the second place, Connecticut water in October was below freezing, and nobody but a damned Hepburn would even consider going in it.

Although I had received the job of Postscripts Editor, I still had not achieved my ambition — which was to write for the *Saturday Evening Post*. In many ways, how this came about was as memorable, at least to me, as was how I got the Postscripts Editor job.

The way it happened was that I had worked at the magazine no more than three days when a memorandum came down from the head editor, Mr. Stout, to all the editors. Somehow it had been put on my desk, too. "What would you think," the editor asked in this memorandum, "of an article on Groton School?" All the editors had written in large letters beside their initials, "NO." Now my initials were not on the memorandum. The secretarial work there had been slipshod. As a matter of fact, one of my jobs was to take the memoranda from my desk at one end of the editorial line back to Mr. Stout's desk at the other end of the line. They did not have an office boy.

Nonetheless, I seized the memorandum and wrote in large letters "YES," and beside this I wrote my initials. I then took the memorandum back. I had hardly returned to my desk when my buzzer sounded and Mr. Stout announced that he wished to see me. This time I was barely inside his door when he swung around in a great swivel chair. "Why," he said, "did you put yes on my suggestion for an article on Groton?" He pronounced it Growton. Groton, I corrected him, pronouncing it Grotten. He was obviously a man of limited range. He ignored, however, my correction. "I understand," he said, "there is a remarkable man up there named Dr. Peabody." He pronounced this Pea-body. Once again I corrected him. The name Peabody, I told him slowly, because it would obviously take him time to take it all in, is pronounced in Boston by saying the consonants as rapidly as possible and ignoring all vowels. It's Pbd, Pbd, I said, doing it a second time so that he would get the hang of it.

I then explained to him that Dr. Peabody had built Groton School on the British idea of the American idea of the British public or American private school. I also told him that Dr. Peabody was indeed, as he said, a remarkable man and that he was, though a man in his eighties, still exercising on the Groton campus at recess every morning — with dumbbells. The push-up kind, I quickly added, of course.

I also firmly emphasized how strict Groton was. I told him the story of a young Groton boy, who on being told he would have to see Dr. Peabody at the conclusion of the school day, was manfully being consoled by a classmate. Maybe, he said, it's just a death in the family.

In any case, after I had finished telling Mr. Stout about Groton School, he thought a moment and then spoke. "You know," he said, "I think we will have an article on —" he paused "— that school." This, I realized, was my opportunity. Mr. Stout, I said, I would like to have a chance to do the text of that article. Once more he thought a moment, and then looked up again. "You know," he said, "it might be a rather amusing thing to send a Groton boy back on that article."

This I could not let pass. Mr. Stout, I said, I did not go to Groton. I went to Milton Academy. What I told you about Groton School was common knowledge. Milton Academy was founded in 1797 — we regard Groton as a rather new school. I started telling Mr. Stout all about Milton Academy, but he held up his hand. I had already found, dealing with people outside Boston, that they cannot take too much at any one time. Regular doses, regularly repeated, at regular intervals was far better — otherwise they could become ill.

Even if I did not get to tell Mr. Stout about Milton Academy I did get the chance to do the article on Groton, and the article came out, too — with my name on it, and with color pictures.

It was my very first published work, a landmark in my life. And not a one of you out there remember it, do you? It is just one of the many crosses I have had to bear.

The reason was simple. They had, at the *Saturday Evening Post,* a man whom they called Title Editor. He was the man responsible for putting the titles on the articles after the writers were finished with them. Remember, I had not been there long. It was a large staff, and I had not been able to educate them all. That man would have taken time — he was a man from New Jersey.

In any case the Groton article, my first published work, a landmark, as I say, in my life, appeared in the *Saturday Evening Post* under the title "Goodbye, Mr. Peebs."

After the Groton article I moved to Arizona — the northern part, of course. My father always said that nothing good ever came out of a warm climate.

CHAPTER FOUR

My Last Duchess and 4,000 Other Celebrities

There were many times in my early writing career in which I believe Polar Bear, who had not then of course been born, could have been most useful — if for no other reason than to keep me from getting involved in undertakings which would have far better not been undertaken by anyone at all, even including an undertaker. I do not mean by this that Polar Bear could not always have made me cease and desist from some project which from the beginning held little prospect of success or, from his point of view, was not part of a joint operation which involved, whether successful or not, at least togetherness.

But, given plenty of time, he could, make no mistake, have done so. Indeed, in his devious little way, he could very rapidly concoct some plan which would make what I had wanted to do, and what he did not want me to do, impossible.

In such endeavors not only did he not play by the rules, he was also manifestly unfair. If, for one example, what I wanted to do involved leaving him for some time — which he could tell from suitcases, tickets, etc. — he would immediately feign a desperate and obviously life-threatening illness — one from which, the moment I had cancelled all plans, he could equally immediately feign a complete and miraculous recovery. If, for another example, I had undertaken something which he thought might involve an intimate association with someone who to him was an unseemly and entirely inappropriate other human — such as someone coming for what seemed to him an interminably long visit — he would not even bother with feigning illness, he would simply disappear. At this, it goes without saying, I would immediately be sure he had somehow gotten out the door and I would not only have the job of looking for him outside the apartment, I would also have the job of looking for him inside. And it was amazing how many places to hide he could find in a small apartment. When I eventually did find him in one of those hiding places in the apartment — he never went outside — he would have made his point and, as far as he was concerned, the longer it took the better.

Why then did I undertake a project — be it anything

from a change of career to a human visitor of which he so disapproved? I can only plead that writing is lonely work — and it was particularly so for me in the days before Polar Bear. It was also particularly then not much, if indeed any, fun. The best you can say for writing is that, in retrospect, it can be some fun when someone who has read something you have written has something nice to say about it. But even in this case, remember it doesn't come until later, and even then you still remember the pain of what you went through to begin with before there was any fun. Altogether, I believe Dr. Johnson put it best. "Nobody," he said, "but a blockhead ever wrote except for money" — to which I have always thought he should have added, "or to meet a deadline." I have also thought, however, that there is something about that word "deadline" that to me symbolizes the whole trouble with writing.

Not to put too fine a point, as the English say, upon my point, since writing is the way it is, when you are a writer almost anything except writing seems a far more interesting thing to be doing. Cleaning up the house, sharpening pencils, telephoning, rearranging books, even reading something you have read quite recently — these all seem infinitely superior occupations compared with the job of actually putting your own words on paper. And when someone promises you some excitement — a luncheon, even with someone you do not care that much about, a visit with someone who, for the life of you, you cannot remember where or when you met, or even another job which, although it may demand some writing, at least offers besides the writing a new and possibly amusing change of scenery and people — the chances are a writer will fall for such an opportunity every time. Certainly in one particular example of this I fell for it hook, line and sinker — something which, in another era with Polar Bear on guard, would never have happened.

It all began in the form of a hand-delivered letter to my apartment from the New York Waldorf-Astoria Towers with a large "E" on the front of the envelope. In those days, if you received a hand-delivered letter from the New York Waldorf-Astoria Towers with a large "E" on the envelope, you were some pumpkins. You had gone about as far socially — up or perhaps down, depending on how you looked on it — as it was possible to go.

This was because, not to beat about the bush, what you had done was to receive a letter from no less a personage than His Royal Highness, the Duke of Windsor. In those days there may have been higher mucky-mucks socially, at least in one particular echelon of our Society, than the Duke and Duchess of Windsor, but there were not many and they did not last as long.

Although I had met the Duke and Duchess socially on several occasions, I should say that I did not receive the letter for this reason. What had brought me to their attention was a few paragraphs I had written about them staying at White Sulphur Springs in a book I called *The Last Resorts*. In any case, in the first part of his letter the Duke of Windsor called attention to what I had written about them, and in the second part he went on to invite me to the Waldorf-Astoria Towers for tea.

Of course the fact that the invitation was to tea took some of the social bloom off the rose. I was brought up in Boston by parents who were uncommonly strict about which meals to which it was proper to invite strangers, and which it was not. Dinner, for example, was out of the question — you did not know the people. Luncheon? Possibly, but luncheon could be tricky, too. Cocktails? Certainly not. Cocktails in the Boston of my day had never arrived at the kind of mass media they are today. Assuming people rarely invite anyone to breakfast, except for dubious reasons, that left only tea. Tea was the most democratic of all Boston institutions. You could ask almost anyone to tea — within reason, of course.

In any case, the die had been cast. It was tea to which the Duke of Windsor had invited me, and although I could have, had I wished, taken umbrage that it was not to be luncheon or dinner, tea is what it would be. If nothing else, I reasoned — always favorable to myself of course — after our meeting the Duke would no longer have such a gap in his social knowledge of Boston.

For better or worse, I accepted. And, when I arrived at the Royal Suite of the Waldorf-Astoria Towers at the appointed five o'clock hour, I found not only the Duke of Windsor but also the Duchess of Windsor and three Pug dogs. At this point I should say that I had, before this time, very little acquaintance with Pug dogs except at a distance. And, now that I think of it even today, I do not believe Polar Bear had ever met a Pug in his entire life. Indeed, as a matter of fact I am willing to bet that if he did, he kept it at a distance.

Nonetheless, I was then, and am still, partial to all kinds of animals, even ones I have not met, and I certainly had no wish, particularly early in my relationship with the Windsors, to take either the pro-Pug or anti-Pug side. I know very well there are people who like Pugs and that, conversely, there are Pugs who like people. I also have a theory and that is that people who like a certain kind of dog and have them all their life often grow, in later life, to look more and more like them — or else the kind of dog they like grows to look more and more like them, I am really not quite sure which. Originally I knew the Duke liked Cairn Terriers, and certainly if there was one animal he seemed to me to resemble it was a Cairn Terrier. On the other hand the Duchess liked Pugs, and there was something about the way she did her hair — parted in the middle — or indeed the whole shape of her face, particularly the jaw, that made her seem to resemble a Pug.

One thing I noticed at that very first meeting was that Pugs liked to sleep a lot. They were asleep when I got there, and they were asleep when I left. After I got to know the Windsors better I grew to understand this and I did not blame them. It was, however, a little disconcerting at first. It was also disconcerting in that there were three Pugs, and they all snored — and not in concert, either.

The Duke of Windsor began the conversation by saying that he had written his book and now it was, as he put it, "the Duchess' turn." But the Duchess would need, as he also put it, "some assistance" — to which he added they were looking for someone with humor since she was known to be so witty.

I believe at that even Polar Bear would have smelled a mouse — but for some reason I did not. The only excuse I have is that there was something about being with the Windsors that seemed to make people not think about what they had just heard — either because of the way the Windsors said it or because of the whole strange aura of royalty in which it occurred. As Henry Adams once said about his father, Charles Francis Adams, who was Ambassador to the Court of St. James', "He was one of the exceedingly small number of Americans who were indifferent to Dukes and Duchesses and to whom Queen Victoria was nothing more than a slightly inconvenient person."

I knew I could hardly measure up to Charles Francis Adams' standard, particularly since at this stage I had no idea what kind of assistance the Windsors were looking for. But at least I did not hesitate to explain that I had never been a ghost writer before and I did not particularly like the idea. I did add, though, that if the Duchess' book was to be an autobiography as told to me, that might be a different story.

The Duchess said nothing, which was an ominous sign, but the Duke seemed to indicate that would be all right. My only other question was to ask them if they had any idea what the book might be called. I still had in my mind that experience about "Goodbye Mr. Peebs" and I did not intend to go through that again. Just as I was thinking about this, the Duke said that so far for the Duchess' book they had not come up with a title. Did I have any suggestions? I told him I did not but that I would think about it, and would at least be happy to make a suggestion.

On that note we said goodbye — with the Pugs not only still sleeping but also not giving me the benefit of so much as a parting snore. In between that visit and the next, however, I spent a good deal of time thinking of a possible title for the Duchess of Windsor's memoirs as told to me, and one idea seemed promising — something to do with the controversy over the Duchess not having been given the title Her Royal Highness, which she craved — but instead being given merely the title Her Grace. Both she and the Duke were so upset about this that, though it happened early on after the Duke's abdication, they spent most of the rest of their lives complaining about it.

I had thought a good deal about this, and on my next visit to the Windsors I told them I thought I had a suggestion for a title for the Duchess' book. Both the Duke and the Duchess were very pleased about this, and I think even the Pugs would have been, too, but the butler had taken them out for a walk before they could hear it. The Duke was in fact so pleased that he could hardly wait to hear my suggestion. "What is it?" he asked, "what is it?"

Untitled, I said.

There was a dead silence. I was not surprised. I had already learned that the Windsors were in a very difficult position where humor was concerned. If no one laughed at something or no one told them something somebody said was a joke they would not venture so much as a smile — obviously for fear it was not a joke. In this case, although I hoped my title was humorous, it was not just a joke. Rather it was, I thought, an effective way to ward off, at the very beginning of her book, the criticism of the Duchess being so angry about not getting the title Her Royal Highness — and that, indeed, rather than being angry about it, she thought it was amusing.

Finally, though, the silence was over. "I think, Amory," the Duke said thoughtfully, "we'll have to get some more opinions on this thing."

One thing was certain. Between then and my next visit the Windsors obviously did not just go ask anybody for an opinion on my title — instead they went, at least from their point of view, to the very top opinionated people they knew. First of all, they asked the Duke's own solicitor, Sir George Allen. Next they asked none other than the British press czar, Lord Beaverbrook, whose paper had already contracted for the Duchess' memoirs. And, finally they even asked, as a kind of outside opinion, Lord Astor. But that was okay at that time — the thing that happened to Lord Astor later had not yet happened.

When I arrived to hear about the verdict on my title I knew right away that the news was not good. I had already learned in the time I had been with the Windsors that if there was good news you got it from the Duchess — if there was bad news you got it from the Duke. They had, it seemed, their marriage all worked out. And this time, because the Duchess was not even there — and neither for that matter were the Pugs — there was just the Duke, so I was certain it was bad news.

The Duke was very nice about it. "The trouble, Amory," he said, stammering slightly, "is that the H.R.H., H-her R-royal H-highness, which the D-duchess did not r-receive, is not a t-title, it's an ap-appellation." He paused. "Could you do anything with the word ap-appellation?" It was my turn for a long silence. I did think of *Unappellated,* but frankly the more I thought about it the more I was sure it would not fly.

Still not knowing what my masterpiece — or perhaps I should say *our* masterpiece — was to be called, I left for Paris to meet the Windsors in the early spring. I sailed on the *Queen Mary* and had a delightful crossing, since my tablemates in the Queen's Grill included the famous playwright George S. Kaufman and the consummate humorist actor Clifton Webb. Arriving in Paris, I stayed at the Traveller's Club until I could choose a hotel. I was extremely careful in my selection of this and finally, from a position across the way, chose not only the hotel I wanted, the Hotel Normandy, near the Louvre, but also the very room. I wanted one which I could see from my vantage point had a balcony halfway around the hotel. Even today when I think of the room I realize that this balcony, properly wired of course so that he could not have fallen off, would have been perfect for Polar Bear. In any case, keeping in mind exactly what floor the room was on, I marched into the lobby of the Normandy, found the concierge, and instructed him to follow me — my mind still firmly on the exact room. Getting off at the ninth floor, I took the concierge directly to the door and addressed him in my best Milton Academy French. *Voilà*, I said, putting my finger firmly on the door, *ma chambre*. But the concierge refused to open the door. *"C'est occupé,"* he said. I told him, in that case, to unoccupé it immediately. *"Ah, monsieur,"* he sighed, *"c'est impossible."*

Finally we struck a deal. As soon as the place was unoccupied he was to call me immediately. And, to his credit he did. I moved in on that very day and in short order put to work not only the concierge but also two bellmen and a maid. I really made an incredible number of changes — a standup desk, really a painter's easel, which I had put next to an opened window looking out on the balcony, a king-sized bed instead of the pipsqueak-sized creation they had there, a large stuffed chair, and no wire wastebaskets but real, masterful wastebaskets ready to take a wide variety of mistakes.

At last everything was to my satisfaction, and late that

afternoon all five of us — myself, the concierge, the maid, and the bellmen, sat down in total exhaustion. Once more I turned to my Milton Academy French to break the last impasse. *Ma chambre est parfait,* I said. *Mais il y a encore un peu de difficulté. "Ah non, monsieur,"* the concierge protested, in a voice as exhausted as he was. *"Ce n'est pas possible. Qu'est ce que sait?"* I looked at him sternly. *Qu'est ce que sait est très simple, monsieur,* I replied. *La chambre est un peu trop chère.* The concierge looked stricken. Needless to say, however, after all the rearranging, all the furniture moving, all the new furniture, not to mention the fact that I had mentioned I would be staying there at least until fall, he could do nothing but lower the price — the first and only time I have ever succeeded in accomplishing such a thing in a French hotel. And indeed, once that was settled everything was truly perfect. It was really a wonderful room with a terrific balcony and I looked forward to a delightful spring, summer, and fall.

There was, however, one large fly in the ointment — and that was the job itself. My disillusionment was not long in coming. It happened over a tape recorder which the publishers had sent over for the Duchess to use in dictating to me. In one of my very first sessions with her she said something about her childhood, then in the very next session I had with her she said something that was totally different about exactly the same event. I asked her about this, explaining that I had played both sections back on the recorder to confirm the difference. At this the Duchess became very irritated. "They told me," she said, "that that tape recorder was not for me, it was for you, and I want you to remember that."

One thing I could not fail to notice was that whatever the Duke had given up by his abdication he certainly did not give up his standard of living. The Windsors had two houses and a total of thirty servants — all to look after just two people. Their main residence was a château in the Bois du Boulogne which had formerly been the home of Charles de Gaulle. On the outside the house was formidable enough — complete with a large park, two garages, two greenhouses, a gatekeeper's lodge, and a long driveway including a high black lamppost topped by a gilded crown. But from the inside it was truly breathtaking. One entered a marble hall, on one side of which was a huge sedan chair and on the right an even more huge globe of the Earth. Next to strike a visitor's eye was a huge carving flanked by sconces and swags of the Royal Arms. As if this were not enough, up the marble stairway, from a thick staff, hung the banner of the Knights of the Garter. Moving on to the drawing room, there were two full-length portraits, one of Queen Mary and the other of the Duke as Prince of Wales in his Garter robes. In the east end of this room, which opened onto the dining room, was an enormous portrait of the Duchess, square-faced and square-jawed, of which perhaps the kindest thing was said by Sir Cecil Beaton. "It looks," he said, "nothing like her." In actuality, most people found the portrait looked exactly like her.

Finally, upstairs one came to the Duchess' suite and the Duke's, the Duchess' being distinguished by a huge heap of cushions, each one embroidered with mottoes which included one entitled "My Romance," and another "British Reserve." I also noticed that the only photograph on the Duchess' bedside table was, of all people, Queen Mary. As for the Duke's suite, it was small and Spartan, the only similarity with the Duchess' being a few of the same mottoed cushions. Of these my favorite was the curious one "A Night In Cherbourg." There were also, I was told, two guestrooms and a bath on the top floor, but these were apparently rarely used. The Duchess' excuse for not inviting friends to stay was simple. "There are not," she would say, "enough guest bathrooms."

The Windsors' second home was Le Moulin de la Tuilerie, an old mill on twenty-five acres near the little village of Gif-sur-Yvette in Seine-et-Oise. Bought for $80,000 from Étienne Drian, a fashion artist and stage designer, it was transformed by the Windsors and some million dollars into an English country house. Here the Duke, who loved the house, had a small room with hardly more than an army cot for a bed, while the Duchess, who never liked the house or for that matter living in the country, had a huge bedroom which was all white except for large beams overhead. These were waxed and gilded, and stood over a truly vast four-poster bed.

Actually the mill consisted of four buildings, the main one of which backed up to a millstream and a picturesque waterfall. Inside, while nearly everything seemed to be colored a bright red, which gave the whole house an overly rich-looking motif, it was also dominated by seemingly endless chintz. In one part of the mill, which was the former barn, the Duke had all his personal trophies and souvenirs. In front of the fireplace in this room the Duchess pointed out, especially for my benefit it seemed to me, a funny twisted red stool — one which, she said, the Duke used to like to sit on and rest while elephant hunting in East Africa. She could, I am sure, imagine what appeal this had for me.

The Windsor "day" would begin at ten-thirty, when the Duchess' maid would wake her for breakfast and bring her the newspapers. In most social set-ups of Windsor proportions the mistress of the house would begin her after-breakfast day by giving "the order of performances" first to the butler, then to the head chef, third to the head gardener, and fourth and finally to the head chauffeur. For the Windsors, however, the first to be summoned would be the Duke. This occurred at exactly eleven-thirty, at which time he would literally be given his marching orders for the day. These were almost invariably menial — to tell the first chauffeur to take the chef to market, to tell the second chauffeur about something she wanted him to pick up, or to tell the head gardener something she wished him to look after before he came to see her.

By one o'clock the Windsors' custom-built royal blue Cadillac would be at the front door ready to take the Duchess to lunch either at a friend's house or at a restaurant, then to take her in the afternoon either to a bridge game or one of her daily appointments with a hairdresser, masseuse, chiropodist, or perhaps to view a dress collection at Chanel, Dior, Mainbocher, Balmain, or Givenchy — after which the car would pick her up to be back in time to instruct the servants on how to arrange and place the flowers for the evening. She required at least three hours to prepare herself for dinner.

Meanwhile, of course, the Duke would be either playing golf or, if he had no golf game, gardening. On one day when it was raining, and he could not play golf, he took me to Versailles and gave me a personal tour. For me it was an extremely memorable day because he made interesting comments on just about all the kings — it was one subject which he knew extremely well.

The remarkable thing was that very rarely did the Duke see the Duchess from their eleven-thirty appointment in the morning until the guests arrived — which they did almost every night, unless the Windsors were going out — in the evening. When these guests did arrive, particularly for a formal Bois house dinner, that scene, too, was memorable to me. From the entrance hall, fragrant with incense and dark — it was lit by candelabra only — the guests hardly knew where to go, but in time a butler would escort them to the drawing room where he would bring everybody to "sign in," as it were, in the handsome guest book.

Finally, ushered into the drawing room, the guests would find footmen in full scarlet livery ready to offer them a wide variety of drinks — from cocktails to champagne. These drinks, however, were only offered twice — for good reason. As the Duchess well knew, if the Duke had more than that there would be trouble — he had, to put it gently, an extremely light head. Indeed, the Duchess never allowed the cocktail hour to last more than forty-five minutes and often not until after it did she appear — at the head of the stairs to march down very much like royalty. Most of the guests, I noticed, curtseyed not only to the Duke but also to the Duchess — although, without the Royal Highness appellation, she was not entitled to this. The butler's announcement of dinner was equally pointed. He ignored the Duke altogether and then, bowing low to the Duchess, said in a voice clearly audible to everybody, "Your Royal Highness, dinner is served."

The Duchess did not believe in more than ten at a table.

If there were more than that there were two tables, with the Duchess presiding at one and the Duke at another. The food was truly outstanding, as might be expected from the fact that the Duchess had a chef who had formerly been the chef of the Aga Khan and was rated as one of the best in the world. Again, whatever the Duke had given up by abdicating he did not give up in the gastronomic field — with, that is, the exception of soup. The Duchess could not stand soup. "An interesting liquid," she liked to say, "which gets one nowhere." Nonetheless, other than soup I have never had food at a private house to match what was served at the Windsors'. On one occasion, when I had lunch with the Duchess, just the two of us, no less than nine courses were served. Of these, the Duchess did hardly more than taste each course — somehow, it seemed to me, as if to prove her classic statement, "A woman can never be too rich or too thin."

Speaking of rich, the Windsors were indeed so. The Duke received from the British government over a million pounds a year tax free. He also had a large account at the Morgan Bank in New York which, acting on stock tips from his rich friends including the Dillons, the Mellons, the Biddles, the Paleys, and the Robert Youngs, he had managed to raise to several million dollars. As for the Duchess, the jewels alone which the Duke had given her — many from his family's collection, which were of course not his to give — were worth many millions, and when they were sold at auction after her death went, along with her other effects, for $50 million.

Despite this, the Windsors promoted the idea among their friends that the wolf was almost always at their door. There were countless stories that when they went to visit for a weekend or even to attend a single dinner party they were paid for doing so. This was not true, but the fact is they had an angle on almost everything to do with money. If, for example, a friend said he wanted to give them a present, the Duchess would immediately say, "Don't send anything here — send it in care of the British Embassy. Otherwise we'll have to pay duty." Even the Windsor automobiles were bargains. The royal blue Cadillac, for example, built to the Duke's specifications, was a gift from the Chairman of the Board of General Motors — so was the Buick station wagon with the Royal Crest on it — and both were sent care of the British Embassy. The main house was owned by the City of Paris but was leased to the Windsors for the incredible sum of fifty dollars a year. The French government forgave them all income taxes and, in the end, all death duties. On top of it all, the Duke was reputed to be the largest dealer in French francs on the black market.

Just the same, I never heard either the Duke or the Duchess say one good word about the French. When the Windsors went out late at night to a French nightclub, the Duke delighted in asking for a German song, and at the times when I ate alone with them at a French restaurant I was not only embarrassed about how they would go on with their talk about the French, I was actually concerned that the waiters might have slipped something, if not in the soup, then in some other dish.

The Windsor dinner parties attracted very few French or even English notables, but they did attract a wide variety of all kinds of Americans. The head of the American armed forces — or indeed all Allied forces — was, for example, in regular attendance. So were what seemed to me a rather motley group of American celebrities. The Duchess indeed kept up on all the arrivals of celebrities in Paris by her subscription to *Celebrity Service,* and rarely failed to see that one she wanted received an invitation to dinner. When a prominent American author would arrive in Paris, the Duchess would not only send an invitation but instruct me to get one of his or her books. When I did this, she would ask me to pick out a particularly good line, and then during the dinner when there was total silence she would turn to the author and say, "I really think your line" — and then she would slowly quote the exact line — "is so wonderfully put." After she had done this, at least one guest would always say to a companion, "Isn't that just like the Duchess? She keeps up on everything." On top of something, mind you, that even Polar Bear, in his sleep, could have seen through.

If the dinners were interesting so were the luncheons, particularly those in the spring and summer at the mill. My all-time favorite was a luncheon at which the celebrity guest was none other than Dorothy Kilgallen, then one of the panelists on the famous TV game show, "What's My Line?" The idea of this show was to have the celebrity panelists try to guess the occupation of the non-celebrity guest.

That Saturday morning I was picked up in the Windsors' blue Cadillac — which attracted, as it was obviously supposed to, a large degree of attention. I climbed into the front seat and had hardly settled in when I saw that in the back seat were Ms. Kilgallen and her husband. To say they were not pleased to see me was an understatement. They clearly believed they were on their way to some engagement far grander than one which would be attended by me. And while they were not adverse to having me not-so-subtly clearly understand this, I, in turn, could not resist indicating to them that I went to the Windsors' almost every day.

Nonetheless, when we arrived at our destination and went into lunch, Ms. Kilgallen's spirits were revived when she found herself seated at the Duke's right. She was particularly pleased when she saw that not only was I not on the Duchess' right, but that seated there was none other than the commanding chief of the American forces in Europe. In any case, lunch proceeded in fine form outdoors on the mill grounds until, just after dessert, the Duchess suddenly clapped her hands and asked if anyone could guess what we were all going to do next. No one could. "We are going," said the Duchess with an excited smile, "to play 'What's My Line?' " With that, immediately the waiters whisked away the luncheon dishes, while the footmen set one long table in front of the luncheon tables, and moved the guests' chairs into an audience-like position. While this was going on, as quietly as possible I asked the Duchess how she proposed to play the game. "You'll see," the Duchess said sharply. "Don't be a spoilsport. You're always so negative." The Duchess then turned to the whole audience. "Now," she said, clapping her hands again, "Dorothy and I are going to be two of the panelists, and the General and —" she looked around, I thought a little bit desperately "— Mr. Amory will be the other two."

As we took our seats behind the long table, the Duke, who was sitting in the front row of the audience, suddenly held up his hand. "Can I," he asked, "be the first guest?" How can we guess him, in a low voice I asked the General, seated beside me, he doesn't do anything. I did not, however, keep my voice low enough, for the Duchess, who had obviously been considering the Duke's request, suddenly clapped her hands again. "No, you can't be the first guest," she said, "everybody knows you don't do anything." At this, of course, all the guests burst out laughing. The Duke looked at first very disappointed, then suddenly he brightened. "I know what," he said, "I'll make up being somebody else." Everybody apparently thought this was a terrific idea, and the game was about to begin, when suddenly the Duke spoke again. "I've got it," he said, "I'll be an airline pilot."

There, of course, went game No. 1. Eventually the audience gave up on the Duke as a guest, but a long succession of other people, one after another, attempted to make up being somebody. I have played a lot of games at a lot of parties in my life — in fact I once did a whole article entitled "The Gamey Crowd" — but I do not think that ever in my life, at any house or house party, have I ever seen such determination to keep a really terrible idea going. The worst thing was that nobody could stop until the honored guest — in this case not Ms. Kilgallen but the General — got up to leave. When he finally did the entire audience and panel too, as I recall, burst into loud applause. Actually, it was the only applause "What's My Line?" received all afternoon.

Early on I realized that one of the many problems I faced in the book was how to get rid of the Duchess' previous two husbands prior to the Duke. Both of these were still living at the time I took on the job, and they were of course the real stumbling block to her becoming

Queen of England. An extraordinary number of Americans believed the British would not accept her because she was an American. This, however, was not true. The British would have accepted an American, but they found one with two living ex-husbands, as they would put it, a very sticky wicket.

I suggested to the Duchess that what we should do with these ex-husbands was to assign them faults — faults so terrible that the reader would not only understand why she eventually had to divorce them, but would also understand how, in contrast to them, the Duke who, though he had a fair share of faults of his own, would somehow be believable as the true love of her life. Not just, in other words, because he was a king but because he was such a terrific person.

The Duchess basically liked the idea and, since she had none of her own, we decided to go ahead with it. Her first husband was Lieutenant (j.g.) Earl Winfield Spencer, whom she had met in Pensacola when she had gone to visit her cousin. "Every generation," she told me, "has its own set of heroes, and mine were flyers." Nonetheless, among the many faults we assigned to this hero were selfishness, bossiness, and demandingness, and we also zeroed in on the major fault we assigned him, which was drinking. Indeed, with the Duchess' prodding I soon had Lieutenant (j.g.) Earl Winfield Spencer having a snort on almost every page. When, however, the Duchess was still not satisfied with this but wanted to keep adding to it, I had to protest. I reminded her that if we did not let up a bit we would not be able to stop the reader from wanting to join him.

But even the problem of how much Lieutenant Spencer

should be drinking was as nothing compared to the problem of his job — which, after their marriage, was teaching naval air cadets to fly, first at Pensacola in Florida, and later at the Coronado Air Force base in California. Having that job in those days of extremely primitive planes — and on top of it, being a heavy drinker — was hardly a believable situation. And, if this was not difficult enough, I still faced another problem attendant on it. This was, very simply, the date when all of it was occurring. The Duchess had made very clear to me at our very first meeting that she did not want any dates in the book, but she soon added another injunction — that she did not want any well-known events in the book which the readers could very easily date for themselves.

That left us with such a large problem that it made the others seem modest by comparison. Here we had Lieutenant (j.g.) Earl Winfield Spencer flying around and drinking and at the same time trying to teach young naval air cadets to fly — all in preparation for a war we couldn't mention. Presumably, if it had been World War II it would have worked like a charm. But the fact was, it wasn't — it was World War I.

On one occasion I did manage to pry out of the Duchess a sort of postscript about the final difference she had with Lieutenant Spencer. She expressed it to me as follows:

> One of the things that made my personal life so difficult was that Win did not have my facility for getting to know people. He also did not have the slightest ability at divining people's motives. I most certainly did — in fact, it was at this period in my life that I realized for the first time that I had a real and truly extraordinary gift for

being able to see through people. It irritated me almost beyond endurance that Win could not understand this. I used to warn him, after one meeting with someone, that this man or that woman doesn't like you, that he or she boded him no good, and all he would do would be to laugh it off or say I was exaggerating. But invariably I would turn out to be right. Although I tried to keep my gift to myself, I could not — I would eventually show it to the person, either in my attitude or in some sudden, pointed remark or barbed witticism that I really did not intend to make. I was, of course, trying to protect him, but when I saw that he simply did not possess the perspicacity to see what I was doing for him, I gave up.

Furthermore, I gave up for good. Today I never use my gift any more. I have put it away and locked it up in a closet, so to speak, along with many other troubles of the past. But I know just as surely as I am sitting here that right now, if I wanted to, I could take out my gift, dust it off and use it again. . . . It may be a little rusty but it is still loaded.

If the problems involved in getting rid of the Duchess' husband No. 1 were not easy ones, those involved in getting rid of husband No. 2 were no walk in the park either. His name was Ernest Aldridge Simpson, and he would soon be legendary in English song and story — in the latter, for being known as "The Unimportance of Being Ernest," in the former, for being starred in a revised Christmas carol of the day:

Hark, the herald angels sing,
Mrs. Simpson pinched our King.

Actually Ernest was only half English — he was also half American. On his eighteenth birthday, however, when asked by his father, who was English, to declare himself one way or the other, he declared for being English. Once having so declared, in short order Ernest soon went all the way and later when the Duke, first as Prince of Wales and later as King, began coming regularly to the Simpson house in Bryanston Court, he seemed to have thoroughly subscribed to the good old-fashioned English belief that when the King comes to your house, he not only sits in your place at the head of the table, he also owns everything including, if he wants her, your wife. Indeed, in Ernest's case, when the time came for divorce Ernest not only went out of his way to make himself guilty with the necessary adultery evidence but also seemed, as he always did, to go the second mile. Indeed what he did was to perform the adultery with one of the Duchess' closest friends, whom he afterwards married.

In short order we assigned Ernest a long list of standard English faults — most of them, I was pleased to point out to the Duchess, began, like "standard" itself, with "st" — stuffiness, stuck-upness, stubbornness, and stodginess — most of which were not very fair, because while Ernest was hardly a life-of-the-party type neither was he, to use one more "st," a stick-in-the-mud. A relatively successful man in the shipping business in both America and Britain, he was an excellent host and a congenial, if quiet, guest. From the Duchess' point of view we could not, of course, get into the real fault he had — which was being happily married to someone else.

The latter was an American woman, whom I eventually had the opportunity to meet in person. I asked her to tell me what she thought of the Duchess. She replied, with a wry smile, "The Duchess," she said, "was a very helpful woman. First she helped herself to my apartment and then she helped herself to my clothes, and then she helped herself to my husband." I was also privileged to have, some years later, a particularly memorable meeting with the husband in question. It occurred at a cocktail party in New York, when a man came up to me and said, "I thought you might like to talk to me. My name is Ernest Simpson."

I did indeed enjoy our talk. It was not a long one, but it was long enough for me to learn that the Duchess' version of her life with Ernest was by no means the only one. There was also the matter of his version. And this was, in a word, that there was hardly a word of truth in hers. "She had a terrible temper," Mr. Simpson said quietly. "I really think the Duke was mortally afraid of her. I know most of the time I was."

Almost everyone, to this day, has his or her own opinion of the abdication of King Edward VIII. So much so indeed that, looking back on it, I sometimes think that even Polar Bear, had he been alive at that time, would have had his opinion on it, too. He was, for one thing, a terrific little abdicator. He could abdicate from a party at the drop of a hat — sometimes literally, in fact, at the drop of a hat. He could also abdicate from where I wanted him to be if he had the slightest suspicion that there might be, in the offing, either a pill, an examination of an ear, a bath, or even a toenail cut. He would also abdicate in a split second from the position of being the only possible perpetrator of some kind of total spilling or breakage. One second he would be there, the next he was nowhere to be found.

One thing I believed without any doubt at all, and that is that Polar Bear would not have thought the Windsors played it very smart — and Polar Bear was not only one very smart cat himself, he was also an excellent judge of smartness in both other cats and people. Both the Duke and Duchess liked to tell people that they did not like to talk about the abdication, but this could not have been farther from the truth. Almost every conversation I had with the Duke would have at least one time in it the preface, "When I was King," and then a story about that. As for the Duchess, she did not know the first thing about the British government, nor indeed about the British people. All she knew was how to get a man, and how to get ahead. But when she got both, in the person of the Prince of Wales and then King, and literally got to the head of the class in that department, she was as stubborn as he was in believing everything would turn out the way she wanted it to. The whole trouble about the abdication, she often said to me, was that she and the Duke had no time to organize their defenses, because it all happened so fast.

So fast! According to her, they met late in the fall of 1930. According to the Duke's book, they met in the fall of 1931. I have always thought that it would have been nice if they at least could have gotten together on that fact. But no matter. Whether it was 1930 or 1931, they still had either five or six years — give or take your pick — to figure out what was going to happen. One wonders what they talked about on long winter evenings.

Actually from the first time Prime Minister Baldwin faced the Duke, then King, with the facts of wife about being a British monarch, the die was cast. Ironically, the Royal Marriages Act did not mean that the King could not marry someone who had two living ex-husbands. Constitutionally, in fact, the King was free to marry anyone he liked except a Roman Catholic. All the Royal Marriages Act did was give him the power to prohibit the marriage of any member of his family. But, again, nobody could prohibit the marriage of the King himself. Despite this, on Baldwin's side of the affair he had first of all his Cabinet, who could be counted on not to be enamored with the idea of the Duchess as Queen; second, Parliament, which would certainly react the same way; third, the Dominions, who would have to accede to any such marriage; and fourth and finally, the Church. The Church of England regarded marriage as indissoluble except by death. And although most people in England believed that the monarch was the Head of the Church of England, that was not actually the case. What he was, though, and officially was so designated, was Defender of the Faith. As such, conceivably, he could have been, for making such a marriage, excommunicated. Although this was not likely, the fact was, it was possible. Neither the Duke nor the Duchess was religious. They almost never went to church — and the Duke's relations with the powers-that-be in the Church of England were far from good.

From the beginning the Duke seemed to have no conception of what was ranged against him and, even if he did, stubborn as he was, he was certain he could find a loophole. He particularly persisted in this when the Duchess was with him, staying at Fort Belvedere. When, however, a brick was thrown through a window of the Duchess' home, the Duchess — who was far from a courageous woman — immediately wanted to leave England. In short order she set off, in company with the Duke's equerry, to the home of the Herman Rogerses, friends of hers in Cannes. En route, she stopped from time to time to scream at the Duke over the telephone not to abdicate — which was certainly the last thing she could have wished, or indeed had bargained for.

The Duchess always claimed that Esmond Harmsworth, one of the cabal of British publishers who saw to it that the public never learned about the Duke's dilemma until it was a *fait accompli,* was the first to approach her with the idea of a morganatic marriage. She claimed to me that she had never heard of such a thing. This was, of course, not true — all the Duke's circle had been discussing it for weeks. The *Concise Oxford Dictionary* defines a morganatic marriage as "one between man of exalted rank and woman of lower rank, who remains in her former station." Surely, one hardly needs to reread that definition to know exactly what the Duchess thought about it. Several times, indeed, she expressed herself to me succinctly on this point. "I thought," she said, "it was medieval." Knowing her well by this time, I was not in the least surprised. Having set her cap for a King, she hardly relished the idea of losing the prize when it came so close to her grasp. If she settled for being a morganatic wife, not only would she not be a Queen, she would have settled for something which, to her at least, sounded all too much like being a peasant.

If the Windsors had made a comedy of errors of the abdication, their life afterward came very close to being a farce. Since they could not get married until after the Duchess' Simpson divorce became final — which was not to be for several months — and since they could not either live together or even be seen together during this period for fear of a collusion charge being levelled against the divorce — as if it were not close to a worldwide fact of life that there had been collusion — they chose to live during this period in separate countries. The Duchess remained at Cannes while the Duke chose, of the various places offered to him, the Schloss Engesfeld home of Baron de Rothschild in Austria. And here he stayed for many months while he and the Duchess talked on long distance telephone almost every day, with almost every call being concerned with how furious they both were at his brother, George VI. The Duke had, typically, never given a thought about how difficult the assumption of Kingship would be for his brother, who was a shy, reserved person with a pronounced stammer. From the abdication on, however, he gave a good deal of thought to his brother. I have never forgotten one day when I mentioned something about his brother. The Duke interrupted me. "That stuttering idiot," he said.

As for the Duchess, besides calling the Duke on the phone about his brother, she also wrote numerous letters on the subject to him. On one occasion, she even accused him of having an affair with Baroness Rothschild when the Baron had gone away. This was not true, but it is almost a pity it is not. It would at least have proved that the Duke's anti-Semitism, which obviously did not extend to the Rothschilds, also did not extend to matters of the heart.

It did, however, extend to dinner parties after he and the Duchess were back together again and entertaining in

Paris. On one occasion, he amazed an English friend when the subject of Hitler came up. "I have never thought," the Duke said to the man, "Hitler was such a bad chap." As for myself, I have never forgotten one of the very fanciest dinners I ever attended at the Windsors'. From my seat of some distance to the Duke, I heard the Duke, who was at that time drinking rather heavily, talking loudly to the lady on his left. He was talking loudly enough so that not only did I hear, but so did several other people. The talk between him and the lady was clearly about Hitler, and also clearly involved a disagreement.

Suddenly the Duke took both the lady's hands in his and, closing her fingers together, enclosed his hands over them. By now most of us were watching in amazement, but either because of how loudly they were talking or because of what they were doing with their hands, there occurred one of those curious silences which sometimes happen even at a large table. Suddenly the Duke said to the lady — and very clearly — "You just don't understand. The Jews had Germany in their tentacles. All Hitler tried to do was free the tentacles." With that, he released the lady's hands.

For a very long moment there was literally not a sound at the table. Then, very quietly, a man spoke. "Sir," he said, "with all due respect, I never believed I would ever hear, at a civilized dinner table, a defense of Adolf Hitler."

The Duke turned red but said nothing. Neither, for some time, did anybody else. After the dinner I went over to the man who had said that and it turned out he was Milton Biow, an extremely prominent New York advertising man. I told him that in all the time I had worked with the

Windsors, in my opinion what he had said took more courage than I had seen exhibited by anyone I had ever met in their house.

To be around any couple in which one partner, be it the male or the female, is totally dominant, is not a pleasant experience. In the case of the dominance of the Duchess over the Duke, however, the fawners and the hangers-on, the sycophants and the social climbers, did not seem upset by it. To them, the Windsors were, after all — or at least one of them was — royalty, and for them this was enough. But for anyone with even a modicum of taste or objectivity, the repeated evidence of the Duchess' dominance was so infuriating that at times one could not help feeling sorry for the Duke. One soon realized, though, that this was hardly necessary for the simple reason that he did not just put up with it, he actually liked it. Even Polar Bear could not have stood it — he would have known that a cat could look at a king, but in this case he would certainly have wondered why it was worth it.

The very first working day I had with the Duchess was one on which I saw for the first time this dominance, and I never forgot it. We were having tea and talking about the book when the Duke suddenly wandered in, tea cup in hand. Immediately he started talking about how he and his ghostwriter had worked. Equally immediately the Duchess stepped in. "We're not talking about *your* book," she said, "we're talking about my book. Take your tea in the other room." As I watched him go, I thought of two things — how much he had given up, and then to be treated like that, and also if she spoke to him like that with a relative stranger present — one who, after all, would one day be writing about her — then how did she talk to him when they were alone?

To some extent this question was answered by the Duchess' Aunt Bessie, who was with her almost from the beginning of her courtship by the Duke. She was also with her as a guest at Fort Belvedere during the crucial days of the abdication crisis. On one occasion, after a dinner party, when the other guests had gone the Duchess berated the Duke — who was, after all, now King — about something he had done and continued this berating to such an extent that he finally burst into tears. Later, after the Duchess had gone to her room, Aunt Bessie sat with the Duke for some time, not only commiserating with him but definitely taking an anti-Duchess side of their whole relationship. "You can always get another woman to love," she said. "But you can't get another throne." It was good advice but, unfortunately, like most good advice the Duke received, he did not take it.

By the time the summer was up I had had all of the Windsors I could take. And, if I may be pardoned the expression, I abdicated — and I never regretted the decision. After leaving the job, I sailed back to the U.S. on the same *Queen Mary* I had sailed over on. In New York, after we docked, several reporters came on board — some of whom, since the story of my leaving the Duchess' book had preceded me, had various questions for me. One question, however, they all had — why did I leave the job? I told them I could not make the Duchess of Windsor into Rebecca of Sunnybrook Farm.

I think this satisfied them, but it did not satisfy a young lady who had overheard it. "I don't care what you say," she said, "she got a king, didn't she?"

I had an answer for that, too, but unfortunately the young lady did not wait to hear it. I wanted to tell her that yes, she was right, the Duchess had gotten a king. But I felt the young lady should also know that it had not been all that terrific. And, besides that, I wanted to tell her that I now thought England should put up a monument to the Duchess. She was, after all, responsible for the country getting a change of monarchy just when it needed it most — before the Second World War.

If I had had a chance, I would also have liked to tell her that what the country lost was a man without character or courage, let alone sense of duty, who thought nothing of giving up his throne to a shy and gentle man who was ill-fitted for the job, who stammered, and for whom every public appearance was a painful one.

This is what they lost, I would have told the young lady. And what they got in return was a man who overcame all his difficulties to become one of the greatest wartime leaders in British history.

Surely the woman responsible for that deserved at least a small monument. Even Polar Bear would have seen the reason for that.

If my Windsor ghostwriting experience was a major error in my life and, as "September Song" has it, a plentiful waste of time, it was shortly followed by another error which was also major, and was an even more plentiful waste. And again, like the Windsor debacle, I believe that if Polar Bear had been in the picture, it would not have happened.

Actually, my only excuse is that the first error led directly into the second. What happened was, coming back on the *Queen Mary* from the Windsor story, I had some long, long thoughts — not only about the Windsors in particular, but also about Society in general. Having seen, almost nauseatingly firsthand, what passed for Society in the form of the aforementioned fawners and hangers-on around the Windsors, I became more and more convinced that the word "Society" itself was suspect — that whatever it once was, it certainly was not anymore, and that something new might not be any better but it could hardly be, at worst, worse.

I decided, in a word, that what had supplanted the word "Society" in at least the media world of a new day was the word "Celebrity." With that in mind, I decided to do some research on the subject. And, I soon discovered, that once upon a time there was a day when the word "Celebrity" was used only impersonally — that a person might be said to have celebrity, or fame, but it would have been as meaningless to say "A Celebrity" as it would have been to say "A Fame."

I also discovered that the change in the word as it had come to be used was by no means as modern as most people assume. As far back as 1836, for example, the *American Quarterly Review*, speaking of John Jacob Astor I, declared, "From an obscure stranger he had made himself into one of the 'celebrities' of the country." This was still early enough, it is true, for the word to be used with quotation marks, but what was particularly interesting to me was that it was used in connection with a man whose family would soon become pillars, if not particularly stable ones, of New York Society.

All of which led me to two further observations — the first one being that Society clearly started as Celebrity, but then, in at least some cases, continued as Society, and the second one was that, whatever it was, again in a few cases, it continued on to become Aristocracy. In any case, as far back as 1856, I found no less a "celebrity" than Emerson himself using the word, and without quotation marks, in *English Traits*. And, finally, by the turn of the century, as witnessed by a 1908 article in *Harper's Bazaar* entitled "The Dinner Party," the word was in full flower:

> If one wishes to invite the Van Aspics in order to impress another guest, one must first find someone to impress the Van Aspics. One must find, then, a celebrity.

The question then became, of course, which was more important — the world of the Van Aspics or the world of the celebrities? For a while it seemed, in fact for half a century, the Van Aspics and the celebrities would, in a sense, split the pie — they were both deemed important. But, as time went on, however, there was no question but that the celebrities had overwhelmed the Van Aspics.

Not that Society died easily — it did not. For years it had been carefully tended and looked after, and was finally even given the crowning accolade of being numbered. Since this was exactly what I was proposing to do with celebrities, I took some interest in who these numberers were. And, as it turned out, I should have taken a lot more interest because an extremely smarmy lot they were — and hardly a lot one would wish to join.

The first and most famous of these was a curious Southern gentleman named Ward McAllister. Born in Savannah, Georgia, and married to an heiress, he soon came to New York and attached himself to the then-reigning The Mrs. Astor. Since Mrs. Astor's ballroom held just four hundred people, Mr. McAllister took it upon himself to decide, in 1888, that Society should consist of just that number, thereby giving birth to the famous phrase "The Four Hundred." In explaining this, however, Mr. McAllister invariably went back to Mrs. Astor's ballroom. "If you go outside that number," he said, "you strike people who are either not at ease in a ballroom or else make other people not at ease." Sometimes, though, as Mr. McAllister later admitted, for, as he put it, a large ball, it was possible to go outside what he called "the exclusive, fashionable set" and invite "professional men, doctors, lawyers, editors, artists and the like." But, Mr. McAllister stated sternly, he did not advise doing this often, and in fact recommended it "primarily for New Year's Eve."

Hard on the heels of "Mr. Make-A-Lister," as Mr. McAllister, in his last years, was called, came another numberer named Mr. Louis Keller. Whereas Mr. McAllister had been relatively striking looking, with a Van Dyke beard and odd and rather loud clothes, his successor, Mr. Keller, the son of a New Jersey patent lawyer, was in person extremely unprepossessing. Sandy-haired, with a curious-looking, drooping mustache, and a squeaky, affected voice, he was troubled early in life with deafness — an affliction which seemed to ward off, at least from his point of view, some of the criticism he received for the sole distinction of his life — which was to found the *Social Register*. Growing up on the fringe of Society, Mr. Keller was, like so many numberers and arbiters before him and since, fascinated by it. "The mind of Louis Keller," said one biographer, "never went beyond Society."

Mr. Keller actually got his start by publishing the Society gossip sheet called *Town Topics* — one which proved a predecessor to the latter-day gossip columns. Nor was Mr. Keller by any means the first to publish a listing of Society. There had, in fact, been a host of "Blue Books," as they were called, or "Visiting Lists," before his *Register.* Mr. Keller, however, had two important things going for him: One was that he, as the son of a lawyer, even if just a patent one, knew his way around the law, and somehow managed to protect his *Social Register* from being copied. The other was that he somehow managed to protect himself from large suits which declared that he had copied others — which of course he had.

In any case, by the time of Mr. Keller's death in 1922, his *Social Register* was a success, partly because of its distinctive black-and-red design — one which, in turn, I copied for my book, *Who Killed Society?* Indeed, three weeks after Mr. Keller's death, at the time the ownership had passed to Mr. Charles Beekman, Keller's nephew and heir, the *Register* reached its peak, numbering editions in twenty-one cities. From that time on, however, there was trouble — the start of which was the *Register*'s attempt to invade the South. "Down here," one Richmond lady informed Mr. Beekman, "we know who we are without being told."

The *Register* also met with a similar lack of success when it invaded Minneapolis–St. Paul, and followed this by having to abandon cities like Detroit and Providence for "lack of interest." Nor was it helped when the *Register* found it necessary to combine Philadelphia with Wilmington, and Cleveland with Cincinnati and Dayton. Although Cleveland was later freed of this burden, the *Register* itself, by the 1950's, was down to eleven editions. As was its custom in those days, first they selected a correspondent, then with his or her help chose a thousand or more names, then mailed them all *Registers* with a five-dollar-due bill. Here, and in various other places, the *Register* began having difficulty for its policy of throwing people out because of what the *Register* owners regarded as "poor marriages." This included, among other sins, a gentleman marrying an actress, which often provoked the *Register* to high dudgeon. Even the regular letter one received after a marriage from the so-called "Social Register Association" was something of a stopper, too:

> It has been brought to the Association's attention that Mr. ——— has married recently. Will Mr. ——— therefore kindly inform the Association of the date and place of his marriage and give the full Christian and maiden name of the bride and the names of her parents in order that the customary notice may be entered in the Dilatory Domiciles.
>
> If Mrs. ——— was previously married will Mr. ——— kindly give her former married name and state whether she was a divorcée or a widow and if the latter give the Christian name of her late husband.
>
> The Association would also appreciate receiving some information regarding Mrs. ——— as to her Family background and any other particulars which would be of assistance.

The repetition of the word "Christian," as well as the phrase "Family background," not to mention "Dilatory Domiciles," can be extremely irritating to sensitive bridegrooms, or brides for that matter, and at least half of the newspaper stories about so-and-so being "dropped" for marrying so-and-so could be traced to such simple irritations. The bridegroom just did not return the form, and the *Social Register* staff being what it had always been, the couple was, in the next edition, not present.

The basic way the *Social Register* has always been run is to have correspondents in various cities whose idea of helping the editors in New York as to whom to put in and whom to put out was to clip Society columns and mail them to New York. For many years the Boston correspondent of the *Register* was Mrs. John Jay Attridge. Although a Roman Catholic herself, as was her boss, Mr. Keller, she told me she was more associated with what she called Boston's "Irish political element" than with the "Yankee Social," and yet she had seen her *Register* include, as she told me, "very few Catholics," and, as far as she could recall, "no Jews at all." Mrs. Attridge also told me she received $150 for her first year's work for the *Register* in 1907. In 1975, her fiftieth anniversary, she received, again for the full year, $350. She was, however, philosophical about this. "It came to about a dollar a day at the end," she told me, "and after all, I worked only about two minutes a day."

After a long pause, during which Mrs. Attridge looked at me closely, she told me she had nothing to do with my being dropped from the *Social Register*. She said it had been "handled in New York," and that the editors felt very strongly about the *Register* being criticized, and that she had been told I had definitely criticized it on television. I told her not to worry about it — that somehow I had managed to survive despite being dropped. I did, however, tell her exactly what I had said. I told her it had happened on the old Garroway "Today Show," and what had happened was that Garroway had asked me about the *Social Register*. Since his famous chimpanzee, J. Fred Muggs, was with us, I suggested to Garroway that one way we might understand it was for us to endeavor to get Mr. Muggs into the *Register*. I told him it would not be easy, because Mr. Muggs was in show business, but I would have to know whether or not he was married. Mr. Garroway said he did not know whether he was or not. I told him we would have to get a letter of recommendation from somebody already in the *Register*, and then get him at least five seconding letters. I told him it would take time, but not to worry. If his name was Fred J. Muggs, I said, I doubted it would be possible. But since his name had a nice society sound of J. Fred Muggs, I thought at least we had a chance.

Unfortunately, we failed — Mr. Muggs never made the *Register*. But a young lady friend of mine, using the same tactics we had recommended for Mr. Muggs, did, for one edition at least, manage to get her poodle in. "Pedigreed," she assured me, "of course."

Even this, however, was not my favorite story about the *Register*. That came to me from an assistant editor of *Look* magazine who told me she had been interviewed by two members of the *Register*'s secret "Advisory Board" who told her they were a search committee for a replacement editor of the *Register*. The young lady never forgot the experience, although she asked me not to use her name — something which was, I thought, a large tribute to the curious power the *Register* had over people, even those whom one would think would be above such matters. In any case, I respected the young lady's wishes for anonymity, and told her story, without her name, as follows:

> At first, she recalled, the men "beat around the bush" and were very "hush-hush." Then they finally admitted they needed a new editor and also that the office needed modernization; they said they had only one "badly battered typewriter" and that most of the addresses were still done by hand. By this time the young editor was beginning to have strong doubts herself about wanting the job, but she recalls that the men were determined to know everything about her; they even wanted to see her paintings and were vastly relieved, she said, when they learned they weren't abstract. Since she also wrote for *Look,* she naturally brought up the question, if she took the job, of her writing on the "outside." This caused some consternation. The men wanted to know exactly what kind of writing she might be doing. Each thing she mentioned caused increased consternation. Finally in desperation she asked them what kind of writing they thought she could do. "The best thing for you to be," one of the men said reflectively, "would be a lyric poet."

Some years ago the *Social Register* was bought by, of all people, the late Malcolm Forbes, of *Forbes* magazine. To understand just why Mr. Forbes wanted such a controversial investment is hard to understand, unless one knew Mr. Forbes well enough to know how intrigued he was with matters of the social world, and also how limited he was in certain ramifications of such matters. I recall, for example, crossing on the *Queen Elizabeth II* with him, and asking one evening why he bought the *Register.* "Cleveland," he said to me, very earnestly, "I will tell you anything you want to know about any of my business interests, but I will not tell you about that." Obviously, someone had apprised him that the ownership of such a book could hardly be a plus for his other businesses, let alone for his personal relations. In any case, the *Social Register* was eventually sold again. And today, not only is its advisory board still a secret, so is its ownership.

The *Celebrity Register* was, of course, to be a very different book from the *Social Register.* In the first place, it was not to be a "Blue Book," but a "do" book. Actually, we ended up with half a hundred well-known Society names in it, but just as Society had, at least in my opinion, changed from a how-do-you-do Society to a what-do-you-do, so the whole basis of Celebrity Society was not who somebody was, but who somebody is.

I first took the idea to Earl Blackwell, of Celebrity Service fame, under the impression that he was a book publisher. He was not, but it really did not matter because in the end we published the book ourselves. Later, this was done through different publishers — Harper's, and Simon and Schuster also published it — but they did very little better than we did in publishing it ourselves. And this despite the fact that we had an extraordinarily able group writing the thousands of biographies. There was, for example, R. W. Apple, Jr., formerly of the "Huntley-Brinkley Report," and later a distinguished writer for the *New York Times.* There was also the late Hallowell Bowser, general editor of the *Saturday Review,* and also the late James Fixx, also a *Saturday Review* editor and author of many books on running. Then, too, there was Marian Magid, of *Commentary* magazine, and Andrew Sarris, who became a distinguished critic.

To the best of all our abilities, however, we never had anything but trouble about who should have been in the books and who should not. We learned the hard way that one man's celebrity is another man's nobody. Yet the latter man or woman did have his or her celebrities whom the first man would not know if he fell over them. To the football fan, for one example, half a hundred players are celebrities. To the non-fan, there is Joe Namath, Joe Montana, O. J. Simpson, and possibly Lawrence Taylor. To the rock music fan, there are many more than a hundred world-class celebrities. The non-rock fan would be hard put to name a dozen.

In general, we operated on the theory that to be a celebrity a man or a woman must be known outside his or her field. This failed, however, when we realized that there are whole fields of celebrities which, by their very nature, are known all over — television, for example — and at the same time a great many fields which are also, by their very nature, basically local. We were, however, considerably cheered up by our New Orleans correspondent, Tess Craiger, who gave up the job of deciding who should be in the book from New Orleans. "We are all," she wrote us, "internationally famous locally."

Besides speaking of being known outside one's field, we also had to consider if a celebrity had to be known by his or her face. That sounded like an easy solution, until one begins to realize that there are hundreds of people whose names are household words — writers, for example, or artists, or business executives, or even radio personalities — whose faces would not be known off their own front porches.

Finally, we learned the hard way that we had to distinguish between celebrities and what were then called — an expression which has faded somewhat — VIP's. In those days, however, there was a distinct difference. Both have or had the fame which, to begin with, made his or her name. But the celebrity's fame is his or hers alone — an individual thing — while a VIP's is basically positional. The celebrity's name, in fact, should need no qualifying identification — indeed, that is probably the best definition of a celebrity — but the VIP is likely to need the additional clout of being identified with his or her organization. When Polar Bear came along, I would learn that it was possible to be both a celebrity and a VIP — but to do so, it would help to be a VIC, or Very Important Cat.

Generally speaking, however, the world of the celebrity and the world of the VIP are, well, worlds apart. From the moment they get up in the morning — for the VIP, early, for the celebrity, late — to the time when they go to bed at night — the VIP, early, the celebrity, late — their ways of life are so completely different that if they ever meet — which, except for very large and usually charitable events, they rarely do — they would hardly know what to say to each other. And, if they do, they would undoubtedly slip up right in the introductions, because a celebrity is generally a first-name man or woman, the VIP a Mr., Mrs. or Miss — rarely a Ms.

If not for the celebrity is the world of clubs, boardrooms, and directorships, not for the VIP is the world of television, columns, fan mail, and autographs. If not for the celebrity is the Establishment, not for the VIP is the talk show. If not for the VIP is the street recognition, not for the celebrity is an honorary degree. Indeed, if the celebrity gets an honorary degree, it is likely to be from a college whose chief claim to fame is that it gave him or her one.

The world of the celebrity is the world of ups and downs, of big money periods and almost totally broke periods. The world of the VIP is generally smooth, and generally an upward course. Constantly at the mercy of the press, without a screening shield, the celebrity almost literally lives off his mention in the column, his picture in the paper, and his appearance on TV. If the VIP meets the press at all, it will probably be through a press release. The celebrity has his entourage and his hangers-on, but his life is basically disorganized and is basically a last minute one. He or she is rarely alone, and does not like to be. On the other hand, the VIP has a social life which is so well integrated with his business life that it is hard to tell where one leaves off and the other begins.

The celebrity is probably a Democrat, the VIP is probably a Republican. The VIP will read *The Wall Street Journal, Business Week,* and *Forbes,* while the celebrity will read *Variety, People,* and *Hollywood Reporter.*

The VIP is listed in the telephone book — by his office, and even his home number. The celebrity has a constantly changing and unlisted number. And, if to reach the VIP you have to play "Just a moment, put Mr. so-and-so on the line, please," to reach the celebrity you have to go through his agent, and that is worse. And the irony here is that while the VIP's world is the well-ordered one of the formal letter and the thank-you note, the celebrity does nine-tenths of his business and arranges most of his social engagements by phone.

The personal worlds of the VIP and the celebrity are perhaps the farthest apart of all. The former is generally well ordered and organized; the latter, usually messy. The VIP marries once or, at the most, twice; his children go to private schools and enter the same circumscribed world as their parents'. And when, in the end, the VIP goes to his final reward, he does so via a well-planned service at his church or synagogue. The celebrity, on the other hand, is much married, has different children by different wives and, though not at all averse to pushing them, sometimes unwarrantedly, toward show business, usually finds them difficult to handle, and vice versa. And he goes to his final resting place not via church or synagogue but via extravagant eulogies in a funeral home.

Finally, if you can tell a celebrity from a VIP by the length of his hair (longer), by the width of his tie (wider), by the amount of jewelry (more) and by the cash he carries (much more), you can also tell a VIP from a celebrity by the fact that he drinks more and tips less, plays sports better and tells stories worse.

Some years ago, dining on his fabulous yacht *Christina*, I put to Aristotle Onassis the difference between celebrities and VIP's. "I have done some thinking on the subject," Mr. Onassis said, "and I have come to the conclusion that the way a VIP gets to be a celebrity is to get control of the people's playthings. It's a little like children and their toys. You do not become a celebrity by controlling the people's money, their banks, their natural resources, their raw materials — or even, as in my case, by moving their materials, by shipping. If I had remained just a shipping man, I would have remained comparatively obscure. But the moment I bought Monte Carlo, that was something else again. I then controlled one of the people's playthings. I was like a man who owned motion-picture companies, or a television network, or a racetrack, or horses, or a ball team — they are all celebrities. And since I controlled the most famous casino in the world, I became one of the most famous men in the world."

Certainly, Mr. Onassis' theory would be accurate for many celebrities since his time. A Donald Trump, for example, would hardly be a celebrity as a moderately successful second-generation real estate man, but as the builder of Atlantic City casinos, he was a shoo-in. In the same way, George Steinbrenner, as a second-generation and none too successful shipbuilder, was far from celebritydom. As principal owner of the New York Yankees, albeit the least principled in that club's history, he is, like it or not, a celebrity. Indeed, taking Mr. Onassis' theory a step further, and taking a large list of "the people's playthings" to newspapers and television networks, you have a large list of celebrities, all of whom are VIP's also — from the Hearsts and the Howards and the Sulzbergers to the Paleys and the Sarnoffs and the Tisches.

Curiously, the late Mr. Onassis gave us as much trouble as any celebrity in the book because of his demand to see his finished biography. From the beginning, we had decided the biographee would have nothing to do with his or her biography, and the biographers would try to be fair, if not necessarily reverential. However, Mr. Onassis was not content with this policy, and sent four large men to our modest-sized office to demand the copy. I was doing my best to explain our policy when, seeing that I was getting nowhere, I told the men I would be happy to read them the biography of another Greek, if they would like to hear it. It happened that my assistant, Marian, had just completed the biography of Mr. Spyros Skouras, and dutifully, while the men stood glowering, I read the following:

> "In bed that night I don' sleep," he recalls, of the day he first heard of CinemaScope. "Then I finally sleep and I dream. I am dreamin' of Egypt, of lions outside the streets, of Bens Hur and the Quin of Seba, of Betsy Grabble in colors. Oh, I had sooch wonderful dream." And, later arising, he welcomed the Chairman of Soviet Russia to his studio's dining room. "I yam a pure boy from Gris," he announced. "Where else but in America would I be standing here?" "I am a poor boy from the Ukraine," Khrushchev, understandably heatedly, replied. "In Russia, I run the whole she-bang."
>
> Born 28 March 1893, in Skourohorian, Greece, Spyros (pronounced "Spear-os") Panagiotis Skouras came to America in 1908, and went to work for a St. Louis hotelman who every dawn played the National Anthem to improve the boy's patriotism. And, married to Saroula Bruiglia (five children), with his two astute brothers, Charlie and George, he prospered. ("My only hobby," he says, "is gins rummy.") When TV came, it was he who organized the campaign "MOVIES ARE BETTER THAN EVER," and it was he who declared, "The critics should not be putting the nails in our coffins." The 1953 premiere of *The Robe* opened a new error in Hollywood,

> when Skouras backed the first CinemaScope picture with $30 million. ("The dice is cast," he declared. "We have landed in Normandy.") Then, as Cleopater familias, Skouras stood, presumably, at Dunkirk. In the middle of the worst of it he received a call that Indianapolis was on the phone. "Listen," he shrieked, "I got no damn time to talk to no damn Greek."

I never did find out what the men told Mr. Onassis, but I had the feeling when they left they had at least learned from that biography we were not people to irritate unnecessarily. In any case, the only other sinister demand for advance reading of a biography came from no less a personage than the late J. Edgar Hoover. Once again, our office was penetrated — this time by two of Mr. Hoover's assistants, whom I took to be G-men. Just two of them, however, were somehow even more menacing than Mr. Onassis' four. It is hard to realize today — especially in view of the current anti-Hoover writing — just how much nervousness, if not fear, a visit from Mr. Hoover's men inspired in those days. He was, after all, a man whom nine Presidents had not dared to remove.

One thing was certain. The more the men said "The Director says," and "The Director insists," etc., the crosser I got. It was less bravery than bravado, and in the end, when they stormed out of the office — and storm they did — I still was virtually as nervous as I was when they arrived, and felt sure they would come back. But, fortunately for me, they never did.

One other incident — equally, if not even more menacing — remained. This was a telephone call I received at three in the morning the day before the publication of

Celebrity Register from none other than Walter Winchell. Like Mr. Hoover's power, Mr. Winchell's seems, in retrospect, exaggerated. Let me assure you, at that time it could hardly have been exaggerated. No one before him or since ever had the power and influence he had, not only in his daily newspaper column in the *Mirror* but also on his weekly television and radio shows. Like many others in Winchell's heyday, I seemed to know dozens of people who worked for the man — some worked as press agents who, in return for giving him three interesting or amusing items would get one mention of their client in his column. Others worked not as press agents but just as people who gave him anti-items against somebody they disliked. Unlike Mr. Hoover, Mr. Winchell was not totally anti-Liberal, but he was totally anti-Communist and also against anybody he thought was so inclined. Some people he just disliked for no reason at all.

In any case he made very clear, very quickly, his quarrel with me. The *Celebrity Register* included a biography of one of Mr. Winchell's pet hates — the late Ms. Josephine Baker. With biting sarcasm, and in the familiar, nasal rasping voice that staccattoed out each Sunday night "Good evening, Mr. and Mrs. America and all the ships at sea," he told me, with incredibly increasing rage, just what would happen if the *Register* appeared without that biography of Ms. Baker out — that it would not only be the end of the *Register*, it would also be the end of me.

Once more I could take no credit for being, as I look back on it, remarkably calm. It was really because it was so late at night, and I was so tired and sleepy, that I never really got around to realize what I was risking. Indeed, at one point, when he raged, "Have you any idea to whom you are talking?'' I told him I did indeed, but I wanted to ask him his reasons for not wanting Ms. Baker in the book. Actually, I knew the reason all too well. Mr. Winchell was a great friend of Sherman Billingsly, owner of the famed Stork Club, and Ms. Baker had come into the Stork Club one night and, according to her, was not served — which, judging from the attitude of Mr. Billingsly, an ex-gangster from Oklahoma, was undoubtedly true.

Indeed, as I began to wake up more, I asked Mr. Winchell if the fact that Ms. Baker was black had anything to do with his opinion. At this he still raged, but I noticed with extreme pleasure that he stuttered somewhat in his reply. I also managed to get in that if we measured every celebrity by who liked them or disliked them as a criterion for our book, we would have no book at all. Finally, I somehow managed not to resist telling Mr. Winchell that the opening night book party for the *Celebrity Register* would be held at the Stork Club, and I looked forward to seeing him there. I like to think that, in the end I, not he, slammed down the phone. But in all fair retrospect, I now think it was he.

Winchell or no Winchell, the first edition of the *Celebrity Register*, including a biography of Josephine Baker, had its debut at the Stork Club. And the book was, in the beginning, an extraordinary success. It was, however, basically a Tiffany item — in fact, Tiffany's was one of the first stores to ask for it, and sold hundreds of copies. But it was not similarly successful elsewhere, even though we did our best to get it to the bookstores which asked for it, and even though it went through several editions.

To find the reason for this overall lack of success, I can

only recall the story of Joseph Choate, certainly one of New York's most famous legal celebrities, who was once asked to contribute to a fence for a very social cemetery. Mr. Choate refused on the firm grounds that no fence was needed. "No one who is out," his argument claimed, "wants to get in, and no one who is in wants to get out." The *Celebrity Register,* it turned out, was to be just the opposite of that cemetery. People who were out, and thought they should be in — of whom there were thousands — were utterly furious with the book. And the people who were in were almost equally furious, because the biographies were so less glowing than the stuff to which their publicity people had accustomed them.

As if this were not enough, all of us who had anything to do with the book soon learned a basic truth about human nature, which was perhaps best stated by two extremely celebrated authors, Mark Twain and Somerset Maugham. "There's always something about your success," Twain once said, "that displeases even your best friends." And Mr. Maugham put it just as strongly: "All of us like to see our friends get ahead," he said, "but not too far." I could see Polar Bear agreeing with both those statements, even though you could count the number of cat friends he had on the toes of one of his paws.

We could, of course, find solace in just how ridiculous the whole question of fame could be. This was, perhaps, best illustrated when a columnist during World War II, albeit not Mr. Winchell, took a poll to find the "world's favorite personality." The Pope (Pius XII) finished behind Bing Crosby and Frank Sinatra. Others, in order, were Eisenhower, Father Flanagan, MacArthur, Winchell, Sister Kenny, and Bob Hope. Joseph Stalin finished fifteenth.

We could find solace too when, translated to show-business terms, the story becomes that of Kim Novak, who had just made a film for Columbia Pictures. Arriving in Paris she was driven by a chauffeur who told her he had had many other celebrities in his cab. "I have driven Gloria Swanson," he said, "and Cary Grant, and President Coty. I have even driven your President."

"What!" exclaimed Ms. Novak, delightedly. "Harry Cohn!"

CHAPTER FIVE

Polar Bear and Me and Your TV — Your Guide to the Medium Medium

The Windsors and the celebrities were not the only occupants of my attention in the days before Polar Bear. There was also, and almost right up to the time he came to me, the matter of a whole new job — one being something which I had never really wanted to be — a critic.

It is not that I do not like critics — indeed, when they like something I have written I am inordinately fond of them. It is, rather, that I just never wanted to be one myself.

When I was a columnist for the *Saturday Review,* I remember a sign the editor of that magazine, the late Norman Cousins, kept on his desk. "The Critic," the sign said, "Judges Himself in His Criticism."

I admit that sign made me somewhat nervous, but it did not actually stop me from writing any criticism. Like most authors of books, I was occasionally given a book to review for a newspaper's book review section, and when I wrote one of these I certainly did not let that sign make me think that all the time I was writing that criticism what I was really doing was judging myself. Rather, I always thought of that sign as being more like what I have always thought of the New England conscience — that it did not stop you from doing what you shouldn't, it just stopped you from enjoying it.

As I said, I did not know Polar Bear at that time. But as soon as I did know him, I decided that he would have been a terrific critic, if for no other reason than because it never would have crossed his set little mind that all the time he was criticizing something — which, frankly, was most of the time — that what he was really doing was judging himself.

Come to think of it, I have never known a cat who was not at least part critic, and in Polar Bear's case he was so far from being a part critic that even saying such a thing does him a complete injustice — he was a total critic. Frankly, I believe he was born that way, and although I did not know him when he was a kitten, because he was a stray and was at least one year old when I rescued him, I venture to say, without fear of contradiction even from him, that he was a critic even then. Indeed, although some kittens do not open their eyes until they have reached the incredible age of ten days old, I frankly can, even now in my mind's eye, see Polar Bear during that ten-day period raising an eyebrow, even if he could not raise an eye, at the actions of one of his brothers or sisters. And by the time those ten days were up, and he could actually open his eyes, I would not, from this criticism, exempt even his mother.

Of course, when it came to yours truly, the record will show that Polar Bear was critical of me from the moment he first laid eyes on me or rather, specifically, the moment I grabbed him through the fence on that snowy Christmas Eve a score of years ago. This time there was no raised eyebrow, either. What he did was deal me a straight left cross — he always had a better left cross than a right cross — to my jaw.

From that very moment I knew he was not just a future critic but one to be reckoned with, and I assure you he did not, ever since that time, fail my assessment. Take, for example, that first night when I had taken him back to my apartment and he had disappeared, and neither Marian nor I could find him. In fact nobody could find him, although it was not a very large apartment, until my brother, who had just joined the search and was a very thorough person, dismantled the dishwasher. And there, sure enough, hiding at the bottom, was Polar Bear. Although my brother was one of the three men in the Army in World War II who had ever gone all the way from being a private to being general, and although I assure you he could give and take criticism with the best of them, I very much doubt if he ever received in either his military or his civilian life any more telling criticism than that wary, one-eyed, fishy look he received that night from Polar

Bear. Indeed, I can still remember my brother looking first at that look of Polar Bear's and then at me. "What you have here," he said sternly, "is one very critical cat."

Actually, Polar Bear's criticism of me that I remember best happened the very next day when I went to give him a bath. In Polar Bear's firm opinion no one gave cats baths, cats gave themselves baths, and the look he gave me was so critically expressive that it all but spelled out words. "Wash a cat!" I was sure he was saying. "Boy, have I got my work cut out for me with this one!" If the look was not enough, I also remember that along with it, and still some time before the bath, we went eyeball-to-eyeball — he at six inches and me at six-foot-three. I knew immediately, with the kind of criticism he was giving me, it was going to be a question of who blinked first.

Of course you remember what happened. Although the purist might say that he won the first round, and that I blinked first, the fact is that criticism or no criticism, that blink of mine was really a way of avoiding another left cross. And, after all, and again criticism or no criticism, I did give him a bath.

I did not, however, I admit, fare so well the next time I went *mano a mano* with him. This occurred when I began the process of — well, how do I say it — training him. The problem was that, being a newcomer to cat ownership, I must have given him the distinct impression that I thought he was a dog. In any case, I soon learned that there was one thing Polar Bear surely was not, and that was a dog. Actually, I had never really thought of such a thing, but when he was in a critical frame of mind he did not give me the benefit of the doubt for the simple reason that when he had that critical mind of his made up there was no doubt anywhere in it. All I had wanted, after all, was for him to learn the meaning of the word "come." I knew he would not do it, of course — I had already had him long enough for that — but I did hope, however, that at our very first training lesson he might somehow begin to grasp the basic meaning of the word.

I really never did know whether he had ever learned the meaning of the word or not. All I know is that once I said it, the jig was up. He never wanted to hear it again. Eventually we came to a compromise. I was allowed to ask where he was — "Where is Polar Bear?" — after which there would be a suitable interval — a very suitable interval, I would say. In this he would first sit up, and then start to walk and look around and do whatever else crossed his mind, and then finally continue the journey to me. All of this, mind you, only after it had been made totally clear to me that he was coming only entirely by his own volition. Otherwise, of course, he would have to turn in his union card as a cat.

There were so many other times when he was the consummate critic. There was, for one example, my naming him. I never in his entire life knew whether or not he knew his name, let alone whether he liked it. All I ever knew was he liked even less all the other names I had tried and looking back at some of them — like Whitey and Snowball and Snowflake — I hardly blamed him. Another example of his consummate artistry at the craft of being a critic was the whole episode of my giving him a pill — particularly what I thought was my final victory, when I had grabbed him, shoved open his mouth, popped in the pill, shut his mouth, and then stroked his throat over and over, until I was certain there was not the slightest possibility that he had not swallowed the pill. Only then to see, of course, a bare few moments later, when I was savoring my victory and reminding him what had been won in a fair and open fight, out of the corner of my eye, a tell-tale little white object in the rug behind me. Which was, of course, what you had guessed it was.

Most critics are not known for their smiles, but one I will never forget was the smile Polar Bear gave me after that pill episode. It came after I looked first at the pill and then, slowly, back at him while all the time he was doing exactly what I was doing — first looking at the pill and then, just the way I had done looking back at him, only this time he looked back at me. And if it is possible that a cat's smile could reach from ear to ear — well, that is exactly what his smile, slowly but steadily, did.

One thing I did not make clear, and that was the nature of the job I had undertaken before I had Polar Bear. It was, not to beat around the bush, the job of being a critic of television for, of all magazines, *TV Guide.* But after the job was mercifully over, and Polar Bear had come to me, I often wondered what kind of critic of television he would have been. He would not, of course, have been one as thorough as I was. After all, I had to see each show three times before writing about it, and I do not believe his attention span would have been up to that. Indeed, Polar Bear's attention span at watching television is the shortest I have ever seen for anything except when I was talking to him about something which was very important, for his own good, for him to hear.

It is true there were very few things on television of which he was very fond. One of these was Ping-Pong.

Since Ping-Pong, however, comes on in full force on your TV only once every four years, during the Olympics, it really was not the answer to seeing whether or not he would be a better critic than I was.

Readers with long memories will recall that at one time I even went so far as to try to train Polar Bear for watching television. Training Polar Bear for anything, as I have already pointed out, was not easy, but to train him for watching television was something else again. For one thing, you had to train him to watch it, and before he would do that you had to train him to like it, for the simple reason that he would not do anything he did not like to do unless you were right there to hold him, preferably with both hands around his neck. With that in mind I bought some television videos which were specially produced for training cats to watch television — which certainly seemed a pretty limited field, but everyone to his or her own business, I always say. Anyway, as I have previously written somewhere — I cannot remember where — the most curious of these, put out by PetAvision, came in three sections entitled, in order, "Cheep Thrills," "Mews and Feather Report," and "A Stalk in the Park."

I really could not believe those titles. Sex and violence — there they were, out in the open, and even on cat video where any kitten could see them, and probably right on the mews — or rather, news — and even in any kind of feather, or weather, or whatever.

In any case, even if for the purpose of making Polar Bear a television critic, I certainly did not want to corrupt him. There was, after all, enough sex and violence in everyday life in New York City without subjecting him to any more of it — and particularly on his own Cat TV, which I had to pay for. I did find, however, as I have also mentioned previously, another offering called "Kitty Video" which was put out by Lazy Cat Productions. In this was a pamphlet entitled. "How to Teach Your Cat to Watch TV." "Most cats," this began, "are not accustomed to watching television, and will need some assistance to learn this human skill."

Human *skill* — they had to be kidding, but they were not. Indeed, the pamphlet went on to warn about distractions — loud music, too many people in the room, and other animals — all of which, they said, could "cause a lack of concentration on the cat's part."

With that I surely agreed — it could be a problem. Polar Bear's concentration span, with the exception of when it was addressed to the pigeons on my balcony or something like that, was, if anything, even shorter than his attention span. And, when instruction was involved, particularly with me doing the instruction, it was close to zero. In any case, to get around distractions, the pamphlet advised never forcing a cat to watch TV but rather, and apparently casually, placing him in your lap and then positioning his head toward the television screen. "Strategically," the pamphlet suggested, "scratch under the right cheek to aim head left."

That, frankly, I was never able to accomplish. Nor did I have any better luck with another suggestion the pamphlet had which it said was highly recommended. "Tapping gently on the TV screen, " it stated, "can help bring a cat's attention to the video." I tried this with Polar Bear, but it was no easier this time when I tried to teach him to be a TV critic than it was when I tried to do it just to teach him to watch for the fun of it. I learned that Polar

Bear was already a critic of TV, and already such a stern critic that he wanted no more of it — or else he felt put down by having to watch special cat TV. I always felt Polar Bear infinitely preferred doing something that was not meant for him to do rather than doing something that was.

One thing the pamphlet insisted on was that I should keep close watch on him while all this was going on. In fact, the "Kitty Video" pamphlet had a stern injunction about this, which went as follows:

> Do not leave your cat alone while the video is playing. If the cat should leap at the screen, it could cause damage both to furnishings and to the cat. Your cat must learn to watch TV passively. With practice, your cat can become a harmless couch potato.

Again, I remind you I had been through all this before. And if the first time I had been through it I had said I was not at all sure I had wanted him to be a couch potato, let alone a harmless one that time, the second time, when the job was, after all, to make him a critic of TV, I felt that even if he was going to be a couch potato I would have preferred a little toughness about it.

Curiously, I found that getting Polar Bear to watch what I wanted him to watch on TV was very much like the difficulty I had always had in this regard with Marian. Time after time, when I wanted Marian to watch something I was watching, or watch something I was supposed to be watching but could not because there was a ball game on at the same time or something else I wanted to watch, I found that she just would not do it. She would say that she wanted to watch what she wanted to watch —

which was so thoughtless and selfish of her that though I am a very long-suffering person I have felt it very difficult to deal with.

One day, however, I had a chance to redress those wrongs I had so patiently undergone. I happened to be at Marian's apartment that day when the TV repairman came to repair the remote control. While he was busy either trying to fix it or preparing to sell her another, it suddenly occurred to me to ask him if it would be possible for me to get a remote control for her set which would work from my apartment. It was, after all, a perfectly reasonable request. There were many times when I would see something on TV that I wanted her to see — and right away too — and sometimes there was not even time to call. What I wanted her to look at would be all over by the time I called. Instead, what I wanted was the kind of remote control by which, if she was watching something else on another channel, I could immediately change her set to the channel I wanted her to see. And, if she wasn't watching anything, I could immediately turn her set on to what I wanted her to watch.

I repeat, it was a perfectly reasonable request, and I even pointed out to the man that there were probably thousands if not hundreds of thousands of men who would want the same thing — to have their women friends watch something they were watching. It could, I told him, be a terrific business for the TV people, but the man was not smart enough to see the possibilities. All he did was look first at Marian and then at me as if to say he simply did not believe what he had just heard. Honestly, he never even did me the courtesy of giving me an answer to my request. Some people, it seems, just do not realize when they have been given a great idea on a silver platter.

Even Marian did not seem to understand what a great idea it was. She seemed to take the repairman's side. And, if all this was not hard enough for me to take, there was a postscript to it. A couple of weeks later when I was at my apartment watching a cable channel, all of a sudden a movie came on. It was a new movie, too, a Pay-Per-View one. Very excitedly, I called Marian and told her what had happened — that I was apparently going to get to see a new Pay-Per-View TV movie for nothing.

Then, if you please, Marian explained that it was not quite like that. "You are not going to see it for nothing," she said. "You *are* paying for it. I found out I could order it just by giving them your phone number." At this Marian paused, the way she always does. "It's just like that remote-control thing you wanted," she said, "only they already have this one."

Not content with simply doing something awful like that, Marian also has to have the last word, too. Fortunately, as I have said before, and undoubtedly will have to say again, I have the patience of Job.

All in all, what Polar Bear and I were most of the time reduced to watching were shows which television never had anything to do with — except years later to put them on — old movies. Night after night we would see an old movie, sometimes for the umpteenth time, and never once think of turning it off just because we had seen it so many times before. After all, we had to make sure it came out the same way it always did. Curiously, Polar Bear's and my preoccupation with old movies reminded me of something which had happened long before Polar Bear came to me, at about the time I took on the job of television criticism. It was a statement made by Mr. Mike Dann, at that time vice-president in charge of programming for CBS. "The biggest trouble facing television today," Mr. Dann opined, "is that we are running out of old movies."

Needless to say, this was grist for my mill. Feeling that Mr. Dann had no right to say something like that and then leave us, in the face of that terrible news, with no actual facts, I resolved to take issue with him. Tell us, Mr. Dann, I pleaded both in print and even on the air, just how many old movies we have left. Tell us exactly the number. The American public, I reminded him, had always been able to bear up under terrible news. It had never been found wanting. But, I stated firmly, it had only been able to bear up and not be found wanting when it had been given the facts. And not just some of the facts, but all of the facts. Then and only then, I pointed out, did the American public measure up. They had measured up at Valley Forge, they had measured up in the War of 1812 when the British burned Washington — the city, not George — they had measured up in the Civil War, on both sides, and they had even measured up in the Blizzard of '88 — not 1988, I pointed out, but 1888.

But, I also wanted to make clear to Mr. Dann, the American public had measured up only when it had been given all the facts, and in this new trial this was the least Mr. Dann owed us. Without another day's delay he should tell us just exactly how many old movies we had left. No matter how bad the news, he must give it to us. The truth, the whole truth, and nothing but the truth. And then, once we had that truth, we could start to cut down. We would not, of course, overdo and cut out watching old movies altogether — that would just make us sick. We would cut down slowly. First, we should figure out just how many old movies we watched each week and, whatever that number was, the next week we would watch one old movie less. We would, say, just watch one old movie less in the late afternoon or in the late evening and finally, after nine or ten weeks of cutting down one at a time, we would not watch any old movie at all. We would not even watch Jimmy Stewart in *It's a Wonderful Life,* or John Wayne in *The Quiet Man.* Of course we could, in those cases, if it made us feel better, just turn them on and then turn the sound off and say them to ourselves. It would not be hard. After all, we knew them by heart.

Interestingly, I found, watching with Polar Bear, that just about the only TV which received his full attention was the cat commercials. Short as these were, he watched them and listened to them intently — and even became, in his way, a full-fledged critic of them. How could I tell? It was easy. He either sniffed at them or shook his head. I soon realized what it was, and I had been right about him being, in his way, a critic of them. What he was, was jealous of them — and right to the very depths of his green eyes.

Immediately, I tried to get him to understand that jealousy was a very bad trait in a critic. A critic, I tried to point out to him, had to rise above wondering how he or she would be in an acting part or a commercial or anything else, and must instead compare the performance seen only to the ideal, and certainly not the personal. I did not think Polar Bear grasped this very well. He was just not any good at grasping what he didn't want to grasp — in fact he was awful at it.

Of course, to be fair there were certain animal shows which, if they did not go overboard on dogs, would keep his attention for a while, if not his concentration. But the average, run-of-the-mill television show, I noticed, held very little appeal for him. And, curiously, at the same time I noticed this, I also noticed they held very little appeal for me. Furthermore, all the time I was watching television with Polar Bear to see how he would be as a critic, I was at the same time making a comparison, not only of me as a critic compared to him, but also how the average shows were compared to the average show I had, for some fourteen years, from 1963 through 1976, been reviewing in *TV Guide.* And, frankly, this comparison was easy — generally speaking, those new shows I was watching with Polar Bear were not only not better than the ones I had been reviewing, they were actually worse. And the very worst thing about the comparison was that it held true even when the recent shows were practically carbon copies of the ones I had reviewed.

This comparison could even be carried right to today, as I write this. Take, for example, one of the most popular of today's comedies, "Murphy Brown." This show, obviously deeply indebted to the old "Mary Tyler Moore Show," is nowhere near as well-written, as believable, or as funny as that one was. Even leaving out any comparison between the two stars, compare for a moment the over acting and over active supporting actors from "Murphy Brown" with those, say, of the peerless Ted Baxter of the "Mary Tyler Moore Show" of yesterday.

Today's endless talk and crime shows — sometimes it is hard to tell which is which — are probably the best examples of television not improving. Take, for example, the best crime shows of yesterday. It would seem easy to carbon copy "Columbo," "Kojak," "Ironsides," etc. But obviously it has not been easy for the networks to do so. They cannot seem to do it even when they actually copy the shows with the same characters. Indeed, with exactly the same Peter Falk, today's "Columbo" scripts are a far cry from what they were in the old days, as is the case with Telly Savalas' scripts with "Kojak," or "Perry Mason," or "Ironsides" with the same Raymond Burr. Indeed, about the only shows you can count on to keep the same quality they were when I was reviewing them are actual repeats — say, of shows all the way from "The Honeymooners" to "All in the Family."

This is not to say there have not been efforts made in the quality direction. Notably, the "Civil War" series, not to be confused with "Civil Wars," the network situation comedy. But unfortunately, these are few and far between, and perhaps even more unfortunately, most of them, like the great shows in the days when I was reviewing — like "The Forsythe Saga" or "Upstairs, Downstairs" — were British imports. As for what has happened to TV news, with the exception of PBS's "MacNeil-Lehrer News Hour," it has gone almost steadily downhill. Not so much the three evening network newscasts themselves as what has happened to the total corruption around them, with its barrage of curious efforts like "Real Story," "A Current Affair," "Hard Copy," and "Unsolved Mysteries," all of which seem to have had only one recommendation and that is that they were, next to talk shows, the obviously cheapest thing to produce — something which, watching them, is only too amply demonstrated.

And yet even these are not the worst of all the modern shows. That dubious honor I would reserve for the mini-series and the so-called "movies made for television." Actually, all anyone who thought that television in general had improved had to do was to be around at the end of 1992 and the beginning of 1993 when not one or two but all three major networks outdid themselves in trying to put on a movie about a seventeen-year-old prostitute who shot in the face the wife of a man she said was her lover. Afterwards, when their ratings were found to have gone through the roof, virtually all network executives, who had climbed all over each other to put that trash on the air expressed, of all emotions, shock. "I don't know any-one in the business," said the vice-president of movies for NBC, "who wasn't stunned."

But not so stunned, of course, as not to do it again. Indeed, not long before television had reached that nadir of taste, an equally extraordinary event happened in the industry — which occurred when one of the largest cable television companies announced that they would soon be able to supply, on one person's set, five hundred channels. Considering the fact that at the time they said this an entire network could not adequately supply just one channel with twenty-four hours of reasonably watchable fare, the idea of saying they were about to supply five hundred channels was not even mind-boggling, it was just plain boggling, with no mind involved.

* * *

Looking back to my *TV Guide* days, when I first met with Mr. Merrill Panitt, the then editor of the magazine, I learned that he had chosen me to be his critic because he liked several book reviews I had done for the *New York Times.* I told him firmly that I felt there was a large difference between a book review for the *New York Times* and a TV review for *TV Guide,* but he would not hear of it. Instead, he preferred to tell me how huge my audience would be — in fact, the more he talked about the circulation of the magazine, the more it sounded as if there were more people who read *TV Guide* every week than there were people. Maybe some of them, I suggested, forgot they already had it and go out and buy it again. He ignored this. Instead, he promised me that after I had worked for *TV Guide* only a short time, I would be a household word — and not just all over America, either, but also apparently in parts of Canada.

Curiously, this promise turned out, as a matter of fact, to be all too true. But Mr. Panitt did not tell me that the household word I would be would not be one allowed on a family show. I myself had to find this out, among other ways, from the thousands of letters *TV Guide* readers sent to me, my favorites among these being used in my last column of each reviewing season. These letters were hardly calculated to give one a superiority complex, to wit — and I will warn you, you will have to look hard to find any of that — the following:

> Why doesn't Cleveland Amory go out and get a regular job? These days they can train almost anybody.

Another letter stated:

> You put Cleveland Amory on the next to last page of your magazine. Why don't you put him two more pages back?

But perhaps my favorite was this one:

> I think it is a shame that you have someone like Cleveland Amory to review TV stories. This man hardly ever has anything nice to say. Everyone has their own tatse, but this man has no tatse whatever.

TV Guide did not want me to use that letter in my column. The editors were very sensitive about misspellings or misuses of words in their letters, because they did not want their readers — particularly their advertisers — to think that only children read their magazine. Instead, they wanted me to use only letters which sounded as if they had been written by not only grownups, but intelligent, erudite grownups at that. I was often told, for example, that Henry Kissinger regularly read *TV Guide* — so many times, indeed, that I always meant to ask Mr. Kissinger if it was true. But each time when I was all ready to ask him, there was something about how he looked that stopped me from doing so. In any case, I could not run that particular letter above in my column — I had to re-spell "tatse." It hurt me very much, especially when I received another letter which went as follows:

> You have a taste that is worse than Mary's, the girl that lives down the street from me.

The fact was that a truly extraordinary number of letters both had mistakes and were on the personal side, an example being the following:

> Journalists like you, who distract the truth, are the ones Mr. Agnew refers to.

That one, at least, was signed, "One of the Silent Majority." By far the noisy majority of letters, however, were unsigned. So was perhaps my all-time favorite:

> If "Dirty Sally" goes off the air, I personally will try to get you sued for defamation of character. It's people like you who cause so much child delinquency. . . . What are you, some kind of sex enjoyer?

Finally, there was another letter back to the magazine:

> There is one thing I would very much like to know. Does Cleveland Amory have a degree in criticism?

That one I did answer. Yes, I replied, a Doctorer of Letters. Besides the letters, however, there was one wire which deserves to be included. It came from Sidney Sheldon, at that time producer of a show called "Nancy." About this show I had written, "Except for the fact that the idea is embarrassing, the execution exasperating, the plot silly, the characters stark, and the writing either for or by children, it is a fine show."

Mr. Sheldon's wire was firm:

> I CANNOT STAND PUSSYFOOTERS. DID YOU OR DID YOU NOT LIKE THE SHOW?

Now there, I say, was a producer to conjure with. No wonder he became a writer.

Looking back over my actual reviews during my fourteen years of reviewing, I find that the ones which stand out in my mind stand out not so much for the reviews themselves but for what personally happened to me after writing them. The first was a show called "The Survivors," which began as follows:

> This show is entitled "The Survivors," and with it they should supply a kit. ABC-TV, who hired Mr. Harold Robbins in the first place, got what they deserved — a circumstance which could easily have been avoided if they had been able to persuade someone to read them one of Mr. Robbins' books. Mr. Robbins is a writer only in the sense that a woodpecker is a carpenter. Somewhere along the line he may, by the law of averages, have had an idea. If so the very idea of his having one was apparently so exciting to ABC that they forgot where they put it. In any case, it is not in this show. Our guess is the idea was to show Mr. Robbins' idea of the so-called "in" people. What comes across, unfortunately, is a good deal closer to the "in" people's idea of Mr. Robbins — the show is unbelievable and it is crude. When it isn't trite it's untrue — when it isn't sophomoric, it is soporific. Every character is a caricature, every situation is a cliche. As for the dialogue, it is to die. In fact it is our theory that one of the characters did die of it. On top of it all, the whole thing is endlessly moralizing — which, in a show as tasteless as this one, is the last straw. Somehow the idea of taking one's morals from Mr. Robbins is like taking higher economics from Bonnie and Clyde.

Just after that review appeared I was on Irv Kupcinet's TV show in Chicago, which featured a roundtable of guests. As I took my seat, I looked at my fellow guests and saw, to my amazement, one was none other than Mr. Harold Robbins himself. To say he was just as amazed when he looked and saw me is to put it too mildly. One thing was certain — I learned that for a critic to be a guest on a talk show and to be seated just one person removed from another guest he has said is a writer only in the sense that a woodpecker is a carpenter certainly did not make for airy persiflage. Still another thing was that, pointed as Mr. Robbins' comments were in my direction, they did not go beyond that. Actually, I have always felt that the reason they did not go further was that the man between us, our host Mr. Kupcinet, was, among other distinctions, an ex–professional football player. And, as such, he was used to observing ground rules and foul lines, and on his show at least, was clearly prepared to demand that his guests do the same.

The second review, the aftermath of which I also recall, was of a show called "Playboy After Dark." From it I excerpt the following:

> The Playboy empire got its start by selling not only the American public but also Madison Avenue on the idea that pornography wasn't pornography as long as the editors put to press each month, along with their naked girls, at least a couple of respectable authors. From there on, the empire branched out into a chain of clubs — which equally cleverly sold the American traveling salesman on the idea that the farmer's daughter looked so well when dressed like a trussed rabbit that even if you couldn't touch her, you were a terrific big shot just being there and kidding about her.
>
> From time to time, however, the empire also attempted

television, and here, alas, the success attendant on its previous endeavors has not been forthcoming. Perhaps television is less easy to kid. . . .

The interviews conducted by Hugh Hefner, the host, must be heard to be believed — and since he smokes a pipe and inhales most of his words, they just barely can be. Mr. Hefner, who is obviously amiable enough in person, has a television personality which can perhaps best be described as midway between technical difficulties and a station break. His conversation varies from dead silence to nervous *non sequiturs,* and it does not matter who he is interviewing — Mort Sahl, Melvin Belli, Gore Vidal — you have never heard them worse. On one show, the guest star was Don Rickles. Right from the start, he was unmerciful to Mr. Hefner. "Where," he asked, "is the dummy with the pipe?" Finally Mr. Hefner was pointed out. "Ah," said Rickles, "Charley Personality." Late in the show, Rickles was still at it. "Do you want to say something, Hugh," he asked, "or do you just want to sit there and smoke your pipe until morning?" Replied Mr. Hefner, "I'm just relaxing." "Well," said Rickles, "then don't have a show. Just go on the Titanic and watch the waves rise."

Once again the follow-up was better than the review. I had been privileged to go through the Hefner Playboy mansion in Chicago — a feature of which was a ground-floor bar over which, on the floor directly above, was a swimming pool with a glass bottom in which the Playboy girls disported themselves. In the middle of sitting at this bar, in the late afternoon, I was told that there would be a dinner party that night and would I like to attend? I asked the man who had invited me, the publicity director of the mansion, if they would be dressing. Apparently extremely sensitive on this subject, he immediately took offense. "Of course they'll be dressing," he said firmly. "They'll be dressed real nice."

The third review I chose was, again, less because of the review itself — because it was only one of a seemingly endless number of game shows I had to review — than it was because what happened afterward was something I have never forgotten. In any case, the review began as follows:

> There are several ways you can avoid this show. But you've got to be nimble, because "Let's Make a Deal" has already been on two networks — NBC for four years and now ABC — and it comes at you both day and night. We have, incidentally, heard that the daytime version is worse. That is, however, hearsay. Having survived the evening show, we have no wish to press our luck. In any case, you have to stay alert and look at your TV listings carefully. Watching, that is, not *for* it, but *out* for it. For yourself, our suggestion is to lock your set, remove all connecting wires, leave your home, keep moving and do not talk to strangers. For your loved ones, who are perhaps trapped in your home, you should take all reasonable precautions. These would include the framing of this review on, or immediately adjacent to, the disarmed set.
>
> We wish to be perfectly fair. This is not the worst show in the history of television. . . . Nor is there absolutely nothing which can be said for it. It is, for example, nonviolent — at least the show itself is. Steady viewers

of it, on the other hand, are something else again. They should be paroled carefully and never in a group. Above all else, it is not like other programs, which are interrupted by commercials. In this one, you have commercials interrupted by more commercials. All the prizes are commercial and all the guessing involves commercials; as for the contestants, when they are not taking part in commercials, they do their best to be equally irritating. In fairness, this is not all their fault. Obviously they are selected for their U.Q., or Uninhibited Quotient. They dress in Halloween costumes, and whether they have made a good deal or lost one, they bounce about, giggling, simpering, squirming and, above all, squealing, in a way that can only be described as a poisonous combination of the last stages of TV ague and St. Vitus dance.

The immoderator of all this is Mr. Monty Hall. No other man living and few dead could put up with what he does and still look as if he's enjoying it. Our theory is that it's because he is not looking at it. He's *on* it, and *we're* the ones watching it. Then too he's a card with his ad libs. One contestant was named Janice Hertell. "Do tell, Janice Hertell," he said. Another couple was nervous. "You're shivering and shaking," he said. "No, you're Ronnie and Sharon." And sure enough, they were. Hall, you're a ball.

This time, after the review's appearance, I was in Los Angeles and went to a hockey game during which, at the conclusion of the first period, I went up the aisle to get something to eat. In the concession area I was suddenly accosted by Mr. Monty Hall himself. Without a single word of greeting, he whipped out a copy of the *TV Guide* with my review of his show in it and, with a sizable coterie already around him, and rapidly increasing in both size and anger, he proceeded in a loud voice, line by line, to read the review. Every so often he would pause to ask the people around him, by this time rapidly surrounding me, if there was a word of truth in what I had said — something which they obviously thought there was not — and who then proceeded, in louder and louder unison, and with more and more menace, to tell me so. Never before or since have I had such an experience with anything I have ever written, and I dearly hope not to. Not once during the entire episode did I ever say a single word to Mr. Hall, nor for that matter did he address a single word directly to me. However, when his group at last unsurrounded me I did ask one of them, apparently their leader, if I could go now. And when he seemed to agree, I felt it was my turn to close the agreement. It was a deal, I said wanly.

My fourth and final review I remember also for what happened afterward, albeit mercifully not so personal. The show was called "Queen for a Day." This time I feel free to favor you with my entire review:

> This show, which will shortly go into its 20th year, will soon have played to some 5,000,000 people — in the studio audience alone. Outside of the studio there are, apparently, still a few people who haven't seen it. In case you are one of them, it is, literally, miserable. It is a competition among housewives to see who can get to be Queen by telling the most miserable story — a dying husband, two or three dying children — that sort of thing, only keep it light, of course. Then, whoever

had the most miserable story gets to go to dinner at the best restaurant, the theater, nightclubbing and the rest. She also gets presents. One lady whose husband was out of work, and who had six children below the age of 5, received, for example, a lovely set of claret glasses.

Needless to say, everybody cries with happiness. The Queen cries because she has won and the other candidates cry because they have lost — and the women in the audience cry because their sad story wasn't sad enough to get them up there where the real sadness is. Mr. Jack Bailey, who is pretty sad, too, tries to keep the crying down to a minimum with his rapier repartee. When a Mrs. Margaret Eleck, for example, started to cry because she wanted a bedroom suite because her house and chicken farm had burned down, Mr. Bailey quickly made her see the brighter side. "Ah," he said genially, "you're called Mrs. Eleck. Well, I'm often called that, too. 'Smart' Eleck."

All in all, it's a bawl. "It's the little things," Mr. Bailey says, "that really count with the ladies" — little things, we presume, like ermine capes, station wagons, deep freezers and trips to Africa. Some years ago one woman wanted passage so she could be a missionary. "What kind of missionary?" asked Jack. "Independent," snapped the woman. "I want to go into the interior of Nigeria where no one's heard of the Lord."

The woman meant well, we are sure. But even in the interior of Nigeria they had probably heard of this show — and not well. It is a star chamber of horrors. Commercial after commercial follows plug after plug. Nowadays, not content with a women's fashion show, they have a men's fashion show, too, full of more com-

> mercials — so that a Queen, who if she wins will be able to visit her dying husband, paralyzed by a spinal stroke on an ice floe at the North Pole, can also have the pleasure of knowing that she can take him a king-sized men's deodorant. On one recent show, another frustrated housewife wanted to be Queen because she wanted a new living room suite. She told us that her old one had been taken away by a man who had come to clean it and had taken it, and a $100 deposit, and had never come back. It had all happened on December 31st. "Happy New Year," shouted Jack. But somehow, after all the giving, we were all for the man. We think he had an idea for a brand-new show — a Take-Away, only keep it light, of course.

This time, as I said, I did not receive a personal reaction. Nonetheless, I remembered well that the show itself received, in addition to the minor honor of my review, the major honor of being chosen as the "Worst Program in TV History." This accolade was awarded by no less an authority on the subject than the actual producer of the show, Mr. Howard Blake. Indeed, a book about broadcasting entitled *American Broadcasting: A Sourcebook on the History of Radio and Television,* by Lawrence W. Lichty and Malachi C. Topping, includes an article entitled "An Apologia from the Man Who Produced the Worst TV Show in History," by Mr. Blake himself. "Sure," he wrote, " 'Queen' was vulgar and sleazy and filled with bathos and bad taste. That was why it was so successful: It was exactly what the general public wanted." Mr. Blake did not, however, tell us who it was who said that he did not know his bathos from his pathos.

* * *

There was one area of my job as a TV critic which, as far as I was concerned, cut close to the bone. This was the matter of animal shows. Over the years I reviewed everything from "Wild Kingdom" to "Me and the Chimp," from "Flipper" to "Lassie." But occasionally I would insert other nuggets of information where I thought they should appear as, for example, when I reviewed a show about an attempt, in a TV drama, to rescue a man on a mountain ledge. "Since the man was a hunter," I wrote, "I was cheering for the ledge."

It was not even much of a joke, and it did not make too much sense. Nonetheless, following the appearance of the review I received a call from the editor of the magazine *Field and Stream*. "That," the editor told me, "is the most despicable thing that has ever appeared in a national magazine." I told him I did not agree — that magazines had, after all, been published since the days of ancient Greece and even Egypt, and that surely sometime, somewhere, possibly in the very dim past, something equally "despicable" might have been allowed to slip by. I told him further that what it was, was a joke, and that if *Field and Stream* was all out of jokes perhaps I could persuade the Fund for Animals to lend them a couple.

At this the editor declared that he did not have to sit there and listen to that sort of thing, and that anyway it was not the first time I had written something despicable. "You once said," he continued, "that a hunter was caught in an avalanche, and that you were hoping for the avalanche." I admitted that he had me there — I had indeed so written. But I urged that he remember that avalanches and ledges were two very different things. There were, I told him, very few avalanches left these days — they were virtually an endangered species.

When I came to the job of reviewing a show called "The American Sportsman" I was at first undecided as to whether not to review it at all or to review it more than once. Actually, I ended doing it once and a half. This first half ran in March 1965, and went as follows:

> ABC has come up with a four-episode, hour-long series covering the world of hunting and fishing and called "The American Sportsman." Here the narration is inept, the fishing is boring, the bird shooting pathetic, and the "he-man" exchanges embarrassing ("Look at those ever-lovin' birds! Hey man! Cock-a-baby!"). And everything they kill on those African safaris, of course, they're killing for the good of the poor, fear-maddened natives, all of whom are apparently refugees from the latest Joe Levine picture. In one sequence actor Robert Stack "bravely" shoots, at a distance of approximately one light-year, a feeble old lion who is billed as a "killer" ("The tribe will remember a man named Robert Stack — a friendly, capable man, an American sportsman"). In another, Joe Foss brings down, again a country mile away, an elderly, bewildered one-tusk elephant who is gently trotting along — and Foss, in turn, is billed as "standing in the way of the thundering, massive charge of a rogue elephant." In one show we heard the "Sportsman" defined as "the certain sense of good in each of us." Honestly, Sport, that's what the man said.

My second review was two years later — by which time *bona fide* celebrities were beginning to show marked reluctance to appear on the program. In any case, a part of this review read as follows:

> Out of regard for their families, we will not mention the names of anyone connected with this show. Suffice it to say, however, that we have as host a man whose idea of communicating excitement seems to be to express even the most obvious explanatory remarks in a tone previously reserved for the deaths of heads of state. Along with him each week we have a curious assortment of white hunters in living color, about all of whose fearless exploits we hear *ad nauseam* — particularly as, armed with a full arsenal of weapons, they boldly advance to test wits and match virility with, say, a mourning dove. We also have guest "stars," a preponderance of them non-entities, each of whom apparently has to be identified as a "television personality" because otherwise you wouldn't know he had one, let alone is one. To top it off, as they approach their victims, they invariably speak in such school-girlish stage whispers that the only thing missing is for a house mother to shout "lights out!"

From the time the show first went on the air, animal people had, of course, turned on it in fury. By the time of that review, they were not only writing letters to the network, as well as to the sponsors and the host, but also to the "guests" who shot the animals. One of these guests, the actor Cliff Robertson, received so many letters after shooting another supposedly "rogue" elephant that, "in expiation," he told me, he produced, partly at his own expense, and also appeared in, a pro-elephant special called "Elephant Country." The late Bing Crosby, who, at the beginning of the show, whatever program he was on always seemed to be talking or wisecracking about "The American Sportsman" and promoting it, soon practically disowned the show altogether — for all his previous promotion. "I never hunt anything except birds," he told me, "I just don't believe in it."

Faced with such curious defections, and many more among other celebrities, hunters redoubled their efforts and desperately attempted to bolster "American Sportsman" with cables and letters. It was no use. First, Eastman Kodak dropped its sponsorship of the show after an advertising executive admitted that his company never should have been part of it in the first place, and, perhaps even more important, after admitting that there seldom was a slogan better designed for a company than the nonhunters' slogan for Kodak, "Hunt with a Camera Instead of a Gun." Then the program's other sponsor, Chevrolet, having also received an extraordinary number of complaints, also dropped the show. In the final analysis there were just too many people out there who were too angry — and, at long last, in 1971 "The American Sportsman" had a change in policy. No longer would the hunting of big game be featured — instead, rescue and relocation would be the keynote of all "game" segments. The hunters had lost. Again, in the final analysis, the fact was that their numbers had been exaggerated by everybody — by the network, by the sponsors, and even by the "guests." They could not keep on the air even one program, and that one on only ten times a year, on Sundays, in "ghetto" time.

Despite all this, I could not help ending up with a certain grudging admiration for one of "American Sportsman" 's stalwarts, Robert Stack. I followed his attempt to shoot "bravely," as I had put it, "at a distance of one light-year a feeble old lion" with several examples of his acting work on other programs. After another of these unfavorable reviews he demonstrated what seemed to me, particularly for a hunter, rare class. "Thanks," he wrote me, "for your continued support."

Before the horrors of the old "Sportsman" have been laid to rest, however, one story about it deserves to be remembered. It came to me from Sid Brooks, a writer who did two "Sportsman" shows. The one I remember best was supposedly the story of a "true" tiger hunt in India, with the Maharajah of Bundi. The "television personality" was Craig Stevens.

One of the Maharajah's men located the tiger to be used on the show for the final kill. The tiger was asleep in a cave. The Maharajah's man put a flag on the cave to mark it. A few hundred yards away there was a concrete structure which Brooks promptly named "The Bunker Hill Monument." This had been constructed near the turn of the century by the Maharajah's grandfather. Complete with thick concrete walls, it had slits or small windows from which, safely inside, the hunters could shoot. The Maharajah himself had hired half a hundred "beaters" who were paid the equivalent of thirty cents a day. Equipped with old muskets and tin cans to make noise, they had as their first job to wake the tiger.

Finally, the tiger did wake up and, bewildered, came, yawning, out of the cave. At first he started to move slowly up the hill, then faster and faster as he was spurred on by the shots, shouts, and tin-can banging of the beaters. He headed in the general direction of the bunker, but one of the Maharajah's trained marksmen actually "steered" him — by firing bullets all around him, one of which actually grazed him — directly to the bunker. In this bunker, peering out of the slits, were the Maharajah and Mr. Stevens. There were cameras in there too, behind them, looking over their shoulders. So, while it seemed as if the tiger was actually coming at them, with no bunker at all, the fact was they were, inside, completely safe. When the tiger, frantic to escape, leaped up, Mr. Stevens shot him.

That was what really happened. But, of course, for the program it was just the beginning. They had to go back and "re-create" — as they called it — to make the whole thing look dangerous. First they returned to the Maharajah's palace. Here the Indians had constructed, right on the palace grounds and especially for the show, a *machan* — a leafy tree platform from which, in the jungle, animals are shot. The Maharajah and Mr. Stevens climbed up on it and were told to have a conversation as if they were hunting together for the first time. Mr. Stevens was directed to whisper to the Maharajah as if there were a tiger in the vicinity. His script called for him to say something about being nervous. "Quiet, Mr. Stevens," the Maharajah whispered. "The tiger has ears."

After this, the crew took film of Mr. Stevens shooting, his rifle pointed at nothing at all. This "shooting" was then, of course, spliced in with the actual shots of the tiger leaping in front of the bunker. The impression the television viewer had was that the Maharajah and Mr. Stevens were sitting in a flimsy, open observation post with a fierce tiger attacking them — whereas in reality, the Maharajah and Mr. Stevens were on the *machan* and there was no tiger anywhere around. When they had actually faced the tiger, they had done so from behind thick concrete. In fact, the wildest animals around the Maharajah's estate were peacocks.

No less remarkable was the aftermath to this "true hunt." It occurred when Mr. Brooks and Mr. Stevens were present at the final screening of the show in New York. After seeing it, Stevens turned to Brooks. "That," he said, was the scariest moment of my life." To this day, Brooks does not think Stevens was joking — he thinks rather that Stevens, by that time, actually believed he had really been in danger.

Generally speaking, TV news shows have, over the years, been relatively fair to animal causes. A notable exception to this, however, occurred as recently as the early Spring of 1993 on, of all places, the long-time number one network news show, "60 Minutes." On the Mike Wallace segment of the show, Mr. Wallace went out of his way to defend a highly controversial experimenter who, at Louisiana State University, had shot some seven hundred cats in the head. The idea, ostensibly, was to learn how to treat human head wounds in combat. Although the cats were anesthetized long enough to be shot, virtually no painkillers were given to those who survived, some in excruciating agony, and the whole thing was so obviously cruel that it caused a furor all over the country. It was also extremely controversial scientifically — indeed, one of the so-called "discoveries" the experimenter claimed he had made had actually been made, and published, as far back as 1894. In any case the experimentation, after an investigation by the General Accounting Office, was ordered stopped by the Department of Defense.

All in all, it is difficult to understand why "60 Minutes"

would have resurrected the subject to begin with, unless they had somehow been persuaded to attack critics of animal experimentation. In any case, they certainly left no holds barred. I have myself known Mr. Wallace for some forty years — indeed, as far back as that I used to do a half-hour show with him on the old Dumont network — and had never known him to do such an outrageously lopsided report. What he did, in a word, was first to launch a merciless attack on a pro-animal young woman who could not remember if she had personally heard, or just read about, the cats screaming, second to give hardly more than a minute of time to the one doctor on the program who was knowledgeable about the cruelty, Neal Barnard, and then, third and finally, to give fawning praise not only to the experimenter but also to an American Medical Association spokesperson who castigated the whole animal movement.

A far better critic than I, Howard Rosenberg, of the *Los Angeles Times*, first extolled the virtues of "60 Minutes" in general, and then went on to point out that the show could also be, as he put it, "one of the shiftiest when it comes to tailoring a story to a particular point of view." Among other things, Mr. Rosenberg took Mr. Wallace to task for not once, but twice, misquoting what Mr. Wallace called "a tenet of many in the animal rights movement," that "a rat is a cat is a dog is a pig is a boy." The actual quote was from Ingrid Newkirk, who said that "when it comes to feelings like pain, hunger, and thirst, a rat is a cat is a dog is a pig is a boy." "The difference," Mr. Rosenberg stated, "is more than subtle."

Two weeks after the broadcast, when Leslie Stahl did the mail section of the "60 Minutes" program, she admitted that an extraordinary number of letters had come in about the cat experiment segment — apparently the first time Ms. Stahl had ever realized cats were popular animals. She then said that the same program had aired a segment on the miseries of women in India, and wondered why there had been so many complaints about the cat segment and so few about the Indian women.

It was at least one time when I dearly wished I had been still writing reviews. If I had, I would have tried to explain to Ms. Stahl that, where pain, hunger, and thirst are concerned, a rat is a cat is a dog is a pig is a boy is a woman is an Indian woman is even an American woman TV commentator.

CHAPTER SIX

The Miracles of Modern Medicine — and Some Exceptions to Same

If Polar Bear was not around to save me from the Windsors or the celebrities or even the job of being a critic, he was very much around for something else from which he could not save me either. This was, frankly, an age-old illness of man and cat — and it was, as you may have guessed, arthritis.

Actually Polar Bear and I got arthritis at about the same time. I made clear to him that cats very rarely got arthritis — that dogs did, and that dogs also got things like hip dysplasia — but it did not make any difference to him. He did not like to hear anything about dogs, even bad news about them. The plain fact was he started limping around all over the place — just like me — and not the way he had always done, leaping on things and jumping. For a time I thought he was just making fun of the way I moved, but as time went by I began to see that he really did have a kind of arthritis.

Of course it was not anything like as serious as my arthritis. After all, I had a very important case of arthritis in both hips. But, just the same, he really did have arthritis, even if it was just a little case. Once I could see that, I could also see, all things considered — which I always do — it was necessary for me to repair to books about cat arthritis and find out more about it. And that is just what I did. And there I found out that, although the disease was, as I had already learned, and already told you, relatively uncommon in cats, when it did occur it was often associated, as one medical book put it, "with a variety of underlying problems." These the book went on to list as "congenital, metabolic, infectious, inflammatory, neoplastic."

Frankly, I always have problems with medical books when they begin to throw big words at me. Not that I do not understand those words, mind you, I just do not like to be bothered thinking about what they mean when I am reading something. Anyway, I put that book right down. But with one particular book I persevered. It was called *The New Natural Cat,* by Anitra Frazier with Norma Eckroate, and it had a whole section about cat arthritis. Part of this went as follows:

> Arthritis is a subtle disease. At first, the little stiffness that creeps into the hips or lower back may not be recognized for what it is. "Well, he's not a kitten anymore," or "We can't expect her to jump up and catch the pipe cleaner the way she did when we first got her," may be all that is said to remark the subtle beginning of a downward spiral in the health of a beloved pet.
>
> The disease is augmented by stress. Cats living under stress, such as those who are declawed or forced to live with incompatible humans or animals or those who are frequently caged, are more prone to the disease.

That immediately raised my eyebrow — I only have one I can raise. I was prepared to buy the idea that arthritis in cats could be made worse by living under stress. I knew it made my arthritis worse. I am constantly having to tell Marian, for example, to stop disagreeing with me about things because if she persisted in doing so it could easily make my arthritis worse. Anybody disagreeing with me, as a matter of fact, can set me off. I have found that when somebody disagrees with me in conversation, it is very much like when I eat something that disagrees with me. What happens when you eat something that disagrees with you? You get sick, that's what happens — which is, of course, where we get our word disagreeable.

But, to get back to the quotation from that book I mentioned, the idea of Polar Bear getting more stress and hence more arthritis because he had been declawed, was extremely irritating to me. I would never allow any cat I ever had anything to do with to be declawed. I regard it not only as cruel, but also as dangerous because it renders an outdoor cat virtually defenseless and even if your cat is, as he or she should be, inside, the fact remains that he or she may sometime get outside and then he or she would not have a chance against any dog or other animal.

Remember, please, I was not disagreeing with those authors because of the way stress in cats could be made worse. I was just irritated about this when it was translated to Polar Bear. Take another of their examples — being, as they put it, "frequently caged. Not only had Polar Bear not been "frequently caged," he had never, to my knowledge, been caged from the day I rescued him. He had, it is true, been put in a carrier on his way to the vet, and at the vet's he had, for one night, been caged — on the occasion of his having been neutered. But irritated as I am sure he was at the idea of being neutered, he could hardly have gotten arthritis from that.

That still left the matter of the third of the authors' three reasons — that stress makes a cat's arthritis worse when, as their book put it, cats are "forced to live with incompatible humans or animals." Indeed, where Polar Bear was concerned, I decided to take up the question of incompatible animals first, even though to do this I had to go all the way back to the days when I had brought into my apartment, hoping to have a companion for Polar Bear, a young cat which I described as the Kamikaze Kitten. The idea that Polar Bear could ever make friends with a kitten who bombed him day and night with sneak attacks, from as high an altitude as possible — the kitten's favorite take-off spot being the mantlepiece — turned out to be one of the worst ideas I ever had. All right, I admitted, it had been a terrible failure, but the whole aborted affair — which lasted, after all, only a few days before someone else adopted the kitten — could hardly have been responsible for making Polar Bear's arthritis worse if, for no other reason, because it took place a full twelve years before he ever had arthritis.

There remained only the question of his being "forced to live," as the authors of the book put it, "with incompatible humans." At first I refused to take this personally. I assumed what the authors must have had in mind were people to whom I had introduced Polar Bear. But even this, frankly, I considered, on the authors' part, exaggeration. After all, I did not introduce Polar Bear to just anyone.

As I began to think more about this, however, I realized that a casual observer, seeing some of the people to whom I introduced Polar Bear, might have jumped to the conclusion that those people were incompatible with him. Polar Bear did not, after all, cotton to strangers, and strangers were just what many of these people were. And often on such occasions, it is true, he would immediately go off into what I called his "put-off program." This would involve, to begin with, his pawing the ground in front of me, but looking in the other person's direction and, after that, sniffing the air, still directly in their direction, and then finally, looking squarely back at me, at the same time making very clear he was asking me when, for Pete's sake, was I going to do something about this person. Altogether it certainly was an attitude which, as I say, a casual observer might well have taken to indicate a certain amount of incompatibility. But this would hardly have been fair, because, though people were, to Polar Bear, certainly strangers, the fact remained he was that way to all strangers, both compatible and incompatible. In a word, where all new people were concerned, Polar Bear had already met everyone he wanted to meet. And, in all too many cases, the more they stayed around, the less he wanted them to.

Which left, finally, when you came right down to it, the possibility that the authors of that book meant that the one person who might be incompatible with Polar Bear was, if you please, me. Frankly, at first, I found this idea so preposterous that I had no intention of dignifying it by even mentioning it. I really doubted very much that those authors could, even in their wildest imaginings, have in mind someone as compatible as I am. Why, even under the pressure of some of the most tryingly unjust circumstances you could conjure up — which could easily cause a lesser person to lose his cool completely, and probably end up going off the deep end — I invariably remained the soul of compatibility. I sometimes, it is true, raise my voice at people who get in my way, or do not do something I want them to. But the plain fact is nowadays you have to raise your voice occasionally if you want to go on living.

Nonetheless, the more I thought about such a ridiculous idea, farfetched as it was, that I could personally be responsible for making Polar Bear's arthritis worse, the more I realized that it was up to me to attack the idea head-on and get rid of it once and for all. I even decided, on the remote off chance that a tiny bit of what those authors had the gall to suggest might have a grain of truth in it, to mend my ways, at least enough so that there could not be even a shadow of a doubt about my exemplary behavior. For one thing, I decided to keep my voice down — Polar Bear did not like loud voices from anyone, even me. For another, I decided to stop thinking about myself, and think only about him. It is not easy for me to think about other people, except about their faults, of which most of them have so many, but just the same I tried. Then too I focused on the arthritis question. I found my own arthritis hard enough to bear — the way, for example, it restricted my movements — but the more I thought about it, in my new unselfish way of thinking, the more I realized that to have such a disease inflicted on a cat, whose leaps, jumps, runs, and other acrobatics were, from kittenhood on, the very essence of his being, was ten times worse. In other words, I made the decision that as much as I would like to get over my arthritis, I wanted Polar Bear to get over his even more.

It would not, I discovered, be easy for either of us to get rid of arthritis. Arthritis, I learned from just about every book on the subject, even the medically self-serving ones, is hardly a disease which is any ornament to the miracles of modern medicine. The one thing you can say about it is that it is a disease from which very few people, and presumably even fewer animals, ever die, but once you have said that you have said just about everything. If people and animals do not die from it, neither do they ever get well — in fact, they get steadily worse, until they might as well die from it. I do not have statistics about how many animals have arthritis, but I do have statistics on how many people have it. These statistics say that close to forty million people in this country have at least one form of arthritis or another by the time they are in their fifties. By the time they are in their sixties, 80 percent of them have it, and by the time they get to my age I have no intention of telling you what percent have it any more than I have any intention of repeating to you how old I am. But I will tell you that, by my figuring, it is well over 100 percent.

To begin at the beginning, arthritis comes from the Greek roots *arthr-*, meaning joint, and *-itis*, meaning inflammation. And one thing that is certain about the disease is that, whether in man or beast, it is very old. It goes, indeed, even farther back from the Greeks to the Egyptians and, according to *Arthritis*, by Mike and Nancy Samuels, arthritis has been located in the fossil remains of a swimming reptile who lived 100 million years ago. When I first explained this to Polar Bear, however, he was not very impressed — he is not big on reptiles, whether swimming or not. He was not even impressed when I did my best to make clear to him that the very same kind of arthritis that he and I had — osteoarthritis — was found in Java Man, who lived half a million years ago. Frankly, I was not surprised he was not impressed at this — but one thing we both were sure of was that Java Man didn't get over it, either.

There are, of course, many kinds of arthritis. Some have arthritis of the hips, as Polar Bear and I did, and some have not osteoarthritis at all but rheumatoid arthritis. And, besides these arthritises, people arthritis, if not animal arthritis, can affect just about every conceivable joint, including those mentioned in the old song about everything being connected from the thigh bone to the hip bone or whatever it was. Indeed, arthritis runs the gamut from the neck, the shoulders, the arms, the hands, the wrists, the fingers, the legs, the knees, and even the toes. Indeed, Mike and Nancy Samuels add that secondary or traumatic arthritis can affect any joint that happens to get injured.

Just about the only good piece of news they had — and frankly about the only piece of good news I found about arthritis — was that it rarely affects the ankle. Immediately after I had found this out I carefully looked at Polar Bear's ankles and even went to the trouble of moving them around a little. He thought I was off my rocker, but the fact is he didn't seem to have a trace of arthritis in them.

Curiously enough gout, perhaps the most famous of all the arthritic diseases and the one which, in your granddaddy's day, was even then the recognized granddaddy of all arthritiscs, is perhaps the most extraordinary of all. The reason is that, while it does not involve the ankle, it does involve specifically the feet, or rather just one foot, and for that matter just one toe of one foot, the big toe. "Typically," one arthritis book tells us, "the initial gout attack affects a single joint — usually the big toe — and comes on suddenly, in the middle of the night." Unfortunately, the same book also tells us, "Little is known about what causes a gout attack to end, but all attacks are self-limiting and eventually go away by themselves."

Until they do go away by themselves, however, gout is incredibly miserable. I had an attack one night, and I really could not believe the pain — and all of it in one damned big toe. I tried everything. I tried wiggling the toe. I tried getting up and standing on the toe. I tried getting up on tiptoe. I tried just walking and moving around. But literally nothing did any good. The pain would vary in intensity, and it would come on and go off in waves. But just when you thought it was gone — or was at least really going — then it would come back again. I think Polar Bear thought I had gone completely around the bend, but there was one thing I was thankful for and that was that I had never read anything about cats getting gout. And, in Polar Bear's case, I was doubly thankful for this, because if there was one thing Polar Bear could not stand it was anyone messing with his toes. Even after fifteen years of cutting his toenails, when you would have thought he would have gotten used to it, he never did. Ever since he fixed one of his leery eyes at those clippers, he regarded it as the beginning of not just a brand-new war, but total war.

Although few arthritis pains compare to the pain of gout, the fact remains that in almost all forms of arthritis the pain never really goes away, as at least it does eventually in gout. But one thing is certain. Whatever form of arthritis you have, the chances are the pain will be enough to lead you, sooner or later, to try some of the most bizarre remedies known in the history of medicine.

There are, to begin with, a wide variety of venom remedies. That is right — that is what I said, venom remedies, and I am not kidding. Snake venom, for example, crops up again and again in books about arthritis remedies. And in case you are not happy about trying snake venom on your arthritis, what would you say to having a go at bee venom?

Again, I am not kidding. In one book on arthritis, called *Arthritis: What Works* — which by this time I expected to be a very small volume indeed — authors Dava Sobel and Arthur Klein reported on a couple who had even used bee venom on gout. Their report ran as follows:

> "Bee venom cured the crippling arthritis in my toe joint immediately and completely," says a computer consultant from New Jersey. "My husband and I caught

> a few bees in a mayonnaise jar, and shook them gently 'til they were dizzy and vulnerable. Then we used long tweezers to hold them around the middle and placed them in the circle I had drawn in magic marker to show the area of pain in my foot. Bingo!"

My guess is that woman attended too many church socials. In any case, one thing I certainly did not like was the idea of treating bees like that. I know the woman said she and her husband only shook them gently, but still, keeping them in a mayonnaise jar and then using tweezers to hold them around the middle struck me as something of which I would not want to be a part — particularly when the bee gets just one sting a lifetime.

In any case, another report on bee venom stated that being stung accidentally was not the answer. This report came from a Charles Marz of Middlebury, Vermont, who stated that he had "provided free treatments with live bee stings for fifty years for the many people with arthritis who visit his home." Mr. Marz maintained that to achieve the desired result he had to administer to his patients, in the course of a year, as many as two or three thousand stings.

My feeling about this was that if the treatment did not sound any worse than having arthritis, neither did it sound a whole lot better. And, if there was one thing I was certain of, I would not try bee venom on Polar Bear. Polar Bear was not fond of bees. They made too much noise to suit him, and although, so far as I know, he had never been stung by one, he came awfully close to it one day on his balcony when he was sniffing away at one and I had to come to his rescue and explain to the bee that he should buzz off — an expression which, in view of the circumstances, I felt deserved no apology. I therefore gave it, and to my amazement the bee did what he was told.

Besides the venoms there are literally dozens, if not hundreds, of other curious remedies for arthritis. Many of these involve metals. Copper is easily the most favored of these metals, and people with arthritis have been wearing copper since the time of the Greeks. Indeed the wearing of copper bracelets, whereby some of the copper is supposedly absorbed through the skin to combat the disease, has not only long been touted, it is still highly touted today.

A friend of mine, Ed Kneedler, a fellow arthritis sufferer and a distinguished musical authority who now lives in Palm Springs, recently presented me with a bracelet, and I have worn it faithfully since the day he gave it to me, fearing that if I did not he would see me without it and be hurt. Actually, I have not found it has done me any good, but neither has it done me any harm — which, for an arthritis remedy, is really pretty exciting stuff, as witness the following report from an Arthritis Foundation Self-Help Course instructor from Indiana:

> Sure, I've tried copper bracelets. But other than "psychological relief" you only get green wrists. There's no harm in them, so if they make you "feel better" then it might be worth having green wrists.

I tried a copper bracelet — or rather, copper necklace — on Polar Bear and, finally, after much fussing — both on my part, for trying to get it the right size, and on his, on general principles — I got him to wear it. I watched carefully, however, to see that he did not turn green. If there was one thing I did not need, it was a beautiful white cat with lovely green eyes who turned all green. Fortunately, he never did. Neither, however, did his necklace seem to do him any more good than my bracelet did me.

If copper doesn't do the trick, arthritis sufferers can always take a more expensive step and go for the gold. "Gold," *Arthritis: What Works* tells us in no uncertain terms, "was first used to treat arthritis for the wrong reasons — when the disease was thought to be a chronic infection of the joints." Nonetheless, gold in either injection or pill form did itself proud in an arthritis survey conducted by the authors:

> Several of our participants used gold successfully for long periods of time — 10, 20, or even 30 years — before it finally lost its effectiveness for them. They never developed any side effects, they just woke up one day to find that the treatment didn't work anymore and it was time to try something else. Others got good results for several years before a toxic reaction ended the therapy. "Gold did the best," claims a housewife from Michigan, "but I developed a rash and got ulcers in my mouth. Now I'm on oral gold."

Even the metal uranium figures in arthritic remedies. I noticed it first in the almost endless advice one receives about travelling for arthritis. The best place to go, most books will tell you, is a hot, dry climate — i.e., a desert. But one book claimed the ideally perfect place for an arthritis sufferer to go was to an abandoned uranium mine.

This was perhaps the easiest of the arthritis remedies for me to abandon. I always think of mines, even in hot, dry climates, as cold and damp, and I just could not see Polar Bear and me grubstaking our way West, until we finally put down our stakes in an abandoned uranium mine — only to learn, when we had done all that, that it did not help our arthritis in the slightest. The only good thing I could think of about the whole venture was that, although we might be cold and damp and miserable for a long time, we sure would be in high cotton when the next uranium boom came along.

Curiously, not just patients but doctors, too, when they get arthritis, have resorted to going to extraordinary lengths when searching for a cure. Among these was none other than the world famous heart surgeon Dr. Christiaan Barnard, who travelled from South Africa to Switzerland for fetal lamb cell injections and then to New Zealand for green lipped mussels. Some doctors, too, have placed their hope in perhaps the oldest of all medical sciences — acupuncture. Developed thousands of years ago, acupuncture was discovered accidentally, according to one source, when ancient warriors hit by arrows felt instant relief from pain and illness which they apparently had for a long time before that particular battle. Although this discovery was not something I wanted to go to the bank on, the results favoring acupuncture in the Sobel-Klein survey for arthritis were higher than for any other treatment except gold. Even here, however, there were some dissenting voices. "Acupuncture," said one patient, "was great for my shoulders, but didn't do any good for my hands or feet."

Nonetheless, if acupuncture had its adherents, so too did just plain yoga. Indeed, yoga gave either temporary or lasting relief to thirty-six of forty-one participants, and only two had no relief. "If nothing else," wrote one yoga practitioner from South Dakota, "daily yoga keeps one *thinking* healthy and spry."

Besides the acupuncture and yoga believers, there are also a wide variety of food believers, not the least of whom are the fish oil adherents. Fish oil, taken in large amounts, produced promising results if one did not mind, as one patient noted, "burping up a fish oil taste."

Along with fish oil, there is literally a whole host of arthritis diets. The general idea of losing weight when you have arthritis, to make walking and generally getting around easier — if you are, well, less round — is of course obvious. But as for what specific foods and drinks are best and which are worse, lots of luck. I have personally read many arthritis books which, while generally agreeing on eating more vegetables, fish, and poultry and less meat and salt and fats, go on from there to be almost totally contradictory about specific foods. One book, for example, will tell you that dairy products should be avoided, while another will say that, for arthritis, milk is literally the perfect food. One book will tell you to eat as much fruit as possible, another will tell you to avoid fruit. One will say eat all the vegetables you want, another to eat some vegetables and avoid others. Even this they break down. One, for example, is pro-shade vegetables, another firmly anti-shade.

Along with diets, people with arthritis try an almost unbelievable number of different pills to relieve the day-to-day and particularly night-to-night pain of arthritis. People take aspirin, to name one, in huge doses — three or four five-grain tablets four to six times a day — often only cutting this dosage when, as the Samuels describe it, "Patients begin to experience ringing in their ears."

And aspirin is by no means the only favorite pill. There are literally hundreds of other pills which are taken to relieve arthritis pain. Unfortunately, an extraordinary number of these also have severe side effects. The particular pill I was given, for example, and had taken for years, ended by giving me the worst single ulcer pain, and indeed the worst ulcer I ever had. And as if this was not enough, shortly after I had stopped taking the pill I saw on the front page of the newspapers a story that the drug had just been found in tests to cause ulcers when taken for a five-month period or more. And I, as I say, had been taking it for years.

One of my favorite personal experiences with pills came from a man with whom I occasionally have breakfast at a nearby coffee shop. "You know what you ought to take for that arthritis?" he told me. No, I said wanly, having over the years suffered almost as much from the advice as to what I ought or ought not to do as I have from the disease itself. "Take alfalfa," he said sternly. Sir? I questioned, still pretty wan. "Alfalfa," he repeated. You mean hay? I asked gently. "Not just any hay," he said, "alfalfa hay. It'll do for you just what it does for the horses and the cows."

At last, I thought, I had at least found a possible remedy for Polar Bear. After all, if he was not a horse or a cow he was at least an animal, and an awful lot of animals eat hay. In any case, sure enough, in short order my friend showed up with a huge, wide bottle filled with pills and marked "Alfalfa." The pills were not small, either. I looked at the bottle nervously, still thinking of Polar Bear in size. How often do you take one? I asked. "One!" he exclaimed. "Not one! Take ten in the morning, and ten at night."

I took the bottle without a word. I could not summon the moral fiber to tell my friend I planned to try the pills on Polar Bear, but one look at those pills convinced me that there were few men living, and I presumed not too many dead, who could ever succeed in getting twenty of those monsters a day down Polar Bear, hay or no hay. What I did decide to do instead was to attempt to get just one pill down him. But to say this was a failure would be an understatement. It was a disaster. In the first place, the pill was too big for me to conceal it when I approached him with it. And, in the second place, it was so much bigger than his mouth that he assumed it was not a pill at all, but some kind of Frisbee. He was all for having a go at having a game with it, too, but he never did get so much as one taste of it inside him.

Unfortunately, I did not get any better from the alfalfa, either. But the reference to horses made by the man who gave the alfalfa to me brought to mind many examples of people who have tried various liniments for arthritis. Indeed, more than 70 percent of the participants in the arthritis survey said they used at least some kind of "Rub-on Balms." "Many of these products," the Sobel-Klein book declared, "are counter-irritants — that is, they try to make you forget about pain by irritating your skin to make it feel hot." Whether this is true or not, one thing was certain. Many of these "Rub-on Balms" had remarkably famous names, like Ben-Gay, and Sloan's Liniment, and Absorbine, Jr. "Ben-Gay and Sloan's Liniment are wonderful for me," a shipping clerk from California wrote in the survey. "If I take a scalding hot bath, cover my knees and ankles with liniment and wrap them in Ace bandages, I can sleep for a few hours with no discomfort."

Encouraging as this was to hear, it was not my favorite in the entire survey. This came from a Georgia accountant — about the way he handled his arthritic discomfort. "I find," he wrote, "that making love *after* a hot bath or shower lessens the pain in my hip."

It was good to think about, all right — feeling better without any medicine at all. I could see no reason why it might not be the start of a whole new field of sex science.

Not long after this I tried for myself a brand-new arthritis therapy — at least one new to me — which was written about in the *New York Times.* It was a biomagnetic treatment, and the idea was to bombard the affected joints with magnetic pulses. According to the *Times* article, the therapy had been first tried at a clinic in Waterbury, Connecticut, and now a new clinic had just opened in Melville, Long Island. Also according to the article, seventeen hundred patients had already received the therapy, and 70 percent of these had experienced at least some relief. Excitedly, I drove out to the clinic, although I did not take Polar Bear because I had already decided that if there was to be any bombardment, it had better be against me first and then, if it did any good, I could try it on him. In any case, during my first treatment, which lasted one hour, I lay in one of a long row of coffin-sized beds. If I was not comfortable, however, I did not feel anything from the bombardment of the pulses, which at least relieved my worry about the treatment. My relief was short-lived, however, because it was interrupted by the appearance of Marian. When she first saw me that day in that strange bed, she could not resist coming up and saying softly, albeit in a voice that could be heard by several other patients, "Rest in peace."

I went seventeen more times for the one-hour treatment, because the regime was supposed to be nine hours for each hip. And even after the last treatment, sadly enough, I did not feel any relief. Although I tried hard to maintain an open, if not optimistic, mind, in the end I had to admit, at least to myself, that I had not found that the treatment had to any major extent alleviated my pain.

In fairness to the biomagnetic people, the fact is that arthritis pain is an extremely tough customer. It is not surprising, therefore, that whole books have been written about this alone and, even in the books where all areas of arthritis are discussed, pain is given high prominence. In the book I have mentioned before, by Mike and Nancy Samuels, for example, there is a large listing called "Pain Control Interventions for Arthritis," and under this general heading there is one in particular called "Distraction." Under this are six separate items. The very first caught my eye: "Keep busy," it said, "with passionate interests, hobbies, work."

I certainly liked the sound of that one — at least all but the hobbies and the work. If there is one thing I can always keep busy with, it's passionate interests.

The Samuels' second recommendation was the longest one. "During painful activities," it said, "purposely think of something else that is positive (imagery), and/or mentally repeat positive affirmations (e.g., 'I can do it.')."

Frankly I am not big on repeating "I can do it" when I am not the one who is doing it in the first place. Nonetheless I was willing to give it a try, but I promise you I did it in such a low voice that no one could possibly hear me.

Suggestion number three was simple. "Listen to music, sing." That one I knew I would have no trouble with. In the shower, for example, I can really sing up a storm. Many times I have even gotten Polar Bear listening so closely that he actually got wet.

Fourth was even easier: "Watch television," it said. That one got to me. As I am sure you realized from having read the television chapter, I have heard of a lot of excuses for watching television, but being told to watch it to distract from the pain of arthritis did not seem to me to get the job done. Most of the time, far from distraction, what you would get would be the addition of having to see one of those awful new shows added to the pain of your arthritis.

Number five was perhaps the easiest of all. "Be around people," it said. That one I really jumped on with both feet. I have told you and told you writing is for hermits, and I hate it. It is much more fun to be around anybody, even somebody you cannot stand.

The final one suggested was right down my alley. "Get," it said, " a pet."

The only trouble with that one was what would I tell Polar Bear when he was in pain from *his* arthritis? I could not very well tell him to get a person — he already had one. But I certainly did applaud the idea of telling people to get a pet. One of my favorite animal soapbox speeches involves telling people that I believe in pets for senior citizens not only from the point of view of the increased adoptions for the pets but also from the actual therapeutic benefits for the senior citizens. The plain fact is that a senior citizen with a pet has to do what he or she should be doing for his or her own good — that is, to stop thinking about himself or herself. He or she simply cannot spend every waking moment worrying about his or her own aches and pains when he or she has a pet who needs watering and feeding, and just plain looking at and talking to, not to mention petting and patting, particularly when this is good for not only the pet, but also for the person.

In any case, for the difference in treating cat arthritis and human arthritis, I returned to the remarkable book *The New Natural Cat* by Anitra Frazier and Norma Eckroate. Readers with good memories will recall I have already mentioned this book earlier in this chapter. Readers with poor memories will not remember, of course, so they might as well go back and read that part again. Naturally this is going to keep all the rest of us waiting while they are doing this, so I will take this time to say that one of the things I like best about *The New Natural Cat* book is its subtitle: *A Complete Guide for Finicky Owners*. Everybody is always talking about how finicky their cats are, but they never talk about how finicky they are. And come to think of it, I honestly cannot remember the last time I met a cat owner who, when it came to finickiness, could not give his or her cat cards and spades.

Anyway, now that we are joined by our readers with poor memories, one of the most remarkable things about the book by Misses Frazier and Eckroate is their attention, when it comes to treating your cat for arthritis, to the matter of stress. Indeed, their very first suggestion about what to do when your cat has arthritis, right after "Consult veterinarian for a diagnosis," is "Check environment for stresses such as loud radios, careless children, and pollutants."

I went over these one by one. I never played a loud radio for Polar Bear — in fact, twenty-four hours a day I played for him a radio station which advertises itself as "Soft and Easy." No rock or any other terrible noises. Of course, the station still played a lot of modern music with lyrics which do not rhyme properly, but nowadays what can you expect? In any case, Polar Bear never complained about it and, like me, he was especially fond of Patsy Cline.

With the authors' second cause of cat stress — careless children — I am in wholehearted agreement. There are, in my opinion, three terrible ages of childhood — one to ten, ten to twenty, and twenty to thirty. And whatever age they are, there are very few of them who are not careless and nowadays, at least from my observation, are likely to remain so at least until they are thirty and perhaps longer.

As for the authors' third cause — pollutants — I am also an authority on these, as of course I am on most things. I am very careful, for example, about flowers. Flowers can be very dangerous for cats, in case you do not realize this. In Polar Bear's early days I gave them up completely, and in his later days, although we occasionally had flowers, I made sure to put them in high places well out of Polar Bear's reach.

Make no mistake, though. The authors of this book do not stop with radios and children and pollutants causing cats' stress. They also include grown-ups and partial grown-ups who have parties where, apparently, more people talk than listen. On this subject I agree with the authors completely. If there is anything I cannot stand it is somebody else talking when I want to talk. I know it upset Polar Bear, too, when I was talking to him about not doing something he was doing. Of course he went right on doing it, just as if I was not talking, but I still do not think he ever liked the talking, either. But it was not only talking the authors said gave cats stress. There was a whole list of other things. Their very first one, for example, brought me up short. It was, very simply, "Any surprise."

That certainly covered a multitude of sins for Polar Bear. For one thing, he put everything in the category of a surprise if he himself had not seen it happen before. For another thing, he also put everything in the category of a surprise if it was anything which had happened before whether he had seen it or not. But the authors of *The New Natural Cat* wisely confined their advice to, and I quote, "Announcing your intentions before doing anything — touching the cat, giving medication and so on."

In any case, the very next item the authors placed on their stress list was "Loud Noises." "Caution all visitors," the authors said, "to speak in calm and soothing tones." Sometimes, reading the book, I had the feeling that even the ancient Egyptians, who worshipped the cat, would not pass muster with these authors. But on the subject of stress they certainly knew what they were talking about.

Phil Maggitti, a friend of mine and a distinguished animal author, has, perhaps better than anyone, told the story of cat stress when it particularly pertains to outdoor cats — those without even the benefit of an enclosed wired run. The statistics, he points out, are inarguable — the life span of an average indoor cat is twelve to fifteen years, and that of an average outdoor cat at two to three years. Maggitti went on from there, in his typical humorous style, to number, backwards, his "16 Reasons Why Cats Should Be Kept Indoors":

16. They are less likely to be hit by a car when crossing the living room than they are when crossing the street.
15. Their owners are less apt to have rabies than are free-roaming animals.
14. Their owners are less likely to bite them than are free-roaming animals.
13. Their owners are not as liable to have fleas, fungus, or worms as are free-roaming animals.
12. It's unlikely their owner will transmit to them the Feline Leukemia Virus, Feline Immunodeficiency Virus, and other contagious diseases.
11. There is less chance of getting a leg caught in a steel-jawed trap.
10. When it's ten o'clock at night, their owners will always know where they are.
9. Birds will like them better.
8. Crotchety neighbors will like them better.
7. They'll never come home looking like something the cat dragged in.
6. It will be much more difficult for people to steal them.
5. They won't disappear as often.
4. Their owners will never have to bail them out of the local shelter.
3. They sleep most of the time anyway.
2. Their owners won't have to go calling them all

over the neighborhood when it's time for dinner.

1. They'll live longer, happier lives, and so will their owners.

In the middle of worrying about my arthritis and my stress factors and Polar Bear's arthritis and his stress factors — not to mention indoor and outdoor cats and people who claim the only way their cats can be happy is to be outdoors — I had an accident. I was, in fact, hit by a truck.

Let me begin at the beginning. It all happened when I was on my way to breakfast. Of all the things nowadays which in my opinion are not what they were in the old days I would put women first, and children second. But I would put breakfast a strong third.

Start with your grapefruit — and before you even try to start on it, ask yourself when was the last time you had a really good grapefruit, a delicious, old-fashioned, sweet grapefruit the kind which, when you were a child, was everywhere. And if you do, by pure luck, manage to come upon one, you can be sure it will not be possible to eat it because it will not be properly cut. In the old days the cutting of grapefruit was an art passed on from father to son, from mother to daughter, among waiters and waitresses, busboys and buspersons, marmalade boys and marmalade girls. There was even a special spoon for grapefruit, with one side of the spoon with teeth on it in case someone had made a miscut and you had to correct it. Nowadays, literally no one knows how to cut a grapefruit, and if they do know they will not do it. It was so delicate, that fine cut with a sharp knife not on the outer side of that delicate inner peel, but right along the tender inside section of the fruit. What you have today instead is something done by some idiot with a clumping machine which, I believe, was undoubtedly meant to be used for some outdoor purpose such as baling hay. In any case, that idiot clumps down three or four times on three or more sections of the fruit, and manages to render the whole thing totally inedible.

But enough about grapefruit. Polar Bear, like most cats, did not like fruit and so, when I gave up grapefruit, at least I was doing something of which Polar Bear approved. As for the rest of breakfast — and remember, breakfast was a meal Polar Bear and I particularly enjoyed eating together, he out of one side of my dish or plate and I out of my side. Or at least we started that way, and went on until his side was gone, and then he ate out of my side, too. But even Polar Bear, I believe, in his brief life noticed the decline and fall of breakfast.

One place he would particularly have noticed it, I believe, is at cereal. Look at your average cereal eater today, if you can bear to do it. I do not include children cereal eaters. Please do not look at them — it is too painful. They'll have milk all over their mouths. Polar Bear never had milk all over his mouth when he was eating cereal. But actually milk is one of the things I am talking about when it comes to cereal. Today I see person after person — forget the children — eating cereal, generally cold cereal by the way, with skim milk, that monstrous, blue, anemic, watery milk. In my day, in the good old days, what we had on our cereal was not anything like any kind of milk. There was not even such a thing as half-and-half in those days, either. What we had was good old-fashioned cream, so thick there were times when you had to spoon it out to get it. Of course we ate it on good old-fashioned hot cereal. A decent portion of that hot cereal, too, in a large bowl. None of these cold cereals in those awful little boxes that are so terrible to open — apparently on the theory children will get into them, and in any case boxes which, in case you haven't noticed lately, they are putting less and less cereal in.

All right, after the grapefruit and the cereal came the eggs. The eggs are still perfectly all right nowadays — the trouble is the way they are cooked. When was the last time, for example, you got a correctly timed three-minute boiled egg? You cannot remember, can you, because all you get today is a one-minute slurp of a boiled egg. Actually, I believe Polar Bear could always tell when a boiled egg was not cooked exactly three minutes and was, instead, just that one-minute slurp I mentioned. But that did not mean he liked it that way — he was just putting up with it, as I did, because he knew, too, that everywhere, but particularly at breakfast, we were constantly letting down, down, down.

In any case, forget boiled eggs and ask yourself whatever happened to good old shirred eggs. Today you cannot even find anybody who knows what a shirred egg was, let alone is, and if you do find somebody he or she will not know how to cook them properly. And if you do find somebody who knows what shirred eggs are, and even does know how to cook them properly — well, you are not out of the woods yet because the chances are that person does not know where to find a shirred egg dish. And let me tell you, a shirred egg without a shirred egg dish to cook it in and eat it off is not worthy to be called a shirred egg, let alone eaten as one.

Well, I will not go on. Of course, there were other things

which went with the eggs — kippers and herring, and smoked salmon, and cheeses, and marmalade, and all sorts of things. But there is no use thinking about it. Your old-fashioned breakfast has gone with the wind. My theory is it went that way because breakfast was a man's meal, and therefore was irritating to all the modern women who did not understand it. And let me tell you one more thing — the number of women you know who understand a good breakfast, let alone ever ate one, you can count on the fingers of one hand.

But no matter. Enough of breakfast, except to repeat that on the morning of the fateful day of my accident I was, as I told you, on my way to breakfast — I was going, as a matter of fact, to the New York Athletic Club. It is not a great breakfast at the New York Athletic Club, mind you, but it is a passable breakfast and that, for nowadays, is at least something. But as I say, enough of breakfast. In any case, to get where I was going I had to cross Seventh Avenue at Central Park South, and even as New York City crossings go this was a bad one. You get, for the particular light for that particular crossing — and in that time you are going straight across what amounts to three different streams of traffic — exactly thirteen seconds. First, there is the stream where the traffic from Central Park South goes downtown on Seventh Avenue. Then there is also a stream going the way I was going, east on Central Park South, across Seventh Avenue — but which sometimes decides to turn right to go down Seventh Avenue, and therefore can get you in the back. Third and finally, there is a stream going west on Central Park South which has an arrow which allows turning left to go down Seventh

Avenue. But the whole crosslight lasts, as I say, just thirteen seconds, and then the arrow comes on and the drivers who have been waiting for it have waited a long time, and are in a terrible hurry — particularly in morning rush hour — and they do not bother to be in one line, which they should be, but turn left in two lines. For these drivers, it is open season on anyone caught in the intersection.

That particular morning — at morning rush hour — there was not one but two trucks ready to make that turn left — one from the inside, or right, lane, and one from the outside, or wrong, lane. I had crossed more than three-quarters of the way as fast as I could, but I could not make it. The drivers of those two trucks appeared to me to gun their vehicles as if they were jumping off the starting gate to turn left and cross over that crosswalk as fast as they could. I knew, with my arthritis, I simply was not going to get all the way across, and that I was a goner. At the last moment I turned my head, and even considered that I might try to jump between the two trucks, but I was not up to that maneuver, either. All I can remember is raising my cane and shouting a futile "Stop!"

I do not remember a single other thing because whichever of the two trucks that hit me knocked me out, and the next thing I knew I was lying on the floor of a van. For a while I did not even really know this, but I at last learned it when I partly came to and noticed that someone who seemed to be sitting over me was wiping my face and neck — both of which were bleeding. The next thing I noticed, to my surprise, was that he was a policeman. And the thing I noticed after that — which was a pretty difficult thing not to notice — was that my neck was in a collar holding it to the floor. I asked the policeman if he could please loosen it a little. "No," he told me, "I'm not allowed to. I'm not even supposed to be wiping you the way I am." He then asked me, as he obviously had been for some time, if I knew where I was. I told him I knew then — that I was in some kind of a police car. He then asked me, and kept repeating this too, if I remembered what happened. I told him I thought I had been hit by a truck, and then asked him if this was true. He nodded, and then asked me if I remembered anything else. I told him I did not, but he kept on asking me anyway until finally I told him I did not want to answer any more questions, and why did he keep asking them? He told me he had to keep asking me questions so that I would not go back to sleep and perhaps lapse back into unconsciousness again — which, he said, would be dangerous.

Our conversation was not long, because I was being taken to Roosevelt Hospital, which was only three blocks from where I had been hit. I was also extremely lucky that the police were only two blocks away when they received the call about my being hit. For all the hurry to get me to Roosevelt Hospital, however, the thing I remember most about being there was what seemed to me, as I am sure most people experience at most hospitals, endless waiting. After a while, however, I saw Marian, and I was awfully glad to see her, despite the fact that just when she wanted to ask me about how I felt, they suddenly began what seemed an endless series of examinations and endless X-rays.

Actually the accident had been far tougher on Marian than on me because she had received just one message — which was that I had been hit by a truck and was being taken to Roosevelt Hospital. She had no idea of how serious the accident was. Typically, however, she got to the hospital almost as soon as I did and, awful as I looked, still bleeding, she was obviously relieved. "What hurts most?" she asked. My ribs, I said.

To this day I believe that no one who has not had broken ribs has any idea of how painful they are. It is not serious, they are not even bound as they were in the old days, and they get well by themselves without anything being done about them. But until they do get well, the pain is both constant and severe, and made worse by almost any movement. For at least a week I could not lie down in any kind of comfort, and at night I just sat up in a chair, doing everything I could to try to avoid any movement at all.

Actually, the injuries I received were described by the doctors in the emergency room at the hospital in one, what seemed to me, remarkable sentence:

> Traumatic injury to body resulting in: fracture of the left lateral fifth, sixth, and seventh ribs, resulting in loculated pleural hematoma with contusions and hematomas to chest wall; closed head trauma, cerebral concussion with unconsciousness and post concussion syndrome; facial trauma resulting in contusions and large hematoma of the left forehead and left frontal region with swelling and large periorbital ecchymosis and hematoma of left eye extending to medial right eye, resulting in complete closure of the left eye with purulent conjunctival discharge; unsightly facial scarring and/or discoloration; contusion of the left hand; contusion above and lateral to the left eye with hematoma extending down left cheek to chin and neck.

One thing was certain. After a report like that, I knew that very few friends who asked me how I was would believe me if I answered fine, thank you. So I decided to answer in kind. I had to practice a few times, but finally I got it down pat. Once I get that loculated pleural hematoma under control, I said, and then lick that darned large periorbital ecchymosis, I will be fit as a fiddle.

In any case, when I finally got home I had various nurses of both the day and the night variety, but second only to Marian my best nurse was Polar Bear. He was both watchcat and guardcat. I have a wonderful picture of him, taken just a few days after the accident — he is perched on my chest, right up to my neck, glowering out at someone who was obviously approaching. Polar Bear did not mind walking up and down on my ribs himself — even though he soon figured out there was a problem there, and did it as gently as possible — but he was absolutely certain that he did not want anyone else messing around with me. Even Dr. Anthony Grieco, who looked after my arthritis and came to examine me the very first night, was in Polar Bear's eyes simply one more suspect. As for Dr. Grieco himself, normally extremely cheerful and optimistic, I could see he was very concerned, and I believe that somehow Polar Bear had picked up his vibes.

As for the night nurse, Polar Bear was actually very fond of her, and grew to regard her as, if not his equal, at least his relief guard. He stayed on the bed all day long and did not seem to sleep at all, but from the moment the night nurse appeared, although he stayed on the bed, he went almost immediately to sleep as if it was, then, all right to do so — his relief was on the job.

An extraordinary number of people who came to see

me had stories of people being hit by vehicles. I had never realized how often it happened, and the more stories I heard the more I realized how lucky I had been not to have been killed or at least hurt worse than I was. In many cases, I learned more about automobiles hitting people than I wanted to know. I learned, for example, that while, nationally, the people killed by automobiles are six times more likely to be drivers or passengers than they are pedestrians, in New York pedestrians make up half of all fatalities. On the non-fatal side, which I was lucky enough to be, the fact remains that nationally more than fifty thousand pedestrians are hit by automobiles every year. And although there are no figures on the numbers hit in New York in comparison to other cities, it is not too hard to imagine that New York leads all others by a wide margin.

With all the bad news I heard, I did, however, hear two stories I particularly liked. One was what Marian said to the lawyer working on my lawsuit about being hit. After he told her that money one might receive for an injury like mine would be tax-free, Marian's answer was immediate. "Don't tell Cleveland," she said firmly. "He'll do it again."

The second story was equally hard to forget. It came when I called Walter Anderson, my editor at *Parade*, and broke the news to him that I had been hit by a truck.

Walter was, as always, all heart. "How," he asked, "is the truck?"

L'Envoi

I remember well — as I am sure anyone who has ever been owned by a cat always does — the first time I knew that Polar Bear was seriously ill. I remember it well, as I am sure you remember when you knew your cat was seriously ill. It is like being stabbed.

For months, I had failed to recognize signs I should have recognized — but which I always attributed to his arthritis. For one, there was his increasingly poor movement of his front legs, let alone the continuing problem of his arthritic back legs. For another, there was the matter of his lying down in an obviously not-wholly-comfortable position and not doing anything to rectify it as he surely would have in happier days. For still another, there was the matter of the doorbell ringing. For some time I had noticed that when this happened, he would go more and more slowly to it. But now I noticed there were times, even now most times, when he did not go at all. Just the same, although I recognized all of these signs and many more I put them down, at least at first, when they were not so glaringly apparent, either to his arthritis or to his being not as young as he was. It was not hard to do — he was, after all, no longer a spring chicken, or rather I should say, as better befits a cat, a spring kitten.

But, as I said at the beginning, I remember distinctly the first time I recognized it was something far worse than either arthritis or the mere inevitable gradual encroachment of old age. I was playing chess with Ed Kunz, a Swiss gentleman and a close friend of mine who lives in the same apartment building. Polar Bear was, as usual, lying asleep beside me on my chair, and I was leaning over to pat him from time to time. But chess is a very absorbing game, and one time when I had not looked at him for some moments and reached out to pat him I suddenly realized he was not there. At almost the same moment — or at least so it seemed to me — I heard a thump. Polar Bear had fallen to the floor. Or, rather, what he had done was flop to the floor. Indeed, what I later reconstructed was that he had suddenly woken and then equally suddenly pulled his legs up from under him and then, as best he could, he had tried to jump to the floor. But, as I reconstructed, he had not really done that because he simply could not jump anymore. And by then, since his front legs were almost as bad as his back ones, he had just flopped — and had fallen right on his face.

It was such a sad and awful sight that for a moment both Ed and I could not believe it. I — who, in Polar Bear's heyday had seen him jump down from the mantlepiece with no trouble at all — was now seeing a cat who could not even let himself down from a rather low chair and, indeed, in trying to do so had stunned himself.

As quickly as I could, I reached down and scooped him up and hugged him, and made a big fuss over him, and then carefully put him back down on the floor, in his basket-bed. From that moment on, only when I was right with him and paying close attention to him did I ever put him on the chair beside me — and particularly not when I was playing chess. And never again did I ever put him up on a chair or sofa or anything else when he was alone.

The worst part of what had happened, both Ed and I knew, and spoke about it, was that the same thing must have happened before. Then too, and perhaps many other times, somehow he had gotten up on something when no one else was around — or someone had put him up on something, and then had forgotten about him, and had gone away. And those times, too, he had undoubtedly fallen just the way he had that time with us.

And also, of course, he had not remembered those falls. All in all, looking back on what had happened, it was not just sad and bad, it was also something which made frighteningly clear to me that not only is it awful that animals, when they are sick, cannot tell us or even try to show us what is wrong, they cannot even seem to be able to tell themselves — or at least, in a case such as that falling, to remember exactly what it is they cannot do anymore.

At the same time, something else was beginning to be very clear to me. This was that animals battle whatever infirmity or wound or disability they have with such bravery and lack of complaining that it must actually be seen to be believed. I would see that quality in Polar Bear many times that terrible Spring, and I shall never forget it. Every now and then I would hear one of his small "AEIOU's" — the sound with which I had grown so lovingly familiar — and the only difference I could notice now was that it was, a little eerily, cut short, until it sounded almost like a plain "OW." It was not, of course, but that is what it sounded like.

Anyone who has ever been in a similar position to mine, and who has seen his or her animal carry on a difficult fight, can only love and respect that animal more, particularly when you realize that it takes a very special kind of courage. It takes a courage which is very different from human courage but is, if anything, more worthy of admiration, because human courage comes at least armed with some knowledge, whereas animal courage often comes with no knowledge at all — not even, in the case of disease, knowledge of what it is they fight.

In any case, after that awful flop to the floor I knew it was high time, and probably past high time, for me to take Polar Bear to the vet. I had not taken him for some time largely because it has been my observation that most of the people I know either take their animals to the vet too much — for all too often a purely fancied ailment — or they take them not enough. Unfortunately, after first belonging to the former category, as I wrote in the first chapter I later belonged to the latter category. Also, besides now belonging to that "not-bothering-the-vet" fraternity of cat owners, I was also a member of that almost equally large fraternity of cat owners who have had at least one unforgettably bad experience at the vet's — and so have learned to dread a visit there almost as much as their cats do. These experiences, in the vast majority of cases, are very seldom ones in which the vet behaved badly, or even the owner did — rather, they are most likely to be ones in which their cat did. Yet these experiences, of course, reflect badly not only on the vet and the owner, but also on almost everyone within cat earshot or sightshot, except the cat. The latter, it goes without saying, could not be enjoying himself more — and the worse the experience for others, the more the enjoyment for him.

I did not, however, have such an experience with Polar Bear. I had it, however, with a previous Fund for Animals office cat who shall be nameless not only to spare his friends among the staff, but also to spare him or at least his memory. What he did, and did in fact more than once, was to use the vet's office as a battlefield on which to express his opinion of dogs. The most embarrassing of these forays was the day he chose as his opponent a truly elephantine mixture of an Irish wolfhound and mastiff. On this occasion, he jumped from his carrier not just at the monster, but literally over the monster, his desire apparently being to land on the top of the monster's head. He did not actually achieve this, but managed to land on the top of the dog's head and neck. From this position of advantage he proceeded to rain down blows, with his well-unclawed claws, upon the rest of the dog's head. During this period the dog, with remarkable restraint, merely shut his eyes and then did his best to remove the intruder, first by vigorously shaking his head and neck and then, when that failed, by trying to wipe him off with his paws.

In the end no harm was done, but when I finally got that cat back in his carrier, and clamped the lid shut, I realized I owed a wide variety of apologies to every person and animal in the room, not excepting the dog in question. To the latter, as a final fillip to my apologies, I released an affectionate pat. At this, for the first time the dog's owner spoke to me. "Don't you dare," she said, sharply, "touch my dog."

As I have said, Polar Bear was not like the cat in that story. He was, however, as are almost all cats, extremely wary of a vet office, and regarded it at best as somewhere between a Lebanon and an Iraq. Altogether, although he loved Susan Thompson, his longtime vet, he would not have been a cat if he was not glad of as long a time as possible between visits. But this time, since Dr. Thompson had moved away to Long Island, he was faced with Dr. Fred Tierney, someone who to him was a stranger albeit one who had long shared an office with Dr. Thompson. Although Dr. Tierney could not have been more gentle or more considerate, I could tell from his first examination of Polar Bear, he was concerned. When he finished, I knew from the look in his eye that the news was not good. And it certainly was not. What Polar Bear had was that dreaded age-old disease which afflicts, in their old age, so many animals — uremic poisoning, or kidney failure.

I cannot even now bring myself to go over the day after

day, week after week, step by steps Dr. Tierney tested and tried — the treatments which sometimes seemed to make him suddenly better and then, equally suddenly it seemed, failed, as well as those which seemed at first, and oh so slowly, to help a little and then, just as slowly, also seemed to fail. At home, I could tell he was going steadily downhill by, if nothing else, his failing to eat. Indeed, no matter how many different foods I tried and how many different ways I tried to entice him to eat, he hardly seemed to eat at all. And, as for his drinking, the only water I had managed to get down him was water I administered myself with an eyedropper.

I remember best, toward the end, the intravenous and subcutaneous infusions Dr. Tierney gave him. These infusions, which are basically a form of dialysis, at first seemed to help so much — and indeed sometimes lasted as long as to give him four good days. But then, in between the treatments, it would be three good days, and then just two. And, finally, the treatments would last — at least toward making him better — just one day. And finally, too, there came the day, just before the intravenous infusion, during which I always held him, when Dr. Tierney said quietly, "I am beginning to wonder whether we're doing the little fellow much of a favor."

I did not answer, but I knew the answer. Even Dr. Tierney's calling him a "little fellow" was a tip-off. Polar Bear was a big cat, but somehow his face, once so beautifully round and handsome, was pitifully pinched-looking, and indeed all of him seemed to have shrunk. I knew we had come to what I had allowed myself to think about as little as possible. From the very first visit with Dr. Tierney, I had hounded him with questions about how much pain did Polar Bear have. For if there was one thing about which I was determined, it was that Polar Bear should not suffer pain. I hate to see any animal in pain, but for the cat who had probably done as much as any single cat who ever lived for the cause of cats in general, and adoption of strays in particular, and had done so not only in this country but also in nineteen other countries where the books about him were published — for that cat to suffer pain was simply, to me, unconscionable.

Finally I came up with my answer to Dr. Tierney's question of whether we were doing Polar Bear a favor. I answered by asking him another question — which was, simply, how long could we expect to keep him going with the infusions? "I can keep him going for four or five weeks," Dr. Tierney said, again quietly, "but the last two or three will be very tough on him."

That, for me, was enough. Dr. Tierney and I made a simple agreement. We would see how that particular infusion did. But if it did nothing — as we suspected it would not — we would, the next day, let Polar Bear go.

The day was at least a day off, and so the next morning, when the infusion was obviously failing again, I sent for Polar Bear's close friends to come to say goodbye to him — among them every single one of the staff and volunteers from the Fund for Animals office. Each one of them held him in their lap, and hugged him, and each one of them, when he or she did so, was crying. As for Marian, she of course went with me on Polar Bear's last awful ride to the vet. Neither of us spoke a word.

Vets are not always keen on having the owners hold their animal or even being present in the same room when their animal is being put down, and the reason is that most of them have had experiences with it which do not make it practicable — experiences ranging from hysterics to last-minute changes of mind. In my case, I was pleased that Dr. Tierney never even mentioned it. He knew, without my saying it, that not only did I want to be in the room with Polar Bear, I wanted to be holding Polar Bear. Marian, too, had her hand on him.

The first injection was an anesthetic but then, before the final one, the sodium pentobarbital, something happened which I shall never forget. Polar Bear was lying on a metal-top table, and I was holding his head with both my hands and, as I say, Marian's hands were on him too but, just before the final injection, with what must have been for him, considering his condition, incredible effort, he pushed in a kind of swimming movement on the metal directly toward me. I knew he was trying to get to me, and although Dr. Tierney was already administering the fatal shot, I bent my face down to meet that last valiant effort of his, and with both my hands hugged him as hard as I could.

In what seemed just a few seconds it was all over. Dr. Tierney did a last check. "He's gone," he said quietly. Only then did I release my hugging hold, but, as I say, I still remember that last effort of his, and I shall remember it always. I only hope that someday I shall forget that part of my memory which tells me that I was part of doing something wrong to him, but rather there will remain only the memory that I was part of doing something which had to be done.

Actually, leaving the room, I was good — at least I was good leaving the examination room. When I got to the outer office, however, I saw Dorsey Smith, a dear friend of mine and Polar Bear's too, who was holding her own cat in her hands. "Is it Polar Bear?" she asked me. I nodded. But when she also asked, "Is he all right?" I could not even shake my head. Instead I did something so unknowingly, so un-Bostonian, and so un-Me — something I could not help, not even just in front of Dorsey, but with all those other patients there, too — I burst into tears. It was embarrassing, and I was ashamed, but the worst part was that, for the first time in my life that I can remember, I could not stop crying.

I wasn't too good afterwards, either. My daughter Gaea, who lives in Pittsburgh, had wanted to come to New York for a visit, although I knew she just said that so she could be with me when I lost Polar Bear. She had always been very fond of him. What she wanted to do that very afternoon, she said when I met her, was to go to see the movie *Howards End*. I knew that was something she had made up, too, because she did not want me to go back to the apartment until Marian had had a chance to remove Polar Bear's things, or at least hide them in a closet.

I played along with this deception, although I knew what was going on. I also knew I would not like *Howards End*, and I did not. Whoever Howard was, he certainly had no end and neither, it seemed, did his movie — although I doubt that I am being fair to it, because that particular afternoon I probably would have found fault with even one of my favorite movies, like *All About Eve* or *Double Indemnity*.

In any case, when Gaea and I got back to the apartment, Marian was there, and she had indeed done an excellent job of removing and hiding at least most of Polar Bear's things — the basket-bed, the toys, the scratching post, his dishes, and even his litter pan. Anyone who has had to go through an animal's death — and we all do sooner or later, and many times, too, in our lives — knows what it is like to come upon a favorite toy, a favorite ball of yarn, or indeed a favorite anything, or even something which was not a favorite, but which was still his or hers. Even a dish can do it. Although, as I say, Marian had removed all his regular dishes, I still came upon much later, when neither Marian nor Gaea were there, a little dish I liked to put his nightly snacks on. I took the dish, and sat down with it in my hand. I turned it over and over, and just sat there, and kept sitting there for so long I actually fell asleep with it. It made no sense, but then, at a time like that, more things do not make sense than do. It is the first part of the miserable loneliness which lies ahead for you, because what you are still trying to do, of course, whether you know it or not, is to hold on to your animal.

But even coming across one of your animal's things is not by any means all of what you must go through. You must also go through sitting and looking and listening, and actually thinking you see or hear your animal. At such a time, even a look at one of your animal's favorite places will be too much for you and, during the first few nights, if you are anything like me, you will not only see and hear your animal before you go to sleep — if indeed you can sleep — you will even feel his paws padding on your bed and then, after that, you will dream about him. My dreams were awful — Polar Bear in trouble, and in a place where I could see him but could not get to him — or else me in trouble, where he could see me but for some reason would not come to me. So many dreams had just one or the other of these two plots — so similar they seemed like endless replays.

But for me the worst part was not the sitting and thinking, or the lying and sleeping, or even the dreaming — it was the simple matter of coming home and not finding him at the door. Polar Bear always seemed to know from the time I stepped out of the elevator that it was me, and he would always be walking back and forth just out of reach of the door as it swung open, and yet near enough to rub against my leg. Whereupon, always, I gave him first a pat, then a pull-up, then a hug, and finally a hold-up of him over my head. It was our ritual.

Now, of course, there was nothing. No him, no rub, no pat, no pull-up, no hug, no hold-up, no nothing. Night after night I would come home and just walk in quickly and sit down, still in my coat. The whole apartment had, for me, become an empty nothingness. I can only describe it as living in a void. I did not want to be anywhere else, but neither did I really want to be there. It was not just that Polar Bear was not there — it was the awful, over-powering weight of knowing he was never ever going to be there again.

As I write about it all now, I realize something I did not realize then — how lucky I was compared to so many others who have to face the loss of their animal without other animal people around them. I, at least, was surrounded by animal people. There were calls and letters and cards and wires and even faxes. And they all were so completely understanding, because they had all obviously, at some time or another, been through it themselves. I remember perhaps best a card from my friend

Ingrid Newkirk. "Damn them for dying so young," she wrote, in her inimitable inverse-perverse way. After reading that I laughed — the first real laugh I had had since Polar Bear died.

I compared, during this time, my good fortune in having such understanding friends as against the fortunes of those whose sadness, I knew, must often be greeted with such incredible lines as, "But after all, it was just an animal," or even, "Why don't you just get another?"

Of one thing I was certain. Anyone who ever said either one of those things to me would not be likely ever to say one of them again — at least not in my presence. In any case, during this period I made it my business to learn about the extraordinary number of books and pamphlets about animal loss there are nowadays, not to mention the hundreds of support groups and even hotlines to which those faced with the loss of an animal can turn. Up until the 1970's, I learned, there were almost none of these in existence. Now there is even a group called the Delta Society in Renton, Washington, which, on request, can supply not only a formidable listing of these groups, but also a wide variety of video and audio tapes. Their videos and tapes are fine, too, but somehow when I ordered mine, I was surprised to learn that I should allow up to four weeks for delivery, which seemed to me somewhat tardy for immediate grief sustenance.

Some of the pamphlets on the subject were extraordinarily detailed. One, from the Marin County Humane Society, was called "The Stages of Grief," and proceeded to list five of these. The first was called "Denial" ("Your first reaction to the news that your animal has died or is about to die — you simply do not want to believe it"). The second was "Anger" ("Why did my animal die? Why did you leave me when I needed you most?"). The third stage was "Bargaining" ("You promise to spend more time with your animal, to never forget his/her mealtime again, to shower your animal with gifts, if only he/she will stay with you a little longer"). The fourth was "Depression" ("A time when your tumultuous emotions ebb into one sorrowful expression, when most people feel a lack of motivation and would like to withdraw from the busy, happy world"). The fifth and final one was "Recovery" (one which, it was stated, "Allows you to take a fresh look at yourself and the world around you").

Frankly, I did not find any of those stages held much comfort for me in getting over my grief about Polar Bear. However, among Delta's videotapes I found one particularly helpful. It was about a grief support program at Colorado State University called *Changes*, and it was not authored by a veterinarian, as so many videotapes are, but by a non-professional. His name was Art Batchelder, and in the tape he tells the story of what happened to him when, after fourteen years, he lost his dog, a sheltie-terrier named Dusty — or at least what happened to him until he met a counselor at *Changes* named Carolyn Butler:

> Carolyn and I had a long talk. Carolyn told me that it's O.K. to cry. She told me that grieving isn't going to be over in a week or two or a month or a year. It may take two, three, several years. She was right.
>
> She told me something then I didn't quite understand or believe what she meant, but I know now was absolutely true. She said, "Art, when Dusty died, a part of you went with him." And yes, it did.

She helped me grieve. In my generation, we grew up with the John Wayne syndrome — men don't cry, men don't show emotions, we're macho, we're heroes. So I couldn't let myself cry in front of anybody. I told her, I drive around in that truck and Dusty's not there and I want to talk to him. She said, "Talk to him, Art."

I wanted the veterinarian to tell me the same thing that Carolyn did, that "Art, it's O.K. to cry. Grief is going to be very difficult — you're going to hurt, and you're going to hurt deeply. Don't hold it in. Talk to people. Let people know that you're hurting. Go talk to Dusty's picture, pick up that urn" — I didn't pick up that urn for two or three months, I didn't touch it. My daughter carried it home, I could not touch it.

And I think they've got to let the person know that it's O.K., that grief for a pet *is* acceptable, it *is* normal. I told the group one time that grieving for a pet is far worse than grieving for a human. And one woman said, "What do you mean by that, Art?" I think she was almost offended. What I meant was if you lose a brother or sister or a parent, it's tremendous grief, it's a tremendous loss, but you have a funeral, you have a memorial service, people come, you get cards, people talk to you. I could walk down the street later and somebody might come up and say, "Art, I'm so sorry to hear about your Dad. He was such a nice man," or something like that. Nobody ever came up to me as I was walking down the street and said, "Art, I'm so sorry to hear about Dusty. He was such a nice dog." Nobody ever came and told me they were sorry that I lost Dusty. . . .

I couldn't take my walks any longer because I couldn't walk along the streets where Dusty and I went. But then

I started taking the walks. I went out one Sunday morning — we had special routes we would take on different days of the week — and I went out one Sunday morning, and there were other people walking with their dogs and I said, I can't do this. I went home.

But after talking to Carolyn I went out there one Sunday morning and I walked, and I saw other people with their dogs, and there was a tug on this hand — I felt it — and I visualized Dusty down there. I'm not going to say Dusty was there, but I visualized Dusty there, and we walked down that street and the tears just flowed down my face, and people saw me, and I didn't care. Because I was proud I had that guy with me.

What Mr. Batchelder found helpful in getting over Dusty — talking to him and pretending he was there when he knew he was not — might not be the answer for everyone, but it obviously was helpful for him. It was also helpful for me, and particularly so, perhaps, in my case because Dusty was a dog and not a cat. In any case, I also found helpful a passage in a book entitled *Courage is a Three-Letter Word,* by Walter Anderson, in which he gave "Don'ts" and "Do's" about how to behave around someone who is grieving not for either a dog or a cat, but a person. The reason I found this passage so helpful was that, although Anderson had obviously written it about the passing of a person — in fact, his father — he told me he would not change it if it was for the passing of an animal. In any case, I found Walter's first two "Don'ts" particularly memorable:

**Don't pretend.* Don't make believe you're there for some other reason; do not divert conversation to other, what *you* consider "less painful" subjects. Survivors usually want to talk about their loss, so this should be encouraged.

**Don't try to make the bereaved feel better.* Although this may seem at first like a contradiction, it is not. I don't know how many funerals I've attended where well-meaning people have advised, "Don't take it so hard." It leaves the bereaved no response and encourages them to conceal their grief. The last time, which was the *last* time, I said, "Don't take it so hard," a survivor asked me, "How hard *should* I take it?"

Many times, going through the loss of Polar Bear, when someone said to me, "Don't take it so hard," I would indeed have liked to answer, as Mr. Anderson did, how hard *should* I take it?

Unlike some people who have experienced the loss of an animal, I did not believe, even for a moment, that I would never get another. This is not to say that I joined the people who said either "After all, it's just an animal," or "Why don't you just get another?" either in spirit or in any other way. But I did know full well there were just too many animals out there in need of homes for me to take what I have always regarded as the self-indulgent road of saying the heartbreak of the loss of an animal was too much ever to want to go through with it again. To me, such an admission brought up the far more powerful admission that all the wonderful times you had had with your animal were not worth the unhappiness at the end — and, regardless of what that meant for you, it meant for your animal that his or her life was meaningless. Nor could I take what seemed to me another self-indulgent road — that to get another animal would be too disloyal to your previous animal. To me, that argument seemed equally spurious as the unhappiness one, and for the same reason — that his or her life was, in the end, again, meaningless.

Like most people, however, I did not want to get another animal right away. To the kind of people who offered to go out and buy one for me, I was polite but firm. I told them that I appreciated their generosity, but there were far too many animals at shelters waiting, all too often hopelessly, for homes for me to consider buying one for myself, let alone letting them buy one for me.

Nonetheless, since I myself had brought up the subject of getting another animal at a shelter, I could not help but realize that this was something else again. And, as time passed, I found myself thinking more and more not just about how lonely my apartment was, but rather how nice it would be to have a friend on four paws around. My first choice was Polar Star, who, faithful readers of my second book about Polar Bear will recall, came to me via Anna Belle Washburn and the Martha's Vineyard Shelter. Polar Star was white, and looked very much like Polar Bear except that Polar Bear's eyes were green and Polar Star's were blue, and that Polar Bear had five toes on his front paws, and Polar Star had six. Like Polar Bear, Polar Star too had been a stray — incredibly enough, he had been purposely left behind when a family of no mean means, but certainly no other recommendation, had left him to fend for himself when they went back to the city after their summer vacation.

As I went through the Martha's Vineyard Shelter, Polar Star reached one of his six-toed paws out from one of the upper cages and patted me on the cheek as I started to go by — something I have always felt was a put-up job, carefully arranged by Anna Belle. But it certainly worked — from that moment I was a goner for Polar Star, and he soon became my second-favorite cat in the world — big, beautiful, bear-like, benevolent, and *bonhomous*. He would, however, I knew from the beginning, have to be one of the Fund for Animals' office cats, because Polar Bear was very sensitive about other cats being, first, within several miles of him and, second, within several more miles of me. Now that Polar Bear was gone, however, I would be free to take Polar Star to my apartment.

Or so I thought. I knew everybody in the office was crazy about Polar Star, but I thought their feeling for my loss of Polar Bear would overcome any selfish feeling they might have about parting with Polar Star. If so, I was, as so often one is now with any kind of help, rudely mistaken. To a man — and only one was a man — they drew the line at Polar Star going anywhere. Sean O'Gara was at least reasonable, but not so Lia Albo. Lia thought little of the idea of my taking Polar Star because she felt a cat she had foisted on us would also miss him. That cat, incidentally, was named Freddie, and though he was not named for my editor, Fredi, he well could have been because, although he is a male and my editor is a female, both are two parts panther and one part Bengal tiger. In any case, the strongest opposition to my taking Polar Star away was Amy Ballad, who was closer to the cat in question than anyone — and vice versa — and said nothing as forcefully as I have ever heard nothing said. Even Marian was of little use to me. In her opinion, Polar Star was the Fund for Animals' official greeter — he loved everybody, new people as well as people he already knew — and he belonged where he was.

I was not a happy camper, an expression I have never been fond of — possibly because I was not particularly happy when I was at camp. All of them, I pointed out, had forgotten that it was I, not them, to whom Polar Star had been given. All of them also, I added, had their own animals in their own apartments or homes, and I alone was in solitary confinement. Even this meaningful argument fell upon deaf ears. I could get, they felt, just as much enjoyment from Polar Star as they did, and why was that not enough for me when I could also perfectly well get another cat at home, and still enjoy Polar Star at the office? Infected as they all were — at least except for Marian — with the idea that all modern offices should be democratically run, I stood as much chance for a favorable vote on the issue as the late Herbert Hoover. Suffice it to say that arrayed against me was not only the New York office, but also the Washington office of the Fund for Animals which, as run by national director Wayne Pacelle, I am doing a favor to call democratic. Actually, it is one of the last places on earth in which you experience pure socialism.

Against such odds, in the end, ungraciously as ever, I gave in. At about the time I did so, however, Bo and Natalie Jarnstedt, noted animal rescuers and friends of the Fund, decided to have a party for animal people at their Greenwich, Connecticut, home. During this party Marian was invited by Natalie into a large bathroom in which were ensconced Natalie's latest rescuees. One of these was a tiny, tiger-striped orange tabby with large owl eyes which were purely golden — a kitten who had been born, Natalie informed Marian, in the Greenwich, Connecticut, town dump. The minute Marian laid eyes on the kitten she wanted me to see him and, when I did, I knew full well what Marian and Natalie had been plotting.

Actually, the kitten was as different from Polar Bear as could be — something which is one of my theories, that people looking to "replace" an animal they have lost should not think of looking for something similar. This all too often invites unfair comparisons. At the same time, I should admit that this kitten did have at least one of Polar Bear's prime characteristics. Even at his minuscule size, and at the age of less than a month, he was already incredibly brave. That very first time I saw him he was not only unfazed by, but actually holding his own against, two other larger cats and, on top of this, two dogs. His very bravery named him for me — he would never be anything but Tiger Bear. In any case, once more I was a goner, and in a remarkably short time I had a new cat, or rather, kitten.

The distinction is important. I had never had a kitten as my own animal beforc, and to say they are not the same as full-grown cats is an understatement. From the moment Tiger Bear arrived at the apartment it was close to impossible for anyone, even friends of mine who are not dedicated cat people, to take their eyes off him. He had already had many trips to the vet because of the difficulty of his early life at the dump, and he had many problems, like ear mites, and every kind of worm you could imagine. I knew from his background he would have many more problems, but you would never know to look at him he had a single one of them. His energy, his curiosity, his playfulness, and his spoiling-for-a-fight-fulness were all unbelievable. So was his extraordinary ability not only to leap impossible heights on straightaways, but also to seem to fly from one place to another. I have seen him do acrobatics which would shame a monkey, and the monkey, after all, has hands — and Tiger Bear would shame him with just his paws. He would leap, for example, from the floor to the top of the back of a tall chair, then come, with all four paws somehow on this perilous perch, see-sawing for a moment and land on the top of a tall bookcase. He would also start a run down the living room and literally bank off the back of one chair, onto another chair, and end up on the highest thing he could find. As for his chewing, please do not mention it. There is literally nothing in my apartment he has not tried to chew — from the telephone cord to my sorest finger.

While watching this extraordinary animal grow, I remembered that when he was born in that dump, for ten days he, like most kittens, could not open his eyes and had not, at that age, any sense of smell at all. In fact, the only sensory ability he had was to be able to hear his mother's purr — otherwise he would undoubtedly not have lived. Eventually, however, not only did he live but, such are the accomplishments of Natalie as a rescuer, eventually both his mother and father were also rescued.

Not the least curious thing about my new friend was learning that in his tiny little body he had two-hundred and thirty bones — twenty-four more than we humans have. He also had an unbelievably supple spine, one that can twist and turn and, helped by his tail as a rudder, could always manage a safe landing. I learned, however —

early and often — that there is no such thing as kitten-proofing the home. Wherever you most do not want your kitten to go, that is assuredly where he most dearly wishes to go, and where he will get by hook or by crook, and sometimes both. Scientists would have us believe that cats do not display either what they call "insight learning" or reasoning ability, and maintain that their learning is based entirely on experience. Based entirely on my experience with Tiger Bear the kitten — and remember, he was nowhere near to being a grown cat — he had all the insight learning I could handle, and then some. As for his reasoning ability, let me give the scientists just one example. There is one particular closet where I do not wish him to go except when I am around — there are too many things in there with which he could hurt himself. So, where in the whole apartment does he most want to go? You guessed it. Furthermore, he soon learned that even if he could not handle the closed doorknob, he found out that if he pulled just right on the tote bag which was hanging on the doorknob — not so far out that the bag came off the knob, but far enough so that pulling on it put pressure on the doorknob — he could get the closet open. "Insight learning" nothing — it was pure out-of-sight learning.

Tiger Bear's favorite sport is assassinating anything in the apartment which he regards as having to do with something which people do instead of paying attention to him. Prime among these targets are the chess board and the chess men. He likes best the ruckus it causes when he manages a single-paw assassination of an entire, and hitherto very close, game. But he is not adverse to the capture of single hostages — he prefers a king or a queen — which he imprisons in, and preferably under, as many difficult places as possible.

One of the things he has taken his time learning is saying even a remotely respectable meow. Polar Bear had his crystal-clear AEIOU, but Tiger Bear, either because he did not have enough cats around when he was growing up or for some other reason, makes sounds which do not seem even to be based on any other sound except one made by a not-very-well bird. They are strictly off-key, and off anything but dissonance. It does not bother me, however, because, for all the trouble he has been, for me he makes up for this a hundred times by his constant following of me wherever I go. I put it down to the fact that he must have had so little individual attention in his early life that he has grown very rapidly to be very dependent on it. All in all, when my friend Ogden Nash wrote that awful poem: "The trouble with a kitten is that / Eventually it becomes a cat," all he did was illustrate that he did not know the first thing about either cats or kittens. The fact is there is no trouble with a kitten. And, eventually, it becomes exactly what you always hoped it would.

Finally, there remains, to those who have lost an animal, two large questions. The first of these involves the matter of whether or not to bury your animal. I have always believed that, as I said in the introduction to this book, the best place to bury your animal is in your heart. I believe that fully. At the same time, since so many people knew Polar Bear, and wanted to know where he would be buried, I finally gave in. I chose as his final resting place the Fund for Animals' Black Beauty Ranch which, over the years, has become home to thousands of abused or abandoned animals. To Chris Byrne, the able manager of Black Beauty, as well as to his extraordinary wife, Mary, fell the job of finding the right place, the right headstone, and the right copper plaque. They did it all wonderfully well. The plaque is not only a lovely one, but it is in the very center of life at the Ranch, and is also in the shade of three trees — a place which Polar Bear loved.

In any case, to me fell the job of writing the inscription for the plaque. I did it as follows:

Beneath This Stone
Lie The Mortal Remains of
The Cat Who Came For Christmas
Beloved Polar Bear
1977–1992
'Til We Meet Again

I chose the line " 'Til We Meet Again" from the hymn "May the Good Lord Bless and Keep You." In using that line, it brought up the second large question — do animals go to heaven? I do believe that we and our animals will meet again. If we do not, and where we go is supposed to be heaven, it will not be heaven to me and it will not be where I wish to go.

I remember once having an argument with a Catholic priest. Our argument had started on the subject of cruelty to animals in general, but it soon went on into the matter of whether or not animals went to heaven. I said that I had been told that somewhere in the Bible, it said that Jesus would someday come down from heaven again, leading an army on white horses. If animals did not go to heaven, I asked the good Father, then where did the horses come from?

Unfortunately, I had the wrong man. The good Father was one who believed in the old Catholic dogma that animals have no souls. Having heard this nonsense before, I responded to it, rather crossly and at some length. I said that the Episcopal Church to which I belonged might not be as big on souls as the Catholic Church, but if and when the good Father and I shuffled off this mortal coil, and we were going to some glorious Elysian Fields — and here I added that being Episcopalian, I might get a little better place up there than he did, but that Episcopalians were very democratic, and I would do the best I could for him — but animals were not, according to him, going anywhere, then it seemed to me all the more important that we should at least give them a little better shakes in the one life they did have.

I feel I won the argument — one of the very few I believe I have ever won with someone who was far more learned on all areas of the subject than I was. Of course I realize our argument had not settled the matter of whether or not animals went to heaven. But I had at least settled something — that, if they did not, then we owed them even more.

Certainly in just knowing Polar Bear, let alone being owned by him, I feel I owed him more than I could ever repay, let alone say. To me he was, and will always be, as I said at the beginning of this book, the best cat ever. I called him that, as I also said, in the special moments we had together, and I will always think of him as that.

I also wrote in the inscription on Polar Bear's monument

that we will meet again. I am not deeply religious, and when the subject comes up, it usually makes me nervous. And when something makes me nervous, I am inclined to make a joke about it. Years ago, for example, when I was working for the *Saturday Evening Post* and my job was choosing cartoons for the magazine, one of the first I chose was a drawing of two angels in heaven with one of them saying to the other, "Do you believe in the heretofore?"

Nonetheless, heretofore or hereafter aside, what I wrote on Polar Bear's monument I do believe — that we will meet again. And if I do not always believe it, I always try to believe it, because I also believe that if you try hard enough to believe something you will in time believe it. And one thing I know is that, when Polar Bear and I do meet again, the first thing I will say to him is that he is the best cat ever. And another thing I know is that, wherever we are, he will be the best cat there, too.